The Foundry

Book 1
Dianis, A World In Turmoil

Frank Dravis

This is a work of fiction. All of the characters and events portrayed in this novel are either fictional or are used fictitiously. Any resemblance to actual events or persons, living or dead, is entirely coincidental.

The Foundry
Book One, Dianis World In Turmoil Chronicles

Paperback version ISBN: 9781976911583

https://www.facebook.com/thefoundrybookone/

Cover: Ian Llanas
Isuelt Map: Jerry Mooney

Table of Contents

Cast of Characters

Protagonists

- IDB (Interspecies Development Branch), Avarian Federation
  - Clienen Hor, director of IDB Margel Damansk
  - Achelous Forushen, chief inspector of Civilization Monitoring
  - Baryy Maxmun, Civilization Monitoring agent
  - Outish, astrobiology intern
  - Gail Manner, chief of Solar Surveillance
  - Ivan Darinarishcan, chief of Ready Reaction
  - Jeremy, the IDB Dianis artificial intelligence (AI)

- Mother Dianis (Life Believers)
  - Christina Tara, Al suri Ascalon defender
  - Alex, defender
  - Feolin, defender

- Timberkeeps, Mearsbirch Doromen clan
  - Woodwern, clan chairman
  - Margern, Wedgewood town chairwoman, sister to Woodwern
  - Sedge the Warlord, mercenary, Wedgewood garrison commander
  - Ogden, master weaponsmith, warden of the Second Ward
  - Lettern Stouttree, archer and scout, Second Ward
  - Pottern Stouttree, apprentice to Ogden, brother to Lettern
  - Racheal Stouttree, sixthsense kinetic, sister to Lettern
  - Mergund, apprentice to Ogden
  - Mbecca, master sixthsense healer
  - Cordelei Greenleaf, sixthsense diviner
  - Brookern, sixthsense voyant
  - Bagonen, branch warden, Second Ward
  - Barrigal, mercenary captain
  - Perrin, mercenary captain

- Tivor
  - Aorolmin of Tivor, the duke of Tivor
  - Marisa Pontifract, owner of Marinda Merchants
  - Eliot, huntsmaster for Marinda Merchants
  - Patrace, alchemist for Marinda Merchants

- The Silver Cup Couriers Guild
  - Akallabeth, guild overseer in Tivor
  - Prince Fire Eye, prince of the wryvern nation
  - Celebron, steward of the watch
  - Trishna, sixthsense telepath

The Matrincy

- The Matriarch, the leader of the Matrincy
- Councilor Margrett, special envoy to Dianis
- Councilor Breia, planetary councilor to Dianis

Antagonists

- Nordarken Mining
  - Rocl Binair, senior vice president of Resource Production.
  - Tomkin, aquamarine production director for Nordarken Mining
  - Quorat, contractor

- Empire of Nak Drakas
  - Emperor Elixir Tyr Violorich, supreme leader of the Drakan Empire
  - General Lord Orn Blannach, supreme commander of the Drakan military
  - Commandant Fritach, commander of the Washentrufel, the Drakan secret service
  - Uloch, Drakan decurion and commander of the Drakan expeditionary force
  - Larech, Washentrufel agent
  - Baldor Prairiegrass, Plains Doroman spy

- Diunesis Antiquaria (Paleowrights)
  - Helprig, viscount of Diunesis Antiquaria
  - Captain Irons, captain of the Scarlet Saviors
  - Duck Peren, examiner

Map of the Continent of Isuelt

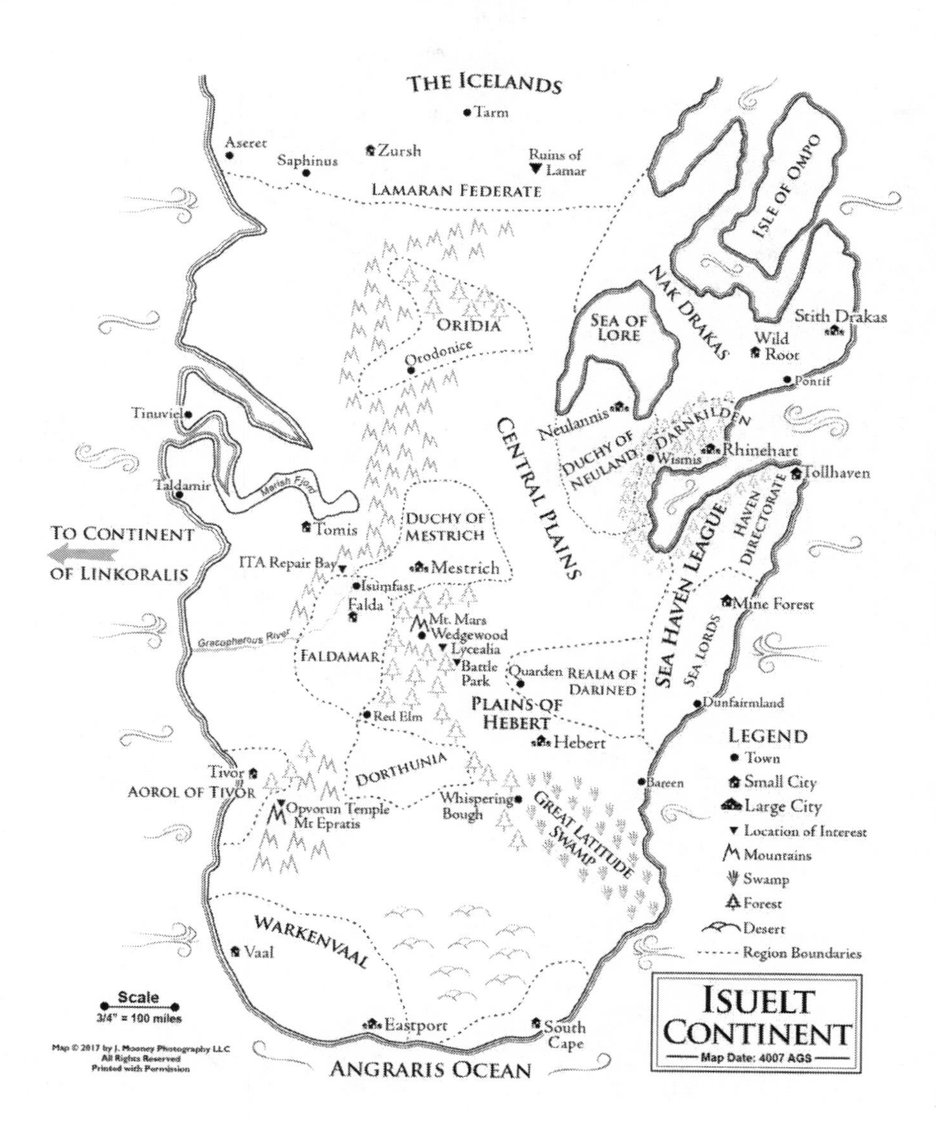

Map of the Margel

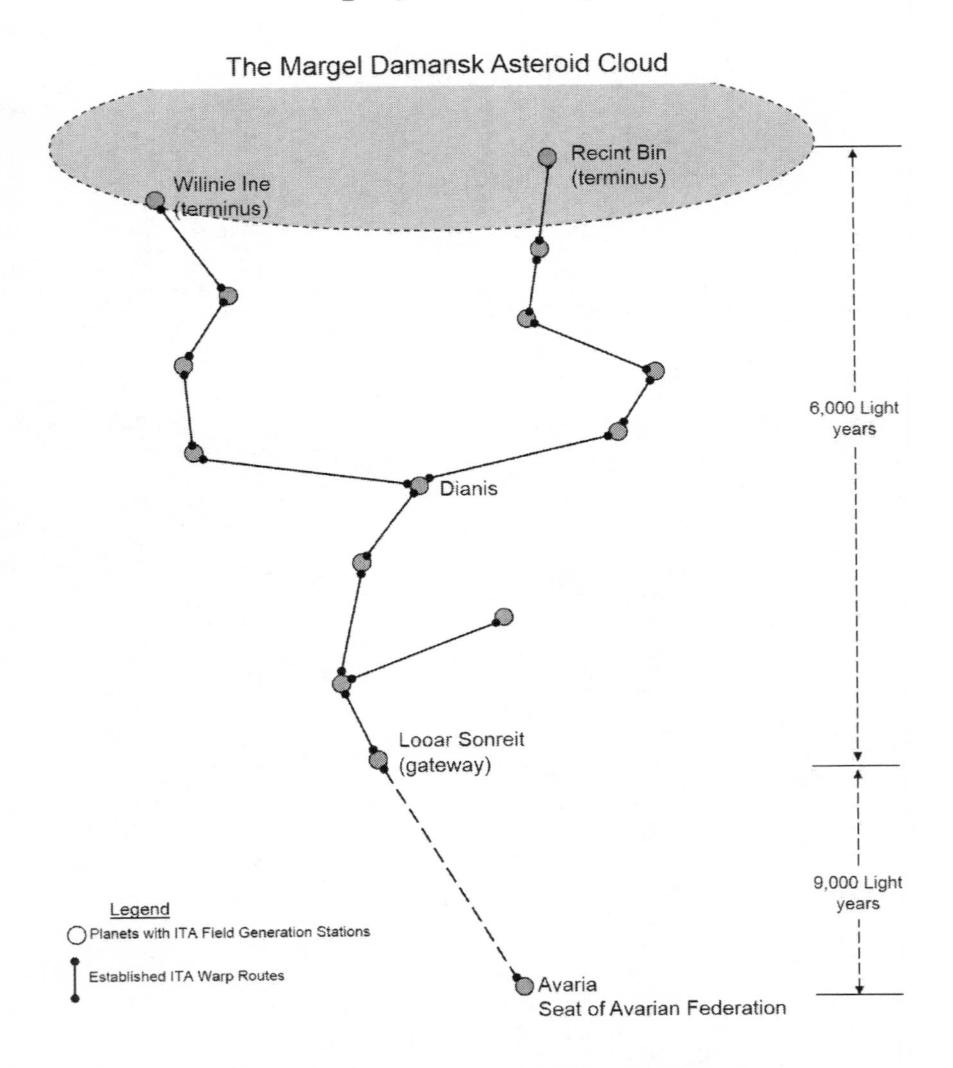

Margel Damansk Arm of ITA Transportation Network

Norma Spiral Arm, Milky Way Galaxy

Prologue

The planet Wespil-IV

He held a hand over the gaping wound in his side. The plasma bolt had gone clean through the enviro suit below his ribs and out the back. The atmosphere on the planet, while breathable, was deadly. *Antibellia bactrial,* prevalent in the air on the bleak world, was infecting the wound, and he would be dead within the hour. Perhaps that's why his pursuers hadn't followed him down into the cave, letting the planet do their work for them. Tomkin lay still, conserving his strength, not believing the turn of events. It still mystified him how his promotion to aquamarine production director for Nordarken Mining, his dream job, had turned into a disaster. But the conclusion was simple and brutal: They needed a fool, someone to sacrifice, and he was both.

A cough wracked him. Pulling out the suit's med pack, he fumbled with the activator and positioned the pack over the entry wound. Pressing the seal around the edges, Tomkin lay back and let the med pack do what it could. Painkillers ebbed into the wound, and the torture from the energy bolt began to fade. The nano-coagulants would attempt to stop the bleeding, but he didn't have another pack to put on the exit wound.

A sharp spasm wracked Tomkin's side. The digestive actions of antibellia bactrial were scouring his open wound. Did he hear a whine? Listening closely, he wondered if his pursuers had sent down a nano recon bot to check on him. Listening, his thoughts wandered. If he could do it over again, he'd never ask that question, the one that landed him here. He felt himself sliding into unconsciousness. He began to dream. He was there, back on Avaria a year ago....

Tomkin resisted the urge to panic. Scanning through the secret production report for Kerrin III, he saw that the proven-reserves trend line sloped downward and, worse, nose-dived in the last two months. He flipped through the production screens for the two other aquamarine mines; both were flat. He sighed with strained relief. It was a sad state when flat was good. As aquamarine production director for Nordarken Mining, his job was to collect, analyze, and report on the vital resource. Tomkin arranged the panels on the hologrid display and juxtaposed the exploration estimates for the past two years against the actual production volumes. The exploration estimates tracked depressingly close to the production actuals. At the current rate of decline, they would have to cut aquamarine-5 quotas by two-thirds to keep their premier mine, Kerrin III, in operation.

Tomkin had waited until today to decide what to do when he received the third set of ground sonar and aural scanning data. He had to be absolutely certain no surprise deposits were located before he posted the new production forecast.

Why did it have to be aquamarine? More importantly, why did he have to be the aquamarine-5 production director? When he'd been promoted to director of the most critical production stream he had been elated, but as time wore on and the numbers grew worse he'd wondered if his predecessor had set him up. Aquamarine-5, the grade-five variety of the mineral, was the key component in any device that manipulated aural energy, and that included field generators. The aural energy fields created by those generators allowed instantaneous communication and travel between generator sites, light years apart. No other grade of aquamarine had the requisite aural-energy properties. A tiny crystal of it was employed in the ubiquitous multi-func devices that people used to connect with each other. Moreover, each day R&D was finding new applications for aural energy in the war against the Turboii. Those technological innovations had only recently stemmed the Turboii advance. He shuddered to think of what would happen to Nordarken Mining if aquamarine production were cut in half. The mining conglomerate was twice the size of its nearest rival, Celestial Navigation, but that margin could evaporate overnight if Nordarken's aqua-5 production cratered. To make matters worse, the upstart TY DeepSpace had recently announced its second aquamarine find, a major one.

Tomkin began to compose a memo to his superior: Rocl Binair, senior vice president of Resource Production. The words flowed across the hologrid but then stopped as Tomkin imagined his boss's reaction when he received the message.

With a determination honed from the surety of his data, Tomkin mentally girded himself and cleared the display. He stood. As of now, he was the only person in Nordarken Mining who had the complete picture of the declining aquamarine production, and it was time to share it -- carefully.

He left his office and walked down the hall. Waving to Binair's executive assistant, he asked, in a somber tone, "Is he free?"

The aide nodded. "You want me to buzz him?"

"Please."

Ushered in and seated in the VP's office, Tomkin took stock of Binair's demeanor, wondering what sort of mood he was in.

The older man was a pale-skinned Avarian with thin lips and a full head of gold hair, the benefit of expensive gene therapy. Binair offered a smile. "Hello, Tomkin, what can I do for you?"

Tomkin steeled himself. He didn't see any point in delaying the inevitable or trying to gloss it over; Binair didn't get to be senior VP in Nordarken Mining by being slow-witted. "I have the most current aquamarine production estimates as of ten minutes ago."

Binair's fixed expression and lack of body movement signaled he had his boss's undivided attention.

"Hmm, judging by your tone, Tomkin...the news isn't good."

"I'm afraid not."

"The new scans came in?"

Tomkin held himself tightly in control. "Yes. Same as before. They've scoured all of Kerrin III, Asteroid field 3123, and the others."

Binair's shoulders gave the barest sign of a slump. "And your research and exploration efforts?" The way Binair said *your* was like twisting a knife in Tomkin's stomach. The message was clear: Finding more aquamarine was Tomkin's problem.

His nerves compelled him to squirm in the chair, but Tomkin held still. "The contractor operations are coming up dry, TY DeepSpace is"—the narrowing of the vice president's eyes told him that trying to blame the dearth of aquamarine reserves on a fifth-rate competitor would buy him no sympathy. "But I did get a hit on one of our research channels."

The executive eased back in his chair. "Oh, which one?"

"Beta."

Pursing his lips, Binair steepled his fingers. Channel Beta was Nordarken trade speak for their secret industrial espionage department. The messages Tomkin received from Channel Beta were anonymous and came stripped of identifying source clues to reduce the chances of exposing informants, some of whom were no doubt federation bureaucrats.

Binair glanced down at his hologrid. He looked up and stared pointedly at the ceiling as if to indicate that someone might be listening. "You want a cup of jorra? Relax a bit?"

Tomkin said, "Certainly."

They stood and left the office, and Binair said to his aide, "I'll be in a comfy room."

Taking the grav lift down thirty floors to the sixth-level basement, Binair and Tomkin stepped into the hall and strode to a sentry station. An armed guard sat behind a console, and another stood next to a full-body scanner. "Step through, please," instructed the guard standing next to the scanner. Binair emptied his pockets, removed his communications link and other items, and dropped them into a personal-property tray. He walked through the scanner, and the console operator said, "Clear."

Tomkin followed the same procedure.

"What room do we have?" asked Binair.

"Bunker G, sir," the operator replied.

Binair moved purposefully past bunkers A through H on each side of the long corridor. The doors to the bunkers were two feet thick and layered with electro, aural, radio, and other shielding. He stepped into G, keeping his eyes carefully averted from the chairs in the room lest a memory scan be able to isolate that particular image. He pulled the door shut and latched it. There was no ventilation in the room. The guards at the security station logged the time the door closed and would warn the occupants if they stayed past the safety threshold. Ventilation ducts in the bunkers were a risk as they opened the potential for security breaches. Binair sat in one of the chairs. They were arranged back to back so that the occupants did not look at each other, another precaution to thwart memory scans.

Tomkin waited outside for Binair to seat himself. Surrounding the door were motion detectors, an additional layer of security designed to detect nanobots. He entered the bunker and made his way to a chair studiously focusing on the ceiling as his security training had taught him.

Staring at the blank black wall in front of him, Binair asked, "You said Channel Beta?"

"Yes, sir." Tomkin had read enough of the secret reports to discern a pattern in them. The Channel Beta people strove to cleanse the reports of markers that would identify the source, but they could only go so far before destroying important contextual information, so subtle clues were always left in the report. This particular message had come from a contact Tomkin suspected was in the Water Survey Department of the Avarian Federation.

"And the planet profile?"

"Class E." Tomkin, even though he couldn't see his boss sitting behind him, could guess the look on Binair's face.

"It's inhabited?"

"Yes, sir, human."

"And the Interspecies Development Branch, are they active?" Binair's voice was as dry as a desert wind.

Tomkin hesitated. "Yes, complete solar system and planetary surveillance. Ground teams are fully staffed, experienced, and embedded in the local culture judging from their operations reports. I checked the declassified IDB reports. There have been incursions planetside, but most were discovered and prosecuted within six months of their landings. I compared the public reports with Channel Beta findings. The IDB has the planet locked down tight."

Binair snorted. "Where is this place?"

"Dianis, it is in the Margel Damansk quadrant."

"Dianis, Dianis," the executive mused aloud. "Why do I know that name?"

"It's the Transportation Authority's central hub for the Margel."

"Oh, that's right, the arm that Celestial Navigation is trying to make a go at. So the IDB there is good?"

"So it would seem. Their chief inspector of Civilization Monitoring is Achelous Forushen."

When the silence stretched on, Tomkin asked, "You remember the chief inspector?"

Finally, Binair said, in a voice heavy with gravel, "Yes, I know Forushen. Though he wasn't a chief inspector then." He paused, the silence oppressive in the dead air of the bunker. "He should have died on Ilos Septi."

Silence dragged on further as Binair soured, thinking of the five long years his career had languished after his encounter with the IDB agent. "So Forushen is on Dianis." He considered the ramifications. "Don't you think it is odd the IDB should have a full surveillance complement on a backwater world like Dianis when there are half a dozen planets needing reclamation from the Turboii?"

Tomkin shrugged even though his boss couldn't see him. "I don't know. If the planet doesn't have any worthwhile aquamarine deposits, I don't pay much attention to it."

A snort came from behind him. "Well it does now, and surprise, it has a full IDB contingent. Do you think that is a coincidence?"

"I—"

Impatient, Binair snapped, "The IDB is stretched thin. And yet here they are on a planet far from the front with a full surveillance team. It seems to me either their priorities are out of alignment or the IDB is protecting something important."

Tomkin considered the argument but hesitated to agree. The IDB was needed to protect primitive populations from extrasolar depredations. Reclaimed worlds were already wrecked, whereas pristine worlds still had a chance to evolve peacefully. It was true reclaimed worlds needed immediate uplift planning for their surviving sentient populations, but the virginal worlds had more people.

"I wonder what the Unclaimed Planets Commission thinks of it? Our friends at ULUP?" Binair scoffed, then stood, but did not turn to look at Tomkin. "So we have a problem. The federation needs aquamarine-5 to continue the war effort, and you need a new source to keep up our production quotas. Dianis might have enough, but it's is a Class E world with an overzealous IDB contingent, and at the same time there are worlds reclaimed from the Turboii War screaming for the IDB's attention. There might be something I can do about that."

Tomkin almost turned to look at Binair. "How can you change IDB deployment orders?"

Binair forced a laugh and moved to the bunker door. "Me?" He held the handle of the door. "Whatever I do my old friend Agent Forushen will never know who has pulled his strings. Sad, but I'll just have to live with it."

Laying in the cold cave Tomkin's life drained away. In his final lucid moment, he came to the realization that he, just like Chief Inspector Achelous Forushen, was an unwitting puppet. Only Tomkin's act was over, and the chief inspector's was just beginning.

Chapter 1
Marisa

The city of Tivor on the planet Dianis

Eliot waited on the wharf in the predawn darkness for the *Wind March* to dock. Torches guttered along the quay, and lanterns lit the gunwales of the vessel. He waved at Marisa standing on the quarterdeck next to the ship's captain. She waved back, but her lack of smile and searching eyes told him that she was disappointed. A boom swung the ship's brow over and settled it on the pier. Marisa was the first across, her secretary and steward following in her wake. She gave Eliot a brief, forced smile. "All's well in Tivor, I take it?"

"Yes, my lady. Nothing untoward. And your hunt for pirates?"

She shook her head, a slight frown matching her gaze as she searched the wharf. "We caught a small one preying on fishing boats, and our good captain put a ballistae bolt through their hull. Where is Achelous? He's here in Tivor, is he not?"

Eliot planned to use a practiced excuse for the trader, but faced with Marisa, his fortitude evaporated. "He is, my lady, but he's leaving for the Auro Na temple. If nothing is keeping you here, I have your carriage ready, and if we hurry, we should be able to catch him."

This time Marisa's smile was genuine. "Very good. And how is Boyd? Has Achelous been with him?"

"Yes, my lady." Eliot waved frantically for the Marinda Merchants carriage to pull up. Drawn by a pair of eenus, it had to thread its way past a knot of stevedores manhandling bales of cotton onto a flatbed wagon. He urged them to hurry as he relished the surprise Achelous was about to get. "He and Boyd are inseparable, truly. It's almost as if he tries to make up—"

"For when he is gone. Yes, I know."

The stable door banged shut. Achelous looked over the saddle of the eenu as he pulled the cinch tight. Marisa stood there in her black knee-high boots, brown fawn-leather breaches, and cape of water-shedding velvet. She had her hands on her hips and a frown on her face. Achelous's heart skipped as it always did when he first saw her. Her raven hair was spun up in a cone bun, her coal-black eyes glinted, and her perfect lips were compressed in a hard line. He sighed. Behind her, Achelous saw Eliot walk past the door sheepishly. He smiled inwardly. *The dog, he brought her here just to spite me.* Achelous ducked behind the eenu's head, to adjust the bridle and avoid Marisa's glare.

"I missed you on the dock. I was hoping you would see me ashore." She came forward. "And yet I find you here. Anxious to be on the road?"

"No," Achelous said heavily. "I just wanted to spare you the disappointment of saying hello and goodbye."

"So you prefer to spare me no words at all?"

He swallowed. Finished with the cinch, he came out from behind the eenu. "No. In truth, I expected the *Wind March* to be delayed. The offing this past day is not fit for entry to Tivor. I expected Eliot to be waiting all morning, and I must be off. Though I am most happy to see you back safe before I leave. I don't see any bandages so..." Achelous let his gaze slide over her figure.

Marisa shook her head. "We missed them. But their luck will not last forever. And what of you," her tone softened, "why must you leave today? Surely the Auro Na monks can wait another day."

"I wish that was true. The high priest and his council adjourn this evening, and I'll have only until sunrise next day to conclude my arrangements."

Marisa's frown returned as she moved closer. "You are going alone?"

"Yes," Achelous said. "Elliot wanted to go with me. He even has his eenu saddled." Achelous tilted his head in the direction of the steed tied to a stable post, saddled, bridled, and ready to go. "But you know, Marisa," he said forcefully. "I do these trips alone. Period."

A woman of patience and discipline tempered from running a successful trading enterprise, Marisa was usually composed and thoughtful. This morning, however, her temper was up, stoked by long frustration. "Why?" she snapped. "You take Baryy and the other traders and guards with you on most of your ventures, why go into the Coldpeaks alone?"

"Marisa, we've been through this. There are things I need to do myself. Others would just get in the way."

She shook her head, not buying a word of it and glared at Eliot who had come in through the cargo doors.

Eliot held her stare, some message passing between them. Marissa sighed, the purse of her lips softening just a touch. She moved to stand next to Achelous and stroked the soft brown fur of the eenu. The stables, animals, the buildings around her, Marinda Merchants, they were all hers. She was the most influential woman in Tivor, and yet she had no control over the man she loved.

She reached up and held the eenu's muzzle in her hands, and it snuffled them searching for a treat. Echo had been Marisa's gift to Achelous. The steed was calm, well trained, and, most important, as swift as the wind. Marisa had asked Achelous to take Echo whenever he was lame-minded enough to go off venturing by himself. It was the most she could do to keep him safe. "Have you said goodbye to Boyd?" she asked, moderating her tone.

Achelous did not meet her gaze. "I was going to. I just didn't want to wake him."

Marisa glared at him. "He's your son. Don't make me cope with his disappointment when he finds you've left without saying goodbye."

He nodded and left Echo in Marisa's hands as he headed into the crisp morning, dawn staining the eastern sky. Crunching along the frost-hardened path, he steeled himself for yet another departure. Not for the first time did he regret the layers of his life, the complexity. If he were just a trader, he could forgo the trip into the mountains. But he had other matters driving him.

"I can follow him again," offered Eliot.

Her ebony eyes glinted hard. The shake of her head almost imperceptible. "He'd just spot you again and take you on a dolphin chase and end up losing you."

Eliot dug at the dirt with a booted toe. "I don't know how he does it," he said, with exasperation in his voice. "No one else can just vanish like that. I follow the tracks across the rock escarpment; they are faint, but I can follow the sign, and then they just disappear!"

Marisa studied Eliot; she'd heard this before and was wary of what he'd say next.

"I don't know." Eliot shook his head. The huntsman's weathered face bore deep crags along both cheeks, a small snow-white goatee tried to hide a prominent chin, and gray eyes reflected decades of time in the wilderness. "I'll say again I think he's an—"

"Shush." She unconsciously looked around, though the prospect of a Paleowright informant lurking in her stables was remote. "I told you, don't say that word. The Paleowrights will never give us rest. Do you want a Paleowright inquisitor claiming you are an obstructionist or even an abettor?"

Eliot shook his head fervently. Even though Paleowrights were a small minority in Tivor, there were still people, regardless of their religious beliefs, willing to earn the artifact bounty the Paleowrights offered. A bounty that included information about anyone who might know of or have access to Ancient artifacts.

Marisa drew herself up to her full height. "Tell Achelous you'll go with him to the Broken Stones crossroads. If there are ill folk about, they'll be lurking in the forest near the crossroads. Beyond there, he can go on by himself. You can also tell him I'll start charging a fee to carry his goods on my ships if he refuses."

Eliot grinned. "I'll offer to share a flask of carvareen, and then watch his back trail."

"Boyd?" Achelous sat on the side of his son's bed; the young boy snuggled under a mound of blankets. The wood stove, freshly stoked in the alcove outside the chamber, popped and pinged as it heated up.

The boy's gray eyes, those of his father, opened and focused. "Papa?"

Achelous bent forward and kissed the boy on the forehead. "Papa has to go; I'll be back soon." He steeled himself for the reaction.

The gray eyes darkened, his mother lurking in their depths. "But you come just back?"

"I know, I know." Achelous brushed the brown locks from the boy's face. "But when I get back, we'll go to the tide pools and hunt crabs. The big red ones your mama likes. I'll even wrap their claws so you can hold them."

"Promise?"

He smiled. "Promise." A point of pride, he'd never broken his word to his son, and never would.

He stood and went to the door. The boy's eyes, big and searching, followed him to the door. Achelous smiled bravely, turned, and left.

The sun formed long shadows in the small meadow as their eenus made clear tracks in the morning frost on the woodland carpet. Achelous and Eliot were at the crossroads. A set of old Auro Na monoliths lay scattered about like thrown dice. Achelous turned in his saddle, suspicion on his face. "You'll not follow me from here?"

Eliot shook his head. "No, you have my word."

Achelous sat back in his saddle feeling the comforting warmth and strength of Echo beneath him. "I have my horn. If I get into trouble, I'll sound two blasts and spur Echo back here faster than a sailor to a brothel."

Eliot smiled. "I'll wait here for a spell just the same. There might be some radix growing under them awnings. The price is up, and it might pay for me to get off my eenu and root around a bit."

Achelous nodded. He bought and sold radix as a trade good, one of the many expensive roots and spices he purveyed. Buying herbs from collectors gave him access to the valuable rumor network of backwoods hunters, farmers, and nomadic tribes. If any strange phenomenon occurred in the hinterlands, they were the first to boast about it. "I'll be back in a week." He set his heels to Echo and rode into the deep shadows.

Eliot waited. There may be radix growing under the eaves, but it was spring and the ground still cold; the root hadn't sprouted yet, as Achelous would know. Tempted as he was to follow, Eliot had given his word he wouldn't. He sat in the saddle while his curiosity gnawed at him. There was more to Achelous than what he let on. Eliot understood why the trader preferred to remain independent from Marisa's Marinda Merchants, but the solitary trips into the Coldpeaks packing only the barest trade goods were at odds with all of his other trading expeditions. When questioned, Achelous refused to give more than a terse explanation. He claimed his sojourns were to meditate with the monks of Auro Na, but if that was true, then why not let Eliot ride with him to the gates of the temple? It was also odd that Achelous rarely quoted Auro Na beliefs, and Achelous seemed to have a calm understanding of what everyone else took to be fearful and mysterious. When the last big earth-shaker had hit, and smoke rose from Mount Epratis, Eliot remembered people running into the street screaming and fearing for their lives. Whereas Achelous had calmly walked out the door of Marinda Hall, looked up at the mountain, and said, "Glad I'm not living on the eastern slope." When Marisa asked him why he looked surprised and mumbled something about lava and went back in the hall.

Achelous halted Echo in the transit zone. He pulled out the Auro Na bible and flipped to chapter twelve, verse three. He knew the passage by heart:

"...as where rays of the heavens shine upon the world in holy aura endowing all the land's keepers with strength to move thy spirit upon the nether."

The text was particularly apropos for what he intended to do. To any casual or even educated observer, the book was a genuine Auro Na bible. In reality, it was a cleverly camouflaged IDB multi-function aural controller. Achelous brushed the printed words with his fingertip and unlocked the control screen. The paper turned glossy, and the text shimmered into the user interface for the area scanner. He tapped the magnify button, and the display showed an infrared scan of a hundred-meter radius centered on the transit zone. The multi-func linked to an external scanner camouflaged to look like a pinecone on the rock ledge above the zone. The scan showed signatures of squirrels, birds, two roe, but no humans or other sentient life.

Satisfied he was alone with Echo, Achelous turned to chapter three and brought up the field-generator interface. He tapped the initiate button and waited for the ready indicator to turn green.

Beneath his feet in a secure cavern hollowed out in the mountain, a small aural field generator spun up. He could feel the hair on the nape of his neck rise as the invisible aural field enveloped him and Echo. The eenu shuffled and piped, but calmed under her master's reassurance. She'd been through this before.

The ready indicator turned green, and the display depicted a human rider and mount. He tapped the shift button and disappeared.

Eenu and rider stood motionless waiting for the decontamination mist to evaporate. Achelous rubbed Echo's snout. It piped and wanted to dance around but finally calmed down. Unbeknownst to Marisa, the swift and steady steed had learned its way around the IDB facilities. Eenus were one of the few native Dianis species to have crossed the extraplanetary boundary between the iron-age world of Dianis and the space-faring realm of the Avarian Federation. It took time and patience for the IDB trainers to get Echo and the other eenus accustomed to the sudden change in scenery that accompanied phase-shift travel. But now Echo clopped along the concrete and metallic surroundings of IDB Central Station, Dianis, as if it were a barn in Tivor. Robotic cleaners immediately sanitized and disposed of any indiscretions Echo might leave along the way.

The decontamination mist cleared, and the bay doors slid open. The transport bay was enclosed in an irradiation-and-decontamination chamber because it connected to a primitive Class E world. Under the Universal Law of Unclaimed Planets, Dianis and extraterrestrial contact was not allowed, which included pathogens. The exception being the IDB agents necessary to conduct in-country surveillance. It was one thing for Achelous or Echo to bring a virus into IDB Central Station, constructed deep within Dianis, where automated detection and decontamination systems could destroy the agent. It was another, substantially more complex, problem if Achelous carried a disease onto Dianis.

Outish, a young astrobiology intern, stood waiting on the ramp. Echo's ears pricked up immediately. The short dark brown Halorite held out his fur-covered hand holding a carrot. Outish smiled as the eenu snuffled his hand then nipped at the treat. "How's in-country, sir?"

"Good, Outish. It's spring. Still a bit cold, but the flowers are starting to bloom, and the natives are peaceful."

Outish's expression clouded. "If the natives are so peaceful, why can't I go into the field with you?"

Achelous rolled his eyes. "Because you're a Halorite and you look like a Halorite. There are no Halorites on Dianis."

"But Field Outfitting said they could transmute my appearance to look human, like a Nakish or a Doroman." Broad-shouldered, covered in short coarse fur from head to foot, Outish stood the height of a human, though his pointed ears and black nose compounded his alienness. Halorites shared 99.8 percent of the same genes with humans, but somewhere in the dim past Human-Halorite evolution had diverged.

Achelous laughed. "A Doroman?"

"Yes." Outish glared back. "A Timberkeep Doroman." Across the continent of Isuelt, the Doroman race of mankind had divided itself into clans that were culturally adapted to unique environments. The Timberkeeps preferred woodlands and deep forests, much the same as Halorites did on their homeworld, and Outish felt a particular affinity for the Timberkeep boreal ethic.

Achelous paused, examining Outish critically. "If Field Outfitting thinks they can do it, they're probably right. But you don't have the training."

“Yes, but I can take the injection-learning courses. My astrobiologist training prequalifies me, and I have to log a year in-country to get my accreditation.”

Achelous nodded absently as he handed the reigns over to Outish. “We’ll talk about it. But first I’ve got to file my reports and find out why this emergency all-hands meeting was called.” He walked down the ramp and stopped. “I’d need to see you as a human, Doroman or otherwise before I would even consider the idea. And watch out for those Field Outfitting boys. Make sure they get it right. You don’t want to come out looking like a Trapazid Gorundig.”

Outish swallowed hard. *A Trapazid Gorundig? That would hurt!*

Chapter 2
The Withdrawal

The planet Dianis, IDB Central Station

IDB personnel congregated at the entrance to the ops-mission gallery. Many of the three hundred staff were there. Some, from Ready Reaction, Civilization Monitoring, and others were dressed like Achelous, still wearing their in-country garb. Voices rose as acquaintances were renewed, and the gathering funneled through the doors for the director's briefing. For many of the IDB staffers, the rare all-hands meetings were the few times they saw one another.

"Atch." A soft touch plucked at his elbow. "Still pounding ground?"

Achelous turned. Gail Manner, chief of Solar Surveillance, smiled at him. It was the first time he'd seen her in person since the last all-hands meeting though they often spoke via A-wave. He noticed that she'd cut her hair to just above the shoulder, but her eyebrows, finely shaped nose, high cheekbones, and green eyes were still as timeless as the first day they met. "Hello, Gail." He reached an arm around her waist and kissed her on the cheek.

"Hey, you two, are you licensed for having children?" Ivan Darinarishcan from Ready Reaction stood behind them. "Clear the door, and I'll ignore this obvious infraction."

Gail made a face at him, and Ivan grinned mischievously as he said, "Old loves never die, eh?"

Achelous smirked. "You just wish you had friends in high places." Gail smiled at the reference to her headquarters on Dianis's moon.

"Yeah?" Ivan said as he found a seat in the gallery. "The only friends you need are the ones that wear these." He pointed to the Ready Reaction Force emblem on the shoulder of his fatigues. Twice in the past year, Ivan and his team had gone in-country to back up Achelous when things looked dicey. On both occasions, the sudden appearance of reaction force personnel had averted bloodshed.

"So how's Marisa?" Gail whispered into his ear.

Achelous turned back to her. "Doing well. Feisty as ever. Still can't believe I traded in a beautiful galactic for a provincial merchant." With Gail in charge of all the optical and aural surveillance equipment orbiting Dianis, it was hard to keep a secret from her. And what woman wasn't curious about who her ex was fooling around with? The fact that Marisa was an indigenous native on a ULUP Class E planet hadn't fazed Gail. She was human like Achelous and knew that neural conditioning, IDB policy, and ULUP regulations could only go so far in curbing passion.

"Well, if you hadn't chased every skirt in town we might have lasted longer." She gave him a teasing smile.

Achelous could never forget those lips, and he was tempted to give them a kiss, but the director began making noises from the podium. "Let's take our seats people, we've business to attend to." As they sat down, Achelous reflected for the thousandth time how things might have been had Gail not stationed out-system for three years. By the time she returned to Dianis, their nuptial contract had expired. Neither person had solicited to renew it, both waiting for what they found when they were back together. But by then, the fire had waned stressed by careers and dampened by the war, but their friendship had grown. In the three years Gail had been gone, Achelous had not pursued another woman, and Gail knew it. It wasn't until after they mutually agreed on the lapsed contract that Achelous had taken up with Marisa.

Clienen Hor, the director of IDB Margel Damansk, brought the meeting to order. Balding, trim of build, crisp in his IDB khakis, Clienen waited until his staff was quiet, his gaze serious but open. Spread around the walls of the gallery were the video screens that connected remote IDB staff based on space stations or other planets in the Margel Damansk quadrant. After wading through some administrivia, the director came to the point of the meeting. "I'm sure you have all heard different rumors. No point in commenting on them as I'm here to inform you of what is official. At the request of the government of the planet Looar Sonreit, the federation has decided to shut down the Margel Damansk transportation arm."

A murmur circled the room, some heads nodding as if they expected this. The Margel Damansk arm bridged fourteen solar systems and covered six thousand light years along its main axis; it afforded access to the heavy metals in the great Margel Damansk asteroid belt. Exploration of the inhabitable planets along the route had been a bonus.

"There is concern from Looar Sonreit that the arm's exposed location makes it an inviting target for the Turboii and their minions.

The fear, rational or not, is that the Turboii might try an end run and sweep this way."

Another low murmur traveled around the room; this time more heads were shaking than nodding. Avaria and its allies were in a death-grip war with the Turboii. Only in the past year had the Avarian Federation finally developed a strategy to halt the advance of the Turboii through federation space. An unpredictable war of strike and counterstrike now prevailed, which was far better than the previous wholesale loss of eighty-four billion humans. Human lives harvested as food for the Turboii and their minion armies. A hand went up in the audience. The director acknowledged it. "Yes?"

"We are nine thousand light years away from the nearest Turboii incursion," the speaker said. "If they wanted to attack the Margel, if they even know where we are, their shift technology is archaic. Their generators are wholly inefficient. We know that. Trying to reach here would be like sailing across an ocean in a bathtub. They're not bringing an army."

The director's nod was ever so slight. "Right. I'm not here to debate Galactic Command risk assessments. Perhaps they would be interested in your opinion?" He paused to let his point sink in. "This is what I'm being told, and I am just passing it on to you. Furthermore," he took a breath, "there is the threat that if the Turboii found the Margel transportation arm functioning, they would somehow be able to infiltrate the transportation network and use it to shift their armies straight to Looar Sonreit, effectively bypassing all of our defenses." In support of his point, the director posted a well-known system diagram of the Margel Damansk transportation arm on the holographic display pedestals distributed around the auditorium. The 3-D graphic showed a large Y-shaped transit system replete with planetary nodes, field-generator stations, and commercial-access zones. The planet of Looar Sonreit sat at the very foot of the Y serving as the gateway to the arm, with Dianis situated at the crucial juncture of the Y. Fourteen solar systems dotted the six-thousand-light-year length of the network. An amorphous cloud hovered at the top of the Y—the immense commercially exploitable Margel Damansk asteroid cloud.

The noise in the chamber rose, and an edge crept into it. More hands shot up, and multiple conversation icons were flashing on the video panels. One person burst out, "And how are the Turboii going to do that? They would need the control codes to get in, and we can change the control codes instantaneously. They would need the codes and signatures for every transportation node they planned to use at transmit time." The voice, belonging to the senior network security manager, became strident. "We already change signatures and codes hourly."

The director's frown deepened. He waited a full minute for the hubbub to subside. Finally, he met the undaunted gaze of the questioner. "As I said, these are the risks that have been expressed to me." Before he could be interrupted again, he held up his hand, and said, "Save your comments for the end and make them useful. I have the same reservations as you do. I took them up with Branch headquarters. They admitted have some of the same issues as you, but I'm told the decision is now final and has been conveyed to Looar Sonreit."

"Final?" The word rang out above the resulting commotion. "Crazy, work lost, extrasolars will run wild, how did this happen so fast," were snippets that reached the director.

He went on. "There were economic considerations as well. The Margel transportation arm has been losing money since the start. With only one mining conglomerate using the system to ship freight, the receipts have been low, and the Transportation Authority wants to close it. The system has also been a substantial burden on IDB resources, and this is a time of war. The IDB is stretched thin. With the war at a crossroads, we've been able to go back into some of the worlds we've freed. But for the IDB, it means evaluating, monitoring, and reconstituting more war-ravaged planets."

Achelous turned to Gail, consternation brewing. She returned his expression with the same surprise. Sensing where the director was going, Achelous stood up. "Clienen," he called out. "Since when has the Margel Damansk been a burden to the IDB? This is what we do. We're not here because we're forced to be here. We're here because we need to be. These planets need our protection and monitoring. ULUP was enacted to prevent—"

"I know why ULUP was enacted, Atch," Clienen responded. "And you are right, it was a poor choice of words, but that is the attitude of many in the government. There is a war on. IDB resources are scarce. We've been recently tasked to reconnoiter and assess three new worlds liberated from the Turboii. Those worlds are a mess. They need our help and assistance the same as Dianis."

The reference to Dianis caught him off guard. Then Achelous waved his arm to take in the audience. "I think we all understand the grave situations those people and planets are in. But the risk to Dianis has not abated. Some might say the need here is greater because Dianis is following its own natural growth and hasn't been decimated by the Turboii. Clienen, closing down the Margel arm is one thing, assuming the security threat is real, but what does that have to do with Dianis?"

"Unfortunately," Clienen said, "with the closing of the transportation nodes, we will be drawing down Margel Damansk IDB resources as well. We will be closing Dianis station and curtailing all operations here. Most of you will be reassigned to new systems and worlds. Probably in assessment and recovery operations. It's not official yet, but I've proposed the entire Margel IDB staff be reassigned to Dominicus sector."

The room erupted: people standing, shouting, staff on the remote monitors gesticulating, and people waving their hands to be heard. Achelous was stunned. It was worse than he expected, much worse. He leaned close to Gail to be heard over the noise. "I thought they might close the arm to commercial traffic. I knew there would be changes, but to shut down all operations including Civilization Monitoring on Dianis is, is just...irresponsible!"

She shook her head slowly. "They can't mean solar recon, too?"

Achelous glanced to where the director was attempting to make some point while surrounded by IDB staff from at least three different departments. "I don't know. I will talk to Clienen after the meeting."

Gail nodded quickly. Achelous had been recruited for the Margel Damansk IDB director's position, but had turned the position down and had recommended Clienen. Achelous believed IDB should be in the field and any job at a holodesk was for administrators, not for field-ops staff. Knowing Achelous had a special motivation to stay on Dianis, Gail said, "I have some contacts I can call, too. The head of the Solar Surveillance data center will know what is going on; he is responsible for allocation of surveillance assets outside of the arm."

Achelous listened to the director's attempts to calm the nerves of the IDB personnel. His reassuring words told them they all still had jobs and the transition out of the Margel would be made with the greatest consideration for the Dianis provincials, and that automated monitoring would be left in place.

But Achelous knew that leaving the planet physically unguarded, even with the sensor grid in auto, would expose the ignorant, unsophisticated population to the depredations of extrasolars.

Achelous felt Gail's hand on his arm. "What are you going to do about Marisa and Boyd?"

"I don't know," he replied, the sinking feeling in the pit of his stomach so intense he felt a wave of vertigo. The sudden realization that his life faced a chasm of calamity overwhelmed him. He had long known that he could not continue his double life forever and that a choice would have to be made. Up to now, he planned to resign and go native. *But now is too soon! I am not ready!* He thought. He was sworn to protect indigenous populations from outside influence, and yet here he was, an outside influence living, loving, and having a child with a provincial. The ULUP penalties for consorting with an indigenous native were steep. Achelous attempted to reconcile his behavior by rationalizing that he was in no way subverting, advancing, or otherwise artificially affecting even the smallest part of Dianis society. To Marisa, Boyd, and even Eliot, he was just an Isuelt trader.

Achelous slouched deep into his chair. The cold reality was that he was living on borrowed time and the bank credits were just about gone. Each sunrise with Marisa brought him one day closer to his time of reckoning. Then his mind leaped at the possibility of bringing Marisa and Boyd off-planet with him and immediately his spirits rose. There were the practical issues of sneaking them off the planet and establishing their Avarian Federation citizenships, but he knew how to do that. He was expert at the system's strengths and weaknesses. They could start a new life on another world, perhaps even on his home world even though he'd not lived there for almost thirty years. Reality, though, was something else. Achelous scowled, he was deluding himself.

"What?" asked Gail.

The crowd in the auditorium began to filter out while Achelous stared at the ceiling. The image of Marisa floated before him. She had built Marinda Merchants and her trading fleet into the largest trading enterprise in Tivor. "She'll never leave," he whispered.

Gail leaned closer. "What was that?"

Achelous groaned and turned to face her. "Marisa, her life is in Tivor. She's like a flower blooming in the spring prairie, pushing through the last snow, a pioneer, the first to face challenges. Others look to her for leadership and inspiration. Marisa needs no invitation for an audience with the aorolmin, the ruler of Tivor. His hall is always open to her, and when she counsels, he listens." It was, he reflected, one of the reasons he had made Tivor his base of operations.

Tivor welcomed all traders regardless of race or creed as long as they were honest. No small part of that came from a culture fostered by Marisa. Miraculously, she had fallen in love with him, of all people, a man twenty years her senior, a man with no known past and a predilection for wandering and resistance to marriage. "Marisa will never leave Dianis. And even if she would, how can I ask it of her?"

Appalled at the notion of extracting a pair of provincials off-planet, Gail stammered, "Oh, and what you would tell her? Um, honey dearest, I'm really an IDB agent, which means Interspecies Development Branch. I'm from an advanced space-faring federation, and I've been reassigned to a new star system. Will you come with me? And, oh, by the way, no one must know you came from Dianis because it's a Class E planet and I'm not supposed to be sleeping with you because you are an indigin." Gail quickly glanced around to ensure no one was eavesdropping. She smiled cynically. "Yeah, right. Can I be around when you tell her? I'd pay to see it."

The gloom around Achelous became palpable. Realizing she had hurt rather than helped, Gail softened her tone. "You'll figure out what to do. And in time she'll understand, just ease her into it. If she gets mad, you'll just have to trust that her love can temper her anger."

Achelous nodded, watching Ivan converse with Clienen. Those two friends of his would factor prominently in any plan he devised. First, he had to decide about Marisa. Explaining the situation to her had its perils, all of which was compounded by the plight of his son if the boy's existence became known. The ULUP rules were clear. Boyd was by birth an extrasolar and subject to extradition. The deportation would happen in the night, conducted by a Ready Reaction team. The child removed from his bed with no alarm. His mother would find the bed empty in the morning and to the end of her miserable days would never know what became of him, destined to search and never find. The pain it would cause her— Achelous swore that under no situation would he allow that to happen.

Chapter 3
Solar Surveillance

IDB Central Station

"That went well," said Achelous, as he caught up with Clienen in the hallway outside the conference room.

The director snorted. "If you call being jumped by an angry mob as going well. And you didn't help things."

"How did you expect us to take it? We spend decades guarding and nurturing this planet only to have much of our life's work rendered irrelevant at the stroke of a bureaucrat's pen."

Clienen stopped, glancing behind him. The hallway was empty. "I knew how they would take it. I knew how I took it. It's not good." He looked at Achelous, who was still dressed in his in-country garb, soft leather boots, baggy trousers, empty handbolt holster at his hip, worn leather vest over a loose, coarse-weave shirt. Achelous's hair was streaked with gray and cropped short for easy keeping in the field. "Achelous, you've lived on this world. I know what it means to you for us to shut down operations."

Achelous averted his eyes and tried to keep from swallowing. "Yes, well, you have to admit this is all quite sudden. What stirred the government on Looar? It's not as if the Turboii threat materialized overnight. They should have been scared witless when we were losing this war. Now that we're pushing the Turboii back, Looar starts peeing puddles on the floor. Why now?"

Clienen resumed walking, and Achelous stayed in step. "Yes, I know. It's a mystery to me as to what rattled Looar Sonreit now. They're in less danger today than they were two or even three years ago."

Feeling like he was coming off the bench to play in a game long underway, Achelous posited, "Doesn't this move have to be approved by the ULUP Board of Control?"

"Yes, and it was. The Looar representatives found allies on the board who were lobbying the federation congress to increase support on the reclaimed worlds. Existing programs and planets that were supposed to be protected were sacrificed. Closing the Margel played right into their hands."

That evening Gail sat at a table in an alcove of the Central Station dining hall. "Looks good," Achelous said, eyeing her dinner as he sat down at the table, "Roast berga?"

"Yes," she said, "it is. I ordered what you asked for, the water muffin. Is it the right season for it?"

He poked the large-shelled crustacean with an appreciative stab of his fork. "No, it's late, but this is firm as I knew it would be. There's a river, a cold river, that flows into the Angraris, south of Mineforest, where the where the water muffins stay firm into early summer. I told our chef about it, and he sends Ready Reaction to the market there to buy them." He savored a bite, trying to forget the turmoil of emotions caused by Clienen's announcement. The water muffin was excellent. "It still amazes me that Class E planets can create products superior to those from the galactic worlds."

She nodded as she cut off a slice of the roast berga.

"We get the domesticated berga from a rancher in Zursh. He takes unstamped 50-penny silver ingots, no questions asked. I suspect he melts the ingots down and pours them as Lamaran pennies and then trades them at a premium. But if he knew how little the silver actually costs us he wouldn't think he was getting such a good deal."

Gail smiled at that. The IDB purchased silver on the local Transportation Authority exchange from miners working the asteroid belt. Silver was not a widely used commodity in the federation, but it was on Dianis. Three-days of harvesting by a contract miner reaped enough silver to fund a year's worth of IDB in-country expenses.

She cut the berga steak, pink and juicy, just the sort of delicacy she couldn't get on Avaria thanks to the loss of so many federation worlds. Her mind returned to the dismal thought of leaving the Margel Damansk and Dianis. "I talked to my friends at Branch headquarters.

Achelous chewed his food thoughtfully, waiting.

"They said to get the definitive word I should contact Resource Planning, so I did."

Achelous swallowed. That Gail had held back her news until now worried him.

"All orbital assets are being withdrawn."

Achelous's eyes grew wide. He put his fork down. "All of them? Why?"

Gail nodded, a sadness in her eyes, a slump to her shoulders. "Yes. They were very open about it, no secret there. The order is in. All surveillance assets orbiting Dianis are to be captured and reallocated. Even the old Century Mark IVs that have been floating around here for seventy-five years. Can you believe it? It will cost more to capture them, shift them back to the refurb lab, and then shift them to a new world than what it would cost to buy a new Sunbird. Someone's math is really bad."

"All of them?" he asked again. "Why?" He knew he was unfair, but Gail was the head of Solar Surveillance for all IDB operations in the Arm.

She shook her head. "I don't know."

"What about ground-based assets? Sensors, generators, nanobots, supply depots..."

"That's not their area, but they heard it would be too much work to pull them out and the potential for cultural disruption too high."

Achelous threw up his arms. "I should bloody well think so!"

Gail looked around at the other diners. "Quiet."

But Achelous's blood was boiling. "Too much work to pull them out? None of them should be pulled out. Nothing. Not the satellites, deep space probes, shift sensors, or ground arrays. They are all needed. We can draw down the staff, mothball Central Station, cancel field ops, but how are we supposed to remotely monitor Dianis if they strip out the sensors?"

"They don't intend to remotely monitor Dianis."

The enormity of the statement flattened him. Sitting for a long moment, his emotions ran the gamut of denial, anger, and finally resolution. Seeking to find the logic in the situation, a logic that eluded him, Achelous said, "Okay, hold the thought about the remoting monitoring, because that can't be true, I won't let it be true. Answer me this, you think it will cost more to refurb and reposition the old Century's than it would to buy and orbit new Sunbirds?"

"Yes," Gail said.

"So why would the IDB go through the trouble and cost to pull the ancient big eyes and yet have the sense to leave the dirt pods intact?"

Gail didn't answer. They both quietly speculated as to the reason. The best strategy to catch sophisticated corsairs was a layered system of deep space, orbital, and ground arrays. Deep space arrays detected spacecraft shifting into the system. Orbital satellites detected ships entering high orbit around the planet. Ground sensors tracked and monitored surface movement. Detection by one layer might be averted, but continually avoiding all three was exceedingly difficult. However, if only the ground sensors were functional evading exposure would be much easier. Thinking that Achelous was implying that the IDB might be complicit in aiding such circumvention, Gail said, "You're not suggesting that the IDB secretly intends to open Dianis?"

"No," he said earnestly. "But the effect is the same. Dianis will be open to incursions. I just want the facts so we can establish the real rationale for this decision. The actions of Looar and Branch headquarters appear illogical. When something seems illogical, it is only because the evaluator does not have all the facts and proper context. Even the ravings of a madman become explicable once you know how his thought processes work."

Irritated, Gail leaned across the table, keeping her voice low. "Why would the IDB purposely open Dianis to extrasolar intervention?"

"Maybe it's not us. Maybe we're being forced to do it from the federation."

"Oh, Achelous now you're seeing rift wraiths." She twirled a finger in the air. "It's been three years since the last corsair was caught in Dianis near-space and a year since one was intercepted in the Margel. What has changed to make Dianis suddenly so popular that someone with that kind of power would conspire to pull the IDB?"

He ignored her question and pressed on. "The location and zones of detection for the ground sensors are secret, but anyone with enough influence to get the IDB to pull solar-surveillance gear would have the ability to get access to the Dianis sensor grid maps. They wouldn't need to pull the ground sensors if they knew how to avoid them."

"Who? And what lever do they have on the IDB? We've been immune to those attempts. There are checks and balances, oversight, reporting. Smokes, Achelous, it takes approval by the ULUP board, even if they subverted IDB priorities."

He nodded. "I'll admit it's far-fetched. But maybe the Matrincy is involved. They might have their own reasons—"

"Damn, Achelous, now you think the Matrincy is involved!" For Gail, the Matrincy was the bulwark against all that could go bad in government. The Matrincy was the differentiator that set the fifty-planet Avarian Federation apart from other galactic democracies. The order of sixthsense adepts guided federation politicians through the pitfalls of special interests, lobbyists, flawed legislation, and the corrupting influence of power and money. It wasn't perfect; its failures were sometimes spectacular, but many cosmic sociologists believed the Matrincy was the critical apparatus that enabled the federation to climb past the many evolutionary ceilings that constrained civilization and cultural progression. From her vantage point of observing primitive societies, Gail fervently agreed with the sociologists that without the Matrincy the Avarian Federation would have collapsed hundreds of years ago.

"I don't know if the Matrincy is involved, but you said it didn't make sense to refurb antiquated satellites instead of manufacturing new surveillance platforms. So we have to keep digging." Achelous toyed with his half-eaten water muffin. "There's something you should know that I haven't told you."

"Oh?"

"Well, I couldn't really. It's classified and restricted to Civilization Monitoring." He shoved his plate aside, his appetite gone.

"What level?" Gail arched an eyebrow.

"Top secret, critical."

Gail blinked. "What subject and who classified it?" The edge to her voice came from her own security clearance, which was top secret, with all subgroups.

"A strategic-findings report. And I classified it."

Gail's eyes widened. "What on Dianis can be deemed top secret and critical?"

Achelous answered, "Did you know there is an aquamarine deposit near Mount Mars?"

Gail's platinum hair shimmered in the sconce lighting as she flicked it back. "Mount Mars? Yes, but it's not commercially useful. Everything I've read in our geological surveys indicates low-grade aquamarine only. No type 5."

"That's why I classified the report critical. Mount Mars is type 5 with beryllium concentrations above the flux-clouding threshold," Achelous said with finality. "There are at least two type-5 deposits that we know of. The other one is on the continent of Linkoralis. The provincials there discovered it while digging a silver mine. It didn't take long for the Linkoralis Paleowright archbishop to get involved."

"There's type 5 on Dianis?" She sat back. "Oh. That's a problem." Struggling with the notion, she asked, "And what about the Paleowrights? Aren't they the least of our problems? What are the Paleowrights going to do with aquamarine-5? It's not as if they can build an aural field generator. They think aquamarine is a status symbol, good for making expensive jewelry. They don't even know the difference between the base version and the type 5 variant, let alone how aquamarine-5 emits aural energy." She laughed in frustration, "Stimulating it with an electron charge is far beyond their comprehension."

"Yes, but this could cause serious problems for the people on Dianis. The Paleowrights are aquamarine-crazy. They'll start digging it up everywhere, and then a simple solar system fly-by scan of a contract miner pinging the planet will light up the ship's aural sensors. The type 5 will be exposed on the surface, not buried and concealed in hard-rock deposits."

"Well, it's not like the Paleowrights will find it everywhere," she was hedging, and they both knew it."

"Gail, one mine is enough."

They sat there staring at each other.

Finally, Achelous broke the silence. "Marisa...," he paused, "when the Paleowrights hear about the aquamarine on Mount Mars, they'll persuade their Drakan allies to intervene. Given where Mount Mars sits, it may not take much to convince the Drakan Empire to move. Your own orbital surveillance has tracked the buildup of their forces on the Western frontier. They are getting ready for a fight with the Western Alliance. This could be a trigger. No one on the continent will be safe."

Gail suspected that Achelous was forming a thesis. She knew how his mind worked. "Okay, we're IDB, there's nothing we can do about the Paleowrights and the Drakan Empire. Provincial free will, that's what we're here to protect. If the Drakans go to war for the Paleowrights—" they locked eyes, "then war it is. But extrasolars we can do something about. It's us versus them." She thought about the rarity of aquamarine-5. The governments of the few non–Class E worlds that had type 5 licensed the mining rights to it for exorbitant prices. "I agree; a new aquamarine-5 source—even on a Class E world—would attract galactic attention.

Relieved she agreed with him, Achelous said, "With the state of the federation commodities market and the demands the war is putting on resources, Clienen and I decided to file the strategic-findings report as top secret and critical so we wouldn't attract attention to Dianis. But we did have to record our assessment of provincial mining activities per ULUP, so we filed the aquamarine discoveries in the monthly ops journal and left out any mention of type-5. Which has me concerned."

She arched an eyebrow. "Does anyone ever read the monthly journals? They're diaries of some introverted sociologist or cultural anthropologist like you slogging through the mud with indigenous primitives. Agent Footsore reports increased starvation rates on planet Alpha Xray due to the summer's crop failure. Who cares beyond us?"

"That was my original thought, and we did need to account for our actions and document the deposits somehow. Dianis won't be Class E forever." Achelous scowled. "But if someone is interested and gains access to the Dianis IDB ops journals they can scan for aquamarine. They'd find the references easily enough even though we kept the exact locations of the deposits out of the journal." Achelous paused. It occurred to him if there was to be conflict over aquamarine amongst the provincials, uglier still would be the conflict between extrasolars and provincials. And the most likely location would be the mine on Mount Mars as the provincial powers were the most concentrated in that region. A potential conflict that reminded him of the psychological scars he still bore from an encounter with a clandestine Nordarken Mining operation on Ilos Septi.

"So I respect your need for secrecy," Gail said, "but Solar Surveillance should know about these sites so we can prioritize them."

"Well, you know now, and in truth, we've been sidetracked. When we were assessing the aquamarine-5 deposits, Baryy Maxmun came across a clan of Timberkeeps at the foot of Mount Mars that has sixthsense."

Gail shifted in her chair. Blonde hair slid from behind an ear, and she brushed it back. "The whole clan?"

"No..."

"Well—how many?" Gail personally knew only two adepts. One in a thousand humans had measurable sixthsense abilities, and of those, only one in ten could call upon the ability in a rudimentary fashion after gene therapy unlocked the ability. Those few who exhibited any talent after unlock were recruited by the Matrincy and sent to their school for adepts on Avaria.

"Baryy did a survey and found 20 percent of the population had what he thought was at least class-two sensitivity."

"Twenty percent! How did Baryy figure that? How did he get involved enough with the clan to conduct such a survey?"

"I know, I know. I was surprised, too. That's two hundred times normal. So I tasked him to set up a trading post in Wedgewood, the town on Mt Mars, and learn everything he could. He's created a database of individuals, their ages, sex, and skills he's seen firsthand. He has data for three hundred of the eighteen hundred members of the clan. I went there on a trading mission to restock his trade goods because I had to see for myself. At his cabin, I watched kinetic kids playing a form of plot-smack without actually touching the ball with their feet. The kids explained the rules to me. They can only smack the plot using a *twip*, a flick of their mind. In other words, they were using telekinesis."

"Kinetic kids?"

"Yeah. That's what Baryy calls them."

"This is fantastic," Gail said breathlessly. "If the news of this..." Gail took a deep breath. "You were serious about the Matrincy. You do think they are a threat."

Achelous's frown said everything Gail needed to know.

"As a Class E world the Matrincy cannot recruit—smokes they can't even contact the sensitives on Dianis," she said. "But are you trying to say that if we aren't here to enforce ULUP, the Matrincy would..."

Achelous's multi-func chimed, and the recombinant chip embedded in his thigh buzzed. He held up his hand to stop her, opened the device, and scanned the message. "I have an alert from our communication center. They have a priority message for me from an in-country courier. In this case one of our messenger pigeons."

Gail slid her plate aside and pressed the dish-retrieval command on the table control. Achelous's Civilization Monitoring teams used messenger pigeons as one means to communicate with provincial contacts. She waited while he scanned the message, something he refrained from doing unless it was important. "It's in code, of course. The first letter is M, which stands for you know who."

A faint smile crossed Gail's lips. "A little love note?"

Intent on deciphering the message with the one-time pad he and Marisa agreed on, a code not privy to the IDB, Achelous said, "Hmm, unfortunately, no. I don't get many love letters nowadays." He almost said being married with kids turned romance into responsibility, but he was, of course, not married. Looking up, “She says pirates have attacked one of her ships, and she is sailing on the *Wind March* to intercept them.”

“Why does she have to go?” Gail asked with a frown. “I mean, doesn't she have—”

“Captains who can do the job for her?” Achelous shook his head and smiled sadly. “The war with the pirates is personal to her. She thinks they are sponsored by the Paleowrights. That they’re being paid to deliberately attack her ships because she convinced the aorolmin of Tivor to reject Paleowright demands to embargo trade with Linkoralis. It goes back to aquamarine, of course, everything eventually does. The Paleowrights wanted to set up a customs operation in Tivor to inspect cargo that they suspect might have come from the Linkoralis continent. He turned them down. Ever since then there’s been a big increase in piracy, most of it targeting Tivor shipping. The aorolmin's fleet is in the fight against the pirates too, but Marisa has as many ships as they do.” Achelous glanced back down at the decoded message. “She wants me to come home to be with Boyd while she is gone.” *Home, what a strange word,* he reflected. *Was Tivor truly his home? Or was it Central Station? What is home? Where is it?*

“So the Paleowrights want to inflict retribution on Marisa through the pirates?”

“Yes, they do that out of habit when anyone defies them, but in this case, I think it is also for economics,” he said, not looking up.

“Economics? Since when are the Paleowrights interested in economics?”

Achelous laughed, looking up from his multi-func. “Beneath all their pomp, blustering, arrogance, and pontificating, they are all about economics.”

Looking at Gail’s confused expression, Achelous realized he should explain, but apologized instead. “I have to get down to the shift station, and ride for Tivor, but when I get back, we can discuss what drives the church of our good Paleowrights.”

“If you think she's at risk, I can put a tracker on her. The *Wind March*?”

He nodded.

“I'll have Orbital track the ship. We have Marisa’s aural signature on file.”

He smiled gratefully. “Thanks.” Gail’s knowing that Solar Surveillance had Marisa’s aural signature did not bother him. He had scanned it himself and provided it for just this eventuality.

As he stood, about to leave, Gail said, “And Atch. We need to talk about the Matrincy. I think it is ridiculous that,” she stopped and confirmed the tables nearby were empty, “they would be complicit in our departure just so they could recruit sixthsense adepts.”

He shrugged and walked away.

Chapter 4
Far Shore

City of Tivor

"My lady," a servant called, trying to get Marisa's attention over the noise of bookkeepers, trade negotiators, and ship's officers hard at work in the office of Marinda Merchants. Marisa stood next to a caravanserai who was wearing striped pantaloons and a baggy blouse tied tight with a purple sash, his bivouac cap festooned with a jaunty feather. Marisa held Boyd on her hip taking a moment out of her busy day as Boyd's nanny hovered nearby. She listened to the caravanserai, still dusty from his journey, explain the exchange rate he'd managed on the trade goods from Falda, all the while ignoring Boyd's sticky, candy-coated hand on her chiffon blouse. Her raven hair secured in a coiled bun framed her arched eyebrows. Boyd waved his hand at her perfectly sculpted nose. Marisa shushed him, twisting her full lips in a mother's smile.

"My lady," the servant called louder. A pause settled across the room. A senior ship's captain looked up from his crew's list and refit schedule. Marisa turned slowly, saying, "No, no," removing Boyd's gooey hand. The nanny moved deftly with a towel to wipe his hand.

"A messenger has arrived from the harbormaster, he is quite out of breath and says it is urgent."

"Here, Bec," Marisa said, as she started to hand Boyd to his nanny, but he made a face. "No, mama, no go."

Marisa sighed and stalked off to the door with Boyd still on her hip and Bec in tow.

The messenger, a gangling lamp-lighter, twelve-year-old, stood in the hall foyer, cap in hand.

Before Marisa could say anything, the boy burst out, "Lady, the harbormaster, has received word from the *Far Shore*, they are being chased by pirates."

"The *Far Shore*? There must be some mistake."

"No, ma'am," The boy rung his cap in his hands. "Bolivour said the message came from the *Far Shore*. He's in contact with them now."

Marisa's frown deepened. "How can that be? There's no telepath onboard the *Far Shore.*" Telepaths were too rare to crew them on long, dull trade routes.

The boy looked uncertain about contradicting the mistress. "Bolivour said the Silver Cup sent him the message."

Marisa's scowl transformed into surprise then acknowledgment. She lifted Boyd off her hip and passed him to the nanny. When he threatened to throw a fit, she was firm. "Mamma must go. I will be back." She kissed Boyd to shush him and turned to a servant. "Fetch my fast carriage." She gave one last fleeting smile to Boyd as the nanny hustled him off, then she walked outside with the messenger.

"So the Silver Cup booked passage for a telepath on the *Far Shore*?" she asked him.

The messenger shrugged his bony shoulders. "Dunno, ma'am, but there's one aboard."

Marissa considered the implications. The *Far Shore,* one of her largest trading barques, was the pride of her fleet. Never before had pirates been so bold as to attack a vessel so large and presumably so far out to sea, preying instead on coastal schooners running supplies along the coast. It was fortuitous indeed that a Silver Cup telepath was onboard as a passenger. The aorolmin kept his expensive telepath Bolivour stationed with the harbormaster to help in routing ship traffic. *And today,* Marisa thought, *that is a good thing.*

Marisa tapped her foot impatiently until her carriage came clattering out of the stables pulled by two black matching eenus.

"Shall I go, ma'am?" The boy was fidgeting with something in his pocket and shuffling his sandaled feet; his eyes on the traffic on the road.

"If you're going to the harbor master's shack, I can give you a ride."

The boy said, "No, ma'am, uh, I mean, yes, ma'am, but I'd rather run." And with that, he darted off like an uncoiled spring, weaving his way between carts, pedestrians, and eenus at a full run.

Marisa climbed into the carriage and wondered who would get to the wharf first, the runner or the carriage. The main avenue was so crowded she ordered the driver to take side streets. "And don't mind the ruts or bumps. Make haste." The wharf was a mile away, and she composed herself to the wait.

Pulling up to the harbor master's shack, she saw the runner leave the building and scamper off on another errand.

"Master Volden, you have word for me?" Marisa inquired, as she strode into the cramped quarters of the master's office. The room smelled of wet hemp, canvas, mold, and tar. The harbormaster sat behind a makeshift desk of three planks resting on two barrels standing on end. A young man, a scribe, sat cross-legged atop a coil of four-inch hawser in the corner scribbling in the harbor journal. She didn't particularly like Volden; he was grossly fat, unkempt, and wore his lunch on the front of his faded captain's jacket. As crude as he appeared, however, he managed to run a tidy harbor and didn't waste the aorolmin's funds on frivolities. How he managed to keep the harbor orderly Marisa could not fathom.

"Aye," Volden grumbled, not bothering to rise or remove the smoking pipe from his mouth. He nodded at a door off to the side. Marisa let a tinge of distaste twitch her lips, but she turned the knob and pushed the door open. It was dark inside; shades were drawn down tightly on the windows; incense hung heavy in the air. The room was little more than a cubby with another barrel desk, a stool, and an unmade cot. Bolivour sat hunched over the barrel, a quill pen in hand and papers scattered about. *Why do these telepaths always have incense?* Marisa mused, as she stepped in and shut the door. Bolivour had a distant look on his face as he stared blankly at the drawn shade in front of him. Occasionally, he would scrawl distractedly on a page. Furtively, Marisa peered at the parchment. Most of Bolivour's notes were doodles and idle scribblings, but "Far Shore, lateen-rigged, three miles, and full sail" stood out. She knew better than to interrupt a telepath when they were "engaged." So with a wrinkle to her nose, and two fingers plucked the corner of the blanket and pulled it to cover the cot. She drew her cloak tight and sat down to wait.

Time passed. Bolivour finally exhaled a long sigh, set his pen down, and stretched.

"Well?" Marisa asked, outwardly patient, though her insides resembled tangled lines on a dock.

Bolivour jumped, letting out a yelp. "Oh, you frightened me. I sensed you had come in, but I forgot you were here. Quiet as a sail mouse you are." He looked ancient and wore wire-bound round spectacles over his rummy eyes. His long hawkish nose was almost as thin as he was.

"You're in contact with the *Far Shore*?" Marisa prompted.

Bolivour nodded vigorously, cracking a broad smile and showing a surprisingly full set of even white teeth.

At least he's friendly, she thought, *compared to the grump outside.*

"Yes, they are being chased by three pirate sloops. Big ones though, three masts each. The captain suspected something was amiss and put on full sail about midmorning. Fortunately, the wind has been picking up, and the pirates had to reduce sail. Otherwise, they would be gaining on him every hour. The waves are rising to thirteen feet, so he's hoping he can leave them in the heavy seas."

"You're talking with a Silver Cup telepath?"

He bobbed enthusiastically. "Yes, I'm touching with her. We know each other, so it was easy for her to reach me."

His head shook in a manner Marisa suspected was involuntary. *Nerves,* she thought, *like frayed rope.* "Does the captain think he can evade them?" she asked.

He shook his head unsteadily. "He hopes he can avoid them till nightfall. He mentioned changing course in the dark."

There was a knock on the door and none other than Commodore Sharper, the commander of the Tivorian navy, stuck his head in. "Ah, there you are lady, in touch with the *Far Shore* are we?" Before she could reply, he said to Bolivour, "Did you get word to the *Sea Bright*?"

"Yes, the captain said he would come about and make best speed to intercept the *Far Shore.* Though if the *Far Shore* changes course in the night, the *Sea Bright* will miss her."

The commodore eased his bulk into the tiny room and shut the door, leaning against it. Resplendent in his naval uniform with gold braid and tassels, the fleet commander star pinned on his breast, the commodore gave a sigh. "Right, ask the telepath on the *Sea Bright* for the best course for the *Far Shore* to shift to at, say, two bells. Coordinate that with the *Far Shore*. Tell them both that the tide is right, and the *Intrepid* will sail within the hour. With this easterly blow, she should be able to rendezvous with them at first light tomorrow."

Concern clouded Marisa's face. "Commodore, if I recall, the *Intrepid* is a ketch and the *Sea Bright* a light brig. Do you think you might be outmanned? The larger pirate ships can carry well over a hundred men."

The commodore let out another sigh. "Our other ships are to the north, the *Far Shore* is a day to the south, and the *Sea Bright* is the only one within reach that has a telepath. Our crews are well armed. We'll not shirk from a fight." He paused then added, "Pirates are hawks when chasing merchantmen, but there's nothing to be gained by tangling with a man-o-war. I reckon they'll change course the minute they see our pennants."

Marisa stood, forcing Bolivour to lean back on his stool lest his long nose brush her bosom. "The *Wind March* is in port, she's twice the size of the *Intrepid,* and in these seas probably faster. I can have her captain ready to sail with the *Intrepid*. Perhaps we can do more than just chase them away."

The commodore quickly nodded. "The *Wind March* has six ballistae that will come in handy. Can you put warriors on her, or shall I roust my marines and ask the aorolmin for a company of archers?"

Marissa looked at Bolivour. "I will ask the Silver Cup for assistance. They'll want to rescue their precious telepath." She exchanged a grin with him. Then to the commodore, "Make your request for archers from the aorolmin, I'll have the *Wind March* ready to receive them."

Chapter 5
Wind March

At Sea

The wind buffeted Marisa, rocking her with the motion of the canted deck. Her long black hair tied in a bun sequestered under the hood of her sea-cape. An errant wisp of a hair caught in the breeze. She braced her arm against the gunwale and rode the surge of the deck beneath her feet. The *Wind March* raced with a following sea; the grey overcast sky low with scudding clouds. Dawn was thirty minutes past, but the sea and horizon were still dark shades of grey. The sails, the few the captain dared carried, were stretched taught in the gale. The foremast yards were bare lest the pressure on the hull force the bow deep in the running swells and cause her to broach. The barque took a wave on her port bow, rose, and shuddered through it, green water breaking over the bowsprit. Marisa blinked from salt spray pelting her face but held her focus on the dark horizon.

"The lookout will see them before we do," Akallabeth said as he shuffled up beside her, grasping a lifeline strung from the forward mast.

Marisa nodded absently.

Akallabeth, the overseer of the Silver Cup Courier's Guild, peered back over his shoulder. The aorolmin's *Intrepid,* a smaller two-masted ketch, continued to fall astern, unable to carry as much cloth or cope as strongly in the pitching seas. Earlier, the commodore, embarked aboard the *Intrepid,* had signaled to the *Wind March* to reduce sail so they could maintain station. But Marisa, owner of the *Wind March,* had instructed her captain to make all due haste. The *Far Shore,* sister to the *'March,* was in dire straits.

Not for the first time did Akallabeth consider chastising the lady for venturing out to sea, in a storm, in the face of what might be a bloody fight, but he knew her reputation. No shrinking violet, Marisa had become the proprietor of the largest, west-coast trading firm by solving her own problems. A cutlass dangled from her hip, and he'd seen an expensive chain mail hauberk under her green velvet cape.

A sailor came weaving up the deck, stopping behind a mast, and then again behind the capstan to wait for a gust and a wash of water to slosh past. He made it up to them at the forepeak. "Captain's respects my Lady, we've had word from the aorolmin's *Sea Bright,* she's been forced to heave-to and launch a boat for a man overboard. The *Sea Bright's* captain expects they'll be delayed by half a glass or more." The sailor was breathing hard, water dripping copiously from his slicker.

Marisa flashed him a concerned look, then her gaze hardened and she said to Akallabeth, "Are your men ready?" It was her way of saying they would go alone.

Akallabeth gave her a level stare, a slight smile forming, "Aye, Lady. Fire Eye and me lads are ready. Lieutenant Rayamars and his archers are looking a bit green, but their bows are strung, though in this wind I don't know how much good they'll be. Master-At-Arms Sifle and his marines are, well, calm as rocks in a pond. Been through this before they have. They'll all be spoiling for a fight soon."

The barest flicker of a smile crossed Marisa's lips, her dark eyes flashing. She said to the sailor, "Thank you. You may go."

"We should go below and get out of the wind and water, so we're not chilled to the bone when the fighting starts," Akallabeth offered.

Her smile deepened. "What... don't you have storms on the plains?"

He laughed, and the gale whipped it away. The lady made reference to his Plains Doroman heritage. Like all Doromen he was a half-hand shorter than the average human, broader in the chest, and thicker in the leg. Unlike other Doromen, the Plains tribes wore arm-rings of silver, one for each battle they'd won. Underneath Akallabeth's

oilskin, he had seventeen arm rings. "Storms yes, waves no."

The bow descended into a deep trough and Marisa called, "Brace yourself." She turned to face aft, pulled up her hood, and squatted down, one hand holding onto the lifeline, and the other the port railing.

Akallabeth, intent on watching her take precaution, almost didn't react in time. He caught sight of the wall of green water and ducked, clutching the foremast just as the wave crashed over them. For a moment, he couldn't breathe, and then the dregs were swirling at his feet, and coruscating aft as the bow rose, heaving the maidenhead high over the wave crest.

Marisa stood and grasped him by the arm. "Come on; let's get to the captain's cabin before you drown."

"Aye," he said lurching down the deck, following the retreating water, "that's a bloody good idea."

They shut the door to the passageway and headed to the captain's cabin when the first mate intercepted them. "Word from the *Far Shore,* they've engaged the pirates with their aft ballistae. She has the wind with her, and they have range on the pirates, but that'll not last long."

Marisa digested the news. "How long until we close on them?"

Knowing the lady, the mate had anticipated the question, "They're just north of Palisade Point, and are tacking northwest. Captain says we're twenty minutes north of the point ourselves."

Marisa drew back her hood. "Then we should see them now, but the visibility..."

The mate nodded, "With these squalls, it's down to less than a mile. We'll be right on top of them by the time we spot her."

Marisa turned to Akallabeth, "Better alert your men—"

The first mate, interrupted, "I've already passed word to the lieutenant and the master at arms. They're bringing their men on deck."

Through the door window, she could see warriors climbing up through the hatches. "May Mother keep them safe. We'll not be wanting a man overboard."

"Aye," agreed Akallabeth.

Then the seven-foot form of Prince Fire Eye emerged from the companion hatch. He wore an oilskin cloak under which he had a breechclout and a wool vest studded with steel plates, but was otherwise naked. He caught sight of Marisa and Akallabeth standing in the passage door and sauntered over to them. The deck heaved in a sudden pitch, and the prince set his toe claws into the deck just in time to spread his arms and hit the doorframe with heavy, leathery palms. His snout came within inches of Marisa. Curious, his forked tongue flicked out to test her scent.

Marisa recoiled in surprise, never having been that close to a wryvern, let alone licked by one. Akallabeth laughed. The wryvern—commonly known as a lizardman--turned his head and gave her a long baleful stare, the golden eye was bisected by a vertical, black pupil. He was so close Marisa could see striations in the gold orb. She felt a shiver as if he were sizing her up for dinner. Then with a flare of his nostrils, he pivoted and trotted back along the rolling and pitching deck as if he were anywhere but on a storm-tossed sea. She caught herself, fascinated by how the reptilian held his tail just above the planking, snaking it back and forth, somehow able to avoided bashing against the myriad of objects along the passage.

Marisa, recovering from her surprise, said, "Mother's Spirit, he's a monster."

"Aye, that he is my lady, that he is." Akallabeth gave a chuckled born from experience as an overseer for the Silver Cup and long friendship with the reptile. "But, he's our monster."

Even to the well-traveled Marisa Fire Eye was an anomaly, one of a handful of lizardmen she had ever seen. One of three sentient reptile species on Dianis, lizardmen were the rarest, and to the uneducated easily confused with troglodytes.

"Tell me, how did you ever recruit him to your guild?" she asked, brushing dried sea salt from her face.

"Ah," Akallabeth said with meaningful inflection, watching the men marshal on deck, "he's an outcast from his nation, forced to flee under penalty of death. His oldest brother, King Aregû-lemo-tăk, assumed their father's throne under dubious conditions and killed Fire Eye's next older brother when the brother charged Aregû with their father's murder. Fire Eye, as is his want to wander, was away. When he returned to Horic ăk a Zûn, their ancestral homeland deep in the southeast, the only place they live, he was warned that Aregû-lemo-tăk was no longer approachable and had ordered the imprisonment of all his father's councilors. Fire Eye ignored the warnings, and when he entered the palace, the guards attempted to take him prisoner." The overseer chuckled. "Fire Eye is not average, not even for a lizardman. He fought his way clear of the lodge and escaped. He's been in exile ever since; that was three years ago."

"Does he harbor revenge? To lose your homeland, everything..." Marisa searched Akallabeth's face for signs of Fire Eye's pain. But the bravo admitted no emotion, not for himself or his friend.

"He's no talker, but if you win his trust, you win his loyalty. He's saved my life twice now. I offered to help him bring his brother, the king, to justice." Akallabeth scuffed a nailed boot on the deck. "I remember he gave me that look of his, the one he gave you just now. That inscrutable look. Then he flicked his tongue twice which means yes." Akallabeth kept scuffing the deck. "Who knows what goes on in that reptilian brain of his? They're definitely not human thoughts. But

I dare say he will hold me to my offer. With lizardmen, watch what you say, they have no thoughts of lying, and hence no tolerance for even the smallest fib."

A long silence ensued as they watched the soldiers seek refuge from the wind and spray as best they could.

"Sail ho!" Came the call from the quarterdeck, relayed from the lookout in the crow's nest.

Marisa made to step on deck when the third mate came pounding up the ladder from below where Bolivour was sequestered. Marisa caught the mate by the arm, "You have word?"

The young officer stopped, "Huh?" Belatedly he recognized their merchant princess under her hood and heavy cloak, "Uh, sorry me Lady. Yes, I come from Bolivour, he has word from the *Far Shore*."

"Then speak it and hurry on your way," Marissa said.

"They've put a harpoon fair through the bow of the lead pirate, below the water line. Timed it perfectly, caught her cresting a wave. The pirate vessel has veered off. The other two pirates are closing in. A half mile separates them, and they are exchanging fire."

Marisa released her grasp, thanked him, and followed up the ladder after him.

The wind tugged at her hood as she looked aft over the mountainous grey seas. Something came and went, in the far distance. *Did I imagine that?* She wondered. *Or was that the barest flicker of Intrepid's topmast?* She turned forward. Surprised, she tapped Akallabeth on the shoulder and pointed.

He took stock. "Aye, we'll be fighting the pirates by ourselves."

Out of a squall, the white sails of the *Far Shore* rose, and Marisa's heart rose with them, as the ship crested a wave. Over the wave, the bow sank into a deep trough. The copper plating of *Far Shore's* stern, tarnished a pale green, came clear of the sea. Her captain had all the lower courses spread regardless of the gale. The port-quarter ballistae fired, marked by a long black dart arching away at a low-slung sloop. The *Far Shore* was in the fight.

Three pirate vessels were heaving and yawing, one, off to the port, appeared to be veering away, while the other two made to close on the merchantman. Marisa had hoped the sight of two ships, one a warship, bearing down on the pirates would scare them off, but the *Intrepid* would be out of sight to the pirates.

She spotted a midshipman and bid him fetch her coif, helmet, and shield.

Akallabeth was gesticulating with the captain, neither of whom could she hear over the gusting wind. Akallabeth stepped back to her, "He says there's no sign of the *Sea Bright,* but he didn't expect any, not for another half glass or so."

In the flat light, Marisa's her eyes were black holes beneath her hood. "Then it's up to us." She approached the captain. "Signal *Far Shore*. We'll cover their escape. They're to make for the *Intrepid."*

The captain, stationed close to the helm, gave the orders to the signalman. "We'll be running straight down on the bastards and were not carrying a cargo of sheep!" He called out over the gale.

Akallabeth gave a quick nod to Marisa and weaved his way to the ladder. Down on the foredeck, Prince Fire Eye waited with the other Silver Cup bravos and the Tivor Marines.

Each time *Wind March* crested a wave green water broke across the bow and ran down the deck, washing the soldiers up to their knees. Now the *Far Shore* was healing hard over to starboard as she made her turn to backtrack past the *Wind March.* The sea between the two vessels churned a field of foaming white caps. To either side of the *Far Shore,* a three-masted pirate sloop stalked her, no doubt preparing to board. In the distance, obscured by mist and cloud, lay the coast of Isuelt. As long as the wind remained out of the northeast the ships were safe from running aground, but it was threatening to veer, and if it should, while the ships were grappled, the shoals off the headland would rip their keels out.

At the crest of the next wave Lieutenant Rayamars, in his first sea battle, took in the breathtaking sight of the *Far Shore,* the big merchantman, heeled over, her sails half furled and tight against the wind as she cut across the bow of the *Wind March* a half-mile distant. Immediately to her starboard, a pirate sloop was overtaking her. Ballistae were firing back and forth between the ships. Riding low in the water, the pirate ships cut through the waves like javelins, but they were taking deep water on their decks. Often completely inundated, Rayamars marveled that none of the pirates were washed over the side as the seas spilled back into the ocean. The sloop nearest to them was crammed with armed men, its sails were cut in a triangular lateen shape foreign to the square-riggers of the northern traders, marking the pirate of Warkenvaal origin. The second marauder was attempting a run at the *Far Shore's* starboard side. The rain had let up, and the wind was beginning to slacken, but the sea churned, a cresting tumult of wild water. As Rayamars watched the merchantman begin hoisting more sail; the two portside ballistae fired hammer harpoons, designed to smash planking. Now the *Far Shore* began taking the worst of it as the catapults on the lead pirate threw shrapnel, and doused the quarterdeck in blood and carnage. Their position untenable, the captain and helm were forced down the after hatch to pilot the ship from below.

The *Wind March* veered to starboard, placing her on a collision course with the *Far Shore*, caught in between them was the lead marauder. The distance closed perceptibly. "Archer's! On my command!" Rayamars yelled, his voice carrying clearly to the Marisa on the quarterdeck. Forty Tivorian archers, hiding below the railing, stood lining the port side and notched their arrows.

"Alright lads, time teach these bastards that Tivor fights for its own," called Master-at-Arms Sifle, the aorolmin's senior Guard commander.

Not only was this was Rayamars first sea battle, but it was also his first battle as a lieutenant after being promoted. It was his first true command, whereas Sifle was a grizzled veteran of over two decades serving three different aorolmin. His forty marines arrayed themselves in four neat platoons with grapples and boarding ladders. Among them Prince Fire Eye stood at the very peak of the bow, the tip of his tail flicking back and forth. Every wave doused him, but he stood there unmoving and resolute like the maidenhead perched below, impervious to weather, ignorant of fear. Fire Eye's focus was on one thing: the leap.

Akallabeth crouched beside the capstan with the six other Silver Cap bravos. As spray dripped from their helms and soaked their cloaks, they talked about mundane things like sanding and oiling their chainmail, seemingly uncaring to their task ahead. Their objective in the operation was to kill or capture the pirate captain while Sifle and the Marines, backed by the sailors, attacked the pirate crew. The railing of the long, sleek pirate sloops rode substantially lower than the merchantmen. That added height meant the archers could shoot down, and the Marines could swing on lines from above.

"Port bow, fire!" Bellowed the second mate in charge of the *Wind March's* ballistae. A heavy, iron-tipped, five-foot-long bolt sprang from the mount with a loud *ka-chunk*. The bolt barely arched before it thudded audibly into the deck of the pirate. Splinters flew, and the pirate crew scrambled for cover like agitated ants.

"Hurray!" came an enthusiastic cheer from the *Wind March* crew.

A pirate standing in the bow of the sloop, holding a grappling hook in his hand aimed to heave it at the railing of the *Far Shore,* paused, peering back at his captain.

"Portside fire!" A *ka-chunk* sounded from the port amidships ballistae mount, and a harpoon sprang away. The amidships harpoon struck solidly in a closed rowing port and smashed it to smithereens. A loud ratchet clacking came from the forward mount as its crew cranked back the arms for another shot. The *Wind March* lumbered on the pirate like a surfing whale, black-hulled and irresistible; steep seas assailed her tall sides.

With white sails billowing and cracking in the wind the *Far Shore* completed her turn and began to pull away.

"Archers, ready!" Rayamars voice carried plainly to the pirate vessel. Forty bows in unison were drawn back and aim towards the sky. The ballistae were firing independently now, and the pirate's own starboard catapult side shot back at *Wind March.* A boulder came straight for Fire Eye who calmly swayed out of its path. His only sign of emotion belayed by the twitching tail.

Amidst the heavy bolts firing back and forth came the command "Loose!" Forty arrows leapt away and vaulted in a graceful arch punctuating the scudding sky. The crews on all the ships watched transfixed.

The cloud of arrows rained down in unison, thudding into the side and deck of the pirate ship. Sailors were feathered, struck, and spun around.

Seconds later, the ships rushing together, Rayamars issued his command, "Ready, Aim!"

The pirate captain, on his flush-decked man-of-war, yammered in the language of the Warkenvaal, and suddenly the vessel turned hard to port. The bow gave way fast, swinging the stern in close, and suddenly Fire Eye was in motion, loping aft, keeping pace with the pirate's stern, the closest point to the *Wind March.*

"What the devil--" The *Wind March* captain cursed.

"He's running!" Marisa called.

The captain did a double take between her and the pirate vessel and shouldered the helmsman aside as he watched the pirate's stern first sweep closer, near enough to splash a bucket of chum on her deck, and then angle off as the enemy captain kept his rudder hard over.

In that instance of time, with the wind snapping sails and the sea crashing against hulls, the opposing crews stood transfixed, neither side shooting. Amidst the cacophony of the storm, silence reined, each side spell bound by the proximity of the other. Only Fire Eye moved, oblivious to the pause, immune to the respite. There came an instance when the pirate's stern was a mere boat's length distant. Waves tossed tall between, and both crews stood in silence, yellow-skinned pirates faced tan-skinned Tivorians. They were close enough to fling insults, but not a word was muttered. They had come for battle, but battle had not come for them.

As the ships heaved and rolled past the quarterdecks came abreast; the pirate captain grinned monkey-faced, his helmet-turban tight upon his head.

Marisa stepped to the quarterdeck rail, doffed her helmet and shook out her long raven hair, streaming it in the wind. A sailor next to the pirate captain pointed at her and gesticulated wildly, stomping on the deck, imploring his captain to action.

The pirate captain merely shook his head and bowed to Marisa.

Marisa's lips tilted with satisfaction: on the stern of the sloop the vessel's name shown clear and damning across the transom, *Uktik Baktar*.

Prince Fire Eye came to stand behind her, his tail twitching. Marisa turned to him. "He's a sneaky bastard. Should we have grappled him and held tight, this veering wind would have carried our ships upon the shoals. We ride deeper and would have grounded first. Then he would have signaled the other two pirates to board us." She scowled at the image.

"Do you know that pirate?" The captain asked.

Her countenance shifted, gloom replaced with a sardonic smile. "No. We've not been introduced." She looked up at Fire Eye. His gaze made long and primordial by the coarse reptilian snout, the yellow fangs, and wide nostrils. She pointed at the retreating pirate, "I have twenty Tivorian gold for you if you find their home port, wherever that rat hole should be."

Fire Eye flicked his tongue twice. They had a deal.

Chapter 6
Water Survey Unit

IDB Central Station

A ringtone sounded from behind him. It came from the shelf behind his chair. It sounded again. That's familiar, he thought, but he could not quite place it. He swiveled his chair careful not to bump the box of samples and specimens stacked beside the holodesk. Distracted, he tried to concentrate on one of the six things he had in motion. The urgent message from Marisa forced a sudden trip in-country, and he was in a hurry to get ready. His office in Central Station was small and cramped, festooned with accouterments and trade goods he'd dragged in from planet-side and not bothered to log them in with Provincial Artifacts. Central Station was located in a former Transportation Authority ore mine beneath the surface of Dianis, and adding office space to the subterranean warren hadn't been a priority. Rifling through the debris of a career he hunted for the incessant ringing. Buried under a stack of parchment maps he found the annoyance, his old Spark Constellation communicator. *Who is calling me on this?* He wondered, amazed the power cell still cooked. On the device's screen showed the face of a man with the title of "Director Annet".

No one ever called him on any of his communicators. Instead, they pinged him through the A-wave channel synced to his multi-func and the A-wave chip embedded in his thigh. Everyone in Dianis IDB knew that was the best way to contact a field operative: buzz them through their embeds, they were always attached to them.

He hit the "accept" button. "Hello?" It was a lucky coincidence for this Director Annet that he was in his office at all, he used it more like a storage closet. He glanced at the network address for the caller. It started with a prefix he didn't recognize which put the caller somewhere in federation space, but not in the Margel.

"Hello, is this Achelous Forushen?" a pause, "Chief Inspector Civilization Monitoring, IDB Dianis?"

"Yes," drawled Achelous, not liking the use of his formal title or the official tone of the caller's voice. Though on the screen the man had a friendly smile if it weren't an avatar.

"Excellent, I'm glad I've gotten a hold of you. Our admin has been trying to reach you for the past day. On a whim, I thought I'd try you myself, and here you are!"

Achelous thumbed the message display on the Spark, and sure enough, there were three pending messages in the past day, all from the same prefix. "What can I do for you, ah, Director Annet?"“

"Yes, thanks. I'm Philip Annet, director of IDB operations for Dominicus III and I just want to welcome you aboard."

"Aboard?"

The director chuckled. "What? You don't know? IDB Bureau of Personnel has posted you to Dominicus III, and I can tell you Achelous we really need you. The Turboii have left this place a real mess. Fifty million dead, another twenty million frozen in cryostasis. Of course, there are still some of the cloned Turboii minions here, about a million or so roaming around the planet, but their Turboii handlers have fled which leaves the warrior drones pretty much aimless, rudderless if you will. Which is why all our field teams go in-country with armor and plasmas, escorted by the 12th Infantry..." the director went on, but Achelous wasn't listening. The pit of his stomach felt like it lay on the floor. *Posted to Dominicus III? Already?* Marisa and Boyd loomed in front of him. His heart wrenched. He tried to think of something else. He had so much work to do. So many decisions to make.

"Chief, I can see this is a surprise to you, but I assure you we really need you. I've looked at your service stellar record and your thirty years of experience..."

Frustration began to grow. *Why didn't Clienen tell me?* Where were his orders? Why did he hear this from a total stranger? Someone who thought he was his new boss!

"So I was hoping you could get out here in two weeks. Field assets are starting to come in, and I need you to take over. Get the logistics in order, the teams organized. Tasking roles established. You know the drill."

"Two weeks?" he croaked, though he'd not meant it to sound that bleak.

The director paused, intent on Achelous. "Well sure. Is there a problem?"

"Um, director, I'm going to have to call you back. I have my own teams here on Dianis to manage. I need to clear this with Margel IDB. Let me call you back."

The director was about to say something when Achelous terminated the call and threw the Spark in a corner. He stared at it hoping it was broken, but they built those old Sparks tough. Then, on second thought, he scrambled for the communicator and did a total power shut it down before it could ring again and deliver more bad news.

He leaned back in his chair stewing, confused, distracted, and depressed. He mentally triggered an adrenalin hormone injection through his embed and waited to feel better, and for his head to clear. He had a serious decision to make.

Achelous strode into the Central Station admin area. Ready to go back in-country he was dressed accordingly, baggy canvas pants, tall leather boots, linen tunic, and a Tivorian robe. Field Outfitting had Echo and his gear at the field generator station ready to go. He stopped at a wall hologrid and brought up Civilization Monitoring's artificial intelligence program. "Jeremy, locate Clienen please."

"The director is in his office," came the AI's immediate reply.

"Thank you," he said, a simmering angst driving an edge to his voice.

"Achelous, is there anything I can do?" Even though Jeremy was just a computer program, a complex one, he -- it -- was trained to perceive human emotions and respond appropriately. The AI recognized Achelous by his voice, image, and aural signature. Undoubtedly, Jeremy detected stress tones in the chief inspector's voice and flux radiations in his aural signature.

"No, not now thank you." It always paid to be polite to an AI, especially his own AI. They had a long memory and stored responses and actions with each individual effectively forming unique relationships with the person. Supposedly, an AI was programmed to ignore slights or provocations, not allowing them to affect the quality of services it rendered to a person. However, Achelous had seen enough examples where he didn't think the objectivity programming was completely effective.

In the hologrid, Jeremy's avatar waited patiently. The AI's image was a human from Calinextra III, the originals who built and staffed IDB Margel. Calinextras bore a purplish tint to their skin, laced with dark veins. Their broad flat ears clung closely to the side of their head. They had black, almost purple hair and unusually large upper and lower canines attesting to their vampiric genes. Jeremy wore the classic Calinextra tunic: black, tight fitting, and with a red sash over his shoulder. If a person looked closely, they could see the details of the Calinextra Civilization Monitoring crest on the embroidered patch on Jeremy's shoulder. Achelous had left it there in honor of the IDB's rich past.

"I need to speak with Clienen," Achelous said. Walking past the glass-walled data center beside Clienen's office, a data analyst in the center stood up and waved at him through the glass. Achelous stopped and waited for the analyst to come to the door. "Hey chief, do you have a minute?"

"Sorry, I need to speak with Clienen, and I'm due to shift in-country."

"Okay. But can you send me the geo coordinates for your aquamarine finds?"

The director's office was a few paces away, and the door stood open, he could see the director was in. Achelous cocked his head. "What aquamarine finds?"

"Well, these." The data analyst led him to his holodesk in the data center. Achelous could see on the hologrid that Jeremy had alerted the analyst. Apparently, the subject was important enough for the analyst to set an aural tracker on him.

"The aqua finds you listed in your 2.52.4007 operations journal. Why didn't you include the geo coordinates? It would have saved me a lot of time. I couldn't find them. Do you have them?"

An overwhelming sense of déjà vu struck Achelous, like falling into deep water and unable to breath. He feigned insouciance and leaned over the desk. "Why do you need them?"

"I received a data request from Branch headquarters on Avaria. It came with a complaint that the report did not follow field report guidelines. In this case, missing standard data."

"What, was it a program check, AI scan, or a human query?"

"Oh, definitely human, an analyst in Sector Resources." Mitch slid into his seat. He was an energetic, diligent sort, and despite gene therapy, his forehead was creased with care lines.

Achelous's sense of déjà vu was complete. *Didn't I just talk to Gail about this last night? It was just last night!* Taking a deep breath, he said, "Okay. Give me their network number; I'll take care of it."

"Uh, alright, but what should I do with the request?" The analyst looked perplexed.

"Flag it as data unavailable and close it out."

"Uh, I don't know if I can do that."

Achelous fixed him with a stare, his lips set. "You can either let yourself be hounded by the request, or you can close it out. Either way the coordinates--" he paused. He wanted to say he would not divulge them unless the request came as a formal inquiry. Instead, he said, "I'll have to retrieve them from the surveyor system and figure out which site you are referencing, so we don't confuse coordinates. So give me the network number and in the meanwhile reassign the request to me."

Mitch appeared to think about it, then shrugged. "Okay, fine with me." He reached across his work panel and tapped a series of grids on the display. "It's in your in-box along with a copy of the request."

"Thank you." Achelous thumbed to the communicator page of his multi-func. He indexed to the newest message and called the network number at Branch headquarters.

He waited for the call to connect at its destination some twenty thousand light years away on Avaria. An older woman, with grey hair--quaint considering gene therapy took care of that--appeared on the screen. Her title showed Penni Donia, Senior Analyst, Sector Resources. "Hi, this Penni, what can I do for you handsome?"

Achelous cocked his head. *Okay.* Experience at interviewing provincials kicked in, and he decided to follow her lead even though he didn't know her. "Hi Penni, how's life at HQ?"

"Fast and non-stop, just like my men." There was a twinkle in her eye. "Let's see—" she looked away from the imager at something on her desk hologrid. "I know your name, and that's not usually a good thing—Ah yes, Chief Inspector Forushen, you've been a bad boy. You left out information in one of your ops journals."

"Yes Penni, I was curious about that." He turned to look at the analyst who was all ears. "We've filed numerous ops journals with reports of sensitive finds and depending on the situation we either included the geo-coordinates or left them out for security. I've never been asked afterwards to provide the data. We keep that here on-site. And Penni, I'm quite surprised someone even fact-scanned the journal. Most of them just get filed."

"But inspector, you know the reports are on our secure servers, and only personnel with the proper clearance have access to them. There is no real need to exclude the data from the journals."

"Actually, there is a real need. We are decommissioning IDB Margel and Dianis with it. There'll be no one here to monitor access to the sites." If Penni were a simple analyst, putting in her time, she wouldn't care. If she were devoted to the IDB cause, she would. Either way, he was curious as to what she would say next.

"Oh-- they're shutting down the Margel Arm?" Penni's posture changed.

"Yes, they confirmed it yesterday. So you can see why I'm concerned with this sudden request for omitted data in an ops journal submitted two months ago. Longer actually."

She looked distant, then admitted, "You're right, not many managers have ops journals on their distribution lists, and a fact scan on the journal would have triggered immediately after the journal was posted. And this scan," she tapped in the hologrid, "was initiated last week."

"Hmm, so you personally didn't set the scan for aquamarine in our field reports?"

"No--" Penni was working her hologrid, swiping the command screens fast, the way she liked her men.

"Which tells me someone has a particular interest in aquamarine on Dianis," Achelous asserted.

"Hmm, I have your answer dear."

"And?"

She was frowning. "The data request didn't come from IDB, It came from the federation office of Galactic Resources, the Water Survey unit."

Achelous could feel his jaw tighten. "Water Survey unit?"

She looked up from the readout. "Yes. I can forward the request to you."

"Thank you. Would they have clearance to scan IDB classified reports?"

She pursed her lips. "That would depend on the level of classification you assigned the report. Water--especially saline and contaminant free--as you know is also a strategic resource we track closely, and the location of those resources is also classified. Although, why the water unit would want to know about aquamarine is beyond me."

He nodded. "Until I identify the source of the data request and they provide an explicit answer as to why they need the geo-coordinates I will not be releasing the information."

She inclined her head, peering from beneath her eyebrows. "I understand."

"So you can close this request and make a note to the originator that the request for more data must come directly to me."

She smirked. "Whatever you say, Chief Inspector."

He ended the call and opened the Water Survey data request in his message queue. His sense of trepidation percolated. *Who in Water Survey is interested in aquamarine on Dianis?*

Staring at the requestor's network address, he tapped the network address, and his multi-func placed a call to the entity in Water Survey.

The call went through. The contact information indicated *AI Matadraxal*, and then the AI's avatar came on the screen wearing a pristine white tunic with gold buttons. The tunic collar looked impossibly snug, but it was, after all, just an image of what the AI was programmed to present itself as: a man of olive skin, slanted eyes, shaved and polished pate, and a slight smile. "Office of Galactic Resources, Water Survey Department, how may I help you, Chief Inspector?"

He wasn't surprised an AI answered his call, but was disappointed nonetheless. He explained his question and waited for the AI to track back through the system and locate the data request sent to Penni.

"Yes, I have it. The data request was submitted by a staff researcher.

Achelous was encouraged. "Can I have their name?"

"I'm sorry, Chief Inspector, but the log only lists *staff researcher*."

Achelous frowned. "Why is that?"

"Scan requests can come directly from nineteen different applications, not all of them forward the ID of the requestor."

"Fine, if we provide the data where will it go?"

"It will be posted to the findings section of the scan report."

"And where will that go?"

The AI paused a moment, "There are three hundred and twenty-two user accounts that have direct access to those scan reports."

Okay, thought Achelous, *this is getting me nowhere.* "Matadraxal, are there any active projects in the Water Survey Department where aquamarine-5 is listed as an item of interest? Like it is needed for the completion of the project?"

"Do you mind if I check your security clearance, Chief Inspector?"

"No, go right ahead." While he waited for the AI to return he glanced at the analyst who caught his attention. The analyst came to stand next to him but was careful to stay out of the communicator's camera field. "Mute it," he whispered.

Achelous did so.

"Analysts can submit anonymous queries through any number of applications. There can be hundreds of information scans, maybe even thousands in a batched set of queries. Slipping in an extraneous query in a batch is easy. If you have the right security clearance, you can use an admin account for the query and your ID will not appear in the report. I knew a guy, an analyst in—" he hesitated, "well, who did a trace on his wife's aural signature as she went about her business during the day. Strictly illegal of course, unless authorized by Internal Security, which it wasn't. Found out she'd been visiting a hotel on a regular basis with another person, always the same opposing aural signature. The agency never knew he was using their data system for his own detective work."

Achelous pursed his lips, "And?" He could see Matadraxal was waiting for him to come back on the line.

"The way you unravel this particular knot is ask the AI to scan A-wave communication packets with the key words from the scan results. Whoever issued the query, if they are an analyst like me, would forward it on to someone else. We all use A-wave. We never think about it. I bet they used A-wave to send it."

Achelous nodded. It made sense. He thumbed the mute button, "Yes, Matadraxal. Sorry for the delay, I'm doing a bit of multi-tasking. What did you find?"

"I scanned all projects and programs for which your security clearance can access, and there are no records of aquamarine-5 listed as an element of interest."

"I see. Are there any projects above my security clearance?"

Matadraxal titled his head, made an apologetic smile, "I'm sorry, I'm not allowed to say."

"Okay, how about this. My director has a class A4 security clearance. I know because his position was offered to me. I'm sure that's as high as any Water Survey project would go. If there are any projects above my clearance that have interest in aquamarine, will you confirm with him? This is of extreme interest to IDB, and he needs to know."

"Yes, if there are any, I will message him."

Achelous thought about it. "Send him a message immediately, regardless of the answer, yes or no. He'll be waiting for it."

The AI, even though it was a program, pursed its lips and nodded. "I will message him immediately."

"Good. And one last request. Please search all A-wave communications in Water Survey that occurred in the day after the alert triggered; search for the text of the scan results."

Matadraxal actually arched an eyebrow.

Achelous smiled, "And of course, please apply Internal Security decryption routines."

When the AI just stared at him, he offered, "This is an official request, and I can escalate to IDB Headquarters Avaria."

The avatar visibly relaxed. "I will comply."

While the query progressed, time passed, and the AI, for Achelous's sake, appeared to be working his own workstation performing other tasks, an absorbing if visual charade. The AI constantly multi-tasked and didn't use hands to interact with a hologrid. "Still checking," Matadraxal reported. Almost another minute passed. "Still checking." Then his – its -- face brightened. "I have results for you. The scan results were transmitted, via encrypted A-wave ninety three minutes after the search triggered."

"Encrypted?"

"Yes, using a new commercial shifting band multiplexer."

"And you were able to crack it?"

"Yes. It is unusual for anyone to use a non-Internal Security encryption method, so I immediately targeted that message. Internal Security acquires rights to all commercial encryption methods, which by the way, Chief Inspector," the AI accentuated the title, "is classified."

Achelous nodded, hoping the analyst was cleared for the information. "Thank you." It always paid to be polite to AIs. While they weren't human, their developers were, and they tended to be a quirky bunch. “Please forward the message ID and send the destination address to me.”

“I can put a call through if you wish. I have already checked locator domain. It is not registered to a federation agency.”

He considered this new piece of the puzzle. “No. that won’t be necessary. Send me the network address and message ID, and I will have Internal Security take it from here.”

The AI bobbed its head. “As you wish.”

After he closed the connection, he turned to the analyst. “Your data request came from somewhere outside of the federation government.”

“Too bad you didn't ask for the decrypted message. It would have saved time.”

Achelous smirked. “Yes, well, I’d need an Internal Security privacy release order for that. My authority and security clearance allows me to trace communication packets, but I’ll have to bump it up a level to view private correspondences.”

“What are you going to do?”

The chief inspector smiled. “Before I take this to Clienen and we involve Internal Security I have one more thing I want to try.” He called up Jeremy.

“Yes Chief Inspector?”

“Jeremy, there is a network address in my message queue from an AI in Water Survey. It is not a federation agency number. I am curious as to who or what is using that number. Can you check the number’s registry without tipping off the owners as to your inquiry? I do not want them to know who is asking.”

Jeremy’s programing immediately registered the delicacy of the situation. He, like the CivMon agents he served, was trained, or more appropriately – programmed -- for counter espionage. “Certainly. I can route my inquiry through my affiliated AI network and have it appear as marketing search for prospects of water filtration equipment.”

Achelous smiled at the logic of it. “That will work.”

“Shall I run it now?”

“Go ahead.”

The results came back swiftly, “The address belongs to a pool of a thousand A-Wave channel accounts registered to a firm called Tangent Assets.”

“And what does Tangent do? What type of business are they in?”

"They are a private company, and do asset planning and strategy development."

"What sort of assets?"

"Sorry, our records don't say. And there is no listing for any Tangent Assets publications on the Fednet Interconn, which is odd. No marketing materials, nothing."

Achelous scowled, but Jeremy just stared back. "Okay, try dialing the number, see what you get. Act like you're a pushy AI trying a hard sell from that equipment company."

"Will do. I will use one of my alternate avatars. Marionette should suffice. Connecting networks now." The call was opened by what seemed to be another AI, but the screen remained blank, not even the courtesy of flashing the Tangent corporate logo. A simple voice said, "Hello?"

Jeremy opened a second voice channel so Achelous could converse with him without the knowledge of the other party. "Guidance as to how I should proceed?"

"Give them your marketing spiel."

Jeremy was two sentences into his marketing pitch and request to speak to an equipment procurement manager when the channel closed.

"Oh, that was abrupt." Jeremy sounded miffed. "I can usually keep them engaged to at least the fourth sentence. Marionette is quite seductive."

Achelous smiled. He'd seen Jeremy's alter female persona.

"I know it has a low probability of success, but I could reconnect and simply ask if they are interested in data regarding aquamarine deposits on Dianis."

Achelous chuckled. "Yea, that would get the results we want. They receive an encrypted message from a federation agency containing classified data, and then you call them in the clear ask them if they want some more." Jeremy feigned a hurt expression.

"No, we'll turn this over to Internal Security."

"You got a minute boss?"

"Sure, Atch, come on in." Clienen Hor leaned back in his chair. He was out of uniform, wearing a plain, long sleeve shirt opened at the collar. His eyes were those of a man who hadn't slept.

"Mind if I—" Achelous indicated a chair in front of the director's workstation.

The pained look on the director's face gave Achelous the impression that Clienen expected another bitch session on the closure of the Arm, but to Clienen's credit he said, "Sure."

Achelous shut the door, which alerted the director this was no casual visit. "I got a call today, from the director of IDB operations for Dominicus III."

"Oh?"

"He wanted to know if I could be on-site in two weeks."

Clienen shook his head, confused. "Two weeks? For what?"

"To complete my transfer and take over Dominicus."

"What?" Clienen leaned forward.

"That's what I said. Bureau of Personnel has already cut my orders."

"Achelous," Clienen shook his head, "I knew part of Margel was headed to Dominicus, but I told them I needed two months to shut down operations and they agreed. Any orders to be issued would come through me. I would check them, validate the assignments, and notify the teams. "

It was Achelous's turn to look frustrated. "Well, Clienen that's not the way it's working."

After a minute Clienen asked, "What did you tell him?"

"That I'd have to talk to you and get back to him. I have my own teams here to take care of."

Clienen nodded. "That's fair. I'll call personnel and ask them why the hell the orders didn't come to me first and what happened to my two-month ramp down."

Achelous tried to keep his face from being pensive, but the mere thought of leaving Dianis at all, let alone in two months put him in a dour mood. He would deal with the details of a ramp-down later. Too much was happening for him to think about it. He felt trapped, pinned between forces that were moving inexorably against each other. "On a different subject, maybe more important, the Data Center tracked me down and wanted me to respond to a data request." He explained the situation.

"Oh, so that's what the high security message is about in my message queue."

AI's could always be counted on to follow through with a request, unlike some of their human counter parts. Achelous asked, "What did it say?"

“Simple. Water Survey has no projects classified or otherwise that have a correlation to aquamarine-5.” Clienen turned to his hologrid and brought the message up. “But the AI did include a network address, in case Internal Security grants permission to decrypt the personal message.”

Achelous perched on the edge of the seat. “Can you get IS to give clearance to read the message?"

Federation personal privacy laws were as strict as ULUP. Aural scanning infringements were always in the news on the Fednet. “On what grounds?” Clienen asked innocently.

Achelous looked at the ceiling and scanned the room, acting as if he was searching for a reason, “Oh, how about unauthorized released of classified information, intent to violate ULUP, conspiracy to exploit Class E resources--

“You can’t prove all that.”

“I can prove unauthorized passing of classified information. Smokes, Clienen, the information should never have gone to Water Survey, that’s a breach right there. Clearly, they do not have a need to know. Water Survey should have filed an official request before they issued the query. Let’s find out what the message says and then have Internal Security investigate this Tangent Assets. Then I can prove my other charges.”

Clienen tapped a finger against the hologrid worktop. He looked at Achelous, then at a holograph on the wall. It was of his wife and children at home on Metatarsis 4. Even though it was seven hundred light years away, Clienen went home every week. As director, he could afford the shift charges. “We don’t need to read the message to do a check on Tangent. We can do that check now.”

“I already had Jeremy do a commercial markets on Tangent. It’s a private firm. No public information.”

Clienen grinned, perhaps the first time in a week. “Atch, you’re good at catching extrasolars, but when it comes to financial archeology leave that to me.” He went to work at the hologrid and started aligning information objects and search routines.

"Jeremy did the checking," Achelous offered lamely. Clienen ignored the comment and Achelous smiled inwardly. He’d forgotten that before joining the IDB Clienen had been a supervisor with the Equities and Instruments Galactic Exchange, in the fraud division. He regularly tracked and conducted forensics on financial transactions across firms, planets, and inter-species agreements.

"First thing you have to appreciate, Atch, is that every firm, public or not, has expenses."

Achelous waited for Clienen to elaborate.

"Most investigators attempt to unravel the legal ownership knot." The director moved and initiated another search routine. "And while that can be done it takes time and usually requires a magistrate's petition from Internal Security." He added two more information objects to a different query, sat back, and waited for Jeremy to finish constructing the query network. "But, right now we're not trying to build a case against Tangent; we just want to know their business relationships. Tangent can be under contract with another firm to collect natural resource data, which is possible, or it can be acting on behalf of its ultimate owner."

Achelous nodded. He knew this.

"However, with something as sensitive as illegally acquiring classified information it's risky to trust a contract firm. You never really know how good they are at keeping secrets. And while ULUP does allow for transparency of information on Class E worlds, it is the domain of IDB to classify and release that information, not to have it stolen from us."

"So what does that have to do with expenses?"

"Simple. Everyone wants to save money, reduce operational costs, and they do it through leveraging, piggybacking on the service contracts of their corporate parents. You get a better deal through higher volumes, and you don't have the overhead of having to negotiate the contracts yourself."

"And?" prompted Achelous.

"And what is one service all firms use nowadays?" Before Achelous could answer, Clienen continued, "among other things, A-wave multi-band."

"Yes, but aren't those billing records confidential?"

Clienen smiled, "They are, but a little known fact is the A-wave charge accounts are kept by the Federation Media Commission, and the IDB is authorized to access those files. The trick is to find them; there are literally billions of them."

While they waited, they discussed an idea Achelous was forming. "I need to do an audit of IDB and Transportation Authority facilities ground-side. We have the facilities report, and the site monitors give us a good status of most of the eighty facilities, but some of the sites don't have modern monitors. We'll need to complete the audit to do a ground-side shut down."

Clienen was guarded. "How long will it take?"

Achelous hedged, "I don't know. There is the bigger problem that my teams have relations with the provincials, and it won't do to just disappear. We may need those relationships if we come back, in a hurry."

Clienen pursed his lips. "So you're going to have the CivMon teams feed the provincials a cover story about their departure?"

Just as Achelous said, "Yes," Jeremy presented the results of Clienen's A-wave account search. The director arched an eyebrow and looked at his chief inspector. He tapped a control on the hologrid, and the results appeared the air above the holodesk.

Achelous read the A-wave Communications Channel Usage and Billing report for Tangent Assets. A thousand channels were listed, but the display zoomed to the one flagged in red. All the channels showed Tangent as the user, Empirium Bark as the billing servicer, Perrien Enterprises as the billing agent, Majorette Mining as the billing parent, and there at the long end of the expense chain was the billing ultimate: *Nordarken Mining*.

Achelous's mouth slowly opened, and then he asked, "Nordarken Mining owns Tangent Assets?"

Clienen clasped his hands and held them close to his chest as he read the data in the holograph. "That's assuming a number of factors. Nordarken is certainly allowing Tangent to use their A-wave communication channels. We haven't proved ownership, but for you and me..." he paused, "I think we have what we need. Classified information about Dianis resources is likely being fed to Nordarken Mining." The director knew the evidence wouldn't stand in front of a magistrate, not by itself. Just because Tangent was using A-wave channels paid by Nordarken Mining did not mean Nordarken was the final recipient of the information, but everyone knew the reputation of Nordarken Mining. He and Achelous had personally seen them at work. He also knew the Nordarken data-gathering network to be superb, and if a corporate subsidiary of theirs had the data, then Nordarken senior management had it too. Clienen stared hard at his chief. "Now comes the difficult part. Depending on the methods we use to probe further, a query may tip off one of their AI sentinels, and they'll go into damage control, and that data will disappear like spit in a furnace."

Achelous weighed the alternatives. "We can attack this from multiple directions. We don't have to risk a further billings probe today. We can do that later."

Clienen's lips thinned, but his eyes said yes. "I'll forward a request to Internal Security for permission to read the message. I can also have them investigate how the query for aquamarine-5 on Dianis came to be submitted in Water Survey."

"Wait," Achelous had a brainstorm. "I mean yes, get permission to decrypt the message, but don't have any investigators probe Water Survey, yet."

Clienen looked blank.

Slowly, a calculating smile formed. "Let's feed them false coordinates first, and have Internal Security ready to track the subsequent message stream."

Clienen hesitated, then slowly nodded.

Achelous had ulterior motives, and he dare not expose them to Clienen regardless of how close their friendship, but it would serve his purposes if the mining conglomerate were both lured and misdirected at the same time. He was now convinced Nordarken was focused on Dianis and its aquamarine-5, but how far would they take their interest? "Clienen, you know they won't stop in their enquiries of aqua-5 on Dianis. I checked the markets. The price of aquamarine is up based on speculation one of the big three miners has only a six month supply remaining. Nordarken will keep probing our networks until they get the coordinates. It would be best for in-country surveillance to feed Nordarken Mining a false location that is far away from the actual aqua-5 mines."

"Atch," Clienen said, "I agree with the logic to feed them false information, but regardless of what coordinates you use, fake or not, it's stupid to think Nordarken Mining will land on Dianis and blithely begin mining operations based on a set of unsubstantiated coordinates."

"What do you mean unsubstantiated? The whole mining industry knows how accurate our geo-assessments are."

Clienen nodded quickly. "Yes, yes, but you're not telling them how much, how deep, or how dense. They'd send in a survey team first. A stealth team to be sure and they'd scout around. What do you think they will do if they come up empty?" He let Achelous ponder that for a moment. He understood Achelous was not happy about shutting down Dianis, but if he were looking for some plot to justify keeping CivMon in-country, he'd have to do better than this. Either that or Achelous genuinely feared a Nordarken Mining incursion. There was another thought, one that Clienen had no proof of, but could not be discounted, and that was Achelous had personal interests planet-side.

In the end, to Clienen it almost didn't matter: the IDB would be gone from Dianis, he couldn't control that, and the planet would be exposed. He deplored the situation, but he knew the tradeoffs, and his responsibility was to ensure the scant IDB resources were effective no matter where assigned. Unfortunately, the provincials would be on Dianis on their own.

Chapter 7
Sixthsense

Central Station

Having hurried from Clienen's office, Achelous stood in an equipment room down the hall from the field generator bay where Echo and his gear waited. "Hi Gail, I have a favor to ask."

Gail's three-dimensional image stared back at him from the holofield projector on his multi-func, as it sat on the repair bench. "Sure. You still in Central Station? I thought you'd be halfway to Tivor by now."

"Yes," he drew out the syllable in frustration. "Things are happening. I'm getting orders to ship out to Dominicus III. They want me there in two weeks. A data request has come through a different agency asking for the coordinates of our aquamarine-5 sites. Nordarken Mining is behind the request. I have no time to plan the ramp down of my teams, and Barry needs me in Wedgewood."

Gail's holographic image stared at him. Not knowing what to say, she drawled out, "Okay. "

"You can help me with Nordarken Mining, and them wanting the coordinates of the aquamarine mines."

She briefly looked away and then said, "Okay, but are you sure it's Nordarken Mining?"

"Yes," Achelous answered tersely. "Clienen and I have confirmed. And this is where you come in. I'm going to feed them false coordinates by updating the operations journal with bogus data, but not just any location. I need the exact coordinates of two functional gold or silver mines. And I need you to pick them. Make sure they are situated in territory where we can deploy a full ground sensor suite around them, and in terrain that makes the sensors hard to detect. And," he stressed, "see if you can find sites that can be observed, at least part of the time by your lunar observatory on Lonely Soul."

"Oh," she said. Then slowly nodded. "I get it. They can pull out our satellites, but they can't pull out the moon."

His strained expression softened into a grin. "I know it's not perfect, but at least we'll have partial visual coverage of Dianis sometime during each day."

Gail mentally ran through the possibility of programming of the observatory on Lonely Soul, Dianis's single moon. "You know, the observatory is scheduled to be shut down. There are too many dust storms up here to leave all these expensive optics and sensors functioning without a maintenance team." But before Achelous could interject, she added, "What I can do instead is have my engineering department, before they pack up, build you a special little surveillance rig that will give you the coverage you want, and we can place it somewhere environmentally protected in the main installation here. You don't need a multi-optic array that can see a million light years. That's kind of overkill. I'll get you something though that can count fingers at million miles. That should be good enough."

"Thanks, Gail."

"And Atch."

"Yes?" he answered before closing the connection.

"You said Baryy needs you in Wedgewood? Is that because the aquamarine mine is there, or because of the Timberkeep sensitives?"

"Uh, both," he hedged.

Gail twitched her lips in the way she usually did when she though Achelous was being evasive. He saw the twitch and knew what was coming.

"Atch, I agree Nordarken Mining is a threat, but to lump the Matrincy in with them is ludicrous. What gives you such an insane idea?"

"Timing."

Gail's aggravation settled to consternation. "Timing? How so?"

"Their behavior," he said. "And their interest."

"Explain," she kept at him.

Even though he was pressed for time and the shift bay operator waited for him, he explained his logic.

Gail narrowed her gaze, stewing. She opened up her hologrid and began comparing calendars, aligning events. "We started hearing rumors of a possible shutdown, what, say a month ago?" She didn't want to feed Achelous's paranoia, but math was math.

He nodded, waiting for her conclusion.

"Why did you classify the Timberkeeps as Critical?"

He answered, "It was the cause of the phenomenon, not the phenomenon itself. The heightened sixthsense abilities are not based on heredity. The cause is environmental."

She waited for him to elaborate. "Baryy, working with epidemiology, postulates the cause of the genetic mutation is in the soil. Something absorbed by specific crops." He let her think about that, and then said, "About a year ago I began hearing rumors of a clan of Doromen with strange powers, and then one day I came across a Timberkeep Doroman who was acting as a telepath for a trading caravan."

"A telepath?"

"Yes. A telepath. He was with the caravan passing trading instructions back and forth between the caravan master and his trading partners back in Neuland. Apparently, the trading master had visited with the Timberkeeps and learned how they used a telepathic early-warning network to alert the clan to threats around their borders. That's why the courier guilds, like the Silver Cup, have been hiring the few telepaths there are."

Surprised, Gail said, "I didn't know telepaths were hiring out."

"You need to come down off that rock of yours more often," he said joking.

"How did epidemiology narrow the increased sensitivity to genetic mutation?"

"We did two autopsies," Achelous answered. "And unfortunately, it was easy enough to get access to a corpse. The Timberkeep mortality rate is climbing. Baryy suspects something toxic is building up in their systems. They have the typical symptoms of gene damage. What usually kills them first is a form of brain cancer. Their clan calls it the Timber's Curse. The cancer rate is twenty times normal, and their reproductive rates are down."

"But Atch, we can repair DNA damage, cure the cancer, and isolate the mutation. Hell, we probably have a cure for that brain cancer now. This could be huge! Think about it, a gene therapy for sixthsense. The Matrincy has been looking for this. It could be crucial to the war effort. We could–" When she saw his sad smile, she clamped her jaw shut.

He let the pause between them grow.

He deliberately shifted the subject from the Matrincy. "Rumors of the Timberkeeps and their extraordinary sixthsense are spreading among the provincials. Barry is worried someone like the

Paleowrights may try to exploit them. Or enslave them. A group of people with these abilities could even become a threat to us. Sometimes I think Baryy might be getting too close to his subjects--"

"Voyants," Gail said interrupting him. "If the Timberkeeps have sixthsense that means they have clairvoyance and precognition. Distance viewing and divining the future. Smokes, Atch, if this is true, they could see us."

He shifted uneasily. "Well, I'm a cultural anthropologist, not a parapsychologist, but I thought clairvoyance only works when the viewer has been to the physical location or has some sort of connection with the object they are viewing. I agree that precognition is a possible threat to us, but without anyone knowledgeable to interpret what they are seeing... They have no way to distinguish between fact and fantasy. For clairvoyance to be truly useful, the adept must have a frame of reference to make sense of what they see."

"Do you really believe that?" she challenged. "Maybe it's true. But eventually the more voyants and diviners they have comparing visions they'll begin to figure it out. Figure us out. And then what happens?"

Chapter 8
The Offer

Tivor

Standing on the quay, Achelous helped Marisa up the ladder from the *Wind March's* captain's gig. He recognized four Silver Cup bravos in the boat below. One of them, Akallabeth, he knew. Another, Prince Fire Eye, he recognized from his IDB dossier, but the creature was a nettlesome enigma. The wryvern sat in the stern of the gig silently surveying the activity on the wharfs in what must be an alien world to him.

Grasping Marisa's hand Achelous sensed the wryvern's inspection, not of Marisa but of him. The golden orbs focused on him like searchlights in the dark. *Is the reptile a sensitive? Can he tell my Avarian aura is different?* The outcast prince of the lizardmen nation was the closest the IDB had come to communicating with any reptile leader. The reptiles on Dianis were a huge gap in the uplift planning for the planet, particularly as they were the native sentient species, not the humans. To uplift Dianis, the three reptilian species would need to be organized.

Pulling Marisa up, "Welcome ashore," he said after a brief but meaningful kiss. He stepped back to look at her, "No bandages. Boyd will be glad to know that mummy is back from chasing pirates. As am I."

She gave him a bright smile, "You made it back. Did you leave as soon as you got my message?"

He shrugged. "I see the *Far Shore* followed you in." Concern crossed his face, "Where's the *Intrepid*?"

Accustomed to his non-answers, Marisa linked her arm in his and recounted the sea action as they walked from the landing.

"So the commodore is chasing the pirates?"

"Yes," she nodded, leaning into him as she skirted around a crate of newly harvested beets. "He waited to rendezvous with the *Sea Bright*. They should be able to catch one of them, the *Far Shore* put the harpoon through its bow." Her face clouded, remembering the gay expression of the *Uktik Baktar's* captain. "I offered a bounty to the Silver Cup to find their home base."

He arched an eyebrow, taking in the lustrous black hair as she leaned against his shoulder. She looked wan and tired; the weather had been abysmal, the seas high. He suspected she was running on little sleep for days. "I think that's the right thing to do. You need to find the pirate base. You can react to their attacks, but they will always have the initiative. You need to take it from them. Besides, if the Paleowrights set the pirates on you, then setting the Silver Cup on the pirates is only fair. Harsh application of force is the only thing pirates understand." He'd learned that the hard way in his own dealings with caravan raiders. "With them, you are either predator or prey, one or the other."

"Yes," she said simply.

"Did you learn what they were after?" Achelous knew what the pirates were after. The IDB had surveillance bots in the cathedral in Hebert, right in the archbishop's private chambers. Civilization Monitoring had the video recordings of the archbishop directing his clergy to hire the pirates. He couldn't tell that to Marisa, but he could chum the water and lure the shark she was.

She pulled her head away, but still held his arm. "The pirates? I know what they are after. It's the Paleowrights I'm afraid we underestimated. I had no idea that trade with Linkoralis was so disruptive to them. I must speak with the aorolmin. Neither of us thought the Paleowrights would actually try to cut off access to the other continent and pay, Mother knows how much, to the pirates..." her voice trailed away.

"Think about it," he guided her slowly along the quay, her carriage driver pulling out to follow them. "They actually convinced the Tomis port authority, the largest port on this coast to allow their examiners to inspect and confiscate all cargos the Church deemed to be contraband. Whatever they wanted."

"Yes, but the Paleowrights own the Tomis city council, you've said as much yourself."

"Yes," Achelous answered, "but they still have to compensate the Maritime Board for the lost tariff fees and pay the cargo owners fair value. Own the council or not, that can be a lot of money. Ask yourself why they would do that?"

They strolled past a ship tied to the quay, a decaying schooner with a cargo of salted fish. Gulls wheeled overhead and a cormorant squatted on a bolster. In a tired voice, Marisa answered, "They wanted a cut of the trade?" She shrugged her shoulders. "The bastards are greedy and arrogant."

"Okay, but what trade?" Achelous pressed. "The Tomis Maritime Board didn't give free confiscation rights for all cargoes, not even the Paleowrights can afford that. What cargoes are they really interested in?"

Thinking it through, she stopped and slowly turned to him. "The Paleowrights want the same thing in Tomis that they want here. Ancient artifacts. And..." her eyes narrowed, "aquamarine?"

He pressed his lips into a tight smile.

"But that trade is miniscule," she exclaimed. "The movement in aquamarine between the Linkoralis and here just started."

Achelous kept his smile. "Just started, and now just stopped. What was the market in aquamarine like, here on the continent of Isuelt before the route to Linkoralis was opened?"

"Well, there was none." Marisa shook her head. "The Paleowrights here hold all the Ancient artifacts and the..." she stopped.

Achelous slowly nodded. "Until the archbishop in Linkoralis started selling aquamarine from his new mine the only source of it, in this entire world, was in the equipment the Ancients brought to the planet." He wanted to say the early Transportation Authority engineers brought the equipment, but that would be the truth, and the truth would have to wait. "The Diunesis Antiquarian Church has acquired or confiscated all Ancient artifacts, and that includes every gem of aquamarine. And they use that store of artifacts to control their faithful and to influence the Drakan Empire by promising knowledge and amazing new technologies. The Isuelt Paleowrights will not share Ancient artifacts or aquamarine with anyone, it would destroy their monopoly."

"Alright, so they want the aquamarine from Linkoralis," Marisa said. "Then Tivor is stuck in the middle, for a time."

"What do you mean for a time? Achelous asked.

"You told me before, that another source of aquamarine was discovered. A vein of it in a gold mine in the mountains somewhere."

He dug his hands into his coat pockets. "Yes. And those people will have the same problems. The Paleowrights will try to take the mine. You watch. It's hard for the Church here in Isuelt to attack their brothers in Linkoralis. It would be bad form. Plus there's an ocean in between. But here on Isuelt, with heathens, it's different. The Church here will fight to save their monopoly on Ancient artifacts, including aquamarine."

She turned away from him, facing the city, she resumed walking. "How do you know this?"

He sniffed. "It's what I trade in. Gems, spices, and weapons. Low volume, high profit items. I have to keep aware of prices."

"And you get to ask questions."

He smirked and nodded.

"You get to learn things, see people, and investigate things."

His smirk slipped. He wasn't quite certain where this was going or if she was leading him somewhere, so he changed the subject. "Things might have been different if the Linkoralis archbishop had decided to cooperate with his peer in Hebert, but instead he decided to sell his Ancient artifacts to the highest bidder. It created quite a rift."

"Why, why would he do that?" she asked, her arm tight against his.

"The word is the Linkoralis Church is bankrupt trying to build their cathedral, and the archbishop is desperate for funds to finish it."

She stared out over the harbor in the direction of the Padmarjar Ocean and the far, far continent of Linkoralis.

He let her ponder the pieces of the puzzle. Fitting them together as she would.

"Now I know why they were so adamant in trying to get the aorolmin to embargo shipping with Linkoralis," Marisa said. "We thought they were after all trade, but in truth, they are only really interested in the aquamarine and artifacts."

Achelous peered down at the rusty nail heads in the worn planking of the quay. He gauged his words carefully. "The Paleowrights don't want it known how dependent the power of the Church is on the absolute control of all things Ancient."

They resumed walking; Marisa's carriage driver kept the coach a discreet distance behind.

Navigating past several coils of heavy anchor line, Marisa said, "There aren't that many ships big enough with crews skilled enough to make the long crossing of the Padmarjar. I've only done it once myself, and there are only two ports on this coast that harbor those ships."

You would know. Achelous thought. *You're the daughter of a sea captain, the founder of Marinda Merchants. You were even born on a ship.*

"And with the Paleowrights controlling Tomis, that leaves only us."

"*Us* as in Marinda Merchants," he added. "You own all the right ships the Paleowrights can't inspect."

"But ships from Myryhn, Mineforest, or Dunfairmland could make it," she said, but judging by his sad smile, he discounted the idea.

"You and I both know the pirates attacking your ships are probably based out of some hole-in-the-wall cove near Myryhn. They're not going to anger their new patron. No," Achelous went on, "the Paleowrights are coming after you, Lace." He used his favorite name for her. "They want to stop you."

He met her gaze directly. "All they really want to do is make it too expensive for you to continue. If you stopped the Padmarjar route, the Paleowrights would probably quit paying the pirates. And the pirates don't like attacking your big, fast, well-armed ships. Without payments from the Paleowrights, my guess is the pirates would find the cost too high. You could send a message to the Church and tell them you won't carry any cargo from the archbishop."

He got his answer when she asked, "What would the Paleowrights do if we beat the pirates. If we defeat them and destroy their bases?"

Defeat them? Outright? The notion caught him by surprise. He stared at her, her jet-black hair, ebon eyes, perfect nose, and olive skin.

She watched him, waiting.

He saw that glint. Achelous knew what was lurking behind that gaze, that diamond-hard glint. "Well," he sought an explanation, "it would depend on if you carried through on importing any artifacts or aquamarine. Of course, one cargo is one too many for the Church. The Paleowright's hold on their faithful, and more importantly on Nak Drakas would slip."

"And then?" she prodded.

"And then the Paleowrights would act. They would come after you Lace, and maybe the aorolmin directly, personally. I don't know how, but I can tell you the Paleowrights are religious zealots. The worst kind. They don't care about losses. They will attack, attack, and keep attacking until the fire of their religious fervor is quenched by your blood. Or," he added, "you beat them totally."

She raised her hand to his face and held her palm against his cheek.

He sighed. She was telling him not to worry. "Promise me this. That you will be prepared. If you decide to go this route, you and the aorolmin cannot underestimate them. The Church holds sway over half the continent."

She lowered her hand and moved in to hold him close. "What's the P-word you use?"

"Paranoid?"

"That's it."

He shook his head, her hair against his chin. "Do you know the difference between intuition and paranoia?"

"No," she said, her face against his neck.

"One is right, and one is wrong."

He held her, watching stevedores unloading bales of tea from an island trader. Marisa bade her waiting carriage to return to the hall. They would walk the rest of the way. The sun was shining; the spring air warming. Tivor was bustling; piles of bricks, stacks of lumber, scaffolding, and ox-drawn carts of building supplies dotted construction sites along the Korvastall, the main avenue leading through Tivor. Occasionally a carter driving by would wave and call out, "Ho there, Lady!" Or a passerby would bid a quick nod accompanied by, "Milady." Marisa would always offer greetings in return. Stopping at an emporium, they procured two hot spiced-ciders.

"So have you considered my offer?" Marisa asked, sipping from her cup, studying him from over the rim.

In the walk from the harbor, the tension of the day's stresses had ebbed away. *But like the tide,* Achelous reflected, *it would always return.* There was other business between them, and he'd been avoiding the subject, but now Marisa came straight to it. He returned her gaze. Between the three forces acting on his life, Marisa was the one he most wanted to placate. No—what she wanted he wanted, to embrace it wholeheartedly, and yet it would make him an outlaw and oath breaker, a criminal from the service he'd devoted the past decades of his life.

He attempted to keep the pain from his face; Marisa did not know the gravity of what she asked. From where she stood, and to any other observer in Tivor, she offered financial freedom, an opportunity for Achelous to settle down, live with her and Boyd, and perhaps be wedded. Her offer to purchase of Achelous' trading business came with a handsome premium. In a twist of fate, he normally would have no other choice but to decline. The trading business was not his to sell; it existed only as a manifestation of Civilization Monitoring operations on Dianis. The caravans, supplies, and provincial workers were all financed by IDB silver. But with the impending departure of the IDB, he could do exactly what she wanted, almost.

Only because of the IDB withdrawal could he even consider going native. For whatever the cause, removing IDB CivMon and Solar Surveillance from Dianis not only benefited extrasolars but Achelous as well. He would be an extrasolar. Removing the satellites with their aural scanners and facial recognition actually helped him more than anyone. His personal profile was prioritized in the IDB signature recognition system in case he needed immediate assistance.

His cider forgotten, Achelous answered, "I have considered your offer. It's very generous. Thank you." He tried to smile, but the import of what he was about to say distressed his stomach like rotting cabbage. "I'm considering starting a new business. Leaving trading." He realized Marisa's every sense was focused on him, absorbing the set of his jaw, the tone of his voice, the shift of his eyes. "Lace, give me a month or so to work out the idea. Don't worry, Marinda Merchants figures prominently in it. I'll give you first rights to invest in the business, at the least you can supply me with the materials I'll need."

She lowered her cup. Emotions flickered across her face like lightning in the sky. Consternation gave way to questioning. "Why so mysterious? Tell me what it is so I can help you. You don't have to do it by yourself."

Waiting for an emporium patron to amble past, he guided Marisa out the door of the store. "It's a," he hesitated, "if I told you now before I fully vetted it for myself you'd probably think I'm crazy. I have to put some pieces together and meet with my people in Wedgewood." He shrugged. "If I can't convince myself it is a good idea, then I'm certainly not going to bother you with it."

She knitted her brows, "Bother?" She rolled her eyes. "You can be so obtuse."

He smiled and leaned in close, "indulge me."

She squinted at that. Then she finally sighed, and a reluctant smile ghosted across her lips. "When have I not indulged you?"

Chapter 9
Ilos Septi

Tivor

"Separation complete, we're clear of the *Westerbrook*." Agent Jonas, pilot of the six-man assault lander, banked the craft away from the mother ship and set it for a re-entry trajectory well below the horizon of the target site.

Marisa woke up. Achelous had thrown off the covers and was mumbling something in his sleep. She reached to pull the blankets back up. In the dim moonlight sifting through the blinds, she could see him working his jaw.

Achelous, in his third year as a field operative, sat in the rear of the assault lander at the sensors control station monitoring the planet-side activity. Behind him, the lights of the cargo bay of the IDB *Westerbrook* receded in the blackness of space.

Ilos Septi spread out below them. A terrestrial planet with major continents, dark blue oceans, tropical forests at the equator, and partial snow cover in the northern hemisphere. A grey smudge comingled with the northern jet stream marking an area of substantial volcanic activity. Ilos Septi had a human population of about two million, another regenerative colony from the Lock Norim legacy, hence the planet's classification as Class E.

"How're our bogeys doing, Atch?" asked Chief Inspector Leggas.

"Still working chief. No change in comm signals. The ore carrier is waiting for another load." He tuned the aural band imager and saw the unmistakable pattern of the portable field generator ramping up for another outbound shift. He mentally shook his head, *amazing the audacity of those miners. Did they really think they wouldn't be caught?*

The assault craft bucked as Jonas angled it into the atmosphere for the steep descent, the anti-grav impellers gaining efficiency as the craft descended the intensifying gravity well.

"Target site below the horizon," Achelous reported. In his third year with the IDB, he loved his work, but the assault landings he could do without. His stomach churned; the inertial dampeners and motion sickness meds worked only so well. He could never dispel the feeling they were falling into an abyss and would hit like an egg. Splat. His butt sank deeper into the seat as Jonas pulled the craft out of the dive and shot between two mountain peaks, the rush of air past the stubby wings louder than the exhaust of the single fusion drive.

Marisa covered them both and leaned in close, her breath on his cheek.

"Landing zone, landing zone" he mumbled, his eyes closed and twitching.

"Landing zone in five minutes," reported Jonas. Conducting an enforcement run on a Class E planet was a tricky operation. They needed to surprise the corsairs, and they needed to avoid alarming the natives. It was, after all, the reason the planet was protected from outside influences. Seeing alien craft flying about the skies fanned the hysteria of the provincials, propagating perverse mythologies that lead to all sorts of irrational behaviors. Because of this, the *Westerbrook's* AI had selected an assault track taking the lander away from populated areas, a route that did nothing for Achelous's stomach.

Using telemetry data fed to them from the AI in the *Westerbrook,* Achelous called out mining site status, "No change at the site; ops still in progress." The *Westerbrook* was on autopilot controlled by the AI. The entire IDB crew, the six of them, were onboard the assault craft.

Marisa figured out that Achelous's nightmares came in chains. Sometimes he'd go for a month sleeping soundly, and sometimes they came every night. She agonized when to wake him. It spared him the torture of the nightmare, but he was never happy with himself afterwards.

Snow-covered treetops blew by the canopy in a blur. Achelous stayed focused on the sensor panel trying to ignore what was going on outside. A vast plume of snow, stripped from the trees, trailed behind the lander. The lander broke into a clearing that turned out to be a lake, and with an abrupt and unsettling dip, the craft dove to the surface, skimming three meters above the water. Racing to the end of the lake Jonas plunged down a deep waterfall that caused Achelous to clench his sphincter.

"Wow!" called Archer, the agent sitting next to Achelous. Archer twisted in his seat looking out the back of the canopy. "Look at that!"

Achelous grimaced and held on waiting for the crash at the bottom.

Jonas jinked the craft around the twists and turns of the riverbed. Abruptly he halted the craft –Achelous's stomach lurched -- and hovered over a clearing in the forest. Jonas sedately brought the assault lander to the ground like parking a passenger car in the garage after the commute from work.

Agent Archer punched the cargo bay control, opened the cargo bay door, and the lander's cargo—the air car--slid down the ramp on its auto loader. Achelous unstrapped from his seat in the lander and was about to follow Archer down the ramp when Jonas, rising from the pilot's chair, clasped him on the shoulder. "Was that better?" he asked, half-hiding a smirk.

Achelous gave him a sidelong look. "What? Were you trying to go easy for me?"

"Well, I just thought with your nervous stomach and all..."

"And what part, exactly, did you go easy on?"

Jonas thought about it. "Um, well..."

Achelous nodded. "Yeah, that's what I thought."

Archer opened the weapons locker and handed out the plasma pulse rifles, deflector shields, and helmets. Achelous buckled on the helmet and connected the data cable to his energy-dissipating body armor. They didn't expect trouble from the miners, but those first few moments of an enforcement action were predictably tense. If the mission threat profile had predicted a high possibility of a firefight, they would have donned projectile armor, brought a Ready Reaction platoon, and stationed a federation corvette in orbit for fire support.

The seating arrangements in the vehicle were the same as in the assault craft. Chief Inspector Leggas sat up front with pilot Jonas, followed by agents Dagatilloori and Bwn, and followed by Archer and Forushen in the rear most seats. Later, Achelous would agree with the investigators that sitting in the rear seats saved his life.

Jonas revved up the anti-grav impellers, angled the pitch forward, and scooted the car out from behind the hulking lander and into the forest. Sleek in design, the air car had a retractable, stealth-enhancing canopy that was now open, though the air was cold and snow blanketed the ground. The team preferred to ride with an open canopy. They liked to disembark quickly when confronting extrasolars even though the open canopy increased their radar and aural profiles. The vehicle's landing wheels and the anti-grav impellers were fully encased within the craft's plexite body. One of plexite's admirable properties, in addition to being radar dispersing, was it could take a good whack, as it did just now, bouncing back with just scuff marks.

Jonas didn't bother apologizing about the scrape with the tree. The team rather expected it. He was the kind of pilot who didn't sweat the small stuff. He got you there quickly and effectively, and if you banged into a few things along the way, it made for entertainment.

"I'm going up top. Tree cover is too thick," came Jonas's voice over the team net. Achelous dialed-up the VR display in his helmet and connected to the laser downlink from the *Westerbrook*.

"Watch our radar signature," Chief Leggas said over the net.

The air car flowed between treetops like water in a river valley. Most of the trees were conifers, and their needles whispered against the car's hull when Jonas hugged them tight.

"Achelous, sensor read out."

"On it boss. We're three mils out. Mining is continuing." At this rate, they'd cover the three mils in four minutes. Then in his helmet's heads-up display, two red circles appeared, each at an approximate corner of the mining site. "Popup radar, popup radar," Achelous called out.

Jonas immediately trimmed the impeller angle and slowed the craft. He let the car settle in a deep hollow between the shoulders of the trees.

"Where'd they come from?" Archer asked.

"Don't know," Achelous replied, checking the sensor readouts from the *Westerbrook*. "You don't think they had ground sensors along our approach?" The car was powered with a hydrogen converter cell, which gave off almost no heat. The impeller drive was silent. The only clue the corsairs could have of the team's approach was the sound of the car's passing, like hitting the tree, or aural signature leakage from the open canopy. The direct connect laser signal to the *Westerbrook* was pencil thin and impossible to intercept unless you passed physically through it.

"Be damned anal of them if they did," Leggas said. No one voiced the obvious. If the miners were careful enough to place ground sensors around the perimeter of the mining site the threat model escalated and the nature of the engagement shifted from enforcement to interdiction. Presence of ground sensors indicated the miners were there to stay, and the corsairs were willing to defend the mine. Defend against what was the question. Fights between rival contract miners were common enough, but were they willing to fight an IDB enforcement unit? The miners were freelancers interested in quick credits, contracted by a shady bulk-resourcing broker who in turn was contracted by one of the galactic commodity conglomerates. Most of the miners never knew for whom they actually worked. The conglomerates preferred keeping their hands clean, so they hired freelancers with plausible deniability through a resource broker. A broker, in the case of an interdiction, who would never be seen again.

"What's the site activity?" Leggas asked.

"Mining ops have halted," replied Achelous.

"Are they bugging out?" asked Bwn.

"They don't appear to be. But work at the site has stopped."

Jonas turned to Leggas. They could see each other through their face shields.

Finally, Jonas said, "If they're suspicious, they may call for a scout ship to do an orbital sweep." The implication being that if the scout ship were properly equipped, it would likely detect the *Westerbrook* in her geosynchronous orbit. No matter how well cloaked the IDB enforcement cutter was, stuck in geosynchronous orbit over the mine site and unable to maneuver lest it lose contact with the ground team, the *Westerbrook's* midnight hull would be seen against the sky of Ilos Septi.

Time was ticking.

"Radar sites are off. Mining ops resuming," said Achelous.

Still, the hover car snuggled in its concealment. Jonas and the entire team loath to surrender their camouflage.

"Well boss," asked Archer, "is it a ruse or is it real?" Referring to the resumption of mining activity. They all knew the story of Ten-Five Alpha where an IDB team had succumbed to just such a ruse. Two of the six were killed and one wounded in the ensuing ambush. At the inquest, the corsairs claimed they were so busy defending themselves from attacks from rivals that they didn't know they were shooting at IDB.

"Button up," said Chief Leggas. "Slide us around to the north. Go slow."

Jonas did as instructed. He closed the canopy, turned the car ninety degrees to the north, and dropped beneath the treetops. This time, unusually careful, not disturbing the barest twig, he swished them along. It took them a full thirty minutes to circumnavigate the site and reposition on the northern edge of the periphery. The only words during the ride were occasional steering suggestions by Leggas and site updates from Achelous.

In position for the high-speed blitz into camp, Leggas popped a site map up on the team's helmet displays. He drew the assault arrow, landing zone, area objectives, and team array. "I don't like how these guys are acting. Three man fire discipline, combat spread. Bwn, be ready with the missile launcher. If someone takes off, you have weapons free. When we've secured the site, we'll disperse in standard search and seize."

Achelous mentally sighed. The boss meant business. Usually, in engagements like these, Bwn did not disembark with a loaded the missile launcher with permission to shoot.

"Ready?" Leggas asked.

"Ready," replied Jonas. "Approach set, guidance locked." Using the downloaded visual mappings from the *Westerbrook,* Jonas programmed the approach into the car's AI. He would leave the hard acceleration, jinking between treetops, and diving between buildings to the autopilot. He needed to be ready with his pulse rifle, prepared to jump out the moment the AI popped the canopy. Flying was fun, but shooting was serious.

"Let's go."

Jonas tapped the engage button, and the autopilot took over. The car shot out from its concealment. Green foliage streaked past, and Achelous instinctively held on. Even though theoretically, the AI was more reliable than a human, he'd come to trust Jonas's instincts more than silicate programming.

The car jinked, dived, banked, and cleared the last trees just as the missile warning blared.

There, just at the tree line stood a concealed auto launcher, its camouflage panels dropped on the ground and a white vapor trail streaking straight for the car. Jonas had just enough time to grab the controls before the missile struck. The warhead exploded beneath the bow tossing the car to the right. Rolling like a log, the car smashed into the roof of a temporary prefab building and deflected up. Totally out of control, the car tumbled end over end through the air and across the mining site. Landing in the snow at the far side of the clearing, it bounced once, twice, and slid across the snow, dropping into a creek bed just deep enough to conceal the wreckage.

Marisa woke up. She'd drifted asleep thinking his nightmare over. Exasperated, she shook him gently, "Atch, Atch."

Achelous dimly heard a woman's voice. It was Marisa. He was in Tivor lying in bed, or was he? Struggling, he tried to get free. A monotone voice intruded. Something about injection--. The drugs of the crash cocktail entered his system, and his eyes shot open. The sudden shock of realizing he was no longer at home with Marisa was eclipsed by the realization he was an IDB agent in a crashed air car, shot down in the midst of serving a search and seize order. "Smokes," he cursed. Fumbling with his restraining harness, he released it and pushed open the canopy section. He needn't have bothered; most of the canopy glass was missing, and only the structural-impact cage remained. He climbed out onto the hull and then fell into the shallow creek. Struggling, consciousness wafting away from him, he hefted himself up and kneeled in the cold water. He could sense the water flowing around his hands and past his legs, but feeling the chill was beyond his faculties. He took deep breaths, trying to sort through the combination of crash trauma and the effects of the shock-suppression drugs the car seat injected into him. Adrenaline, one of the drugs, finally got hold of him and he stood and staggered against the car. He glanced to where Jonas sat, but the bow was either sheared off or completely crushed. In his current state, he couldn't tell which. He called over the team net, not knowing if it worked, if his helmet functioned, or if anyone was still alive.

"What, Atch? What is it? I'm here." Marisa answered.

Amazingly, Archer responded. "Trapped. I'm trapped! Out, need out!"

For Achelous, the rising panic in Archer's voice drove clarity and purpose into his concussion-fogged brain.

The car was upright with its bow in the far bank of the creek bed and the stern propped up on the near bank. Achelous stumbled and then crawled under the car and came up on Archer's side. Slowly, his mind began to clear, and he became aware of a terrible pulsing headache and fractured vision. He grabbed the door release and yanked. As he feared, the door was wedged. Fumbling around the underside of the car, he found the emergency access port. He popped open the fist-size door. Inside, the door-charge-light glowed red having been armed by the impact. The door charges would blow all six access doors, or those that remained. Normally, one took precaution to ensure the door charges were seated properly, so they detonated outward, but all Achelous could think about was rescuing Archer and retrieving a weapon.

The security sergeant signaled a halt to his three-man squad. Multiple small pops and detonations sounded from the creek bed. Then smoke drifted up in the cold air to be whisked away in the breeze. For the umpteenth time, he cursed the foreman for ordering first-attack mode for the missile launchers. They didn't even know what they shot down. It could have been one of their own hover cars coming in from an ore survey mission, though he knew all the cars were accounted for, except of course the car belonging to the geologists from Nordarken Mining. Their car now sat crushed in the collapsed garage the low-flyer hit when it crash-landed. He could hear chaos on the communications net. The foreman barking orders, the excavator boss demanding first priority for field shift out of here, the Nordarken Mining geologists demanding help to load their test and sampling equipment on a grav sled so they could shift out as well. The corporate stiffs were loath to risk any connection with illicit mining operations, but everyone did it. This rhodium mine was working well. So well the production analysts in Nordarken finance didn't believe the projections and sent a team of their own geologists to inspect the operation, and now they were stuck here in the midst of the chaos.

He signaled his two teammates to keep advancing. He'd feel more comfortable with a full team of five, but more bodies were just more pockets to split tonnage bonuses, and the owners were driving the foreman to keep costs down.

Shuffling through the snow, he stepped into the track left by the vehicle when it slid into the ditch. In places, soft unfrozen ground was churned up with the frozen topsoil. He waited until the foreman quit talking on the net, "It's probably an intrusion contractor who came to sniff our ops. So it's no problem. We got them."

The sergeant had to agree, but it was still no telling what outfit tried crashing their party, Mckenz, Po, Lite Rock. Whoever it was they'd finish them off and set a plasma mine booby-trap to kill whoever came to rescue them. One thing bothered him though: why come so close? Why do a fly over? Usually, they just landed in the distance and sent in a recon bot.

His rifle at the ready, he stepped over the stump of a tree sheered clean off at the ground. The rear of the hover car pointed up at him. He signaled one man to move left, the other to move right, both of them to cover the wreckage while he stooped low and peaked into the shallow ravine.

Crouching in the snow, he noticed the car was pearl white with black numbering in an official-looking font on the rear quarter panel. Where have I seen that before? His memory was trying to tell him something.

Sliding through the calf-deep snow, he got his first good look at the car and choked. "Blazes—"

The foreman was monitoring the progress of the security team and the active scanning of the four popup radars waiting for signs of more intruders. "What is it?"

"Uh—"

"Well?" Demanded the foreman, "I haven't all smoking day, are we pulling out or not?" Not that the foreman would let the security sergeant make that call. The mine was running at full capacity, and the ore vein had forked into three other veins. There was money to be made.

"Uh, it's an IDB enforcer car."

Silence on the net.

The foreman came back. "Whaaaaat? Are you bloody daft?"

"No. It's IDB."

Silence again on the net and then everyone starting squawking. Then the sergeant heard the foreman, "Shiren. Spirits damned and hell screw me!"

He winced at the foreman's cursing. Any calm there may have been left in the camp evaporated.

The foreman ordered an emergency evacuation. Everything would be left behind except for the excavators and their accompanying ionizers, and those would be the last to leave. There were three excavators, and it would take time to cycle them through the shift zone. "Get back here and set the demolition charges," the foreman ordered.

"What about the IDB? The car doors are open. Looks like some of them got out."

"Kill them. And do it quickly. They'll have Ready Reaction down on us in—" the foreman looked at the missile log checking the time of the launch, "Smokes, they could be shifting in minutes."

"Why don't the team and I just come back now?" He was worried about the mob of people trying to shift out. He'd didn't want to be at the end of the line. "These boys have got to be toast."

"No! If any are alive, they'll try to take out the field generator, or start zapping us. Anyone who gets zapped stays behind."

"Right, okay guys," the sergeant called to his men, "shoot anyone you see. I'm going to check the car, so don't shoot me!" The sergeant had been zap-stunned before, and the memory compelled him to take caution.

Achelous adjusted the wound seals around Archer's legs; they were a mangled mess. He'd activated the suit's med kit, and for the moment it was the most he could do for him. The agent was fading in and out of consciousness. Achelous had him propped up against the root ball of a huge tree that was toppled in the creek. Water flowed just at the agent's feet. They were down river from the crashed car and around a bend, out of sight. He laid Archer's rifle on the agent's lap. At least he'd have it if he stayed awake long enough to use it. He turned to go back for Bwn who was alive but worse than Archer. Dagatilloori was dead. Both Leggas and Jonas were missing, apparently jettisoned from the car when the bow hit the building. He'd go looking for them as soon as Bwn was safe.

He shouldered his plasma pulse rifle. Actually, it was Dagatilloori's, but his own was inop after the crash. It had taken a frustrating minute to first remember and then enter the clearance code with his trembling fingers so Dagatilloori's rifle would accept his aural signature.

Peering around the bend his helmet's infrared sensor immediately picked up a target crouching behind a tree and another on the other side of the car. Most of that person was obscured, but the bogey's legs were clearly visible beneath the undercarriage. He zoomed in on the target by the tree. Definitely a hostile with a weapon trained on the car. That settled that question, the camp personnel didn't come to rescue them. He thumbed the pulse rifle to electro-stun mode. Like all IDB agents, he'd undergone extensive combat training and did the scheduled injection learning refreshers, but he'd never actually had to shoot someone.

Suddenly two plasma blasts came from the car.

Achelous stared. *What?*

Another two bursts flashed in the car, and he could see Bwn's helmet exploded.

They're killing us! Achelous thumbed the rifle to plasma-pulse and drew on the assailant by the tree. The target indicator in his heads-up display signaled a lock, and he fired once, twice. His injection training took over, and he ran in a crouch up the streambed not bothering to check the assailant.

"IDB *Eider* to IDB *Westerbrook* assault team, do you copy, over."

Achelous watched the legs of the bogey behind the car. He contemplated shooting them, but then they moved out of sight towards the front of the car.

Achelous steadied his targeting pip just above the front of the car.

"IDB *Eider* to IDB *Westerbrook* assault team, do you copy, over."

Just when the bogey peered over the car, Achelous fired.

"Damn," the hurried shot missed, and the bogey ducked out of sight. "I read you IDB *Eider*. This is Agent Forushen."

"Report status." The request was short and to the point. Ready Reaction Force didn't waste time.

"I'm in a fire fight right now." He scuttled forward and kept his targeting pip aimed below the undercarriage hoping for a leg shot. He waited for movement. Moments passed, and he heard splashing in the stream.

"Forushen, be advised we're picking up a detonator signal. They've set a timed charge near your location. We have two humans moving away from your position heading for the field generator. No other targets near you."

Oh oh. "Roger that. Thanks, *Eider!*" Achelous wheeled and ran back down the creek as fast as he dared on the treacherous ice covered rocks. He turned the bend, splashed through the water, breathing heavy. Running to Archer the flash of a terrific blast beat him. He dove for cover behind the toppled tree as dirt, water, and debris rained down on him. A part of the plexite body, perhaps a fender, hit the tree and sprung up and over, splashing into the creek.

"What the hell did you do?"

Achelous looked up from his prone position, mud smeared his cracked face shield. Archer was sitting with his back against the bank. The agent appeared to be alert, but immobile. "The bastards set a timed charge hoping they could lure me in. The *Eider* warned me." He didn't tell him Dagatilloori and Bwn were dead. Although, with the explosion, Archer would figure it out.

"Ready Reaction is here?" Archer asked leaning his head back against the frozen bank.

"Yea. They're on their way down."

"Oh. I can't hear anything on the net. My helmet must be broken."

Achelous rolled onto his back and sat up, scanning the brush between him and the camp. "*Westerbrook* assault team to *Eider,* you coming down?" He tried to keep his voice steady though panic hovered at the edge.

"ETA ninety seconds," came a female voice, sounding just like Marisa. He could tell by the background noise and shudder in her voice that she was aboard an assault lander and not in the *Eider* in orbit. What was Marisa doing on an assault lander? The lander was coming down hard and fast.

"Be advised they have missile launchers and other defenses."

"Roger that," she replied.

Achelous looked up. There, directly above him was the fireball of an assault lander coming straight down. So fast its heat dissipating shell was blazing. The sight galvanized him. Anger replaced panic. Marisa called to him. He'd not let her down. He leapt up. He wanted to find the bastard who blew up the air car, the same person who shot Bwn, unconscious and defenseless. Turning to Archer, "I'll be back. You going to be okay?"

The agent's eyes were closed, but he waved a hand weakly. "Go."

Achelous dashed across the stream and climbed up the bank. Before him, a hundred meters distant, a concealed missile launcher sat with a missile in its firing tray. Radar and missile were pointed directly at the incoming assault craft. A sudden, brilliant flash blew the anti-aircraft battery into a thousand pieces. Heated air and a concussion wave assailed him. He staggered then kneeled against the gale; his helmet sound suppressors clamped down. Two more flashes struck at the compound.

Achelous ran for the destroyed battery, his rifle at the ready. He halted near the wreckage of the missile launcher, now marked by a crater created from the particle cannon onboard the *Eider*. The frozen ground soft and oozing, the dirt in the crater slagged. He stood and ran along the tree line skirting the compound heading to where he remembered the field generator and shift zone were located. The pounding in his head threatened unconsciousness, so he stopped and knelt to let the swaying and flashes subside.

With a whoosh and blast of hot draft air, a heavy-assault lander came down like a hawk on a rabbit, its 30-millimeter plasma cannon and twin laser turrets firing at anything that moved, notably the two ore extractors lumbering toward the shift zone. A laser hit the track of one, slicing the tread in two; the track rolled off the drive wheels like a broken conveyor belt. The extractor spun in a circle on its one good tread until a plasma bolt hit the engine putting it out of the operator's misery. The operator and mechanic jumped out of the cab and made a run for the shift zone.

Achelous crawled over to a stout tree and watched the destruction. The heavy-assault lander carried a crew of two and a Ready Reaction platoon of ten. Ready Reaction troopers, five from each side, disembarked the lander hitting the ground running, immediately disbursing in teams of two. Suddenly a missile ripped away from a retractable rack on the lander. Achelous watched as it streaked across the clearing and then up into the sky. There, a hover car was making good its escape until the missile blossomed yellow just behind it. The car spun in the air; smoking, it dropped into the distant forest with a crash of shattered trees.

"Agent Forushen?"

Startled and in a fog, Achelous turned. Two Ready Reaction troopers stood there, one with a field-portable, wound-stabilizer lab slung over his shoulder.

"Aural scanning shows you are seriously injured."

"Huh? But Archer, Archer is worse." Torn, he wanted to find the person who booby-trapped their car, but right now saving Archer took precedence. "I'll take you to him."

"Atch, Atch!" One of the Ready Reaction troopers was Marisa. She had her helmet off.

"What, what," he said groggily, slowly surfacing.

"You were dreaming. Nightmares again."

"Uh?" He could feel Marisa close to him, her face next to his. He was in the master's chamber at Marinda hall. The sound of her voice was a welcomed relief to the nightmare of Ilos Septi, her warm breath a delicious comfort.

He sighed, then sat up in bed trying to focus. Marisa was snuggled under a pile of silk quilts, and her body heat leaked out from where he sat exposed. His mind spun, part of it still reliving the Ilos Septi interdiction from twenty-seven years ago, and part of it coming to grips with where he was. The fire in the stove was out, but it warmed the room enough, so he didn't bother with it. Feeling the way he did, a simple thing like answering whether he should load the stove or not, helped center him back to reality. Finally, knowing Marisa watched him, he leaned over and kissed her on the cheek. "I'll go check on Boyd."

Achelous sat a lamp, turned down low, on the nightstand next to his son's bed. Collapsing in the large comfortable reading chair, he swallowed deeply from a glass of water. Boyd lay there sleeping like all young boys, dead to the world and innocent of all its crimes. Sliding down in the chair, he considered how Ilos Septi, a single event, had shaped his life and more importantly, his values. Guarding civilizations was no longer just a job, or a career, or even a passion, it was an obsession. Unscrupulous operators proved they were willing to kill for profit. He'd seen one of his team members shot dead, point blank. Never mind another three were dead from the crash. The shooter was never caught, though a suspect was identified. Achelous suspected the shooter's body drifted in some asteroid belt, insurance against being mem-scanned.

Leggas and Jonas died in the collision with the aircar garage. Ironically, it was the collision that sealed the fate of Nordarken Mining that day. The contract miners interdicted on Ilos Septi had no direct ties to Nordarken. Most personnel except for the two extractor crews escaped through the shift zone before a demolition charge destroyed the field generator and its log of shift targets. The extractor crews, heads-down in the mine, were unaware the geologists were even at the site. The trans-shipment of ore was arranged on a free credit basis. Until the Nordarken Mining geologist team arrived, the site supervisor was the only person with a clue as to which conglomerate they were working for. The subterfuge and standard plan to conceal the identity of the contract host would have worked, as usual, except for a single piece of evidence. The spotlight that exposed the true perpetrators was found in the collapsed garage. In it, partially crushed, sat a Maglev Streamer passenger car with the Nordarken Mining company logo emblazoned boldly on its side. Registration of the vehicle tied it directly to the Resource Production department at Nordarken corporate. Fingerprints and residual aural signatures identified two Nordarken employees, a senior geologist, and a field intern.

In the end, after years of legal wrangling, Nordarken suffered fines and the loss of mining rights equivalent to the sum of thirty million Avarian Federation credits, a net reduction of five percent of annual corporate profits. Hardly a devastating blow, but the loss of the mining access rights caused them, back in those days to fall from second to third largest galactic resource conglomerate.

Since then they recovered their position and more. Today they were the largest resource-harvesting firm in human space regarding both ore tonnage and revenue. They were more ruthless, cunning, and meticulously careful to conceal their exploitation of non-sanctioned zones. Sitting there in the dark Achelous shook his head. It was a running joke amongst IDB agents that they should form a support group of agents who'd encountered Nordarken Mining. Unfortunately, it was a small subset of agents who'd successfully brought a case against them. Achelous was one of the few, and because of Ilos Septi, he was forever a person "of interest" in the Nordarken intelligence system. He'd heard it from ex-Nordarken employees, particularly those who'd joined Celestial Navigations, the number-two strategic resource conglomerate, and main competitor. Anything Celestial could do to hamper Nordarken Mining they would, including passing information to the IDB.

Staring at Boyd's tiny form beneath the quilts he admitted *I'm no closer to making a decision and events are accelerating away without me. I can be drug along behind them, or I can get out in front of them. Soon, Clienen will order me to set the transfer date to Dominicus III.* He sipped the water. The clear taste bringing clarity of thought. *There are few absolutes in life, but this one is certain, I will never leave Marisa and Boyd.* He took a deep breath, exhaling slowly. *What else is there? How does career compare to love and family?* And though his mind shied away from it, he finally conceded, *even my oath does not compare.* His thoughts slipped into dark shadows, deeper, blacker, treacherous and malignant. *The only way I can save my oath, my honor, and leave my family is to kill myself.* He focused on his breathing, each breath soundless in the night. His chest rose and fell. A melancholy settled on him like dirt thrown in a grave, cold, heavy, and implacable. Death lay within, three simple command sequences to his embed chip and he was gone. Simple, he didn't even need to move. Marisa would carry on, Boyd would be taken care of, and the violations of his oath would end here.

"Papa?"

He froze.

"Papa, you sleep with me?"

He turned his head to stare at the pale face. *Can he read my thoughts?*

Boyd slid out of bed dragging a quilt with him. He tossed it in a heap on his father's lap and climbed up the chair. Snuggling close, he pulled up the blanket and said, “Papa we go sleepy."

Achelous finally moved. The devils of his dark thoughts dispelled by a small voice in the night. He wrapped his arm around the boy's boney shoulders and laid his head back. In the morning, he would start planning.

The embed alarm woke him. Marisa would be up soon, and he needed to place a call. He carried Boyd to their room and tucked him next to his mother. Marisa stirred, but he leaned in close, "shush, go back to sleep, it's not time yet."

He padded silently through the hall and up the stairs to the solar. On the deck outside, he climbed up to the observatory.

An idea he mulled was to keep the Auro Na temple field generator operational after the Dianis shut down. With it, he could come and go between Dominicus and Dianis. Wiping the transmit logs would be a problem, but he knew it could be done, but was it sustainable? How long could he travel back and forth before being caught?

The primary problem with that idea was it did little to counter the Nordarken threat. He could sneak into Dianis to visit Marisa and Boyd, but he'd have no time for other activities. The image of a Nordarken surrogate drilling and excavating on Dianis and invariably dominating the local populace came to his mind's eye. He fumed. He was certain they were the cause of his predicament, though he had no incontrovertible proof of their involvement, he did have four basic facts.

He leaned forward on the observatory railing not seeing the dawn creeping up the shoulder of Mount Epratis or the early teamsters delivering cargoes on the street four stories below. Pulling out the Auro Na bible, he opened a secure document and titled it simply: Planning. He needed to make a decision, and the four relevant facts were first--aquamarine-5--a critical strategic resource found on Dianis, was in short supply across the galaxy. Second, Nordarken Mining needed the resource, not just for profit, but to retain entire contract chains in the face of competitors. Third, Nordarken Mining knew of aquamarine-5 deposits on Dianis. Fourth, Nordarken Mining had repeatedly demonstrated they were willing to violate Class E sanctions, particularly when surrogate miners were willing to take the risk. The question was not if they would come, but when and how? He didn't have the proverbial glowing plasma, the one piece of evidence that told him they were coming, but he had an idea of how to get it.

He thumbed to the communicator screen in the bible and readied a call. Short of Internal Security finding the analyst from Water Resources and chasing the lead deep into Nordarken itself, he didn't know how else he'd get his evidence.

Letting the aural selector bring up Baryy Maxmun's A-wave locator, he placed the call. A-wave direct-direct was untraceable.

The call went through. The geo identifier placed Baryy in Wedgewood.

"Yea chief," came the agent's voice and mind's eye image.

Achelous could see tall trees in the dark background, snow still on the boughs. Spring came late to the mountains. "Did I get you at a bad time?"

"No, just hauling firewood to the cabin. I'm clear. What's up?"

"Well, I've got to make some inspection rounds in preparation for shutting down operations."

"Oh. It's going forward huh?"

He tried to keep from appearing as depressed as he felt, his voice business-like. "Yes," he nodded to the holograph imager, then forced a chuckle, "The director from Dominicus III called and wanted me there in two weeks."

"Two weeks!" Baryy looked around making sure no one saw him. "How are you going to do that?"

"I'm not, I've put him off for a while."

Baryy appeared relieved. "Oh good."

"How are you doing with the Timberkeep sensitives?"

Baryy cocked his head, "We've been making good progress."

"Can you wrap up your research in three weeks?"

Achelous could see the sociologist's jaw tighten. A long pause settled as the agent apparently dropped the load of firewood next to the door of a squat cabin. Snow was shoveled clear of the steps. "Yes, but it won't be as good. There is just so much to learn."

Achelous leaned back. "I understand. I don't think I can give you more time than that. But I do have an idea I want to run by you, it may help our cause." He laid out the idea, expanding and refining it as he went.

Baryy listened without interruption; a slight frown began to form halfway through the plot. Finally, after considerable hesitation, he brought himself to ask, “Is that legal?”

Achelous took a deep breath, not hiding his own discomfort with the idea. He would need the agent’s assistance if he were going to pull this off. “If you think there is someone we can work with, we can mind-wipe them afterwards.”

The agent’s frown deepened to a scowl. “I don’t know chief, this sounds sketchy.”

“Baryy, look at this way. What happens if I’m right? Rumors are already spreading about the aquamarine finds, both in-country and off planet. Who do you think will be first to be exploited if Nordarken sends a deep-cover research team?”

“Well, the Timberkeeps. But I don’t know, that’s a lot of ifs. If they really have the information, if they learn of the Timbers and sixthsense, if they send a deep-cover team to evaluate, if they contract with extrasolars.”

Listening to Baryy's skepticism, he had to agree the scheme seemed implausible, so he tried a different tack. “You can’t debate the aquamarine though. They’re hurting for it real bad, and have broken exclusions to get it before.”

Baryy sighed. “Yes, you’re right. It is a problem.”

“So let's try my idea as an insurance policy. If we don’t learn anything or they don’t see anything, then I’m just being paranoid, and we can button things up and head for Dominicus III.”

Baryy thought about it. As close to violating ULUP as Atch’s idea came, he was right that they should know if Nordarken Mining, or if other extrasolars had intentions on Dianis. The idea would actually aid his research, potentially propelling it far beyond what he originally planned, if it worked; and if the mind wipe took, and it usually did, then it would be no harm, no foul. Still, if the director or someone above him found out about the little escapade, the chief would have lots of explaining to do.

“Okay, but this is your idea.”

Achelous pursed his lips. “Absolutely. If it goes in the ditch, I take full responsibility. You were just following orders.”

Baryy smirked. "Yea, well, I'm a big boy. The sociologist in me tells me this is a good research project and good for the Timbers and maybe Dianis. The agent in me says it’s bad for ULUP, but that's your problem."

Chapter 10
Whispering Bough

Foothills of Mount Mars

Achelous met Outish outside the shift chamber. Their three eenus stood tethered at the entry ramp. Echo piped when it saw Achelous, and he went to check its harness and saddle. The steed fidgeted, restless to get back into open country. He patted her neck. “We'll be going soon.”

“So you've been certified by Field Outfitting?” He looked the young astrobiologist up and down, giving him a visual inspection. The reversible genetic alteration from Halorite to human was complete. His fur replaced by smooth, pinkish skin, and he sported the beginnings of a Doroman beard. His long hair covered by a typical Timberkeep stocking cap that hung to his shoulders. He suspected under the hat were signs of Doroman early pattern baldness. The big nose and prominent cheekbones fit, but the largish ears, a Halorite artifact Field Outfitting apparently could not compensate for, were an anomaly. Achelous smiled inwardly, the Timberkeeps would give him flak over those. The baggy britches, thick-soled sandals—another Timberkeep preference--heavy leather belt, leather vest over a linen shirt, and a heavy draw-tight cape completed Outish's authentic Doroman appearance.

“Yep, I have the gear you recommended, plus some things they suggested.”

Achelous cocked his head. “Have you gotten used to the physiological changes?”

Outish averted his gaze, “Uh, yes, but it's been a little weird, no fur and all. Very drafty. Just walking is windy. I need lots of clothes to stay warm. And this, this hair—“ he scratched his scruffy beard, it itches!"

Achelous gave him a sympathetic smirk, “We wear clothes. We don't run around half-naked like you Halorites.“ He opened the internist's cape, it was double lined with wool over flannel. “Let me check your gear.” He first examined the bags and packs on Outish's eenu, an older, well-broken steed with the patience of a long summer's day, and named Tulip. Satisfied, "Okay, so empty your pockets and your satchel."

"Uh? What for?"

"I need to check and see what you are bringing in-country."

Outish shoved his hands in his pockets. "But I've been cleared by Field Outfitting."

Achelous smiled like a patient parent. Exaggerating his motions, he looked around the bay area. "Funny, I don't see anyone from Field Outfitting here."

"But they checked me," he whined, "we went through the list."

The patient smile never wavered. "You haven't been cleared for insertion unless your team leader clears you, and today your team leader is Chief of CivMon, now dump your pockets."

Outish caught the edge in the word *dump*. "Okay, okay." On the stainless table next to the field operator's station, he emptied his pockets and satchel. The field generator operator, a grizzled technician who looked like he'd been around since they discovered aural energy, gave a tired smirk to Achelous. Achelous rolled his eyes.

Picking up a Transgenix multi-func from the items emptied on the table, Achelous asked, "What's this?"

"That's my multi-func."

Out of the corner of his eye, Achelous saw the operator turn away, shaking his head. The man would probably laugh, but he'd seen it too many times before.

"And you were going to carry it onto a Class E world?"

"But it has all of my music!"

This time the operator did laugh.

Achelous regained his patient smile. "Your music stays home. Take up the flute, they travel well." Achelous tossed the Transgenix into a holding bin for Outish to retrieve on his return. "You have your camo carbon-wafer multi-func, that's more than enough."

"But— it doesn't play music," Outish exclaimed loudly.

"On purpose," retorted Achelous. Then the chief inspector saw something peeking above the neckline of Outish's shirt. He opened the intern's vest and started unbuttoning his shirt. "Hey, what are you doing?" Outish complained, trying to slap away the questing hands.

"Undo your shirt."

"Why?" he asked petulantly.

Achelous arched an eyebrow, his patient smile gone.

"Okay, okay." He undid his shirt.

The patient smile returned. He pulled the hem of the undershirt out from Outish's pants and saw a label. "Hey Wian," he asked the operator, "do we allow Terestian Mica II on Dianis?"

"Without looking up from his hologrid, the operator responded, "Nope. Banned on all Class E."

"But I'll get cold!"

"You wanted to go in-country so bad," said Achelous. "Welcome to Dianis. You can wear leather, duck, silk, wool, shearcloth—"

"But wool itches," Outish grumbled.

"That's what the shearcloth is for. I don't recommend silk; it will mark you as a rich man, which you aren't, so someone would think you stole it. Where we're going, we want the respect of the locals, not their suspicion."

With their gear packed and Outish finally passing inspection, they shifted in-country. Achelous lead the way, quickly clearing the shift zone, cutting through the brush and intersected a trail heading north. He remembered the trail from his previous visit to Wedgewood, it was clearly mapped on the multi-func positioning system. He could call up a positioning transponder with his Auro Na bible, but it wasn't necessary.

They stopped at a promontory overlooking a broad plain and Achelous dismounted. In one hand he held Echo's reigns; the eenu contentedly browsed the fresh spring shoots. Eenu were always eating. Stop for thirty seconds, and the herbivore would find something to eat.

Taking a deep breath, he let the stress of shift-in ebb away. *I love going in-country.* He exhaled slowly and reflected on how long it took him to make the mental transition from Central Station and modern civilization to Dianis and its pristine wilderness. The air was crisp and cold, the sun rising behind them. He felt at peace. More than ever, he knew this is where he belonged.

Outish squirmed in his saddle like he had a case of hemorrhoids. Achelous, aware of the young intern's discomfort, tore himself from the view and went to check their pack eenu. Seeing Outish wriggle he chuckled as he tightened the pack straps. "What is it, that eenu not fit you?"

"No," Outish said defensively, "It's just that, well, with no fur down there, you know, on my butt, I'm not used to this saddle. It feels like I'm going to fall off."

Achelous checked the pack girth and satisfied, mounted up on Echo with the pack eenu tethered behind. "Well, you'll get used to it. Tulip there is about as broke as they come." Then on second thought, he turned to look at the young Halorite, "You did take the injection learning courses for riding eenu's?"

"Yes!" But he immediately demonstrated his poor riding skills by needlessly sawing on Tulip's reigns. Regardless, the old steed correctly interpreted the message and without complaint, and with considerable tolerance for her young charge, moved out to the trail.

Achelous waited for the young intern to get some distance down the trail before he remounted. The panorama before him lifted his spirits like the eagle he spied soaring above the plain. Letting the view fill his soul he smiled. Backing Echo, he gave her a slight squeeze, and she trotted after Tulip.

They halted near the forest rendezvous. This time Achelous checked their positioning in his bible. Baryy and a party of six Timberkeeps from Wedgewood were to meet them and escort them into Wedgewood. IDB tactics, contributed by Achelous, ensured they did not meet near the shift zone to reduce the chances someone could accidently locate the concealed entrance to the underground field generator bay. Some generator bays couldn't be physically entered from the planet's surface, like the one near the Auro Na temple, they were shift-ins only. The Wedgewood generator site, however, had a concealed exterior door and a supply cache, and could double as a cramped, but welcomed sanctuary in time of need.

"How could an eenu make that?" asked Outish.

Closing his bible, Achelous looked up. "What?"

"Over there," Outish pointed at a tree trunk. "It's the right height for eenu rub, but how could a bull make that sort of carving with its antlers?"

Achelous cocked his head. He moseyed Echo over to the Twitter Olen, a tall, smooth-bark tree with a pale blue sheen. "That's not eenu rub. That's a trog glyph."

"Trog?" Outish contorted his Doroman face getting used to the changes in facial muscles. "Oh, you mean *Nexisamaphibia Isueltai*?"

"Yes," acknowledged Achelous. "Otherwise known in the Dianis vernacular as troglodyte."

"Uh, well, that's hardly a precise term. Troglodyte can refer to so many species."

Achelous gave the astrobiologist intern a sidelong look. "Don't worry, we're on Dianis, and on Dianis troglodyte refers to big, ornery, warm-blooded lizard. Now get out your multi-func and scan that glyph. I need to know what it says."

Happy to oblige as he was actually doing work that applied to his astrobiology certification he pulled out a book, *The Lore of the Woods* that doubled as his carbon-wafer multi-func, and flipped to the correct page and enabled the scanner.

Relieved that the intern might actually know what he was doing, Achelous watched Outish nudge Tulip closer to the tree with just knee pressure as he used both hands to hold the book and run the scanner. *Guess the kid did take injection learning for eenu riding.*

"It's processing," said Outish. "It says—oh, this can't be good."

"What?"

"It says Spinex Tribe. Stump man die."

His eyebrows narrowing, Achelous moved closer to study the marking. "You're the biologist. Tell me how long the carving has been there."

"Well, depending on the levels of oxidation, subsequent discoloration, the onset of new growth, and the extent of overgrowth we should be able to calculate—"

"Outish, there's running sap draining from the scar. The bloody trogs carved it yesterday."

"Yes, I was going to get to that."

"It's a warning glyph. The trogs have expanded their range, and they've declared war on the Timberkeeps."

"How do you know that?"

"Because stump man is the derogatory form for Timberkeep. The trogs are insulting the Timberkeeps by referring to trees as stumps."

Outish swallowed. He began to regret the idea of masquerading as a Doroman changeling. Looking around, the forest took on more of an ominous aspect, the bucolic image it held for him just moments before evaporated with the translation of an innocuous carving. Instead of being pillars of nature, the tree boles were signposts of threats. He shivered and looked around for more glyphs. "Why are we meeting Baryy and the Timberkeeps so far from the entry point?"

Achelous pulled out his handbolt, a compact crossbow with a clever cocking mechanism. A hidden detent in the grip responded to his finger pressure and aural signature. The charge status indicator glowed, showing fifty. He released the detent, and the indicator resumed the appearance of wood. "Your weapon charged?"

"Uh, yes, Field Outfitting checked it before we left."

"Check it again," he said holstering his weapon and wheeling Echo about. "What are the rules for using the laser?"

"Uh, only in the last resort when the life of yourself or fellow agent is at immediate risk of great harm. A conventional indigenous weapon should be used in all cases until it proves ineffective in deterring the threat. Discharge of a non-indigenous weapon, regardless of need, shall be reported to IDB headquarters at the earliest practical time."

"Very good," Achelous smiled, trying to reassure the young intern as he fumbled with enabling the charge indicator on his handbolt. "Remove your glove and try it. Sometimes the aural scanner in a new weapon won't recognize your signature if it doesn't have enough reference scans. The glove may be attenuating your signature just enough to fail authentication, especially if you haven't handled the weapon before."

Outish removed his glove, and the cheery glow of the charge indicator showed eighty.

Seeing the number, Achelous started. "Eighty? What model is that?"

"Um, the guy in outfitting said it was the latest, a Seventy-Two T."

"Hmm, I'll have to get me one of those. I wonder if the laser's bigger?"

Outish shrugged. Weapons weren't his thing. Animals, plants, bugs, anything alive is what interested him.

"The reason we didn't meet Baryy at the shift point is we don't want to take the risk of anyone thinking there might be something special there. I wouldn't put it past the Paleos to dig up the place." He started Echo down the trail. "If they dug enough they'd eventually find the generator bunker. They know the Ancients liked to bury things, so the Paleowrights are mad about digging. I swear to the spirits that every inquisitor and examiner has a shovel strapped to their eenu."

Nearing the rendezvous with Baryy and the Timbers, Achelous pulled out his bible and brought up the inventory panel for the IDB cache at the shift point. It might be the last time -- with six pairs of prying eyes watching his movements -- to interface with the in-country cache system. He scrolled down through the inventory. Hmm,

I see Baryy has been there ahead of me. The Wedgewood cache was small, and its inventory made smaller by withdrawals assigned to Baryy Maxmun. Ten surveillance and five defense nanobots were checked out. Forty of the recon, surveillance, and defense bots remained. They were expensive little toys, and the IDB was fortunate to get an allotment as the bulk of the bots were going to the war effort.

He programmed ten recon bots and five defense bots and set them to launch on an intercept course for him and Outish. Five of the recon bots he set to seek concealment and bivouac halfway between here and Wedgewood, a good day's ride north. The remaining recon bots were to circle three hundred meters out from him with an equal interval between each. No bigger than a fly, and looking remarkably like one, it would take the bots some time to reach their position. If needed he could set them to emergency power, but their tiny electromotive engines would overheat in less than two miles. A marvel of nanotechnology, their filament wings could beat many millions of times before wearing out, collecting solar energy with each stroke.

The defense bots he set to trail his position by fifty meters and loiter when possible. They would find a tree branch or blade of grass to perch on to reduce wear and avoid attracting the attention of birds. He set the primary threat signature to troglodyte and threat priority to self-preservation, unless the primary threat entered the spotter search radius. Then action programming would change to agent preservation. They'd lost more than few of the bots to the Pomericia Fly Catcher, a beautiful teal, and scarlet bird. Unfortunately, for the IDB, the spirited little bird was adept at not only catching flies and moths but nanobots too. Sadly, because bots destined to Class E worlds were programmed to release nano-dissemblers that would cause self destruction in case of power failure or capture, once the bot was consumed by the bird, the decomposing bot would kill it.

Nearing the rendezvous Outish never noticed, nor could he, the presence of five defense bots trailing behind them or the invisible surveillance ring that orbited about their vector.

The two parties met at the rendezvous. Baryy made the introductions between them and Ogden, the leader of the Timberkeep party. The Timberkeeps, as a whole, were curious about Outish, his clan, and lineage. His official, carefully crafted story, placed him as a runner for Achelous and as a member of a Plains Doroman tribe from south of Tomis, far from Wedgewood. Back at Central Station, Outish had drilled on the Doroman injection learning modules and supplemented them with further research.

"Tork River? I hear there is good fishing there?"

"You guys build boats?"

"Any cute girls in that clan?"

"Yea, how many?"

The questions from the Timberkeeps came fast, and Outish handled all of them, sometimes with his imagination when they went way off script.

Amidst the questions, Achelous noticed one of the younger Timbers, Mergund, staring at Outish's ears. Achelous turned away, trying to suppress a smile. The young Halorite was in for some ribbing. *Oh well, the lad wanted to come in-country.*

"Ogden," Achelous addressed the leader of the Timberkeep party, "we came across a warning glyph about a mile back, along the trail. Are you having problems with trogs?"

Standing a half-hand shorter than Achelous--as was normal for Doromen-- completely bald, with bushy eyebrows, a mustache, and a thick brown beard that hung to his chest, Ogden's eyes were cheery, a twinkle of mirth hovering at the corners. A blacksmith by trade, his hands were heavily callused and scarred. "Oi, the loglards are up to their usual connivances, flustering and blustering about. We've set Lord Sedge on them. He's out here somewhere abouts."

"Lord Sedge?" Achelous asked. "You mean Sedge the Warlord?"

"Oi! That's him," chimed a younger Timber who possessed all of his hair, but whose beard resembled peach fuzz.

Achelous glanced at Baryy, who nodded. He couldn't help notice the agent sported a Timberkeep earring. Evidently, he'd settled comfortably in Wedgewood with the Timbers.

"Oi. They call him Lord Sedge."

Achelous noticed Baryy's use of the Timberkeep slang. *He's definitely lived with them long enough.* Facing Ogden, a man he instinctively trusted, he shared a candid opinion. "No vested lord would hire himself out as a mercenary captain, and Sedge is not a lord." He tilted his head. "But still, I'm surprised he's signed on with you. Sedge has led armies. The King of Mestrich did indeed offer him a lordship, but only if he would take a permanent seat at the king's table and lead the kingdom's forces. Sedge turned him down. He loathes being a barracks boss, he's a field commander." The IDB Dianis database on influential individuals, human or otherwise, went into detail, even to foibles. Which proved useful for when a field agent encountered the person. Much of the data came from Achelous and his CivMon teams, and Sedge the Warlord had an interesting dossier starting just before his arrival in Mestrich. "How many men did he bring with him?"

"Two companies," replied Ogden, "and I know he's no lord, but the boys like to refer to him as such."

"Two companies?" Achelous said surprised. "That's two hundred men give or take and a lot of expense for a clan your size. He usually contracts for a whole season. I'm surprised you can afford him."

Achelous read the guarded expression now dueling with Ogden's normally cheerful countenance. "We can afford it. And he's been good for us. He's out here now with a company running a sweep for the troglodytes defacing our trees."

"Oh, is that why you hired him? To fend off troglodyte incursions?"

Ogden hedged, "That and to organize and train our lads to fight better. He's running patrols to keep watch on our borders."

"This is farther north, and higher than what I think the trogs are accustomed to and the glyph on the tree singled out Timberkeeps. I know men and trogs are not friends, but we usually just avoid each other. If the trogs are coming up here, I would think, well, it's almost as if they are after you."

The intrigue surrounding the troglodytes was lost on Outish. He just wanted to see one in real life, not as a holovid. For the moment, he forgot he looked like a Doroman. His insatiable curiosity combined with the genetic oddity of warm-blooded reptiles was a combination ready for his insatiable curiosity about anything living. He'd taken time back at Central Station to study them in-depth. Unlike the non-sentient reptiles on Dianis, the sentient species of earlking, lizardmen, and troglodytes were warm-blooded. True, their heat regulatory systems were inefficient compared to humans, but they could still sustain their own body temperatures. He agreed with Achelous though. In his study of Dianis fauna, he would have thought this oak-pine habitat zone too cold for the troglodytes, at least in the spring. Yet the glyph was recently carved. *Could the trogs have a more efficient heat chemistry than first assumed? If so, does that make them more intelligent than the other reptiles?* Current science presented a compelling case for linking the ability to regulate body temperature in bi-pedal reptiles to their cognitive capacities.

Ogden hooked his thumbs in his belt. He ignored Achelous's implied question. "Our feud with the Great Swamp trogs goes back three generations, before my time, when we were living in the Southern Forest, a day's ride from the Great Latitudes Swamp. In those years, we traded freely with Hebert, and like you said, trogs and men aren't meant to mix. But back then, we didn't fight the way we do now. We even managed to trade tork eggs and marshcat. The Hebert city folk have a taste for marshcat bloom. They grind it up and smoke it in their pipes."

Achelous nodded. Tangential to his spice business he'd received requests for marshcat, but IDB doctrine forbade merchandizing psychoactive drugs as part of in-country operations. He preferred trading in edible spices, gemstones, and weapons. Weapons for the captains and generals so he'd know where the next war was brewing. Gems for the kings and merchant's wives so he'd know where the next coup was forming. Finally, spices for the cooks and chefs because they were always bragging about who was coming to the ball, so he'd know what alliances were forming.

"So what happened?" asked Baryy.

A variety of emotions played on the blacksmith's face. He started once, then twice, and finally settled on "I don't think anyone really knows. Just that the trogs grew increasingly hostile, until one night, they attacked. The clan expected trouble and were ready for them, almost. Trogs are devilishly good climbers and were over the walls even as the alarm bells rang. It was a bad fight; the clan lost heavily trying to hold the wall, but in the city center the clan council had ordered three great bonfires readied, with hundreds of naphtha arrows stacked nearby—"

Outish looked at Achelous, "Naphtha?"

"Trogs don't like fire."

Ogden chuckled, "No boy, they don't. While their hides are thick, and in places tough as plate armor, the skin oil burns easily. So our archers shot their burning arrows and drove the screeching trogs back into the swamp to sooth their scorched hides in the muck water.

"For some months an uneasy stalemate settled in with the trogs constantly raiding our villages outside the Bough and the Timbers mounting patrols. Then word reached the Bough from the Life Believers in Hebert that the Church had grown frustrated with the constant warring in the countryside and was preparing to march its regiments to settle the dispute. No one can explain why, but the

Paleowrights had sided with the trogs against us, their own kind, and the churchmen were coming to demand the Timberkeeps leave, at the point of two thousand spears." Ogden's fellow Timberkeeps were solemn listening to the tale. The story of Whispering Bough chronicled their exile from their ancestral homelands and defined their existence. While life was good in Wedgewood, it would always be the place they fled to out of fear and not settled out of choice.

"When the clan elders met to discuss the treachery the clan chose the better of two bad fates. They chose to immediately evacuate Whispering Bough and the outlying communities--on their terms--not some farce dictated by the Church. That night Azerorn Talltree, the clan's greatest warrior led a surprise night attack on the trog war camp.

"Life is about small favors," he said, twisting the end of his beard, thick and smoked with grey, "and The Mother herself granted one to Azerorn that night, for the wind blew out of the east, carrying with it the sea air and smells of the Angraris. The trog's keen sense of smell was for naught. With kindling, naphtha, and spark boxes, our warriors launched their attack. Outnumbered heavily, Azerorn planned to surprise, confuse, and shock the trogs into disarray and then quickly retreat, hoping to buy time for the clan to flee north.

"And success flowered there that night, but in the years since has withered. The troglodyte chieftain and a stout band of his warriors pursued the retreating Azerorn through the flaming arrows and there in the swamp did battle our Whispering Bough champion.

"They say the ring of axe against axe could be heard in the highest minarets of Hebert, three leagues distant. The troglodyte chief was fast and powerful as are all trogs, but Azerorn was filled with conviction and the stalwart blood of Doromen. In the end, sacrifice for friend and family conquered hatred and revenge. Azerorn smote the trog chieftain and left his bloody corpse to stain the Great Latitude."

The Timberkeeps were silent, even Ogden brooded.

"Uh—" Outish stirred, befuddled, searching the Timberkeeps, "Why so sad?"

"Tis simple, lad," said the blacksmith, "We believe had Azerorn made good his escape without killing the chieftain there'd be no feud. To the trogs, a great wrong was done to them, and rather than let our clan flee beyond their ill will, the troglodytes issued a *kurchka,* a blood oath, that they would never rest until their chieftain was avenged. And here we stand today, sixty years later, fretting over warning glyphs. For the trogs are unavenged, and never will be." With the last, he put his hand on the hand axe holstered at his belt.

Achelous, a trader of weapons, out of habit glanced at Ogden's eenu, and sure enough, a broad double-headed battle-axe lay strapped behind the saddle.

"And that be the cause of the Timber's Curse, the sickness that dogs our every step," Mergund challenged.

"There's no proof the brain-galls are from a trog curse," retorted Ogden.

"There could be other causes for the malady," Baryy interjected, "and probably are. It could be something in the soil or water in Wedgewood that was not present in Whispering Bough."

Achelous calmly turned to Baryy, his expression flat. Baryy looked away, his face suffused. The agent was treading dangerously close to violating ULUP. Providing information or direct assistance to an indigenous population, in this case the Timberkeeps, with knowledge of how to fight the Timber's Curse was strictly forbidden. He made to change the subject. "Ogden—"

"Please, you may call me Og."

Achelous nodded, "Og, we are some distance from the Great Latitude. I make it almost seventy leagues. Moreover, we are much higher here than in the swamp. Something just doesn't smell right. How did the trogs know to find you here?"

"The Paleo's told them," blurted Mergund.

Ogden looked pained. "We don't know that-- for certain."

Achelous rubbed his chin. "Okay, it's been sixty years. Word would get to the trogs eventually." He shook his head dismissively, "They probably learned you settled here not long after you cut your first log and split your first shingle. And," he nodded at Mergund, "the Paleowrights could have told them, so what. It doesn't really matter. This is cold country for trogs, why come now? And it's only spring; if the trogs are here now, there will certainly be trouble by summer." He left it unsaid as to how hot and dry it could actually get. "They could, "he hesitated, not wanting to be alarmist, "reach Wedgewood. What's happened in the Great Latitude to cause them to come here now?" Achelous, of course, knew exactly why the troglodytes were this far from the Great Latitudes. He and Baryy exchanged a glance. The question he wanted answered was did the Timberkeeps know the true connection between the troglodytes and Paleowrights. What did the

Timberkeeps suspect? While the pirates were a tool of the Paleowrights, the troglodytes were their thralls.

"What are you saying?" Ogden guarded his expression.

"I'm saying troglodytes have proven to be easily manipulated. They're primal creatures, quick to take offense. I could see, not that it is true, the Paleowrights encouraging the trogs to harass you. But like you said, it's been sixty years, what's fanning the flames now?"

"Those Paleos, they hate us too," chided another of the Timberkeeps.

"What would the Paleos have to gain from sending the troglodytes after us?" Ogden gruffed.

Exasperated, lacking the patience of Achelous, Baryy interjected "Gold Og, your gold." Baryy waved his arm in the direction of Wedgewood. "You have a gold mine up there. The Paleos need money for all the churches they're building and Ancient sites they are guarding. Those Scarlet Saviors don't come cheap." Both Achelous and Baryy knew it wasn't the gold that drove the Paleowrights, but the yellow metal served as a useful surrogate.

Ogden shook his head. "Noi, trogs don't trade in gold. It has no value to them. What would the Paleos offer the trogs for them to invade Mount Mars and attack cold Wedgewood?" He shook his baldhead dismissively.

If only you knew Og, and apparently you don't. "Does it matter?" asked Achelous. "With control of your gold mine, the Paleowrights could buy whatever they promised the trogs." He arched an eyebrow, "Og, perhaps it's not the gold in your gold mine that they want, but the aquamarine you found."

The Timber's eyes widened. "You know about that?"

Achelous turned to Baryy, who supplied "Og, it's not much of a secret, there's a whopping great pegmatite sitting on the floor in Murali's." This was even news to Achelous whose eyes gave away his alarm.

"And Murali's," Baryy went on, "is not exactly the sleepy little tavern it used to be, with all the gold miners, prospectors, and carpenters flocking to Wedgewood. Sometimes you can't even get a stool at Husher's DinDin, and you know how greasy that place is. Murali's is the best pub between here and Hebert. Anyone who walks in there half-schooled in the lore of the Ancients will have an idea of what that blue slab of hex crystal is."

Achelous finally asked, his voice a harsh whisper, "How big is it?"

Baryy, his expression neutral, said nonchalantly “Standing on the floor, it reaches your waist.”

Achelous gaped at Ogden, “And you’ve got that sitting in the open?”

Chapter 11
Troglodytes

Foothills of Mount Mars

The trail meandered through the olems and firs hugging the shoulder of the ridgeline. To their left, a wide park settled into a bowl shaped by the opposing ridge. The party followed the trail as it kept within a few paces of the tree line, close enough to the open spaces so they could spy any movement across the expanse, but deep enough in the forest, so their movement was broken by the trees. The Twitter Olems were still bare, just budding out, but the occasional stands of firs and spruce offered better concealment. Lettern, one of the two female Timbers, rode point in the party of nine. Ogden praised her abilities as a scout and claimed she had the eyes of a hawk, to which Lettern calmly demurred, her shoulder length hair braided under a leather headband stamped with the clan's scrollwork. Whenever the trail rose to a crest, she would slow their pace, and as they approached a dark stand of firs, she would halt them entirely, testing the wind, checking for tracks.

"Why don't we just ride out there?" Outish asked Baryy, pointing at the park. He and Baryy were near the end of the pack train. "Because we'd be seen for miles" Baryy replied over his shoulder." Outish gazed out at the wide expanse. He could see a raven sitting on a rock clear across the field. Relishing his first foray into a class E world, he pondered the many differences and similarities, comparing them to his own experiences and what he'd learned so far in his young astrobiologist career. "So why are you so sure the Paleowrights are able to control the troglodytes? I mean they are reptiles, they are so different from humans or Halorites." He said it quietly, keeping out of earshot from the nearest Timberkeep.

Rocking gently in the saddle as the eenu hooves crunched through the dry olem leaves, Achelous answered, "You did your research on the troglodytes, or should I say Nexisamaphibia Isueltai. You must have read about their dependency on sage-rose."

"Yes, but it is only a dependency if they get hooked on it. It's like abusing any psychoactive substance. Besides, sage-rose doesn't grow around here. How could they get hooked on it?"

"The Paleowrights give it to them," said Baryy, riding behind.

"Huh?"

"Yep. They grind it up, dissolve it in alcohol, and inject it into tork eggs."

"What? That's ridiculous!"

"Shsssh," hissed Achelous. "Not so loud. And why is it ridiculous?"

"Well," Outish sought for a reason, "how would the Paleowrights even know to do that? And why would they want to do that?"

"The answer to your first question is simple," Achelous replied. "They learned it from the Ancients."

Outish twisted in his saddle and mouthed in a whisper "They learned it from us? How?"

"You probably read the book, *Dianis, the Zoological Perspective of the Lock Norim Legacy?"*

"Yea, it's the guide on Dianis flora and fauna. A bit dated, only four hundred years old," he snorted. "It was written as a reference for the transportation engineers."

"Yep, and the Paleowrights have a copy of it."

"No," breathed Outish.

"And they made copies of it too, or we would have lifted it from them," said Baryy.

Achelous rose up in the saddle, stretching his legs. "The book does a credible job of laying out the physiology of warm-blooded reptiles. The author paid particular attention to troglodytes because they represented the biggest risk to the construction crews. The Paleowrights found a copy of the book in some long-buried Transportation Authority dorm they excavated. They have some very talented archivists. They read it and started experimenting. Eventually, decades ago they started injecting tork eggs with the sage-rose. Tork eggs are a delicacy to the trogs. They didn't need to get all the trogs high on sage-rose of course, just the chieftains, subalterns, and their mates. Pretty soon, the trog chieftains refused the plain tork eggs. They'd only eat the spiked ones. Eventually, the Paleowrights quit bothering with tork eggs as the delivery mechanism and just offered ground sage-rose as a snuff in little pouches. It's how you can tell if the trog is someone important by the little leather snuff pouch hanging from their neck."

"Seriously?" Outish said amazed. "But why would they want to do that?"

Achelous took a deep breath and thought about the Diunesis Antiquarian Church's long history of population manipulation and cultural influence. "Who knows why they did it in the beginning, and the part about injecting tork eggs is all Paleowright ingenuity. The book does not say how to get the trogs hooked, just that it was physiologically possible."

"Devious bastards," said Baryy staring out at the park.

"The Paleowrights have subterranean halls filled with archivists and examiners pouring over every Ancient artifact they have." He paused and considered Paleowright motives. "The interesting thing about sage-rose is you can't get it locally. It grows on the Isle of Ompo, in the Drakan Empire, and yet, to my knowledge, the Drakans have no idea of the real reason, the secret reason the Paleowrights buy it from them. To hold troglodytes in thrall. It's just part of the Paleowright's larger strategy of manipulating Nak Drakas. They constantly promise the emperor new weapons, new technologies that the empire could use against the Western Alliance, and yet they rarely deliver. Instead, they keep all that knowledge to themselves."

"In a way, they are doing our job for us."

Achelous agreed, "Yep, they are controlling the propagation of extrasolar influence."

"Okay, okay, so if you guys are right and the Paleowrights can actually tell the trogs what to do by just waving a bag of hooch in front of their nose, do you think it was the Paleowrights who instigated the attack on Whispering Bough? If the trog chieftains were high on sage-rose, it would explain their erratic behavior."

Neither Baryy nor Achelous answered.

Outish looked at them. "What? You guys aren't talking."

Baryy finally said, "The Timberkeeps have no hard proof, but the circumstantial evidence fits. The Timberkeeps are Life Believers, and they resisted conversion to the Church. Living so close to Hebert at the time we know the Paleos considered it an affront, a very public rejection of everything the Paleowrights stood for, and they just couldn't let go."

"But we have hard proof," injected Achelous.

"What? What proof?" asked Outish.

Pitching his voice to just above the clomp of hooves on the pine needles, Achelous said, "Outish, often, for a person to act natural when under cover it is best they don't know the truth, that way they are not living a lie."

"Yea, so."

"So there are many of things you don't know, so you can act natural when dealing with the Timberkeeps. It takes a lot of time and practice to live a lie, as we do, without getting caught."

"Yea, so."

"So we seeded the Hebert cathedral with surveillance bots. In the archbishop's private chambers specifically."

Outish rode along, quiet, considering the implications. "What did you learn?"

Achelous sniffed. "Lots."

"The bots have only been there for a few years," said Baryy. "So we don't know—yet—what were Paleowright's specific involvement was sixty years ago in Whispering Bough, but we do know, they have a sophisticated and well adapted method of manipulating the troglodytes via the distribution of marshcat."

Outish squinted in the sun slanting through the trees. The confusion and complication between the various factions and species were beyond, way beyond what he expected. He thought he'd be touring peaceful villages, visiting locals, and updating the IDB database on indigenous species.

Not wanting to give up his pastoral vision of peacefully collecting data for his astrobiology certification, Outish asked, "Why would the Paleowrights send the troglodytes up here, so far from the swamps?"

"The same reason they got Tomis to issue an embargo against Linkoralis. The same reason they are paying pirates to raid Tivor shipping. They can't have anyone but the Church controlling the collection and distribution of aquamarine, any aquamarine. No one on this continent, or even Linkoralis, holds an aquamarine amulet or another artifact without a certificate of ownership from the nearest Antiquarian bishop. No one. And if they are suspected of holding aquamarine the Church sends a squad of Scarlet Savior goons after them." A tingle in Achelous's thigh brought his attention back to the surrounding forest. The embedded recombinant crystal buzzed with a warning frequency. He looked around and quickly brought out his bible. Holding it close to his chest so no one else could see he cracked it open just far enough to view the screen of the surveillance monitor. "Damn," he swore under his breath and snapped the bible shut. "Uh, Og," he called out loudly, "we need to stop."

Echo halted, as did Baryy and Outish but the rest of the party continued.

"Ogden, Lettern—stop!"

They halted and turned in their saddles. He had to think of something fast. "Did you smell that?"

Ogden had a blank look, and Lettern frowned, shaking her head.

He spurred Echo beside the trail and stopped abreast of Lettern. "Trogs," he whispered, though he suspected his yell had given them away.

Again, she shook her head. "I didn't smell anything, and the mounts aren't shying."

Agitated, he stood in the stirrups. "I've smelled them before; I just now caught a good whiff." Troglodytes were renowned for their thick, musky odor: a combination of urine salts and fish guts. "Do you mind if I take point, just for a bit?"

Her brows knit into a tight band and he belatedly realized he'd insulted her. But there was nothing for it, the spotter bots were orbiting three hundred meters out and reporting multiple targets. "I'm sorry, maybe I'm just paranoid. Humor me." And before either she or Ogden could disagree, he spurred Echo and pulled out his handbolt holding it up so everyone could see. Baryy, at the back of the pack, wondering at the commotion saw Achelous hold up his weapon. He immediately turned to Outish, "Weapon up, Atch has bandits." Drawing his own handbolt, he one handed his wallet, dropping the reigns and letting his mount follow the other in front. With a practiced motion, he called up the sensor display guessing that Achelous had surveillance bots orbiting the trail.

"How does he know?" hissed Outish.

Checking the screen, *Oh, oh,* thought Baryy. "Recon bots," he whispered at the intern.

Achelous knew they were in a pickle. His instincts screamed bolt left and lead the party out into the park away from the impending ambush, but if he didn't spring the trap and the troglodytes stayed put, he'd look the fool and wouldn't be trusted. Churning through the variables his dilemma was solved for him when Echo suddenly set her hooves and skidded to a stop. A stand of dark timber loomed ahead of them, the trail snaking through the center of it. While he couldn't smell anything himself, he knew Echo could. The warning tingle from his thigh embed escalated to buzz; the trogs were moving closer.

Seeing the eenu stop short Lettern pulled her bow and notched an arrow. Signaling a halt, she eased up beside Achelous, her own steed piped and made to back-pedal. She calmed it with a reassuring "Shush."

"Well," asked Achelous, "do you want to go in there?"

She gave a quick shake of her head, "Left." She kicked her eenu into a trot, waving for the team to follow her as the eenu threaded the distance to the tree line.

Achelous held his position until Baryy rode by and he then fell in behind Outish. "If they attack don't stop, just keep going, Baryy and I will hold them off. We'll call Ready Reaction if—"

"*Karaaaaga dulaaaa!*" The hoarse, guttural cry sounded from the dark timber, and a troglodyte sprang into view hefting a spear. Outish gaped. The thing was scarier than the ones in the holovids, it was bigger, taller than a man, uglier, with fangs protruding up from the lower jaws and short horns sprouting from the side of its head. Two huge flaring nostrils contrasted with its small piggish eyes. Its skin, what he could see of it beneath the crude jerkin, was an olive drab. More trogs appeared and one holding a spear heaved it at Lettern. She ducked low in the saddle as it arched overhead.

"Go!" Achelous smacked Tulip on the rump. "This is not a biology experiment, quit gawking and ride!" Echo needed no urging and literally vaulted away. Trees rushed by as branches whipped at him and reached for his eyes. Achelous squatted low in the saddle. In a brief flashing instant, frozen in time as Echo hurdled a dead fall, Achelous could see a swarm of ten-plus trogs bounding after them in their odd, loping run, their long muscular tails pointing out behind them in counter balance to the forward lean of their bodies. Echo landed its vault and dug in with all fours, dirt flying.

The defense bots, alerted by their surveillance cousins, lifted off from their loiter and shifted modes from self-preservation to agent preservation. Bot Five, per bot protocol, assumed the master bot role. It designated targets and set threat thresholds. Agent number Three—Outish--was immediately assessed as highest risk, and the defense bots sped after him.

The on-duty Solar Surveillance agent was pouring a cup of jorra from the autoserv when his multi-func chimed with an alert. Sipping from his cup, he checked the status. Chief Inspector Forushen's in-country team showed red. The agent thumbed through readout. Feeds were streaming in from five surveillance bots. He read them, "Shiren!" He dropped the cup in the sink and hit the alert button. Running to the command center, he contacted the Ready Reaction team in the Ready Room.

Ivan Darinarishcan answered, "Ready Room."

"Hey Ivan, are you Ready Team leader?" He was surprised to get the chief of Ready Reaction himself.

"Yes, I'm in the rotation. What do you have?"

"I have a threat Level Charlie reported by surveillance drones attached to the Forushen party."

"Composition?"

"Twenty troglodytes in pursuit of the party, there are nine members in the party, six provincials, three IDB, all on eenuback." The agent could almost hear the chief assessing the situation, principal amongst the considerations was when and if Forushen would trigger his talisman and escalate to threat Level to Bravo—danger imminent--requesting an immediate and direct intervention by Ready Reaction. Ivan could if so inclined, preempt by shifting in-country before escalation to threat Bravo and be in a better position to intervene. The problem was his team would be committed while other in-country CivMon parties would be exposed with no immediate Ready Reaction coverage.

"I'm alerting the backup team."

"Roger that," responded the agent, "Connecting you to the surveillance feed now."

Outish hung on for dear life. Eenu riding via injection learning was one thing, the actual experience of flying past trees and galloping across the rock-strewn landscape, dirt clods flying from hooves, and watching the riders ahead of him dig into their mounts was way too realistic. Tulip dodged a large sage bush and sprung over another catching Outish by surprise. He nearly fell off clutching tightly to the saddle pommel and Tulip's mane. In his tunnel-vision death grip on the saddle, he barely glimpsed the hand-axe fly by, spinning end over end, and thud into the turf ahead of him. Comprehension dawned, *whoa, was that meant for me?* He tried closing his eyes, but it only made the terror worse. At least Tulip knew to follow Echo even though Achelous was visibly pulling away, leaving a growing hole in the pit of the intern's stomach.

Defense bot One, on direction from Five, targeted the lead troglodyte that had the speed and angle to intercept agent Three. The trog was far ahead of the pack and made to leap at the haunches of agent Three's mount. Bot One zipped in and struck the target in the ear, the designated target zone for troglodytes, and the thinnest for the tiny nanobot stinger to penetrate.

The troglodyte screeched, grabbing its ear and went down in a hard rolling heap.

Outish twisted in alarm. A trog sprawled in the dirt, barely an arm's reach behind. His eyes widened, and he grabbed the reigns tight and for the first time urged Tulip to, "Go! Go! Go!"

A horn sounded from behind Lettern. Then, to her dismay, it was answered by another on the opposing ridge to her left. Lettern drove her eenu over a creek that clove deep into the park's soft soil. She cleared the landing and wheeled about. Achelous crossed behind her and pulled up.

Ivan watched the feed from Solar Surveillance. The agent had a satellite coming into position; visuals, aurals, and infrared would be up in a minute.

"One of five deployed defense bots has successfully executed an attack. Surveillance bots are detecting sound signatures of a second aggressor force approaching from the west." The agent's image showed to the right of the multiple sensor panels on Ivan's holodesk.

"Acknowledged," replied Ivan. "Come on, Atch, don't wait all day to pull the cord. Call danger imminent. We don't want to rescue a corpse."

Sergeant Horalznick and the rest of the five-man team stood behind Ivan watching the action. "You ready to go?" asked Ivan without looking back, not so much as a question, but as a clue he was about to take matters into his own hands.

"Say the word," Horalznick checked the team status display on the rear wall. "Back-up team is arriving now."

Ogden's mount jumped the creek, and he pulled it up from its headlong rush to stand chafing next to Lettern. "We've got company," he pointed to the western ridgeline, a group of troglodytes swarmed down through the olem boles running in their odd, undulating lope, their long thick tails held parallel to the ground as their torsos angled steeply forward. Some carried weapons: clubs, axes, and spears. Most ran naked except for decorations of chains, bones, little leather pouches, and teeth necklaces rattling against their chest. Others wore crude tunics sew with bits of bone.

Just then, a third horn sounded from a wooded knoll situated near the head of the broad valley but more to the east.

"Ula! We can't fight them all!" exclaimed Lettern.

"You're right," said Achelous. He clasped his IDB talisman and signaled danger imminent. Alarm bells were ringing in IDB Central Station, Ready Reaction command, and Solar Surveillance high overhead. Beacons in the embeds of agents all over Isuelt were buzzing. He was about to yell "follow me," when Outish came thundering past on Tulip bellowing "Go, go, go, go—" the old steed had her ears back and digging turf for all she was worth. Whether it was fear of the troglodytes or a desire to be rid of Outish was uncertain. Achelous gaped. The intern clung to the saddle, reigns slack, eyes wide, and definitely not in control, but Achelous realized Tulip had a purpose. Alert to her surroundings, the wise old steed galloped for a gap between the trogs in the west and the blaring horn in the east. "Follow Outish!"

Wheeling Echo about he gave her a hard kick, and she launched after Tulip. He prayed the nanobots' early detection of the ambush afforded them enough edge to let them flee the park before the trogs could move to block their escape. The eenus, encumbered by their riders, were still faster than troglodytes, but only just. It would be a close thing. Tulip followed a natural angle that kept her between the trogs running on their left, and the band emerging from the knoll on the right. The wind rushing by, Achelous predicted the eenu's course; *if we can just get past them, we'll be in the clear.*

The troglodytes on the knoll saw the humans change direction and angled their pursuit. Both eenus and troglodytes raced through the sage and scrub grass, flitting past treacherous gopher holes, and dodging rocky outcroppings.

Achelous gradually caught up with and drew abreast of Outish. The intern did a double take. Fearing he would be passed and left behind he resumed his chant, "Go, go, go, go, go!" Poor Tulip laid her ears down afresh and redoubled her efforts to quell her irksome charge.

With dread, Achelous heard a wail from behind. "Batar is down, Batar is down!"

He turned in the saddle in time to see a hapless Timberkeep in a twisted sprawl. His mountain pony thrashing in the dirt with a broken foreleg, victim of a gopher hole. The other Timbers were turning to rescue their fallen comrade.

"Blast!" Achelous leaned back and hauled on the reigns. He tried to turn Echo about, but she had the bit and wanted to beat Tulip. "Woa! Woa!" He sawed the reigns and pulled hard right forcing Echo to claw her hooves and skid. "Outish, keep going!" he yelled as if the intern had plans to the contrary. Achelous prodded Echo around, its flanks hot, beginning to steam. He eased her into a gallop then raced back to the fallen warrior.

"Baryy! Attack the trogs! Achelous spurred at the nearest trog just in range of his handbolt. It was a jarring ride galloping over the broken ground and the troglodyte's undulating run made for a difficult target. The distance closed quickly, and Achelous veered left. Bringing the crossbow up, he fired.

The trog stumbled and fell; a quarrel in its hip.

Swiftly, two-handed, reigns free, Achelous reloaded the handbolt and took aim at another troglodyte when a massive weight slammed him from behind, and he catapulted off the saddle. Flying through the air, he caught a whiff of trog breath and saw the ground. Hitting hard, they tumbled through the sagebrush a mass of arms, legs, and tail.

Bot Five designated Agent One as highest risk.

Ogden waved his axe and bellowed "Charge!" He lead four Timbers in a line abreast past Baryy who sat astride his mount shooting his crossbow as fast has he could set, lever, and aim.

Ogden despaired their charge wouldn't reach Achelous in time. The Tivor trader was doomed, a mace blow his sure death. Inexplicably the trog wielding the mace screeched and clutched at an ear while the trader rolled clear. Two other trogs swarming to the trader similarly fell. Not questioning how or who killed the assailants, the blacksmith led his riders through the troglodyte pack. He hoped to drive them away and extricate themselves before they were overrun by the other groups.

Achelous ducked and rolled not letting his fourth attacker get a grip and rake him with rancid claws. He held on grimly to the handbolt though the quarrel was long lost. Pulling back from a snap of the trog's jaws, he armed the laser via its aural connector, stuck the handbolt in the monster's ribs, and fired.

A look of surprise dawned on the trog's slobbering face, and then another laser pulse turned it to agony.

Achelous rolled the beast away and staggered up. A trog charged him with an axe, and he fired the laser square between its eyes.

Shaking off his shock and gathering himself, he saw the Timberkeeps in a melee about him. A Timberkeep was being dragged from their mount only to have her attacker feathered by Lettern's arrow.

Recon bot Five assigned a target to the last defense bot. The bot sped past the running and galloping forms fixing on a troglodyte swinging around behind Agent Two. The bot skimmed past Agent Two on a collision course and struck the troglodyte's ear. It latched on with micro grapplers, raised its abdomen, and jabbed the one-shot stinger of *terratetrohydiboro* into the nerve endings of the reptile. With a wail, the creature succumbed to the last of the defense bots.

"Achelous! Get on your eenu! We ride!" Ogden waved at Echo behind the temporary battle line of Timberkeeps.

Achelous staggered past Mergund and grabbed Echo's reigns.

A new sound, different from the trog horns, came from the east. It carried to them again, this time a distinct trumpet, refined, holding an ululating pattern as it floated over the prairie grass. Baryy recognized it immediately, having heard it on the Wedgewood practice grounds. "Follow me!" he waved. Heaving the unconscious Batar up in front of his saddle he remounted and spurred toward the trumpet.

The two packs of trogs from the ambush and western ridge were nearly upon them. Achelous knew Baryy could not outrun them while riding with the extra weight. He pulled up behind Baryy's eenu and prepared to fire a quarrel at the nearest pursuer. Ogden and the other riders charged past and wheeled waiting for him and Baryy to catch up.

Not managing more than a trot with the extra weight, Baryy called back to Achelous, "Leave me! Go ride ahead!"

Achelous pulled up to Baryy's flank and gave him a stern look. He was there to stay.

Baryy turned away and fired a quarrel at a wyvern coming up on his right. Slowing Echo, Achelous pulled behind Baryy and then sped up on his right, firing a shaft into the same trog's leg, causing it to crash into the powdery dirt. He peered out across the park and was disheartened to see the three packs merge into one, green, undulating, growling mass of pumping arms, slavering to close the distance.

"Go, go, go!" Outish called, but gradually slowing Tulip came to a halt. "Huh?" A trumpet called from the park. Then a chorus of peeps and pipes echoed back. Outish slapped the reigns on the eenu's neck and kicked, but the animal refused to budge. Instead, paying him no heed, she turned about and stared with her big brown eyes. “Hey! No, no, no, this way!” He pulled the reigns hard left and instead of turning, she reared. “Woa, eenu, hold on.” She dropped back down, and he gave her slack, frightened, yet greatly relieved he still sat in the saddle. More piping came, and Tulip piped herself, and then let out a screech that made him blanch.

Far down the field, an answering clarion call came bright and clear.

What? Are there eenu’s calling to her? He wondered. In the distance, down the gentle incline, two opposing lines of combatants formed. On the left, he was surprised to see a long staggered line of cavalry charge across the plain. On the right, a dull green mass of loping troglodytes surged, the two groups on a collision. In between were two lone riders heading towards of the cavalry. Whence the cavalry came, Outish had no idea, but another warbling eenu call came to them, and this time he saw six other riders galloping in from the right, closing on the rear of the troglodytes. *Who the spirits...are they? Six riders against thirty?*

Tulip pawed the ground twice, shied a bit, and then launched herself back down the park.

“What the—“ Outish exclaimed, trying to slow her, but the eenu ignored him.

“Well met!” Ogden yelled over the thunder of hooves and the shouts of the riders. They galloped side-by-side, tall grasses blowing between them, the cold wind tearing their eyes.

"Nearly dropped on you, did they?” Sedge called back, smiling grimly across the gap. “You’ve found my quarry!”

“Oi! Not by choice.”

Achelous aimed for a gap in the oncoming line of eenumen, and as the riders pounded past he heard the immediate crash of steel, keening of mounts, grunts of men, and snarls of reptiles.

He slowed Echo, now lathered and heaving. Turning her about, he took stock. Baryy halted nearby and dismounted, carefully lowering the unconscious Timber to the ground. The cavalry and trogs were fully engaged with the eenumen sweeping through the horde lopping and chopping as they went. Breaking through, the cavalry whirled, and the trumpeter called to form up. Bracing for the charge, the troglodytes formed their own line. A rising note from the trumpet sent the eenumen into a gallop.

"Ready?" Achelous asked Baryy as he loaded his handbolt.

Baryy quickly nodded and struggled back on his skittish animal as it shied from the chaos. Getting it pointed at the fracas he called, "Ready."

"Ha! Look there!" Achelous pointed with his weapon.

Ivan and the Ready Reaction team skirted past the edge of the battle and came at Achelous and Baryy at full gallop.

Achelous waved his arm, indicating they should join the fight, and before Ivan could countermand, Achelous sent Echo at the melee.

Oh, oh, thought Baryy, *This isn't good, Ivan is going to be livid.* Directly aiding one sentient species against another, regardless of troglodyte versus human, was strictly forbidden. Moreover, CivMon doctrine clearly stated agents were to avoid combat and extricate themselves from danger at the earliest opportunity. Compounding the problem, Achelous was about to drag a Ready Reaction team into the fight; a team that should instead be preserving its strength in case other in-country teams needed assistance.

Achelous at first looked like he was about to drive Echo straight into the melee when he pulled up and fired his handbolt.

The trogs, overwhelmed by a full company of cavalry, broke and ran for the western ridgeline.

Achelous fired twice more, and then he and Baryy were joined by the Ready Reaction crew. He noticed with relief that the reaction team had Outish in tow. He grinned at Ivan's scowl. "We had to make it look like we wanted to help. We're going to Wedgewood, and we need their cooperation."

Ivan let his expression go neutral. He gripped the saddle pommel and sheathed his long sword. "Good to see you too, Atch."

Achelous's smile turned into a smirk. "Thanks for picking up my intern. Thought for sure he'd be in Lamar tonight."

Sergeant Horalznick laughed.

"No, I was not," Outish protested. "I turned around and was coming back to help."

Skeptical, Achelous was tempted to ask how Outish came by the sudden fortitude but thought better of it. For some reason, Tulip drew his attention. The steed returned his inspection with a sorrowful gaze, the huge brown eyes at once innocent and ageless. Whatever transpired, it wasn't talking.

Suddenly afraid Achelous may somehow guess the truth, Outish turned Tulip away. For better or worse, they were now co-conspirators.

Achelous went to holster his handbolt when Ivan asked, "Did you discharge that?"

Thinking the chief of Ready Reaction was going to remind him of the regulations to file a report for discharging a non-sanctioned weapon, he replied, "Yes, three times. It was either them or me." *And that's a problem,* he thought. *If the Timberkeeps bother to check my victims, they won't find any crossbow bolts, and in one trog they'll see a neat, cauterized hole, dead center in a bony forehead.*

Horalznick said, "Better you alive than otherwise."

But Ivan, serious as ever, replied, "There's dried blood on the aperture."

A troop of the Timberkeep cavalry was returning, and Achelous had to turn away quickly to inspect the weapon. Sure enough, at the end of the fore stock, where the spiral aperture was situated as part of the advanced cocking mechanism, charred blood caked around the camouflage shielding so it could not close, exposing the aperture. He jammed it into his holster as Ogden and another fellow rode up.

"Achelous, are you hurt?" Ogden asked concerned.

"No, roughed up maybe," but when he stretched, his grimace told otherwise. "Nothing that won't heal, after it complains long enough. Baryy has one of your warriors over there," he pointed.

Ogden signaled to Lettern and Mergund to help their fallen comrade. Mergund led two other mounts, one draped with a body, mute testimony to the savagery of life on Dianis.

Outish swallowed.

"And this here be Sedge," Ogden said in his simple way of introduction.

Achelous had never met Sedge but had seen images of him in his IDB file. The mercenary commander looked younger in real-life. He held his helmet in the crook of an arm exposing shoulder-length grey hair tied off in a ponytail. He had side burns, a close-cropped goatee, mustache, and a natural arch in his left eyebrow. An old scar angled along the left side of the jaw. His face was ruddy from exertion, but Achelous guessed he was a Lamaran. His IDB personnel file went back only ten years or so and didn't list his heritage. Before those ten years, Sedge was an enigma. "I'm glad you found us. How did you know we were here?"

"What? With all that ballyhooing? Bloody sounded like a trog festival with all the horns and howling. Couldn't help but come and have a look see." In truth, Sedge and the company of his mercenaries had been trailing the larger band of trogs. "And you," he dipped his chin at Ivan, "I see their horns brought more than just bees to the honey," he took in the six tough, capable looking men. Their eenus were well fed, which was odd for mercenaries. Even Sedge's own mount showed ribs compared to theirs, but mercenaries they were judging by their thick studded armor and well-oiled swords. The armor was mismatched among the men, no badge or insignia visible; the tack and harness were as varied as the armor. He assumed them men of a free company, but he had watched them angle in from behind the trogs, and by the way they kept their order and efficiently cut down the trogs in their path he knew them well trained and disciplined. Yet, curiously, they lacked the lean, hungry look of men living from one client to another. These men were calm, confident, self-assured. "Kind of odd for mercs to come running to a fight with no guaranteed pay."

Before Ivan could respond Achelous said, "It was a fortuitous circumstance. I've hired Ivan and his men in the past to guard my caravans that travel this route." Then to Ivan, "I gather you recognized Outish, my runner, though how you came to be here now is a mystery..." Achelous arched an eyebrow, doing his best to appear curious while knowing the truth. It was a game they played in front of the provincials: who could spin the most creative story.

"Word has it," Ivan said, "the Wedgewood council pays a bounty for loglard horns. Am I not right?"

Achelous blinked, now how did he know that? Ivan ever so faintly smiled at him. Baryy must have filed it, and to Ivan's credit, he'd downloaded the information before the insertion.

"True," said Sedge, "but you boys will not be claiming a bounty today. This was our fight, we carried the day." The last he said daring Ivan to contradict.

Unperturbed, Ivan casually pointed, "There are four trogs over there that bare our handiwork. We'll claim the bounty for them."

Sedge appeared to size up Ivan. The merc was unblinking, his expression even. "They were fair kills, true enough, but my lads would have had them anyway." Competition amongst mercenaries was fierce, and Sedge brooked no bounty poaching from his men.

"Perhaps," acceded Ivan, "but not before the youngster there..." He tilted his head towards Outish. "Was laid bare for some trog's trophy rack," referring to the troglodyte's preponderance for skinning their victims.

Sedge turned pointedly to Achelous. "What say you, trader, you owning up for your youngling?"

Caught off guard, Achelous took the hint nonetheless and feigned a grumble, "How much?" He squinted at Outish.

"What?" the intern carped.

"Four silver pennies, Lamaran, Faldan, or Wedgy, makes no difference," smiled Ogden cheerfully. "One for each loglard."

"Plus two more for saving his life," chided Ivan.

"Six silver pennies! That's more than two week's wages," Achelous griped at Outish.

The intern's jaw dropped, taken aback. The thought of Achelous not wanting to pay six measly pennies for saving his life unnerved him. Or was the chief inspector just acting?

Achelous reached into his purse, counted out six silver pennies, counterfeit of course, but real silver, and of the correct weight nonetheless. Fresh from the Margel Damansk. "These will be coming out of your pay Outish. It's your skin they saved."

Ivan pocketed the coins, hiding a secret smile. The IDB giveth and the IDB taketh away.

"I figure you to be from a free company. Who are you riding with?" asked Sedge.

"No one," answered Ivan. "We're on our way to Taldamir. Signing on as guards for a wealthy merchant. Though picking off a few trog hides," and he jingled his purse, acknowledging Achelous, "helps pay for our meals and fodder along the way."

This was code to Achelous. Depending on the cover story offered by Ivan, Achelous was to respond in a specific way, indicating whether it was safe for the Ready Reaction team to leave, stay, or be ready to attack. "That wouldn't happen to be Deuel?"

Ivan nodded. "Yes, you know of him?"

"I've traded with him." Which was Ivan's cue that he could leave.

"So his promise of silver is good?"

Achelous shrugged. "He's always traded fairly with me."

“Well, in that case, I think my men and I will bid you gentlemen farewell and go in search of more lucrative opportunities.”

“You could sign on with me,” offered Sedge. “As you’ve heard, the Timbers are paying.”

Ivan averred, “Thanks for the offer, but Deuel is expecting us, and...” He waved his hand at the bodies of the dead trogs and that of four Timberkeep troopers, “I suspect Taldamir might be a bit quieter than here.”

Sedge smiled sarcastically, “Don’t tell me you’re running from a fight?”

Ivan laughed at the warlord’s bald attempt to incite his ego and spur his professional pride. "There's easy money, and there's hard money." He signaled his men to move out. “Keep your silver Sedge. If I need hard money, I know where to find you."

Chapter 12
Lock Norim

The ruins of Lycealia

Having spent the night in the relative safety of the mercenary camp, the party bid their farewells to Sedge at dawn. The mercenary commander planned to pursue the stragglers of the ambush and make a wider sweep beyond the park for more troglodytes infiltrating the foothills of Mount Mars. The sun climbed bright and cheery in the east melting off the prairie frost from the budding catsclaw bushes and tufts of willow grass.

An hour of riding in silence behind them, Achelous succumbed to his duty to collect intelligence and prodded Ogden into the conversation. "So what brings a blacksmith out here to shepherd a couple of traders?"

"Blacksmith? Ha!" I leave the blacksmithing to my apprentices. They make the nails, hinges, and latches. Sure, some of the work is intricate and technical. So I'll help the lads with the design and processes, but I reserve the bulk of my time for weapons and armor. Armor saves lives, and oi, I make some of the best."

The way Ogden said the last so simply and without airs, Achelous took him at his word. "Oh," he apologized. Seeking common ground he went on, "I trade in weapons; armor can be bulky and expensive to transport. Plus, as you know, the best armor is custom fitted. With weapons, the attraction is greater. Not as profitable, but I can sell more. Warriors and bravos tend to collect weapons, but they usually can only afford one set of armor."

"Oi, I forge weapons too, and you're right about them. What's the first thing a man buys to defend himself, a shield, or a sword?"

"If she's an archer she'll make her own bow, forsake the shield, and shoot her enemies long before they come in arm's reach." Lettern, riding behind Ogden, smiled brightly when the two turned to look at her.

"Right," acknowledge Ogden, "But a bow takes more skill. A farmer defending his livestock from thieves will pick up the sword first."

"Or pitchfork," interjected Lettern, grinning mischievously. As a member of Ogden's Second Ward, she knew the armorer well. He loved to say "Pitchforks are for hay, and hay is for eenus." So he left the pitchforks to his journeymen.

"Because," Ogden continued unfazed, "the threat of injury dealt by the sword is as good a defense as the shield or hauberk. And," he emphasized, "you can attack with the sword."

"The sword only defends on its edge. Don't miss the parry." Commented Achelous.

Ogden nodded, his beard rubbing on his chest, "After you've traded a few sword blows then you appreciate a good shield. And because a man has only two arms, he needs a helmet. And because he can only look one way, he needs pauldrons, and so it goes. But that's why a good armorer always has a ready stock of weapons because the bravos come looking for weapons first and buy your mail later. And, oi, if the sword you sold them breaks or takes a nick when it should have cut they'll not be buying your armor. So you can't sell them any old piece of sharp tin." Turning, he glanced at the handbolt holstered on the trader's hip. "You can tell a lot about a man, or..." he winked at Lettern who appeared to not notice, but smiled nonetheless, "a woman, what kind of weapon they carry, and what kind of weapon they want. Those two are different."

Achelous began to appreciate Ogden's sense of business. "So you use weapons to bring the bravos into your shop where they will appreciate your armor, and if you did a good job on their sword, they'll buy your chain mail."

"Well, that's a bit harsh, but not too far off the mark. Fine chain mail is the most expensive item in my shop. One full chain mail hauberk costs as much as ten good swords."

"He doesn't need to lure them, trader," Lettern said. "Any fool on Mount Mars or leagues around knows there is only one forge to trust your life to, even if I am an archer."

Ogden grunted and pointed a gloved hand, "Now that crossbow of yours, interesting design—where did you get it?"

Achelous casually glanced down and suddenly remembered he'd failed to clean the burnt blood off the fore stock: As long as it stayed in the holster, no one would notice. "I traded for them at a bazaar in Eastport. Why do you ask?"

"Oi, because until we met at the park, I thought Baryy's was unique. One-of a kind. Some lost Ancient design I'd suspected. But now I see yours, and your lad Outish has one, and even that merc captain, Ivan had one. Makes me think they can be manufactured in quantity. May I look at it?"

Not for the first time did Achelous consider it ill advised that so many CivMon agents armed themselves with the handbolt. But the weapon was well-designed, passed ULUP certification for in-country use, and efficiently concealed the deadly little laser. Abruptly he pulled Echo out of line, "Baryy, can I see your handbolt? I'm curious if it is the same exact design as mine. I thought perhaps it was different."

Baryy, immediately on alert, rode to him, "Yea, sure," he leaned down to pull it free, "What's up?" he whispered.

Achelous held out his hand, counting on Baryy to trust him and follow his lead. He inspected Baryy's handbolt. "Hmm, they're identical, though yours is cleaner, mine is dirty and has blood on it." Baryy's eye's flickered, getting the message. "Og is curious about their design. Ogden, want to try it?"

Ogden came to Achelous and signaled to Lettern to keep going, they fell in behind. "Oi, you read my mind. It's heavy!" He examined the cocking and spanning mechanism that set the handbolt apart from other crossbows. Rather than made of wood, the limbs were made of layers of spring steel. Little did he know, the steel accounted for only some of the extra weight. The laser power cell being the primary culprit. The spanning lever nested along one side of the forearm and stock. "May I?" asked Ogden as he instinctively brought it up two handed. As its name implied, the weapon was usually fired one-handed, but two-handed it was deadly accurate. Achelous handed him a quarrel. Riding his eenu Ogden imitated the motions he'd seen of during the trog fight. Ratcheting the lever forward, pinioned on the front of the forearm, he cranked it back, watching as the twin cams pulled the bow and cable tight in the process. He set the quarrel and took aim at one of the huge anthills that dotted the park and pulled the trigger. The dart sprang away with a satisfying twang. Ogden grinned, seeing the quarrel buried in the anthill. "Oi, those oblong wheels are ingenious, that's why you can lever it with one hand! And all from eenuback. I didn't have to dismount." He eyed the weapon appreciatively.

And a fifty-shot pulsar laser concealed in the stock was a bonus, thought Achelous. Should the stock become damaged, exposing the internal casing to air, oxygen would activate nano-dissemblers in the casing and immediately consume the laser componentry turning the hollow stock into a gooey mess.

“We could make these. It would take some doing, but I think we could devise the casts necessary to make most of the parts, and I can forge the steel limb sheaves, though I admit, I admire whoever built these. Those limb sheaves are fine, fine work." He looked up, "Eastport you say? Is that where the armorer is?" A look of professional concern and jealousy crossing his countenance.

Achelous ignored the question. “Do you have a blast furnace?” An idea he'd been nurturing, a grand idea, something with so many challenges he couldn't know them all, suddenly had an ally. Unwitting perhaps, but an ally nonetheless.

Ogden peered at him quizzically, “I don’t know about a blast furnace, but we have a furnace. It’s a small one, but I have a design for one bigger one. Large enough to produce five hundred pounds of molten iron per day.” His pride in the vision reflected off Achelous. He gave the weaponsmith credit, erecting a large foundry in Wedgewood without the supporting infrastructure of a large city like Tomis, Zursh, or even Tivor was a huge undertaking. Unfortunately, he’d have to grow it considerably bigger in both capacity and capability for what Achelous had in mind. Yet Ogden’s knowledge and existing abilities were on par with the blacksmiths in Tivor. Tivor was by far a larger city, it had a major port for shipping raw materials and finished goods, and there was, of course, Marisa, Marinda Merchants, and her close connections with the aorolmin. However, neither she nor the aorolmin stood to lose or gain what Ogden did. For Ogden, Achelous’s idea may very well mean survival for their entire clan.

Ogden interrupted his thoughts. "What did you mean by a blast furnace?"

Achelous arched an eyebrow. *Don’t they have blast furnaces on Dianis? I thought they did?* He tried to remember foundry capabilities across the globe, but without the aid of his multi-func, he couldn't run a query. He decided to risk bending ULUP. "Ah, well, it's just what the name implies. It builds on what a bellows does, but makes the entire process continuous. Instead of smelting pig iron in small batches, you get a steady output stream of molten metal, within limits."

Taken aback, Ogden asked skeptically, "Ula. How does it work?"

"Well, I'm no expert, but I know coal, iron ore, and limestone are continuously dumped into the top of the furnace while an air-compressor of some sort, could be from a water wheel, pumps air into the bottom of the furnace. The outflow of the furnace is driven by the amount of fuel and ore dumped in the top and the volume of air pumped in the bottom. If you can keep the firebox hot enough with the jet of air, you basically have a stream of molten iron. There is a gating mechanism you open periodically to let the molten iron flow out."

Ogden nodded slowly at first and then became animated. "Oi! I can see how it could be done. You can have a stone cauldron with a sluice gate to moderate flow--" and he launched into monologue conversation with himself working through the details of how to build such a furnace.

Listening to him ramble about conveyors and lifts and a steel-frame fan, Achelous grew impressed by the weaponsmith's agile mind and his infectious can-do attitude. He decided to offer him a deal, more of a test, but a deal nonetheless. "I tell you what, if you can convince me you can make the parts and build fifty of these handbolts, I'll give you one to disassemble and copy. We can talk about the terms of the partnership later."

Riding behind, Baryy eyed Achelous. *What is he up to? Why would he go out of his way to have non-laser handbolts manufactured in-country? He'll have to place a requisition to Field Outfitting to make a handbolt without the laser components. Why?*

"Oi, outstanding! Let me take a peek at the one you have when we get to Wedgewood, and I'll make any part you want. That should convince you." Ogden beamed, and clasped Achelous on the shoulder.

They rode further along. The trail, a hard packed course wide enough for a wagon, wound higher and higher into the foothills, the sage and chaparral growing thinner, giving way to varied grasses and patches of a low flowering ivy with tiny orange buds. Stands of olem, firs, and now pines intermixed amongst hidden parks. Ahead in the distance Mount Mars loomed, snow draped its flanks.

"There's still snow in Wedgewood?" Achelous asked. They had most of a day's ride left and a solid climb ahead of them. Snow in any quantity would slow them, forcing another camp.

"Oi." Ogden pointed to a notch in the mountain's left shoulder. "There be our dale, sheltered from much of the bad weather that roams about the mountain. We get our fair share of snow though, to be sure. We still have piles of it under the eaves, but else it's mostly gone."

Achelous let his head bob with the easy gate of Echo. "You never did tell me what brought an armorer out here to the low-lands, as an escort. Surely you have enough work to do managing your foundry."

"Oi. I'm a warden in the clan militia. We've never forgotten the loss of Whispering Bough. With loglards spreading further west and higher up the clan council decided we needed to organize better. Instead of just sounding the gong and expecting every able bodied Timber to come with axe in hand – which we still do—the council, at Sedge's advice, thought it good to muster out wards and assign each ward a set of patrol duties and watches. I be the warden for my ward. I have forty fighters, men and women, drawn from me foundry, Erv's stables, Morgat's tanning operation and a few other businesses along our stretch of road. Sedge organized the entire militia, and the clan appointed him as the commander of the garrison. He has an ops officer that runs the duty roster, watch rotation, patrol schedule, and the like. It was my ward's turn to patrol the main road, all the way down to the park, so here we are. Though now I wish we'd brought more troopers." He didn't mention the pain he felt at returning home with one dead Timberkeep, one badly injured, and three dead mercenaries. There would be grief to pay. Erv would sorely miss his wrangler, as will the lad's mother. He thanked Mother the lad wasn't married and with younglings. The loglards were becoming a painful problem.

Achelous sensed the unspoken. "You have our gratitude for your protection."

It was simply said, simply offered, and simply accepted.

Ogden stared at the trail; then raised his eyes to the horizon. "If we didn't run patrols the loglards would choke off our trade. And that be no good. Oil for our lamps, flour for bread, hops for ale, and all manner of supplies come by wagon. If the loglards..." he let it go without saying. They'd have to abandon Wedgewood. It would be devastating. He had no idea where they would go. Where ever, the clan would be forced into a vassal role, renting land, becoming holden to landlords and no longer true stewards of the forest or their fate.

Achelous pondered the predicament. "Do the trogs know they are that much of a threat? I mean, do you think they are marshalling in such a way as to purposely force you out?"

Ogden pursed his lips, then shook his head. "Noi, their raids are more of a nuisance." He clamped his jaw. The fact was the foothill raids were an increasing nuisance, and the higher into the foothills they came, the more nuisance became a disruption. Already the clan was forced to pay gold from their mine to Sedge and his mercenaries. Regardless of the youngling's age, Mergund's earlier comments echoed in his ears: *Why now, after sixty years, are they clawing our trees with their crude obscenities?*

Ahead, Outish and Mergund rode beside each other. The similarities between the two drew them together, at least until they understood each other. Each was a young Doroman apprentice in their master's business, and each had a firm idea of how they would manage things should they be put in charge. Mergund yearned to forge his own axe but complained to Outish "I spend so much time stoking the forges, shoveling coal, and clearing the water wheel of debris that I can only practice at castings and work on the anvil at the end of the day when most of the contract work is finished. By then my arms ache, and my eyes burn."

After a silence, Outish realized Mergund was staring at him. "What?"

"Huh? Oh." Mergund turned away and pretended to stare off into the distance.

"What is it?" prompted Outish. This was his first time in-country and the first opportunity to interact one-on-one with a provincial, and he was nervous. Could he do it without blowing his cover? Would he say something wrong like blab about the Turboii, or expose knowledge that would have him labeled as an Ancient? The CivMon rules for speaking with provincials seemed fraught with all sorts of opportunities for slip-ups. Fortunately, the native language if the Doromen was easy to master, a variation of Avarian Galactic adopted by the clans and many of the western Isuelt cultures during the seventy-five years Transportation Authority engineers roamed about Dianis before ULUP, and without discretion. But navigating the culture and norms of Doromen was trickier. He didn't entirely know when something was normal or amiss, and it weighed on him.

Mergund turned back quickly, happy to be prodded. "I was just wondering, can you hear better with them?"

Outish blinked several times, attempting to fathom what Mergund meant. Then, aghast, "What do you mean?!"

"Those," Mergund stared, "your ears."

Outish started. He desperately refrained from reaching up and covering them. "What do you mean? They're normal!"

Mergund Laughed, “For a rabbit maybe.”

Outish glared and was about to offer a scathing retort when he remembered from injection learning it was custom amongst young Doroman males to find a physical fault with others of their peer group. It signaled acceptance and established the mechanism by which each would tease the other, thereby setting limits as to what was fair game. If a Doroman was a cripple but had largish lips his friends would tease him about his lips, studiously avoiding the more obvious and painful detriment. The trick was, in return, finding the physical abnormality of the antagonist to use in the by-play. Failure to find the same flaw meant exclusion until you did. Most young males got around this by waiting to hear how other people teased the person. On the trail, Outish didn’t have that convenience. However, Mergund’s physical oddity stared him in the face. “Well, I’d rather have rabbit ears and hear my enemies sooner than have that peach face of yours. Is that a naked baby’s butt? I'd freeze on a summer’s day. Honestly, how do you survive?”

Rather than look crestfallen, Mergund reached into a saddlebag and proudly pulled out a striped scarf that matched his knit cap. “I don’t ever freeze, winter or summer,” and he shoved the scarf back in the pack. “But those ears-- do you tie yourself down in a gale? You could take flight!”

“No, I tuck them under my cap, it keeps them from flapping. I can see with your peach face that you at least don't have to shave, but does your nanny get confused about what end she needs to wipe?”

"You hide them under your cap? What is it, a tent?"

They kept at it, one teasing the other until they’d firmly established the bounds of their ridicule, although, being young men, Mergund's fictional nanny became a topic of discussion. "Is your nanny cute? She'd have to be if she were going to wipe my butt."

The trail came to a cross road where it met a larger way. A stout sign pointed in two directions; the "Wedgewood" arrow pointed at the north road angling uphill through thickening pines and firs. The other arrow, pointing east, read “Lycealia.”

As Lettern, on point, was about to go north Achelous called out, “Hold up a minute.” He turned to Ogden, “I’ve been to Lycealia before, but Baryy and Outish have never seen it. I think it’s about an hour, do you mind if we take a detour?” It would indeed be good for the two other CivMon agents to see the site, but Achelous had been apprised of new activity there, and so he had ulterior motives.

"Oi. You want to?" Ogden offered.

"Yes." Registered on the federation's Galactic List of Protected Historical Sites Achelous considered it one of the best surviving examples of Lock Norim culture on Dianis.

"Good. We can be there and back and still make town before dinner."

"You sure? I'd not want to make it much of a bother." He glanced back at Baryy who said, "I'd like to see it too, for all my time up here I've never made it there."

"No bother," said Ogden, "been there enough times myself, but I can always stand to see it again. A mysterious place it is. I always get a feeling of being watched while I'm there. Can't quite explain it, but it is grand, truly different."

"Grand? How so?" asked Baryy. He suspected Ogden felt watched because as a protected site it was under direct IDB surveillance.

"The Ancients of course; they built it. Though why they would build it out of marble and not concrete like they built everything else, is a mystery. And there's not a nail in the place. It's not as if it was scavenged either. There's none of the usual damage you see in old ruins, like bolt holes torn loose or rusting studs staining the stone." He scratched his beard. "The Ancients loved their metal too, yet there's not a brace or bolt to be seen."

"Excellent, an enigma." Achelous smiled at Ogden.

Behind him, Baryy smiled inwardly at his chief's ability to act the role. *He wears the cover of a trader like his own skin.*

They rode the distance to Lycealia until the marble edifice began to emerge from the surrounding forest.

"The Paleos are here of course," grumped Ogden, slowing his mount. "Lettern, hold up," he trotted ahead, and Achelous followed him. The warden desired to take the lead and be the first to meet the new occupants of the site.

"Why are the Paleowrights here?" asked Achelous coming up beside Lettern and Ogden. Video and satellite surveillance had detected their presence, but he'd not had the time to send a team to assess the visitor's intent. If they'd come and gone CivMon would have ignored them, but they'd apparently taken up permanent residence. Not that the IDB could do anything, the rights of provincials under ULUP trumped any federation protection of historical sites. They could, if they wanted to, raze the ruins. It had happened. The most CivMon could do was watch and record the event.

"Oi," he spat, "Their high and mighty archbishop in Hebert declared it a mission. Built a little hovel with a guard shack of all things. There's a priest that will probably demand a tithe from us just for looking." Uncharacteristically Ogden scowled. He stood in his stirrups scanning the area ahead.

"Oh-- I can pay the tithe for us, all of us," offered Achelous.

Ogden shook his head. "Ula. I won't pay it, nor will I let you pay it. Out of principal. It has sat here silent and serene for eons. Who are the Paleos in their hubris to think they can just move in and claim it for their own? And demand a toll besides? They have no right. No Paleo hand shaped those blocks nor set those stones. Bah, no Scarlet Warrior could ever build such magnificence; the stones fit so tight a blade of grass will not grow between them. It is a work of art that has become part of the land itself. Would you charge to view the mountain? Of course not. Lycealia has been here so long its bones are those of the world. No man can claim ownership."

Ogden struck a deep chord, and Achelous wasn't about to disagree with him. The Paleowrights, on the other hand, held a deep-seated belief they were the protectors of all things Ancient and fervently attested that without their stewardship the rich heritage and history of the Ancients would be lost to scavengers, antiquity traders, and fading memories. A point Achelous couldn't argue either; they were both right. However, what he could argue against were the methods the Paleowrights used and dogma they propagated to bolster their image and coffers. But that was his personal opinion, not his professional duty. Control of Lycealia was strictly an indigenous issue. The IDB could intervene against extrasolar depredations or excavations but were powerless to against provincial souvenir hunters.

Ogden spurred his mount forward and trotted into the clearing surrounding the ruins.

Outish halted in the line abreast, formed as the travelers came out of the forest. "Incredible," he breathed to no one in particular, but Mergund heard him and nodded, mute. Like Outish, this was the Timber's first visit.

Out of the surrounding forest, the marble structure rose six stories in its white-turned-grey height. There were two parts to the site. A large open-air amphitheater was dug into the earth facing the soaring rise of Mount Mars; the pine and fir forest framed the view. The marble seats were deep set so a spectator could rest their back as they gazed upon a raised stage. The construction was a perfect semi-circle, the depth of the seating allowed for seating of five hundred spectators. Hosting large spectator crowds apparently not the objective, but more so the quality of the experience. When the site was built, an age ago, the Lock Norim population on the planet was miniscule. The second and grander feature of the site gleamed brightly in the sun. Compared to the sublevel amphitheater, the marble building bulked like a perfectly symmetrical iceberg. Crowned with a gleaming white dome -- half of the edifice's total height -- the structure resembled a temple, though no statues or religious icons adorned its facade. "What's in it?" asked Outish. History, in general, was his weak point, except when it came to genetic evolution.

"An indoor theater," replied Lettern. Do you want to go look?"

Outish shifted uneasily in his saddle. Darting off with a Doroman, a female no less, without Baryy or the chief's guidance unnerved him, but before he could frame his reply Mergund said, "Oi, come on floppy ears, let's go have a look," and Mergund trotted his eenu into the clearing and onto the marble apron surrounding the site.

Lettern dismounted with her bow, passing her reigns to the Timberkeep beside her. Stepping softly onto the apron she paused, glancing back to Ogden.

The warden simply nodded.

Not to be out done Outish slid out of his saddle and made to join Mergund who was now dismounted and peering into an open door.

"Outish, take your weapon." Achelous, followed by Baryy, dismounted and drew their handbolts from the saddle holsters. "You coming?" he asked Ogden.

"Oi, my lads and I will stand guard. I'm waiting for that priest to show himself.

Achelous nodded sagely. He swept his cloak open so he could reach his quarrels and cautiously walked forward. He saw Lettern had an arrow notched. The video monitors back in Central Station were probably recording their actions, though he couldn't remember the camera angles. Certainly one of Gail's big birds had a lens fixed on them.

"Your first time here, what do you think?" Achelous asked Baryy.

"It's beautiful. Perfectly architected to fit the dale. It's as if it belongs here. Always was here, and forever shall be. The carvings on the edifice even draw out the harmony of the wilderness."

Achelous peered at the carvings that adorned the header just below the dome. Woodland sprites, pirogies, toadstool gnomes, and dancing dwarves cavorted amongst marble ferns, forest lilies, and regal spruces. Achelous casually glanced about, ensuring they were out of earshot. Referring to the carvings, he said, "Only the trees are native to Dianis, the rest is from off-planet." Achelous smirked, and Baryy nodded vigorously. "You'd have thought the Locks would have been more parochial, respect the local culture. It's like—"

"You are trespassing on holy ground! This land is under the protection of Diunesis Antiquaria, and none shall pass without my permission!"

Achelous pivoted and out from the building behind the amphitheater stage a priest shuffled into view leaning on a well-worn staff of gnarled wood.

Outish froze in place, but Mergund gave the priest one look and ducked mischievously into the theater.

"You there!" The priest brandished his staff, "I'll have you out of there you miscreant blasphemer!" Striding up to Outish, his shuffle now a strong gate, the priest jabbed the intern in the chest with the staff, "You are trespassing. Leave at once!"

"Hey you old geezer, watch your stick!" Outish backed away from his antagonist, who's stubble-strewn, sunken cheeks, pale skin, and prominent cheekbones reminded him of cadaver just raised from the dead. He had grey eyes and lank white hair that contrasted starkly with his red, four-cornered cap. His white priest's vestments were smudged with wood ash, particularly at the hem. He wore black slippers. Around his waist was a wide, red sash that matched his cap. Tied around the sash was a rope belt of green silk.

"You dare to chide me!?" The priest's eyes flared, and he raised his staff to strike.

Outish instinctively stepped further back. "Woa grampy, you off your meds?"

Achelous blanched. Baryy mouthed to him "Meds?"

The priest vaulted forward, neither age nor infirmity impairing his step. He swung the staff aiming its gnarled handle straight at the apprentice's head.

A loud "thwack" sounded, Lettern parried the staff with the arch of her bow and took the shock in her outstretched arm.

The priest seeing her for the first time glared incandescently and drew back.

Lettern's other hand held an arrow, and she sprang forward jabbing it at the priest's neck. The honed edge of the broadhead stopped just at his jaw. She held it there, the steel point pressing into his skin.

The priest stood rooted, his glare turning to shock as he stared her in the eyes. Cold danger, unrelenting as the stone beneath their feet lurked in Lettern's green eyes whose pupils were tiny dots in the morning sun. She didn't waver.

Achelous came forward. "I'd be careful sir. I've seen her kill, she's quite good. Lower the staff, nice and slowly."

Anger flared anew on the priest's visage, but when he tried to face this new speaker Lettern thrust harder, keeping the arrowhead firmly under his chin. A thin trickle of blood began to seep down the stubble.

"That's my apprentice you tried to bash the brains out of," Achelous said in a calm but firm voice. "And he was doing you no harm. After you lower your staff, you can tell me how we are trespassing."

Slowly at first, then swiftly, the priest let the staff fall to his side.

"Smokes, put that geezer's cane in a bio processor and him with it," Outish mumbled under his breath.

Achelous signaled to Lettern, and she pulled back, taking three quick steps, knocking the arrow as she moved.

The priest had no doubt she could draw and release before he could get to her. "You'll pay for this," he hissed. "My guards will be back soon, and then you will pay."

Having quite enough of the drama, Ogden rode his eenu forward and looked down on the priest. "Then bring on your guards so we can be done with this farce, priest. Tis a free land and no one has claim to Lycealia. You had no call to attack young Outish here, and under Clan Law, I as a Warden of the Wood may arrest you for willful mayhem."

"A Timmy are you," the priest sneered. "I should have seen it right away."

"That's because you were too busy wailing at me with your stick!" enjoined Outish.

Achelous darted him a warning look, and Outish pouted. He grumped something unintelligible and stalked away, heading toward the theater.

"I'll have the Saviors on you I will," called the priest. "I'll have the lot of you arrested for defiling an Ancient site."

Achelous hooked his thumbs in his belt. "How much?"

The priest shook his head, "Huh?"

"How much to let him have a look?" and he tilted his head towards Outish.

"No. We shall not pay," blurted Ogden. "I came here when I was a lad. There were no," and he fairly spat the word "Paleos then and there should be no Paleos now. Lycealia belongs to all men. It is no one's to charge for."

The priest's expression hardened, and he was about to launch a tirade when Achelous rolled his eyes and interrupted. "Fine, how much for some information?"

"Information?" The priest rested his staff on the ground, leaning on it. The tension of the conflict clearly weighing on him.

"Yes, information. I want to buy information. That's why you are out here right? To earn money for the bishopric back in Hebert. Let me guess, they're banging the pulpits of the temples proclaiming that Antiquarian faithful should go on a pilgrimage to Lycealia and worship. And when they get here, you levy a tithe. Or does the Church have something grander in mind? Hmm, let's see, there is both an outdoor and indoor amphitheater... a perfect place for indoctrinating the ignorant masses."

The priest began to look wary, his jaw working.

While Achelous interrogated the priest, Baryy took the opportunity to drift away. He casually inspected the façade of the dome, marveling at the perfect, hairline joints between the marble blocks.

When the priest turned to rail at Baryy, Achelous pulled a coin out of his purse and thumbed it into the air. "This is a Lamaran Durket." The silver caught the sun's glare and flashed as it spun back down. Achelous caught it and showed it to the priest. It was newly IDB-minted, not a nick on its pristine silver surface. He often thought they should mint them to look old, but life's work was never done.

Baryy slipped into the massive building through a side portal, the columned archway had no door. He was looking for something in particular. Running his hand over the smooth, cold, polished stone, he could not help but admire shrewd and intricate inlay. He counted gold, silver, and copper in the scrollwork. Like many Lock Norim ruins scattered across the human reaches of the galaxy, this ruin was saved from depredations because of the low human population. No wars had been fought in this part of Isuelt, and both humans and reptiles had ignored Mount Mars until, of course, the Timberkeeps settled Wedgewood. He examined the scenes depicted by the inlays. From his sociologist perspective, they were important clues as to how the Lock Norim regarded Isuelt. Did the stylistic rendition of woodland lore, fairies, will-o-the-wisps, and prancing unicorns represent their attitude toward the entire planet or just Mount Mars?

The sound of voices came from a passageway. Through it found what amounted to an auditorium. A concourse, ten paces wide, encircled the chamber. In the center, marble seats stepped down to the bottom where Mergund and Outish loitered on the stage. There was a circular balcony above with more seating. High above, at the center of the dome, a glass iris impervious to a thousand years of weather let glorious sunlight flood the chamber. The prismatic effect of the iris radiated more light than what he thought possible. *I wonder what material the Lock Norim used--*

"Whahoo!" Mergund tested the perfect acoustics.

Achelous held the coin. "I'm surprised your guards are not here, with all the trogs roaming about." He deduced the value of the durket to be substantially more than the tithe for the entire party. The avarice in the priest's demeanor and his clutching hand proved it. Every time the priest reached for the coin, Achelous asked another string of questions.

Ogden's original distaste at paying the tithe turned to bemusement as he witnessed the trader at his art.

"Ack. We don't have troubles with troglodytes," the priest waved his wrinkled hand dismissively. "They know better than to bother us here at Lycealia."

"Oh?" Achelous wondered if the priest was more than just an obdurate old fool. "We had a skirmish with them yesterday, not more than a half-day's ride from here. Must have been a good sixty of them."

The priest leaned hard on his staff and gave him a piercing, knowing stare. “If you were riding with the Timmies I’d not be surprised. Tis well known the trogs want Timmy blood,” he smirked at Lettern.

“Yes,” noted Achelous, “but what’s to stop a band of them from killing you and your guards just for sport or better yet, food?”

The priest shook his head, religious fervor powering his words, “They’ll not bother us here. Of that I am sure.”

So the knowledge of Paleowright power over the troglodytes extends to the ranks of the priests. But do the priests know how? Achelous considered the ramifications. If it became public that the Church controlled the troglodytes, the scheme would backfire on them.

Baryy walked through an archway to the outside. In front of him was a large, marble patio bordered by a stone balustrade. In the center of the patio, he saw two perpendicular lines of black marble that quartered the open space. Another circle of black marble overlaid it as a bull’s-eye. He instantly knew the significance of the circle. Moving to the balustrade, he surveyed the forest beyond. In the thousand years the site had sat abandoned, storms, erosion, and the continual frost-thaw cycle had attempted their work, but the foundations of Lycealia were little moved. There were cracks in the paving stones, and the polish of the external marble was etched and degraded, but the place was eerily unchanged. Almost as if it were ready to receive its old masters.

"Is that true?" Achelous asked in mock surprise. He knew the troglodytes were enthralled to the Paleowrights, but the Timberkeeps didn’t, in this case, Lettern and Ogden, and it was good for them to hear the evidence first hand.

"As true as this be the work of the Ancients!" retorted the priest.

Achelous smiled at the priest's choice of metaphors. The Ancients, as worshipped by the Paleowrights, did not create Lycealia, the Lock Norim had. "Fine." He flipped the durket to the priest.

"Your grandness," the priest said, reminding him of the Paleowright honorific for priests, as he drew a pocketknife and gouged the surface of the coin to test its authenticity.

Achelous blanched. "You know, that coin was in perfect condition. You could have bartered it in the market in Hebert for more than its face value."

The priest shrugged half-heartedly, "It all goes to the Church."

A clattering of hooves turned Baryy's attention to the road. Achelous and Ogden waved to him. Outish led Baryy's mount, followed by the rest of the Timberkeeps.

Baryy hurried down a set of steps and caught up with the party.

"Quite the place isn't it?" Ogden said, reigning in his mount. "As if Mother herself carved it from the stone of the mountain."

Baryy climbed into his saddle. Even knowing the truth about the Lycealia, he agreed with the warden. Softly, he asked Achelous, "Where do you think they quarried the marble from? I'm surprised none of it has been scavenged for building materials."

Achelous answered, "The Paleowrights in Hebert would consider it sacrilege." Then, as the party began to move out, he said louder so everyone could hear, "What do you think Ogden, are there any marble quarries hereabouts?"

"Oi, there is an old quarry on the back side of the mountain, but that's nigh on forty miles from here."

Achelous nodded to Baryy. Forty miles to the Lock Norim was trivial, it came down to energy, something the Lock Norim had plenty of. He waved the rest of the Timberkeeps to ride past so Outish, Baryy, and he could ride at the rear.

When a gap opened in the column, Baryy said, "The patio was the landing zone. No tool, burn, or skid marks on the pavement, so they used anti-grav. The stone was definitely laser cut."

Outish chimed in, "Why would the Lock's build it in the first place? It's out here in the middle of nowhere."

Achelous let Echo's comfortable gait massage his hips and joints; the carpet of pine needles lended a spongy quality to the hoof steps and muffled the sound. "The Lock Norims may have been human, but why they did what they did is often beyond us. I think there is an even more important Lock Norim site up there," he pointed to the top of Mount Mars. Snow was blowing off the peak in a long contrail. The white contrasted starkly against the royal blue of the sky.

"Why, what's up there?" asked Outish.

Achelous stared at the peak, watching the jet-stream scour snow from the high crag. "Just a hunch. But forty miles would put the marble quarry just on the backside of the peak. Solar Surveillance has confirmed there are ruins up there, near the peak. We currently have them listed as Lock Norim-possible in origin, but no one has been up there to confirm."

Outish perked up. "Another Lock Norim site? Do you know what that would mean for my astrobiology certification if I did the bio--"

Baryy smacked him on the shoulder, "Not so loud moron," he hissed.

"Ouch! You didn't have to hit me."

Mergund turned in the saddle at the fuss, hoping he could join in.

Baryy smiled sweetly, "Got a keep the youngins in line."

Achelous let his mount crop the fresh spring shoots as the gap opened further. He said softly, "It would be the seventh Lock Norim site on Dianis. They could have used the same quarry to build the facility on the mountaintop. And yes, it would look good on a list of credits to be on the first survey team. But more importantly, we're not quite sure what role Dianis served for the Lock Norim. Zursh, we know, was an outpost of the colony. We suspect it was a surveyor's base for resource exploration in the northern hemisphere."

"Was it a big colony?" Outish asked. Human history beyond genetic evolution was as boring to Outish as dust on a bookshelf. It only interested him when, like now, it mattered to his studies.

"Probably less than a million, total, for the whole planet. Dianis was established late in their expansion, but for us, it is important as we think Dianis was the primary colony in this reach of the galaxy."

"Do you think we will ever find them?" Outish asked, reverence in his voice.

"You mean if the Turboii didn't get them?" Baryy grumped, giving him a sidelong look.

And so goes the debate, thought Achelous. *What happened to the Lock Norim? And did the appearance of the Turboii with their minions mean they had destroyed the Lock Norim along the way, or did it mean the Lock Norim were driving the Turboii back, forcing them into this sector of the galaxy?* Either way, the advent of the Turboii offered plausible explanations for what some speculated was a temporary, albeit a millennium's long retreat of humanity's progenitors. "We've found no evidence the Turboii and Lock Norim ever met each other. It's pretty clear the Turboii have come after, long after, the Lock Norim."

"In our arm of the galaxy," said Baryy. "We don't know what happened beyond here, but we do know the Lock Norim and Turboii came from the center of the galaxy." He shut up before he strayed out on thin ice. Achelous was the cultural anthropologist, and it was his specialization to know the history of cultures and evaluate the potential outcomes of interactions between societies, but that was where anthropology overlapped with Baryy's own sociology.

Achelous' reply came well worn, honed from centuries of debate. "The colonization path of the Lock Norim in this arm does point back to the core, but only so far as we've measured it. What, ten thousand light years?"

The party fell silent as they caught up with the Timberkeeps. Baryy idly pondered the Lock Norim enigma. Astrobiologists, like Outish, debated the cause of human physiological regression on Dianis since the collapse of the Dianis Lock Norim colony. They argued, and were supported by a substantial body of knowledge, that much of humanity on Dianis had regressed in mental and physical abilities in the fifteen hundred years since the disappearance of the Lock Norim. The theory posited that much of the Lock Norim advanced physiology and mental abilities were artificially sustained by gene therapy, as the Avarians themselves were practicing now, and that the therapy did not represent an engineered leap in evolution, but merely an artificial elevation quickly lost. This was contrary to evidence that types of Avarian DNA modifications were passed on through birth, at least through the first and second generations.

Conversely, Baryy a sociologist preferred to examine the regression and progression of societies rather than species, which was why he requested a posting to Dianis. Here he could investigate the cultural phenomenon of the decayed Lock Norim society while monitoring the growth of the subsequent provincial society. With the fifteen hundred year difference between the collapse of the one and the growth of the other, he could compare and assess how the human race socially evolved after the dissolution of technological and cultural norms.

Where Baryy and Achelous's two sciences came together, sociology and cultural anthropology, was in the Theory of Reverse Colonization. Baryy glanced at the chief, then off to a squirrel shredding a cone. Modern history provided clear documentation. The Avarian Federation spawned from the planet Avaria, the first world in this galactic reach to rise from the bones of the Lock Norim skeleton.

Avaria began its galactic exploration. That expansion followed in reverse order the previous Lock Norim colonization route, planet by planet. Just as the Lock Norim expanded out from the center of the galaxy, leaving stepping stones of colonies and outposts along the way, now did Avaria expand inward from the rim of the galaxy. It was like seeking out decaying, moss covered stepping-stones, finding worlds populated with humans ignorant of their past, most believing that they were the sole humans in the galaxy.

Baryy thought, *I'm glad I'm not a cosmologist because some of their questions would drive me nuts: Who came before the Lock Norims? How long had the tidal ebb and flow galactic civilization occurred? I have my own questions. Of all the evolutionary ceilings that doomed a civilization to stagnation and death, which was the greatest threat to Avaria? What caused the demise of the Lock Norim?*

Chapter 13
Wedgewood

The town of Wedgewood

Taking the trail from Lycealia, the party rode into an area interspersed with small farms in woodland clearings. Occasionally Outish would get a view up the mountain. The trees there appeared to be much larger than the firs and spruce covering the lower reaches. "Those are big! He said to the Timberkeep warrior who rode beside him.

"Oi, those are Ungerngerist. Some of them are over five hundred years old. They are why we live here."

"Ungerngerist?" Outish turned to the warrior. The man's name was Bagonen and had been introduced as the branch warden, second in command, of Ogden's Second Ward.

Bagonen plaited his black beard into two short braids, each salted with grey. His ruddy cheeks were a warm contrast to his somber brown eyes and bushy brows. The warrior was heavy set, but Outish knew he was swift with the axe having witnessed him in action against the trogs. Little did he suspect, however, that Bagonen would be dead before summer, killed defending his home: Wedgewood.

"Oi, Ungerngerist is the tallest tree that grows on Mount Mars." Bagonen tilted his chin at the mountain, "That dark green band across the shoulder be Ungerns. Wait till you're beneath them, you'd think they were holding up the sky."

Outish had seen holovids of the Ungerns in his injection learning courses. Part of his qualifying to go in-country, and their plans to travel to Wedgewood he'd studied the local ecosystem as it was of more interest to him than the town itself. Not only was the Ungerngerist the largest tree on Mount Mars it was the largest tree on Dianis. Truly a monumental adaptation to the montane and lower subalpine ecozones. They were claimed as a tourist attraction by the Transportation Authority engineers three hundred and fifty years ago. *Wow,* he thought, *some of those trees would have been alive then!*

The region of farmland gradually gave way to the forest proper as the party entered an area of pure moss birch. Here and there, remnants of winter – crusty snow --lay in shade underneath fallen logs. The pure grove of white birch reflected brightly against the yellows and browns of withered grass and sodden leaves awaiting the rebirth of spring. The grove stretched for as far as the eye could reach on the straight trail, always angling upward. The white trunks were festooned with tufts of black moss and cast the world into a black and white monochrome devoid of all color except for the browns of the eenus and clothing of the riders. Moving past a tree Outish plucked a clump of moss from a trunk. It was charcoal black and dry to the touch. When he rubbed it between his fingers, it crumbled.

"We make a poultice out of that," said Bagonen. "Good for all sorts of infections. Lousy for drinking though," he shivered, screwing up his ruddy face. "But you can ferment the birch sap; it makes a fine rakia that puts fire to your toes."

Outish examined the stalks of the moss closely, identifying its structure, then blew it from his palm. "I don't drink alcohol, so I wouldn't know."

Bagonen tilted his head. He stared at Outish from beneath his busy eyebrows, sizing him up. A long moment passed when he finally said, "And why would that be?"

He shrugged. "It's not good for you." He was going to launch into a description of the physiological effects but remembered he was supposed to be a simple trade runner who wouldn't know much, especially about biology.

Bagonen smiled then chuckled. "Lad, there are a lot of things that are no good for you in this world. Like hunting barefoot in the snow, or logging a tree in a stiff wind, or swinging a dull axe at a loglard. And I'll grant you that drinking does you no good in the morning, but drinking is like a wife. You take the good with the bad and hope you get more good than bad. A shot of rakia won't maim you like frost bite, crush you like a tree, or eat you like a trog."

The party continued to climb through the different ecozones and their corresponding forest communities, each with its dominant flora and fauna species. Outish kept careful note comparing what he'd learned to what he actually saw. He'd grown accustomed to the berriu stags with their black chests and white rumps, but his heart leapt in surprise when he saw his first tiracu, a wolverine-like mammal with long fangs, even longer claws, a black mask for a face, and thickly mottled-brown fur. It was busy digging out a hollow log, shredded wood flying. Lettern stopped beside Outish as he watched the animal excavate the log. The tiracu pulled its big badger head from the log, sniffed the air, and squinted in their direction with its beady eyes.

"Not afraid of us, is he?" noted Lettern laconically. The animal was only ten paces off the trail. "No..." whispered Outish, consumed by the creature's behavior, "it's not."

The tiracu sniffed again, then ducked his head back in the log and more wood chips flew.

"Ornery varmints," she said evenly. "They nest in the Ungerns, not in burrows. If you mess with their tree, they are down to the ground in a hurry, and you'll wish you were on a fast eenu."

A little further, the understory along the trail abruptly receded, and the forest dramatically changed. Outish gaped, craning his head. They were now in a pure stand of the most massive trees he'd ever seen. The lowest branches started some forty feet above his head. The trunks were as wide as two eenus put end-to-end and deeply furrowed with what looked to be a red, corky bark. Moss adorned the tall, muscular root mounds, and spring ferns dappled the floor with their fiddleheads. Around the trunks and across the ground a millennia of pine needles carpeted the land in a thick loam that muffled hoof steps and choked out all but the hardiest undergrowth. "Those are--" he gaped.

"Ungerngerist," answered Ogden, riding behind. The gargantuan pillars stretched away into the distance, their limbs forming countless arches.

Achelous smiled knowingly, riding behind Ogden. "We have them outside of Tivor, on the flanks of Mount Epratis."

"Oi? You do?"

He gave a nod, "Yes, but there are no Timbers there. I've always wondered that they've never been colonized."

"I didn't know they were there," replied the weaponsmith, surprise in his voice.

They came to an Ungern with a sentry platform constructed high above the ground supported by the lowest rung of branches. The platform and railing completely encircled the bole. Two guards with bows waved; Ogden waved back. A third sentry emerged from a tree house above the platform and walked down a circular set of stairs to sentry walk. He leaned on the railing with the other two. "Oi Ogden."

"Oi Tuskhammer, good to be home."

The man smiled broadly until he saw the four canvas-covered bodies draped over the trailing eenus. His expression went grim. “Trogs?” he asked.

Ogden’s cheer slipped. "Sedge is at them."

In the distance, they heard hammering, sawing, and the sound of men at work. As the party came in view of the workers, Lettern waved to a guard in a newly erected stone gatehouse. To either side of the bastion, a twenty-foot high stonewall stretched for about thirty yards and abruptly ended at a scaffold. Stonemasons with their carts, cranes, wagons drawn by oxen, and laborers hauling rock were busily at work.

As Lettern proceeded through the gate, Baryy spurred forward to Achelous. “This is the wall I told you about. They’ve started on the rear gate as well, but they have a long way to go to enclose the whole town.”

“Those are interesting,” Achelous pointed at sharpened stakes set into slots in the parapet and angled steeply down. “How can those stop a ladder? The ladders will lay on top.”

“They’re not for ladders,” said Ogden. “They’re for trogs.”

“Oh... so they can’t scale the wall.”

Beyond the gate, Wedgewood spread out, and Achelous was surprised. There were many more people than he’d expected. New buildings were going up, and carters were hauling construction materials. Achelous's trained anthropologist eye and ear caught the cosmopolitan feel. He’d expected to see mostly Timberkeep Doromen, but there were Plains Doromen judging by their beards and armbands, and Rock Doromen were marked by their heavy black leathers and pale skin. Lamarans, Oridians, Mestricans, and even some Darnkilden strolled about as Achelous waited for a wealthy Mestrican to clear his path. The only member of the Western Alliance he didn’t see yet was the SeaHaven League, and he looked for their nautical fashions.

Conspicuously absent from the foot and rider traffic were Nakish and Herberians from Hebert the capital of the Church, Diunesis Antiquaria.

“Down there is my foundry and armory,” pointed Ogden, aiming at a street that led off to the left. “Make sure you come by so I can show you my goods, and we can talk about fabricating that crossbow of yours.”

Achelous agreed, and the three traders took leave of their escorts.

They turned right at a lane and rode higher up the mountain leaving the bustle of the town behind, entering an area where small cabins, dugouts, and tree houses snuggled in the forest. Outish pointed, gawping, "What are those?" Just then, the occupant of Outish's curiosity stepped out the door and caught the young intern inadvertently pointing him. He was an old codger with a grey beard tucked into his belt, he wore a greasy pair of leather pants and a red long-sleeve woolen undershirt.

"You have a problem with that finger of yours youngin?" The codger called. "Or does it just point wherever the wind blows? Try putting it in your nose if you don't know what to do with it."

Embarrassed, Outish dropped his arm and quickly looked away.

Baryy grinned at Outish's discomfiture as they rode by, ignoring the hermit's glare, whom he knew. "Those...," he said, once they were beyond earshot of belt-beard, "...huts that you were pointing at are bivwacs." He waved at a handful that dotted the slope-side, most being higher up the slope than the more comfortable and respectable cottages and cabins.

Outish studied them intensely. The nearby bivwacs resembled the size of a two-stall outhouse. What set them apart from any outhouse Outish had ever seen were the steeply pitched shake roofs that looked more like tall conical hats. A thin, crooked stovepipe punctuated the roof skewering the air with its own little peaked cap. The sidewalls of the huts flared outwards. Some of the fancier bivwacs had a little flower box mounted under a tiny four-pane window set beside the narrow door. He yearned to look inside, but settled with, "Do people live in those? What do they do in them? They're tiny! They must be shitters, I mean outhouses, but there are too many. Do you really need that many outhouses?"

Baryy laughed. "No, they're not shitters. People live in them. Mergund lives in one. You should ask him to give you a tour. It won't take long."

"But..."

Baryy expected the question, "They sleep in a hammock strung between the walls. They have a tiny stove and maybe a chair. That's it."

"But where do they put their stuff?"

Baryy smirked. "Oh they are quite creative, wait till you see one, they hang all sorts of things on pegs and nails. At first, I thought the peaked roof was just for snow, but the space is used for dangling their gear." He paused. "There are two types of people who live in bivvies: young men and hermits, usually male. In Timber society young men generally leave home when they come of age and live by themselves until they can afford a dowry for a wife." They turned aside onto a narrow lane snaking between the huge Ungerngerists, slanting up the mountain. "Probably the best feature of a bivwac is they are built on skids. You can drag them anywhere. Makes for a mobile culture. The young men get their friends together and drag their bivvies to where they work, like outside the gold mine where a bivill, a bivwac village is.

"In the winter the hermits will buy a fire-wood pile and then have their bivvy hauled to it."

It was Achelous's turn to smirk, "Instead of hauling firewood they haul the house."

"Yep. Makes it easy to leave if you don't like your neighbors. You can literally pick up and move in the middle of the night, which is sometimes the reverse problem when you wake up in the morning and find a hermit camped just beyond your boundary stones."

They pulled up to a quaint cottage set back into the slope. There were a few other abodes nestled on the hillside amongst the tall ocher trunks, the perfect place for an in-country operative to live in quiet obscurity. The cottage had a shake roof covered by mounds of moss and a fern or two. The walls were of cut stone, square and exact, the eves wide, and the ornate fluted gutters routed rainwater to the ubiquitous rain barrels, one at either corner of the cottage. "Well here we are, my cabin, courtesy—" and he looked over his shoulder for any eavesdroppers, "of the IDB. I rent it from a sweet old grandmother who moved in with her eldest son. Apologies in advance, but it'll be a little cramped with the three of us. After you store your kits, we'll take the eenus down to the stable and get dinner at Murali's. And there," he paused for emphasis, "you'll get to see the largest block of aquamarine-5 outside the vaults of the Avaria Strategic Reserve."

Dusk deepened the shadows beneath the pine boughs as the trio led their eenu's down to the stables. Outish noticed a flicker of light high up in the gloom of an Ungerngerist. A woman was lighting a lantern. He stopped, and she waved when she saw the young intern's attention. "Is that—"

"Lettern," Baryy answered.

She smiled. She had changed out of her archer's garb and wore a simple shift baring her arms and legs. Turning she went inside a one-room tree house that connected via a rope bridge to an adjoining tree fort.

"Wow, it would be awesome to live in a tree house," said Outish. The view has to be great. You'd be up with the birds and the squirrels. You could study without distraction. There are animals up there you seldom see because they don't come down to the ground."

"That's basically what Lettern does up there," Baryy motioned. "When she's not rangering for the clan she's a poet and song writer. Uses her loft as a study. Sometimes when you are near you can hear her and others playing their latest renditions. But, counter to what some people think, Timberkeeps prefer to live on the ground."

Outish frowned and Achelous said, "I'd heard that."

"Yes. It's a matter of convenience. With tree houses, Timbers can't use their favorite building material, which is stone, not wood. Besides, it takes more work to build a livable tree house and when you do there is just a fraction of the space you'd get if you built it on the ground." The sociologist in Baryy warmed to his subject. "But convenience is the real issue. Who wants to haul food, water, furnishings, and other necessities forty feet into the air? You have to drop your nightsoil buckets down." He shook his head in distaste. "Some people will do it, but it's usually the romantics or someone willing to pay for the crank service. Lettern is allowed to live in her tree house for free because it is connected to the Perrty tree fort. That big Ungerngerist next to her tree is called Perrty. Part of Sedge's new clan defense doctrine is to have half of all tree forts manned at all times. So the clan pays the rent for archers willing to live in tree houses attached to forts."

"I would also think," Achelous eyed the long rope ladder leading to Lettern's high house, "that people don't want to climb a rope ladder every day. For some of these, you have to be part squirrel to get up there. Access has to be an issue."

Outish began to pay attention to the fine art of lofting and the numerous new tree forts. Some lofts had crank lifts, some had iron ladders mounted to the tree, and a very few had wooden staircases that wrapped around the trunks like huge coiled snakes. Rope ladders seemed to be a common way up. That Lettern could climb that rope ladder with ease, he had no doubt. She was built like a cat.

Baryy went on. "Which is why Sedge likes tree forts. If they are hard to get into they are easy to defend." Baryy pointed at a fort over the stables. It had the same downward-facing stakes as the new wall, these encircled the tree just below the loft decking, and the railing around the structure was covered with planking providing protection for a crouching archer. The access ladder climbed through a trap door between the spikes. In a time of battle, the ladder could be drawn up and the section of spikes lowered and locked into place. "Through the clan council Sedge has decreed there should be enough temporary loft space for six full wards of archers, which is why you see so many new tree forts being built."

"It looks like Sedge has thought about ways to move forces from tree to tree," Achelous said. "I can see from here rope and plank bridges between the trees. Like an aerial trail network."

"That's been a topic of debate in the council. Do they need all those swinging bridges? Some people think they are unsightly. Personally, I think the tree forts are the way to go. And the Ungerngerist bark is fire resistant, though trogs don't use fire."

As Achelous led Echo over a creek-side footbridge, he said, "So to defend the town they need enough warning to man the tree forts before the trogs get into town."

Baryy turned and offered a grim expression. "And we know trogs are fast."

Pipe smoke wafted past them as they entered Murali's. The inn's tavern held a swath of tables, almost all of them taken. Men and women crowded around a long bar, and a trio of musicians sat on stools between the bar and entrance. Achelous looked around, and Baryy caught the question in his eyes. He nodded in the direction of the musicians and then leaned close to be heard over the noise of the patrons. "Look what the flute player has his ale mug sitting on."

Concealed behind the trio, next to the stack of split-wood for the fireplace, a crock of ale sat perched on the largest aquamarine crystal Achelous had ever seen. Three feet tall the pegmatite rested on a low polished oak table. Bluish green and roughly octagonal, a million or more Avarian Federation credits were being used as a decoration, Achelous gaped. *Only in Wedgewood,* he breathed. Properly assayed, cut, magnafluxed, and polished there was enough pure aquamarine-5 to energize seven, maybe eight ship-sized field generators. Not small ships, but battle cruisers. They knew it was aquamarine-5 because you could stand in Baryy's cabin and ping it with the aural scanner in their multi-funcs. The rebounding signal came back so amplified that the scan meter pegged at omega--unmeasurable.

Before his boss's open mouth attracted attention, Baryy tugged him by the sleeve and hustled them over to the last available table stuck in a corner.

While Achelous overcame his shock, Outish, oblivious to the pegmatite, surveyed the pub with the expectancy of young boy invited to his first clan gathering. Indeed, this was only his second in-country establishment he'd entered, and definitely the most interesting. Stag, boar, bear, and tork trophies adorned the walls and over the mantels of the two opposing fireplaces. The long richly lacquered bar ran the length of the back wall where an imposing array of clientele guffawed, tilted fired mugs, and blew pipe smoke rings. The low ceiling added to the din. An attractive serving maid swung past their table with four frothing mugs on her tray. She wore a green woodland dress; the bodice cut low, her blonde hair done in a high bun. She winked at Baryy, "Be right back."

Outish missed it, but Achelous caught the cue. He peered at his apprentice trader and Baryy turned away.

The two fiddle pickers and flute player offered a snappy tune adding to the general din. Outish shifted his feet on the tightly laid, but well-worn wood planking. In the space between trophies, embossed brass plates hung along with cracked shields, dented helms, notched axes, and other weapons retired from the battlefield.

"Yo Baryy!" A patron called from the bar. He lifted his mug in greeting. Baryy smiled and raised his hand. Another man from two tables over looked up, "Oi Baryy, up for a game of tubric? We're meeting at Balsam's."

"Uh, maybe later. Got the boss in town." And he tilted his head in Achelous's direction.

The man looked past his friends to Achelous. "Well bring him too. He's got coin ain't he?"

Baryy laughed, "Yeah, more than me."

"Hi Baryy, you weren't gone long."

The agent turned, and the serving maid was back. Her skin clear and smooth. She had high cheekbones and eyes that twinkled. Outish endeavored to not stare at her bosom but failed.

"Yes," responded Baryy, "I tried to keep it short. Hey, what's on the dinner board for tonight? It's packed in here."

“Well, we have berga stew or roast boar. Loins, chops, and hams. You pick.”

He turned to the others, and they debated their tastes. In the end, Outish really didn’t care what he was fed as long as it was true provincial. He was finally in-country and wanted to live that way.

After taking their drink orders, water for Outish and Bash-me-Brains ale for Achelous and Baryy, the maid asked, “Aren’t you going to introduce me to your two friends? Honestly Baryy, for someone as smart as you, you forget your manners." She smiled, teasing him with her feigned impatience.

Outish nodded vigorously, “And he’s a sociologist—“

Achelous kicked him under the table. He humored the server, “Don’t mind my runner here. He babbles like a creek at spring flood. Don’t know why I brought him. Next time I’ll leave him tied up with the eenus.” He turned to Outish, his eyes narrow.

“Oh don’t do that,” she quipped, “unless he eats hay and likes to roll.” Outish began to color.

Baryy intervened before he completely lost control of the conversation. “Atch, Outish, meet Daryan.”

She locked Achelous with a direct, appraising gaze. “Oh, please to meet you, sir. Baryy has mentioned you.” She held out her hand Doroman fashion. Achelous grasped the fingers in the requisite response.

Then she turned her mirthful gaze on Outish, “You, however” she put a finger to her lips and looked away, fluttering her long eyelashes, “hmm, nope. Baryy’s never mentioned you. But since you’ll be dinning in the stables I’ll bring the water over, so you don’t have to drink from the troughs." She smiled tartly, turned with a swoosh of her long skirt and headed off for the bar.

Smitten, Outish asked, “Who was that?”

Before Baryy could form a response, he spied a man approaching their table and made to catch Achelous’s attention.

“Oi, brought some strangers with ye?” Without asking, the Doroman pulled a chair from an adjoining table and sat down.

“Hello, Baldor.” Baryy turned to Achelous, “Achelous friend, this is Baldor Prairiegrass.”

Baryy said it so smoothly even the most perceptive spy would not have caught the cue. However, both Outish and Achelous were instantly on guard. The use of the word “friend” following the formal form of an agent's name was CivMon code for *beware, trouble is near*.

The man hunched over the table and leaned toward Baryy like a long-time confidant. Without preamble and barely a glance at Achelous, Baldor said, "I've meant to tell you, Barro, I like your way of things. You keep a level head about you, and you see the Timmies for what they are."

Achelous frowned inwardly, his expression impassive as stone. The man had a cheery face, but his tone of voice spoke otherwise. His ruddy skin, pointed beard, accent, and most of all, his surname, placed him as a Plains Doroman though he wore no arm rings. His shearling vest appeared new, and his britches and wool shirt were in good shape. He bore a strange tattoo on his left forearm.

"Oh—I don't treat them any differently than my other customers," he said, leaning away, his concern open.

Baldor smiled tightly, compressing his thin lips, "And you don't. You don't treat them special like they think they are."

Outish shifted uncomfortably, but Baryy didn't react. Achelous nudged the young intern with his foot.

"Other traders will cut them deals just because they run Wedgeville here and own all the farms, but you've got the nerve to stand up to them." Baldor turned his honey-sweet smirk on Achelous, pointedly ignoring Outish. The intern gave a twitch when he realized he'd just been dismissed as irrelevant and by a fellow Plains Doroman no less. "Something I'm sure Mister Achelous here can understand, being the master trader that he is. And how did you like your ride into town?" He laughed with a weak "he, he." Then went on, "The Timmies attracted a bit of trouble did they? There will be more of that, sure as the grass grows. Ever since Sedge Highbrow came, there's been trouble with the loglards. Stoked them up he has. And who wouldn't retaliate when attacked unawares. Them loglards don't want to be up here, but if they have to attack Sedge just to feel safe in their own weed huts whose to blame them?"

Conscious of other patrons looking their way Achelous began to wonder if the sudden appearance of the Doroman at their table was a calculated act, a display of some sort to convey a message or start rumors.

"You came all the way from Tivor? Pretty country down there, a bit warm and wet for my liking, but pretty. The Tivors know what they are doing."

Achelous cleared his throat, “Yes, speaking of wet, I’m a bit thirsty, you know, coming all the way from Tivor.” He waved to Daryan to keep coming; she’d halted halfway across the bar with their mugs when she saw Baldor seated at their table, a blank expression on her face.

Baryy went to help her. Whispered something in her ear and brought the drinks himself. “Sorry Baldor old cone,” he used the term “cone” which meant many things to a Timberkeep, one of them being a prickly object under foot, "but it seems I've only ordered three drinks." He sat down and passed out the mugs when he could have instead asked Daryan to fetch more.

“Oh, that be fine. My drink is over at the bar.” He eyed the frothy crocks and returned his attention back to the master trader “So I hear you saved the day in the fight with the loglards. You and them merc friends of yours.”

Achelous kept his breathing even and slouched in his chair. “You’re well informed Mister Prairiegrass, what is it you do for an occupation?”

“Oi, I do a bit of mining, coaling, and even wall building.” He leaned across the table and lowered his voice to conspire, “Worked on the clan’s farce of a wall. As if it could keep out a gecko.” He leaned back and waved his hand in a circle, “Truth be known, if it weren't for old Sedge the Kledge chasing the loglards we wouldn’t have to build no wall, and I wouldn’t have lost my farm.” The sweet smirk was gone, replaced by an acidic twist.

Taken aback Baryy stammered, “You think the Timbers are responsible for the loss of your farm?”

Baldor wheeled on him. “Of bloody course they are," he hissed. "A whole lot of us had to flee when the loglards came out of their swamp. They’d still be there if the Timmies had stayed in Whispering Bough.”

Achelous sensed an age-old argument brewing, one that Baryy had no place being in the middle of. “Be that as it may...Baldor, Wedgewood is here now, and I don’t see it packing up and leaving any time soon, so the best we can do is profit from it.“ On a hunch, he let the word *profit* hang over the table.

Something clicked in Baldor, and his smirk was back on, though his countenance was still dark. “Speaking of profit, I heard you stopped at Lycealia." He waited for Achelous to react. "You and the Paleo priest struck a bargain for information.”

Achelous felt a distinct irritation at Baldor knowing so much. The fight with the trogs he could understand as there were a good many mercenaries with Sedge, but knowing about their visit to Lycealia and his dealings with the priest troubled him. "I'm a trader," he said noncommittally, "I need information to know what to buy or sell. What are you selling?"

The man shrugged, "You went out of your way to Lycealia; mayhap you're looking for Ancient artifacts?" His lips cracked to show teeth.

Achelous's irritation escalated. The last thing they needed was for this rumormonger to spread the word they were artifact hunters. He needed a way to get rid of Baldor and confer with Baryy. Fortuitously it showed up in the form of roast loin of boar. "Well, I don't know about Ancient artifacts. I prefer spices, gems, and arms. But my dinner is here, and I am far famished. Shall we continue this some other time?" He gave his own version of a sickly sweet smirk, communicating in Baldor's language. The man rose, bid the three a good evening and made his way past the other tables to the front door, apparently forgetting his tankard at the bar.

A tense silence settled on the table. Achelous stared at Baryy, creases at the corner of his eyes. Constrained by what he could say in public, Achelous simply stated, "He's well informed."

Baryy nodded, slicing up his loin chops as he replied just above a whisper, "I'm pretty sure his odd jobs are just a cover for him to meet and grouse with people. His real business is selling information."

"What sort and to whom."

He shrugged, "Anything really, but I know he's cozy with the Paleowrights and the Nakish traders that come through."

Achelous had a dozen other questions to ask, but he figured they could wait until they were back at the cabin. Suddenly he felt very tired, hungry, and in dire need of more than one ale. He hefted his mug and quaffed the stout dark fluid, the coldness cascading smoothly down his throat. Seeing Outish, subdued, sitting beside him he felt a twinge of guilt. The intern had been excited and in awe of his first visit to a provincial town and the Wedgewood tavern until Baldor had effectively cast a pall over it. Achelous nudged him with an elbow. "If you want, we'll get you a tumbler of local favorite, fermented birch sap: rakia. It's like sipping crystal mint spiced with raspberries, but with an eenu's kick. And dig into your stew, I'm sure those peppers you had them add will strip the bark off your tongue." He smiled at

Baryy. "When in-country, live country." He lifted his mug of Bash-Me-Brains in toast and Baryy agreed, "Here, here. To Wedgwood and the Woodlife." They held up their mugs until Outish got the hint.

He grabbed his own mug and clinked the others a bit too hard, sloshing beer and water onto the table, but Atch and Baryy didn't seem to notice. A group of miners at the table nearest theirs raised their mugs, toasting Outish "Like the Turfy says, to the Woodlife!"

More patrons raised their mugs, and the cheer spread around the tavern like a flock of geese taking to the air. "To the Woodlife!"

Outish quickly glanced at Achelous, wide eyed. The lute player started up leading the fiddlers in rousing mining song. The pipe smoke no longer seemed to bother Outish. The crowd noise resolved into a song as miners, millers, and masons alike started to chant and stamp to the tune. For once Outish began to feel, maybe not at home, but at least welcomed in his surroundings. He dug into the berga stew and found it to be blistering hot. It was so good.

Baryy raised his mug in a second toast, "To fine women and finer food."

"Here, here," Achelous enjoined.

Outish beamed and raised his mug. *Life as a CivMon agent might not be so bad after all.* "Maybe I will try some of that rakia."

The flutist and fiddlers packed up their instruments and left for home. Achelous rose from the table and waved to Outish and Baryy that it was time to leave. CivMon doctrine dictated one member of the party must stay sober at all times, and that no agent could become "inebriated." Well, Achelous figured, he wasn't inebriated, but someone, most likely him, had forgotten to assign the duty sobriety watch. As they weaved their way past the emptying tables, he stopped. With the musicians and bar-standers gone, the aquamarine-5 pegmatite stood in plain sight. Achelous swayed and squinted, able to see the artifact in all its glory. "Smokes," he breathed, "A million?" He shook his head steering Outish for the door. *More like thirty million Avarian credits,* he thought. With *those riches at stake, a corsair team could come in, ignoring every security layer the IDB had in place, and do a swoop and scoop. Simple brute force. Blast the few provincials that got in their way, dart for orbital escape, and hit the shift generator for deep space.* He sighed, trying not to think of the mayhem. *Hell, ULUP be damned, we should confiscate it just to save Wedgewood from being attacked.*

Being a *virolmir*, as they said in Northwren, had its advantages. In the Isuelt common tongue virolmir translated to wisdom thief, or more loosely-- a spy. Baldor did not consider himself a spy, he'd sell information to anyone, even the Timmies if they paid him enough. As of now the *Washentrufel,* the Nak Drakas secret service, was the most interested in what he had to sell: updates on the construction of Wedgewood fortifications, the training and arming of the militia by Sedge, and how much gold the Timmies were extracting from their mine. *The cheap Antiquarian bastards aren't paying much, and the arrogant morons act like they know everything I tell them, but at least they are buying,* he thought with satisfaction. In his experience, people didn't pay for information they didn't need; which told him a lot about the Drakans. The one good nugget of information he held back, waiting for its value to appreciate. There was a risk the Washenfoofel fools would learn it themselves, but he doubted it. *Most people don't know the huge crystal in Murali's' was aquamarine. Quartz they say. Bah! Blue-green quartz? Such idiots.* That little surprise he saved for a special moment when there was a premium price to be had. It confounded him that the Paleowrights cared more for the worthless crystal than gold itself, but he never bothered himself with motives of clients. He just focused on what they wanted and sold it.

A cat bounded in the hayloft above. Listening to the sounds of the struggle while Baldor peeked through the crack in the stable door, he could visualize the mouse being toyed with. More scampering; the little pitter of rodent feet followed by the whisper padding of the barn mouser. He huddled under his cloak; the cold mountain air penetrated his bones, a bale of hay served as a seat. He'd long reconciled himself to a life of a virolmir, both the good and bad sides. Shifting on the bale, more to generate heat that to get a better view through the crack between the stable doors, his breath frosted in the darkness. For the umpteenth time he considered searching the stables for an eenu blanket to keep warm, but finally, Baryy and his boss and the lackey came out from the inn. *Grass fire and gopher holes you've made me wait long enough, you drunken morons. What's it been? Three hours?* The big-eared lackey stumbled on the stoop, but the boss caught him by the collar. Baldor smiled in the dark. The pickings would be easy tonight. Of his methods for gathering information, eavesdropping was his favorite. Properly positioned, usually out of sight, it was amazing what he heard, and it was free! Early on in his career, he'd learned that information begat information. Learning who was dorking who opened wide the door to blackmail, not just for money, but for more dirty secrets about others. It became a fine art of knowing when to blackmail and when to wait for the future victim to rise up the social ladder and then threaten with revelations. There were other ways he picked up rumors and tidbits leading to bigger stories. Like grousing with fellow workers and buying drinks – though he was too cheap to have any fun at it – or scrounging garbage. Of late, his emerging clairvoyance had proved a boon. It came with a price though: skull-splitting headaches where his ears would pound and ring, sensitivity to light, and nausea so bad he'd vomit till his throat hurt. The Timber's Curse. Somehow, the bastards had given it to him, and now he was suffering, but he'd make the most of it. That was how he'd gleaned the trader's visit to Lycealia. Not through any paid informant or idle chatter amongst the wardens, but through a vision that came first as a driftless daydream and then resolved to vivid clarity: a trader in Lycealia, haggling with a Paleowright priest. While he couldn't hear, only envision the encounter, he could tell by the way the trader tempted the priest with the silver Durket that he was extracting information. At first, the augur didn't make sense till Baryy, the sneak that he was, shifted into view. It was an educated guess that the boss was involved in Ancient artifacts as his sudden aloofness at the table attested. The bugger was trading in them, of that he was sure, and that useful news he could sell to the Churchies.

Squinting in the dark, he saw the boss shut some sort of book and put it away. *Odd, what would he be reading now, at night, standing on the stoop?* He thrust the thought aside. Waiting until the trio walked down the street and around a corner, Baldor slipped out of the stables like satisfied barn mouser.

"Oh gosh, humm oi, am I drunk." Outish staggered, his head spinning, up seemed down and down up, and then he realized he was lying flat on his back. From far away he saw the chief inspector lean down from a great height. Then his stomach lurched. He rolled and heaved his guts into the dirt. "Ugh," phlegm and other noxious fluids covered his mouth.

Baryy asked, "Atch, do you think his metamorphosis treatment is reacting to the alcohol?"

"I don't think so, I've never heard of any cross effects or negative interactions. Unfortunately, our astrobiologist, the one we should ask is the one lying in the dirt. When we get back to the cabin, I'll give him some *ataflourazene.*"

Together they lifted the Halorite-Doroman, each taking an arm, careful to avoid his slime, and began to drag him back to the cabin. "Oh, am so, so, so, so, sorry boss. I--" a dry heave interrupted his rambling. "Oh spirits, I will never drink again."

Achelous laughed, a bit loudly he realized. "Yeah, sure. What you need to do is learn how to drink. In our line of business, you never know who you'll be sitting across from and what will insult them. If a Darnkilden Ranger offers you a skin of maysparkle wine and you refuse they'll treat you queer."

Baldor slipped past the hitching post where the lackey had collapsed in the dirt. The sharp odor of vomit mixed with eenu piss tainted the air like fresh skunk. Waiting by the post, ignoring the smell, he kept a good distance behind, just far enough to hear them. *What was an astrobiologist? Some sort of trader slang? Metamorphosis treatment? Was that a hazing ritual?*

A large fly or perhaps a humming bird orbited above his head for a moment then whisked away. He barely paid it any attention so focused he was on the traders. Not a thought did he give to the oddity of an insect buzzing by on the cold, starless night.

Achelous stopped; Baryy nearly dropped Outish face first when the inspector let his arm slip free. "Smokes," he cursed and fumbled for his bible. Then he thought better of it. He bent down and grabbed the arm.

"What?" asked Baryy.

"Nothing friend."

Baryy twitched, standing straighter. His training took over, and he casually pulled Outish's arm higher over his shoulder looking ahead, to his side, and behind, following the chief inspector's lead. They trudged on in silence.

Baryy coughed loudly, and said, "Outish you smell like a latrine," then whispered, "how many?"

"Yea, I think I peed my pants."

Achelous responded clearly, "Don't know about you Outish. Might have to get you a diaper."

"Don't need no diaper," he slurred, "I already peed. It's warm."

At the cabin, Baryy unlocked the door, and they deposited Outish on the floor in the tiny kitchen. In the dark, away from the window, Achelous opened up his bible. "Looks like we have one bogey," he said softly. "Trailed us from Murali's. The aural pattern matches an older human male. He's circling the cabin, looks like he's angling for your back window." He moved to the front door. "Light the lamp. Act natural. Then draw the blinds on the windows. Whoever it is, is snooping. I'll go out for an I.D."

"Back up?" Baryy hissed, fussing with the lantern.

A curt nod from Achelous told him they'd both go out.

Lantern lit, and blinds drawn, Achelous cocked and loaded his handbolt. According to the short-range aural scanner in the multi-func and the telemetry data from the surveillance bot, the intruder stood against the back wall near the rear window.

They casually opened the front door, and Achelous asked in a normal voice that carried in the still darkness, "Where's the privy?"

"Out back," said Baryy.

Achelous promptly stepped off the front porch and made his way directly around the rear of the cabin. He heard a noise at the rear and hurried his pace, then called loudly "Hey! Who's there? Baryy, someone's using your privy!"

Keeping up the act, Baryy ran forward, "What! He can help me dig a new one!"

By the sound of running footsteps and cracking of underbrush, the intruder was bolting.

Achelous held his position.

"Should we chase him?"

"No," Achelous murmured. "We've got his aural signature. But someone is interested in us. We need to find out who, and why."

There was silence while they watched their breaths steam away into the night. Baryy wondered what Atch was thinking. "Should I post a surveillance request with Solar? I'm sure they'd get a lock on the signature."

For a moment he didn't think the inspector heard him, but then Achelous replied, "We could do that, but Solar has orders to bring down the network. We might be better served running a few surveillance bots in town. Post one at Murali's, another at the stables, and another at the general store. If the spook is in town, he'll turn up."

Chapter 14
Fileas Faugh

Wedgewood

The pain extended from between his eyes to the back of his skull in a crescendo of drums that battered his mind into dull mush. He wanted to move faster, but his body swam in a pervasive malaise. Outish now had first-hand evidence of why Halorites should not drink. The glorious late morning sun filtering through the green boughs, the smell of pine needles and amber sap, the call of Worl Woodpeckers and Threedee Wrens did nothing to lighten his mood as he trudged back from the latrine. Oh, to have modern facilities right now. Mercifully, the effects of ataflourazene tablet began to take hold, and the impact of the alcohol in his system drained away with each trip to the latrine. Ataflourazene, the alcohol antidote, required the person to consume copious amounts of water to dilute and remove the agent's reactors.

Inside the cabin, a fire cracked and popped in the hearth. The smell of tea drew Outish to the table where the chief inspector and Baryy were in discussion over the events of the previous evening. Pouring himself a mug of the steeped tea and dolloping in plenty of honey, he wedged himself in at the tiny table.

"We've had a hit on our visitor from last night."

Outish's head swam in a fog. He peered bleary eyed at Baryy. "Oh?"

"A surveillance bot posted in the rafters above the front door at Husher's DinDin picked up his signature. We got a good picture of him." Baryy slid his purse over and opened to an imager screen. Climbing up the steps of the diner was Baldor Prariegrass.

Outish blinked. "Why--he was the guy at our table last night! The snoop!"

Baryy nodded, pulling the purse back. "Yep. He's a snoop alright."

When the agent said no more, Outish shook his head, even though it hurt. "What are you going to do? Er, what are we going to do?"

"He's got a rider," answered Achelous. "We'll keep an eye on him. I've got an alert set to trigger all of our embedds should he come close."

"Rider? What's a rider?" Outish was feeling so slow.

"For the next five days, our friend mister Prairiegrass will have his very own surveillance bot. It will take pictures and an aural scan of everyone he meets." He tilted his head. "That may be a lot of people the way our friend gets around, but if he's working for someone, we'll find out who and they'll get their own rider."

Outish sat his cup down and rubbed his face wishing he had his old fur back. "So chief, I've been wondering why the IDB doesn't just use nanobots for all in-country surveillance. Why send us out at all? Whenever Solar Surveillance detects unusual ground activity, we could just release a cloud of nanobots to fly in, hover around, and be flies on the wall. It would be a lot safer for us. No fighting trogs, getting spied on. We could sit in Central Station, and monitor and direct the bots. I've watched the sensor operators. It's really cool when they take control of a bot and start chasing a bee or buzz a squirrel."

Achelous gave him a flat stare, and Baryy rolled his eyes.

"What?" Outish complained. "It's true!"

Achelous emitted a tired, but patient sigh. "Baryy?"

"What, you want me to explain?"

"Sure, you helped catch Fileas. That's a good example."

He sat back and looked pained as if to say, "Do I really need to?" Before he could beg off, Achelous said, "Start at the beginning, consider it part of our Astrobiologist's field training. He may be your next Assessment of Cultural Disruption partner." To that, Baryy nodded grudgingly.

"Fileas?" asked Outish.

"Yes, Fileas Faugh," answered Baryy, dredging up his memories. He could just as well make Outish view the file on the hologrid, but somehow telling the story carried more weight. Which was important in the field. "Fileas was an architect, and his federation records indicate a good one too. He had a flourishing construction business on Wikdim IV. That is until his partner embezzled most of their money and fled to the outer reaches. Fileas was left high and dry; cash flow problems killed his business. But then, just as tax collection was about to put his firm into receivership Fileas was approached by a friend of a friend. The guy's name was Latro Binar-something or other." He shook his head not worrying about the detail. "Latro had the idea of setting himself up as a wealthy businessman on a Class E world. Typical story. Latro wanted the easy life and didn't like that in the modern world he woefully lacked in skills, education, and pluck. He dreamed of setting himself up as a prince on a primitive world where even his meager determination and paltry knowledge of the universe would instantly establish him as a wise man, or so he hoped."

Outish nodded. He'd heard these stories before, it was why the IDB and ULUP existed--to keep the would-be princes and demigods from invading the primitive worlds and exploiting the ignorance of the natives, or worse, corrupting the local culture with regressive behaviors born from destructive cults.

"Latro had a couple of things right. He understood that knowledge is power, especially if your knowledge was vastly superior to everyone else's. And he knew he needed a real expert with a real skill that could be easily brokered into success on a primitive world. So Latro did his research. Lazy as he was, he was committed to having it easy and was willing to work to get there.

"As per ULUP, the IDB, in exchange for not allowing people to land on Class E worlds, is responsible for publishing news of how the various indigenous civilizations are faring. Call it an Uplift scorecard. Each planet gets its own annual grade. Latro seized on a series of documentaries on Dianis created by the *Galactic Explorer* based on our own reports, nanobot films, and solar and in-country surveillance.

"There are gaps in what we know since Latro died in the crash, but we do know that he acquired a ship and two business partners, set off for Dianis, and promptly pancaked when they landed.

"One of Latro's partners, Fileas Faugh, was nearly suicidal over the prospect of losing his business. To fund Latro's wild idea, he decided to sell the remaining assets in his business before the government could take over. He took the credits and with a shady pilot, whom Latro knew, rented an aging Moonstreak yacht, and made the shift to Dianis. Clearly a desperation move on Fileas's part and a grand adventure for Latro."

"When was this?" asked Outish.

"Four years ago. We picked them up with our orbital arrays when they shifted in and began to make their approach."

Achelous chuckled. "We did better than that. Their pilot, a guy called Rock Jock, thought he had mapped a hole in our recon net. He was wrong."

"What happened?"

"Gail shot him down." Baryy sat back.

"She did?" Outish's eyes grew wide.

"Sure did. When Solar Surveillance tried to hail them, instead of aborting and shifting out, they broke for the surface under power."

Baryy shifted his cramped feet under the table. "Protocol is if you are forced to orbit a Class E world, for whatever reason, engine failure, medical emergency, whatever, you are to hail the IDB immediately. We will come to your assistance. Any attempt to land on the planet will be taken as an overt sign you intend to violate ULUP, and you will be attacked and disabled. In the case of Rock Jock, there was no doubt he was on a final trajectory for landing. He was under full power with electronic and aural shielding in place."

"So she shot them down," said Outish.

"Well it was easy," replied Achelous, "the damn fools almost displaced an aggressor satellite when they shifted in."

"Then what happened?"

"The craft was disabled, but Rock Jock managed to crash it within a hundred miles of their intended landing site."

"Where was that?" Outish, thanks to the growing effects of the ataflour, was feeling more alive.

"Zursh, in the Lamaran Free Cities."

Achelous added, "But Rock Jock wound up killing Latro in the crash. Fileas survived unharmed."

A confused expression started to spread on Outish. "So the guy who planned the mission is now dead?"

Baryy couldn't help but smile, then turned serious. "So by the time Ivan and his Ready Reaction team get to the crash site Rock Jock had set off a thermite charge and incinerated the wreckage."

"But isn't that good?" asked Outish, "Ready Reaction would have had to do it themselves?" Corsairs or not, you couldn't just leave discernable wreckage of a space ship on a Class E world. The cultural impact could last decades if not centuries.

Achelous shook his head. "Old Rocky knew what he was doing. He slagged anything that could hold an aural signature, and they were wearing personal aural dampeners. We didn't know who we were hunting."

"Oh."

Baryy nodded his head. "With no aural signature, you can't do orbital, ground sensor, or nanobot aural scanning. No way to I.D. the corsairs in the general populace."

Achelous pursed his lips. "Even though Fileas and Rock only had a twenty minute head start on the Ready Reaction team it was enough. Later, Fileas told us they shipped a shielded anti-grav cargo sled with them. It doesn't leave any tracks to follow."

"So we were kind of stuck," interjected Baryy. "Cloud cover prevented direct visual observation from the satellites, and the bad guys were gone from the crash site by the time the recon pod and enforcement cutter arrived. So we had to wait for the extrasolars to show themselves, which can be a while, depending on how good they are. As much as Ivan and Reading Reaction wanted to go into Saphinus, the town Fileas and Rocky scooted off to, and root them out it was Farmer's day. The town was bursting with visitors to the market. The population was normally four thousand, but on Farmer's day, it grows to more than seven. So the extrasolars caught a lucky break."

Achelous shifted his chair back to stretch his legs out from beneath the table. "I had to make the call: send them in or not. They would have gone in quietly enough, though six heavily armed mercenaries always attract attention. At the time, we didn't know how many people we were looking for, though we knew it was less than four. The yacht was a four-seater with a cargo hold, and we'd already found parts of Latro's body. During that time period, we had four other CivMon teams in the field, and I needed to make sure we had enough Ready Reaction to back them up, so I held off committing the extraction team."

Baryy went on, "So we waited. We even did as you said, we sent in a swarm of nanobots in recon pods every time Solar thought they detected peculiar road traffic, congregations, anything that might look like, from space, an emerging new center of influence. But nothing, the nano's would hover about, listen, but nothing."

"You see," noted Achelous, "Bots can't interrogate. They can't ask questions; they can only minimally interact with their environment. Hence, their intel gathering is limited to what they can observe and even in a town the size of Saphinus there is a lot to observe. Our job is a lot easier when the Class E world evolves to the electrical age, and they have radio, television, or even satellites for us to monitor. Telecommunications are easier to tap compared to deploying expensive bots buzzing around attempting to listen to every conversation. Telecommunications use finite conduits for streaming data."

Baryy took a sip of tea, the cup gone cool to the touch. "A month goes by, usually the amount of time it takes for a corsair to get settled in and have their strange mannerisms, weird customs, or odd accents draw attention to them. I went on a mission with Ready Reaction into Saphinus and then later to Zursh to perform the Assessment of Cultural Disruption. Nothing. Normal as snow in winter. Though, we didn't expect to get lucky on the first pass anyway. But, even for a corsair with the knowledge of the galaxy, there is no guarantee they are going to be a success. An extrasolar is just as vulnerable to a knife in the ribs in some dark alley as your local provincial.

"We performed three more cultural disruption assessments before we hit on something. A year after the crash we discerned the Auro Na were building a new astral monastery in Zursh. They'd broken ground, were digging foundations, cutting stone, and erecting the cranes."

Achelous smiled at the memory. Baryy caught the smile. Nodding his head, he agreed, "Yes, it was one of those few times where the Paleos actually helped us. I was in Zursh treating one of the local Paleowright priests to an expensive lunch. Paleos can be excessive gossips and are particularly scornful of the Auro Na, not to mention the Life Believers. They will blab all day spewing out their demagoguery, extolling the sins and wickedness of their competition. That's when the priest told me of the grand plans of the Auro Na to build a monastery in Zursh. He said it was doomed to failure, that no one had ever been able to build a cathedral that tall, and that the newfangled flying buttresses wouldn't work."

Achelous added, "The priest was jealous."

"Yes," said Baryy emphatically. "Dark green with envy. Any time we hear of a new innovation, it's a trigger for us whether we suspect corsairs or not. We try to investigate every significant technological or social advancement and document the event because it helps us to refine our cultural evolution model and Uplift plan for that society. Event logging provides input to our evolutionary models so we can validate them.

"So I went to visit the builder. Ironically, extrasolars face significant challenges when establishing themselves. Just trying to fit in, adopt the culture, and understand the society can be daunting. If you get it wrong, it can get you killed. They are just as likely to do something that will alienate them as endear them. And there is one complication in particular that you can count on to expose an extrasolar."

"What?" Feeling better, Outish wanted to know more.

"Extrasolars, all of us, are loathe to reverse our gene therapy. After spending all that money on perfect hair, perfect teeth, perfect noses, perfect sight, elastometric joints, etc., we are just too vain to give it up when we go in-country."

"Ohhh—"

Baryy chuckled. "The first I saw Fileas I knew he was extrasolar. No receding hairline, hair brown as the day he was born, perfect teeth--which in-country is a dead giveaway—and after I spoke with him for a few moments I could tell he was a lot older than he looked. He had a grasp of engineering, structural capacities, and load dynamics way beyond mine. When I asked him where he'd learn how to build monasteries and where he worked before, he became evasive and tried to obfuscate. I pressed him, and he became offended and ordered one of his foremen to shoo me off the site."

"At this point," said Achelous, "We did deploy a pod of nanobots to monitor our good builder. Hoping he would lead us to his fellow corsairs."

Baryy added, "But the problem is the extrasolar may have severed ties with their partners or have too infrequent contact, so you have to prod the interloper into action and yet not press him so hard that he runs. So, I waited for the builder to leave the building site and I scanned his aural signature in the market. We sent a copy of it to Federation Citizen's Rights, and they came back with a hit on Mister Fileas Faugh, former owner of Registry Construction and an architect of some note.

"With the identity, Internal Security started a search for known associates and came up with Latro. Latro's data trail led them to the lease of the yacht and a pilot by the name of Jorgen Olzyk who was wanted for three counts of piracy, two counts of asteroid claim jumping, and another count of reckless endangerment for a low-orbit collision."

"Wow."

Baryy nodded at Outish's surprise. "In the end, we settled for less subtle means of extracting information from Mister Faugh. We sent Ivan in one night to extradite him. We have the vid back in Central Station. The look on Fileas's face when he opens the door and Ivan announces IDB is precious."

“Makes what we do worth it,” growled Achelous.

Baryy stood up. “So Ivan brought Fileas back to Central Station where we memory scanned him. That’s when we learned that Rock Jock—Jorgen Olzyk--was killed when the patrons of the gambling house he owned learned his dice were loaded.”

Achelous shook his head. “The whole escapade demonstrates two things. First, any determined corsair with resources can breach and elude the surveillance system. With the right equipment, intel, and planning they could do it virtually undetected. All they need to do is search long and hard enough, and they will find the holes. If we leave Dianis, dismantle the thin solar surveillance network, the planet will be wide open to exploitation. Fileas didn't have a lot of resources. There are sophisticated multi-solar companies out there with not only the financial resources but the technology and the staff to build robust secret planet-side operations, right under our noses.”

“What was the second thing you learned?” Outish whispered.

“The damage that just two extrasolars can do. Fileas, by bringing advanced building techniques to Dianis essentially started a building war between the Auro Na and the Paleowrights. Now instead of using their precious resources for building practical structures like schools or a hospital, both of them have embarked on building needless, exorbitantly expensive and grandiose monasteries and cathedrals. Other builders have come to Zursh to learn the methods and have only partially mastered them. Not having the advanced math skills they’ve taken the theories back to their homelands sometimes with disastrous results.”

Baryy chimed in. “For six months after arresting Fileas we were flying around the Lamaran Free Cities buying, stealing, and destroying the contraband articles they brought in-country.”

Achelous snorted. “Like the anti-grav sled, the Paleos took from a Lamaran farmer who was using it to haul his hay. He and his magic carpet were the talk of the land.”

“Or the dice controller and six pairs of dice that Rock was killed over. They were being used in yet another gambling house,” Baryy smirked. “Or the solar-powered multi-func Fileas allowed his assistant to use as a calculator.”

Achelous added, “Counter intuitively, the Paleowrights suffered the most from the episode. The people who came into possession of the contraband items saw Rock and Fileas for what they were, not as all-powerful Ancients, but as opportunists at best and swindlers at worst. Some of those provincials were devout Paleowrights, and when they saw the cavalier attitude of Rock and Fileas, they abandoned their faith. They said if this is what the Ancients were like they are not worthy of worship, which greatly disturbed the local Antiquaria clergy."

Baryy nodded. "You know what the Paleowrights did?"

Outish shook his head.

"The Paleos purged them," Baryy said, his expression challenging. "They brought in squads of un-badged Scarlet Saviors, assassins actually, and started killing anyone who had an Ancient artifact and anyone with ties or direct knowledge of Rock or Fileas. They didn't want the general population thinking this was how Ancients acted. They wanted to maintain the mystique and aura of the Ancients as gods and not as normal human beings with foibles."

Outish stammered, "But what about the town, didn't they try to stop it?"

The agent shook his head with a grim smile. "By the time the Governor of Zursh perceived the scope of the atrocities seventy people were dead, and another hundred or so, across the Free Cities, were killed later. The governor sent the City Watch in search of the murderers and tried to stop the killing, but by then the assassins had done their work."

Outish swallowed.

Achelous scratched an itch under his shirt he hoped wasn't a tick. "Suffice to say the locals in Zursh now want nothing to do with Ancient artifacts. They won't touch them." He'd laugh if it weren't so sad. "The Paleowrights wound up doing our work for us. Instead of trumpeting the existence of Ancients and offering Rock and Fileas up as proof, albeit as poor examples, they went out of their way to hide the identities of two real Ancients. During the six months after the arrest of Fileas, it became a race between the Scarlet Saviors and us to round up the remaining extrasolar gear. We even contracted with the Silver Cup, posing as private collectors, to help find artifacts. Every person we found holding an artifact we warned of what the Paleowrights were doing. We even relocated a peasant who had a chunk of the wreckage. One of Ivan's teams arrived at the peasant's hovel just ahead of a squad of Scarlet Saviors. There was an ugly confrontation, but the Saviors withdrew vowing the peasant would face judgment."

"Just so they could continue to propagate the belief in Diunesis Antiquaria," Baryy said. "It wasn't about getting the facts or history right. It was about maintaining the status quo, the belief system, the power structure. And because of Rock and Fileas at least a hundred and seventy people lost their lives."

Chapter 15
Cordelei

Wedgewood

The walk-lanterns were lit, as were ladder and porch lights in the tree houses and forts. Seen from afar they looked like giant Will-O-the-Wisps hovering high in the trees. Baryy stood at the front window of his cabin. The low ceiling gave him bare room to stand, but he'd since become used to it.

Outish turned to wave as he headed out on the path from the cabin and Baryy grimaced as the intern backed into the low gate and fell over it. "Oh smokes—" he reached for the door when Outish quickly sprung up and signaled, "I'm okay!" he dusted himself off under the walk-lamp. "Nothing broken!" He waved again and hurried off into the night, embarrassment evident in the tilt of his head.

"What did he do?" Achelous asked, pulling his muse from the fire.

"Oh, nimrod turned to wave and fell over the gate.

The chief inspector sniffed in humor.

"I thought he smacked his skull. Those Halorites are tough." Baryy took a chair in front of the fire, but his rigid posture, elbows on knees, and the way he elevated his heels belied his tension. "Well, at least he's gone for a while; we won't have to worry about him."

Achelous pursed his lips and gave the barest nod. They'd sent Outish to Murali's to play dice with Mergund and Lettern with strict orders to drink spiced cider only, to which he fervently agreed. The trio had taken to wandering Wedgewood together, Lettern as the de facto chaperone, or at least steady rudder. "You have the bots ready?"

"I do." Baryy eased off his elbows. "Atch, is there no other way to do this?"

Achelous continued to stare into the low fire, taking the chill out of the cabin as the thin mountain air gave up its heat to the spring night. "There are other ways, but believe me, I think this is the easiest, and potentially the most accurate." He gave the agent a smirk, the firelight reflecting in his brown eyes, "And it is certainly the most creative. Besides," he reached for the iron poker, "we have a deal. I get to test Cordelei, and you get to steer Mbecca."

Baryy let out a long sigh, bouncing his heels. The fire popped, and a log hissed, steam bubbling out its end--the wood not quite dry. Achelous let him stew with his thoughts. Baryy needed to reconcile their situation to his own satisfaction, at least to his own grudging avowal. Baryy could continue to suffer through his angst watching passively as people he knew suffered and died around him while he held the knowledge to cure their ill, or he could do something. Helping Daryan's father had been simple enough. A dose of plaque-eating bacteria followed by a dose of the arresting agent had cleared his heart blockage. The former Warden of the Seventh had even, on this day, returned to the practice field for the first time in a year cutting and hacking with his axe like he'd never left. Unfortunately, Daryan's mother, a woman of only forty years, was a different story. Firmly in the grips of the Timber's Curse, she languished in their blacked-out lodge, hiding from the blinding daylight. She was dying, and Daryan knew it. The pain in Daryan's eyes when she fled to him for a few hours of respite agonized Baryy to the core. When her mother died -- and die of the tumor she most certainly would -- how could he look Daryan in the eyes?

His supervisor was offering the opportunity, opening the door for him to help Daryan's mother and all the Timberkeeps, and yet he was bound by the same oath that Achelous had taken: to uphold ULUP and protect native societies from outside influence and depredations of extrasolars. The problem was his sense of values were at war with each other. He knew what he wanted to do was fundamentally right. Saving human lives from disease on Dianis, according to his values, was equal to saving humans from Turboii food factories. Perhaps more so as death by a curable disease was a waste of life, a travesty upon the human conscience. Death by Turboii harvesting, while a travesty upon the Turboii Empire, was, unfortunately, often not within human control. On the one side, the Avarian Federation spent huge sums of money to fight the Turboii, and on the other side they spent significant resources enforcing ULUP, and ULUP essentially said if the provincials couldn't care for themselves, let them die. Whereas the war against the Turboii was exactly the opposite—where the provincials can't defend themselves from the Turboii the federation would help. The Avarian Federation was attempting to save as many human worlds from annihilation as possible, partly to keep the fighting away from Avarian core worlds, and partly to prevent human extinction.

Yes, he understood the argument, the question of where do you draw the line? On primitive worlds whose indigenous populations are at odds with each other, how do you prevent aid to one society from causing the detriment and sometimes annihilation of the other? Rather than establish a court to manage an unworkable set of laws that attempted to weigh and balance actions for the total benefit of all life on the planet, ULUP imposed an infinitely more workable, fair, if harsh, system of complete isolation. The imposition of free will without interference. Let nature's course take its direction, let the strongest survive. The problem was Baryy could not, would not, sit idly by as someone died when he had the power to save them. He sighed. He could agree with the argument that if he helped humans in Wedgewood, then the troglodytes would likely suffer in some small way. Yes, Wedgewood may be stronger to stave off an attack from other provincial nations, and again he would be guilty of aiding and abetting one side over the other, but war was out of his control. He couldn't control societies or cultures, but he could save lives of those around him.

So Achelous struck a bargain with Baryy. He needed Baryy's help, and Baryy needed him. Achelous would cover for Baryy while the agent worked with Mbecca to surreptitiously expose the cause of Timber's Curse and develop a cure. In return, they would visit Cordelei Greenleaf.

"Okay," said Baryy, looking straight at Achelous. "It's dark now. I'm sure she's waiting for us."

An owl piped in the evening. A promising mate answered back with a warble. Baryy listened as they waited below the eves of Cordelei's cottage, away from the well of illumination cast by her walk-lantern. A light showed through the shutters in her windows. Achelous toggled through the displays in his multi-func, flipping pages in the Auro Na bible as he did so. He set the aural signifier to scan and found three aural signatures in the target radius: his, Baryy's, and a female target whom he assumed was Cordelei. He zoomed in on the female subject and set the signifier to "Monitor." He waited while the signifier calibrated to the woman's steady state. Her aural readings were nominal: well within the parameters for a calm, unalerted person, with – according to the scan – a mild case of depression. Her biorhythms were down, but nothing of concern. Tapping the *Transmit to Embed* icon, he closed the bible. "All set." In the dark, he noted the bob of Baryy's head. The multi-func was now programmed to monitor the female within the cottage and transmit to Achelous a variety of signals indicating the target's emotional state. The embed in his thigh picked up the signal and would vibrate when the woman's baseline state changed. Should she become alarmed, happy, angry, even tell a lie or attempt to conceal information the multi-func would detect the variations in her aural signature and cue his embed to relay the change to him. Achelous knew most of the signals by heart, particularly the ones that indicated lying or concealment. Admittedly, and with some shame he'd used the tactic on Marisa. Once or twice as an experiment when they were in bed. He was an undercover agent in a potentially hostile environment, and he could not risk being double-crossed.

They knocked on the door and made their introductions. Cordelei Greenleaf fit her nick name: Sour Dour. The corners of her mouth were turned down in severe arcs, her lips were thin, and her jaw set in a firm clamp. Sadness veritably wept from her eyes, as if all the world's sorrows bore witness through their lenses. She had a slow, deliberate manner as she crossed to her viewing table and sat, carefully arranging her long woolen skirt. In stark contrast, and in some odd attempt to obviate her character, she wore a colorful Doroman scarf over her white linen blouse. If Achelous were to guess he'd say she was fifty years native, though life on Dianis was harder than on a federation world so he could be wrong. She could be much younger. *Sour Dour, I bet you are.*

She came straight to the point, "Baryy tells me you have need of a reading?"

"I do," said the chief inspector. He withdrew the required coins from his purse and placed them on the table.

She reached her hand out to his, stopping him. "Please, I will collect my payment afterwards."

He shrugged. In the adjoining kitchen, a lamp, turned low, emitted a feeble flame; only coals glowed in the fireplace, and one single, tall candle in an elaborate glass holder sat on the viewing table off to one side. Otherwise, the cottage was dark. Incense, a rich aromatic version he'd never smelled before, burned in an incense pot somewhere. Baryy's chair creaked as he shifted beside him. "Yes, well, before we get started, do you mind if I ask you some questions?"

Her eyebrow gave the barest twitch. "That is why you are here. You come bearing questions, I divine their answers. It belongs to you to issue questions worth my fee."

"State your name for me."

She arched her eyebrow, but answered "Cordelei Greenleaf."

"Where do you live?"

The eyebrow stayed in place, "Wedgewood."

Achelous needed to ask a series of calibration questions to make sure his multi-func interpreted her answers correctly.

"Have you ever seen me in any of your dreams before?" He was concerned about what the diviner may already know about them. Her auguries could potentially wander anywhere, in Wedgewood or the galaxy, and according to Gail, they may even be able to expose the IDB.

"No," she said perfunctorily as if he were bothering her with useless questions. The attitude tone in his thigh shifted up, reflecting her mild annoyance.

"Give me your hand." He reached out, and she grasped it. Her fingers were cold.

"Tell me a lie." He asked, "I need to know how you react. Tell me you are going on a voyage tomorrow and try to make me believe you."

This time the tone in his hip elevated to mild agitation, but her only visual cue was a shift in her jaw. She complied, painting a remarkably vivid picture of a sailing ship leaving the SeaHaven League. At first, his embed buzzed with distinct tones of lying and untruths, but as she went on the tones started to mute. "Okay, that's good," he didn't want her to get carried away with a flight of fancy. Apparently, she was a dreamer in more than one fashion. He deliberately paused to let the hum settle back to baseline, and then asked, "Have you ever dreamed of Baryy."

The agent shifted uncomfortably in his chair, not liking the potential implications of his boss's question.

Cordelei looked hard at Baryy but made no move to retrieve her hand from his grasp. "Yes."

"What was the dream about?"

She backed off, her face became cloudy in the glow of the candle. If possible, her jaw tightened further, and she gave a brief shake. "I don't remember."

The embed tone changed. Cordelei wasn't exactly lying, but she wasn't trying to answer, perhaps she couldn't express what dream contained. Achelous would have to ponder the implications later. “Thank you." He let her hand go. "Your patience is appreciated. Now for my questions about the future. I have four to start with.” Cordelei charged by the half hour, not the number of questions, and she gave no guarantee that she could or would see the future on behalf of the client. If she became exhausted by the client’s questions before the half hour was up, the client still paid the full fee. In the dim light, Achelous noticed an hourglass on the dresser behind the woman. Judging by the sand in the bottom glass, she had turned it when she answered the door. Hmm, no loose book keeping here.

From his satchel, he withdrew five pieces of parchment and sat them face down on the table, blank sides up. Cordelei’s attention riveted on them. He felt the buzz in his thigh spike to something akin to a mixture of fear and excitement. By the way her eyes danced across the blank pages, even though the drawings were face down, the woman already saw something. *Genuine, she is a real sensitive,* he thought, relieved. *At least Baryy is on target so far. But what kind of sensitive is she? And how good?*

She lifted an arm and turned her shoulders to the dresser. In a practiced motion, not taking her eyes from the parchment, she withdrew a pipe, a taper, and a leather pouch. Opening the pouch, she extracted a pinch of a dried green herb and packed her pipe. Tearing her gaze from the paper, she held the taper over the candle and lit it. Then bringing the pipe to her mouth, she stoked it with the taper and puffed. She shook the taper out while puffing contentedly on the pipe, all the while transfixed on the first blank page. Smoke curled out of her nostrils and drifted up into her hair. The smell assailed him. He leaned next to Baryy. “Marshcat.”

Her eyes flickered between them, grey orbs in the glimmer.

“Shall we begin?” Achelous held the corner of the first page, and Cordelei gave a quick nod.

He turned the page over, revealing a stylized, hand-painted picture--unbeknownst to Cordelei--the company logo of an obscure equipment manufacturer. It was a control glyph, the icon of a real entity, but the probabilities of the dreamer having seen it or anything similar should be miniscule.

The prescient’s brows knit, and a frustration hum registered in his thigh. *That’s interesting,* he thought. “Do you recognize this drawing? It is a rendering of a company shingle, it is like a coat of arms. It represents the firm and its interests.” She looked up from the glyph. “I’m not a child, I know what it is. And no, I have not seen this one. Please continue.”

Achelous glanced askance at Baryy who shrugged.

He turned the next page. It was a picture of an emblazoned comet flying through a stylized compass against a black background dusted with silver stars.

Cordelei picked it up and scrutinized it. At length, she handed it back. “These will come later.”

It was the chief inspector’s turn to knit his brows. Out of the corner of his eye, he caught Baryy looking at him. “What do you mean, later?”

She shook her head impatiently, “Not now, later. They are of no concern.” The logo belonged to Celestial Navigations. He mulled the implication of Celestial Navigation becoming involved on Dianis, either now or later. It fit with a plan he stewed over, but he couldn't decide if that was good or bad.

As Achelous made to turn the third page, the prescient took another hit of her pipe. Smoke drifted in the air like a marsh wraith, irritating his eyes. He flipped it over.

She shook her head. “These come in name only. This image, but not the men behind it.” She tapped the logo of three intermeshed gears and the menacing maw of a mechanical beast. Baryy's rendition of an ore extractor.

“This image, but not the men behind it?” Achelous repeated, almost to himself. She glanced up as if a new thought came to her. “Imposters.”

“You mean someone will come imposing as them?”

Her gaze stared past him, the permanent frown deepening to a hard grimace. "Replacements. No--" she shook her head, the distant gaze unwavering. "Agents, mercenaries. Paid men." The tingle in his thigh told him she was giving it to him straight, unfiltered, as best she could interpret what the combined vision of the marshcat and her skill unveiled. The embed even added tones of excitement and expectation.

“Fine,” he said, turning over the fourth page revealing a strange sailing ship at anchor in the background, and a man in armor, holding a sword standing on a beach. A provincial, similar to a Plains Doroman farmer, stood facing the warrior. “What about them?" He pointed to the soldier, "Do you see them in the future? Do you see them here on Isuelt?” He knew he was reaching and was prepared to offer more explanation, but it was important for Baryy to hear what Cordelei had to say with as little prompting as possible.

She lifted the page, and then took the page with the gears. "These," the prescient said of the ship and soldier, will come as these," and she waved the glyph of the gears.

"You mean those," and he pointed, "will come masquerading as those?" Again he pointed but to the gears.

She nodded tentatively. The buzz in Achelous' hip told him she spoke the truth but still struggled with what she saw.

"When do they come, and where? Can you tell us that?"

She set them down and picked up her pipe, puffing thoughtfully. The fog drifted to the taper then swirled up and away. "Soon."

"What is soon?" he demanded, a note of exasperation creeping in.

She stared at the drawing as if it held her spell bound. Dreams, drug induced most likely, dancing before her vision. Breaking her trance, facing Achelous directly, "Soon, but not as soon as you would like. Much will change and happen before then." A shudder ran through her.

Achelous sat back. Then Baryy asked, "Can you tell us where? Where will they land?"

Prying her eyes from the page and she looked at him with newfound interest, as if he were finally worthy of attention. "North. In Mestrich."

Finally a definitive answer. Baryy hissed at Achelous, "The false coordinates. The bastards have access to our data system. We set them for Mestrich, in that played-out silver mine."

Achelous riveted on Baryy. "Cordelei sees the future, a possible outcome of the future. One, albeit strong, thread of Fate. But even fate can be changed. I've not yet filed the exact geo coordinates for our little ruse."

"Huh? Why?"

"Because without them it stalls any extrasolar incursion and gives us time to prepare. Time to set the trap. She sees what will happen after we post the false coordinates. Now that we know they will take the bait, I will update the reports with the fake sites and alert Clienen."

"And here."

Achelous looked at the voyant. "And here what?"

"They will come here as well," she said simply, her gaze off in the dark, the candle casting her to a yellow hue.

"Here? Come here as well?" He was stumped.

She slowly swiveled her unfocused eyes to him and narrowed their aperture. "Wedgewood."

"Shiren," Baryy cursed heavily.

This was going too far. Achelous made to retrieve the fifth and last page, but Cordelei slapped her hand down. Her index finger pinioned the paper. Achelous looked up. She stared hard at him, unyielding. The buzz in his thigh told him anger, and she looked at him and Baryy him as if seeing new images and the hum turned to sorrow, sadness. Achelous noted the time in the hourglass drain away with the last grain of sand. She kept her gaze on him, boring in.

Achelous sat well back in his chair, half expecting a violent outburst. The buzz in his thigh giving off a confusing array signals. "Baryy—"

"Yes?"

"Arm the bot."

"Now?"

"Yes, now. Time's up." Achelous held the stony gaze of Cordelei as she said, "You haven't asked any questions about this one," Ice dripped from her tongue as she pinioned the page beneath her finger.

Baryy got a clue something was seriously amiss. Puzzled, it dawned on him he didn't know what was on the fifth chart. Achelous had added it just before they left the cabin. Baryy stood, shoving back his chair and opening his purse. He heard Achelous say, "What question should I ask?"

She took the image of the gears and placed it beside the sheet under her finger. She could not see its image with her eyes. She didn't need to. "Will you live to fight Nordarken Mining?"

Baryy fumbled his purse, dropping it on the floor. "Nordarken Mining?" he hissed. "No one said that name."

In the dim light, Achelous knew he'd gone pale. A deep-seated paranoia about learning his future gripped his heart. He fervently believed no one should ever learn their own future, whether they lived, loved, cried, or died. "Baryy, trigger the blasted bot." His voice came out a croak. If he leaned back any further, he'd tip the chair over. To keep her distracted while Baryy set and armed the Probuteral bot, he sought to say something, and by some morbid volition, he asked, though his instincts screamed not to, "Will I live to fight the Nordarken Mining?"

Cordelei squinted into the gloom. "There is a woman, you love her. She will plead for your life with another far, far away." Achelous could hear the tiny whine of the nanobot's wings spin up.

"I see a ship, in the heavens" and she pointed at the ceiling. "A silver cup and sticks that shoot fire." The bot was airborne. "Many will die. She will---" Cordelei jerked upright, held stock still for an instant, then collapsed with the solid thunk of her forehead on the table.

The transition so sudden, both Achelous and Baryy remained rooted.

"Uh, what was that about you dying?"

"Oh no. Oh no." Achelous shook his head. *That's not right! She needed to finish!* He stared at the unconscious form of the prescient, her head, shoulders, and arms sprawled out across the viewing table. "She didn't get a chance to finish that part!"

Baryy let out an exasperated groan. There was no chance of asking her now. The probuteral would wipe her memory and short circuit her aural repository going back at least a day if not two. When she woke, she would find herself with a nasty bruise on her forehead, four silver durkets richer, and no clue as to how she came by them. They could, of course, try to rerun the test, but sixthsense was a quirky thing. Her readings of the charts would be different because she had already seen them, even if she didn't remember them.

Achelous retrieved the five drawings and tossed them one by one unto the coals of the brazier where they flared, casting a garish light across the gloom. He was about to throw in the last one when Baryy asked, "I know the logos we agreed to, what as the fifth?"

The inspector paused, his hand halfway to the fire, "It was another control glyph, but it turns out I didn't need to show it to her. She read all of them face down before I flipped them."

"What is it?"

He turned it over. The image was of two fists, a lightning bolt in one, and a twisting vine in the other. Between them was the figure of a farmer guiding an ox-drawn plow. Emblazoned above the farmer were the initials I.D.B. "I wanted to know, given the right trigger or clues, if she could augur us. Apparently, Gail was right. The Dianis sensitives can see us."

Baryy's eyes were wide and black in the fire light. "She went from the IDB control glyph to Nordarken Mining without you turning the chart."

Achelous said nothing.

Baryy said it for him, "That's not good. We're not the only thing they can see."

Chapter 16
Mbecca

Wedgewood

The next day Achelous and Baryy, accompanied by their astrobiologist, visited Mbecca Yuletree, the preeminent sixthsense healer in Wedgewood. Her abode, a rambling two-story stone lodge had repeatedly been added onto since the very founding of the town. The house, if it could be called that, sat well up-slope from Wedgewood proper, and a wide thickly mulched path led to her front door. Walk-lamps hung on poles the entire way. The lodge itself housed a twelve-bed infirmary where Mbecca and her assistants treated patients. On the second floor the newest edition, an exposed staircase rose into the reaches of a massive Ungerngerist. At the third rung of branches, an expansive observatory encircled the bole. Though the view of the night sky was largely obstructed by the living branches above it, the observatory served well as the local sensitive's den, a place of solitude, reflection, and meditation—scrying and augury. It doubled as the unofficial meeting place for the clan's emerging social group of sixthsense adepts.

Achelous and Baryy followed Mbecca up the winding staircase, through a door in the observatory, and into a cozy kitchen, or more likely a pantry with tables and chairs. It was Achelous's turn to uphold the arrangement he'd struck with Baryy. Outish had been given strict orders to contain himself and observe. If he had questions, which Achelous was certain would spout like a fountain, Outish was to feign idiocy and put them as stupidly as he could. Otherwise, Achelous would give him the "cease and desist" signal.

The four of them sat a corner bench in the kitchen whose walls and cupboard doors were elaborately decorated with colorful scrollwork and renditions of woodland flowers. An assistant readied a serving of tea. Immediately, counter to Achelous's wishes, Outish started to fidget; he stood and began wandering from nook to nook peering, lifting, and otherwise inspecting anything that struck his fancy, which was everything.

Anxious that Outish would blow their careful script, Baryy said, "Outish, sit down, you're a guest, not a chipmunk hunting for nuts."

Mbecca laughed. She looked at Outish with the eyes of a teacher, understanding written in her gaze. She followed his movements from article to article. "He doesn't get out much, does he?"

"No," replied Achelous, "this is his trade first mission. I'm trying him out as a runner."

"Oh he's way too intelligent for that," she swirled her tea with a spoon, "look at him, he's cataloging and noting everything of interest, quickly and efficiently. You really should make him a market surveyor. Send him out, he'll tell you what people are buying, what they are using." She looked at Achelous, "And perhaps more important, what they are not."

Outish's ears turned pink at the praise.

"Find anything of interest?" she asked, lifting her chin.

He held a glass jar, examining the contents of dried berries. "These. Even dried their aroma is quite strong." He asked Mbecca's assistant, "Are you putting these in the tea?"

Mbecca turned a satisfied smile on Achelous. "Bring them here," she said to Outish. "They're kdel berries, we pick them in the fall."

Achelous watched Mbecca pour them into a bowl and eat one.

"Here, have some," she passed Achelous the bowl. "I'll warn you, they're an acquired taste."

The color of amber and crinkled like a raisin the chief inspector popped one in his mouth. The tough skin yielded to his chewing and then an intense flavor assaulted his tongue. He almost spit it out.

Mbecca laughed. "Told you. They take some getting used to."

The flavor reminded him of a cross between raspberries and onions, at once repulsive and yet oddly soothing. She handed him a cup of water. He drank from it washing the offending berry down. Baryy and Outish each tried one, Baryy blanched, but Outish chewed his thoughtfully.

"More?" She waved the bowl at them.

Mouth firmly shut, Baryy shook his head.

"Yes, we make tea out of it. It's better than eating the berries straight. I have a pot steeping." She stood with an effort, the joints in her knees giving an audible creak, and shuffled to a small oil-fueled cook stove. The assistant made to intervene, but Mbecca waved her away. "Oi, the vagaries of age, but by Mother's fortune I still have my mind." Mbecca was a plump woman, her coarse black hair cropped in a vague shape about her head. Her skin darker than most Timberkeeps: an oak brown with big dark freckles like walnut stains.

She wore an unglamorous frock and a plainly embroidered vest, both in stark contrast to a woman of her obvious means. She trudged back across the floor in thick, shearling slippers, holding the teapot in her hands.

She poured the tea. The crockery was chipped, the handle of Achelous's cup reattached with glue. She noticed his examination and offered, "It's my special set. Been passed down for generations. Came with us from Whispering Bough. Many a famous Timber and other people have partaken from these cups."

He nodded seriously. "I'm honored," then the aroma of the tea wafted to his nose. "Oh—," he sniffed, "this is good," breathing deep the aroma's essence went straight through his sinuses and into his brain, "How lovely."

She smiled. "Taste it."

Achelous took a sip. "Hmm, sweet, yet tart, no—acerbic." He sipped again. "There's that raspberry-onion taste, only in the tea it's much more tolerable, quite enjoyable."

Her eyebrow arched, "I don't know what a raspberry is, but I know what an onion is. And you're right it does have a hint of it."

Achelous hid his consternation. That was a peril of his job, relating to a provincial an experience remembered on a different world. Low-level memories were hard to compartmentalize by planet. *Where did I learn about raspberries? Earth?* "How come I've not heard of kdel before now? I trade in herbs and spices. This is quite good. Did it come with you from the Great Latitudes?" The marsh was a prodigious producer of all sorts of unique herbs, not just marshcat for which it was best known.

"Mmm, no," she stared into her crock; the sediment drifting in the eddies. "It's native here to Mount Mars. I don't know that it grows anywhere else."

Achelous paused, holding the crock halfway to his lips. "Nowhere else?"

She met gaze. "No, not that I know of."

His brows began to knit, "Do you grow it or pick it wild?"

She began a grin. "Why? Are looking to trade it? There is barely enough for those of us who can afford it."

He swallowed and set the cup down. Baryy said the Timberkeep cancer rates were elevated in two tiers, the first tier being the long-time Wedgewood inhabitants, and the second higher incidence tier comprised of families of the more affluent and well-to-do

Timberkeeps. They suspected the second tier, the wealthy, had access to something not available to the general populace.

He stammered, “No, no. I wasn’t looking to trade it. But I am curious. Do you cultivate it or harvest it wild?”

“Both. Although, it’s only been in the last few seasons that our cultivated plots have begun to produce in substantial quantities. It takes years for a bush to grow large enough to bear a reasonable harvest. ”

Something was nagging him. It was at the edge of his consciousness; the sense that niggled him when he knew something, but his mind was slow making the connection. “Where do you grow them, certainly not under the Ungerns? I wouldn’t think there’d be enough light for a bush to bear much fruit.

She nodded as she popped one in her mouth. “True, we grow them on the terraces above the Ungerns. There’s plenty of light up there.”

“Terraces? You dug terraces?”

She shook her head and waved a hand “Noi, they’re natural, or at least they were there before us.”

Achelous blinked. *Natural terraces? Did they show on satellite imagery? Did we miss them?* It was yet another reason they should mount an expedition to the mysterious peak. He filed it away.

“Were the plants, the bushes already growing on the terraces?” Outish asked, peering out an open window. Three Tiny Tot humming birds, resplendent in their violet plumage, buzzed about a red cup suspended from the eves. Occasionally one would perch on the rim and sip from the cup.

Mbecca glanced at the runner who appeared engrossed in the feeder. She studied him, “Why yes, that’s where we initially found them.”

Seeking to draw attention away from Outish, Baryy asked, “Mbecca, on a different subject, have you attempted to treat victims of the Timber’s Curse?”

Her happy face clouded. She picked up a spoon and stirred her tea in slow circles. After a lengthy wait, “Yes, yes I have, but sadly to little effect.”

“What do you think is causing it?” he prodded.

She rolled her eyes. “If I knew that I would treat it.”

Then Achelous recounted their planned fictional story of a healer managing to cure a brain tumor of a rich merchant by the name of

Com. The story, while fictional on Dianis, would be true in practice on federation worlds.

She shook her head. “What makes you think they are dying of a brain tumor?”

The Timberkeep tradition of burning their dead went hand in hand with a cultural aversion to dissecting the dead bodies. The headaches, nausea, weakness, blindness, and loss of motor controls could be associated with a tumor, but you had to be trained to recognize them as such. Achelous decided to take a risk, just one of many he'd taken lately, and decided to connect the dots for the healer. “What I've seen and heard is the symptoms are remarkably similar. Baryy,” and he tilted his head in the agent's direction, “my trading firm has an account with Com," he lied smoothly, "We supply him all sorts of herbs.” It was a cover story of course, but he needed to establish Baryy's credentials for helping Mbecca.

Baryy picked up the thread. “Com's son was not the first. The healer treated others.”

Mbecca was intrigued and probed with more questions.

Achelous sat back and listened to Baryy plant the first seeds with Mbecca on how sixthsense might be used to locate, arrest, and potentially shrink the tumors. He mused on what Mbecca shared. *The coincidences are accumulating. Ruins near the top of Mount Mars, terraces, soil contamination, dramatically heightened aural sensitivity, proven Lock Norim artifacts at Lycealia, just a day's ride away. They all coincide with the dislocation of the Timberkeeps from Whispering Bough, the construction of Wedgewood. They have to be linked? We need to send a survey team to Mount Mars, take soil samples, map the growth zones of plants unique to this area, and moreover, search for Lock Norim artifacts. But when? We are running out of time.*

Chapter 17
Game On

The planet Avaria

Rocl Binair, Senior Vice President of Resource Production met his director in Bunker H of the safe room complex. They sat in their chairs facing away from each other. The thick entry door sealed tight. The wan room lighting coming from the overhead sealed-cell fixture, completely self-contained, no external wiring.

The new Aquamarine Production Director for Nordarken Mining came straight to the point. “The IDB withdrawal from Dianis is on track. Everyone is leaving. They’ll be gone in thirteen days.”

“Everyone?” Came Rocl’s surprised voice.

“Everyone.”

“What about the surveillance satellites?” Rocl asked, staring at the blank wall, but not seeing it.

“Those are mostly gone now. The rest will be captured in days.”

Rocl chuckled. Then his mirth turned into a solid laugh. “Are you serious? They took all the satellites too?”

Even though the vice president couldn’t see it, the director smiled and nodded. “Yes, even the eighty-five-year-old satellites.”

Rocl shook his head. “Amazing. And the ground crews? Surface monitoring?”

The director replied, “We think all the surface sensors are still in place and operating.”

“Well, they had to leave something behind, if for no other reason than appearances,” Rocl laughed again.

This time the director joined in. “Yes, if only for appearances.”

A moment passed then Rocl asked, “Have you passed the request to contracting?”

“I have. The agency has found two contractors interested in our,” he hesitated, “our venture.”

“Excellent.”

“One is willing to go directly to the two sites we have coordinates for, but they need thirty days to survey and disable the ground sensors. The other contractor thinks those sites are too hot but is willing to conduct a geologic survey to identify other sources on the planet, at their cost. They think if there are two, two found by the indigins, that there must be more." The director let that sink in. "I'm inclined to agree with them."

"Hmm," Rocl mused out loud, "so what do you propose?"

"I think we should do both. Contract with both of them."

Rocl liked this director. Just over ninety days on the job and he was proving to be more aggressive, more direct and less squeamish than Tomkin. He might even prove useful, for a while. "And how will you keep them from fighting each other?"

The director knew the question was coming. Independent mining contractors, particularly those willing to jump a Class E, were notoriously predatory and predisposed to "outing" a competitor working the same claim. "We will assign strict operating zones with clearly defined coordinates. They are not to stray beyond those zones."

"And when they do, because you know they will."

The director waggled his head, a common idiom to his nationality. "Not our problem. If they shoot each other, why do we care? We are paying for a commodity. Contractor casualties are their overhead, not ours."

In spite of himself, Rocl smiled.

Chapter 18
Transponder

Central Station

That's done, Achelous thought ruefully. He'd taken a certain step into an uncertain future. Like walking in a thick fog, able to see only few yards at a time, each foot forward exposed new grey shapes looming in the mist. He'd submitted his IDB resignation, and like walking in the swirling mist on the dunes by Tivor, what came next surprised him. Settling into Clienen's office, he'd told the director he was tendering his resignation and fully expected that would be the end. Instead, Clienen talked him out of it, citing among other points compulsory war service, something Achelous never dwelled upon. Under the Articles of War, all able-bodied men and women between the ages of twenty and ninety must be fully employed, unless on approved sabbatical. Moreover, if the manner of employment was not directly linked to the war effort, able-bodied men and women of the specified age group must be assigned a war-related activity for a minimum of thirty days a year. Such was the dire state of the Turboii War. Thoughts of compulsory war service had eluded him because a career in the IDB was considered in direct support of the war effort. He had never planned to leave the IDB.

Sitting in his cramped Central Station office, he scanned the long, hand-written list — he couldn't risk keeping an electronic copy on his multi-func -- of things he needed to do. At the top of it was resign from the IDB.

Clienen had reasoned with him: why resign from the IDB when he'd just have to find another job or be assigned one? It was better to take a sabbatical and when the period expired then consider resigning. Sadly, Achelous didn't believe the two and a half years of leave would be long enough for what he needed to accomplish. Under the Articles of War, as compensation for being denied career intermissions or outright retirement, people of war service age were allowed to take a six-month sabbatical for every five years of service. He'd never taken a sabbatical and so the time accrued, and he was due two and a half years. A more immediate problem was Baryy's five years of service entitled him to only six months. Another nuisance, however, was solved and he crossed it off his list. Clienen had provided the solution. Achelous replayed the conversation in his head. "My heart's just not into going to Dominicus III. Not while there is so much to do here. It may be selfish, but I don't see how the provincials on Dominicus III are more important than those on Dianis." The conversation from ten minutes ago vivid in Achelous's mind, and he went over it and over it, analyzing every detail, assessing the implications of the change in his plans.

"So how is quitting the IDB going to help?" Clienen had asked with concern. "I can understand going on sabbatical, spirits know you deserve a break, but quitting the IDB?"

Achelous chaffed in his chair. The conversation was not going the way he'd planned.

"And how is quitting the IDB going to solve the problems on Dianis?"

Achelous framed his answer. At least this part of the conversation he was prepared for, but it was still rife with risk. He moved forward like treading on thin ice, wary of plunging through, his trust in Clienen paramount. "I want to pursue my own investigations of Nordarken Mining without interference from the IDB."

The director sat back.

Going over the meeting in his mind Achelous saw Clienen's stunned reaction. On the director's hologrid the decoded message from Water Survey, as authorized by Internal Security, was displayed, the message that triggered Achelous's suspicions when he first met with the director. It was in clear-text, sent from Water Survey to someone at Tangent Assets, and it read, *Article of strategic interest found on Dianis, Isuelt continent. Specific location is unknown. Will provide report. Request Lamp meeting, 4007.2.57.*

To Achelous, it meant the spy had met with a contact just five days after Achelous had filed the initial field report, and that the spy passed the report to their contact. The meeting date of 4007.2.57 was three months ago, and that was the size of their head start.

"Are you concerned someone may try to stop you? Or are you worried the Water Survey spy may track your activities?" Clienen asked. "Because if you are, Internal Security has narrowed down the Water Survey suspect list to three people. All of which are under surveillance. To take it any further they'd have to make more overt inquiries, and you and I both agreed to not do that until after we seeded the false coordinates."

"Fine. I think it's time to file a new field report with an update on the aquamarine-5 finds listing a second and richer deposit, and in this report, we'll include the coordinates." Achelous smiled. It was like dabbing a cherry on top of whipped cream.

Clienen appreciated the idea. "So if we do this, and Internal Security catches the mole, and we can track the information back to their contacts, will you still want to conduct your own investigation without interference from the IDB? Or should I say would you then be willing to go to Dominicus III?"

A deep frown set on his visage as Achelous became impatient. "It depends on who the mole is and who those contacts are. Clienen, busting one of Nordarken Mining's spy rings is not going to stop them. You and I both know their intelligence network has firewalls to maintain plausible deniability. We'll never tie this leak to anyone important at Nordarken headquarters. We'll eliminate the mole, which is good, but it does not change the fact that the IDB is leaving Dianis, that Dianis has aquamarine-5, and Nordarken Mining knows it."

"Okay, so what can you possibly do to stop them? Assuming, and it is a big assumption, they intend to launch a corsair operation once we pull out."

Achelous's frustration boiled over. He made a snap decision, reached into his satchel, and pulled out five sheets of paper. "I conducted a field trial experiment on one of the Timberkeep sensitives. A dreamer." It was a ruse to dress up his unsanctioned, interventionist interview with Cordelei, portraying it as an innocent evaluation of emerging native sixthsense capabilities. With anyone other than Clienen, the story would make plausible sense.

As expected, Clienen reacted skeptically, on the verge of being offended that Achelous would stoop to con him.

"I showed her this logo and asked her if there was any relationship between it and Dianis." He slid the first sheet across the desk.

The director turned it over, peered at it, and then shook his head. "What is it?"

"The company logo of an obscure equipment manufacturer. Of course, I used parchment and hand-sketched the logo. The sensitive came up cold."

Clienen nodded at the other sheets, and Achelous handed them to him. The director flipped each page, in turn, asking questions about what turned out to be stylized glyphs, some for logos for Avarian entities. When they came to Nordarken Mining, the director grunted. When he saw the IDB glyph, he asked, "What did she say about this?"

"I wasn't going to show it to her. It was face down, and when I tried to retrieve it, she stuck her finger on it and glared at me, quite angry. She wanted to know if I thought I'd be alive to fight the Nordarks. And—" he paused for emphasis, "Clienen, neither Baryy nor I had mentioned any names up to that point. She picked Nordarken Mining out of the ether."

"What do you mean, live to fight the Nordarks?"

Having nothing to say, Achelous shrugged.

"She prophesied you're going to die before the Nordarks arrive, and they are coming soon?"

He grimaced at Clienen taking the prediction to the extreme. "There may be a situation where my life is in danger, but I think she wanted me to ask the question just to see me squirm."

The director shuffled the papers then handed them back. "You shot her with Probuteral?"

"Via nanobot."

A faint smile creased Clienen's lips. "Nasty little bug. Never know when you're going to get stung and forget what you're doing."

Achelous smiled himself. "They're so focused on you it never dawns on them to watch out for a bug."

The director took a deep breath. He sighed, then idly tapped the hologrid, his mental wheels spinning. "This adds a new dimension. I could ask the Matrincy to send a team to do their own evaluation, perhaps even cross verify the visions of this Cordelei Greenleaf. But what would that get us? You did the test correctly. The veracity of the Timber prescients is documented and proven. The Matrincy would want to know why you performed the test in the first place. Which would lead us down a muddy hill greased with pig shit. Aside from possible accusations of interventionism, we'd get into your theories of why the IDB is really being pulled out of Dianis." He let the unvoiced suspicion hang between them. Was the Matrincy involved in clearing the way for extrasolar intervention on Dianis? All for the war effort, to facilitate the extraction of a strategic resource not only crucial to the movement of military assets, but the creation of new aura-based technologies that could tip the balance of the technology in Avaria's favor. Such a conspiracy was one way of circumventing ULUP without having to go through the arduous and public process of granting an exclusion. The possibility was far-fetched. It was the Matrincy that championed the rights of indigenous peoples. Yet...

Clienen continued to tap his finger. Achelous and now Baryy, were willing to invest their own time investigating the Nordarken threat and they clearly would rather do that than go to Dominicus III. The only way they could continue their investigations was to either resign from the IDB or go on sabbatical. In any case, they would not be planet-side to monitor-- Then clarity of the situation rolled over Clienen like a wave. He thought it through. He didn't know whether to be angry or admire them.

Achelous watched the director as he pondered something. Clienen stopped tapping his finger on the table, his face alternating between a distant look and a piercing glare that made Achelous want to squirm. Achelous held himself still, waiting.

Imperial Sanctum. Clienen thought back to the brief, sole meeting he'd ever had with the Matriarch herself. She had asked him a simple riddle, and at the time, he wondered why she asked it: "If you had to do what was right, and it was wrong, would you do it?" Upon retrospect, he realized she had been referring to the concept of *ultimate cause*, whose official term in the federate legal system was Imperial Sanctum. It was a high-risk defense used for when an entity broke the law, usually an archaic helplessly obsolete law, in favor of the future good. Unfortunately for the defendants, the courts rarely agreed with people who arbitrarily, and for their own benefit, declared a law obsolete.

Conflicted, Clienen settled on a pragmatic approach. Neither Achelous nor Baryy were guilty of anything, yet. If they should violate ULUP then they'd have to defend themselves. Perhaps with ultimate cause. By then Clienen would be at his new post at IDB headquarters. Both Achelous and Baryy were scheduled for transfer to IDB Dominicus within sixty days, unless they took leave, but their Dianis charters would expire nonetheless. Staring at Achelous, he was tempted to ask him what he intended to do in the next two and a half years. It would be an awkward moment, and Clienen didn't really need to know, not professionally. Instead, he pursued a tangent. "So is there anything I can do for you while you are on sabbatical?"

Achelous eased. "Well I do have one thing you could help with."

"Yes?"

For what he planned to do, he needed the use of the recombinant crystal chip embedded in his thigh. He could make do without if it was removed, but it would mean procuring a commercial embed and a few other gadgets to replace lost critical functionality. He still wouldn't have all of his existing capabilities, the most crucial being he could not interface with IDB facilities or CivMon field assets. "When I'm on leave I'd like to think I was, you know, off the radar."

"Oh?" Clienen didn't have a clue where this was going.

"That means not being on the tracking leash twenty-six hours a day."

"Oh--" now Clienen had a clue.

"Can you have the locator transponder turned off?" Achelous could turn off the aural transmitter in the embed that signaled his position to Solar Surveillance satellites and ground monitoring equipment, but he could not turn off the signal responder that would send back a response should it get pinged by a search array.

Clienen rubbed his jaw. "Sure, but do you think that is safe? If you are incapacitated..."

"Yes, well, it may not be the IDB that does the pinging."

Clienen sniffed. The implication being with the transponder enabled anyone with access to the secret transponder codes, the Matrincy, Internal Security, IDB Affairs, or an industrial spy, could learn exactly where he was.

"Fine, your transponder will be disabled the day you go on leave. But I have a different question. Do you want an AI? Jeremy will be either archived or his servers replicated elsewhere. Dianis Central Station will be dark. Will you need an AI?"

Shocked, Achelous asked, "Are you offering me the use of Jeremy?"

"Hmm," Clienen hedged. "I need to check my authorizations, but I might be able to get you a specialized clone of Jeremy."

Achelous cocked his head. "What sort of specialization?"

"Counter espionage?"

Chapter 19
Outish

Central Station

The three of them huddled at a table in the Central Station dining hall. It was, Achelous mused, one of the few times in recent memory that he, Baryy, and Outish were all Central Station at the same time. Usually one of them was in-country. It felt odd to be drinking Temerish Orbit and sitting under the holovid ceiling, and not draining Bash-Me-Brains and listening to fiddlers at Murali's. The 3D holovid of the spectacular Gnomegeron Chasm on Avaria was so vivid it gave him vertigo to look into the canyon, but Achelous preferred the primitive and real, to the galactic and illusionary. His thoughts turned to Boyd's laughing face and Marisa hugging him close. Dispelling the blissful visions and his brooding drift, he turned to the onerous business at hand. "Outish, you know that when the IDB leaves Dianis, your internship contract will terminate."

Judging by his expression, Outish either hadn't considered that eventuality or didn't think it applied to him. The lad was drinking a benign herbal concoction he'd drummed up through the autoserv.

"And it is official; Dianis IDB will cease planet-side operations in forty five days."

"You mean..." Outish struggled, whether he was under false perceptions or he'd chosen to ignore stories of CivMon's departure, he was unprepared for reality. "You mean I'll have to leave?"

Achelous knitted his brows. *What was Outish thinking?*

"But-- no! That can't happen; we're on the verge of a major breakthrough. If we can isolate the chemical interaction in the kdel plant and prove it stimulates activation of the thalamus it would be the biggest breakthrough in sixthsense since the discovery of the thalamus as the aural nexus." Scientific debate still resonated in neuroscience circles as to the exact role of the thalamus in aural processing within in the brain, but the indisputable fact remained that the thalamus was the key to coordinating sixthsense abilities and controlling aural energy.

Achelous appeared unmoved.

“Atch, come on. The density of sixthsense in the Wedgewood population is a thousand times normal and their capability graphs range from five to a hundred times normal. This is the only place in the federation with those numbers. Smokes, the Matrincy scours the galaxy for adepts a quarter as good as those here, and they find only a half dozen each year.”

Achelous drummed his fingers, which he never did unless he was stressed. “The Matrincy knows that Dianis, because of the Timberkeeps, has the highest concentration of human sensitives in the galaxy.”

Baryy stayed impassive, and regardless of how compelled he felt to aid the intern with the arguments, he'd been briefed by Achelous beforehand and told to stay out of it. So he sat on his hands and tried not to fidget.

“Yes," Outish nodded fervently, "but they don’t know why! Is it genetics? We’ve proven it’s not replicatable outside of Wedgewood; the population is highly localized. The symptoms point to environmental contamination and that means a chemical. A chemical if isolated and controlled that could be used on other populations.” He paused and scratched at the table. “Assuming the cancers and DNA damage can be mitigated.”

Achelous hedged, “You think it is caused by chemical contamination. It could be a prion or some other pathogen.”

“That’s because we haven’t looked,” exasperation ruled Outish’s tone. “No one knows we should be looking. Except us.”

Reluctantly Baryy weighed in, on Achelous’s side. “The source of the brain tumors and increased sixthsense sensitivity could be coincidental, and not related.”

Outish quickly rebutted, “Uh, I don’t think so. The odds of them not being related are astronomical. However, I will give you that perhaps the increased sensitivity is overcharging the brain and the thalamus is mutating, and thus we have the cancers. The agent may cause the stimulation and the stimulated activity is causing the DNA damage.”

Listening to Outish’s argument, Baryy had an idea, *if we could do an autopsy, we could run a chemical analysis on both the thalamus and the tumor.*

As if on cue Outish completed Baryy’s thought, “We need so much more testing. A molecular scan of a live sensitive’s brain will tell us much of what we need to know about the effects on the brain and any chemical build up."

"That's a good idea," said Baryy. "It's not something I've considered, but I suppose that's why he's the astrobiologist, and I'm the sociologist."

"Now is not the time to leave," the intern pleaded, "if I can isolate the causal agent not only would I get my astrobiologist certification, I'd get an accreditation."

Achelous smiled inwardly. He couldn't blame the young internist, new to the field, unproven, and unlettered, for having a hearty amount of self-interest. In fact, he was counting on it. Now was the time to fan the flames. It bothered his conscience that he was manipulating the young man, but in the quest to face and defeat the Nordarken Mining, the end justified the means. Imperial Sanctum, ultimate cause. "If you were to find the cause of the increase in Timberkeep adepts the Matrincy would probably give you the Federation Insight Prize."

Outish's eyes popped out. "You think so?!"

Baryy covered his face and rubbed his hairline. He didn't know whether to grimace or laugh. *Although, it would just be the intern's dumb luck...*

Achelous nodded, "It's the Matrincy adepts, the few we possess, that have changed our tactics against the Turboii's cloned minions. Being able to telepathically intercept the Turboii command messages has proven to be a decisive battlefield advantage." Outish drank in every word. "That's why at every opportunity the Turboii single-out and attack our adepts." Achelous changed subjects. "Baryy and I are taking a sabbatical. We're not going to Dominicus III, at least not now. And you, since you are an internist to IDB Dianis will have your contract terminated."

Outish's brown eyes started to well up, and he dropped his head. "You'll still have your intern commission from your institute, of course, but you just won't be able to fulfill it with us."

Outish mumbled, "I'll have to start all over on my certification. My time here will be zip. I'll have to find another research program." He lifted up his head, tears in his eyes, "Do you know how hard it is to find an astrobiologist research billet on the human side? All the astrobiologist's coming out of school are being fed into Turboii and minion anatomy studies. It's grunt work, counting and cataloging genes, DNA sequencing. The research directors are getting all the glory."

Achelous nodded. He'd been the one to approve Outish's application to Dianis. "Well fortunately for you, just because your intern contract expires does not mean you immediately have to find employment." He looked at Baryy, then back to Outish. "You have time to find another program."

"But I've been here a year and a half! I was just now getting into the field. Learning real stuff. Seeing firsthand the natives interacting within their biosphere!" For Outish, to give up on his dream and start over was a crushing blow. He'd even sacrificed and undergone gene translation into the physical appearance of a human, a physiology he was only now growing accustomed to.

It pained Achelous to watch the lad squirm and suffer, but he had to make sure when he made the offer that Outish was committed and would not renege. Too much was at stake. He sensed Baryy beside him was becoming exasperated with his treatment of the intern, but it had to be done this way. "Interesting thing about information systems. You would think with Ether storage, X-Light data transfer, and AI control, that the systems would have evolved over the years, but they still have the same problems."

Outish blinked, wondering what data had to do with his predicament.

"Your internship is registered against Dianis under the ULUP Authorized and Licensed Agents Registry.

"Yeah," Outish said uncertainly.

"The agency through which you gained the authorization is IDB Dianis."

"Yes?"

"If the link between your ULUP authorization record and the agency responsible for administering your activities were dropped, there'd be nothing to connect you with us."

He frowned, trying to comprehend what Achelous was saying.

Baryy spelled it out for him. "You'd be what they call an orphaned actor, able to roam about Dianis at will, without fear of prosecution until someone found you, checked your authorization, and discovered you had no supervising agency. At that time, they would have no recourse but to assign you to IDB Sector Operations. Sector Ops who would then rescind your authorization because they won't have a Dianis billet."

"You would immediately be escorted off the planet," supplied Achelous, "they'd probably yell and threaten, but there'd be nothing else they could officially do."

"Except for bitch at the Chief Inspector of Dianis CivMon and ask him how an intern was allowed to roam about a Class E world without a supervising agency." Baryy smiled at Achelous.

"Yes, and they'd first have to find Outish, follow his credentials records, and then find me."

A gleam resurrected in the intern's eyes. "How do I get this link dropped?"

Achelous shrugged, "Things happen. Data is moved around, edits are made, transformations loaded. Data can be corrupted, even in the Ether. There can be unintended side effects of modeling changes. Stuff happens."

Outish peered at the chief inspector. He decided it was best not to know too much, especially if someone conducted a memory scan. He chewed on it some more. "So I'd be able to write the research paper and file the findings?"

Baryy nodded. "Yes. But you'd have to do it before your presence planet-side was discovered. You'd have to keep a low profile and be very discrete." *In other words, operate in secret,* but he didn't say that. "The minute you publish the paper all attention will be focused on you and the Matrincy will come looking. So the paper had better be complete. You'll get one shot at it. Nail the research; get your facts validated."

"But I'll need access to a lab. I'll be alone. All my data will be anecdotal. How will I live on the planet and do my research?" He downcast his gaze, overwhelmed by the complexity of what lay before him. Being planet-side and working with the Timberkeeps was only half the challenge. Without the analysis of the chemical compounds and thorough evaluation of the interactions within the human body, anyone could label his findings as preliminary, or worse, conjecture, and then launch their own clinical research and take the glory.

Achelous slid a sheet of old-fashioned paper across the table, along with an ink pen. "On that paper, nowhere else," Achelous stressed, "Write down everything you need to conduct your analysis. Equipment, materials, infocubes, whatever." He looked at the intern whose hopes and aspirations were plainly etched upon his visage. "What we seek to do Outish is transformative. For Dianis, for the Timberkeeps, for humans, and for the Turboii War. Baryy wants to save the Timberkeeps from dying out. You want to publish the findings of Timberkeep sensitivity, which will have far reaching implications for the Turboii War and humanity in general." He paused. "And I want to protect Dianis, like all of us, from the depredations of the extrasolars that we know are coming. To do all that, we'll need each other."

Outish stopped breathing, he deciphered the ramifications of what Achelous just said. *The team is staying on Dianis, without the IDB's permission.* A chill ran down his back and would have raised his hackles if he were still in Halorite form. *Achelous and Baryy have it all planned out. The chief, arch enforcer of ULUP, the master pursuer of extrasolars is breaking the rules and going off station.* Outish had the stark feeling that Achelous was something other than the distracted and distant cultural anthropologist he'd taken him to be. The word *zealot* came to mind. *Does that bother me?* He thought about his research and what it would mean to his career. He considered the alternative of having to find another research billet and starting over, knowing the secret of aural activation was his to pursue. He could not accept leaving it for someone else to discover. *No, it doesn't bother me that Atch is a zealot. Maybe that's a good thing.*

Not one to assess risk or even care, Outish was all in.

Chapter 20
Isumfast

Transportation Authority Repair Bay at Isumfast

Outish smacked his lips, his face contorting in different directions. "How old did you say this was?"

"The machine or the carva grounds?" answered Baryy.

Achelous punched his carvareen order into the Ancient autoserv. It was indeed ancient in more ways than one. Order entry was an actual keypad, and the serial number indicated the machine was three hundred and forty years old, left behind when the Transportation Authority engineers finished the installation of the last interplanetary transshipment field generator, the colossal generators with the capacity to shift three hundred thousand tons in one lift. "Welcome to Isumfast," Achelous said, "be thankful there is an autoserv, otherwise, you would be the cook."

A new set of contortions, most of them negative, conveyed Outish's feelings.

"You said you needed a lab. Well, here it is, complete with a terrestrial bore driller." Baryy smiled. It took a bit of research to recommission the old autoserv, but it had been brand new when the engineers had turned it off, so it was a relatively simple matter of finding compatible protein, carbo, and nutrient packs to stock it. Beyond the autoserv, the old ITA repair bay included few creature comforts. The bay's purpose, last used three hundred and thirty two years ago, had been to service and repair heavy equipment. A half dozen of the construction machines sat in the cavernous garage under three centuries of dust, some on flat tires--the ones that used tires instead of tracks--but most, he suspected were in running condition. The excavation machines were so old they pre-dated anti-grav repellers, but the engineers made due. The vehicles were designed to sit patiently through long periods of inaction, stationed planet-side to save on shift costs. At the time the Dianis transportation node was built, it was cheaper to leave the equipment in place rather than transport it around the arm. He could understand why, given the antiquity of the repair bay's field generator: serviceable, but incredibly energy inefficient. To supply the power, the repair bay sat on top of its own geothermal energy plant. Located in the mountains fifty miles north of Falda, along the Gracopherous River, a short aircar ride from the sleepy town of Isumfast. The repair bay was one of those forgotten artifacts of the frenzied build-out era when the Transportation Authority was rabid with expansion.

Outish, stared at his surroundings in the underground cavern, still uncertain about what the first batch of carvareen was doing to his belly. "How did you find this place?"

"Pictures," Achelous said.

"Pictures?"

"Yes. Transportation Authority engineers, when this station was built, were more interested in digging and powering up, rather than keeping records. They had a lot of money to get the Margel up and running, and little time. This bay was used intensively for two years, according to a paper manifest we found in the office over there." He pointed at Outish's potential lab. "When the construction teams moved to the next planet node, they quite literally jumped in the shift zone, shifted out, and only as an afterthought, sent someone back to turn off the lights. Backfilling with paper work, documenting the facility, and logging its equipment was left to some over worked accountant, and with money bursting budgets, there was not much interest in keeping track of the few credits invested in a dusty, dirty place called Isumfast. Hence, we can't find any records for the repair bay in the master facility manifest. There are vague hints: a planning document for its design, some archived message traffic approving the project, but it appeared once the green light was given for construction all thoughts of accounting for the facility were lost against the noisy progress of building out the nodes.

"What's that got to do with pictures?" Outish asked. Sometimes the chief took his time getting to the point, but he always had a reason for it.

"We were on a cultural anthropology mission to Isumfast exploring and documenting the impacts of Transportation Authority construction. The research question that spawned the mission was why did Isumfast have such a strong pro-Ancient culture? Through survey data acquired by interviewing local populations, and empirical evidence gathered by CivMon we constructed a cultural impact heat map."

Outish nodded. He'd used those heat maps for comparing biological anomalies. Anthropologists like Achelous created the maps to show the varying degrees of "cultural impact" for extrasolar influence, and identify where the relative hot spots existed across the world. On the Ancients cultural heat map, Isumfast stood out as an anomaly. Not only because its population fervently believed in Ancients, but because Paleowright religious representation showed bright red as well.

"I was with the team when we discovered, at an inn in the town of Isumfast, a collection of artifacts including actual pictures. The few inns and taverns of the village had been popular with the mechanics from the repair bay. Picking up on local legend the team followed a trail of clues, mostly the scenes in the pictures, up the Gracopherous River to a box canyon formed by an impenetrable wall of rock. Just the place transportation engineers would put a repair bay. In truth, the site was selected for its geothermal energy source. The team suspected as much when they saw hot springs feeding into the river, giving the box canyon a vaguely sulfurous odor.

"That's when the team brought in SONAR mapping gear and located the facility and a probable entrance concealed by a landslide. I had the team file a report. The source of Isumfast's Ancient cultural sensitivity was solved, and the team moved onto to its next assignment."

"Wait," said Outish, "how long ago was that?"

Achelous shrugged a shoulder. "Twenty years ago, maybe."

Outish looked to Baryy. "So who's been in here since then?"

"No one's been in here. We're the first since the engineers left."

"But, but," Outish stammered, "chief you said we shifted in unanchored. You gave virtual coordinates to the field generator at Battle Park. There's no one there! How are we going to get back? How did you know we weren't shifting into solid rock? How--"

Achelous held up a hand to calm the intern. "After we met at Central Station and discussed our, or rather your accreditation predicament, I felt I needed to pursue some options. So I went to Battle Park, shifted a manipulator drone into the bay here. It was programmed to find and, if possible, restart power. It was successful. I then shifted in myself, with Baryy running the field generator at Battle Park. I was able to recommission the field generator here in the bay."

"And brought in the carva grounds." Baryy smiled, holding up his cup. "The entrance is still blocked by the landslide, and we'll need to clear that, at least enough to crawl in through, but all the equipment and systems here predate the IDB. So none of it is on the Margel comms grid." He paused, "This site is off the IDB systems network. We're operating in the darknet."

"Even though there is a record of us using the Battle Park field gen station to get here," added Achelous, "the teams use those local site generators to go a lot of places, every day. Our initial hops into the bay here will be lost in the noise. From now on though, we'll use the three-hundred-thousand-ton shift generator to get in and out. It's overkill, but with the power dialed way down it won't attract much attention."

"We can start shifting in all the gear we need." Baryy pointed to a worn, but functional holodesk, which stood out from mining and repair gear as easily the most modern piece of equipment. "Including your lab test equipment."

"You can get A-wave here? Fednet Interconn?" For the first time, Outish seemed hopeful.

Achelous walked over to the holodesk. "Yep. Anonymous accounts only, using multi-node bounces to disrupt source traces. As long as we don't ping an Avarian federation site, or trigger an AI sentinel, we should be able to get out. The connection will be slow because of the multi-node translation..." he shrugged his shoulders.

Outish looked at the hologrid Achelous already had up. There were multiple image frames. One of them had a banner that read *Chemistry Department, University of Wisconsin, Madison.* "You're already out on the Fednet," Outish said, able to read the text the desk translated to Avarian. He squinted, trying to make sense of what he was seeing. "What is that stuff?" The 3-D frame showed a page explaining a list of chemicals, kerning techniques, hot-rolling methods, cup pressures, and bi-sectional densities.

"Stuff we'll need," Achelous answered, his voice distant.

"Where are you?" The intern persisted.

Finally, Achelous pulled his attention from the hologrid and looked at Outish. "What?" he asked confused.

Outish pointed at the grid. "Where is that?"

"Earth. It's another Class E. In the Orion Arm. I did my anthropology internship there. They have technology we'll need."

"How can they have A-wave on Earth if they are Class E?"

"The same way we have it here," answered Baryy. "There's a federation A-wave communications satellite orbiting Earth."

Achelous was scrolling through the on-line document. "The federation has it piggybacked onto one of Earth's own communications satellites. We are piped into what the people on Earth call the Internet, very similar in concept to the Fednet Interconn, but way more primitive. That's how I got to this library site. It's been invaluable for my research."

Baryy and Outish went to plan the layout the biology lab.

Achelous read the text on the hologrid. "Need to avoid $Ca(NO_3)_2$ as it absorbs too much water. The preferred nitrate is formulated on potassium." *Hmm, I wonder if a provincial alchemist would appreciate the difference?* He downloaded the information into his multi-func and sent sections of his notes to the artifact synthesizer he'd brought from Central Station for just this purpose. The printer module scrawled pseudo-handwritten text onto sheets of coarse-fibered Dianis paper, purchased directly from a Tivorian merchant. Marisa would need the instructions for Eliot and Patrace, the alchemist she'd hired for their new joint venture, the project he hinted to Marisa that day in Tivor, on the quay when he escorted her off the *Far Shore*. He retrieved the papers from the synthesizer, wondering at the irony. The text came all the way from Earth in real-time, via stealth A-wave satellites linked to the IDB monitoring station on Saturn's moon, Titan. The data was about to be shared from one Class E world to another, from a chemistry professor on one end to an alchemist on the other, fifty thousand light years apart, and neither would know the distance their information had traveled.

He walked to the control panel for the antique field generator and set the destination for the Tivor shift point. He had rendezvous to make with Marisa, to deliver the plans. He'd spend the day with Boyd before plunging head long into what would be the most important thing he'd ever done, or the biggest mistake, or perhaps both.

Chapter 21
First Shot

Tivor

The morning's dew, heavy on the grass, was marred by the wagon tracks and eenu hooves. Eliot and Derek, Eliot's apprentice from Marinda Merchants blacksmith's shop, pulled the tarp off the wagon exposing their work to daylight for the first time. At Akallabeth's bidding, the participants to the experiment arrived at the forest clearing outside of Tivor from different directions and at different times. The Silver Cup, contracted to maintain security, posted scouts on the two trails that lead to the old abandoned Hafflin farmstead. The farmhouse, its sides weather-stripped to grey wood, sat at the far end of what had been a tilled field and pasture, now wild with briars, stag horns, and other pioneers. The farmhouse sagged under the weight of its decaying roof like a swaybacked mule. Morning hens flew out of the gaping holes in the shake shingles.

Marisa and Patrace, Marisa's new alchemist, gawked at the contraption lashed on top of the flat bed wagon. Marisa had seen the drawings Achelous sketched, but until today had not seen the results.

"Take the eenus well away," instructed Achelous, "and tie them securely. We don't want them bolting." He motioned at Derek, the young blacksmith's apprentice, and pointed at the edge of the clearing opposite from the house. "Well away." Eliot paused at hearing this and exchanged glances with Marisa. Patrace walked over to the wagon and peered into the gaping hole at the end of the log tube. She noted the thick ropes that secured the log onto the wagon. Turning to Achelous as he inspected his project, she said, "Do you really need all these ropes? It won't be coming off anytime soon!" She pointed a thin-lipped scowl at Eliot, "Did you get these off a ship? They look like hawsers?"

Eliot shrugged, neutral, he wasn't about to take credit for something he didn't understand. Marisa came to his aid, "Yes, that's exactly where they came from. "

Achelous inspected the thick iron bands that bound the hollowed-out log, followed closely by Patrace. The alchemist, intensely curious about everything, never seemed to stop her stream of acidic quips. Her hair was a wild, grey mop; a comb stuck randomly in above an ear. She wore a long frock over which she adorned it with a leather apron, shiny with much use. Her keen blue eyes didn't miss a detail, and her strong chin wasn't afraid of fronting an opinion.

Checking the bands that encircled the ten-foot log at one-foot intervals, Achelous nodded to himself. They fit tight, the welded seams of the rings filed flat, nary a crack to be seen. The bark had been peeled cleanly from the log; the gaping hole in the end deep and smooth. Derek had done a decent job, especially for being an apprentice and having to work in the secret makeshift forge they'd constructed, the land and buildings procured by Marinda Merchants as part of Marisa and Achelous's new joint venture. While Achelous had been forced to turn down Marisa's offer to buy his business, she had willingly accepted his offer of investing in a new enterprise of which she knew very little. Until today, he'd been vague, even secretive as to the nature of their joint venture, asking her to take it on faith until he could arrange a demonstration. The fewer the people involved, the better. Security for their "project" was paramount.

Prince Fire Eye came trotting across the field in his loping, undulating run, tail held out behind him. He halted beside Akallabeth, tilted his head up, and flicked his tongue. "Clearss," he hissed.

"Sentries in place?" asked Akallabeth.

Fire Eye did a double flick of his tongue.

"You know of course this concoction you've had me make is extremely volatile," said Patrace. "The sulfur by itself—"

"Eh hem," interrupted Akallabeth. "Your work, as all of this project, is secret. You know that. Which includes discussing your formula with anyone but Marisa or Achelous."

"Well honestly, do we need to be so—"

"Yes," snapped Achelous. "You know the terms, and you accepted them."

Patrace bit her tongue. The look in the trader's eye told her he meant to abide by the terms. The last chilling sentence of that written contract was, "If the signatory should divulge or otherwise represent activities of the project or contents of the formula to anyone without expressed written release of the countersigned, the signatory's life will be forfeit." She glanced nervously at the wryvern. Those baleful eyes gave her the willies. The reptile's tongue flicked, tasting her scent and the fear-tinted pheromones her breath spewed into the air.

Finished with inspecting the smaller vertical borehole at the closed end of the log, Achelous asked, “Where’s the powder?”

Patrace pointed a long boney finger at a box on the side of the wagon.

Eliot added, “We followed your instructions to the letter as you requested. Patrace has mixed the powder, two different grain sizes, and we’ve kept it dry. We have the marble balls that fit the tube as closely as possible. Boring out the trunk was a bit of work, but Derek forged an auger to do the job. It’s the same diameter all the way in and stops two feet from the other end. We tested the bore by rolling the balls down. One of them got stuck, but we hoisted the log on end, bounced it on the ground, and it came out.”

A mass of thin, dry hemp line lay coiled on another tarp on the ground, protected from the dew.

Patrace said, “The coarse grain is in the brown sacks. The fine grain is in the smaller white bags marked with red twine.”

Achelous opened a brown sack. The powder inside was black; the smell a distinctive mixture of rotten eggs and something more malodorous, *a latrine perhaps?* Each of the brown bags was the same size and appeared to match his specifications in weight. Up to this point, everything was theoretical. His knowledge of mixtures, korning, and weights all gleaned off the Fednet Interconn, connecting back to Earth. He took a deep breath. The Earthlings employed this technology for hundreds of years. *It should work, if it doesn’t blow us all up.* The powder appeared peacefully benign, sifting through his fingers like the sands of an hourglass. He doubted any of the spectators appreciated what sort of controlled violence lurked within those grains, other than Patrace who watched him like a reproachful nanny.

Reaching into the box, he hefted one of the marble stones. Roughly the size of a grapefruit, the weight surprised him. “Eliot, did you bring the scale?”

Eliot retrieved the scale from a second box and set it up. Placing the stone on the pan, they marked the measurement.

“Measure out fifteen percent of the stone’s weight in the course powder.”

Marisa and the others watched in silence, completely engrossed. Even Patrace held her tongue.

While the coarse powder was weighed and placed in a new sack, Achelous opened a bag of the fine powder and poured a quantity on the hemp twine. He made sure to thoroughly embed the fibers of the twine with particles of the mixture. "Derek, stand well away, kindle the torch, and stay there. Don't come near."

Finally, unable to contain herself Patrace asked, "Are you sure you know what you are doing? Mixing fire and that powder is unwise. I cannot be held responsible."

Achelous merely cast her a sidelong glance.

"Powder bag is ready," called Eliot.

"Bring it here." Achelous went to the bored-out end of the log and calculated the aiming of the wagon. It was pointed at the house. The end of the log raised off the wagon bed by a block of wood. "Hmm," he had no idea if the elevation was too much or too little, but they would find out. "Go ahead and use that pole you brought along and carefully stuff the powder sack down the bore hole. All the way to the end. Make sure it is all the way in."

"Atch," Marisa asked, compelled by Patrace's warning, "Where did you get this idea? What is it supposed to do?" Up to now, she'd been engrossed in a plan to defeat the pirates and had not paid much attention to Achelous's "project." As long as it kept him at Marinda Hall, that's all that mattered, until now.

Eliot paused in his loading, intent on the trader's answer.

Achelous expected this moment and dreaded it. He disliked lying to Marisa, and longed for the day when there would be no more secrets between them, but that day was still in the future, so he lied yet again. "It's amazing what you can learn when you trade with enough people. I bartered, out of curiosity, for some of this powder, from an old alchemist in the north country. It wasn't until later when I went back to him that he gave me the formula, for a favor. As for what this does," he patted the log, "We shall soon see. Maybe nothing."

Before they could ask more questions, he quickly measured and cut the twine into three equal lengths. Retrieving a skin of the fine powder, he mounted the wagon and with a marlinspike thrust down through the vertical hole and pierced the sack Eliot had rammed down the barrel. "Eliot, go ahead and load one of those balls. Push it all the way in."

Patrace had a deep frown on her face. Marisa asked, "What?" The alchemist just gave a slight shake of her head, trying to understand the forces and mechanics of the device Achelous was assembling. He poured an amount of the fine powder down the vertical hole then stuffed the end of a length of impregnated hemp into the hole.

He jumped lightly off the wagon and inspected the experiment. His blood was pumping. He was about to do something that would forever change the course of Dianis history. It wasn't too late to stop. He could still disassemble the contraption and tell everyone it was a joke, but no, he was committed, ULUP or not. Oddly he relished the moment, the last moment where the innocence and ignorance of the bystanders still held sway. "Stand back everyone, get way back." Almost giddy, even light headed, he strode to Derek and retrieved the torch from him. Tunnel vision set in. The loose end of the hemp twine lay along the tarp. The sun climbed; birds circled the peaceful prairie calling to one another completely unaware.

"Get back," he snapped and waved vigorously with his arm when the others barely moved. He hurried towards the fuse afraid he'd lose his nerve, fearful that common sense would smite him and the awful realization of what he was about to do stricken him immobile.

He bent down, holding the torch just inches from the fuse, and turned to look at the group. They heeded his advice and moved almost all the way back to the forest. Everyone intent on his every motion, even Fire Eye's tail lay motionless.

He torched the fuse. It sizzled a bit and then suddenly flared to life, and in a billowing cloud of sparks and white smoke streaked across the grass to the wagon. Achelous's eyes grew wide, "Oh—!" He threw the torch and ran.

He got five steps when a thundering explosion announced the dawn of the Gunpowder Age on Dianis.

As one, the spectators blanched and cowered. The eenu's tethered at the forest stamped and piped, rearing on the hitching line.

Achelous halted next to Marisa. Breathing heavy, sweating more from stress than exertion, he thought, *well, I'm still alive.*

"That was a bloody stupid thing to do!" screeched Patrace.

Achelous turned and looked at the wagon. Smoke rolled across the field, but the cannon appeared to be intact. Then he looked at the house. He let out a "Yes!" He yelled and shoved a fist at the sky: "It works!"

"Works!? My ears are ringing because of you!" came the alchemist's rejoinder.

"What works?" asked Marisa confused. "The explosion? It was supposed to explode?" But then she saw where Akallabeth was pointing. Fire Eye's tail bounced like an agitated rattle.

"Oh Mother," breathed Eliot. "The tube did that?" A large hole nearly twice the size of the cannon ball shown in the side of the farmhouse.

Achelous took off running like a schoolboy, and the spectators quickly followed suit. Even Patrace ran, hiking her smock up to her thighs.

The ball had gone through the outer wall, through two rotten interior walls and clean out the other side of the house.

Marisa stared through the four perfectly aligned holes and suddenly had a vision of a monkey-faced pirate captain grinning at her as he made his way to safety. "Oh Atch," she breathed, "What I could do with one of these."

"I'll not be standing in front of that anytime soon," marked Eliot.

"It's a catapult," exclaimed Derek. "We've made a whopping catapult. Doesn't look like a catapult, but it's a whopping catapult sure enough! And a good one too! Never seen one shoot a rock in a straight line before. No arc. Just boom, straight through. Straight through a whole house. And just a small rock, nothing so big as what you think you'd need. Gawd."

Marisa stepped aside to let Akallabeth enter the house and inspect the damage. Achelous stood back, oddly aloof, detached. She noticed him watching the reactions of the others, his initial excitement replaced by his typically inscrutable, knowing expression. *With this,* she thought, *I'd be able to wipe that silly smirk off that bastard pirates' face.* They'd attacked twice more since her rescue of the *Wind March,* each raid bolder than the last. However, the notion of having to confront the bandits cast her mood into a funk. That Tivor, Marinda Merchants, and the other trading houses even had to deal with pirates seemed unfair. She put her arm around Achelous when she sensed him beside her, her ruminations far away. The power to make your enemies quail, to keep the pirates at bay, came at a price. You had to invoke power to create fear, and the ability to create fear was the only thing the pirates respected. That meant, she leaned into Achelous, inevitably sowing death and destruction. Warning shots across the bow carried no weight unless you proved willing to put a shot *through* the bow. She looked back across the unplowed field gradually going back to nature, back to Mother. "What do you call that?"

He followed her gaze, settling on the wagon. He hesitated.

"Tell me truly, what is it called?"

"A cannon." He let the sound of that sink in. "We are now in the cannon business."

She nodded ever so slightly, her raven hair glossy in the sun, her ebon eyes depthless pools. Wisdom, sadness, determination were dusted like blush across her face. She understood what the cannon was: a weapon of war. *You don't bring a weapon of war to the battlefield to plant daisies. Once this machine is carried forward, either the next captain or I will unleash it.* Grasping him by the shoulder, she asked, struggling to get her mind around all implications, "Is it safe?" The power, enormity of change, and the dread of destruction was overwhelming. "Do we really need this? I mean..." for a moment she was at a loss for words. "I mean this could be devastating. What happens if others learn of this?"

He held her gently by the elbow and led her away from the house. "That's why we must keep this a secret. Eventually, word will get out, people will come snooping around, and by that time we must be far enough along that we have an insurmountable lead on them."

"Lead on them for what?"

"Marisa, a log cannon bound with iron rings and hand scraping saltpeter from latrines will not suffice. We have much to do before this weapon is practical. We're shooting marble balls for Spirit's sake."

She absorbed his intensity. "But that's not what I meant." Achelous had missed her point completely, his concerns so different from hers. He assumed others would learn of the invention and that both friend and foe alike would eventually come to possess it; a shocking revelation of itself. It bespoke a vision of the future far in advance of what a normal person might see. *How does he know this? Is he prescient? Does he have sixthsense? He's never admitted to it. No--If he did have sixthsense Akallabeth's people would have said something. He's as dead-sensitive as I am. But how does he know the future so well? Things that worry us never seem to worry him. I know he has a plan for this cannon. What is it?* But she was afraid to ask. Her suspicions made her shy away from the subject like an eenu from a snake. Instead, she tried circumspection. "Why, Atch? Why do we need this? Why us? Why now?" She figured if she asked enough questions he'd pick the easy one to answer and that in itself would tell her much.

He avoided her gaze and made to turn away, but she grabbed his sleeve, "Atch, you're a successful trader. I know you trade in arms, but this—" and she pointed at the hole in the wall, and saw Akallabeth watching them. She struggled to voice the confusion, awe, and dread she felt welling up. "This is big, maybe bigger than all of us. I agree, there will be others, good and bad that will come for it. They'll offer huge sums. I know. This can sink ships! But do you really want to sell this?" Behind her question was the entreaty to stop right there and walk away.

"Marisa, I've seen and learned things that will come to be known across this land. I will tell you this now and then must hold my tongue. There is an ill wind coming to Isuelt. A wave of men and machines bent on stealing the riches of this land. Your people, our people, will rise up and attempt to stop them, but against those—" and he searched for a safe description, "interlopers, swords and arrows are but fly bites on a bull's hide. This weapon is our only hope of hurting them."

She arched an eyebrow. Not for a moment doubting him, just freighted of how he knew it. She reached up and touched his cheek. "Who, Atch? Who are these people?" He shook his head, tightening his jaw.

Derek came running "Achelous sir, can we try that again?" He was wild eyed, having witnessed something first hand that was shocking, mysterious, and devastating all rolled up in a non-descript stone ball. He wanted to see it again, believe it really happened and to prove they could duplicate it at will.

Akallabeth had reservations about firing the device again, but he too wanted a repeat performance. To be double sure that the first round wasn't just a fluke or strange parlor trick. "Fire Eye, check the sentries. Make sure they are at their posts. We may have attracted attention. One more bang like that and we'll have the Spring Carnival down around our heads, so we'll need to pull up stakes fast." Fire Eye slurped twice and was off at a dead run.

"Yes, we should try it once more," said Achelous, glancing sidelong at Marisa. "Eliot, measure out the powder carefully." Not for the first time did he wish Baryy or Outish were here to help him, but they were in Isumfast or Wedgewood, on their own assignments. Baryy had delivered a handbolt, minus the laser circuitry, to Ogden as a test of weaponsmith's skills and capabilities to replicate the weapon, and then produce it in quantity as a trade good. Baryy's other task was to aid Mbecca, as discretely as he could, in devising a psychic treatment for the Timber's Curse. Outish would be the consultant, but his inexperience working with natives precluded him from interacting at length with Mbecca. Instead, he'd have to funnel his suggestions through Baryy who would know what to say and how to say it without arousing overt suspicions or causing rumors. Outish had a project of his own to collect plant and soil samples and prepare the test lab at Isumfast. They needed to make sure the facility was adequately provisioned before the Margel went dark.

The mushroom hunter sniffed the air. It didn't smell like rain, yet he was sure he heard thunder. The eenus kept looking east, in the direction of the old Hafflin farmstead, their nostrils flaring. *Must be smelling the rain before my tired old nose,* he thought. Though the weather should be coming out of the west, not the east. He hoisted the sack of first-crop tilooms and tied it to the pack eenu. He reckoned he had enough to make a trip into Jiren's worthwhile, so he saddled up, setting a course through the woods for the main road into Tivor.

Eliot loaded the powder while Achelous examined the barrel of the cannon. He didn't know what exactly to look for, but the vid he downloaded showed the professors taking great care to check for stress and cracks between each firing. The muzzle was satisfyingly scorched. The black residue and smell of burnt powder exhilarated him. It was proof positive the grand scheme would work. Every small successful step meant attainment of the ultimate goal. He took comfort in it, patted the barrel, and continued the inspection. The welds on the iron rings were sound, but there did appear to be a few hairline cracks in the trunk. He could not remember if they were there before. They could be from the natural drying process of the wood. He mentally filed away the location of each crack. The fact that he couldn't see directly underneath the log where it rested on the wagon bothered him a little, but he figured they could live with one more test firing.

"Ready," called Eliot.

Achelous retrieved the torch from Derek. This time the entire party was well back to start. "Cover your ears if you want to be hearing tomorrow," yelled Patrace.

The mushroom hunter navigated his eenu's around the deadfall. He reckoned the road to Tivor should be just ahead. Ducking under a limb, he heard a deep booming thunder. This time the sound louder, sharper. His mount's ears pricked up and the eenu stopped, the ears twitching back and forth. "What is it girl, what do you hear?"

The change in the wind carried the smoke like a veil across their view, but before it obscured the field, they'd all seen a greyish streak hit the peak of the farm house roof, crush the shake shingles, and caromed off into the blue. When the pall of acrid smoke drifted lazily away Achelous frowned. He turned to Patrace, "Is all the powder the same?"

"Well of course it is," she reacted, "I mixed it in one batch. I'm not an idiot; I know what I'm about."

His lip twitched, a retort coming to mind, but he bit it back. "Eliot how much powder did you use?"

"Eighteen percent of the ball weight, as you instructed."

"Uh, no, I said fifteen percent." But that shouldn't have made that big a difference.

"Was the ball the same weight as the first one?"

Eliot's expression went blank. He looked to Derek, "Do you know?" Derek shrugged.

A dry cracking and crashing sound came from the branches above, and the mushroom hunter craned his neck expecting to see a large bird or even a startled forest monkey. Instead, a round, grayish object smacked into the ground, bounced twice and rolled away. The eenus immediately started, eyeing the underbrush suspiciously. "What the Spirits..." He peered back up at the sky expecting to see more raining down on him. Tentatively, his curiosity getting the better of him, he dismounted and tied his pack train off to a tree. With a hand on his knife, more of a short sword actually, he edged through the brush. Twice he glanced up fearful. He'd seen hail as large as his fist knock a man cold, but this thing, while it resembled a hailstone, was larger. Searching through the ferns and briars, and pushing aside the prickly tine, he spied a grayish, domed object that looked more like a puffball mushroom. Creeping up on it, and peering about, he reached the knife out and tapped the object. *Hard, no, stone hard. Stone?* He picked it up. The ball, for that's what it was, was round, and man-made, of that he was certain. He could see tool marks where someone had chiseled it into shape. It felt warm to the touch, which was odd, and a blackish, almost sootish residue covered it. It even smelled as if it came from a chimney, but different. He hefted it with an appraising feel. "I'll have to show this to Jiren, see what he thinks of it." *Strangest thing I'll tell him. It fell right out of the sky. He'll love hearing that.*

"I gather you wanted the ball to hit in the same spot," said Akallabeth.

Achelous nodded, "I'd prefer it. Just like shooting a bow."

"Fire Eye says the wagon moved back. Could it be that moving the wagon backwards actually gives the ball more time to rise?" Akallabeth stroked his beard. "As you say, even an arrow has an arc. Perhaps we haven't reached the peak of the arc." He pondered the implications. Then he said to Marisa, "Oi, I wonder how far that log can shoot? Judging by the arc of that ricochet it can go a long way."

"I think you're right," She agreed.

Achelous almost said *a mile,* but he held his tongue in check. He was way out on a limb as it was, and the more Akallabeth and Marisa and the others –the provincials-- discovered and learned on their own the better. The more they invested their own energies and intellect into the endeavor, the more the origins of the cannon and gunpowder would be obscured. He needed the provincials to adopt the weapon and carry its development, in part to obfuscate who was responsible for its invention should the day come when an IDB assessment team came planet-side to investigate the rumors of a leap in technological development. Cultural anthropologists were polishing the theory of Development Discontinuity, a theory that could actually predict, through a chain of mathematical equations, the probability that a disruptive or vastly innovative cultural or technological advancement would occur in a given civilization and even in a given generation. If they learned of the invention of gunpowder on Dianis, they might very well target it as a case study to compare their formulas against. The problem was, the Dianis advancement was artificial and wouldn't fit their models. He smiled inwardly, picturing a befuddled anthropologist in some far off lab squinting at a computer readout that made no sense. All sorts of consternation would set in. He went to throw the tarp over the wagon. Of course, since the discontinuity formulas were essentially correct, it would lead them to one of two conclusions: an aberration had occurred, or there was outside influence. Either finding would attract attention from the IDB, ULUP anthropologists, or the Matrincy, or perhaps all three. He sighed. *I'll deal with that if it happens.* Until then, he had work to do.

Chapter 22
Duck

Tivor

Jiren leaned back on two legs of his chair, propping it against the wall of his fur and feed store. Inside, his daughter weighed the morning's crop of tilooms, paying off the hunters. Townsfolk, most of whom he recognized, strolled by on the Korvastall. Some would nod, and some would stop and gossip. He was no fool. The reason a group of his customers patronized his business was for the rumors they might hear, or what he called the *early news*. The town criers, bulletins, and the *Tivor Literal* being what they were, only went so far. It was well known to those in the know, that if you wanted the real word before everyone else, then you did business at Jiren's Fur, Feed, and Furnishings. The prices might be higher, but so was the cost of not being informed.

"Morning Jiren." Duck Peren, holding two mugs in his hands, squeezed his bulk into his customary chair, and settled down with a sigh.

"Morning Duck," Jiren gave him a casual glance. The kind of recognition due an acquaintance you've known many years, but never progressed beyond the incidental relationship. They were repeating their long-standing morning ritual. Every third and sixth day of the week Duck would visit Jiren, hand him a mug of steaming carvareen purchased three shops down the way and settled in to hear the word on the street. Duck handed him a steaming mug, "Care for some carva?"

"Oh, thanks, Duck." Jiren acted genuinely surprised and pleased, as he did every third and sixth day of the week.

"Fine morning for business," prompted Duck. "I see traffic is up."

Jiren appraised the traffic on the Korvastall, as he did every morning his shop was open. He knew the wagons, riders, watchmen, soldiers, and carters so well, along with their patterns that he could instantly gauge when anything was different. "Yep, Barney's had to make three runs this morning. He usually makes two."

For mundane information, or confirmation of what Duck might already know, the delivered mug of carva was adequate payment.

"How about Marinda, they shipping anything new?"

That was Duck, always wanting to know about Marinda Merchants ever since the Paleowright viscount had come to Tivor. A mighty source of gossip that visit was. Of course, Duck wasn't just interested in Marisa Pontifract. He wanted to hear about anything new, different, or *odd*. How he loved odd. He'd buy a whole bundle of stag furs at inflated prices just for weird, or very strange. What he did with those pelts Jiren had no idea, nor did he care; Duck was a miller. What a grain miller needed with all the random stuff he bought, or why he was so insatiably curious was none of Jiren's business, as long as Jiren's business was good. Paleowright clergy though—not that Duck was a Paleowright, and if he was it was none of his business—were always interested in the abnormal, and their devouts fed on it. Anthing odd, to them, meant Ancient. While he and Duck never spoke about religion, they'd gossiped long enough for the fat man to provide ample hints as to the direction of his moral and philosophical leanings. Conspiracies were king. "Nope. Shipments and buyers look to be the same. Lots of cotton, bale-cloth, iron ingots, copper pandits, and finished goods from the South. I expect Marisa to be sending over my order of porcelain today." He liked dropping Marisa's name and implying that she personally handled his account, even though they seldom spoke. Her business carried every trade good shipped up and down the coast, across the ocean, and she bartered in quantity; anyone in Tivor who bought from the wharves could claim Marisa Pontifract as a confidant, and they would be a person to know.

"How about that beau of hers? Seen him about?"

There he is, always asking about that trader. Jiren half expected the question. For some reason, Duck was fascinated by the trader's comings and goings. Jiren's shop was located two blocks down from Marinda Hall, which afforded a good view of deliveries to their warehouse but a poor view of the entrance to the Hall itself. Jiren wasn't interested in the comings and goings of a person not active in Tivor politics or not an influence in its business. Achelous did all his trading with Marinda Hall--no surprise there, so Jiren couldn't comment on what trade goods the outlander dealt in. "I don't pay much attention to him, but I did hear he was in town." Jiren figured he'd give Duck something to chew on lest the fat man keep badgering him with inane questions, so he offered "I heard the Silver Cup is working on some sort of contract in town. They've brought in more bravos from outside. Tight-lipped bunch they are."

"Oh?"

"Yea, Harriet came by, said six of them were in for dinner last night. Said the wryvern was with them. Gives her the creeps. Yellow eyes, slurping tongue. Stares at you like you're food. Doesn't take a crap like men, goes out and shits with the eenus.

"Harriet said the Silvers usually let a room from her for a couple of days and then ride out on contract, but these are hanging on. Good for her business, even if one of them is a rep-tile. People have been coming to her place just to gawk at him. "

"Oh." Duck leaned back, satisfied. The chair gave an ominous creak.

Jiren glanced over, calculating the cost of the chair in case the fat man broke it.

Chapter 23
The Foundry

Wedgewood

Achelous sighted on the target and squeezed the trigger. A satisfying and surprisingly familiar thump sounded. The quarrel flew sweetly and struck the target dead on at forty yards. "Hmm, impressive." He went to cock the handbolt—

"Be careful with that." Ogden hovered close by like a new father. "We've not quite perfected the lever trap and spring mechanism yet. A devilish piece of work that is."

"Oh..." Achelous turned the handbolt over and examined it. The weaponsmith and his foundry had done a superb job of replicating the inert version of the handbolt. Ogden's replica was made of real wood, not whortresin, steel not duraloy, and the bow string was some sort of natural fiber he didn't recognize. The laser aperture with its camouflaged port was missing, of course.

"You wouldn't happen to know where those lads that built the hand-bolt you have obtained their steel, would you?"

Achelous glanced over. Baryy and Outish stood by with Mergund. Baryy kept his face blank and Outish, learning more and more how to work with provincials, looked down and scuffed the dirt with a booted toe. "No, I'm sorry. I traded for them. Why, is there a problem?"

"Well no. It's just that our first try at the cocking mechanism failed after five shots. The iron cracked; the mechanism is an intricate design. We switched to more expensive steel and played with the composition and tempering process. We managed to improve the failure rate to over twenty five shots, but our steel is still too soft. But don't worry, we're headed in the right direction, I'm sure we'll get the knack of it soon."

As he hoped and had expected, by introducing Ogden, Patrace, Eliot and the others to new and challenging projects, they were compelled to innovate, to spawn their own solutions, and directly drive—in their own right--the advancement of Isuelt society and industrialization. As a cultural anthropologist, he'd seen and studied the results of external vectors, such as the introduction of a disruptive technology like gunpowder. However, not just any culture or society could benefit from the introduction of outworlder science. Giving fusion power to cavemen wouldn't work because of the comprehension gap -- in this case a gaping chasm -- was too far for the cavemen to bridge. When conducting cultural and societal engineering, a thorough assessment had to be made of the society's current state, including economic, religious, and technological parameters, and then the assessment mapped to a list of portable technologies that fit the developmental environment. Precise mathematical models were used to gauge a society's capacity to absorb the change, the magnitude of change, and the technological differential. The IDB's purpose on the more advanced Class E worlds, such as Earth, was to conduct societal engineering as a part of the Uplift process. However, Achelous didn't need a yearlong assessment to tell him that Dianis was primed for black powder; he knew it instinctively the same way a farmer walks a fallow field and knows what will grow there. "When you have it working let Baryy know, in the interval I've something else I need to discuss with you." He moved towards the door of the foundry, but Ogden hung back. The weaponsmith had a downcast expression on him, only partially concealed by his long beard. He ran a hand over his bald pate.

"Oi, but we've been working long and hard on this Achelous, and I've spent a fair bit of coin too." Mergund peered at him expectantly. "We planned to finish the second casting tomorrow with improved tempering and be ready for another demonstration day after that."

It dawned on Achelous that Ogden and his foundry crew had put their hearts into replicating the weapon. For him to not share in their excitement, their accomplishment, was a tremendous let down. To say they would talk about it later and walk away must have been demoralizing. How could he explain to them he never intended to sell the handbolts in any quantity, but instead used it as a test of the smith's skills to determine if he was capable of the *real* project. To that end, the trail proved a success, but now he had to invoke damage control: the interpersonal variety. The kind he was least capable of. "I tell you what, how many handbolts have you built so far?"

Mergund brightened, "Three!"

Ogden shook his head, "No, they're the old castings, be lucky if they don't break before thirty cockings."

"Okay, I'll contract for fifty of the handbolts with the new castings, sight unseen. You've got to guarantee they'll last for a hundred shots though. Anything less and my customers will complain, and my reputation for selling quality will snap like brittle pot mettle."

Still staring at the ground, Ogden massaged his chin. Then slowly, "Alright, a guarantee of one hundred shots."

Achelous's selection of weaponsmith was confirmed by Ogden's thoughtful consideration of the guarantee before he agreed to it. Clearly, the man intended to deliver on it. The smith was just as concerned with his own reputation as was Achelous. "Done, I'll pay a third down now to help you cover your development costs. *And* I'll take the one you have in your hand." Achelous held out his. "How many times has it been fired?"

"That'll make three times," blurted Mergund.

"Fine," he took the weapon from Ogden. Thinking about how much silver Baryy had stashed in his cabin and if they'd have to make a shift to the Isumfast repair bay for more. "I'll keep it as a backup until you replace it with a new model." He smiled.

Ogden, still tenuous, perhaps because he was letting a customer walk away with a weak prototype, just nodded.

"Now come on Og," Achelous waved, "let's go to your draft room and let Mergund and your other smiths get to work, I have something else we need to talk about."

Achelous closed the door to the drafting room and made sure it was secure. Outish and Baryy leaned against the back wall of the small space making room around the drafting table. Achelous and Ogden stood at the table with the newcomer, Celebron. He'd introduced Celebron to Ogden at the handbolt demonstration, but now he explained what Celebron did. "Og, Celebron is from the Silver Cup Courier's Guild, I suspect you've heard of it?"

"Oi, we've one or two lads from the clan working for your outfit."

"Three," replied Celebron.

The man's shoulder-length, snow-white hair was pulled back into a ponytail. It gave Ogden a queasy feeling to be close to him in the confined space. Celebron's pale complexion and beardless face conjured visions of wraiths. Ogden knew well enough from what land Celebron hailed for the winter-rinds of Darnkilden were fabled in fact and fiction, more fiction than fact, he hoped. Even here in on the slopes of Mount Mars tales were told of far off Darnkilden Rangers and their exploits against Drakan invaders and their Ompean allies.

The Rangers were a bulwark against the Drakan Emperor's grandiose visions of continental conquest; dreams that dissipated like morning fog against the stark reality of Darnkilden forests. Containing the Drakans was once a chore belonging to the Lamaran Empire, itself now a mere shadow of former glory in the guise of the Lamaran Free Cities. Judging by the manner of his dress Celebron was a Ranger, garbed head to toe in tree-bark-grey buckskin with the signature hood to cover his beacon hair.

"Celebron is a Steward of the Watch for the guild."

Ogden peered at him from under his bushy eyebrows. That meant the man was head of security. For a guild specialized in delivering confidential messages and packages, security was a principal function.

"I've brought Celebron here because what we're about to discuss must remain a secret for as long as possible. Eventually, the word of it will get out, but it must not before we are ready. Is that understood?" Achelous had Ogden's full attention. "Do I have your word that you will speak of this to no one unless I release you?"

Ogden jutted out his chin. He didn't give his word lightly, nor did he like doing it when he didn't know what secret he was being asked to keep. "And what be this about?"

"I have something I want you to build for me. A weapon. Eventually, I'll need at least five hundred of them. As you are doing now with the handbolt, we'll need to work on a series of prototypes before we get to the first production model. And that model will be the springboard to a whole series of models. If you can forge this first prototype and successfully shoot it, then you will be making this weapon for the rest of your life. It will transform your business. You will become the preeminent weaponsmith in all of Isuelt." He would have said all of Dianis, but the smith surely would have thought that a flight of whimsy.

Ogden saw the gleam in his friend's eye, heard the passion and conviction in his voice. It was worth his word to hear more. "But what of the handbolts? Will you not be needing them?" Again, the trader saw the look of a craftsman whose creation teetered on the edge of failure. He tried to be gentle.

"Ogden, as important as the handbolts are, what we have here," and he pointed at a scroll sitting on the table, "is revolutionary. Yes, I need you to finish the handbolts, but this is bigger. And don't worry about the silver to build the prototypes. Keep proper accounting and submit your costs to me each month and I will reimburse you. For everything.

"Do I have your word?"

"Oi. You have my word. You don't swing at a log with just one stroke."

Achelous cleared a space on the drafting table and looked to Celebron. The bravo opened the door and stepped out, shutting it behind him. "Celebron and two of his companions will ensure we are not overheard." He unrolled a scroll on the table. It was a drawing, a careful sketch of a weapon the likes never before seen on Dianis.

Ogden peered at it intently. Aware of the stillness, he glanced up at Outish and Baryy and realized the two were in the know. One leaned against the wall, and the other sat on a chair not caring about the drawing, but instead observing his reaction with keen interest, like an armorer pouring molten iron into a mold. They'd evidently made the same promise he did, but as to their roles, he had no clue.

"What is it?" he asked in a hoarse whisper, his beard wagging above the scroll.

"A gun. A smoothbore flintlock."

He blinked, comprehension failing him.

Achelous pulled a small bag, no larger than a purse, from his satchel. He undid the drawstring and poured a fine black powder into his hand. Sitting the bag on the table, with his other hand he withdrew a small lead ball from his pocket. "You pour this powder down the muzzle of the gun." He indicated the hole at the end of the barrel on the drawing. "Then you wrap this ball, or bullet, with a patch of leather, ram it down the muzzle, and fire it."

Seeing Ogden's puzzlement grow deeper he said, "Here, kindle that paper for me." He pointed to a crumpled note.

Ogden dutifully turned up the damped lantern, caught the edge of the paper on fire, and dropped it in his pipe tray.

Achelous retrieved Ogden's expensive ivory pipe from the lip of the tray and tossed the palm of gunpowder onto the flaming paper. It whooshed in a flash of light, belching a cloud of smoke. Ogden, too late to step back, caught the acrid fumes. His eyes were wide, and he started coughing, waving at the smoke. Baryy and Outish flapped at the air.

"That," said Achelous, "is gunpowder. Don't ask me what it is made of because I won't tell you, but what I can tell you is," and he pointed at the drawing, "this firing hammer holds a flint. When the trigger is pulled," he pointed to the curved pull, "the spring-loaded hammer is released, and the flint strikes this pan, it sparks the priming powder into a brief fire, which flashes into this chamber and ignites the powder charge. The powder burns so fast it literally explodes. Then all that smoke and gas you see in this room forces the bullet down the barrel, burning as it goes, accelerating the ball to incredible speeds when it finally leaves the muzzle."

Ogden stared at Achelous, awestruck.

"This little ball," and Achelous held out his palm again to show him, "will travel so fast and contain so much force that it will penetrate plate armor and kill a man at a hundred paces. It will kill at two hundred paces if the man is not wearing armor, such as a trog."

Ogden blinked.

"Imagine Og, what this could do for the defense of Wedgewood if your warders had them in the tree forts."

The Timberkeep knitted his brows and waved at still drifting soot lingering in the lamp-dim room.

"Ula, who has made such a thing? How do you know it works?"

Achelous shrugged. "I have the silver. Do you want to find out?"

Chapter 24
Emperor Tyr Violorich

Stith Drakas, capital of Nak Drakas

Emperor Elixir Tyr Violorich peered at the rain lashing the windows of the Planning Room. Wind from the last vestiges of an Angraris hurricane buffeted the Trufel Citadel on its perch high in the center of Stith Drakas, the capital of the Drakan Empire. He clasped his hands behind his back, hands hidden in the long sleeves of a rich purple robe adorned with gold filigree along the shoulders and hem, and contrasting rubies and emeralds embedded in the high-necked collar. The dome-cloth of his gold crown matched the robe, which meant he had multiple sets of matching crowns and varied color robes. Crackling in the fireplace the fire and lamp light from various wall sconces caught on his earrings, aquamarine earrings. The earrings matched the aquamarine pendant that hung on his chest. The keen brown eyes looked past his hooked nose that dominated his perfectly groomed and dyed goatee. "It will take forever to get a trading fleet to Linkoralis," he growled. "Have you seen the weather?" He pointed to the window. "Just sailing to the Warkenvaal will take what?" He looked to Commandant Fritach, the commander of the Washentrufel--the secret police, for the answer.

"Three weeks your majesty."

His eyes narrowed. "If they get there," he snarled. "Damned Paleowrights. They will forever be the thorn of me, them, and every Ancient to ever walk the earth."

"Regardless, highness, we should send them on their way, and while they are enroute we can pursue other means." The voice of reason came from Lord Orn Blannach, overlord of the Nak Drakas Militaristrium--the entire military of the mighty Drakan Empire, army, cavalry, and navy. Lord Blannach wanted the mission to succeed as much as the emperor. The Antiquarian Church had finally decided to sell, openly, its stores of aquamarine, and most importantly its Ancient artifacts, and with those relics the promise of technological advancements. Unfortunately, the Isuelt branch of the Church had taken issue with the largess of the Linkoralis branch and had so far successfully blocked all attempts to import goods from

Linkoralis such was the power of the Isuelt Paleowrights. The Linkoralis Paleowrights were not nearly as strong or as well funded, hence their need to liquidate their Ancient artifacts and sell the ore from their as yet small aquamarine mine. He suspected the Linkoralis archbishop to be shrewder than what his Hebert counterparts gave him credit for. As Commandant Fritach had privately confided with him, Blannach expected they would copy the Ancient manuals, books, drawings, and offer to sell copies only. Regardless, at this point, a copy of an original was much better than a rumor of an original.

"Fritach has already said the Paleowrights are paying pirates to raid Tivor shipping bound for Linkoralis, the blockade appears to be working. What do you want us to do when our own fleet lands in Tivor to make the crossing? Attack the pirates, give aid to Tivor?" Shaking his head, "neither of which we can do because the hell-spawned Ancient-worshipers are our allies!"

Commandant Fritach mentally grimaced at the emperor's vehement cursing of the Paleowrights. Fritach himself was a Paleowright, as were most Nakish. The month of Thomsa the Electrician was upon them, and that was Fritach's patron Ancient. If only the archbishop in Hebert weren't so ridiculously greedy with their archives, hoarding and lording over every little shred of paper, every useless scrap of metal. The whole thing was ludicrous and with it their dealings with the empire. The single thing Fritach feared was the emperor would one day lose his temper and order an assault on Antiquarian archives. He tried not to think about it because he was unsure of how many of his own men would follow him in that crime. Fritach himself was first and foremost loyal to the empire and the emperor, but that could not be said for the average Nakish. The Nakish loved their Ancients.

Blannach moved to the planning board, a table the length and width of a hay wagon. On it, painstaking crafted and agonizingly accurate, was a map, a diorama really, of the continent of Isuelt. Beside it, in a new extension to the Planning Room was a similar map of Linkoralis, but it was mostly blank, with the edges gradually taking on detail. "Certainly your highness. We are the trusted and faithful servants of the Ancients, and the Church is our spiritual standard and our guide toward Ancient greatness." He smiled to himself as he leaned out over the map. He knew the emperor was fuming, but someone had to say the words. In a land full of Paleowrights, one could never let the façade slip. "We know we've been outmaneuvered in Tomis. The bishop there will be looking for any attempts to restart trade."

"And what other course of action do we have Blannach? Do not toy with me. My patience is naught." The emperor stood his ground not willing to be lured to the table.

Blannach reached out and put his finger on the side of a mountain just south of the east-west centerline of the diorama, some eight hundred miles from Stith Drakas. There, represented by a cluster of tiny plaster hovels, under his finger was a fair sized town. "That is our other course of action," he said.

Arching an eyebrow the emperor took the bait and came to the table.

"Commandant," Blannach said looking past the emperor's shoulder. "Inform the emperor as to your latest intelligence."

"Very well." Fritach had been expecting this. It was the whole point of the briefing.

The emperor listened to Fritach's briefing. Slowly his perpetual scowl melted until he too was leaning out over the table peering at the mountain-side town with a label flag pinned next to it. "Wedgewood," he said to himself.

The emperor leaned back from the table when Fritach finished. "And your plan Blannach? You always have a plan."

Lord Orn couldn't tell if that was an accusation or a compliment. It didn't matter. As the overlord of the Militaristrium, the Marshal of the Army, he was the emperor's closest advisor. "If the people of Wedgewood accede to the Paleowright demands, we could take a page out of the Church's own gospel and hire mercenaries to attack the town and gain control of the mine. It would be mercenaries versus Church pikemen and Scarlet Saviors. The Scarlet Saviors individually are good," he said grudgingly, "but mostly they are bullies. Regardless, it clearly it is too far for us to directly intervene."

"Yet," interrupted the emperor.

"The other case, and for me the more interesting, is if the town chooses the resist the Paleowright demands."

"We've interrogated traders and caravanserai who have been there," Fritach commented. "The town is mostly Life Believers and was built by a clan of Doromen. Though we don't see many of them here in the northeast word is they are notoriously independent. To the point of being touchy about it."

“So we’ve suggested to our ecclesiastical brethren that Wedgewood might make a good forward base of operations for the army.” Lord Orn saw the storm coming on the emperor’s countenance and braced for it.

“Wedgewood,” The emperor growled and pointed at the town and waved his hand towards the east indicating the eight hundred miles between there and the Drakan frontier. “You can’t be serious.”

“Of course not your highness. But the Paleowrights need not know. All we want is for our Washentrufel agents to be invited to tag along, to offer guidance and perspective.”

“Ah.” The emperor almost smiled. “Then tell them whatever you want. Tell them the sky is green and the Ancients are returning tomorrow. I want that aquamarine mine. I want the whole thing, and I don’t want to share it. I want to dig aquamarine out of the ground, ride to Hebert, and sprinkle it like pixie dust in the streets. I want to look that sniveling archbishop in the eye with a bucket full aquamarine and tell him I will sell it cheap, to everyone in the land, so they can all have their own part of the Ancients.”

“Unless,” said Fritach.

The emperor scowled. “Yes. Unless they start dealing and open the archives. Wide open.”

Chapter 25
Bells

Wedgewood

The three of them with a newcomer stood in the sunlight on the stoop of Baryy's cabin. It was the only time of day for the sun to beam through the sole gap in the canopy over the cabin. "We've had someone lurking around the cabin, I'm sure they were eavesdropping," said Baryy. "So watch our back-trail as we head up the mountain. We want to know if someone follows us."

Trishna, a Silver Cup telepath, said, "I'll wait here for a few minutes, then drift along behind you—keeping a good distance." As a bravo assigned to Celebron's team, Trishna's role in the guild was courier telepath responsible for relaying messages across Isuelt through the Silver Cup's network of adepts. Reassigned from her post in the Stronghold of Darnkilden, Celebron also used her for her tracking and surveillance skills. A rule for anyone recruited into the guild was they must be able to defend themselves, and Trishna was no exception. The long bow slung over her shoulder and the bo staff she carried identified her weapons of choice. Like her Darnkilden brethren, she wore dark green leather britches, knee-high boots, and a long calf-length coat. Her shoulder length red hair, with side braids, was tied back with a simple purple ribbon. The silver locket about her neck and a Cartesian Scroll ring were her simple adornments. Her face was unremarkable except for a narrow nose and thoughtful green eyes, and in the fashion of all pathics, she kept her red hair well back from her forehead. Of a modest build, she had the air of a woman who could roam all day, yet save notice for special moments.

Outish, Baryy, and Achelous set off up the mountain taking the trail behind Baryy's abode, their intent to inspect the concealed terraces below the summit. Outish steered them to a nearby brook and began to follow its twisting, gurgling climb over moss-slick rocks and ankle deep sedge. The early ephemeral blooms of trillium dotted the banks. Pitching his voice low, "I've found wild kdel berries growing along the sides of the creeks coming down from the peak. As near as I can tell, the plant is unique to Isuelt, probably all of Dianis. The berries are quite good. I can see why the Timberkeeps are trying to domesticate them." They hiked up the hill beside the brook. "I've started taking soil samples from the creek beds and using the soil analyzer." The soil analyzer was camouflaged to look like a log of firewood that Baryy kept stacked next to the fireplace. It was not standard Field Outfitting issue, but the product of a special order placed by Achelous. Today Outish carried it in his pack. "So far everything is pretty much as you would expect in a pristine boreal forest except that I found a trace of two unidentified minerals. One looks close to calcium carbonate, but not exactly. A larger, better equipped lab should be able to help with that mystery."

Trishna followed the three traders at a discreet distance. She ambled about; to the watchful observer, she appeared more interested in sniffing the spring blooms of the woodland plants, picking moss for herbs, and unearthing the occasional root to be dried and ground for medicines. The picture of a Darnkilden Ranger, a denizen of the forest, partaking of its hidden bounty.

The higher they climbed the taller and more vigorous the understory became as the massive Ungerngerists shrank in size and began to thin. Harvesting the sun, the ferns, bracken, and love-me-nots grew more authoritatively. She examined and identified each mushroom she came upon, and tip toed around the cucumber slugs, and plucked snails the size of her fist, dropping them in her sack. Later, she'd feed them a diet of fiddleheads, clean them out, and cook them in goat butter. Careful to conceal her intent, she often paused to stop and listen, not for audible sounds, but for telepathic emanations. In the forest, away from the town and its background noise of busy minds churning over mundane worries, it was easy to sense if someone were watching. Though it was difficult to catch thoughts directed at the traders, she could do it in the barren aural field of the forest, but she had to concentrate. She couldn't actually read thoughts unless the person was another trained –awakened-- telepath who could express their thinking in pathic form. But like a lantern glowing on a moonless night, focused thought was hard to miss, if directed at you.

They continued to climb, their first destination the lowest terrace where the Timberkeep berry farmers planted their kdel crop.

"Atch...I was wondering..."

Achelous trudged behind Outish on the steepening slope. "Yes?" He stopped, appreciating the respite, though Outish showed no sign of flagging.

"How can the provincials defend Dianis against the Nordarks or any other corsairs? The Nordarks have plasma assault rifles and energy armor; they'll have infrared detectors and ground radar. Won't the muzzleloaders just get the provincials killed quicker?"

Achelous and Baryy exchanged glances, and Baryy shrugged as if to say he'd tried to explain the strategy to the intern, but Outish either didn't understand or wasn't buying it.

"Hmm," Achelous said, letting his breath catch up, "you have to challenge your assumptions. As I've said, we're not trying to arm the natives so they can defend Dianis. We just want to make it too expensive for the Nordarks or anyone else to exploit the land. The Nordarks are all about profit. They'll ignore the most strategic resource in the galaxy if they can't extract it profitably."

"So what do muzzleloaders have to do with Nordarken profits?"

Achelous was surprised by the question. He had to remind himself that the young intern's education and realm of life experiences were narrowly defined by biology and had little to do with economics, though he thought the connection was self-evident. "If we can increase the cost of extracting aquamarine beyond the margin the Nordarks need to profitably extract the mineral they'll leave. The way we do that is increase their security burden, otherwise known as overhead. The Nordarks usually contract with small, independent resource extractors when they first attempt to crash a Class E. It's been their model time and again and has worked well for them. Nineteen out of twenty cases we are never able to pin charges on the Nordarks themselves. Slippery bastards. The contracting goes through layers of middle men who conveniently disappear when we bust an extractor if we even get the extractor." He thought back to Ilos Septi, the rare time they did pin Nordarken Mining. "They use the independent contractors as a litmus test. Send them in, see if the IDB has a trap set, sample the quality of the ore deposit or resource load, test the passivity of the natives, discover any new bacteria or pathogens, etcetera. If the mine proves productive enough and the extraction cost sustainable, meaning few security concerns and a hospitable geology, they'll buy out or cancel the contract with the independent and force them off the site -- an accident or two with their managers helps, as does blackmail. Then they take over the dig with their own non-badged personnel. Remember, middlemen, the independents increase costs. The Nordarks like to be what they call, vertically integrated. They want to own the entire supply chain from extraction through refining to finished product.

"So these independents usually come on site with a few tough guys, shoot some plasmas, run over a village or two with their heavy equipment, and generally terrorize the locals into submission, or better yet, force them to flee the area. Then they get to work. The independents are even more penny-wise than the Nordarks because the 'Darks negotiate lean contracts with tight margins. So the independents, after their first landing, can't afford a lot of security. Certainly, they can't afford shock troops like you are referring to. These guys will be lightly armored, if at all. They'll have plasmas, but they won't be willing to die for their company if the action gets rough. After all, they can just bug out and head to the next planet where the diggings are safer.

"Think of it this way: it's like burglar proofing your home. You don't need to make it burglar-proof; you just need to make it more secure than your neighbor."

"But why do these independents rely on the Nordarks at all. Why don't they just mine for themselves and not contract with the big conglomerates?"

"A host of reasons, intel being one. The Nordarks do all the planning, scanning of IDB surveillance systems, selecting insertion points. It's the Nordarks that find the resource deposits in the first place. Most independents are diggers. They lease one or two ore extractors, run the snot out of them, and keep moving from job to job. They don't have the staff or equipment to do geological surveys. You might think it's as easy as renting a deep crust radar imager and scanning every lump of rock in Federation space, but iron, nickel, and copper we have. And the IDB doesn't let anyone come within scanning range of a Class E, let alone orbit it.

"Then there's the other end of the equation, after the dirty work of violating ULUP and stealing the minerals, the independents don't want to go shopping for buyers. Buyers ask questions, especially for the certificate of origin for strategic resources. The Nordarks are there to receive the materials and process it, no questions asked. It gets back to the power of owning the supply chain and being vertically integrated. Their operations are so large they can distribute the origin accounting across many holdings, more than a few of which have been marginal producers for years and are only kept operating to do the laundering."

"Okay, I get it, but Atch, what's to prevent the security forces, even the cheap independents from donning their energy armor at the first sign of trouble and smoking any provincial they see?"

To this Achelous gave a wry smile. "You seem to be missing some history lessons. Your assumption is obsolete chemical projectiles, such as firearms, are ineffective against modern armor, and that provincial guerilla forces can't win against trained security forces."

Outish creased his brows. "But it's why we're here. You have cited all those cases where extrasolars have terrorized, subjugated, and exterminated whole native populations!"

Achelous nodded. His mind wandered to when the Spanish on Earth crossed the Atlantic Ocean and wiped out the Incas. In that case, the contemporaries were not separated by historical epochs but evolved on the same planet in the same era, and hence their technological gaps were narrower but no less decisive. "If all the Diesians had to fight with is what they have now, arrows, swords, and spears, and they had no knowledge of the enemy, then I would agree with you. They would be doomed. But that is not the case. Baryy--what is the energy, the foot-pounds, needed to penetrate energy armor with a solid projectile?"

Having done the calculation before when Achelous first introduced him to the idea, Baryy readily pulled out his purse and activated the multi-func. "What is the surface area of the projectile?" He didn't remember the specs his boss used.

"A third of an inch in diameter, the cross section of one of those bullets I gave Ogden."

Baryy punched in the numbers. "I'm assuming you want the typical energy armor profile of police and security forces, not front line infantry or heavy assault?"

"That'll do for starters."

"Mass of the projectile?"

"One hundred eighty grains should do."

Baryy punched in the one eighty. "Thirteen hundred foot pounds."

Achelous nodded. "A rifled muzzleloader with a hundred and eighty grain conical projectile and fast burning powder can generate more than eighteen hundred foot pounds at one hundred yards. When you compare that to a plasma bolt at hundred yards, because of attenuation due to the atmosphere, the chemical projectile holds more energy."

Outish shook his head, "But, chemical projectile weapons are obsolete."

"It depends on who is doing the classifying. And never confuse obsolete with effective. Energy weapons came into vogue for three reasons." Achelous held up three fingers. "First, they're light-weight. They don't rely on heavy materials, such as steel for their construction, so they take less energy to shift around the galaxy and boost in our sub-light drives and therefore cost less to use. Second, they are cheap to manufacture. Flash-pressing the circuitry, plasma generator, and particle concentrators cost less in both raw materials and time compared to the heavy manufacturing needed for metal barrels, breaches, and trigger mechanisms. Third, you can rearm anywhere; all you need is a suitable particle element and an energy source to recharge the power packs. You don't need to worry about shipping tons and tons of ammo from planet to planet. The supply chains are simpler, field repair is simpler, and plasmas aren't sensitive to dirt. Energy weapons are the choice of the modern space-born military."

He went on, "To counter energy weapons energy armor was developed to absorb, deflect, and dissipate laser and plasma bolts. Tuning the energy field concentrators even allowed the armor to cope with low velocity, physical weapons like clubs, spears, and arrows. But energy armor has never been able to cope with high velocity bullets. It's why medium and heavy infantry must wear albuminum hard armor in addition to energy armor."

Refusing to cede that modern security forces could be vulnerable to provincials, Outish tried "Right! The security teams could don hard armor or vibrolux when they learn the natives have chemical projectiles."

Achelous concealed his growing irritation. *Is Outish being deliberately obstinate?* "Yes, those commercial armors can stop several classes of projectile if the security forces are equipped with them. But remember hard body armor is designed to prevent critical injuries and save lives. We don't necessarily need or want to kill any of the security forces." He caught himself, did he just say *we*? "All the provincials have to do is shoot them in the leg. Force an evacuation. Drive up the security costs to an unprofitable level. You see Outish, the Nordarks or whoever they send will certainly adapt to the provincials initial tactics. We, *I,* will help the plan those tactics, assuming a progression, always staying one step ahead of the security forces, forcing them to adapt again and again until they give up and go home. And we'll keep that up until the Nordarks quit. Because this planet belongs to—" he almost said *us,* "the provincials. When you live where you fight, when it's your home you are defending, your tenacity, your staying power is only limited by, sad to say, birth rate. It's their home Outish. They've no other place to go, whereas the Nordarks will eventually lose their appetite when they keep having to funnel in men and resources.

"I'll give you another example of adapting. The provincials don't need to have a direct confrontation with security forces. All we have to do is damage their miners and ore extractors. Those machines are not armored. One bullet to the operator's bubble or to a neutrino energy cell and the machine is out of action. Even if the Nordarks hang on through a bitter, protracted guerilla war, the fight need only last until we get the attention of the Matrincy and the evidence of a corsair incursion is irrefutable. Then the IDB will be back, and the Nordarks exposed for what they are."

"Atch, when you say we, who is we?"

They stood looking at him, the three of them on a narrow rocky outcropping in the forest. Neither Outish nor Baryy had signed up to join a guerilla war against extrasolars. Aside from the personal danger they might face, each had his own motivation for staying in-country, and while their interests were aligned for now, eventually they would accomplish their individual goals and what then? Would their relationship evolve around new common interests, or would it be time to go their own directions? Achelous accepted them as volunteers and appreciated any help they could provide. Beyond that, he could ask for no more. "We is me, and whoever joins the cause. You two are welcomed to help in whatever capacity you desire. There is far more at stake here than thwarting a Nordarken incursion. The Timbers are dying, aquamarine should be a strategic resource for Dianis, and--" he thought of Marisa and Boyd. Quickly, he pushed visions of them away. He needed to focus on what was relevant to Outish and Baryy. "The primary disadvantage any primitive society suffers when faced with an invasion of a technologically superior force is the lack of knowledge, not the lack of technology. A galactic truism applies: knowledge is power. Corsairs take advantage of this. They rely on awe, mystery, and fear as much as physical force. The provincials become so terrorized, with no basis for understanding, they often just give up and flee, or worse, pursue some sort of ritual suicide or other fruitless act born out of ignorance. Remove that ignorance and physical resistance becomes possible. Imagine if the provincials on Teran Ky had just a few advisors when the Turboii first landed. They could have crushed early scouting missions. Which is why now we put advisors into all Turboii frontier worlds. An advisor here on Dianis can prepare the natives, and when the time comes, the advisor can separate fact from fiction, dispel the fear and quell the panic that is the coin of corsairs everywhere. Corsairs count on their sudden god-like appearance to sow dismay and reap their aura of mythical invincibility. They would much rather shoot a fleeing native in the back than face a surprise attack at night." He turned to look out over the forest, appreciating the natural beauty and peace however fleeting of the world around them. Neither Baryy nor Outish knew he had a son, his most closely guarded secret. Baryy certainly suspected that Achelous was keen on Marisa, but he had no idea the depths of their relationship or the lengths to which Achelous would go to defend her, his son, and their way of life. In his subconscious, Achelous had come to an agreement that he would never leave Dianis. He was there to stay. Moreover, a new idea was forming: a loftier vision, one much grander than defending against extrasolars. He wanted to live to see the day when Dianis was Uplifted, formally accepted into the Avarian Federation. To do that he would have to vastly accelerate the Uplift process and that meant unifying over half of the native population. "If I can delay by just one day the advent of corsair tyranny, save just one life from a Nordarken incursion then I will have succeeded. So when I say we, I mean myself and anyone who will help me for however long they choose."

Trishna surreptitiously watched the three traders from behind a bole. They were deep in discussion, so she found a log to sit on and idle her time. Picking absently at the rotting wood she day-dreamed for a moment of home and her betrothed in distant Rhinehart. She reached down to break off an edible shell fungus growing on the trunk. The variety was bland tasting but worked well in soup. She froze.

Oh, you stupid fool. Slowly Trishna sat up, her inner mind in a frenzy deciphering how long she'd been watched. The thoughts were alien, either that or the person, no —persons-- were too distant to telegraph the nature of their intellects. She stood and feigned a stretch, purposely turning to align her mind's directional sense to what was resolving into an aggressive and alien thought pattern. Fear crept down her back. The overtones were hostile, sharp edged. A powerful urge compelled her to run, but instead, she remained outwardly calm and scanned the forest as if she were bird watching. Facing up hill, she started out in a nonchalant stride. The watchers were lurking hidden in a dense grove of cedars to her right, about a hundred paces away. They must have crept into the cover while she was sitting on the log. It was the only explanation for not sensing their presence sooner.

Increasing her pace, she absorbed the images floating around her, images taken by alien eyes as the lenses were vertically slit. The colors of the mental pictures were oddly distorted with heat, blue for cool, redder for warmth. She could now grasp and sample the harsh intents of the thoughts. The emanations were sentient, not the shallow patterns of lower life animals, and they were decidedly not human.

Skipping to a boulder and then springing to the top of a Ungern log, she had a commanding view of the thinning forest. Achelous and his two assistants were directly up slope from her by two hundred paces or so. She felt tempted to wave, but whoever was stalking her might not be aware of her clients. The fact she was in plain sight and no longer attempting to be unobtrusive should give the traders a clue as something was amiss.

In the far distance, a bell began to ring. It was down in the valley beyond the town walls. Not familiar with the ways of Wedgewood Trishna pondered its meaning. Then the bell was echoed by another, closer this time inside Wedgewood itself. More bells began to ring. A harsh guttural horn blared to her left, opposite and away from the tolling.

The emanations concentrating on her spiked, taking on the pulsing pattern of minds managing movement. She whirled. Three troglodytes emerged from the cedar thicket at a dead run. She stood directly in the path they'd take if they were heading to the horn.

Baryy moved to a rock outcropping, listening intently. "It's an attack. Wedgewood is under attack." He waved his arm for them to follow. "Come on, we'll need to help. They'll expect us to help." Without further ado, he began running downhill. After their surprise, Achelous and Outish followed suit. Baryy in his haste crashed through the ferns, skirted boulders, and leaped a shallow depression, outdistancing his fellows.

Trishna pulled the bowstring tight against her cheek, the thick calluses on her fingertips were iron. She let fly, the arrow thudding soundly into the shoulder of snarling troglodyte. It stumbled, fell, rolled, and stood up scratching at the shaft. Trishna's heart pounded, and her hands trembled with sudden tension, *these are big troglodytes.* She notched a second arrow, the practiced motions a salve to her nerves. She brought the bow up more by muscle memory than conscious thought. Clearing her mind, she found a target, sighted, and loosed.

Baryy, trying to focus on the ground ahead as he ducked branches and careened around a tree--gravity propelling him--saw troglodytes closing on their Silver Cup bravo. He caught a glimpse of her shooting. *Troglodytes? Up here? The bells are ringing down in Wedgewood?* At risk of running past Trishna, he slowed his headlong rush down the slope. *How many trogs are there? How close?* He stopped in a low clump of fiddleheads and cocked his handbolt. Trogs were running across his front. Breathing heavy and beginning to sweat, he ran to where he could get a shot.

She had time for one more arrow. A pluck of her fingers and the grey and white fletching zipped away; the broad head went straight into an open trog mouth and sprouted out the back of the head. Trishna tossed her bow safely away and freed her quarterstaff. The trog with the arrow in its shoulder came at her shaking and twisting its head, saliva and gore dripping from its jaws. She hopped back, spun, and brought the hornbeam staff around in a whistling arc that cracked loudly against the trog's skull. The beast's forward momentum took it past her where it stumbled, and rolled in a heap.

"Ha!" she dropped into a bracing stance and jabbed the end of the staff into the chest of the next reptile. The end of the staff thrust hard against the oncoming chest elicited a reptilian, "yowl." The force of the impact deflected the troglodyte and spun Trishna completely around. Out of position and unprepared, it was all she could do to duck a clawed swipe.

Baryy saw a wounded troglodyte, a broken arrow protruding from its bloodied shoulder, swing at their bravo and knock her sprawling off the log. He aimed his handbolt. It was a difficult shot, branches, bracken, and ferns in the way, but he had no choice; he fired at the attacker's spinal ridge vanes.

“Fire Outish! Shoot!” Achelous yelled to the intern. It was no time to be fussy about choosing sides.

Achelous came up beside Baryy, sighting on anything that looked green and scale-like. An olive-drab movement rustled the bright green ferns; a ridge vane sharked through the foliage. Achelous squeezed the iron trigger of Ogden’s handbolt.

Outish in his haste had not loaded the handbolt. Breathing hard, disoriented by the sudden action, he fumbled with the cocking lever and dropped the quarrel.

Trishna scrabbled through the underbrush. She’d tumbled a distance down slope. Her hair loosened and tangled in her face; her shoulder throbbed and burned. She could feel something wet and sticky in her armpit. She had no idea where her staff was. Grimly, she pulled her short sword. Not her favorite weapon, it was more a large hunting knife. She held still and waited for the foul beast to come for her.

“Blast,” frustrated and embarrassed, not wanting to disappoint the senior agents, Outish grabbed the quarrel and ran down slope. Beneath his skin-deep human metamorphosis, Outish was still a Halorite. He vaulted to an old stump and sprang forward landing on both feet with a loud thump. Not hesitating, knowing Baryy and Achelous were just to his left, or so he hoped, he ran to a huge log, scrambled up the side and peered over.

A grotesque trog with two arrows protruding from it was kicking at the undergrowth, growling, and snuffling. The alarm bells from Wedgwood had ceased, but voices could be heard. Men were mounting their tree forts and pulling up the trap doors. Outish ducked down behind the log, he blinked, trying to concentrate on loading the weapon. He slotted the bolt and cranked the lever back. Taking a deep breath, he crawled up the log and looked for the trog. The insanity of the situation was not lost on him. He was an astrobiologist; he should be studying alien organisms and researching mutation paths, not battling massive reptiles that wanted to eat you. On Halor his father was a computer scientist and his mother an academy director, neither had any military experience.

Trishna feigned death. She could hear the trod of the beast close by, the rustle of undergrowth an arm's reach away. Surely it could smell her. Waiting, her body pins and needles, her shoulder stiffening like a hitching post, she gripped the leather wrapping of the sword hilt, her palm slippery with sweat.

The trog stopped. It heard the sounds of humans coming from Wedgewood.

Achelous creeping up from behind whispered into Outish's ear, "Aim carefully and shoot. It's a big one."

Outish's eyes grew wide when the trog whirled around and set its gaze on him. It emitted a low rumble and charged up slope. Outish aimed at the body, no place in particular, and fired, but already the beast was arching backward.

Stuck in the spinal joint between its backbone and tail was a short sword with Trishna hanging on with one hand.

"Smokes," Outish said, "that's a big trog."

They stood over the body of the reptile and waited for a ward of Timberkeeps to sweep the area of stragglers.

"It's a boar," supplied Achelous. "A big one."

Baryy shook his head. "All that muscle. Trishna, you did well today."

Trishna's arm was in a sling, her shoulder bound and wrapped. She swallowed, still a bit dizzy. "I stabbed and dared not let go."

Outish nodded dumbly. He could only imagine her courage.

A warden hailed them from the trail.

When they met the man, he said, "We'll be needing to build two or three sentry forts up here. We spotted the loglards below, and that worked well enough, but we didn't expect them to be sweeping around and coming in from behind."

"Best to find that out now," said Achelous, "How many were there?"

The warden shrugged, "Dunno. More of a scouting mission, maybe. But I dare say they put the fear of life into the town. By my count, this is the third different tribe we've seen. Never have the trogs come this close."

"They're growing them big, too," said Baryy.

"Oi, so I see." The warden doffed his helmet; it was smeared with a greenish-brown paste so it wouldn't glint in the sun. He rubbed a mailed-sleeve across his sweaty forehead, the iron links cooling his skin. "It's going to be a long hot summer."

Chapter 26
Saltpeter

Tivor

"Impressive." Marisa inspected the old flourmill converted to grind gunpowder. The millstone, as tall as she, rolled around the race driven by a set of wooden gears propelled by a water wheel.

Patrace, never happy, never satisfied, eyed it with her perpetual scowl. "I don't know how he expects us to make five hundred pounds of powder a day! The man is daft." She checked herself, "Sorry mi'lady, no disrespect."

Marisa smiled in her professional way. She understood Patrace. In building Marinda Merchants, Marisa had to deal with all sorts of personalities: thugs, liars, cheats, pirates, princes, and prickly alchemists. Honed by long years trading, Marisa enjoyed a hard-earned talent of persuading people to follow her. Achelous, though, was her toughest challenge yet. Compared to him, Patrace was easy. "I'm sure you can do it. Once you have this mill working to its fullest, we'll build another one."

"But the money mi'lady and the mill house. We'll have to construct the next one from scratch, and where do we find the sites?"

Marisa kept to her smile, strolling over to a mound of yellow powder, dumped unceremoniously on a tarp. She stood there while Derek shoveled it into a vat filled with a noxious solution. "Achelous says he has the silver, and he has certainly made good on what we've needed so far." *And according to his plans, we'll soon be selling it to the aorolmin,* she thought. "As for the next mill and site, tell Eliot what you need, and he'll find it."

If possible, Patrace's expression soured even more put off by Marisa's steadfast attitude that nothing was impossible. Though Patrace would never admit it to anyone, she was happiest when she could complain about everything and yet have the time and tools to solve the hardest problems. Marisa made the process both infuriating and liberating. Infuriating that she refused to be surprised by anything Patrace did -- no matter how substantial the accomplishment. Liberating in that Marisa had no doubts about

Patrace's ability to deliver. She expected Patrace to be as expert as Patrace presumed to be, but Patrace would never allow that to mellow her disposition. She liked being cranky. It kept morons from trying to be friends.

"So you are digging the sulfur from the mountain?" The mill and much of the aorolmin's realm lay in the shadow of Mount Epratis, an active volcano. Hot springs and gas vents dotted the slopes.

A curt nod and the alchemist twisted her countenance into a rendition of a storm cloud. "We have to develop a rectification process for it. It's sulphur all right, but you'd never know it to look at it. It's impure and rife with other chemicals."

Satisfied with his shoveling, Derek began to stir the solution with a large wooden paddle.

"But you found it right where Achelous said?"

The way Patrace jammed her fists on her hips made Marisa smile. She had to turn away lest the alchemist throw a childish fit. Mentioning Achelous's name usually caused the wild-haired woman to balk, pout, or stalk off in a huff, her skirts billowing behind. Marisa was still puzzling out the dynamics behind Patrace's strong reaction to Achelous, and she half wondered if Patrace was jealous. The fact that Achelous's suggestions and plans made the work easier just caused the alchemist to get angrier. She detested giving the trader, a mere merchant, credit for anything, and certainly nothing remotely scientific. How could a caravanserai know more about earth science than her? Then there was the woman's drive to develop her own solutions. Achelous called it the "not invented here syndrome." Marisa sighed. She'd taken to funneling Achelous's ideas through Eliot. For some reason, the alchemist tolerated Eliot and was even marginally polite with him. Eliot's talents at organizing and running Marinda Merchant's operations were dragging him deeper into the gunpowder project, and Marisa was afraid she would have to find a new huntsmaster.

"I see you've set up charcoaling furnaces." Gunpowder had three components, the first two, sulfur and charcoal, were the easiest to come by, and as long as they were mixed in their proper ratios: ten percent sulfur and fifteen percent charcoal, their roles in the equation were straightforward.

Patrace replied, "We're experimenting with different wood."

Judging by the shift in Patrace's stance, they were venturing into a subject free of Achelous's taint, an operation where Patrace was left to her own designs.

"I'm measuring the mixtures and ratios to and see which wood species makes the finest carbon grains. A fine grain charcoal burns hotter, releasing the greatest energy. Of course, the heat and fire from the furnaces is a constant risk; we have to keep the coaling operation well apart from the mill. One spark and you'll blow me and all the grinders into the harbor."

Marisa nodded absently. With Patrace, it was all about her. The eternal martyr suffering a lack of humility, impatiently enduring the indignity of the buffoons who surrounded her. "And have you solved the problem of the saltpeter?" That was the question, the reason Marisa had ridden out to the mill. Everything else she gleaned from Patrace's frequent missives. Marisa kept her tone even and continued to wander about the mill like a damsel in a boutique. Achelous had dumped the problem into their laps, without apology, saying simply it would take creativity to find a solution for it. As if he knew the answer to the puzzle but wanted them to solve it.

In Patrace's early efforts to supply powder for the log cannon she'd resorted to secretly scraping the white salt crystals from old cellars and latrines, well away from the prying eyes of outsiders. After enough encounters with rats and venomous spiders, and sinking up to her knees in excrement, she'd wisely contracted with the reclusive Coasters to finish the job, but it was a laborious way to make the thirty pounds of required explosive. The problem became all the more daunting when she faced a production goal of five hundred pounds of gunpowder a day, with saltpeter making up seventy-five percent of the total. Patrace had to find a source or method capable of supplying over four hundred pounds of the precious chemical a day. *A day!*

Marisa turned when the alchemist's normally quick response failed to sound.

Dragging a hand through her flyaway grey locks, Patrace said, "I have an idea you may not like much."

"Try me."

"Saltpeter is a mineral that crystallizes from organic matter as it decomposes over time. We know this from the notes Ach--, well the notes *he* provided. The best environment to grow saltpeter is a hot place with seasonal rain and then extended dry spells." She glared at Marisa. "Sound familiar?"

"The Warkenvaal," Marisa said, looking away. Marisa's encounters with the pirates was well known; many of them hailed from Warkenvaal ports.

"Eastport and South Cape. I'd wager their dung heaps are covered with it."

Marisa wrinkled her nose. "What are you suggesting?"

"That among other ideas, we send someone down to the southland and buy it or collect it. Have Achelous do it. He trades in spices. A caravanserai I spoke to told me they use saltpeter to season and cure their meat."

"You said other ideas?"

Patrace answered, "Yes, well, long term we create our own saltpeter plantations. An idea I have is for you or his nibs to buy up the surrounding poultry farms and build shelters for the dung to decompose. Do what you want with the chickens, but I need their poop. Pigs will do too. It will take time, as much as a year for the first harvest. In the mean while we can search the caves in the mountains."

Unbeknownst to Marisa and the alchemist, Achelous's entire strategy of arming Dianis to prevent extrasolars from exploiting the world relied on Patrace's creativity to leech potassium nitrate from manure.

"Caves?"

Patrace rolled her eyes, the visual equivalent of saying *must I explain everything*. "Bat droppings, you know scat. The caves are perfect. They're fecund, humid, and protected from rain. Even better, the caverns are heated by volcanic vents. The heat will accelerate decomposition." Then she had an idea, "Maybe we can haul pig or cow dung to the caves?"

What neither woman understood was how the saltpeter "appeared" in dung heaps, cellars, and cesspools. Nor could Achelous divulge the process and still maintain the plausibility of self-invention in the face of a future IDB cultural assessment. Diesian medical science had not evolved to the point of discovering bacteria and how certain bacteria fed on decaying organic matter giving off waste nitrogen, which combined with trace salts or metals – potassium -- formed potassium nitrate, i.e., saltpeter. While the pre-ULUP transportation engineers unintentionally educated and accelerated Diesian science in some fields, biology was not one of them.

Patrace idly toyed with the grease brush used to lubricate the millstone gears, "I suppose we could go around scraping everyone's latrine walls and pigeon coops like I had the Coaster's do at Marinda Merchants..."

Marisa turned in surprise, but Patrace just gave her a tight-lipped frown, "But then that ugly fellow Master Beth would be all over us for carelessly exposing the operation."

"Oh, so 'Kalla has been here to see you?"

"Ha!" Patrace threw up her arms. "He and his goons practically live here. You must have seen the guard when you rode up!"

Marisa shook her cocked head, doubtful, "No, I didn't."

"Well, I bet he or she is out there. Sneaky bunch they are."

"What did Akallabeth have to say about the Coasters?"

"It was *his* idea!" she nearly screeched. Calming a bit, she added, "I can see why he likes them. They're mum and frugal. Ask them questions, and you get grunts and stares for answers. Like prying open a clam with a toothpick." Then she grudgingly acknowledged, "But they do what you tell them with no fuss."

Unlike you, Marisa thought. "The Coasters would be perfect for running your saltpeter plantations. They *are* secretive, don't seem to mind dirty jobs, and guard their lands like mad hermits. Few people get near their villages without being challenged."

"Though I don't know why, those shores are all gloomy fens, sand dunes, and mucky tidal swamps."

Marisa wandered over to a stack of small wooden casks, one of which was sealed and in her idle musings was about to pull the lid to peek inside when Patrace issued a sharp rebuke, "Don't do that! It's damp enough in here with the water wheel." Marisa froze, twisting her head at the alchemist, a quizzical look betraying her ignorance.

"It's our first test batch. And depending on the source of the saltpeter, the gunpowder soaks up water like a sponge." She waved her hand in a circle, "That's why I need the separate dry storage."

Marisa removed her hands from the barrel and brushed them off. Smiling brightly, "Tell us what you need, and you shall have it. We need to see a plan and alternatives for reaching the production goal of five hundred pounds a day by the end of the year." She said *we,* but in truth, those were her demands. Achelous and Marisa were joint partners, but she was the one managing the operations.

Crossing her arms over her chest, Patrace fumed, "And what exactly does Atch--, er, *he* needs all that powder for?"

Marisa arched an eyebrow, "Who says it's what *he* needs? Remember Patrace, Achelous and I are partners. According to our testing, how much powder is needed to shoot a one pound ball?"

"Three quarters of a pound," she said without stopping to think.

"And if the *Wind March* as ten cannons to a side and fires ten broadsides in a fight with pirates, how much powder has it consumed in one skirmish?"

"Seventy-five pounds."

"And if I want enough powder to see the ship through a trading route, there and back, with powder to spare how much will I need?"

Patrace halted, not knowing how to calculate the answer, and was annoyed at being asked such a question.

Marisa shrugged, "Three thousand pounds—I hope—should do it." She ran a finger around the rim of the barrel, "And if I want to put cannons on every one of my ships and those of the aorolmin too, and stock them all with enough powder—" She let the statement hang and turned to the alchemist who picked up the thread.

"Forty five thousand pounds."

Marisa nodded quietly, her dark eyes taking on a flinty aspect. "Forty five thousand pounds should do for starters. I want to sink the bastards. That should make it economically impractical for them." She smiled at her own joke, recalling Atch's lesson on pirate economics. "And then," she said more to herself, "we'll deal with the Paleowrights."

Chapter 27
Defender

Wedgewood

Amidst the clamor and commotion of wards returning from chasing troglodytes, archers disembarking their tree forts, and villagers emerging from safe havens, a tall warrior rode her eenu sedately down the middle of Wide Lane. Two fellow warriors trailed her, leading a pack train of eenus. A half-ward, trooping back to their assembly station, made to cross in front of the warrior when the branch warden held out his arm. They halted. A shield on one of the pack eenus caught his eye. He stared at the shield, and then to the woman. Her worn greaves, gauntlets, and bastard sword sheathed on the eenu told him she was the real thing. The branch warden offered a short bow, holding the troop in place, waiting.

She returned his nod and issued the barest smile. Continuing on her way, she had the air of a local, when in reality this was her first mission to Wedgewood.

One of her fellow warriors touched two fingers to his temple in salute to the ward.

A Timberkeep trooper nudged another and pointed to the painted shields, scarred, and dented, yet the symbol on the shields shone bright in the morning sun: a white lily upon a field of green against a sky of blue. The emblem universal amongst all Life Believers, the worshippers of Mother Dianis, the faith of Timberkeeps. The lily represented life blossoming in a harsh world; the green field portrayed the plain upon which life flourished, and the blue sky described where life aspired. When the icon was emblazoned upon a shield, it meant one thing.

"Life Defenders," said one trooper. He gulped. "We're in the turds now."

"Ula, Defenders never show unless there be real trouble. Who called them?"

"Must've been the clan council," offered the branch warden. "I'll take one of them Defenders for every five Savior pukes."

"Oi," murmurs accented all around. The reputation of the Life Defenders lived far and wide. Though few in numbers, their renown as guardians of the Mother Dianis Faithful was well deserved. They defended the lowly peasant and impoverished farmer with great zeal, having an affinity for those who worked the land and practiced honest stewardship.

The tall warrior dismounted in front of Ogden's foundry and tied her mount's reigns to a hitching post. Stepping inside the iron works, she found the weaponsmith stripping off his chainmail hauberk, fresh from leading a scouting patrol. "Hello," she called.

Ogden blinked, standing at the weapons racks at the back of the foundry; the bright glare from the street cast the warrior in shadow. He could see by outline the person was a woman, her long hair bound and thrown over a shoulder. She carried something on her back. He grunted, pulling the heavy mail over his head and draped it on the mannequin. Squinting against the light, "Hello yourself. I'm a wee busy now. The shop's closed on account of the trog attack," he huffed, "if that's what you call it. Rode half way to Lycealia and didn't see a tail of the bastards."

"Of course."

"Uh? Of course what?"

"You're right to question it as an attack. The reptiles were scouting."

Ogden paused, he wanted to strip off his greaves and armor, but his respect for a visitor, no matter how untimely, prompted him to trudge to where he could get a better look at her.

"Scouting eh? You think they're scouting us for a real attack?" He walked into the light and stopped. An amulet of a white lily hung on a chain about the woman's neck, resting atop her breastplate. His surprise met her gaze. "Oh." He swallowed. "Are you just visiting? Or," he paused, "were you called?"

She gave him a broad, yet tight-lipped smile. "Sedge called me."

"Ula," he exclaimed. Sedge had evoked the Mother Dianis summons for the devoted, in this case, a Defender. Now Ogden was concerned. He eyed her up and down, curious as to what a real Defender looked like, not one from a legend. She wore burnished brass greaves glinting gold in the sun, a chain mail skirt over tight leather britches, a sanded steel breastplate with attached mail sleeves, and matching steel gauntlets. At one hip, she carried a sword, short for her, average for others, and a long sword in a sheath over her shoulder. The weaponsmith in him wanted to peer at her eenu. He'd bet there was a two handed broadsword, a mighty death reaper, strapped to the mount. Her long hair was the color of summer wheat, her eyes a startling leaf green. Even with the scar over her right eyebrow and another on the left cheek, he'd call her beautiful. The old wounds added to her unassailable looks. She towered over him by nearly half a hand, and he was glad she was on his side.

"Sedge called in the Life Defenders?" he asked.

"Not because of the trogs though," she said, and Ogden caught a hint of tiredness, or perhaps disinterest in her voice. "I suspect you can handle them."

"Oh?" he asked.

"Sedge has asked me to muster with your ward for a time. We have a special task."

"We do? Does the head warden know this?"

She smiled, a gentle ghost flitting away. "I don't know. Does it matter?"

Ogden shrugged. She had a point. Being a devout Life Believer, he readily accepted a Life Defender as his leader. "Just as long as he knows to make changes in the watch rotation, I'm okay with it."

The ghost smile came back; her lips pale against the sun-darkened skin.

"Oi, I should mind my manners." He stuck out his hand Timber fashion, palm up, "I'm Ogden Snowbirch, weaponsmith, warden of the Second Ward."

The warrior clasped his hand. "Christina Tara, Defender, *Al suri Ascalon.*"

Ogden froze, his grip turning to lead. An *Ascalon.* He attempted to conceal his awe and surprise. For her part, Christina merely shook his hand and let it go. She began to explain her presence and connection with Sedge, but Ogden's mind was in a fog. An Ascalon Defender? He'd heard, a time back, there was a new Ascalon, but the last real Ascalon chronicled in the clan Mother Dianis histories was Timothea the Rain. Timothea died at the battle of Galatia over twenty years ago and had been the last of his rank. To suddenly have an Ascalon standing in his shop shaking his hand was enough to shiver his forge.

"My compatriots and I passed a Paleowright camp on our way here," she said, as her gaze took in the forge and weapons racks. "Curious, they were pitched less than a league away while the trogs were roaming about. Their behavior belied nary a concern nor did they post a watch. Either their arrogance has led them to think they can defeat any and all comers," she paused to return her attention to him, "which I can believe, or they had nothing to fear, even though their numbers counted less than twenty. Alex and Feolin--my companions—and I encountered a band of the troglodytes circling back from Wedgewood. We drove them off handily enough for there was no fight in them; they were running to their recall. Yet the band was only an arrow's flight from the Paleowright's camp. The churchmen treated the trogs as if they were merely loose squirrels harvesting pine nuts. Don't you think that odd?"

"Odd? Paleowrights?" Ogden laughed.

Christina smiled at Ogden's jest.

He clamped his jaw. "What of the Paleos? You've come here because of them?"

She turned to walk into the warm sunshine, out from under the shadows of the smithy and drew him along with a glance. "An emissary is coming, a viscount. He has two squads of Scarlet Saviors with him. We met with Sedge after coming into town. Sedge says his cup is full organizing the expanded patrol schedule against the troglodytes. He wants to push them further out, at least two days ride in any direction from Wedgewood. No more surprises. But he needs someone to watch, shadow if you like, the Antiquarians while they're in town. Ensure they stay out of trouble. He," Christina's green eyes glinted in the sun as she sought the right expression, "questions their motives and timing for sending such high ranking clergy. If they make any move to inspect the mines we're to," she put a hand on Ogden's shoulder and leveled a steady gaze, "dissuade them."

His beard twitched, registering a smirk, "Oi, no good ever comes from the Scarlet Britches. A little dissuading we can do."

"To be safe, I will provide instruction to your ward on how to fight your Scarlet Britches. I've met them before; they all attend the same gladiator school."

"What?" He made a face. "You expect trouble? Here in Wedgewood?"

Sighing, she tilted her head to the sunlight. "I don't know Master Ogden.

There is an old saying, perhaps you know it: *When a troubled wind trembles the bough—*"

“—*The storm soon follows*,” he said peering out from thick brows.

Chapter 28
Sedge

Wedgewood

Outish banged open the door to the cabin and rushed in, heading to the in-country weapons chest. "There's going to be trouble," he said, lifting open the heavy, iron-bound lid. He pulled out a helmet and chain mail hauberk.

Achelous stood up from the tiny kitchen table where he and Baryy were playing a game of Hunter-Killer in the diffused, greenish sunlight slanting through the kitchen window. Spring was warming, and finches were building a nest above the window.

"What do you mean trouble?" Achelous asked as Outish fumbled with an axe.

"There's an Ascalon Defender in town, and she's marshalling Ogden's ward."

Achelous blinked. Baryy stood up from the table, careful not to disrupt the game pieces; he was winning. "An *Ascalon*." Baryy said frowning, "I didn't think there was such a thing."

"Oh. Well, there is! And she's here," said Outish trying on the helmet. Up to now, he'd donned his armor only twice, both times at Central Station, once to confirm it fit, and the second for his single day of in-country weapons training with Field Outfitting. He never expected to wear it for actual protection. As an intern, he was not expected to be proficient with period weapons and fighting styles, nor was it part of his Dianis astro-b indoctrination. "She's going to train us on how to fight Paleowrights."

Eyes widening Achelous started to form a response when Baryy beat him to it. "You can't be serious."

Bent over with the helmet on his head, an axe in hand, and the hauberk draped over a shoulder, Outish looked up. "Well, of course, she's serious. She's a bloody great Ascalon!" His eyes took on the glow of stars. "She's awesome," he breathed.

"Hang on there son, we don't get to pick sides in domestic affairs. We have a mission and a set of objectives. Picking a fight with the Paleowrights is way out of bounds." Achelous placed a hand on his hip.

Outish stood straight. "And what about the fight with the trogs? What do you call that?"

"Self-defense," Achelous replied evenly.

Outish shook his head. "They've just as much right, maybe even more to this planet as the humans. Yet we have no problem killing *them.*"

Achelous narrowed his focus. "It doesn't matter if they are trogs or mosquitoes. If the life form attacks us, we are authorized to defend ourselves. What have the Paleowrights done to you?"

Outish hesitated. "Well—nothing."

"Fine, then put the armor and weapons down."

The sudden storm brewing across the intern's face put the chief inspector in a mood more apt for dealing with brigands than a fellow agent. Baryy eyed the double-bladed axe, the edges gleaming dully. It was just like Achelous to furnish a neophyte with a first class weapon.

"But—"

"Yes?"

He looked away. "I told Mergund and Lettern I'd help."

The chief inspector slowly shook his head.

"But we're staying here, Atch. We're going to be living with these people. When the IDB leaves we'll depend on them. They'll be our friends. They are our friends."

Outish's passionate reasoning caused Achelous to squint. Finding or making friends on a hostile alien world often meant the difference between life and death for IDB agents. The trick was not compromising the mission in the process. Achelous softened his expression. Pursing his lips, he walked towards the door. "Help how?"

Outish mumbled, "Help fight the Paleowrights if they cause trouble." With the general hostility between Diunesis Antiquaria and Mother Dianis, and the memories of Paleowright treachery at Whispering bough, Timberkeep anti-Paleowright fervor was dry tinder in a hot summer forest. One spark...

"Outish, we're in Wedgewood. How many Paleowrights are there and where did they come from? How can they be a graver threat than the trogs?"

Then Outish explained that he'd seen ten Scarlet Saviors escorting a coach carrying three people, one of them a Paleowright viscount. There were rumors and speculation that hundreds more might be gathering at Lycealia. He explained that Sedge had summoned the Life Defenders, and for the moment they were tasked with watching the Paleowrights, that the Ascalon was going to provide tactics and weapons training to Ogden's ward, and Mergund and Lettern expected him to join them.

Baryy had his wallet out. "What's the Ascalon's name?"

"Christina Tara."

The agent entered the name into the multi-func. He waited for it to retrieve the data from Central Station, and read the display. He arched an eyebrow. Showing it to Outish, "Is that her?"

Outish peered at the holograph, "That's her, though she has a scar on her left jaw now."

He showed Achelous, who read the caption below the name: *The sole Al suri Ascalon Life Defender. Champion of Mother Dianis, spiritual leader of their warrior elite.* He handed the device back, thinking. "We should visit with Sedge—for trade discussions of course -- Odgen will be pleased if I can sell his future inventory of handbolts. And while we're at it ask Sedge about the Defenders and these Paleowrights you've seen. How do you know it was a viscount in the coach?"

"Ogden said so."

Achelous breathed deep and exhaled. "Paleowright viscounts don't just wander around paying homage to the faithful in the countryside; it's not in their DNA. And they certainly don't slum—their words--with Timberkeeps in Wedgewood."

Taking advantage of the chief inspector's quandary, Outish asked, "So, can I go?"

"And do what?" he asked. "Scarlet Saviors are the warrior elite of the Paleowrights. Remember your cover story: you are a trade runner bonded to a master trader. You cannot enlist in a Wedgewood ward and still serve as a trade runner, for that reason Ogden would be surprised if I allowed it. He will know as a trade runner I may send you anywhere in Isuelt at any time. He probably wouldn't accept you as a permanent shield-man, not unless you lived near Wedgewood. And think about this, one swipe of a Paleowright rachier, and you could be dead. This is not a grand adventure led by some vixen goddess, Outish. This is a primitive land where supporting life is a heavy cost and death comes quickly. For certain while you are an IDB intern you will not be marching with Timberkeeps against Paleowrights."

"This is a chance to keep tabs on the Timbers though," Baryy mused. "We're already learning things from Outish we might not have heard otherwise. If the Timbers adopt Outish as their own, and it appears they've taken a shine to him, it will help with our research later on. In their eyes, he's a Doroman and we're just pasty-faced Isonians."

Outish hefted the axe. "I've used an axe on Halor for wood chopping, but I was kind of looking forward to learning how to use it as a weapon." He turned sheepish, "After the fight in Battle Park against the trogs when Sedge came with the cavalry I've felt more like baggage than help."

Achelous didn't agree. The intern had acquitted himself well enough when they faced the troglodytes, even if he fumbled loading the handbolt. He gave it more thought. "This is what I want you to do, tell Mergund and Lettern I don't care if you attend training with them, time permitting, but your duties to me come first. Then you can stay in touch what is happening between the Timbers and the Paleowrights. Keep Baryy, and I informed. I'll make it clear to Ogden that I can't let you muster with his ward unless Wedgewood is under direct attack. At that point, we all may be mustering. Of course, it will never come to that, not while the IDB is here, we'll shift out first, or Clienen will send Ready Reaction to pull us out." He stared hard at the young intern and using his knuckles tapped him on the conical helmet. "Don't fight the Paleowrights Outish. Don't even get close. If we have to call Ready Reaction a board of inquiry will be interested to know what you were doing in the middle of a provincial fight. Suffice to say that's attention we don't need."

Baryy pulled on the bell cord. A delicate tinkling sound came from far above. He and Achelous looked up as a sentry called down from the tree walk, "State your business."

"Baryy Maximum and Achelous Forushen to see Sedge. He's expecting us."

The sentry waved his arm to an unseen person, and the equipment lift lowered on a stout hemp rope. The two traders stepped onto the platform and held on the railing as the elevator was cranked up the height of the tall trunk. With each crank they gained a better view of Wedgewood. Bivvies dotted the upper slopes, lodges and cabins the lower slopes, and Wide Lane, the main street, stretched from the Main Gate to Timber Hall at the far end of town. The panorama closed in as the lift rose amongst the branches. Nearing the top, they could hear the clanking of a gear pawl as the winch mechanism hoisted them through an opening in the floor of the tree walk. An archer wearing a studded leather vest and green woolen leggings eyed them critically, then without a word signaled for them to follow. The archer moved along the fortified tree walk around the bole until it came to a rope foot-bridge with wooden planking. The span crossed between two massive Ungerngerist citizens. Baryy noticed that earlier in their lives the trees had reached massive limbs across the gulf but had those had been delicately removed at the trunks. Making their way across the void, the bridge swayed with the tread of the three men, Achelous glanced down. Towns' folk walking Wide Lane were the size of mice. Across the bridge, he spied the capture pins for the structure. There were four, one for each supporting cable. A wooden mallet hung on one of the cable mounts. *A single good whack on each of those pins,* he thought, *and the bridge will drop like a trap door.*

They mounted a spiral staircase and climbed through yet another floor opening, emerging into a broad, expansive loft completely circling the tree. The roof overhead as the floor beneath was supported by the limbs of the Ungerngerist.

Sedge, his grey hair braided, turned from a telescope, and gave them a brief cocked smiled. His sharp eyes glinted from beneath his craggy brows. "Afternoon gents," he waved to a table with chairs, "I'm just spying on our Washentrufel friends." He wore a handsome brown cape that matched his pants in color and fabric. They were tucked into knee-high boots made of supple leather. His white linen shirt was open exposing a muscled chest and a thick mass of grey hair. A silver chain and large medallion hung amongst the mat. Achelous settled into his chair and reflected on the change in venue when last he saw the warlord in Battle Park.

"Washentrufel?" Baryy asked looking at Achelous then back to Sedge.

Sedge set the telescope down on a stand and waved to a guard, "Water for us, please."

He sat in a chair. "Yes. They're not advertising who they are, but my Scout's boss is certain one of them is a Washnen agent, and if true, so too is the other. Both of them are Nakish with Stith Drakas accents, and the younger one flaunts a rapier made by the premier sword maker in Nak Drakas. They're the kind of traveling companions I would expect a viscount to have, particularly when he comes to Wedgewood." He gave a wry smirk. "They're Washentrufel all right."

A troubled notion crinkled Achelous's eye. "Even so, we're far from the Frontier. It's not as if the Timbers are a threat to the Empire. What is the Washentrufel doing in Wedgewood?" The appearance of the Drakan secret service in Wedgewood was a new and unmodeled variable in the socio-economic calculus for Isuelt.

Sedge sniffed. "Riding herd on their Paleowright puppets I'll wager, and taking time to snoop around. His lordship the viscount has requested a meeting in front of the Clan Council. Probably wants to issue another of Hebert's inane decrees."

"How so?"

Sedge smiled, the one he reserved for knowing the unknown. "You've been around the continent once or twice master trader. I can assume you are no novice trade runner. Why do you think the Paleowrights have deigned to come to lowly Wedgewood in the form of a viscount, second only to the archbishop in Hebert, with two Washentrufel agents no less? The squads of Scarlet Saviors are for intimidation of course."

The chief inspector hesitated, debating whether he should tell Sedge what he really suspected or feign ignorance. Attempting to act nescient would only be disingenuous, and he needed Sedge's cooperation. "Your mine?"

"Yes, and what about our mine?"

"The aquamarine?"

The seasoned warlord gave an almost imperceptible nod. "The Paleowrights are bloody fanatics. I curse the day the Timbers found aquamarine down that hole."

Achelous had his own problems with aquamarine discoveries on Dianis. It was ironic that both he and Sedge were faced with the same threat but from different quarters. Not wanting to dwell on those tribulations he said, "As my message said, Ogden is developing a crossbow under license to me. It's a new design I came across in my travels. I'm wondering if perhaps we can organize a demonstration?" He withdrew Ogden's steel and wood handbolt from his holster and set it on the table.

The warlord looked, then reached across the table. "This is the one you gents were using against the trogs out in the park?"

Baryy nodded, "Works good."

Sedge stood, his movements quick and cat like, bearing no reflection of his grey hair and weathered cheeks. He held out a hand, "Quarrel?"

Baryy pulled one from an inside sheath and handed it fletchings-first. "You cock it by—"

"I see how the mechanism works," he said casually, half-distracted as he examined the craftsmanship. "Ogden forged my sword, and arms most of the wards. Men come from leagues around to armor up with him. We're lucky to have him." He slotted the quarrel, walked to the railing and cranked the lever back. Baryy jumped up to witness the shot. Sedge leaned over the platform railing and sighted down the length of the shaft. The steel arms thumped with their release. Baryy watched the white and black fletchings streak in a shallow arc as they followed the iron head into a rain cistern at the corner of a guard shack far below.

The warlord grunted. "A tad light to shoot at loglards from up here, but I saw you lads use it up close and personal. I've seen the Caltracks of Lamar, and the Assinians of the Warkenvaal use short bows from eenu-back to good effect. Bastards. All they did was run away when we got close, shooting at us while we took casualties. How many do you have?"

"Will have," answered Achelous from back at the table. "Og is putting the finishing touches on the third prototype. He's fabricating fifty for me."

"Yes, well tell the old goat to quit polishing his chamber pot and build the lot of them. I have a nasty foe to fight and for once would like to have eenu archers on my side." He handed the 'bolt to Baryy. Gazing off into the boughs, "A troop mounted with those would do well to scout and harass the trogs. It'll confuse the stink out of them. And confusion is a condition to exploit."

Achelous grinned. "Speaking of confusion. You remember my runner? The one rescued by those mercenaries in Battle Park?"

Sedge sat back down at the table, "You mean the one that ran his eenu to a lather?"

Achelous appreciated the warlord's discretion at not stating the obvious, that Outish had run for the hills with shameless abandon. It wasn't all of Outish's fault. Achelous had told him to ride for safety; he just didn't expect him to do with such zeal.

"Yes, well, he's made friends with shield-bearers in Ogden's ward. And he even helped us drive off a few troglodytes during the incursion yesterday. So now he's chafing at the bit to join your Ascalon Defender and fight those Scarlet Saviors you mentioned."

Sedge laughed. "From one extreme to the other. Your lad is better off staying on his fast eenu than facing the Red Rapers." He smirked knowingly, "'Course, he wouldn't be the first young buck bedazzled by the likes of Christina."

Baryy chimed in, "Be it peer pressure or the guises of that warrior goddess, he's training with them now. Even wearing his armor, which before he treated like pots and pans in the bottom of a cook's trunk."

Sedge laughed again. "Dare say I'm not surprised. I've known Christina since she was a Defender second class. While we can all agree about her womanly charms, she has an innate ability to lead, an astute sense of her surroundings, and is nigh unbeatable with a sword, the longer the better. Many a gruesome brute who took fun terrorizing Life Believers has regretted the sight of her. Most of them made the mistake men usually do: stared at her bosom while they should be swinging. She's earned the rank of Ascalon. And she's the only one there is. The Life Believers are hard pressed keeping new Defenders alive, and I doubt they have the wherewithal to test for another Ascalon soon. They're supposed to have a witan of three."

Achelous pursed his lips. "My runner told me you brought her here, along with two other Defenders. Surely the Mother's Faithful have need of her elsewhere? Wedgewood is protected. Compared to those who live in the hinterlands I doubt the Life Believers here are in any serious risk, aside from troglodyte incursions. I don't see how a Defender triad will add appreciably to your ten wards and two mercenary companies."

It was Sedge's turn to sit back and consider what he would or should share with the two traders. True enough, they'd spilt trog blood together and the trader's assistant, so his scouts told him, was no friend of that sneak Baldor. But he was careful in sharing information with men not of his command, non-Timbers, and particularly with outsiders. These two were traders and talked to many people, which cut both ways. It could be an advantage to Sedge if he cultivated and recruited them as part of his intelligence network and a disadvantage if they let their lips waggle. On balance, however, he'd have to share information if he expected the trader to offer any in return. Achelous and his apprentice were inquisitive, asking many questions according to his reports, more so than the usual traveling trinket seller looking to offload their wares. "This visit of the viscount's has been a long time coming. The day they hauled that aquamarine pegmatite out of the mine I knew we were in for trouble." A speckled magpie swooped through the veranda alighting on a massive branch near the railing. It dropped down on a platform feeder and ruffled around in the seeds pecking for just the right one. Having found a large acorn remnant, it cast a critical eye at the trio, pondered their meaning, and dove off the platform swooping in an undulating flight to the tree next door. Sedge resumed. "Not everyone in Hebert is an Antiquarian. We have friends. When word reached us that the viscount was lobbying the archbishop for action and the Washentrufel was in attendance at those meetings, well, I told Woodwern we'd better start preparing. You see Achelous, it's a mine. It can't be moved."

"So you called the Alon," Baryy said, using colloquial for Ascalon.

"Yes, among other things." He pointed at a tree fort. "We've built more of those. A lot more."

Chapter 29
Timber Hall

Wedgewood

Christina slowed her pace. Spectators lined the lane to Timber Hall, the seat of the Mearsbirch Clan Council. They were two, three, and more ranks deep near the hall. Word had spread quickly of Viscount Helprig's demand for an audience with the Town Board. He was about to face a joint a session of both the Town Board and the Clan Council. Never having been to Wedgwood before, Ogden had advised the Defenders on the backdrop of the gathering. Of the two committees, the council wielded the most power as Wedgewood would be little more than a squirrel den without the clan, but the Town Board handled all of the administrative tasks, planned construction projects, collected levies, managed the town facilities, and set ordinances for its inhabitants. Usually, a harmonious relationship reigned between the two due to the Town Board being comprised entirely of Timberkeeps. Nepotism between the two bodies an established norm: a wife may be on the council and the husband on the board or vice versa. If dispute occurred between the assemblies it moved into the kitchens, dens, and bedrooms where conflict resolution was mediated.

Each administrative body held eleven members. Each member was allowed two assistants to attend them at their meetings. Each member and their assistants were also allowed to invite four concerned or interested parties to either witness or bare testimony at the hearing. Those invitations came in the form of writs, and those writs were in popular demand for the viscount's visit.

Dutifully carrying Ogden's writs, the four approached the Hall. "Perhaps we should find a side entrance," offered Alex, one of Christina's two fellow Defenders. "We'll attract less attention." Alex was echoing an unspoken creed amongst his brethren: Never glory in the renown of one's deeds.

To which Ogden laughed heartily. "Be too late for that. Half these people have come hoping to see you and care not one cone for the Paleos. They want to see Defenders, and they want to see her." He smiled at Christina as they kept their pace. "We go in the front door.

They've already spotted us. If we try for a side door, they will just follow us."

Ignoring the growing crowd of townsfolk following in their wake Christina viewed Timber Hall and what must be one of the oldest and undoubtedly the grandest building in Wedgewood. It stood at the end of Wide Lane, the very end of Main Street, in a cul-de-sac ringed by massive Ungerngerists. The exterior stone walls were grown over by lichen and vines. More lichen and moss grew on the shake shingles. The gracious symmetry of the edifice was accentuated by the numerous gable ends.

"Look at all those windows," breathed Feolin, the third Defender in the trio.

"Oi," admitted Ogden, "there be twenty two porches, I know, in me youth as a novice apprentice I made the hinges for all those windows. Each one lets light into the chamber of each of the twenty two council and board members. Those are on the third and fourth floors. The second floor, with that row of vertical windows down the two sides, is where the assistants have their desks, and is open in the center so you can look down into the council camber. You'll see when we get in there."

As the four approached the steps leading to the expansive deck, the crowd lined on either side of the walk grew silent.

Christina followed behind Ogden as he led the way up the steps. A hand, palm up, thrust out from the crowd, "Please Alon, bless me youngin, she's been sickly and can use all the help you can give her."

Christina turned, and the mother, wispy brown hair poking out from a colorful woolen bonnet, thrust her child out in outstretched arms.

She peered down at the child, Christina shoved her gauntlets under her belt. A hundred eyes in the throng watched her every move. Stepping forward she lifted the girl to her face. The nose was running, eyes watery, cheeks red against the light chill. Concern darkened Christina's countenance, she asked, "I have heard..." she paused, looking at the mother, "is it...?"

The mother looked down, nodded once and sobbed. "Oi, the Curse."

Christina cradled the child and said, "Mother loves you. Her heart beats in you. All things have their place and you my precious child have yours. Mother watches." Standing on the steps, towering above the woman she reached a hand and rested it upon her bonnet.

"Bring her to me after this day's affairs. There are things I can do. I would learn more of this Curse."

Depositing the child with her mother Christina turned to the crowd and met their stares with her piercing gaze. These were her people, and she was fiercely proud of them.

Ogden coughed. "Excuse me, Alon," he said clearly and respectfully, "they are waiting for us to enter the Hall."

"We come to Wedgewood, my fellows, Alex and Feolin," she addressed them each. "The north wind blows, but I have found a brilliant folk here, and my heart warms in the spirit and love they have shown us. Over these coming days, you will see us amongst you. I want to know each and every one of your names." She surveyed the throng, a smile drifting and fleeting as she met the gaze of those who offered it.

Christina turned, hope plain on her countenance, and they approached the massive doors where the Master at Arms stood with two fearsome guards with tall halberds.

Ogden made his apology, "Alon, the rules are no weapons in the Hall except those carried by the Master at Arms and his deputies."

"Oi," replied the barrel chested master. His black beard thick as coal, the conical helm on his head bearing the crest of Clan Mearsbirch. He paused to let the trio of Defenders understand the import, but then he added, "However, Darry here," indicating a deputy sheriff, "will be glad to carry your arms and will be at your side all the while."

A deputy standing behind the master bowed deeply. "Be my honor to bear the weapons that have defended so many Believers. My true honor indeed."

Alex smiled broadly, "As generous an offer as we could ever ask." He unbuckled his sword.

The Hall interior smelled of ancient pine. Christina raised her head taking in the massive wooden beams supporting the roof high above. Every inch richly lacquered and aged to a dark caramel from decades of pipe smoke, fireplaces, and the hot air of constituents. Family banners of each clan holder hung from the rafters, their colorful and varied patterns adding a riot of relief to the timber atmosphere. Nestled between the pennants were tapestries depicting momentous events in the history of Clan Mearsbirch.

The Hall was packed. Windows were thrown open to vent the heat of so many bodies. People thronged the second and third floor mezzanines, and the youngins, who did not need a writ, were admonished to show respect and refrain from throwing spit wads onto the crowd below.

Usually, the joint Board-Council Meeting was an annual event. Today was an exception. During the year the two groups communicated with each other through the numerous family ties amongst the members.

Following the precedent of the Annual Meeting the two committees, with their respective chairmen sitting side-by-side, sat in twenty two chairs in a single row near the rear of the Hall. The chairs were placed behind one long set of tables stretching half the width of the Hall forming a solid front of administrators. However, there the precedent ended. Instead of the normal tiers of assistants, witnesses, and writ-holder chairs placed directly in front of the administrators an aisle was made to lead directly from the enormous doors of the Hall, straight to the witness box, an area designated in front of the phalanx. A potentially hostile phalanx to the witnesses to be sure. To either side of that aisle temporary, elevated bench works had been erected. Timberkeeps, if anything, were mindful of one's comfort during tedious council meetings. Everyone in the Hall would have a seat with a view.

Christina, Alex, and Feolin were given seats of honor: The first three chairs, at ground level, immediately to the right of the eleventh clan council member.

The hubbub of the gathering diminished to an expectant murmur as the board and council members filed in order from the rear vestibule. Each body proceeded along the left or right wall, taking their assigned chairs, with the chairmen leading the way. The junior most members sat the farthest from the center. Once all members were seated, both chairpersons raised their gavels and said, "I hereby call this joint session of Town Wedgewood and Clan Mearsbirch to order," and then struck their dockets.

Woodwern, the clan chairman, turned jovially to his Town Board counterpart, a woman, and said loudly, "Ula, we've quite the witness gallery here today Margern, did you exceed your quota?"

Margern, famous for blushing at the slightest provocation, did so. "Why no Woodwern, but is that your whole family I see in the second loft?"

The chairman, acting surprised, looked up. "Why it is indeed! How did they get in here?" And with that the crowd roared with laughter, some cheering, others hooting, for the chairman and chairwoman were brother and sister.

The pair waited till the throng subsided. Then the chairwoman said with a long sigh, "I guess Woodwern... we should get to the business at hand."

At that, the chairman appeared to steel himself and brought his gavel down again. In a loud voice, the timbre practiced from commanding many a raucous clan hoot and moot, the chairman said, "The council summons the petitioner."

Viscount Helprig was furious. He has been told the meeting would start at the top of the hour and so he purposefully arrived with his escort late, a quarter past. Not enough to cause insult, but enough to let the Timmies know who was in command. Instead of being immediately ushered into the presence of the council, he was forced to wait outside in the lane with his aide, flanked by two rows of Scarlet Saviors.

Finally, the tall ironbound doors, whose raised and weathered grain attested to the ferocity of Mount Mars winters, swung open and the Master-at-Arms called from the portal, "His Viscount, the exalted Lorentis Helprig, second to the archbishop of Hebert, Paleowright Seat of all Isuelt, servant to the soul of Diunesis Antiquaria, you are summoned to appear before the Mearsbirch-Wedgewood elders."

"At least the moron recited my title correctly," fumed Helprig. He, his aide – an astute middle-aged priest -- and his escort of ten Scarlet Saviors marched forward toward the high, broad stone steps that led to a veranda that lay before the doors. Perhaps their pace was a bit fast, but he would be glad to be rid of the gawking crowd of peasants as they pressed in from all sides, completely unpoliced, not a watch or guard in sight! How deplorably uncivilized. As he trudged up the stone steps, he saw a rank of armored halberdiers flanking the doors. Their existence became evident when the spectators in front of them stepped back, as if on cue. Two guardsmen, each with halberds half again as long as the men were tall, stood at either side of the opening. The weapon shafts planted hard on the deck with their gleaming blades straight up.

"Well, at last, a sign of respect that I am due," he whispered to his aide.

The first two of the Scarlet Saviors, resplendent in their yellow and crimson plate armor, led the viscount to the portal, but then the two guardsmen dropped their Halberds at an angle baring the opening. The Master-at-Arms broke from his position at attention and looked with alarm at the armed ranks of liveried warriors. "My lordship, when we granted your request for an audience your aide was advised of our tenants. No armed men are allowed in the Hall, except in time of war."

The aide, a Paleowright predicant, arched an eyebrow, but when he saw the sergeant unrelenting, he frowned. The viscount, however, held no restraint. "Your rules do not apply to me. I am beholden to no authority other than the archbishop."

The Master-At-Arms smiled, obsequious. "I am most sorry for the misunderstanding." He took a step back and appeared ready to signal the guardsmen back to attention when he said instead, "We wish you no distress. Since you are unable to enter our premises without your armed escort, this council meeting is closed." And with that, he signaled for the portal doors to close.

As the mighty doors swung slowly closed the eyes of both the aide and viscount widened in dismay. Even the helmeted heads of the lead Saviors tilted up as they watched with surprise the portal closing.

"Wait!" called the aide. The doors stopped without command from the sergeant. The aide and viscount had a hurried, whispered conversation, hardly private in the midst of the crowd before the portal.

"We've traveled at great person expense in time and monies to come to this—" the aide waved a hand at a loss for a polite description of his surroundings, "you cannot bar the way! We demand admittance!"

The sheriff stood stone faced.

"This is an affront!" declared the priest.

The Master-at-Arms signaled for the doors to close. "Affront or no. No weapons in the Hall."

Another hurried discussion with the viscount and the aid said to the Master-at-Arms, "Do you guarantee his Excellency's exalted life in your hall, under penalty of forfeiture of all properties in Wedgewood to the holy throne of Hebert?"

The Master-at-Arms, without conferring with the administrators, said, "Of course. All folk, great or small, are under the council's protection whilst between these walls."

The two Paleowright clergy conferred again, and then the viscount said, “We shall proceed. My honor guard will remain here. Captain Irons, you will attend us.”

With a flourish and a bow, the Master-at-Arms signaled for the guardsmen to raise their weapons and he stood aside.

The viscount entered the packed hall with his aide trailing to the right and the Scarlet Savior, Captain Irons, to his left, bereft of his weapons. The lord’s red robe, trimmed with gold, and his scarlet pantaloons tucked into white lace-topped hose made a stark contrast to the surrounding mass of tans, browns, blacks, and greens of the simple woodland folk who’d come to gawk. And gawk they did. The teenagers pointed at the viscount’s hat: the tall mitre and rear covering that flowed down his back matched his robe. The mitre was split in the middle so that its gold interior was exposed to view. The viscount walked in a peculiar synchronized manner tied to the tap of his ceremonial staff mounted with a bluish green gem that could be nothing other than aquamarine. The predicant beside him matched his master’s gate, but the Scarlet Savior walked stiffly, his sword hand fidgeting at his hip.

A youngin in the mezzanine turned is head away so his mother couldn’t see. He inserted a juicy spit wad in a reed tube and took careful aim at the viscount’s hat. Just as he inhaled, his mother screeched and snatched the boy’s arm no one the wiser amidst hubbub except for lad’s friends who laughed and giggled, having put him up to it.

Traversing the long aisle, the focus of so many curious and judgmental eyes, the predicant took the lead from his master and positioned himself before the council. He made the same introduction of the viscount as the Master-at-Arms, but somehow managed it to last twice as long and seem thrice as grand. The viscount, in recognition of the council, gave the barest nod the occasion would allow.

Making a point of it, the aide cast about looking for a chair for his liege. He spied a three-legged stool off to one side, but that plainly would not do. They would be forced to stand and suffer the oversight of their hosts.

“Well, eh hem,” the clan chairman cleared his throat, “We all here at Wedgewood—“

“Sir,” the predicant interrupted him. While the aid’s own vestments paled in comparison to his master’s, his attitude was up to the task. "It is customary that you and your council should rise in the presence of the viscount and present yourself for his inspection."

The chairman blinked, then blinked again, his jaw working while the council members stirred and a murmur rippled through the attendance. "Uh, inspection?" he choked.

Margern placed a hand on his arm, "Woodwern, may I?"

The chairman eased himself back and grumbled something.

"Sir, it would be our pleasure to present ourselves to your lordly master if it were but our custom. We are unfortunately simple folk," she waved a graceful hand to her left and right indicating the two ranks of administrators, "not accustomed to the attentions of those in such high and lofty offices. Our own councils as you must understand are bound by long tradition, tradition governed by clan law and town ordinances. As you are within the *Town* Hall," and she emphasized the word, smiling sweetly and fluttering her lashes at the clan chairman in reference to some internal debate, "the Town Board decides the protocol upon which our meetings will be governed, and that includes to whom and when we will bow, genuflect, salute, or otherwise present ourselves." Without taking a breath, she went on. "It is your good fortune that I am the town chairwoman and I, by obvious happenstance, have the entire Town Board with me. So if it be by your choosing, we could adjourn this meeting, and I could reconvene the Town Board, and we could discuss this matter of presentation and inspection. I would subsequently ask the board to put it to a debate whereby we would thereafter vote on the motion. Now—"and she demurred sweetly at the aide, "If you are amenable we wouldst call yourself to bear witness and present to us all of the customs and necessaries of presentation and inspection so that our debate reflected on all the pertinent facts—"

"No, that shall not be necessary chairwoman," the aide said, slinging the title out like it were a dirty dishrag. He leaned over to the viscount, said a few words and the viscount nodded.

"We will allow this deviance of Church protocol in light that Wedgewood is so far removed and isolated from the civilized world."

"Are you sure?" she asked. "It wouldn't be a bother. We would love to hear about how you do things in Hebert. We could have tea and—"

"I am sure madam chairwoman."

The use of the honorific in front of her title seemed to appease the matron, though by her disappointed expression, she looked like a badger parted from her favorite log. An afternoon of tea and polite conversation as to the world's affairs would have been so much fun. "Very well," she said, reluctance heavy in her tone.

"Eh hem, shall we get back to business?" queried the chairman. "You've come a long way. I'm sure we are all interested in what you have to say." He pointed at the throng seated on the stacked benches.

Up to this moment, the viscount's expression had remained a benign mask. He took in everything and missed no nuance. The chairman realized this and suspected that one-on-one in a public debate the patriarch would be more than his match, but Woodwern had not risen to the most powerful position in Wedgewood by being a fool. Margern was where she was, on purpose.

The viscount spoke, "Yes, we shall come to business as I have more pressing matters to attend. We have traveled here on a side errand to express and safeguard our interests."

The chairman steeled himself, mentally ticking off the possibilities and kept coming back to the same conclusion the joint planning session had arrived at that morning. He could feel is blood rising, again. With practiced diplomacy, he responded, "And those interests are?"

"Ah. I am so glad you asked. It has come to our attention that you have a mine here in Wedgewood." The noise of bored feet and restless chairs in the hall had been rising, but at that moment not a creak nor shuffle could be heard.

"We have a number of mines. What of them?"

"There is one mine, in particular, the Tolkroft mine." The silent crowd turned to ranks of glaring statues.

The chairman's gaze shifted from the audience back to the viscount; the two locked eyes. Taking a page from Margern's book, he said innocently, "Ah yes, everyone has an interest in Tolkroft. You'll be in the majority there."

"It is reported the Tolkroft mine is producing aquamarine. Do you deny that?"

"Deny?" The chairman waved a dismissive hand, "The aquamarine is of little use to us. As a bauble, it has its virtue like the aquamarine gemstone on your lordship's staff. If you be wanting the aquamarine, we can arrange a fair price for it. You needn't have traveled so far; our works manager can negotiate—"

"Ah," interrupted the viscount, "but alas you miss a fine point of Antiquaria law."

Rolling his jaw before he spoke, the chairman asked, "And that is?"

"You understand of course that Diunesis Antiquaria is the protector and administrator of all things Ancient. And that aquamarine was brought to Isuelt by the Ancients for use in their star-spanning commerce. Aquamarine is at the very core of their divine powers. The sanctum of all things they held holy. And when the Ancients departed Isuelt they left it in trust to us, the Paleowrights, in safe keeping for their eventual return, including all their artifacts, in their original state, to pave the way for the greater glories of our world."

The chairman, a devout of Mother Dianis, recalled in a vague corner of his mind some of what the priest said. Now the man's words brought the subject to perfect clarity. As a past magistrate, he had a disturbing sense of where the priest was leading. The bored-crowd noise began to rise again, but the chairman was intent. "Your point is?"

"The aquamarine is the property of Diunesis Antiquaria; it belongs to the church. We shall safeguard it. The Ancients stored it in the mountain, and we've come to reclaim it." The murmur in the Hall took a decidedly different tone.

Woodwern wanted to rise up out his chair and begin pacing as was his wont when he aimed to interrogate a witness during examination, but he sensed Margern calm and contemplative, and it settled him. He knew his sister to be coldly calculating the outcomes, and his job was to get her all the information the Paleowrights would divulge.

On cue, the predicant said, "We are prepared to compensate you for your efforts in removing the aquamarine from the mountain. We are willing to offer you a silver durket for every thousand weight delivered to Hebert." Hearing his aide's smooth delivery of the offer the viscount assumed a smug expression.

Woodwern leaned back. He was on familiar ground now: negotiating with a cut-rate chinster who wanted everything for nothing, the usual starting position of an unscrupulous buyer with no interest in building a long-term partnership. Always bad for business, chinsters were the kind where you flipped the *open* sign to *closed* when you saw them coming. "A silver durket wouldn't pay for the eenu feed to haul it there."

"And then there is the matter of the gold," the aid went on as if the chairman hadn't spoken.

His brows furrowed. "Gold?" Woodwern asked. The Hall was again quiet enough to hear a squishy baby fart in the upper gallery.

"Any gold deposited or encased with the aquamarine is a gift of the Ancients and is therefore under Paleowright domain." The crowd exploded in jeers. Spit wads rained down. A rotten potato arched over the viscount's mitre nearly hitting Margern who merely ducked aside, willing to suffer friendly fire in the name of a good cause if poor aim.

A burly man in the upper row of the main floor gallery stood with rock and took careful aim. Sedge, seated in his First Assistant's chair leapt up and in his best parade ground tenor, roared "Enough!" The Hall fell instantly silent, pregnant with expectation and yet with an air of disappointment. The two clergy turned to look at him. The man with the rock looked around like a truant child, then sat down with a thump.

From his chair in the front row, closest to council, Sedge put his hands on hips and bowed to the committee. "Apologies dear sirs and ladies for my outburst." He dropped his hands letting his cloak fall open, purposefully exposing the ivory-hilted short sword. He remained standing as was customary for an assistant offering testimony.

Margern said, "My Lord Viscount, may I introduce our warlord, Sedge the Steadfast, Victor of Blummington, Holder of the King's Warrant, and—" she stopped and peered at Sedge, blushing, "I'm sorry, I've forgotten your other titles."

He gave her a bow. "You honor me with my name alone madam chairwoman."

The predicant leaned over and whispered into the viscount's ear. "Ah yes," said the viscount aloud. Then, "I was apprised the Timmies had engaged your services." For a moment the two men eyed each other like adversaries before the prize fight. Then dismissing Sedge with a flippant wave, he turned back to the council and said, "You have been served notice by an official of the Church as to our claim against Tolkroft Mine. I give you one day to consider your response and deliver it to my aide. After which I will offer my observances and advice to the archbishop with or without your response." Abruptly the viscount pivoted in a practiced motion summarily terminating the interview and strode from the hall; all pretenses with his staff forgotten, his aide hurrying to keep pace.

"Bah! Did you see them? They were like toads on a stump. Buffoons," fumed the viscount.

"What did you expect?" Larech, the Washentrufel agent asked. "You didn't exactly open the door to negotiations." He and the other agent, not having writs, and not wanting to be seen in the Hall with the Paleowrights, had gained entry via a scullery entrance in the basement.

The viscount waved dismissively at the agent and turned a gloomy expression out the window. His aide rented the whole second floor of the dark, moss-covered, back-woods inn. He thought it incredibly dingy, but the Timmies, the toady fools, thought it the height of hospitality. A scarlet trooper stood watch at the head of the stairs. No Timmy allowed to pass, not even the inn keeper.

"Fortunately this little excursion has been productive on our end," Larech said, sitting patiently in a bentwood rocker, a teacher attempting to instruct a student in the finer points of intelligence gathering. "My assistant made acquaintance with a group sensitives who are bound for a secluded conclave. It offers—"

"Honestly Larech, why do you persist in this farce? Your superiors are twisting your tail. These tree sods are vulgar louts. Find other more suitable subjects to study. It's a waste of time I tell you." The viscount spoke to the gauze curtains as he watched a young girl skip down the street.

Larech's professional detachment never wavered. "As your lord well knows, the Timbers have been contracting out their sixthsense skills. There are more adepts here than anywhere else on Isuelt. The emperor is concerned they could be used against us. We must evaluate their capabilities."

Helprig deigned to look over his should at the senior agent, "And if they pose a risk?"

Larech had ridden in the stuffy coach with the viscount all the way from Hebert. Helprig had insisted on keeping the curtains sealed to keep out the dust out. He had dined with the priest more times than he cared to think. The man's constant baiting and clumsy probing for information was fundamental to his nature and as relentless as a mouse hunting seeds. "Then we will inform Commandant Fritach, and if compelling will present the evidence to the emperor. He will decide on a course of action."

Unfazed by Drakan bureaucracy, it didn't compare to the Antiquarian Church, the viscount cut to the chase "I'd recommend you exterminate the lot of them. Bring your vaunted Marshall Blannach here to chop their trees down and root out their badger burrows."

Unfazed, the agent tilted his head. Razing Wedgewood would be convenient for the Paleowrights as they would have their aquamarine mine and the deaths of a few thousand souls attributed to the emperor. "Be that as it may, I still need to collect our test subjects. The professors at the academy are most insistent. They have the emperor's ear."

"And if your little group of sensitives refuse to go willingly?"

The viscount sought every opportunity to engage the Washentrufel and by extension the Drakan military against the Timberkeeps. Anything to shift the cost and burden from the Antiquarian coffers. "Then I will have to borrow the services of your honor guard and compel our pigeons to come with us."

"Ha! Finally, you show some backbone. Force is all these morons understand, and I will show them force."

There was a polite nock at the door.

"Enter!" snapped Helprig.

A Scarlet Savior in full armor opened the door. "Sire, a messenger has delivered a packet for Agent Larech."

The agent held out his hand and the guard advanced into the room. Sitting in the rocker, he opened the envelope. He waited for the guard to leave before retrieving one of two messages from the packet.

He read the first message. "Seems an informant of ours, a creature by the name of Baldor Prairiegrass has an aquamarine crystal as long as your leg that he'd like to show us. Price is four silver durkets." He held the note out to Helprig who turned from the window. "Interested?"

The viscount snatched the note and eyed the agent suspiciously. Larech just smiled.

The viscount read the message then tossed it onto the agent's lap. "He says it's not his to sell, but we might want to see it. It's your silver. Pay him what you want. We've nothing else to do for the moment. I assume you know how to reach this, this, cutpurse?"

"I do." Larech read the second message. "Hmm, it appears for another sum he's willing to sell us information on a trader by the name of Achelous. Seems the man is guilty of interrogating your

Lycealia curate when the site guards were away, then blocked the curate from enforcing Antiquarian law on the site by allowing his companions to inspect the ruins unaccompanied. He says that later he overheard numerous strange conversations with the other weapons traders in his group."

Helprig's aide, the predicant, who'd been drafting dispatches sitting at a tiny desk in the corner of the room, set his quill down and looked up.

Exasperation flared anew, and the viscount snatched the missive and read it, seemingly distrusting every word of the agent. He read it and harrumphed, "We hear this drivel morning, evening, and on the privy. Yokels will sell their insane babbling grandmother for a few silver believing she's been touched by the Ancients." He reread the missive. "The curate did complain to me about an insolent Tivorian who forced him under penalty of death to stand aside and let his men trample through the ruins. At the minimum, we should bring charges and have the trader publicly flogged for desecrating a holy site. We need to trumpet from the parapets that when we declare a ruin under our protection it is with the full might and authority of Antiquarian Law!"

"Tivorian?" asked the predicant. He arched a brow and went to draw open the door to the adjoining room. Into the room he said, "Captain, a moment please."

"What is the meaning of this?" Helprig snapped.

Captain Irons came in.

Ignoring the prelate, the predicant asked, "Captain, did the Lycealia curate say the trader was Tivorian?"

"Bah, what of it," scoffed Helprig.

Irons replied, "Yes."

Turning to Helprig, the predicant offered, "A Tivorian trader by the name of Achelous is here in Wedgewood?"

Befuddled for the moment, Helprig's jaw hung slack, but Captain Irons caught on. "Here in Wedgewood? What is the Mother's spawn doing here?"

Helprig swiveled to the Scarlet Savior still missing the meaning.

"Exactly," said the predicant.

Larech, not to be left out of any intrigue asked, "And this man is of some import?"

“If it is the same trader Achelous from Tivor, and I’ve not heard that name before, then he is the aide to none other than Marisa Pontifract, of Marinda Merchants.”

The viscount’s jaw clicked shut. Then he growled, “That whore bitch?”

The predicant smiled. “None other than.”

“And she is a whore bitch because?” Larech prodded.

“She’s the one who convinced the aorolmin of Tivor to refuse our demands for Tivor to cease trade with Linkoralis.”

“Oh,” Larech said. He knew well of the flap between the Linkoralis and Isuelt Paleowright branches. On the surface, the disagreement was about aquamarine trade across the ocean and the bishop of Linkoralis wanting to sell Ancient artifacts. At the heart of the dispute, however, was control. The Antiquarian Church on Isuelt was on a mighty tear to halt any aquamarine or artifact trafficking not of their own design.

Helprig handed the message back, more thoughtfully this time. “Your informant may be more than the typical clawing beggar. Pay him half of what he wants and learn everything he knows. Traders are a chin flapping lot, always quick with the rumor. But if this is the same Achelous, and you need to confirm it is, then we shall want...” he paused, seeking a suitable description, “a private interview with him, here, without interference, before we leave.” Then he thought upon it further. “No-- I think we should have him accompany us to Herbert. I will have our captain here arrange it.”

Chapter 30
Murali's

Wedgewood

Achelous watched Ogden's deft hammer blows pound rhythmically at the task, driven seemingly by machine rather than man. Mergund handled the mandrel, a long straight steel rod that Ogden hammered the orange-hot iron bar around. With each strike of the hammer more of the bar enveloped the rod as it lay on the black anvil. Mergund, wearing heavy gloves, carefully rotated the rod to keep it from sticking to and being welded to the bar. Even with the heat of the glowing metal and the repeated swings of the hammer, a scarce bead of sweat crowned Ogden's brow. His arms rippled with corded muscles; each hammer stroke welded the malleable iron around the steel mandrel, shaping it into a long tube and bringing the gun barrel closer to completion.

"Oi, mind you," Ogden said as he used stout iron tongs to twist the molten bar and aimed fresh blows, "If you want five hundred of these," he looked at Achelous for confirmation, "I'll be needing to try some of your ideas to speed up the work, but for now, for our first go, this will have to do."

Achelous stood staring at the anvil yet conscious of the Ascalon sitting cross-legged on an armor chest in the corner. While Achelous and Celebron initially vetoed the idea of bringing anyone else in on the project, Ogden stood firm. His beliefs and his trust in Christina so complete he was willing to walk away from the project rather than offend her. Moreover, the Ascalon Defender was assisting his ward, and she was often at the armory. Ogden refused to curtail her movements or keep any secret from her. So Achelous and Celebron met with the flaxen-haired paragon and struck a bargain. Christina had professed little interest in their secret endeavor. Her own mission and obligations to Sedge the subject of her attentions. Ogden was a Life Believer, and she had intimated to Ogden, she would honor his wishes of secrecy in the matter. Ogden was appalled when Achelous suggested she give an oath to not divulge the clandestine work. Ogden replied, "Life Defenders are naught but their word. She has said she will stay silent and so she will to her grave."

Achelous, glancing over to where Christina sat atop the chest incongruously weaving a basket, acknowledged that she was one of the most capable warriors he'd ever met, firmly in the company of Prince Fire Eye. Yet the two beings couldn't be more different. One human, one reptile, they were the kind of champion that you didn't need to see them in action to know they were fearsome. The woman exuded a latent, controlled skill akin to an autoban mechwarrior. Moreover, his trader savvy and experience told him she was not a person to be swayed by physical threats or immoral advances.

Achelous's thoughts turned to other matters. Ogden was in for a surprise when he learned they would eventually need thousands of the rifles, each model successively superior to the last, but it was best to let the weaponsmith work his way into the realization, one hammer blow at a time.

Against the sharp pulse of each strike, the occasional spark of molten metal flying, Achelous' attention turned back to Christina and her timeless art of weaving the basket. The practice of token bestowal was something neither he nor Baryy was aware of. He'd have to make an entry in the Life Believer's practices journal. Life Defenders bestowed small favors upon their charges, blessings of their passings, tokens of attention for other Believers to take heart from. Christina weaved baskets in a distinctive pattern and then branded her name and title to them. The talismans were highly treasured by Life Believers and displayed proudly, hallowed by a servitor of the Mother herself. Foes who sought to avail themselves of the holder of such a memento thought twice about it as Defenders were quick to avenge those they favored. Curious, Achelous asked, "Why weave baskets?" She paused and looked up. "I mean wood carving, painting..."

"Baskets are vessels that serve. Every person needs one. They should be strong to carry their charge yet appealing to the one who bears it." Christina threaded a blue wicket into the emerging bin. "In truth master trader, I find it soothing to weave while I contemplate the world and those around me."

Her green eyes, cast dark in the foundry, seemed to see through his soul. He wanted to pull away, but stood rooted.

"Were you at the council meeting today master trader?" she asked.

Sitting atop the weapons chest, her hands busy, she studied him, and Achelous had an itch at the nape of his neck. He wanted to reach up and scratch it; he wondered with suspicion if the Ascalon was an adept. There was no record of it in her file. "No, but my assistant told me about it." In truth, Baryy had recorded the event with his multi-func via a nanobot perched in the rafters and replayed the holovid at the cabin. The recording was a useful historical artifact documenting a moment in the cultural development of Dianis and even now sat archived in the IDB Dianis knowledge base.

Christina uncoiled from her perch, leaving her basket behind. "What do think you of the Paleowright demands?"

Ogden gave the barrel a vicious blow, and Mergund groaned. "Easy master, you'll dent the barrel. I fear bending of the mandrel. It's heating up and becoming soft."

Achelous ignored Ogden's angst. "I think it's typical of the Paleowrights."

"How so?" she asked.

"They make unreasonable demands they know you have no intention of meeting and start negotiating from there."

She watched a spark fly from the bar, and a black smudge appear as Ogden lifted the hammer. The smudge faded back to orange.

"So then what are their real terms? What negotiating tactics do think they will," she ran a hand across the hafts of halberds stacked in the weapons rack, "employ."

Achelous stared at her, wondering her intent. "Their real terms?" His breath heavy, he chose not to answer. "As for tactics, certainly they will offer silver, but probably not much. Trinket trade, blockade, and armed aggression are more their style. Paleowrights are not subtle. They have too much power and power corrupts. There must be three hundred Scarlet Saviors in and around Hebert they can call upon. If the archbishop wanted he could march the Hebert foot battalions. I bet he could put a thousand men in the field, easy." He didn't want to excite or alarm his hosts, it was even counter to IDB doctrine to offer guidance to one party over another, but he'd seen the recording of the meeting in the Hall. Baryy had run the viscount's speech pattern, intonation, and body language through the IDB behavior analyzer, and as puffy as the clergyman seemed to be, there was real malice behind his meaning. Ogden should be warned of it.

"But would their clergy pursue a war, over a mine?"

Now the Ascalon asked the important question. She came to it so quickly Achelous guessed she'd been stewing over it. He shrugged, "It's not just a mine, its aquamarine, the jewel of the Ancients." The last he could not say without a wry smile, parroting back Paleowright dogma that was both fact and folklore, and absolutely irrelevant to anyone incapable of building a field generator. He tried a different tack. "They like wearing and showing off their aquamarine baubles, but gold pays the freight. Since they hold a monopoly in in the aquamarine trade, and tightly control the sale of every gem, they can't very well have you digging it out of the ground and selling it as jewelry. But never mind that, Scarlet Saviors, churches, and even viscounts, don't come cheap. It may all be a ruse to get your gold. And they don't have to launch an overt war to get it; they could do something more devious."

"As such?" she prodded, all the while Ogden and Mergund alternately heated the iron bars wrapped around the mandrel and then hammer-welded them into a seamless tube, slowly working their way toward the end.

"There are many beautiful things of value. The Paleowrights could threaten any of them. Take for example the Ungerngerist."

Odgen paused in his work and glanced up with a quizzical expression.

"The Paleowright's could force you to attack them, at the time and place of their choosing."

"The clan would fight," she said now standing by the forge, staring into its coals, oblivious to the heat.

He nodded, the coals glinted orange from her eyes. "What's to keep them from coming to Mount Mars, setting up a logging camp, and start chopping these magnificent trees down and leaving them to rot?"

"They wouldn't!" gasped Mergund, holding onto the steel rod.

"I've seen more devious acts lad. You Timberkeeps would howl in fury. You can't protect the entire forest. You'd be forced to attack, and the Paleowrights would be ready for you." He let the ramifications sink in. "An ugly alternative is to meet them at the bargaining table on their terms." Achelous shook his head, "Once the enemy knows what you value they have leverage on you and will find a way to use it."

"Bastards," growled Ogden. "Greedy bastards."

"Ogden! Oh—boss." Outish appeared in the doorway with Celebron looming behind. "Yes?" both men responded.

Out of breath, Outish took a moment. "The Scarlet Britches, er, Paleowrights are at Murali's."

Returning his focus on the forge, Ogden indicated to Mergund to lift the mandrel and the barrel up to the light.

"How many?" asked Christina.

"All of them. Even the viscount and his priest."

As if she were waiting for this, the Ascalon turned away and strode into the dim recesses of the foundry. "Oi, me thinks we're done with this for today," said Ogden tight lipped, examining the work. "We've finished with the hard part." Mergund carried the mandrel away to separate it from the barrel. "What be the 'Britches about?" asked Ogden, stripping off his heavy leather apron stained black from the forge.

Outish stammered, "Uh, I don't know, they're not letting anyone in or out. Daryan snuck out back, through the kitchen before they could stop her."

Achelous watched Ogden's neutral expression turned to a frown.

"Bagonen thinks we should summon the ward," Outish added.

Ogden's frown deepened, and then he nodded, his beard dipping in the orange glow. Outish wheeled and darted away before Achelous could call out. He didn't expect his astrobiologist to be the one volunteering to gather the ward's fighters.

Christina strode past and into the daylight of the foundry doors. Her shield on her shoulder, her bastard sword slung across her back, and her long sword at her hip. She was fully armored except for her helmet under her arm. "Master smith, I will join with my compatriots outside the tavern. Summon your ward, but muster them nearby, out of sight. If there's strife, I want surprise the ally to our side, not theirs."

When he gave her a blank look, she added, "I'll not be wanting the Scarlets taking refuge in the tavern which they most surely will do if confronted with an armed force. You may join us yourself if you wish, but tell your armsmen to stay concealed and watch for your signals."

"Oi," he responded, and Christina left.

Achelous, torn between following Christina and the desire to keep Outish out of trouble went to find a place he could call Outish on his multi-func.

Christina turned the corner and strode down the middle of Wide Lane. At the distant end, Timber Hall rose in grandness. Along the lane, passersby stopped to gawk at the tall, flaxen haired warrior. Immediately they sensed a change in her demeanor. A popular spectator attraction, Christina had up to that time walked through

Wedgewood with a smile, no armor, and only her long sword at her hip. Today her lips were pressed, and her mail sleeves jingled against her gleaming breastplate.

Alex emerged from the door of a boutique where he stayed in the room above. Likewise fully armored he joined Christina without a word on her left. Now the foot and wagon traffic parted, giving the two a wide berth rather than just stare.

At his station Feolin nodded to a woman, thanking her and handed her an empty serving bowl. Seeing the other two armored Defenders, the woman did a double take and scurried into her shop. Feolin's shield, helmet, greaves, and sword belt hung on the hitching post. He collected them, and stepped into the lane, matching Christina's stride on her right.

As the trio approached Murali's where a crowd had formed, word spread ahead of them. Townsfolk and visitors alike turned, nodding and murmuring. More folk, mostly youngins, came running. One Timberkeep was heard to say, "Oi, those Ancient lovers will have *them* to answer to. The Defenders are here."

When the crowd parted, and Christina, Alex, and Feolin strode into the clearing, one of two Scarlet Saviors posted on Murali's porch opened the door and stepped inside. As Christina and her brother Defenders approached the veranda, she saw furtive movement of men amongst the crowd and in the alleys to either side of the street. The unmistakable sound of steel scraping against chainmail came from the stable behind her.

Just then a body crashed through the front windows of Murali's and landed with a hard thump on the wooden porch. Three Scarlet Saviors stepped quickly out the door. From within, through the broken panes, a man's gruff voice could be heard "That'll teach the cheeky bitch." And indeed the inert form was a woman, an archer dressed in woodland garb and bow gauntlets. Her long brown hair obscured her face.

Christina's eye twitched, it could have been the result of an errant breeze. The three Defenders arrayed themselves abreast in front of the two steps leading up to the veranda, Alex on the left, Feolin on the right. Their faces unreadable masks. Each held their helmet under their right arm, and on their left, they bore scarred shields with the field of green, sky of blue, and lily of white.

A Timberkeep made to advance onto the deck to check the woman, but Feolin gestured for the man to stand back.

"Ah, what do we have here?" said one of the Scarlet Saviors, resplendent in his enameled armor, yellow facings with crimson trim. Their helmets, shoulder guards, greaves, and gauntlets had fluted edgings that gave the men an exotic aspect. No other organization on Isuelt could afford such ornate armor for its soldiers. "Life Defenders have come to rescue their children. Well it's too late for her," the man scoffed at the prone body, "it appears she's had an accident."

A scream echoed from within the tavern. A moment later another Savior stepped through the open door. "The mistress of the place doesn't like his lordship confiscating her huge aquamarine crystal." He chuckled behind the cheek plates of his fluted helm.

Christina handed her helm to Alex, shouldered her shield, and reached with both arms behind her and drew her great broadsword over her head in one fluid motion. The sound of the steel scraping free of its scabbard silenced the five saviors standing on the platform. The grey blade was twice as long as a typical sword. As arrogant as they were, Paleowright warriors were well versed in the reputation of Life Defenders. Derisive the Scarlet Saviors may be, but the sight of the amazon swordswoman drawing her weapon stayed their taunts.

Christina walked to the porch steps and calmly drew a line in the sand with the mighty cleaver. "Here you've come in our good graces, here you've defiled our fair places, and here you will pass no further."

Stepping back she and her brothers donned their helms, each a different style suiting that Defender. Alex and Feolin drew their swords, and Christina shifted her shield onto her back, stretching her muscles she made a great sweeping arc over her head with the shimmering blade. In truth, she did not need to excersize her muscles, but instead sought to taunt the Paleowrights. She wanted them out in the open, away from whatever hostages they may have inside.

Captain Irons stepped forward to the edge of the veranda. "You've no right issuing a trespass edict; we are here under the lawful orders of the Viscount Lorentis Helprig and are duly dispatching our charge of collecting Paleowright property. You are to stand aside and surrender your weapons or face the consequences."

"If it is the viscount's orders you are beholden to follow then we've no complaints with you," Christina responded. "Deliver the viscount to us, and we will consider the matter settled." The Ascalon's even, unfettered tone confounded to the Savior in light of the apparent odds the Defenders faced.

Another of the Paleowrights came forward, "You're a foolish heathen if you think you can prevail against the five of us, now stand aside or I will personally shave your pretty head from your shoulders." He stepped down on the first step, one step remained.

A jovial whistling came from the stables across the street where a mute group of bystanders blocked the entrance. A large Timberkeep in a full chainmail hauberk and a steel helmet with ox-horns pressed his way through the crowd. He carried a massive double-bladed war axe and a finely wrought shield engraved with the likeness of an Ungerngerist. He strode up to the Defenders and took his place beside Feolin. "Now don't ye be so hasty counting me friends here alone. Oi, I'm worthy of you five pink twitches, myself."

Feolin glanced over, "Nice shield weapons master, you've brought your parade-best?"

Ogden about to reply saw the body on the veranda. He broke ranks and moved to the edge of the porch and reached out to wipe the woman's hair from her face. His gauntlet rested ever so tenderly on her face while he composed himself, riding the torrent of sudden emotions. Ogden grit his teeth and swallowed. The archer was one of his own: Lettern. Her cheek was cut and bruised, and her mouth bleeding. She'd been struck by an armored fist. A silent growing rage enveloped him. He glanced up at the nearest Savior, hatred pinning the man. Slowly, silently he turned and moved back towards Feolin. Two more Saviors came out onto the veranda, they carried the aquamarine pegmatite between them. They were followed by the predicant and the viscount himself along with the last three Saviors.

Ogden called out in a hoarse bellow, "Bagonen!"

A door at the back of the tavern was thrown open, and the trod of many booted feet sounded from inside. Two of the Saviors turned nervously to peer inside at the noise, but the others stood calm and self-assured.

"What is the meaning of this captain?" The viscount asked, derision dripping from his tone. "Clear these vermin so we may be on our way."

"Sergeant, squad forward."

"Gladly," said the Savior standing on the top step. He took a step, and his foot landed on the deadline.

Mergund, encumbered by his shield, made his way past the tables inside Murali's and looked out the shattered front window. He saw a body lying there and immediately recognized his close friend.

Anger caught him, and before Bagonen could ready the troop to sally, the apprentice grabbed the knee-high sill of the broken window and jumped out.

Bagonen saw him go. "Blast! Perry, Mischief, go after him! The rest of you, follow me!"

The sergeant's reflexes and skill saved him--momentarily. Christina's broadsword blazed a two-handed, storm-driven swing into his hastily thrown shield that crushed it and broke his arm. He staggered to his left and more from luck ducked his head as Alex's sword crumpled the fluting on his helm. The four Saviors of the sergeant's squad surged off the deck.

Mergund reached for Lettern when a Scarlet Savior swung his rachier axe and caught Mergund from behind, aiming for the exposed gap between his helmet and mail.

"Oi, Second Ward to me!" Ogden commanded and heaved a mighty blow at a Savior who tried to fend it with his shield while aiming to stab Ogden in the belly. Behind, the crowd scattered and ten men of Second Ward charged from their hiding place in the stables.

Perry climbed the sill to help Mergund, but a swing by the Savior forced him to dodge back. Mischief thought better of going through the window and notched an arrow.

"Drop that rock" the viscount ordered to the Saviors holding the pegmatite, "go help them," he said seeing armed men issue from the stables. Then Bagonen surged through the front door of Murali's and bulled a Savior off the deck while taking a swipe with his axe at the predicant. The priest yelped, back pedaling.

A Savior feinted with the spear tip of his raichier, spun and came with a vicious back swing. Christina, who'd faced the crimson knights in lonely battles in the grey land between Mother Dianis and Diunesis Antiquaria, was ready for him. She let the back swing come whistling just a hair's breadth from her face and jabbed her brutish weapon taking the Savior in the throat. The spray of blood galvanized his fellow armsmen.

Captain Irons and two of his fellows leaped from the deck and met the surge of Second Ward with a flurry of raichier swings. Three Timber troopers went down with battered shields, a severed arm, and crushed helmet.

Ogden battled in his own fight. His opponent's shield, shattered from Ogden's might, was cast off and now the two men traded cuts and swipes. Ogden's larger war axe easily deflecting the lighter raichier, but the Savior was faster, and Ogden had to use the broad double-blade as a shield to parry the expert cuts of the professional soldier. To Ogden's credit, the Savior was dismayed at the strength the master wielded the imposing weapon.

Perry head-faked and the Savior swung, shattering, then destroying window frame. Mischief, on cue, let loose his arrow. At five feet the iron bodkin punctured the Savior's breast plate; the impact sent him staggering back.

The viscount drew a long dagger and made to stab Bagonen in the neck from behind, but a Timber pushed through the door and smashed the bishop with the haft of his axe. A Savior, aghast, in a frenzied assault, pitched the Timberkeep off the deck in a flurry of blows.

The captain found fighting the Timbers harder than he expected but quickly surmised they were not dedicated, professional soldiers. While they appeared to mysteriously to know some of his arms tactics, they lacked the skill to press home the attack in the face of his onslaught. Already he had killed or wounded three of them, but then he came across a more even match in the Defender wearing timeworn Lamaran Free-Cities armor. The Defender deftly deflected each raichier thrust and slash and offered a withering array of sword counters. Irons, aware of the fighting around him, sensed he was needed elsewhere. He pressed the attack to finish the Defender.

With the fighting drawn close, Christina jammed her broadsword into the dirt and unsheathed her long sword. A second red assailant went to join the fight against the master smith, and Christina intervened with a slash at his shoulder. The combatant took the blow on his armor and came back with a cut of his own. The Ascalon caught it on her blade. Normally, a raichier axe would have driven the lighter long sword down, but Christina's held like a Ungerngerist. She smiled grimly at her adversary's discomfiture. Then she slashed back, spun in close, and gave the man a hammer blow with her armored elbow to the back of his head. He staggered forward, tripped, and sprawled in the dirt. She stepped forward, waiting as the warrior rolled and came up braced for an attack. She waved an armored fist at him, inviting him to attack. He obliged, and they met in a crash. Their shields clashed, she could feel his hot breath on her scared cheek. They pushed away, and in the same move each spun to slice at the other. But Christina, despite her height, crouched lower and as his cut went over her head, her cut caught him behind the knee, cutting through leather, cloth, flesh, and sinew. The man toppled.

"Hold! Hold I say, or there shall be no mercy!"

The Timberkeep combatants, recognizing the voice, immediately disengaged and fell back.

The Scarlet Saviors glanced about for opponents and saw the three Defenders standing as confused as they. Before the Saviors could resume the fight, Sedge, unarmored, carrying only a short sword, bulled through the crowd across the street.

"Paleowrights do as I say, or naught will this be your day." He waved his sword and pointed to the left. A full ward of forty Timberkeep archers were forming up in two ranks. The front line kneeled.

Belligerent to the end, the standing Saviors refused to move.

Sedge made a point of counting. "I see five of you still standing, one of whom is adding his red blood to his red armor." The warlord let the point take. "Understand I will have my archers shoot you down where you stand. Your armor will not save you. At this range, they can't miss your eyes."

Forty bows came up, notched and drawn, taking aim.

Irons peered to where a Timber fighter had the predicant pinned against the tavern wall. The viscount lay on the ground, dead or injured. His first duty was to save the viscount, if possible. He calculated the odds. Their eenus and coach were stabled at the inn, some three hundred paces away. They'd have to fight every inch of the way. "You will grant us free passage?"

"You will surrender your weapons. You will then take your eenu's and ride from here immediately."

"No," gasped a Savior lying on the ground. He rolled over, helmet gone, his head a mass of blood. "No, we do not surrender our weapons." Underneath the gore, Christina recognized the gasping voice of the sergeant.

Sedge gave a short bitter laugh. "Today you do, or I will personally take yours," Sedge pointed his sword at the sergeant, "from your dead fingers."

Irons recognized the situation for what it was. He needed to recover the viscount and extricate themselves. The archbishop in Hebert must know of this atrocity. He tossed his sword-axe into the dirt. "Bring us our eenu's. I must attend our lord."

As if reading the captain's mind, Sedge nodded slowly. "Take this message to your archbishop. If he desires to treat with Clan Mearsbirch, then deliver us a wise man and not a fool. Your viscount is responsible for this carnage. If he is alive, I should charge him with mayhem and murder."

The captain blanched. His eyes narrowed under the brow-guard of his helmet. Weaponless, amidst a host of enemies, his liege incapacitated or worse, he bit back his reply. Instead, he turned his back on the warlord and went to aid the viscount.

Mbecca, dressed in an ordinary smock and her black hair cropped short, walked amongst the fallen, directing the aid of her healers. She bent down and grasped the hand of a Timber warrior who lay with a ghastly neck wound. Her free hand rested on the bloody bandage about his neck. Immediately the man's frightened, searching look calmed to something akin to watchful peace.

Stable hands brought the Paleowright eenus and coach forward, clearing a way through the crowd grown larger by far. They watched the wounded Paleowrights loaded into the chaise, and the diminished troop escorted out of town. Six eenus were led, four of their riders draped over the saddles. The wail of a Timberkeep mother and sobbing of a new widow punctuated the departure, drawing a sharp counter point the disgrace the Paleowrights left in their wake. There was no joy in the withdrawl of the vanquished; the death of seven Timberkeeps cast a pall not soon to lift.

Chapter 31
Pyre

Wedgewood

The Timberkeep sensitives rocked painfully on their bound hands as the Larech drove the covered wagon in a mad dash down the mountain lashing at the team of four eenu's. He prayed with dogged faith to the Ancient Philosecleas. His prayer pleaded for the eenus to see the road better than he. Lonely Soul, half full, was dying behind the shoulder of Mount Mars, and soon even its wan glow would be gone in the midnight darkness. Trees rushed by, their boles caught in the faint silver luminescence of the moonlight. The Washentrufel agent needed to be as far away from the conclave by daybreak as possible. Originally they had planned to lure the six Timberkeep adepts from their conclave with the prospect of establishing a scrying service in Faldamar and then later drawing them to Stith Drakas, but now, with the debacle at Murali's, word would reach the adepts, and they'd refuse to work with either the Paleowrights or Drakans. To salvage their mission the two Washentrufel agents, after rendezvousing with the Scarlet Saviors, had doubled back in the deep of night. Leaving the wounded, including the viscount, behind with the chaise. The three healthy Saviors and the agents stole back into Timberkeep territory to where the six adepts slept in an isolated cabin used for meditation and practice of the arts.

"At least we'll be able to achieve our part of the mission" called Larech over the rush of the wind. Captain Irons sat beside on the bench. A last feeble ray of Lonely Soul slanted through the boughs and splashed on the captain's red and yellow helm. He refused to either admit failure or cast aspersions towards the viscount. His duty was to serve the Faith, to honor the Ancients, guard all that was theirs, and to follow the viscount's orders. The Ancients would provide the foresight, and the viscount need only follow their guidance. That four Saviors had perished – a terrible toll – was justified in their actions to retrieve the incredible Ancient talisman the Timberkeeps so flagrantly abused. Sitting on the floor of a tavern no less!

Larech gave up trying to communicate with the zealous captain; instead, he turned his thoughts eastward and to the experiments that awaited the captives.

The bonfires crackled with blistering heat. Per Doroman custom the funeral pyres were lit at dawn, their flames rising with the sun to release the embodied souls to the light of a new day and thereby seek a path to the nether world before night darkened their way.

Christina, as Ascalon Defender and with the Wedgewood Mother Dianis Chamberlain's blessings, gave the eulogy. Dressed in simple fawn colored robes hanging to their sandaled feet, their deep cowls thrown back, the Defenders presided over the requiem. Seven bonfires consumed a fallen Timberkeep, freeing their soul, converting their body to ashes to be spread amongst the groves of Ungerngerists. Those ashes would, in turn, be consumed by the forest, taken up by the roots and carried skyward so their the essence could strengthen the spirit of the Boreal Steward: Mother Dianis. Some said that woodland sprites were the departed souls of Timberkeeps who chose to stay behind, tiny Boreal Stewards, dancing amongst the tall, gnarled trunks, flittering through the needles, nesting in the pine cones, buzzing with humming birds, and tweaking squirrel tails. But all Lettern could think of was the horror and bury her face in her hands and cry. She had awakened in Mbecca's infirmary covered in blood: not hers, but Mergund's.

Outish, at a loss for words and out of sorts, scuffed his boot in the pine needles. Seeking some form of expression he awkwardly put his arm around her shoulder not knowing the Doroman custom for consoling, but it felt right to him.

"He died because of me," Lettern wept, turning to him. "He was trying to help me, and they killed him." A racking sob shook her.

It was all the more difficult for Outish to cope and offer solace to Lettern, an accomplished fighter who considered herself the protector, the chaperone for the two young men, he and Mergund. Watching the flames crackle and climb, consuming Mergund's body as it lay upon the pyre, Outish felt the disconcerting queasiness of mortality. One moment Mergund was alive, vibrant, laughing, and the next cold, grey, and silent. Up to now in his life, he'd never lost a person he knew. Medical science and extended longevity in the Avarian Federation had spared him the ordeal. Mergund would never again tease him about his ears; he'd never more hear his cawing laugh. The pyre served as a stark warning that life on Dianis was harsh, precarious, and precious. Oddly, even with the pain and confusion, he'd never felt so alive and relevant as in that moment.

He caught Achelous watching him. When the chief inspector refused to turn away, Outish stared back. Outish didn't see a chief inspector concerned about the mental balance of a novice field agent, but the respect and understanding of a person who'd been through the same pain. Whatever Achelous's plans, he would let Outish live his life.

Chapter 32
Holes

Tivor

Jiren Mekant leaned back on two legs of the chair propping it against the wall of his fur and feed store. His daughter Sissy, as usual, was inside minding the store. Today, late season cranips were the hot sellers. The suppliers – herb hunters in most cases – came in the back door, and the buyers – grocers and tavern keepers– entered in the front. Pedestrians, as every day he was open, walked by on the Korvastall, some nodding and some stopping to gossip. They were after what he liked to say, the early news. Jiren opened the morning's twice-weekly edition of the *Tivor Literal* catching up on what his gossip may have missed. When you did business at Jiren's Fur, Feed, and Furnishings you expected Jiren to be in the know, even on the mundane reported by the *Literal.*

"Morning Jiren." Duck Peren, holding two mugs in his hands, sat his mass into the chair beside Jiren and settled with a sigh.

"Morning Duck," Jiren gave the miller a casual glance. And so they repeated their long standing ritual. Duck offered a steaming mug, "Care for some carva?"

"Oh, thanks." Duck was ten minutes late today, and Jiren was getting cranky waiting for his carva.

"Fine morning for business," prompted Duck. "Traffic is the same I think?"

Jiren watched the carts with their eenus and teams of oxen tramp through the mud of last night's heavy rain. He knew the wagons, riders, and carters so well he could gauge when something was different. "About the same for this time of year. Construction lumber is up. Most of it heading to the new quay the Maritime Board is building. And I've seen the first stone shipments for the new tower the aorolmin is putting up."

For Duck, casual information, confirmation of what he might already know, or even an intuitive observation of no shattering import was adequate payment for the delivered mug of carvareen.

"Anything else new? How about Marinda?"

Jiren reached down beside him and hefted a sack. He handed it to the miller. Out of the corner of his eye, he watched the presumed-Paleowright reach into the bag and retrieve a round stone ball eight inches in diameter. He'd made a point of measuring it.

Duck held the ball up. "Heavy. What's it for?"

Jiren shrugged. "A mushroom hunter brought it in a week ago. Been sitting in my store room. Thought you might want it."

Duck ran a hand over the chiseled surface and smelled the black smudge. Wrinkling his nose, his head came back. "What's that smell?"

"Dunno, but you want odd?" Jiren tipped his head at the ball, "that's odd."

"Oh?" Duck brightened, "How so?"

"The 'shroom hunter told Sissy it came crashing down from the sky, like a huge hailstone, only it isn't a hailstone there were no clouds in the sky. Except he'd heard a booming sound just before the ball nearly killed himself and his 'nu."

Duck ogled the stone with new respect. "What, do you think a catapult may have thrown it?" Jiren twitched the corner of his mouth and chuckled. "A catapult? What on Dianis for? Artillerymen don't care if their stones are round, whatever fits in the basket is good enough. And from what I've seen of catapult rocks up on aorolmin's ramparts they are much bigger too. Don't know where that stone came from, but the hunter said he found it just west of the old Hafflin farmstead."

Duck rolled the ball back into the sack and contemplated it. "Might be worth a ride out there."

Jiren leaned back and watched the wagons trundle by. "I just stocked up on lamp oil and I have a new brass lamp that burns bright. You should take a look at them."

He grunted, "I'll do that." Sometimes payment for information meant more than a mug of carva.

In the forest west of the old Hafflin farm Duck watched the Paleowright tracker pick through the leaf litter.

"You say you were standing here when the ball fell through them branches?" The tracker pointed overhead at a tree.

"That's right," replied the mushroom hunter. "I was on my way out to the road when it came crashing down and bounced away through the brush." He pointed westward.

"So it came down at an angle?" the tracker asked.

Duck looked up expectantly.

The shroom hunter pointed up at the tree, a broken branch swinging in the breeze. "Well, yea, I guess. Must'a come from east of here."

"The Hafflin place?" Duck prodded.

The hunter blinked. "From over there?"

"It's in the right direction, and there's nothin' between here and there except woods," supplied the tracker.

"Let's go see," said Duck, chomping to move on.

Having paid the mushroom hunter for his time and send him on his way, the tracker and Duck rode their mounts across the overgrown field.

"See anything?" asked Duck.

"Well, it doesn't take no hound to figure it out Duck. The tracks are plain as day. "About a week old. Someone hauled a wagon through here," he pointed at a path of tramped prairie grass and young sumac. Riding further, the tracker stopped and dismounted. Bending down he plucked a clump of vegetation.

"What you got?" Duck asked dismounting.

The tracker grumped, "Burnt, something burnt a stretch of ground here. Like a hot poker laid on the grass and charred it." He stood and walked a few paces. "Here is where they rolled the wagon back and forth. The end pointing due west."

The examiner stared into the west, trying to imagine what was beyond the old farmhouse, weathered grey, with holes in its roof.

Removing his floppy, wide-brimmed hat the tracker scratched the back of his neck, staring at the farmhouse. After a moment, he went to his eenu, contentedly munching weeds, and set off for the house.

Duck came up. "What? What is it?"

The tracker just shook his head looking at a round hole in the side of the weathered-grey house. Fresh yellow wood shone around the edges of the opening. Climbing down off the eenu, he stepped gingerly inside the decrepit building. Duck nearly peed himself when a flock of pigeons burst out an upper story window.

"What is it? What ya see?" he asked once his heart quit hammering. Wanting to see for himself, he crept in through the farmhouse door. The door lay on the floor; the leather strap hinges long eaten by rodents. The interior ceiling had collapsed. High up on the wall he could see the ragged hole on the wall facing the field and another fresh opening through a flimsy interior partition, and a third circular wound in the opposing outside wall.

"Went clear through," said the tracker. "That stone," and he waved his hand in the direction of Duck's eenu and the canvas sack tied to the saddle, "or one just like it came in through that wall and went clear out that one," he pointed. He stepped to a window in what must have been a kitchen, given the rusting, broken-leg cook stove. He grunted. Fresh splinters of the wall board lay on top the roof of an ancient pigpen. "Be glad you weren't standing in front of it when it came through. It packed a wallop."

Like an excited kid, Duck rushed to the window and elbowed the tracker aside. "Whoa," he gawped.

The tracker chuckled. "Whoa is right. Whatever went through here went in a straight line." He shook his head. "Damndest thing. There's no arc on it."

"No arc?

"Yea, I was in the Tivor militia. We'd go out and collect the launch stones from Wistermen's field so he could plow it. We'd shoot them from the castle catapults for practice. They always had a nice high arc to them when we fired. If there were a catapult on that wagon, the ball would have had an arc. That's why I nearly missed the hole when I walked in here. I was looking down near the floor, not higher up on the ceiling." He glanced at the Paleowright examiner, who seemed to struggle with the concept.

Duck worked his jaw and screwed his face into a frown. "But how did it get out to where the mushroom hunter was? He said it came down from the sky, not through the woods?"

The tracker cocked an eyebrow and thought about it. Turning around he stepped through the broken door and stared out at the field. Duck joined him.

"The hunter said he heard booming, like thunder," mused the tracker. "Whatever was out here was fired more than once. My guess is one of those shots went high and came down in yonder forest. Which I can believe given the *whoomph* it had to carry to pass through two walls in a straight line. Whatever it was, aim it up into the air like an arrow, and I bet it could go quite a ways."

The examiner peered up into the sky imagining the stone ball sailing clear above. But what had shot it? A tingling sensation crawled up his back. Had someone unearthed a lost piece of Ancient technology? Probably not, it was a stone ball after all. Still, whatever mysterious contraption had flung the ball so far and so hard was worth investigating, particularly since whoever done it was keeping it to themselves and that was the most intriguing part of the puzzle.

"Well, here's your silver," Duck dished out the two silver tenpennies, wanting to be free of the tracker before they discovered even more and the man started getting his own ideas. "I'll be expecting you to keep this quiet, and if you hear of anything else bring it straight to me." He put his purse away. "I have some more nosing around to do."

Duck stood outside the house and watched the tracker ride away. Listening to the crickets, his mind turned to the part that bothered him: the burned grass. It had been in a straight line and lead to the supposed wagon, or maybe from the wagon, but the wagon had not caught fire. Why? He loved a good puzzle, the odder, the better, and the Ancients – they were odd.

Chapter 33
Family

Tivor

Achelous draped an arm over his head blocking the late afternoon sun. He lay on the stuffed leather divan in the study, Boyd sound asleep on his chest, drooling on his linen shirt. He forced intruding thoughts away from his groggy mind, clearing it, letting the fuzzy mellowness of his nap seep back and tug him down into unconsciousness. Dimly, through the closed door of the study, Marisa's muffled voice could be heard, probably speaking to a servant. For one of the few instances in recent memory, he was exactly where he wanted to be in the world. No other place in the galaxy held a greater attraction to him than snoozing on the couch with his son.

A startling thump brought him awake. The room was cast in deep shadow, an orange glow low in the window all that remained of the sun. He felt for his son then rolled onto his shoulder. Boyd lay on the rug next to the divan blinking, his dark eyes mirror copies of his mother. "Papa?"

"What? You—"

Marisa opened the door to the study. "I heard a bump?"

Achelous looked past her to the lamp-lit hall behind. She must have been nearby. He reached down and picked up his son before Marisa could intervene. "He's okay," he said, "he just slipped off." He smiled at Boyd, holding him up, "Kids go bumpy in the night?"

Marisa watched the two most important people in her life, one consoling the other. "You two were knocked out. Running around the wharf and kite flying must have worn you out."

He stroked his son's wispy head of hair, "I guess we were."

"Well, it's time for dinner." She left the door open, and Achelous could hear her issuing instructions for placement of the dinner settings. He sat up sitting Boyd next to him, clearing the cobwebs from his consciousness. He could get accustomed to spending the day with his son, napping on the couch, and waking up to a feast served by a beautiful woman. Life should always be so good.

At the dining table, he noted two place settings and Boyd's highchair placed between them. Judging by the preparations he assumed he didn't need to change into proper dinner attire and instead pulled the table top back from the highchair and slid Boyd into it. "Just us three this evening?" he asked a bit surprised.

As trade councilor to the aorolmin and head of the most extensive trading firm in Tivor, Marisa maintained many business contacts, and Marinda Hall was the center of much entertaining. Indeed a rare night passed when no ship captain, storeowner, wealthy customer, Tivor nobleman, or other dignitary enjoyed the hospitality of Marinda Merchants.

"Yes," she gave a relieved sigh, the lamp light accentuating her cheeks and playing on her eyes. "My secretary reminded me of several commitments, but I thought it would be just us tonight."

Achelous nodded contentedly and slouched in his chair. "Good. Then I don't have to go up and get dressed, and Boyd can stay right here." Tivorian custom, especially for nobility and the well-to-do, dictated the children be fed separately, usually by the nanny in the kitchen. Achelous, suffering the detachment from his son, preferred to have him nearby whenever he was home and that included feeding the youngling himself. He'd gone so far as to design an innovation in dinning furniture -- an elevated stool he called a "high chair" complete with an adjustable, toggled table platter that sat in front of the child and restrained him from climbing out. Marisa, originally aghast at the idea of having the boy's father feed the lad himself and in the dining hall no less, immediately saw the practicality of the chair. Since its first appearance in Marinda Hall, the carpenter who'd fashioned it had built a number of them for other well-to-do parents. When pressed as to where he acquired the idea Achelous demurred, "Just makes sense, doesn't it? Sit the kids up high where you can get at them, lock them in with the table top, and let them splatter to their pleasure as they may." That he subverted Dianis parenting and dining norms with a blatant case of extrasolar influence bothered him none in the least. The chair was constructed of wood, and the idea was practical, any father could have thought it.

After his favorite meal of corned berga, cabbage, boiled potatoes, hot honey rolls, and a creamed tuber similar to rutabaga, Achelous sipped his wine feeling entirely at peace. Turmoil may loom a few days in the future, but there in the Hall, at that moment all was serene, stress banished to the shadows, not daring to show its acid self to the comforting glow of the manor lamplights.

"Dearen?"

"Yes, Lace?"

In private, the two slipped into their pet names for each other. Marisa settled her glass of a fine Astur wine delicately on a doily stamped with the Marinda coat of arms. "Ogden lives in Wedgewood?"

In an instant stress surged out from the corners, threw aside the chairs, and climbed straight atop the table. Achelous knew the subject had to come up. Why Marisa had taken until now was only a guess. He swirled the wine in his glass -- a fruity red, of galactic quality -- seeking to keep his blood pressure down. Having made the final promise to himself to lie to Marisa only when her safety demanded it, he was determined to keep the pledge. Now that promise would be tested.

"Yes, you know that." He glanced at her, then leaned over to fuss with Boyd.

"But Wedgewood is almost four hundred miles from here," her voice barely above a whisper. "That's ten days hard ride, thirteen if you spare the whip."

"Yes?"

The corner of her mouth turned up and her brow furrowed. He wondered how many pieces of evidence she would trot out to convince him it was impossible to have gone to Wedgewood and come back in just ten days. The round trip should have taken nearly a month. Echo surely didn't show the strain, which bothered him more as the evidence would not escape Eliot who already had too many odd facts to add together. The truth was, he'd gone other places in those ten days, not just to Wedgewood and back. He normally referred to a program in his multi-func that automatically tracked his in-country travels and set overlay alerts to warn him when he was returning too soon given his stated destinations. But this time, with Lights Out approaching and the need to coordinate a myriad of ramp-down activities, he threw caution to the wind so anxious was he to get back to her and Boyd. After four years of living dual roles, he was getting tired, tired of the acting and the lying. He decided to save her the pain and discomfort of calling him out. "There's a reason why I keep the knowledge of my travels secret. And why you are the only person who knows exactly when I leave, where I go, and when I come back."

She looked at him with an open, yet tentative expression.

"Do you believe in sixthsense?"

She bobbed her head. "Of course." It came in a husky voice.

"Well, there is an aspect of sixthsense called teleportation." There, he'd said it. So far so good, no lying.

Gazing steadily at him, a tilt of challenge to her chin, he realized he'd have to go into detail. "The Ancients created and mapped special locations across Isuelt and called them shift zones. They're for teleporting a person from one place to another instantaneously. When you teleport," and he hesitated, seeking a non-technical, non-galactic description, "you are transported through what is called the ether and back into the real world. I found, through my travels, a map of these shift zones and began to experiment with them." It was all more or less true. "Travels" and "found" could mean many things. That he left out a raft of crucial details was an understatement.

She appeared to struggle with the concept, but then defaulted to asking the easiest of questions. "So you use these -- shift zones -- to travel between here and Wedgewood?"

Her ready acceptance of the idea, that it was somehow as she expected, bothered him. How much did she know and was not letting on to? "Yes. It still takes time though, because the nearest shift zone is up by the Auro Na temple, and the closest shift zone to Wedgewood is a day's ride away."

She nodded and toyed with her fork. Boyd began squirming in his chair, and Marisa rang the serving bell. The maid appeared at the kitchen door, and Marisa asked her to take Boyd for his evening bath. "I'll be there in a minute," she said.

When the maid and Boyd were gone, Marisa asked, "Do you have this map? Can I see it?" Achelous was quick to shake his head. He expected recriminations, perhaps even anger when she realized all his trips to the Auro Na temple were not to meditate, but to use the shift zone; but there was none of that. She was ahead of him, well ahead of him, and it was unnerving, and yet it was a testament to the woman he loved, the mother of his child. "Lace, you don't keep something like that lying around. If the Paleowrights learned of it or found it, it would mean disaster for all free western nations. The Paleos would share it with the Drakans, and then the whole continent would be open to invasion, quick, sudden, and unpredictable. All the good work that Lamar, Darnkilden, and the 'League have been doing to keep the Nakish bottled up would be for naught." He could see the immediate appreciation of the threat in the change to her countenance. "It's why I'm secretive about my travel plans. If it became widely known that I can move about so quickly it would attract the attention of a Paleowright Examiner and then there'd be no rest from their suspicion."

"Who else knows of this?"

Now came the hard part, how was he to tell Marisa that Baryy and Outish were in on the secret, but she, his lover of four years, mother of his child, and gunpowder business partner, had not been taken into his confidence. "I try to keep the list short, to those who absolutely must know and who use the teleports with me."

"And?" The word came with an insistent edge.

"Baryy and Outish. It's proven quite effective," he hurried on, "for my runner to move fast across the continent to check on, you know, trade prices, local conflicts, wars, a duke's new mistress, and other things. You know, the kind of events that can impact demand and prices for arms, spices, and gems."

"Baryy and Outish?" Her eyes began to narrow.

"I can't do business without them. They have to travel with me." Marisa had met other IDB field agents that masqueraded as part of his trading firm, but only in passing, so he chose to ignore them.

"I can imagine," she said dryly. Either professional jealousy or irritation at being excluded from his list of confidants colored her tone, he couldn't tell which. She relaxed her shoulders. "Akallabeth says demand for their telepaths is picking up, particularly for sending trade messages. I've started using them."

Achelous nodded. "So I've heard. The Timbers are becoming a power in that market. With their spate of voyants and telepaths, the Mearsbirch Clan council is talking of setting up their own telepath guild. The Silver Cup doesn't want the competition, so they're coining a partnership with them."

Still struggling with the notion of teleportation, Marisa held those questions at bay surprised by how much he had shared. Emboldened, she took another step and broached her real concern, a subject that had been occupying her thoughts for some time. "Eliot suspects you—" she glanced at the table candles, the flames swirling in the currents of the dining hall, "that you are an An—"

"Yes, well," he cut her off; it was not conversation he was ready for. They were making progress on the tricky issue of his instantly shifting around the continent, and he wanted to stick to it, a concept it would be good to have her understanding and support of in the coming weeks and months. "We should speak with Eliot. I know you trust him completely and I accept that. Explaining the use of the Ancient shift zones, left over from before *Epis Exodi,* will go a long way to resolving his qualms. I'm sure he must be thinking some strange things about me," he chuckled. "Akallabeth will have to know about the teleport zones as well, he may have to use them with me to coordinate security between here and Wedgewood."

"Can he use them without you? How do they work?"

He shifted in his chair, leaning on an elbow. Marisa, an expert trader herself, immediately picked up on the body language. "Well, it's not that simple to use. There is a secret to triggering them. The Ancients, I presume, needed to protect their access so natives like..." he almost said, "you and I" which would have been a lie concerning his heritage. He went on "...wouldn't stumble into them. A secret I am purposefully withholding incase the Paleos, or someone else may learn of the zone's existence. Without the secret that triggers the zones they are just unremarkable places in the forest or mountains that don't attract attention." Again, he told the truth. That the "secret" required a multi-func to call up the generator interface and select a shift route was a detail he would only divulge to her at the last possible moment, if ever. Trying to explain a multi-func and not expose the IDB would be a challenge. The IDB and the other layers of his secret life he would reveal and unwind carefully, as need dictated.

Again, Marisa averred her gaze, seemingly willing to accept the dodge at least for the moment. Turning back, her black eyes pierced him like a spear, "You know a good deal about the Ancients."

He held her gaze, his psychometric training kicking in to keep his pulse even. The biologic triggered a response in his recombinant embed. It interacted with his hormonal system to reduce the spike of cortisol his adrenal gland threatened to dump into his blood stream. He considered giving her his practiced speech of *I've made it my personal obsession to learn about them as much as possible*. Instead, conscious that the pause had lengthened into a long moment of pregnant silence he said, "It's my job."

Her lashes fluttered in a blink. She sat straighter. *His job?* It was not the answer she expected. Not that she knew what to expect. *What is his job?* Already he'd admitted to using some form of Ancient technology that allowed him to flit back and forth across the world at will. That in itself was incredible, but now... She wanted to ask what his job was, but she found she didn't want to know the answer. Not now. It was scary enough that Achelous admitted to knowing of and operating Ancient technology. Her mind shied away from knowing more, like an eenu from a viper. Maybe tomorrow, but not today.

She reached out a hand and covered his. "Dearen—" she breathed, her heart pounding. "I'm afraid. I'm afraid for you."

Blinking, confounded, he asked, "Why?"

She drew her fingers lightly across his skin, "I've heard rumors. Eliot brings the whispers to me. People are—curious about you. There's an Examiner in town." It spilled out in a rush. "Duck Peren. He runs a mill on the Upper Torrent River. He thinks he's coy. He's trying to conceal his true nature since Tivor is mostly Life Believers or agnostics. We're not overly friendly to Diunesis Antiquaria." She continued rubbing her fingers on his hand, thinking. "Akallabeth says Duck has been to the Hafflin Farm, and he's been inquiring about burned grass. He even has one of our stone cannon balls, which by Mother's capricious nature was found by a mushroom hunter, intact!" She shook her head at the wonder of it, then went on, "For some reason, whoever Duck talks to, he always asks about you."

Achelous let his expression collapse to a tight frown and relinquished his grip on the psychometrics. Duck Peren, the same man he and Baryy investigated three years ago for holding Ancient artifacts. Little did they know at the time that Duck was a Paleowright Examiner whose occupation was to find Ancient artifacts. Ever since then Duck had assumed that Achelous was a buyer and seller of Ancient artifacts himself. "Blast. Those damned Paleowrights are such pests!" He pulled his hand away and pushed the chair back, rising. "They're arrogant bastards with no care for the life or dignity of anyone not of their own minds. You heard about Murali's. They dared to think they could just confiscate clan property and stroll away with impunity. They're idiots! Seven Timberkeeps died in that fight. All because of Paleowright arrogance."

She gazed at him, pain in her eyes, fear in her heart. "It's why I'm afraid. What if they should come here?"

"They wouldn't—" then they both shared a look at the kitchen door where Boyd had been carried for his evening bath.

Achelous sat. "Right," he said with a heavy sigh.

"I'm taking precautions," she said. "Eliot has hired guards that Akallabeth recommended. They'll be posted tomorrow."

He nodded. "I think that is wise. I will ask Akallabeth to keep a watch for any Paleowrights entering Tivor. You should also speak with the aorolmin. Tell him the Paleowright behavior in Wedgewood demonstrates how far they are willing to go to protect the aquamarine trade. The City Watch should be alerted."

"But what about you? Are you safe?"

He tilted his head. His own personal security was assured until the Margel went dark in eighteen days. After that, he'd be faced with a new reality when the Ready Reaction force departed for Dominicus III. "There are precautions I can take. Let me think about it." He said the last to ease her concerns. "In the meanwhile," seeking to change subjects, "tell me of Patrace. I haven't heard about her progress with the saltpeter or the granulation process."

Chapter 34
It Kicks

Mount Mars

They met in a secluded dell nearly a full day's ride around the flank of Mount Mars, well away from Wedgewood's hunting grounds, farmsteads, timber groves, and mines. After hearing of Akallabeth concerns about Duck Peren snooping around Hafflin Farm Achelous was determined to redouble their security. Celebron posted his bravos a mile or more outside the approaches to the dell, one higher up the mountain with a commanding view and the other astride the dim game trail that marked the route to the dell. Trishna, her telepathic senses keen to the surrounding sentience of the forest, sat hidden at the entrance to the hollow, her mind wandering through the landscape seeking intelligent thoughts and conscious intentions.

Outish came back from the target, a canvas tarp stretched between two trees fifty paces away. On the center of the tarp, he'd painted a single black dot the size of his fist. Fir trees crowded in on both sides of the natural lane to the target. In an hour the forest would return to its unremarkable and anonymous existence, no one except the chattering squirrels and ratchet-head woodpeckers the wiser. The party stood hushed as Baryy, Ogden, and Ogden's new assistant Pottern made preparations. Marisa, who'd made her first trip through a shift zone, stood off to the side while Achelous hovered close by like a chemistry teacher supervising the latest class experiment. She still wondered in awe at the incredulity of being on Mount Mars. The experience of the actual shift, of moving through a dimensional warp, was rather anti-climactic. One moment she stood in the warm southern forests of Tivor and in the next moment she stood in the chill foothills of Mount Mars. The simplicity was somehow disappointing, but the freedom of the movement thrilled, empowered, and scared her. *What if everyone could do it?* She tried to focus on the test, but her world was changing so fast. She'd never been to Mount Mars or Wedgewood. If you couldn't sail there, she usually didn't go there.

Peering at the weapon that lay on the oilcloth stretched on the ground, she was impressed. Ogden and Achelous had been busy. That too fueled her disquiet. *How did they come up with that? Ogden is an armorer, a blacksmith. That is not armor. Oh Achelous who are you?* Her spirits sank to a new low. The man she loved, the man she thought she knew these past years was gone, transformed overnight to someone different, almost alien. Her fear, her gnawing fear was she might not like the new, real Achelous, whomever that may be. Fortunately, he'd not changed in his apparent love for her or Boyd, but he'd certainly changed in other behaviors these past weeks. In some respects for the better as he was willing to share secrets, *but why now?* Something had changed, and that worried her as well.

Baryy handed Ogden a carefully wrapped packet of premeasured powder marked "A1."

"Oi, I pour this straight down the barrel," Ogden said more as a statement than a question, he knew what to do, but his hand trembled in anticipation and perhaps a tinge of fear. Achelous had warned him what could happen if the powder charge was either too big or the forging of the barrel unsound. "That's right," replied Achelous. "I think the A1 powder is still too coarse for what we ultimately want, but that's okay, it won't pack as much punch, and for today we want to be on the safe side. We'll see if we need to test the B1 and C1 charges. Though I'd rather save intensive testing for the cavern Marisa's alchemist found. We've pan-fired some test batches in the cavern. It's so deep underground you can't hear a thing at the cave entrance." Achelous spoke in part to keep Ogden's mind from obsessing on the potential danger he held in his hand. He wanted to tell Ogden to stick to the procedure and follow the safety precautions they'd outlined, but micromanaging the artisan while he loaded the weapon would only make the man tenser.

Baryy handed him the round lead ball wrapped in a linen patch dolloped with berga grease. The loading operation followed a prescribed sequence. Even the sourcing of the linen patches, right down to fabric thread count and cutting size adhered to a standard to ensure uniform shape and thickness. The supply of the berga grease was chosen for consistency to eliminate any uncontrolled variables in the testing; all under Baryy's tutelage. Rigorous supply chain and quality control processes were alien to the Timberkeeps, but once convinced of the potential danger they were quick students to grasp the basics. Many of the concepts Baryy had to learn himself via injection learning, and he was fond of reminding Achelous, "I'm a sociologist, not an industrial engineer!"

Ogden took the ramrod from Pottern, his new apprentice, a promising lad whose bare face smiled often. Lettern, Pottern's sister, had convinced Ogden to give him a chance. He'd been working as an ironsmith in the Tolkroft mine fashioning the crude, heavy iron brackets for securing support timbers and fabricating lift bucket widgets. Lettern, Pottern, and the little wildcat Rachael were the three Stouttree siblings and had numerous friendships with the troopers of the Second Ward. Only lately had Ogden been able to look Pottern in the eye without thinking of Mergund and the day in front of Murali's. The deck had been cleaned of the blood stains, the front windows repaired, the shattered railing built anew, but for Ogden the memory of the severed neck and those sightless eyes would never dim.

"Seat it hard," reminded Achelous.

Ogden placed the ball and patch on the end of the barrel and rammed the bullet down with the rod. It was a good close fit, the patch gripping the wall of the smooth bore. Pottern had spent time carefully pouring and filing fifty of the forty-caliber bullets. Ogden was learning the jargon and science of building a firearm, but the principals he understood intuitively. When the powder burned it generated gas, building pressure inside the barrel, like a forge bellows, forcing the ball out the muzzle. The patch formed a seal around the ball to prevent the gases from blowing past the ball, maintaining pressure and transferring speed and energy to the mass of the bullet. The berga grease lubricated the patch and ball. Achelous schooled him on the need of forging the barrel and breach plug to withstand enormous pressure. They were about to discover if Ogden's first attempt at forging a barrel met those demands. Failure meant spewing deadly shrapnel from an exploded barrel. Ogden appreciated Achelous's honesty when he said he'd never built a firearm himself, but it did not engender confidence. Achelous said he had read *The Muzzle-loading Cap Lock Rifle* book, an Ancient tome, cover to cover, twice, and he let Ogden review it when a matter of interpreting instructions arose. For security, though, Achelous never allowed the ragged manual out of his sight for fear of it falling into the wrong hands, which hindered Ogden's learning as the trader was often away from the foundry. As far as Ogden knew, only he and Achelous were aware of the book. It was their prized secret. One day, with trepidation, he had asked Achelous where he'd gotten the book, mindful of the answer and its importance to the Paleowrights. To which the trader had said, "That's what I do, I trade for things. It's amazing what people are willing to buy or sell."

The truth was a bit more complicated. Achelous could have printed the book on native Isuelt paper, but the cost in ink and paper was exorbitant. Paper was a rarity in the Federation and expensive on Dianis, particularly in the quantities and quality needed for a machine-printed book. So Baryy had connected via the Avarian Fednet Intercon to the planet Earth's Internet system, and using an on-line purchasing system known as Amazon had ordered a used copy of the book using a credit account funded by the IDB. The book was shipped to an unoccupied IDB safe house in Glendive, Montana, United States of America, Earth. There, an automated cross-shipment system tracked the Fedex barcode on the box. Once the package was delivered to the safe house, it mysteriously vanished, unnoticed, appearing in the shift station of IDB Earth on the planet Mars, where via a preprogramed sequence Earth shifted it to IDB Dianis and flagged it for pick up by Achelous. The first fifteen hundred miles of the journey had taken, with Two-day Shipping, thirty-nine hours. The last twenty-one thousand light years of the trip had taken six minutes; most of that time due to the wait at the Mars shift station for low-priority packages.

Tamping the rod in the barrel, Ogden checked the depth gauge. "Oi, check." Outwardly calm, his inward excitement overcoming the fear of explosion, Ogden brought the smooth-bore muzzle loader to his shoulder in a motion he'd practiced a hundred times getting the fit and feel of the stock. The weapon was brutish and heavy; the long barrel made it seem unwieldy compared the refined swords he specialized in. The detached, professional side of Ogden critically assessed the feel of the musket as if it were any of the thousand weapons he'd forged before. It formed an ugly, menacing extension of his shoulder, a mass of heavy iron and dense wood. Pottern had carefully chiseled, carved, and sanded the hornbeam wood stock and the forearm grip, applying multiple coats of shellac giving the wood a rich sheen. The warrior side of Ogden yearned to test the weapon. He sighted down the barrel at the target. The non-adjustable sights were crude, but they'd suffice for the test. Satisfied he said, "She's ready to go." He lowered the weapon and carefully set it in the gun rest they'd erected, anchored to the ground with iron stakes hammered deep into the earth. Strapping the gun into the rest, he checked the aim, aligning on the canvas target thirty paces away. “Should be good.”

Silence seeped into the forest clearing. Even the noisy woodpeckers fell mute taking their cue from the rigid postures of the observers. A fluffy-tail squirrel sat on a branch above the group transfixed by the tableau below; the nut in its tiny paws forgotten.

Baryy gave Ogden a powder flask with a ribbon. “That’s your priming powder.”

Ogden nodded and uncapped it, pouring a pinch into the flash pan of the breach lock. He’d previously examined the powders and conducted his own “flash and bang” experiments. Nothing big or loud enough to attract attention, but enough to enhance his own understanding of what Achelous termed *the propellant.* “I know this part works,” he said, a nervous edge to his voice. “I tested the flint lock; she’ll spark every time.”

Outish pulled a roll of twine from his pack. “Before you cock it let me attached the draw string.” He bent over the mounted gun, looped the twine around the trigger, and pulled the slipknot snug. Handing the cord to Ogden, Outish scurried to stand with the observers.

Marisa, the only person besides Achelous to witness a test firing, stepped well back and covered her ears. Celebron took notice and retreated too. Achelous signaled all of the party to move back. The group congregated around Marisa.

“All ready?” Ogden asked. Peering down, the squirrel leaned forward dropping its nut. Seeing nods all around, Ogden said, “Oi, ‘ere goes.” He pulled, gently at first, feeling tension on the string and trigger.

The hammer on the flintlock snapped forward and a fizz came from the firing pan – “Bang!” White smoke spewed from the priming pan and grey smoke jetted in a long dirty gout from the muzzle. The squirrel scattered in a blur. Marisa, even though she had prepared for it, gasped and jerked.

The crowd collectively exhaled, waiting. In a distinct anti-climax, the gun sat unchanged upon its stand. The rest and musket had barely moved.

Achelous dropped his hands from his ears and walked towards the musket. He eyed it from a distance, afraid of what he might see: a fractured barrel, a blown breach. The gun lay quiescent, no worse for wear. Without stopping to inspect it, he hurried past and began to jog.

Marisa ran after him. It was all so new and strange. Her heart beating fast, she took a ragged gulp of the high mountain air and ran faster.

Achelous halted in front of the canvas and examined the painted black dot. He scowled. No hole in the target's bull's eye. He scanned the canvas looking for a hole, any hole that might witness the passage of the bullet. His hopes began to dim. Where was the hole? Please, any hole--

"There!" Marisa pointed. A foot high and to the left of the circle was a round piercing the size of her fingertip, a smudge of grey surrounded the edges. The fabric punched through from this side. "Hurray!" she threw her arms around his neck and kissed him. "You did it! Ogden did it! It works." She released him, a surprised and bemused expression on his face. "It works," she repeated, the gravity of the moment toned down the pitch of her voice. She put a finger in the hole, contemplating its meaning. Too overcome by the ramifications, she briefly smiled at him and turned to walk back as the others surged past her to peer at the canvas wound.

Ogden saw the puncture. It was just a wee hole, not like the gaping slash of an axe blade. Twirn't much for the many hours of labor, and iron, and coal that went into making that hole. He wondered what happened after it went through. Did it fall to the ground? How far did it go? He looked above the canvas at the trees behind. Curious, while the others gawked and chattered, he walked around them to behind the target, projecting in his mind the path of the bullet. He scanned the ground then moved further seeing if the projectile chipped one of the boulders beyond laying at the foot of the scree slope. Turning left he faced directly down the path of the shot from the gun through the tarp and beyond, his eyes searched first one boulder then a tree it rested against. He squinted, not sure of what he saw, then his eyes widened. His jaw fell open. Suddenly the gun was no longer ugly and ungainly, nor was it a waste of time, it was dangerous. He burst out laughing, a deep sound rumbling up and pouring out.

"What? What?" exclaimed Pottern coming to his side.

Ogden pointed, and Pottern gawked, "What? Noooo, oh my lards!"

Baryy came around the tarp, saw where Odgen pointed, and said, "Ouch, that would hurt." A hole, the size of a finger, punctured a pine-wood sapling as big in diameter as Ogden's wrist. The round went clean through shredding the backside in a gaping wound. Baryy peered close; around the edges of the entry hole grey flecks of lead darkened the bright yellow sapwood.

Calming his mirth, Ogden savored the moment. Crude and lumpy as it was, the gun was a real weapon. He had created a mechanism that invisibly shot a lead ball with such force that not even three fingers of wood could stop it. Surely no armor could withstand such power, and at sixty paces!

Achelous turned to Outish, recalling their debate about the strategy and feasibility of using gunpowder against extrasolars. “What do you think?”

Outish knew immediately to what he referred and shrugged. “It’s not a plasma.”

Achelous smirked, “No, but it will kill you just the same.”

They returned to the mount and hurried to repeat the test. Ogden aimed the muzzleloader on the stand carefully and pulled the draw cord. Again, through the lingering smoke and with ringing ears the party ran to the canvas. This time the hole was a foot to the right of the bull’s-eye. Handshaking and backslapping went around, another apparent success until Achelous opened the ink bottle he carried for just this purpose and dipped the quill pen. He drew a circle around each hole. The group not quite fathoming the meaning of the circles, but Odgen’s tight lipped countenance told Achelous he got the message.

Back at the test stand, Achelous said, holding the gun, scrutinizing every inch, “The barrel appears sound, shall we try firing the weapon from the shoulder, the way it was intended?”

“I’ll do it,” said Outish stepping forward to unstrap the gun from the mount, but Ogden held out an arm. “Noi, if anyone is to be the first to fire it, it should be me. I forged it. If it is to blow up in a face, then let it be mine.” Achelous thought Pottern might be a better choice, but he couldn’t fault Ogden’s underlying motives. Never ask someone to do something you weren’t prepared to do yourself; there was real physical danger in firing the muzzleloader. And yet Achelous had to weigh the risk of a mishap maiming the weapons master, or worse. The course of history for Dianis was being charted at this very moment, and Ogden was crucial to that success. But the armorer would have none of it; shouldering Outish aside he untied the bindings himself.

Loading the weapon with powder charge, bullet, and practiced ramming motions, Ogden primed the flash pan with the flask and handed it back to Baryy. Kneeling behind the stand, he rested his elbows on the wood and steadied the sights on the black dot of the target.

"Keep the stock tight to your shoulder," said Achelous. "Grip the trigger with the fleshy part of your finger tip. Take a deep breath, let it half way out, and then squeeeeze, the trigger."

Ogden listened to Atch's instructions. They'd gone over them before, but hearing them again calmed him. He concentrated on each step, oblivious to spectators behind him. Closing his left eye, he formed a stable tripod with his elbows on the stand and his knee on the ground. The trigger at first felt like a cold lump of steel, but he took a deep breath and let his calloused finger caress the curved projection. Achelous had tried the trigger back in the foundry and found it too stiff, the pull uneven, so Ogden went about refining it, filing and shaping the mechanism so it pulled evenly. Something the trader said came to him: "For target shooting, we want a short trigger pull. In the field of battle we'll want something more forgiving."

He squeezed the trigger feeling it draw smoothly—"psst Bang!" flame and smoke jetted away from the bench. Ogden flinched. Even with his heavy and well-muscled body, the discharge surprised him. The flash and puff from the pan stung his eye. "Oi!" he exclaimed, "It kicks like an ornery eenu!"

The off-worlders, Baryy, Outish, and Achelous laughed. They expected a reaction, and reasonably suspected the gun would kick even though chemical projectile weapons had long been obsolete in the Avarian arsenal. Only Achelous, in his early tour of duty on Earth, had ever seen one actually used and that was a much more refined automatic weapon with hardly any kick at all.

"Shoot it again," chimed Baryy, "it's like the second time for everything, it gets better."

"If ye say so," Ogden replied skeptically. He wiped his face with his beefy hand; the air around him smelled like burned, rotten eggs.

He loaded the gun again, noting how dirty and soot-smeared the muzzle and priming pan were beginning to look. Mentally shrugging, he took aim and fired. This time he was ready and let his shoulder absorb the kick. Waving at the smoke drifting around him, he set the muzzleloader down, surprised at how he was shaking; the tension had wound him tighter than a barrel stave.

The party went to the target to examine Ogden's marksmanship. Achelous drew two more black circles. At the widest, there were two feet between holes. The closest any two bullets came was a hand.

"Why that be no good," Ogden moaned, saying what was clearly written on Celebron's face. "Lettern would laugh at me. She can put three arrows in a knot-hole at fifty paces," he pointed at the canvas. "Anything smaller than a wagon and you may not hit it."

"That's why I circled them," replied Achelous. "For what you have there," and he angled his head toward the stand and the prototype," is as good as it gets. You see," he chose his words carefully to keep the science and jargon of ballistics from befuddling the provincials in the group, "you're shooting a round ball. When it comes out that barrel it will fly where the barrel is pointed, but just like an arrow *without* fletchings, the ball will wander, pretty much randomly along the line of flight."

Ogden arched an eyebrow and Baryy nodded.

"So your say'n we put feathers on the balls?" Pottern asked incredulously.

Achelous laughed, and Outish piped in, "Yep, you see you use humming bird feathers and a special tree bark glue that won't ignite when the ball shoots down the barrel."

Pottern smirked at Outish. "I have me a better idea, we dig some ear wax out of those ears of yours and use that to glue on your twiddle bird feathers."

Outish turned red, but before he could issue a rejoinder, Achelous interrupted, "In a way, we can accomplish the same thing."

Pottern and Outish stared at him.

"Put a spin on the bullet."

Ogden's brows furrowed. He unconsciously scratched his beard.

"Sure, have you ever skipped a stone on water? You need to impart a spin to it. If we impart a twist to the bullet, it will work like a child's spinning-top to stabilize the bullet during flight."

Nodding sagely Ogden wanted to ask Achelous if he had read that in the *Cap Lock Rifle* book as they'd only covered the portions Ogden needed to complete the project so far. There were chapters he'd not yet seen. However, by their agreement, Ogden could not divulge the existence of the book. So he left his question for later.

"And how do you do that?" asked Marisa, looking between Achelous and Odgen, half expecting the weapons master to ask the question.

"I'll show you." Achelous took the musket and held up the muzzle end. "Per the design the barrel is smooth."

"Oi," the weaponsmith nodded.

"The next thing to do is rifle the barrel. That is cut equally spaced grooves inside the barrel that slowly twist down the length of the tube. The grooves will grip the patch and impart a spin to the bullet as it leaves the muzzle."

"You can do that?" Pottern asked, awe in his voice. "Will that work?"

Achelous smiled at Ogden and a hidden message passed between them. "We can do that and much more. What you need to worry about," and he gave the young intern a straight look, "is how to make more than one rifle a week." He hefted the gun. "And now you know the difference between a rifle and a musket." Handing it to the apprentice, "That is a smooth-bore musket. Once your boss puts grooves in the barrel and it shoots apple-size groups at two hundred paces you'll have yourself what is called a rifle. And while he's figuring out how to cut those grooves, you figure out how to make me a rifle every hour, not every week." The message was more for Ogden than the poor overwhelmed apprentice whose glazed expression testified he had no idea how to productionize firearms manufacturing. Achelous chuckled, "Don't worry lad," and he glanced at Baryy, "maybe my weapons trader can help. He's seen a thing or two in his travels." He handed the gun back to Ogden. "But we've accomplished here today what we needed. We've proven we can build a gun, that we can produce a reliable gun powder, that we can manufacture bullets, and we can even shoot the gun without it exploding." He pointed at the damaged sapling, "And that the gun is lethal, at least at close range." Dropping his arm, "Og, you may complain about accuracy, and I'll give you that, but at ten paces that gun will hit a man square in the chest."

On the ride back, as they neared the Hall Gate, Marisa noticed Ogden's pensive mood. She eased her eenu up beside his. "I think it was worth it for you to not lead the rescue mission."

His head sank lower.

"I've not met her," Marisa admitted, "but I'm sure Christina will find them."

"Oi."

It wasn't exactly the response she was hoping for. Achelous told her that ever since Barrigal and Bagonen had left with Christina and eighty troopers to search for the six missing sensitives, Ogden had been in a deep funk. The only thing that seemed to distract him was the work on the special project. She decided to go to the heart of the matter. "Outish says Lettern is the best tracker you have. She has an incentive to find them."

"Oi, so do I," he gruffed.

At least that's something, she thought. "I think it's a high compliment that Woodwern and Sedge wouldn't let you go. Who can arm and train the new wards as well as you? Besides Og, sometimes you have to let the chicks out of the nest. Bagonen will benefit from riding with the Ascalon and Captain Barrigal."

"It's half of my ward they've taken. I should be leading them."

"That's fine," said Achelous from behind. "But what happens if Wedgewood should get attacked while the expedition is away searching for those missing adepts? Who is Sedge going to call on to lead the field units other than you or Perrin?"

Ogden hedged. "There are other wardens."

Achelous sniffed. "And how many handle notches do they have?" He let the point sink in.

Before Christina left on the expedition, Outish had surreptitiously scanned and recorded the aural signatures of her and most of the departing troopers. During the fight at Murali's, a recon bot had captured the profiles of the viscount and Scarlet Saviors. What Achelous didn't have were the signatures for the missing adepts, so Gail was tracking, with her one remaining aural scanning satellite, the progress of the Scarlet Saviors as they headed east. Intel that could not be shared with the Timberkeeps, but they almost didn't need it as the pathics, voyants, and dreamers in the rescue force were proving effective. Impressively so. While the Paleowright group had separated--one bound for Hebert and the other for the Drakan frontier--it was assumed one of those parties were shepherding the missing adepts. The latest report from Gail showed Christina's expedition had split to follow the separate groups and that they were catching up, but the Paleowrights had a sizeable head start. In the race to the Drakan frontier and Hebert, the Timberkeeps were losing.

Chapter 35
Corsair

In orbit around Dianis

Quorat plotted his course into the inner solar system. Dianis lay ahead, it's only moon, Lonely Soul lay off to the right. The trick was to burn his deceleration out of sight of any of the deep or near space surveillance platforms that the IDB was sure to have. The contract broker said the IDB was dismantling the surveillance systems. Quorat's first job, one of three he had a commission for, was Intrusion Testing. His second job, which paid a higher payout, was to physically verify the existence of one of two aquamarine mines. There was a kicker clause in his contract that boosted the payout if he was able to locate and verify *both* aquamarine mines. Finally, the third payment, that actually tripled his income, came if he was able to obtain an aquamarine-5 sample. He snorted at the idea. *As if.* He grumbled to himself as he manipulated the attitude controls and planned his deceleration burn on the dark side of Lonely Soul. There was an IDB monitoring station on the moon, but supposedly, it was shut down.

They all want samples. Always with the bloody samples. Go down to the planet, walk around, and ask the locals if he could have a rock or two. He shook his head. *It's not as if the locals know the difference between aquamarine and the beryllium-dense variety. As if they care. It's not like they conveniently stack the stuff in neat little piles and label them.* No. He would have to land, gather specimens, run tests, gather more examples, and then be on his way. On the plus side, he didn't care about being caught, except for his own survival. There was no provision in the contract against alerting the IDB to the intrusion. No penalty for shooting any indigins. *They must really want this stuff bad.* He thought. *I wonder who it is.* He steered away from that thought. Better not to ask, not to know. For certain, his gig was not with the end customer, but probably a contract miner. Extrasolar mining outfits needed intrusion prospectors like him to start a project, but they never had enough work to keep an intrusion prospector busy full time, so they contracted them out. He didn't care who he worked for; the bonus for bringing back an aqua-5 sample was enough to let him take off for the whole year. *It's tempting. First, I have to get planet-side without waking half the planet.*

He planned to come in over the southern pole where supposedly the near-space surveillance satellites had been pulled, scan for any airspace surveillance platforms, and drop into the ocean just off the coast of a continent called Isuelt. Once on the bottom, at shallow depth, less than a hundred meters, and near shore he hoped, he'd assess the situation. In general, on a human-inhabited, liquid-water world like Dianis he preferred to go submersible as close to the site as possible, launch a drone recon package, and then--only if necessary--embark in his convertible, specially designed air car, and make his way to the mine site. Pretty standard stuff. He liked this kind of contract. He didn't have to fight with other operators. Recon and sabotage contracts were the worst. Of course, those were some of the most lucrative. Nothing like a quick swoop and boom to rev up the old bank account. In this gig, according to the contract broker, the indigins were mainly bow-and-arrow, sword types. They could be nasty if he let them get close, but generally, they ran for the hills after a few sustained bursts of a plasma rifle. The problem with plasma bursts is the IDB sensors could pick up the radio static from the discharge, even from deep space. And the IDB took a dim view of corsairs using the locals for target practice. *That means if I have to shoot anyone I better do it after I have the samples. If I want to bother with samples. Though it is tempting.* He was trying to talk himself into it. As a practice, he stayed in his ship or air car as much as possible. *When you plant boots on dirt things get messy. For everyone.* He thought of a past encounter with indigins and shrugged the memory aside. *Maybe if I see some ore cars, or buckets, or whatever they use down there, I could come back at night and root around.*

Settling to the bottom of the ocean shelf, he watched the bubbles percolate past the video feeds. The hull popped and pinged as it first cooled, and then compressed from the pressure. Fifty, sixty, seventy, eighty meters and he was down, just below the maximum operating depth for his Trans-Star Hyper-Light Intruder. The Intruder was, after all, a star ship, not a true submarine. A cloud of disturbed sediment drifted past the external cameras.

"Ship secured for submersible operations," said the ship's AI.

“Take us north, up the coast, maintain this depth and keep our wake profile minimal. Ensure the heat diffusers are working.” He went back to examining the course plot and the two mine locations superimposed on a map of Dianis. So far his map data and surveillance intel supplied by the contract broker had been spot on. He planned to follow his original course to the mine site on the continent of Isuelt first, which meant cruising subsurface for nine hundred miles.

“What’s the best speed with minimal wake tracking.”

“Thirty two miles an hour,” was the AI’s prompt response.

He groaned a painful, deep-belly sound. “Twenty seven hours?!”

“Affirmative. It is confirmed by your intrusion plan.”

“Ack. Well, that’s not going to work.” *What was I thinking? Twenty-seven hours? We’re bound to hit something or break something.* His desire for stealth warred with his goal to find the first site and his fear that the Intruder would suffer some sort of failure cruising submerged for so long. He looked at the map. Assuming the IDB surface scanning satellites were gone, and he’d not seen any on his way in, he could surface and rely on the ship’s holofield camouflage to conceal him. There were three indigin ports along the way. He’d wait to pass the first, a place called Warkenvaal Vaal. Then he’d lift to the surface and scoot along until he came up on the second port, a place called Tivor. At that point, he’d submerge again to avoid disturbing any of the local shipping.

He issued the appropriate navigational commands to the AI. Sliding the maglev command chair over to the autoserv he ordered a dropper tube. He swallowed the caplet. “Wake me when we surface. I’ll want to check our projected holofield image with the seagull.”

“Affirmative.”

“Blowing ballast. Rising to the surface. Blowing ballast. Rising to the surface. Forty meters. Blowing ballast--”

“Whaaat?” he said groggily.

“Blowing ballast—“

“Oh shut the hell up!” He reached over and smacked the mute button. “Ack,” he rubbed his face. *Thank Spirits for the mute.* He’d installed and hardwired the button after he learned this particular AI would turn off the mute command on its own volition. It would even ignore verbal commands for silence. The software provider had claimed it was a mandatory safety feature. *I’ll give you a mandatory safety feature,* he grumped to himself, *the mute button. Without it the AI would be dead.*

Nearing the surface, he said, "Let's try a flock of gulls. Project the image to the holofield. Launch the seagull drone."

Watching the video feed from the seagull drone, a unique drone configured just for this operation on Dianis, the bird lifted off from the Intruder and began to circle about the ship.

Quorat smiled. Something he rarely did. *The marvels of modern technology,* he almost laughed. It was the first time his ship ever looked like a swirling flock of seagulls. Watching the image critically from the orbiting seagull drone he eyed the defects in the projection, but at thirty feet who was to complain? "Send the bird out a half mile. Assume a recon flight pattern."

As instructed, the AI repositioned the seagull.

Quorat's smile was back. "Perfect. A freaking flock of seagulls," he laughed.

"What is the average speed of a flock of seagulls?"

Quorat waited for a response. Just when he was about to yell, he saw the mute button flashing yellow. "Ack!" He smacked the button.

"Fifty miles an hour depending on prevailing air currents, ambient humidity, sub-specie of gull—"

"Fine, fine, fine. Set ship's speed to fifty miles per hour and resume course." He settled back in the command chair. At the new speed, the time to destination read sixteen hours. His objective was the end of a long, narrow inlet labeled Marish Fjord. He examined the course in greater detail now that he was actually planet-side. The port of Lucille may be a problem, but he could steer well out to sea from it. Navigating down the fjord would be okay as long as he was skimming the surface. Operating subsurface was best for stealth, but the thought of running submerged in a fjord gave him the willies. He was a space jock, not a sub driver.

"Craft ahead."

Quorat flipped the display from the orbital images of the Isuelt-Mestrich mine site he'd been inspecting to what the ship's passive external sensors were detecting. "What is that?" The video image was indistinct, but at fifty miles an hour it was growing in size.

The AI zoomed the video image, digitized and enhanced it, and a sail appeared. The bulk of the vessel was still below the horizon.

"Hmm, at current course and speed how close will we approach?"

"Three hundred meters."

"Oh. That's too close."

"We are nearing the expected shipping lanes for the port of Tivor. More shipping can be expected."

He'd have to change course, diverting farther out to sea or go submerged. "Any active scanning or other energy sources?"

"Negative. Emissions profile of a pre-steam, humanoid world remains constant."

The ship in the display grew as he hesitated. Now the top three courses were visible. A side of him wanted to test the holofield camouflage against a real indigin target, but the cautious side, the side that had kept him alive this long, wanted to avoid all contact.

"Ship is identified in our Dianis planetary data base as a large three-masted merchant ship; a ninety-two percent probability that it is a barque."

The hull of the vessel rose above the horizon. It was moving north, heeled ten or so degrees to port under full sail. The white sheets tight against the wind. He watched. The sea, while choppy, was not unduly rough, and the ship sailed gracefully like a majestic, snow-capped mountain.

"Shall I change course?"

Quorat ignored the AI for the moment. He owned an island on his home world, and pleasure sailing was a pastime of his neighbors. While he had never sailed himself, he liked watching the catamarans from the deck of his dacha. Here on Dianis, they made a living from sailing, apparently, and it looked like they did it right.

"Shall I change course?"

"No." He wanted to get closer. The ship was mesmerizing. "Slow to thirty and enhance holofield. Get it as sharp as you can."

"Executing."

There was gold lettering on the stern of the ship below what he presumed were main cabin windows. A pale blue and yellow flag flew from the stern post, and another much longer pennant streamed away from the top of the second mast. "Translate the wording on the back of the ship, below that gallery of windows."

"Translating, searching probable languages."

At thirty miles per hour, they would overtake and pass the vessel in three minutes. Then he saw his first live Dianis indigins. There were three on the rear deck, the quarterdeck of the ship, and they were definitely human, and one in particular... "Zoom in on the three humans on the rear deck."

"Translation confirmed. The lettering conforms to Tivorian language standards. Vessel's name is *Far Shore*.

"Zoom in on the woman, the female human."

She was beautiful and staring right at him. He sat back startled. "Can they see us?" Her black hair was coiled on top of her head exposing an exquisite neck and delicate ears. Her black eyes seemed to pierce the holofield and see right into the Intruder. She moved to the railing, her cloak rustling in the wind. Two male crewmembers stood beside her, one pointed at the Intruder. She raised her hand as if to acknowledge it.

"They see the holographic image of our seagull camouflage," noted the AI.

"You mean they can see through it!" he railed. "It's no bloody good! Take us further out to sea. Plot a course to avoid all shipping." He watched the woman watching him. She wasn't fazed one bit, and that worried him. *What's wrong with our holofield? The first indigins we run into aren't even confused. Bah, that's bad. Maybe it's just her. Maybe it's just a coincidence?*

Chapter 36
Lights Out

Continent of Linkoralis, Dianis

The incessant wind scoured the broad, bare plateau. Lichen and small stubborn tufts of grass the only things clinging to the dark, fractured granite. In the high, thin air at thirteen thousand feet elevation, the decommissioning ceremony attendees kept their movements slow and purposeful. Standing at attention in the neat ranks of uniformed IDB personnel, Baryy wondered whose idea was it to hold the ceremony on this lonely patch of rock. The nearest human or sentient being was a hundred miles away confirmed by the sole remaining IDB surveillance satellite, due for shut down within hours. For their last official act, the staff of IDB Dianis Station had lobbied the director to hold the flag lowering outdoors and in-country, not in the cloying, subterranean auditorium. In a way, it was their coming out party. The one time they were all gathered together, in plain sight with no pretense of concealment. *And so they stuck us up here,* he thought morosely. He knew from talking with his melancholy friends they needed no reminder that this was their last time standing together as an elite group, caretakers of an entire world soon to be left on its own to the whim of stellar currents. How--many asked--could the IDB shepherd Dianis for eighty-five years and then abandon it as if those vested years were just sunk costs? Was not the original intent of the ULUP charter inviolate?

Unaccustomed to wearing his uniform Baryy hazarded an itch underneath his combination cap. He dropped his arm when he caught the chief inspector frowning at him. They were at attention. He smiled inwardly, if he was suffering in his uniform, then Atch was faring no better. So he smirked and bared the discomfort. Good company made misery bearable.

The wind tugged at his service braids and medal ribbons. The temporary ear implants negated the noise so Achelous could hear the command adjutant issuing parade ground commands over the wind gusts. If they wanted to have a secure, private site for holding the decommissioning, they found it atop the flat mountain at the far southern end of Linkoralis, one of the four continents of Dianis. It helped to have a field generator station located near the summit, a leftover from the early Transportation Authority days when they used the plateau for receiving heavy equipment landings. Rocket burns and exhaust stains from those bygone operations were faint etchings on the weather-scarred rock. Soon the IDB presence on Dianis would be no more than the same lingering memory.

Facing the podium, an array of IDB, civilian, military, and Matrincy dignitaries were seated under the bright, mid-day sun. At that southern latitude, autumn was in full progression, adding a further chill to the alpine plateau. Director Hor opened with his speech. Gail Manner had reviewed the text beforehand and let her gaze wander to where, by far, the most curious intrigue lie, the three matronens in their dark purple cloaks. Two of the matronens had their hoods up to block the wind, but the third, a striking blonde, let the wind tug at her long hair bundled in a ponytail and wrapped, Avarian fashion, around in front under her cheek. She recognized the councilor from the Interconn news as a former wife of General Marion. The Matrincy did that: arranged two-year marriage contracts between their councilors and promising members of the military and other bureaucracies. Ostensibly, to increase the bond with the Matrincy, but more to the point, to dig Matrincy talons deep into the power centers of society. Gail glanced away and diverted her thoughts before the councilor sensed her attention and plumbed their direction. Three matronens at the decommissioning of a backwater world spoke volumes about Matrincy interests. She would have bet no matronens would have been here. Yet there were three. At a decommissioning? It made more sense if it was a *co*-missioning.

Listening to Clienen recount the history and accomplishments of the IDB teams on Dianis Achelous gravely regarded the three flags on their tall staffs behind the podium. The wind carried them briskly, fluttering like huge butterflies. The center pennon bared the black starscape and white clusters of the Avarian Federation. The left banner exhibited the Avarian-appointed green and blue swirl of Dianis, someday to be replaced by what the Dianis governing body would choose when the planet achieved uplift. On the right streamed the IDB colors showing two fists, one holding tightly to a lightning bolt and the other a twisting vine. Between them was the figure of a farmer guiding an ox-drawn plow. Emblazoned above were the initials I.D.B. Normally, protocol dictated the flag on the right represented the nation hosting the event. That the IDB colors occupied the host-nation staff, and the Dianis green and blue swirl were on the left, signified to the careful observer that Dianis was in caretaker status: ULUP Class E. Achelous could count the minutes that the IDB colors would remain flying on that right staff for he understood Clienen's speech to be short, honest, and heartfelt. He sighed venting his frustrations to the wind. The bright sun high in the clear pristine air did nothing to dispel his gloom. It was a bitter moment. Twenty-five years on Dianis building teams, studying the cultures, cataloging the political dynamics, and evolving a plan for uplift was coming to an end. He tried to convince himself it was not a waste. The work, the research, the knowledge base built were still valid, except that with each passing day their efforts would age, erode, and eventually become hopelessly out of date.

He grumped, chastising himself for worrying about the loss of considerable Uplift work when the real concerns were the extrasolars and the wide-open invitation for them to pillage the planet. Ironically, in a quirk of fate, what he abhorred professionally he applauded personally as it meant he would be going home to Marisa and Boyd. The elation of being with his family warred with the depression of no longer enforcing ULUP and protecting Dianis. It was an internal conflict he could not just turn off with a switch. The battle of logic and emotions waged back and forth, and lately, he felt increasingly guilty that his ethical disappointment withered in the light of his father's glee. The bridge between the two, the link that kept him from emotionally splitting asunder was the plan to go native and salvage the IDB principal by thwarting Nordarken Mining. The thought of Nordarken Mining gave him a calm, grim determination. The Nordarks were the common enemy of his two personas, the unifying villain that kept him whole, the piercing cause legitimizing his going rogue.

Baryy listened as the band played *Last Hurrah* and over the ear implants it sounded remarkably good, even as the wind gusts threatened to carry off his cap. Already one hat had rolled across the irregular rock surface and sailed over the edge. To his amusement, he watched an inspection drone obediently returned with the errant cover. *Can't be leaving evidence of Ancients behind!*

The adjutant called salute and the IDB personnel snapped their right-hand flat across the left breast and held it there while the final cords of *Last Hurrah* played, and the IDB flag descended the staff. Finally, only two banners flew; the third flagpole achingly naked.

"IDB Margel Damansk, IDB Dianis, dismissed!" barked the adjutant.

Achelous swayed in the wind. His thirty-two-year career, the best years of his life had come to an end. The next step he would take would be as a civilian. He tried to rationalize that he was on a two-year sabbatical and that he could return to the service, but he knew the actions he already precipitated and those he planned in the coming months would preclude him from ever returning to the IDB. He took that step. His legs were heavy, a sudden depression seemingly dragging him into the atoms of granite.

Walking, almost stumbling across the uneven rocky surface, he pulled himself together when he saw Baryy heading his way. He noticed the director looking at him blankly. Then, for some reason, Baryy stopped in his tracks.

"Chief Inspector Forushen?"

In his daze, he'd failed to notice their approach. Two of the Matrincy dignitaries, councilors by the cut and shade of their robes, hovered to his left. He focused on their signet pips. The one, a younger male with close-cropped hair, shaved face, and no eyebrows wore the pip of Planetary Councilor. The second and the one who'd addressed him was an attractive blonde woman of indeterminate age and wore the pip of Special Envoy which could mean anything. Her long hair was bundled in a ponytail and draped outside of her robe across her left breast in the fashion of Avarian Cardolors, though she didn't appear to be of Cardolor heredity. As a cultural anthropologist, it was a habit of Achelous to identify race and culture. In his line of business, it helped him navigate interpersonal currents.

He blinked, the polychromatic contact lenses shifted to a darker setting so he could see the pupils of her eyes and so she could not see his. "Yes?"

"My pleasure of joining your spirit Chief Inspector. I'm Councilor Margrett." She held out her bare hand palm down, her sensing ring-signet a lustrous onyx in a gold setting.

He smiled, his lips tight. "I'm sorry councilor, I would normally honor you in joining spirits, but I am a troubled man. I would not bother you with my heavy heart." With his gloved hand, formal dress white gloves, he reached out and caressed her fingertips so she would not lose face at his rejection. "Old habits and training die hard. I watch who I touch on Dianis, you never know who may be an adept." Though he meant no offense, he did indeed mean her, as well as provincial adepts. The councilor undoubtedly was an adept and skin-to-skin contact vastly promoted the extrasensory impulses between sentient beings, particularly sensitives. He in no way would let this woman touch him so confused and raw were his thoughts and emotions.

She maintained her warm smile and searched his eyes with an understanding gaze, whereas her companion shifted ever so slightly and Achelous caught the stiffness in his stance. The councilor went on, "I can appreciate your discomfiture, Chief Inspector. This must be a trying moment for you after twenty-five years here on Dianis." A tiny warning bell tinkled in his brain, she'd read and studied his dossier.

He turned to look at the bare flagpole. While he did so, gathering his wits, Councilor Margrett slid her arm through his and with ever so subtle pressure urged him to walk with her. A step behind and to his right the planetary councilor followed.

Gail witnessed the classic *Matro Press* as non-adepts derisively called it, and instinctively sensed Achelous was in trouble. These were no lightweights, the woman had been a consort to one of the most dynamic generals in the Avarian military, and now she was focused on Achelous. By the way the matronen held Achelous's arm, Gail knew she was angling for skin-to-skin contact. At least the poor sod had kept his gloves on. The other councilor held what they called the "shark" position. Stalking behind he had his aural senses out picking up whatever emotions Atch would leak. As a seasoned in-country operative, Achelous, through his aural defense training, automatically shielded any thoughts from eavesdropping. The matronens would even expect an IDB agent to guard their thoughts and emotions as a matter of course; hence, the blank wall of emanations would not raise their suspicions. Nonetheless, Gail's heart went out to him. They were after something, and their approach suggested interrogation. If the matronens gained any inkling of Marisa or Boyd, they'd not rest until they had it all and then Achelous would be done for.

"I don't believe you've met Councilor Breia," she steered Achelous around so he and the councilor could face each other. Breia bowed. A minimal bow to be sure, but with respect nonetheless. "I've read much of your work, Chief Inspector. Your research findings on

Earth were insightful, particularly for an intern agent. May I ask, were you mentored during the process?"

Achelous gave a bare smile. "I was posted to what the Terrans call a newspaper reporter. In those days the Terrans distributed their news on a printed paper media. Maybe they still do," he shrugged. "I've lost touch. It was a solo posting, strictly embed cultural assessment and monitoring work. Nothing dangerous or intrusive, so I had plenty of time to review the news stories and other research materials and synthesize the monographs you probably read. In truth, my superior, Chief Inspector Giomustafl was a hound for information, not just what the Terrans pumped out on their own but with the Avarian perspective on it. He was constantly badgering me for my opinions, and so, if you like, much of the credit goes to him for establishing the research direction." Giomustafl was long dead. In a twist of fate, Giomustafl was killed in a non-guided automobile accident on Earth, a head-on collision. So many cars, so many drivers, and none of them AI controlled. Such a waste.

Apparently mollified, Breia said, "I would think your experience on Earth prepared you well for Dianis. For my briefings on Dianis, I pulled your situation reports and followed your thoughts on the progression and shifting the balance of power between Lamar and the Drakan Empire with keen interest. On the whole, I would say Dianis and her peoples have substantially benefited from your fostering, or should I say guardianship?"

Guardianship, thought Achelous, the center of his moral contention. *Am I the objective guardian that ULUP requires of me, or am I merely acting in my own self-interest?*

The councilor seemed genuine in his praise. However, Achelous, like all non-adepts wise in the ways of sixthsense, kept the matronen at arm's length. Appreciation and antagonism were typical tactics used to penetrate the Blank Wall. "Thank you for your kind words councilor. It is gratifying to hear the voices of Dianis have reached the Matrincy, but may I ask why? Why now?"

Without affront, Breia replied, "I am the newly appointed planetary councilor. Hence my interest in your work."

Achelous frowned. "I don't understand. Dianis does not have a—"
He let the sentence hang as comprehension dawned.

Breia injected, "Exactly. It does now. It was precisely because of your reports on the Timberkeeps and your security breach alert that prompted my appointment."

"Security breach?"

"Yes, Chief. Your director filed the alert with Internal Security and followed it up with a formal complaint to IDB headquarters. He cited your suspicions of a plot by a galactic mining operation inferring they are somehow behind the withdrawal of the IDB from Dianis." Breia gave him a pointed look. Either the idea was preposterous, or Achelous' suspicions had now come full circle to haunt him. "A conspiracy theory with basis, but whose further thread has been snipped clean."

"Meaning?" Achelous asked tersely.

The councilor gave a faint grin at the chief inspector's directness. "Meaning Internal Security followed the lead to a senior manager of a Nordarken Mining subsidiary, but the man has turned up missing. The subsidiary, Delphi Plots and Exploration is, we believe, a front for Nordarken industrial espionage. The devils are damned crafty. Mineral exploration on hostile worlds is a risky business. An entire survey team can be swallowed up by any number of natural," and Breia shifted his stance, "or man-made disasters. Makes it easy for them to 'lose' someone if memory scanning is in their future."

"So you are taking the threat seriously?" he asked surprised.

"Quite," answered Breia. "Unfortunately, unless the perpetrators instigate another action we can intercept the case has no further leads."

Achelous pursed his lips, he expected as much. No, he expected much less. He was encouraged the investigation went up through all the right bureaucracies, IDB, Internal Security, and the Matrincy, but the result was the same: Stillbirth, dead before it saw the light of the day. "And what of the IDB withdrawal? Councilor I find it highly coincidental that IDB Dianis should be withdrawn along with its orbital surveillance assets within the same period as the security breach. We've all heard the rumors. We don't need the Strategic Resources Council to publish any confidential reports. Nordarken stock has fallen forty percent in the past two months on the aquamarine supply rumors, and I've heard shipments of aural-enabled consumer devices are being curtailed and the aquamarine saved for security-critical applications."

"I was curious about that myself," said Gail. She sidled up to Achelous and placed her right elbow under his left and smiled sweetly across to the Special Envoy. She reached out a gloved hand, "Councilor Margrett I am in awe to make your acquaintance. And here on a desolate mountain, on a far-off Class E. Whatever are you doing on Dianis?"

The aural signet pip on their IDB uniforms emanated their name, rank, and role to those with a multi-func, aural reader implant, or the sixthsense ability to decipher it. Generally, this made the need for introductions a quaint formality, a formality Achelous felt compelled to adhere. "Councilors, this is Gail Manner, Chief of Dianis Solar Surveillance—"

"Ex-chief of Solar Surveillance," she corrected him. "Remember, IDB Dianis ceased to exist five minutes ago."

Councilor Margrett's eyes flickered over their close contact. Her smile, if anything, became warmer. "I'm pleased to meet you in person. I recall from the chief inspector's personnel file that you were contracted."

Gail brushed back a platinum lock the wind had tugged from beneath her uniform beret. "Yes, once renewed," she gave a mischievous smirk, "but then we became too busy with our careers and drifted apart," her voice wistful, but the way she gazed at Achelous underlined her feelings of affection and perhaps, protection.

"You were saying Councilor?" Achelous asked of Breia, hoping Gail would get her answer from the Special Envoy. He didn't want to let Breia off the hook.

"Yes," Breia continued, "The timing was unfortunate. We don't have control over where the IDB sends its assets as they report to the ULUP Board of Control under which the IDB is chartered. I can tell you we, I specifically, reviewed the reassignment decision and found the case beyond question. Dominicus III is in dire need of a cultural assessment, and they need the IDB to form a recommendation for a Class D Uplift. The planet is a wreck, and the sooner we can establish a caretaker government the sooner we can move them towards self-sufficiency and get them back on their feet."

You mean drawn into the Federation so they can help you with the war, thought Achelous dryly. Fundamentally, he didn't have a problem with it, even a shattered world like Dominicus III had something it could contribute to the war effort. He just thought it disingenuous when true intent was cloaked in altruistic purpose. It insulted his intelligence. "The Dominicus III problem is not new councilor; other worlds fit that profile. What we do or did here on Dianis has always been a compromise when stacked against the needs of humans everywhere. What I'm curious about is how did the priorities suddenly change? I fear we have only displaced problems from Dominicus to Dianis."

"And what about my satellites? Some of them are antiques. It will cost more to capture, move, and re-orbit them around Dominicus than what they are worth." Gail frowned at Breia. "Spirits, why move them when they can still be used here? We can put their alert and detection systems in auto, route the telemetry and aural signals to the Central Station AI and let it monitor for intrusions. I know it is far from perfect, but at least it is better than no eyes at all!"

Councilor Margrett interceded on her junior's behalf, "From your perspective, I can see how illogical the situation may appear. However, you must appreciate all assets, even old ones such as your Centuries are invaluable in the face of the Turboii War. Your accounting is correct that the original cost of a Century satellite, with its limited capabilities, is a trifle compared to the effort to shift it across the federation. However, the fact remains that the federation's space dock and aerospace manufacturing is almost completely devoted to building warships, fleet drones, and orbital forts for the war effort. There is simply too little production capacity remaining to build solar surveillance equipment."

"They're building new Sunbird II's at the plant in the Usarian system," Gail countered quickly.

Margrett didn't miss a beat, "Yes, but at ten percent capacity of that single plant and they have a backlog of twenty-four months. We need surveillance satellites on Dominicus now."

Gail's frown turned into an unguarded, open scowl. The special envoy had better information than she did and evidently had done her homework. But Gail wasn't about to let it go and readied her next salvo when Achelous fired it for her.

"Regardless," he said, steering the conversation back to the central question, "someone made the decision the needs of Dominicus outweigh those of Dianis. And perhaps there is a compelling reason to divert IDB resources to formulate an accelerated Class D Uplift for Dominicus. Maybe there always has been. But you cannot tell me," his voice began to rise, "that Dominicus needs our ***all*** of our surveillance satellites, nor can you deny another alternative exists. That of siphoning IDB assets from across other missions in small increments, leaving all IDB engagements modestly shorthanded, rather than completely terminating operations here."

He took a breath and plowed on before they could interrupt. "If I went to Dominicus and I am ***not,*** I would be the one responsible for crafting the E to D uplift program, and I can tell you having eight, maybe twelve orbital assets on Dominicus would be nice, but all twenty-four from Dianis is overkill. The damage is already done to Dominicus; there will be all sorts of revitalization contracts awarded. There'll be more licensed extrasolars coming and going than carts at a farmer's market." Achelous could feel his anger pulsing, his frustration a raw nerve after protecting the planet for twenty-five years. He consciously calmed himself, letting the hormone regulator in his embed do its job.

A signal was beeping in Achelous's earbud while simultaneously the embed chip buzzed with an alert. It was the ringtone for the director. He tipped the earbud to Clienen's channel.

"Achelous, I see you are having a heated debate with our Matrincy guests. Anything I should be aware of?"

Achelous raised a hand to his ear and turned away, a signal to the others nearby that he was in communication with an outside party. "It's my same complaint as before Clienen about us leaving Dianis, only now I have the Matrincy to complain to. I'll talk with you later." He closed the circuit and turned back.

"Your request for a sabbatical is one of the reasons we wanted to speak with you," Margrett said. "We were hoping we could convince you to stay on here at Dianis for a few more months. It would be a single operations team; you could pick whom you need. But the remaining Margel assets would still transfer to Dominicus as scheduled."

His brows furrowed, they didn't answer his question on how the monitoring priorities changed from Dianis to Dominicus. Maybe they didn't know, maybe it was an answer they knew he wouldn't like, or perhaps it was secret. He wanted an answer to the redeployment of all twenty-four Dianis satellites, but at this point, with the IDB leaving and Marisa ramping up gunpowder production the answer wouldn't change his course of action. "What sort of operations team?"

"We need you to complete your work with the Timberkeeps and if you like, to continue to keep an eye on things."

"An eye on things?" he asked arching a brow.

"At least you and your team would be in-country," she said softly.

He dismissed her suggestion out of hand. Without Solar Surveillance or a staffed sensor group to monitor all the sensor suites, a single in-country team could not intercept an incursion unless the extrasolars landed on top of them, and the councilor knew that. He had an idea of the two locations most likely to see an intrusion by the Nordarks, they were at the false geo-coordinates he'd seeded into the reports, but neither site was near Wedgewood. He'd picked those coordinates on purpose, to keep the Nordarks away from Mount Mars. "What is it about the Timberkeeps you need us to research?" He was irritated that now, after the IDB pennon had been struck on Dianis, the Matrincy should show interest in the Timberkeeps. He decided to play dumb. *Do they care about the planet and the rest of the inhabitants after all?*

"Inspector," Councilor Margrett's smile gone. "Four weeks ago my former," she caught herself, disturbed at the lapse, "General Marion, brigade commander for the 1st Air Assault was killed when a Turboii rocket made a direct hit on him. A direct hit Inspector. The brigade's energy shield was down. They were taking artillery rounds across their front. Compare that to the 3rd Delevan another unit in the line with the 1st that fared much better. The 3rd accurately predicted Turboii attacks in their sector and were able to repulse the assaults with heavy losses. Their energy shield never came close to losing its discharge capacity.

"Do you know the difference, the sole key difference between those two units?" she challenged.

To Achelous the difference was clear, the 1st Air Assault was the Avarian Federation's premier assault brigade, the best of the best, whereas the 3rd Delevan was probably a line infantry brigade. You put the 1st where the fighting was the worst.

"The 3rd had three of their own adepts, from Delevan itself. They were the ones who discerned the aural command sequences routed from the Turboii to their minions. They mapped the planned attack vectors, and the 3rd was ready for them every time. The Turboii became so frustrated attempting to attack that unit they threw everything they had at the 1st. Without any adepts to discern the shift in tactics the 1st was nearly overrun. The battle started to go so badly it was almost as if we were back to the early years when the Turboii crushed us in every battle. All for the want of two or three adepts. That is what I want you to do Inspector, find out why the Timberkeeps have such a high preponderance of sixthsense so we can bottle it and furnish sensitives to all our units."

He sighed. At least she was honest with him. He shook his head. “We’ve supplied the field reports. They contain our findings. What more do you want?”

She thrust her hands deep into the pocket-folds of her robe. The wind tugged at the end of her blond ponytail. Councilor Breia interjected, “Your reports suggest their sensitivity is due to their environment, perhaps a chemical contamination. You’ve conducted no hard research. We need soil and water samples tested and analyzed. We need DNA samplings from the populace, Aural scan readings of the entire mountain and villages.”

Achelous’s mind immediately went to Mount Mars and the suspected Lock Norim site they planned to explore the day they were attacked by the troglodytes. *Was there something leaking from that site?*

“We think it is an unlikely coincidence that the Timberkeeps live so close to an aquamarine mine. A mine at the base of a mountain where a known Lock Norim site rests.” Margrett said. “There is no health risk connected to aquamarine, but there are correlative hazards associated with industries that operate near an aquamarine mine.”

He was aware that she was watching for his reaction. *So they know about the Lock Norim site on the top of Mount Mars. What else do they know?* Then his brows knit. *What do they have that I don’t?* “The ruins at the top of Mount Mars are not proven to be of Lock Norim origin. They are listed as probable. We’ve never been up there to confirm. Unless you know something I don’t?”

“We have your own satellite images,” she replied. “Even though the ruins are badly weathered, it is clear the construction techniques are advanced, at least for Dianis provincials, and what provincials on Dianis would build on top of the highest peak on Isuelt over a thousand years ago? The reptiles? They were the only sentient species here then.”

Which is the same logic Gail’s geosurvey team had advocated, and why the site was registered as Lock Norim-probable.

Breia’s countenance remained placid. “If we could get DNA sequencing of the cancer it may be close enough to our existing models that we could develop an antigen for it in weeks if our current cancer treatments do not work.”

“What are you saying councilor? Applying an off-world cancer treatment to the Timberkeeps would be a direct contravention of ULUP. Unless—“

"Unless we gained a special exemption from ULUP?" Breia hinted at a smile.

"If we determined the cause of the heightened sensitivity and attempted to apply it to test subjects we'd need to have the cure for the side-effects ready. Regardless of who the test subjects were." Councilor Margret continued to watch Achelous intently, but then shifted to Gail when she realized the chief inspector's poker face wasn't giving more clues.

"I don't see how I can help much further. Starting with the original Timberkeep settlers, they have been living in that area, eating off the land and drinking the water for sixty years. By all reports, it's only been the last ten years or so that they've exhibited the increased sensitivity. We cited these findings in our field reports. We looked for any significant changes in their lifestyles, eating habits, or environment that may have occurred ten years ago." What he failed to mention was the speculative information they omitted from the reports. The Timberkeep diet had changed over the years. As farms spread, new crops were introduced, and existing harvests improved through better cultivation. One plant, in particular, was relatively new: the kdel berry.

"We want you to return to Wedgewood and—" he looked uncertainly at his superior.

Margrett kept her attention on Achelous, but Gail had the distinct impression they were heading into an area where Gail's presence was no longer welcomed if her presence was wanted in the first place. The councilor glanced her way and then pointedly at the podium and the few IDB personnel who had not taken the lift below and shifted back to Central Station. "I was wondering Chief Manner if we might have a word with the Inspector alone?"

Achelous could feel Gail's grip on his elbow tighten, her cue to take caution. He turned to her and smiled, "I know we have a lunch date. Can you get a table for us in the Atrium? I'll be along in a minute." Gail contained her surprise; they had no lunch appointment. She turned to the Special Envoy, "Okay, but don't keep him long."

Gail sat at the table spinning her fork. She was on her second glass of water and was beginning to feel bloated. The suspense was killing her. What had Atch told them? What did they want him to do?

She was sure Achelous was holding back from her, he'd not taken her into his deepest confidence, at least not on his real plans for leave.

They shared many secrets, but the threat of a memscan bounded the secret sharing and kept communication to non-verbal, non-visual clues. A memscan could not interpret nuance, subtleties, body language, tone, or implications. It was like looking into a barrel of water; the cleaner the water, the sharper the image on the bottom. The murkier and thought-dependent you could make the memories the less accurate the memscan. It was not that he didn't trust her, of that she was also sure. Living with memscan risk honed both a person's ability to drop subtle clues and of interpreting them correctly.

The fork spun around for the twentieth time. Her intuition made her think Achelous was actually planning to take his two-year sabbatical on Dianis. Logic and data pointed in that direction as well. *The other possibility is he intends to spirit Marisa and Boyd off the planet.* She mused idly on that. *Where would he take them? With the Matrincy snooping around and their sudden interest in the Timberkeeps, whatever he planned the Matrincy now made it more complicated.*

She spun the fork and considered the problem with a knife. The risks of staying on Dianis made it almost funny. That Achelous could do it she had no doubt, but the challenges! Of course, if anyone could pull it off it would be the chief inspector. She wondered if he could do it legally. Under ULUP there were exclusions, and she seemed to recall an advanced fellowship for trained and licensed researchers—

Achelous and Baryy entered the Atrium and made their way to her table. She'd been there long enough so when the best table in dining room, the one in the upper observation bubble, opened she requisitioned it. The view out the window at the sea life was incredible. A hundred feet below the surface, built into the side of an immense coral reef off an island uncharted by the provincials, the Atrium afforded the best view on the planet of the multi-colored sea life. Constructed by the early engineers and later re-commissioned by the IDB, the maintenance of the Atrium was only possible because there was no sentient sea life on Dianis and was inaccessible to the surface inhabitants.

Baryy and Achelous sat down. "I thought the Atrium would be closed by now," remarked Baryy.

"Tomorrow is its last day," replied Gail. She reached across the table to shake his hand, Dianis style, fingers clasped to fingers. "How are you doing, Baryy, it is so good to see you again. And by the way, I only know the operating schedule because I've been here for almost an hour." She glared at Achelous.

Achelous sat back in his chair, "Ah yes that. Sorry I'm late, I needed to collect Baryy." He moved the place setting aside to clear the hologrid. He tapped the drinks menu, scrolled down through the alcoholic, beneric, and trium drinks, and selected the Otum vine acid.

"Achelous filled me in on the—" Baryy paused when Achelous double drummed his fingers on the table. Gail knew enough about in-country ops to catch the subtle hand signal. The two used them so blithely it seemed unconscious. She could only guess at the meaning for the double drum, but she dutifully watched in silence as Achelous pulled out his multi-func, attached an unfamiliar emitter to the end, sat it on the table, and touched the broadcast button. He nodded, and Baryy continued unfazed, "...Filled me in on the meeting with the matronens just after the ceremonies." He looked at Gail, "Seems they want us to recruit Timberkeep voyants for further testing." Gail's eyes arched open. "No?"

Achelous grumbled, "And to help with the war effort."

"What?" she rasped.

"Recruit, hire," he waved his hand dismissively, "it all means the same. Any Timber voyant we bring to the Matrincy is not coming back to Dianis the same way he or she left. They'll be mind-wiped. They'll have to be."

"Voyants?" asked Gail.

Achelous nodded, "Voyants and telepaths. They want to test the telepaths for the ability to detect Turboii command signals, and they want the voyants for distance viewing experiments."

Gail blinked, her shoulders tense. "How many?"

"Five each, for starters. Enough for a comprehensive evaluation."

She sat back dismayed.

Baryy nodded. "Can you believe it?" venom dripped from his words. "And I thought the Paleowrights were bad, but they only grabbed six."

"Recruit? What exactly does that mean? And what did you tell them?" She watched as the autoserve door opened and Achelous's Otum vine acid slid out, bubbling and frothing. The lime green liquid churned in the glass and quickly coated the outside with frost. Silent, a deep frown on his face, Achelous waited until the glass was totally frosted before he dumped in the shot glass of neutralizer. The frothing subsided immediately. He grabbed the glass by the insulated handle and took a drink. A puffer fish darted by the Atrium window chased by a long, lethal-looking predator.

"Ug," she said. "I never could drink that stuff. But since you're drinking..." she pulled up her own menu then peered at the multi-func, "I take it that gadget will ward off evil Matrincy spirits?"

Baryy glanced over his shoulder and down at the tables below. "It takes the surrounding aural background and amplifies it. We're not only pathic-proofed, but it has an electronic and subsonic scrambler."

Achelous sat his mug down, feeling the lime green liquid burn-freeze all the way to the pit of his stomach. He shuddered. An average person could only drink one vine acid. "So I told them I would think about it. They were most insistent. While neither Breia nor that Margrett of yours didn't say it, I got the message loud and clear they were not accepting *no's*. I told them, Baryy and I am signed up for an exploration charter out to the Farless Islands on Remus IV. And that we agreed we both needed a break." He looked at Baryy, "I couldn't tell who they wanted more, me, or Baryy. When they learned he was going to Remus as well Breia got agitated, and Margrett went stone still." Remus IV was a sleepy, sparsely populated Class C where, in addition to living in a tropical, white-beach, grass-hut vacationland, a man could readily drop off the aural and information nets. The perfect place to go, disappear, and sneak back to Dianis.

"So they are serious." Her drink appeared at the autoserv. "Atch, what if the Matrincy research can shorten the war? Don't get me wrong, but what if?"

He retorted, "And if it's so bloody important to them then why don't they just send an envoy to the Timbers and open negotiations?"

"Well," and she cocked her head, "because it's against ULUP. Dianis is a Class E."

"Right," shot Achelous, "for a damned good reason." Then he moderated. "They are willing to go for a ULUP exemption, and they hinted a secret exemption, and for that, they would need Baryy and me to testify in front of the ULUP governance committee. They need us to help convince ULUP that A, it is worth the effort, and B that it can be done." He shivered, the vine acid was reaching his extremities. "I'm worried if we don't support them they'll just have Ivan go in and snatch." He waited for the effect of the vine acid to flash to his fingertips and readied for the psychic rush. "They never did acknowledge my assertion that someone made the decision that Dominicus III was more important than Dianis, which it is not, at least not where the surveillance equipment is concerned. And they refused to comment on my idea of pulling IDB resources from a variety of installations instead of totally closing down Dianis. I tell you, Gail, there is something else at work here. Someone is paving the way for Dianis to be mined for the war effort and not just for its aquamarine deposits." He paused, his lips tight.

"Maybe we should—" Baryy's voice trailed off.

"Maybe what?" Gail asked looking between Baryy and Achelous.

Achelous held up his hand, the psychic rush was upon him, and he couldn't talk.

"Tell them about the Lock Norim site on the top of the mountain," Baryy said. "It's not official and completely unsupported by direct evidence – yet -- but we think something may be leaching from a Lock Norim site at the top of Mount Mars."

"Oh," she drew out the syllable, watching Achelous's hand slowly lower. The Otem would completely reset emotional, psychic and hormonal balances. The question was to where. "Well, we did kind of tell them," Baryy corrected, "The location is listed on the Lock Norim probable list, and any mineralogist could track the watershed on the mountain and trace it back to the peak. We just never had the time to go and investigate to confirm the ruins are Lock Norim."

"What good would it do them? As you said it's all speculation," she pointed out.

Achelous shook his head. He took a deep breath and let it out in a long blow. He blinked and picked up the conversation as if nothing had happened. "The councilor knows about the ruins on Mount Mars and is way past thinking they are probable but certain. She thinks there is a connection between the aquamarine mine, the ruins, possible soil contamination, and the Timberkeep sensitivity. But never mind their speculation, just give them time. They'll dig around, do more research, find the right combination of treatments and interactions. And when they do whatever is the cause of the enhanced sensitivity will be the next hot strategic resource, maybe more so than aquamarine. Everyone will be running around seeing the future." He yawned, then shook his head. Paging through the entries, he scanned the hologrid for his next drink. "Until the Matrincy figures it out and can nurture their own adepts, the Timberkeeps on Mount Mars will be at risk."

Baryy huffed, "As if the Timbers don't have enough problems. They already have an aquamarine mine in their backyard."

Achelous shook his head, "Not according to our field reports. And by the way, the Matrincy apparently knows the truth about that too, but the official geo-coordinates put the nearest aquamarine mine sixty miles to the northwest in Mestrich dead center in a ground sensor field."

"You falsified a field report?" Gail gaped at him.

He yawned hugely and smiled at her discomfiture. "Clienen is in on it. We filed the deviation in a double stage report, to be opened by the IDB commissioner only under a carefully controlled set of circumstances. The commissioner reviewed the plan and approved." He wondered if the commissioner did precisely that, and provided the information to Matrincy. *It doesn't matter. I can only control my own actions and the rest I just have to let go.* Achelous scraped some of the frost off his empty mug waiting for his next drink, then smiled at her.

She arched an eyebrow. "You don't want sex, do you? You always were horny after a shot of Otem." Baryy laughed, and Achelous shook his head. "No, no." His smile faded. Even with a phase-shift, Marisa was three hours away. The vine acid wiped clean away the tension of the meeting with the matronens, but Gail was right, it was hard to think of anything but Marisa lying naked in his arms. A Tivor carvareen shot hissed out of the autoserv chute. He downed it in one swift motion. Setting the porcelain cup down slowly, "In the case of Class E's we obscure op reports all the time." *All the time* was an exaggeration, but they'd done it enough where the commissioner ceased to grill them on the need for the excessive precautions.

Gail looked glum.

"What?" Baryy asked.

"But what if this could actually save the lives of troopers in the war? Even shorten the war?"

"Then they should treat with the Timberkeeps as equals and not as specimens." Achelous was unbending.

"There's another reason why they don't want to open official channels to the Timbers," Baryy supplied. "And I'm not as ready to convict the Matrincy of the conspiracy that Atch is painting, although abduction of Timberkeep adepts would do it for me." He paused, then, "For the Matrincy to expose themselves to the Timbers would mean they'd have to officially acknowledge them as a ruling body, no matter how small. And that means honoring any legitimate territorial and property claims the Timbers hold, which in my mind reasonably includes the aquamarine mine and the watershed all the way down from the top of Mount Mars and the terraces where the Timbers are cultivating the kdel. If there is anything in the environment causing heightened sixthsense, then the Timbers should have the first claim to it. The Matrincy is afraid of what they don't know. Even if they could recognize the Timber clan before uplift to Class D and not trigger ULUP lawsuits from every indigenous-rights attorney seeking to protect the claims in absentia of Nak Drakas, Lamar, you name it, they don't know what they'd be giving up. Perhaps the Timbers refused to negotiate? Then the Matrincy would be faced with the messy business of seeking annexation."

Achelous leaned forward, "And we're talking years going that route, not the weeks or few months to conduct clandestine recruitments or even abductions." He was exaggerating, but the lingering effects of the vine acid tingled in his blood. "It's so much easier and expedient, not only for the Matrincy, but the Nordarks as well if Dianis stayed Class E with no officially recognized clan, nation, or whatever. This way any extrasolar with a shift-capable ship can come and go as they wish. We're at the ULUP breakpoint Gail, the point where the economic value locked up on the planet far exceeds the ethical value of enforcing indigenous rights. You know it's happened before. During my tour on Earth working for the Chicago Sun-Times, I wrote a human interest story on how the American Indian ultimately gained compensation through legal gaming casinos after the U.S. Government repeatedly violated treaties with them. Each time gold, oil, or fertile farmland was found on Indian territory the treaties were nulled, the land taken, and the tribes moved until there was no other place to move them and the land they occupied was worthless, or so it was thought."

"Those are the typical actions of Class E governments," she retorted, "We are Class A for Spirit's sake. We can do better. We have done better! We enacted ULUP."

Achelous nodded slowly, waiting for the caffeine to kick in. "Yes, but even Class A Avaria is not immune to greed. As you've pointed out there is a war on, and in times of war the hawks will say sacrifices must be made to ensure survival, and hence we start the long slippery slide towards totalitarianism."

Gail sat there and stewed. Silence descended on the table. Her mind shied away from where Achelous' train of reasoning led. She refused to accept his as the only logical interpretation of events, but she found it hard to argue when her own satellites were begin scavenged. She resolved to herself to learn everything she could behind the decision to move IDB Dianis to Dominicus. There were people, associates and friends in ULUP administration she could speak to.

Having drunk her fill of water and now a glass of wine, Gail excused herself to go to the women's room.

When she was gone, Baryy began to suffer a change of mind. He asked, "Atch, maybe Gail is right? Maybe we should testify in front of the ULUP board. At least that way we would be part of the research and if the Matrincy environmental experiments succeeded the Timberkeeps would be off the hook."

A pained expression clouded the chief inspector's face. "Baryy, your own hereditary research and now the work of Outish shows that only by long-term exposure does the mutation occur. It takes years. " He sat back, feeling more awake. "Success or not, the Matrincy needs Timberkeep adepts to influence the war, today, not ten years from now." He shook his head with one vigorous twist. "I for one will not be part of an abduction and subjugation plot. How would we be any different from the damned Paleowrights? We'd be worse, the Paleos can't brainwash, we can! Forced mind-wiping of innocent provincials makes the Nordarks illegal excavations look like petty theft."

Chapter 37
Nak Drakas

Stith Drakas

Viscount Helprig felt beads of sweat breakout along the rim of his mitre. The emperor's displeasure radiated like a hot torch. Theirs was a foolproof plan, he was sure of it. Just the thing needed to punish the Timberkeeps: an assault on Wedgewood.

"Explain to me again Helprig why the Drakan Empire should march through Darnkilden to punish some upstart Doromen just because you feel slighted?"

"Your Majesty, they did more than slight the Church and my eminence, they murdered most foully four of my personal guard. They did accost me personally, breaking my arm, throwing me to the ground, and rendering me unconscious."

Emperor Exelir Tyr Violorich smirked, the barest twitch of his lips. He'd been briefed on the Wedgewood debacle by Commandant Fritach, head of the Washentrufel. The haughty, bombastic prelate had gone to the Timberkeep enclave expecting the locals to quail in his presence, and instead, they handed him his head. Emperor Violorich sat on the throne in the receiving room, elevated above the petitioners on its lofty dais. Incense burned in the corners of the colonnaded chamber. The sound of booted soldiers echoed on the gold-inlay marble until they tread upon the lush carpet that formed a burgundy pool upon which the throne towered. As the emperor preferred, the sconces on the pillars were damped, casting the room in a perpetual gloom except for the two lamps on tall wrought-iron pedestals either side of the petitioner's box. The emperor liked to see his subjects clearly. On his right stood Commandant Fritach; on his left General Biornach, head of Landwher Strategy for the Drakan Militaristrium. Attired in a purple silk robe, a gold sash, embroidered gold sleeves, gold armor shoulder boards, and matching crown of purple silk and jewel-encrusted gold circlet, the emperor appeared eminently comfortable. His two petitioners were not.

"An attack you say unprovoked and undeserved."

"Indeed your Majesty! We were there in that Ancient-spurned hollow to serve a lawful writ of claim against Ancient property. In the course of pursuing thy writ in the manner of confiscating said property, we were most treacherously ambushed and waylaid without warning. No concern given to the sanctity of Church and clergy. Only through the heroism of my personal guard were we able to fight our way clear and make," he cast his eyes down theatrically, "our most ignominious escape."

The emperor steepled his fingers, resting his elbows on the arms of the throne. "And why bring this to me? If a slight, however egregious, has been committed against the Church your archbishop in Hebert should seek satisfaction. This is an Antiquarian matter. Of what relevance is it to the Empire?"

"Your majesty, are you not abhorred, nay insulted by this assault?" When the regent merely tilted his head, Helprig tried "Sire the obdurate heathen miscreants are hoarding a mine of aquamarine! The wealth of which is untold! The secrets that can be gleaned—"

Shifting on the throne, setting his hands on the arms, the emperor roused himself. "Don't tire me with tales of aquamarine, I've heard nothing but promises of the glories it and your precious Ancient technology should bestow upon the Empire." He gestured as if swatting a fly. "Are you aware of what your debacle has cost us Helprig?"

The viscount blinked. In the dangerous silence, the predicant reminded him, "The adepts, the Timberkeep adepts."

"Oh, yes" Helprig stumbled.

The emperor's eyes glared like coiled vipers. "Commandant, enlighten the priest, but just enough to explain our displeasure. You need not share the details."

The Washentrufel commandant, against his best judgment, said, "As you wish sire." He narrowed his gaze at the churchmen. "We had plans to establish a scrying center and pathic outpost in Mestrich. We intended to staff it with Timberkeeps adepts. You know of course that the Timberkeeps have been supplying telepaths to trader princes and courier guilds?"

When Helprig looked blank, but his predicant bobbed his head and squeaked, "Yes, sir. My lord has been briefed but has many issues to contend with."

"I'm sure," Fritach replied dryly. "Unfortunately with your Scarlet Saviors butchering Timberkeeps at the tavern in Wedgewood our chief agent was forced to abort the plans to peacefully contract with the Doromen adepts and was instead forced to abduct them. You see we had bigger plans than just establishing a telepath message station, but also a scrying and divination observatory."

"But in Mestrich?" asked Helprig. "It's, it's not in Nak Drakas."

"Exactly." Snapped the emperor. "Exactly the point. Not in the empire but in the heart of its enemies." What Violorich did not say was Mestrich sat firmly astride the historical invasion route from the northeast corner of Isuelt to the southwest shore.

"It would have served as a forward listening post if you will," said Fritach, relieving his emperor of the burden of explaining mundane issues to morons. "Now instead the alarm has been issued against us. The Oridians, Darnkilden Rangers, and Defenders have been alerted and are reinforcing patrols all along the frontier.

"That damned Ascalon," growled the viscount, "it's all her fault!"

The emperor actually smiled, a tight-lipped caricature of a snake stalking prey. "That part you have right. She's sent word via the Life Believer pathics, including the Silver Cup." The last he said glaring at Fritach. "When do we expect the sensitives to arrive here in the capitol?"

"We do not know sire. We have a message by carrier pigeon saying they've had to divert numerous times to avoid the patrols. The adepts have attempted to aid their rescuers by communicating telepathically, but our agents have taken measures to thwart them. Drugging, blindfolding, and sleep deprivation chief among them." What Larech had thought to be the most direct route to Nak Drakas--following the main road up the Central Plains--had turned out to be a tortuous carriage journey first through eastern Mestrich and then along the tangled trails of western Darnkilden. The pathic network of the Silver Cup and Life Believers conspired against them at every turn, providing annoyingly accurate guidance to patrols on where to block roads and interdict intersections. Helprig, on the other hand, accompanied by five squads of Scarlet Saviors had taken the longer route traveling through Hebert to the port of Bareen, and booked passage aboard a merchant trading vessel bound on the northern shipping lanes to Stith Drakas. In the four days it took to beat north against the unfavorable winds the ship had been stopped and inspected three times by SeaHaven and Darnkilden warships.

The emperor sat and stewed. He considered punishing the viscount for all the trouble he'd caused, but then another idea began to form. If they couldn't recruit the Timberkeep adepts to their service, they could do something else entirely. Eliminate them, all of them. The fewer adepts in the west, the fewer the Western Alliance would have to deploy against him. An attack on Wedgewood would serve that purpose. Let the viscount think it was about the aquamarine mine. "And what of the Silver Cup Fritach? Have we been able to use them?"

"Only through intermediaries sire. Their senior guild leaders are Oridian and have close ties with the SeaHaven." At that, the emperor wheeled on him. "Yes, sire. They refuse to send official messages for the Drakan Empire. Our agents and spies, of course, can send encoded messages through Silver Cup, but it is laborious to encode the texts, and the pathics eventually catch on."

"Then what good are they to us? We should shut them down. Close all the Silver Cup parlors in Drakan territory."

The commandant nodded his head. "We could sire, but those branches also serve has useful conduits for misinformation."

The emperor spat, "Bah." He turned back to the viscount. "And yet here we sit, at a stalemate with the Western Alliance. Only through the blood of our own has progress been gained against them -- Drakan progress, from the points of our spears and blades of our swords. How has Paleowright knowledge of the Ancients helped us? Not one twit. You and your priests lounge like harem eunuchs in your holy Archives hoarding knowledge, glorying in words while the script crumbles and the ink fades. Have you shared one useful insight, one simple mechanism of advantage to gain us against the League?" The emperor glared, a dangerous gleam in his eye while the viscount emitted a mewling sound. The count's aide whispered something in his ear.

The emperor turned sharply to the guard captain who immediately drew his sword and advanced on the pair of Paleowrights.

Yellow lamp-light glinted off the polished weapon. "There are no secrets before the Emperor. Speak clearly so all may hear or lose your tongue to Drakan silence."

The viscount squeaked, "I, he, he reminded me of recent studies where our monks replicated an Ancient weapon, a device within our means of creation that does not require cursed *electricitum*."

"Electricity," interjected the aide.

"And that is?" asked the Emperor leaning forward. The predicant answered, retreating from the guard captain. "A new bow, your majesty, one with wheels that is easier to pull, hold, and shoots more powerfully. Ordinary men, even weaklings can draw it and shoot as far as the strongest archer."

The regent sat back. "Hmm, how odd it is I hear of this only when you should come begging for my aid, or is it your wits are sharpened by the point of a sword?"

"It was our intention to present you, your majesty, with an actual working version as soon as the monks made a model fit for an emperor."

"Bah," he spat again. "Supply the plans to General Biornach today, we will build it ourselves. Today Helprig or by the Ancients Helprig I'll have you bound in irons and shipped to the Ompo salt mines." He turned, "Fritach how many troops does the Archbishop of Hebert command?"

The commandant answered, "He has two regiments of Church troops, two hundred Scarlet Saviors—"

"But those are for—"the viscount attempted to interrupt, but the emperor deftly snatched up the baton sitting on the stand beside the throne and banged the brass gong that hung between him and General Biornach. The guard captain reacted instantly, drawing his sword and advancing on the viscount, again the keen edge reflected yellow light. The gong stood beside the emperor for the sole purpose of expressing his Excellency's moods, and in this case, his irritation had reached a crescendo. The sword slashed up into the air, and the emperor tapped the gong with the barest touch. The blade hung in the air. "Prelate, tell me why I should spare your arrogant hide one second further," the emperor spoke as a tired master to an errant child. "This is not Hebert, or the cathedral, or Wedgewood. You are in Stith Drakas, home of the Drakan Empire." The last he said with a heavy weight as the empire was the strongest nation on Isuelt, and perhaps all of Dianis. "And," he smiled, a cold, malicious effigy, "you are in my presence. You will stay your flapping tongue till I require any more drivel." Helprig cowed to a pale grey.

The emperor waved to Fritach to continue but did not release the captain from his threatening posture. "And they have a thousand militia in the Hebert barracks for guarding the walls and policing the city."

Sitting back, the emperor steepled his fingers again. Seconds turned into minutes; silence stretched clear to the audience-chamber doors. The guard captain stood patiently, his arm raised, sword aiming straight down the viscount's face while the emperor entertained imperial thoughts. Helprig focused on the point of the blade, transfixed by the prismatic effect of the lamplight reflecting off the beveled edge of the blood groove.

Breaking the brooding silence, Violorich finally asked, "So you would have your troglodytes lead the attack?"

It was not a question but a command, and so the viscount answered: "Yes your majesty."

"Fritach, how many warriors do the Timberkeeps have?"

Without hesitation, the Washentrufel commandant answered, "Ten front line wards of forty men each and four reserve wards. They also have two companies of mercenaries contracted with Sedge, their warlord."

"Hmm, how many troops in a Church regiment?"

Fritach looked to the predicant, "How many men do you have in each of the Hebert Regiments?" He knew the answer, the question was a test.

"Eight hundred, my lord."

The emperor did the math in his head, simple as it was. A thousand or so troglodytes, plus sixteen hundred house troops, plus two hundred Scarlet Saviors against seven hundred Timberkeep militia and mercenaries. Almost a three to one advantage. Professional soldiers arrayed against wood-wrights in an unguarded forest town, and yet here were the Paleowrights asking for his assistance. "General, what you think you of their plan?"

"Is workable my liege. It is obvious the viscount did not plan it himself." The viscount reddened against the glare of the lamplight. "The crux of the plan and its potential undoing is controlling the troglodytes. To my knowledge, no joint human-troglodyte attack has ever been attempted. I'm interested as to how they plan to accomplish it."

"Well, Helprig?" The emperor waited. "Now when you should offer explanations you stand there mute. How do you intend to control the troglodytes? This too I am curious."

The viscount continued to stare at the captain. Another brief touch of the gong and the guard captain lowered his arm. "Stay there Voss and do not shield your sword. The next time I bang the gong just slit his throat."

"Well, Helprig?" asked the general.

The viscount stammered, daring to clear his voice, "I, I am assured the chieftains will do our bidding. They have *ruregurir* with the woodsmen." He said *ruregurir* as if that would be enough, but then added, "We trade with the trogs, and they covet tork eggs. They will be well paid. Our interests are aligned." He omitted why troglodytes craved Paleowright tork eggs above all others: sage-rose. He also did not mention they seldom bothered with infusing tork eggs anymore and instead just supplied the ground sage-rose in snuff bags, a little secret if leaked to the Drakans that would be catastrophic. Helprig waited breathlessly for the emperor to challenge him on why the eggs were so important, more specifically how a small delicacy could guarantee the cooperation of the slavering, primitive reptiles. If the Drakans learned how the Paleowrights controlled the troglodytes they would demand the sage-rose for themselves, it was grown in Ompo, a Drakan vassal. Moreover, they would inquire how the Paleowrights learned of the reptilian dependency on the drug which would take them to Ancient technology, a technology that the Paleowrights withheld from the empire. The emperor, regardless of the backlash from the Nakish faithful, would sack every Paleowright, church, cathedral, archive, and treasury in Nak Drakas, and then he would set his sights on Hebert itself.

The emperor squinted, thinking. Then grunted, "We will provide two centuries, Helprig, no more," Your troglodytes and house troops will lead the attack. The commander of our centuries will have strict orders to remain in reserve until your forces are committed. General," he glanced to his left, "we do not want our centuries wearing Drakan uniforms. Attracting the attention of the Alliance would be premature. Let it remain a surprise that there is a Nakish force in the hinterland. How do you propose to infiltrate them across the border?"

Helprig quietly let his breath out.

"Sire," the general replied, "we have a variety of contingencies in preparation. For this operation, I would suggest we dispatch them by sea. Use our merchant shipping. We will replace some of the ship's crews with our soldiers and over the course of a few weeks assemble them in the port of Bareen and move them in small groups inland to Hebert."

"They will evade the SeaHaven blockade?" asked the emperor.

"We've used the method before sire, successfully, though not with two hundred men."

The emperor turned to scowl at the viscount. "There you have it Helprig. We will aid you in this endeavor under the terms I have imposed. You will feed and provision our men once they land in Bareen, but their commander will not answer to the Church. He will have a Washentrufel advisor and will be under strict orders from General Biornach. And one more thing, you will bring me the plans for this new weapon, regardless of prettiness. And you will bring me more Ancient technology, something to wage war, or I will have you bound in irons and digging salt till your shackles rust from your body. You have until the winter snows Helprig, or I will send the Washentrufel to train you as a salt miner."

"You're sure?"

"Yes, Alon, at least four tribes."

Christina wheeled her mount around. "Barrigal, Bags, your thoughts?" She'd stopped calling them captain, at their request, as they'd become friends on the long hard ride east.

Barrigal, one of Sedge's two mercenary captains, glanced to the SeaHaven scout they met on the border between the SeaHaven and Hebert. "It is not good news."

"That makes over eight hundred troglodytes headed west," said Bagonen.

The scout appeared shocked at the news.

"Oi," Bagonen nodded to the scout. "We've been dodging and fighting trog hunting parties since leaving Lycealia. All the bands were moving west."

"We thought they were hunting parties," said Christina, "but a Faithful in a village south of Hebert said all the troglodyte tidal pens are empty. No live fish stocks. The troglodytes have picked up their nets, huts, and youngins, and are migrating. West."

Bagonen slouched low in the saddle. His face reflected how he felt. "Bad omens for Wedgewood. The loglards are massing." He locked eyes with Christina.

She held her jaw tight. Her mount sensed her agitation and started to fuss. Christina slewed the eenu around to face north. *So close,* she thought. The Oridians had, at first, forced the abductors to stop and hide. Then in an agonizing game of cat and mouse, the Darnkilden Rangers had driven the Washentrufel agents –whose identities they were now sure of-- to flee south, with their captive Timberkeeps. But the Washentrufel agents were good at field craft, and were being aided by Paleowright sympathizers, and supplied with food and fresh mounts.

She had to make a choice: continue the pursuit north and pinch the Drakan agents between her warriors and the SeaHaven League, or turn back west and race the troglodytes home to Wedgewood. Her own force of eighty troopers was spread across a net fifty miles wide. It would take time to gather them, and Wedgewood had to be alerted, soon. Sedge needed to know how many, and from where the trogs were coming. She had two pathics with her communicating with the clan, but the farther east her force rode, the longer it would take to return and aid the town. Worse, if the troglodytes were indeed massing near Wedgewood, they'd have to fight their way back. Outnumbered ten to one, she didn't have nearly enough fighters to take on eight hundred troglodytes.

The eenu piped, restless. Christina turned the mount around again in a full circle and stared north. "So close," she breathed. "So close." Standing in the stirrups, she settled back down and gave the mount right leg. "West," she said without looking at Barrigal or Bagonen. "Sound recall. Send a message to Sedge. Warn him of the new count. Tell him we are coming home."

Chapter 38
Treedog

Wedgewood

The snow was gone, and so too were the spring pioneer blossoms. Late spring flowers were giving ground to fiddle-headed ferns, and Ungerngerist pollen drifted down in great clouds to catch in the hungry open cones.

"So why did Achelous let you join the Wards?" asked Pottern, "I thought you were too busy running trade missions?" Pottern gave Outish a teasing sneer.

"We've enough business around Mount Mars to keep me busy," replied Outish. "I—" Lettern held up her hand, waving them to silence. She was lean and tan, fresh from the Alon's rescue mission to the east. The gauntlet scars on her cheek, from the fight at Murali's, were fading from angry purple to blush red. Their witness to that outrage would have been more livid if not for Mbecca's healing touch. Lettern seldom spoke of that day in front of Murali's, but Outish sensed she burned with the shame of it.

In the distance, a dog could be heard baying. "Is it Noodles?"

Pottern listened carefully. Aloft in the forward watch-stand on Ungern Way, the main road into Wedgewood, they had a good view beneath the canopy to the next ridge where the road tipped out of sight and descended down the mountain. "Sounds like her." The baying stopped. Curiosity crossed Pottern's face. "Maybe I should go see what she's gotten into." It was something to do other than being stuck in the watch-stand.

Lettern held out her arm, stopping him. "I never heard a treedog bay like that. I thought you taught her to track troglodytes?"

Pottern nodded, "Yep. She'll chatter when she's on the scent."

Just then, Writing, one of the ward's two telepaths, came running on the trail from her post at the main watch-stand, between them and the Main Gate at Wedgewood. Outish dropped the rope ladder, and Writing came scrambling up, on the fly. Rolling through the trap door, she asked breathlessly, "Pottern, where's your dog?"

“Out there,” he pointed, “she’s been roaming, and caught the scent of something.”

“Yes I know,” said Writing, “she’s onto trogs.”

“What?” exclaimed Outish.

Writing nodded. While human pathics could not communicate with animals, the tight human-canine bond offered a rudimentary form of shared visualizations, and if the dog trained with its handlers, like Noodles did with the ward, then the images could be sharpened into a proper connection. “She’s onto them. They might try to kill her.”

Suddenly worried, Pottern stammered, “Maybe I should call her back?”

Lettern shook her head. “Not without letting the trogs know we’re here.” She asked Writing, “Did you send a message back to the gate pathic?”

“No, I wanted to make sure first.” Sending a trog alert to the telepath at the Main Gate would stir Wedgwood into a frenzy.

Lettern turned back to the distant baying. A false alarm would not do.

Noodles appeared at the top of the far ridge still barking, her attention riveted on something to the east. “I’m going down,” said Pottern.

“No you’re not Pots, you’re staying right here.” Lettern grabbed her bow from the bow rest and in one practiced motion bent and strung the hornbeam bow like it was matchwood. Taking a cue, Outish loaded his handbolt.

“Writing,” Lettern instructed, “go back down and wait. If I signal with two fingers it’s trogs, and you send a message to the gate pathic and get back to Main Stand. One finger means it’s just a badger or wolf or something.”

The pathic climbed down the rope ladder and backed away from the massive tree to get a head start to Wedgewood. Moments ticked by. From the ground, Writing couldn’t see the far ridgeline where the dog barked. The sound stopped. The mental images from the dog were confusing compounded by the fact they came from a visual perspective of a foot off the ground, ferns and grasses blocked much of the view. The dog didn’t need to see the troglodytes, its sense of smell more than sufficed. Maybe the images of the trogs were from the dog’s memory? A clear vision came to her of the dog with its nose high in the air, nostrils flared as the nose waved back and forth seeking scent. Writing began to relax. She felt her heart beat slower; the dog was probably just agitated over something that might have smelled like a trog, and it conjured up the image from memory. Then a motion from the watch stand caught her eye.

Outish frantically waved a hand with two fingers up.

Writing bolted, calling to the gate pathic as she fled.

"What do we do now?" whispered Pottern. A lone troglodyte stood in the center of the ridge surveying the road, testing the air.

"We blow our horn," said Outish.

"Not yet," hissed Lettern, "our camouflage is working. He doesn't see us. Writing has gotten off her message, and she'll carry the word to Main Stand. Let's watch a bit before we spook it."

Chattering like a squirrel, Noodles scrambled up the tree to the watch stand. Standing on the railing, panting, tail wagging, her tongue lolling out, the dog looked at Pottern for approval. "You did good, good girl," he whispered, petting her profusely.

Outish tapped him on a shoulder and pointed. Three more trogs stood in the road. Another appeared off to the right in the forest.

"Shiren," Lettern cursed. "Time to go boys, where there's four there's a whole lot more."

Pottern and Outish scrambled down the ladder and Noodles followed behind them on her raccoon-like claws. Lettern saw another trog to the right, three more to the left and the ones on the road began to move forward. "Outish." As he looked up, Lettern dropped her bow to him. She straddled the railing and used the repelling rope to descend in two bounds. Hitting the ground, she commanded, "Go! Run!" She raised the watchhorn to her lips.

Ogden assembled the Second Ward beneath Main Stand. The operations officer was holding off on sounding the general alarm until Ogden confirmed with his own eyes the presence of trogs. The two had argued over the decision, but the ops officer was firm. Ogden complained what good was it to have lookouts if you didn't believe them? The captain countered that with the town being tense from the last incursion calling a tree-up for an invasion would spin the citizens into a tizzy so they would wait to confirm. Sending the whole town to hard-points and tree forts, shuttering businesses, and escorting children and old folk caused a substantial disruption to the clan. Ogden had left the confrontation in disgust and rode forward with his ward. Over the soft beats of the eenu hooves, three sharp watchhorn notes sounded down the road. Two blasts meant enemy sighted. Three blasts meant enemy sighted and the watch was falling back.

The trumpeter, in the Main Watch stand above where Ogden dismounted and arrayed his ward across the road, blew one note followed by three more. His was the relay call to Wedgewood a mile away.

As much as Ogden preferred to meet the trogs on eenuback, the forest turf was too spongy and riven with roots to make for anything but treacherous galloping when they left the road. "Two ranks. Ottern, Milarn, Boden, Torden, flankers left and right." Giving the commands to position his ward across the Way, he could see to where the pine-needle lane ran a twisting course through the forest and around the enormous trees. They'd pick that watch location because the understory was low, so except for the tall, cathedral-like arches of the trees, his view was unrestricted. Three figures emerged on the road at a run. It was his forward watch post.

"Flanking watch are vacated," reported Bagonen, the branch warden.

"Aye," acknowledged Ogden.

The sound of a galloping eenu came from behind. Ogden turned and saw the Scout's captain.

"What do you have Ogden? I hear a lot of horns, but don't see any green scales."

Ogden turned back and focused on the three approaching runners.

Lettern stopped in front of the ward, all three Timberkeeps were panting heavy, encumbered by their weapons. "Skirmish," Lettern, gulped air, "skirmish line," she pointed back, "they're coming through the forest."

"How many?" asked Scouts.

At the end of the road, a group of trogs appeared, loping. The force grew and did not hesitate when they saw the line of warriors barring their path. Turning into an accountable mass, it continued to lengthen.

"That answer your question?" asked Ogden.

Scout's captain paled when he saw the charging horde. Without a word, he turned towards Wedgewood and whipped his mount to a gallop.

"What now?" asked Bagonen an edge to his voice.

"Pull Main Stand. Send riders to the outer posts, tell them to fall back on the town." Ogden gritted his teeth.

"And us?" asked Bagonen.

"Mount up. We'll fight them at the wall."

Every bell in Wedgewood rang, some with more fervor than others. The bell in the Mother Dianis chapel rang so hard Sedge expected it lose its clapper. "Silence those bleeding bells! I think the town knows we have visitors. All except for Timber Hall, it's far enough away, it can ring for the outlands."

From his vantage in Tall Lofty, the gigantic Ungerngerist tree that housed the Command Post, he watched the twelve wards muster. Towns-folk and other non-combatants walked, some ran, to their safe houses. Crews of the forty-plus tree forts donned their armor, strung their bows, stacked their arrows and quivers, unlimbered rock boxes, and pulled up their entry lifts, ladders, and ropes. Some of the largest of the tree forts like Tall Lofty could house forty men, and others less than five. Many of the wards had dual duty posts: first on the wall and then in a tree fort should the wall fall. Twice a week for the past month the clan, at his urging, had called surprise "tree ups" as they had become known.

The bells, one by one, stopped ringing and the welcoming silence, except for Timber Hall, was filled with the murmurs of the pedestrians below. Sedge watched in satisfaction as the drills paid off and Wedgewood became an armed camp in just ten minutes.

Off in the distance to the east, beyond the Main Gate and somewhere along the Ungern came the clarion note of a brass wardhorn, purposely different in tone from the ox-sticker watch horns. A second note immediately followed the first, and the town held its collective breath, waiting. Then the third note.

What the bells, with all their tolling clangor, failed to accomplish by causing alarm, that one lone distant trumpet more than made up. Those who were nonchalantly mustering to their safe houses now broke into a run.

"Ward in retreat commander!"

"I hear it," answered Sedge. In his two years as Mearsbirch warlord, he'd come to respect and even admire the doughty warriors who volunteered to defend their clan and town. They trained hard, fought well when their time came, and were loath to surrender one tree to an enemy. A ward sounding retreat was in dire straits. "Who has the watch?" he asked.

"Second Ward sir."

Sedge grunted. He visualized the plight of their commander. "Stay wise Ogden," he said to himself. "Don't get your bravos trapped."

Christina, just recently returned from the east, strode purposely towards the gate, her Defender shield upon her arm and plain to those all around. She wore her full armor, bastard sword slung over her back, longsword at her hip. At the gate, she met Alex and Feolin. A half-company of Sedge's mercenaries were arrayed in two ranks before the portal, and the wall, such as it was, was fully manned with five wards. The problem was, even in their haste to finish the rampart the stonewall encompassed only half of Wedgwood. Where the wall ended, a wooden palisade had been erected. She gazed to where the barricade met stone, at least the trogs couldn't just walk in.

"Open the gate!" called the gate captain.

On the road, eenumen galloped, a full squadron of mounted infantry. While they rode with haste, their form was good and discipline evident in the two columns riding close with no gaps. They came through the gate, and their leader swung aside directing the troop to the stables. Christina recognized him under his distinctive horned helmet and brass shield. "You have word weapons master?"

Ogden looked up to where Christina paraded on the wall-walk. "Oi, they've bloody emptied the Great Swamp, so they have. I'll wager every trog buck between here and the Angraris is slathering on the Ungern. Coming fast they are."

She turned, peering out beyond the wall, her hand resting on the granite block cut fresh from the mountain. She could hear the troglodytes before she saw them. The thud of their feet pounded into the carpeted road and through the foundations of the wall. The jingle and clash of harness grew, and then the trog host hove into view. Her eyes narrowed. "Mother..." Alex breathed. Christina could feel her heart beat beneath her breastplate. The sight sent a chill along the wall. "So many," one archer said. The troglodyte host came at the wall at a dead run, one long, sinuous, reptilian battering ram aimed at the gate over which Christina, Alex, and Feolin stood.

"Captain, you have orders for your archers?" Christina asked, stirring the gate captain from his shock.

He stammered, then called out, his voice carrying, "Archers! Ready!" Bows and crossbows came up.

So rapid their advance the trogs were already in range. The captain called, "Loose!" Before the first flight thudded home, he called again "Archers!" The first ranks of trogs, tightly packed on the narrow road, fell sprawling in a gnarling, twisting mass of leather jerkins, green scales, and all manner of spiked weapons, tripping and entangling the rearward ranks. But in their reptilian agility, the troglodytes overcame the obstacles leaping their fallen hatchren in great vaulting arcs.

"Loose!"

More attackers fell, stumbling and rolling in the pine needles.

"Loose!"

The archers were now firing point blank down the open mouths of the reptiles as they stacked up at the foot of the wall and began climbing. Christina watched in detached professionalism as a trog reached the first of the sharpened stakes embedded in the wall, pointing downward. The beast grabbed the stake and tried to pull it free. Mounted solidly the spike resisted and the animal attempted to maneuver around when a quarrel pinioned its shoulder dropping it into the thrashing mass below. A reptile's javelin sailed past, and Christina made ready her shield. More javelins came, and she moved along the wall deflecting the projectiles while their targets, the archers, emptied full quivers. An archer gargled behind her, and she turned. A trog, climbing up and over its hatchren in writhing reptilian ladder, was through the spikes and ripping out the throat of the warrior. She drew her bastard sword and cleaved the foe's jaw clean away.

"They're on the wall, sir!"

"I see them," said Sedge, watching through his telescope, "Damn that was fast. Sound Tree Mount."

The Tall Lofty bugle sounded two short blasts followed by two long.

Ogden hustled to his assigned post and called out "Second Ward! Form skirmish line!" To his right, Barrigal was assembling half of his hundred and eighty-man mercenary company, the center of the line, and to the right of them, the Seventh Ward formed the right of the skirmish line. Their task to hold back the assault giving the wall defenders time to quit the ramparts and gain their respective tree forts. They had practiced the move, but never really expected to do it.

Ogden watched as Alex the Defender, the last on his section of wall, jumped from the wall-walk and landed in a hay wagon piled high with straw. Alex rolled off the wagon and jogged to the waiting skirmish line. Alex, not particular as to where he fought, nodded to Ogden and squeezed in beside him. "Mind if I join you weapons master?"

"Oi, happy to have your sword any day Defender. We'll be falling back to the Perrty and Coarky Forts as soon as the wall is cleared."

"Then we'll be parting company along the way. Defenders are assigned to the Hall." Christina and Feolin had the use of parapet steps to descend the wall and fought a delaying action against trogs pushing down from above. The two used the cover of the arrow barrage from the three supporting tree forts and hustled to the waiting line of mercenaries.

The Defenders, their shields freshly painted, courtesy of the artist's guild, heartened all Timbers in the skirmish line. To have a Defender -- three of them and an Ascalon -- was a tremendous boon. Timberkeeps believed that somehow, no matter the odds, no matter the fear, the doubt, and blood, that they would prevail if Mother herself were at their side.

Troglodytes streamed down the wall steps taking five or six at a bound. Their hoarse, guttural croaks and squawks added a strange alien sound to the ordinarily peaceful woodland town. They waved spiked clubs, hammers, and flails; the myriad of weapons was confounding. One trog wielded a pitchfork purloined from a Timber farm, and another hefted a useless plow blade.

"Sheild wall! Shields up! Lock shields," called Barrigal the mercenary captain in command of the battle line. They need not hold long, but they were only one rank deep.

"Blast these shield walls," Feolin whispered to Christina, and her helm dipped.

Christina sheathed her bastard sword and drew the shorter long sword. "Aye," she replied.

Feolin added, "Never was one for the oyster can. No room to swing and you have to stand like a tree."

The trogs came at them in a scattered group unprepared as to what to do once they were over the wall. As one, the warriors in the shield wall readied for Barrigal's next command. "Three steps forward. Ready... Now!" Together the line surged forward and smashed their shields into the leading reptiles. The tactic was designed to stall the initial surge causing it to jam up and stifle the mass of warriors now coming over the ramparts in a flood. They need not hold them long, but stop them once they had to do. Christina planted the boss of her shield square in the open maw of a fiend and felt the crunch of teeth while simultaneously stabbing with her sword from below. She twisted her sword free of the sucking flesh and jabbed at the face of a reptile attacking the Timberkeep warder beside her.

A stream of arrows slanted down from the surrounding tree forts growing into a hail as more defenders made it into the tops. Dead and wounded Troglodytes began blocking the way of the others behind, but still, the shield wall was only one rank deep.

The attackers at first attempted to bull their way through by sheer mass but the defenders were packed shoulder to shoulder, and the trogs succumbed to right-handed sword cuts from below the shields. The smarter reptiles, rapidly learning to adapt to shield-wall warfare, tried to grapple with the shields and drag them down blocking the sword thrusts while snapping at the warriors with their jaws.

"Back three!" Barrigal called, and the merc bugler sounded the call.

"Back three!"

Retreating steadily down the street, Ogden saw they were between Murali's on the left and the stables on the right. The farther into town they withdrew, the more tree forts came into bow range of the shield wall. Some troglodytes, distracted by the new surroundings, split off from the nasty fight in the shield wall to rampage, ransacking buildings, assaulting tree forts, or just committing mayhem. While the trog host was numerous, their discipline within the town nonexistent. It was almost as if they assumed the capture of the wall and invasion of the city would end the matter, but it was in the streets where Sedge intended to fight the real battle. Having listened to the accounts of Whispering Bough, he doubted any wall could withstand a determined trog rush unless it was triple the height of his, and even then it wouldn't take them long to learn half the barrier was a wooden palisade.

Baryy cranked back the cocking lever of his handbolt and fired at a troglodyte climbing the trunk of the Perrty tree fort. "Did you get the message off?" he asked Trishna. She pulled her bowstring, sighted at the distant shield wall as it bent backward from Murali's. Her arrow struck in the thinning mass of troglodytes. "Yes, Marisa is with Achelous. They know."

Baryy watched the line of warriors, depleted by ones and twos, continue to backpedal. Stretching from the gate were the bodies of the shield warriors, fallen wherever Barrigal had ordered a stand. Baryy sought out Outish, but couldn't tell his armor from the others. Today there would be no Ready Reaction to the rescue. As far as the IDB knew, Outish had gone home to Halor, and he and Achelous were on Remus IV. His message to Achelous in Tivor warned of the attack and alerted him against traveling to Wedgewood until, until... he dispelled the dark thought and loaded another bolt. So far, no trogs had directly attacked their fort, but there were enough of the green bastards running around below to make everyone nervous. Per the fort defense doctrine of overlapping and layered fields of fire the redoubts farthest from the fighting directed their bows at forts closer to the main enemy body so those bastions could, in turn, aim their fire further in. And so it went, with the epicenter of the battle being the Main Gate and spreading ever westward as the trogs spread out.

"Buckthorn has fallen sir."

Sedge took the news with a clenched jaw. "Did they make it off?" he asked twisting his head at the messenger.

"No reports yet, sir, but twelve made it off of Hollowmeade." All the tree forts were connected to at least one other if not two by rope bridges. The fort defenders drilled on how and when to surrender a fort, retreating across a bridge and then pulling the support pins as the enemy followed them across. As long as the center forts held, the outer bastions would have positions to fall back to. Sedge didn't need to look at the fortification map of Wedgwood. He often lay awake at night, sleepless, tossing and turning over the plan, the positioning, and the manning of the forts. Hollowmeade and Buckthorn were the two forts nearest the Main Gate.

Her eyes burned with sweat, her hair plastered beneath her helmet. Christina backed and felt the first step of Timber Hall with her heel. It had been a long, slow, painful slog, watching her care die in ones and twos, but they'd made it without the line being broken and overrun. Second and Seventh Wards had split off to their respective tree redoubts, and now Barrigal and his merc company along with Christina and Alex were finally at their destination, a half mile of hard fighting and back stepping from the gate the whole way.

Feolin had gone down under a sudden rush only to be dragged back to their line at the last moment. Christina personally fought a way clear for him to be locked into one of the safe houses they passed, brimming with spear points and snarling Timberkeeps, guarded from above by the archery of five tree forts. The trog assault had degenerated into roving bands of reptiles bouncing from one hard-point to another, always seeking a weak, easy target, but finding only determined resistance from behind barricaded doors.

Barrigal limped, bleeding from a spike wound to his thigh, the blood draining into his boot so that it squished. He grasped the rail at the top of the stairs. "Right. 'Ere they come lads."

Unlike the Clan Mearsbirch wards, Barrigal's merc company had no women. Christina accepted his bias. It was his unit to command and pay, and it didn't bother her to be called a lad.

A throng of seventy or so trogs led by a chieftain came straight at the Hall.

"No shield wall," she said.

"Finally," grumped Alex. The remaining sixty mercs and Defenders were arrayed in a loose line across the front of the hall. They were bait.

"Back to back?" he asked.

"Yes," she said, unlimbering her bastard sword.

The trogs came in a heaving, grunting rush. Then the barricaded windows flew open, and a cascade of arrows sang forth on the twang of bowstrings and thump of crossbows, and trogs fell in a wave-like surf rebounding from a spume-covered cliff. Blood splattered across her face, sweat trickled down her back and between her breasts. In a terse mood, Christina swung her greatsword, finally free of its sheath, to wreak Mother's Vengeance. She swept left and right in efficient motions, conserving her ebbing strength. Once again, the fighting enveloped them. Alex stabbed low from a crouch as Christina's two-handed sword came whistling overhead, slicing, maiming, evoking gruesome wreckage to all it touched. Alex and Christina fought attuned. She swung hard left, and Alex knowing her backswing would expose her, gutted the attacker seeking the opening. She saw a trog aiming a massive club at her shoulder. The trog's eyes bulged, blood sprouted from its nose, and the club fell free. She brought her blade around driving a trog back from Alex. He followed her around in the pivot like a shadow slashing anything that drifted into her wake. Another trog lost an eye before it reached her, but Alex was at her right hip? The attacker staggered away clutching a paw to its face. Christina looked up the steps. “Rachael! Get back inside child!”

On the veranda, a girl in a plaid dress, knee-high deerskin boots, and a braided ponytail, pulled something from a leather foundry sack and threw it at a trog. The instant the object left her fingers it accelerated and swerved unerringly for the beast’s eyes. It struck with a hard, squishy thump.

“Rachael! Inside!”

“No!” she yelled back. “I want to be a Defender!”

Barrigal made to lay a hand on the girl, but she danced nimbly away and threw another lead musket ball. She might never be a pitcher for the Pinecone lobcaller team, but what her arm lacked in accuracy her kinetic mind more than made up. The projectile swerved from its downward angle and caught a trog in the ear with a solid thwack. The iron pellet sunk into the ear like a stone in water and Racheal let out a whoop.

Alex bashed his shield into the bloody snout of a troglodyte, smearing it with gore and drove the animal back over several bodies and stabbed it in the groin. The attack broke. Their chieftain dead, the troglodytes skulked away. Alex watched as a few slaked their thirst in an eenu trough. Exhausted, adrenalin draining away like a mountain stream, he stumbled backward, drawn to the steps by Christina. Sheathing his sword, he watched as a Timber matron burst out from the doors and pursued Racheal, intent on dragging her back inside. He smiled at the girl’s determination to avoid capture. “Who is that?”

Christina shook her head in concern, tired green eyes seeing the future of Wedgewood. “Rachael Stouttree, Lettern and Pottern Stouttree’s younger sister.

He laughed as the matron grasped a handful of Rachael’s shawl, but the girl pulled free, surrendering the garment. “Please, please,” she said running to him, “I want to be a Defender!”

He smiled mirthfully as the matron with Barrigal’s wounded help caught the girl and hauled her up the steps. She beseeched him. “Please!”

“When we’re through with this, come see me.” He called as the girl was carried away and the Hall door thudded shut with her safely inside. Barrigal limped to the head of the stairs. “Damned handy with pellets that one is. I wonder if all those Kinetic Kids are that good.”

Alex grunted and turned to watch the roving bands of troglodytes seek easy targets while at the same time trying to stay out of range of the tree forts.

“Rock Lichen has fallen sir. The trogs scaled the trunk and managed to swing out to the edge of the parapet and climb in on the rope bridge. They trapped the garrison when Long Needle pulled the pins.”

Sedge didn’t need to be told what that meant. All six of the fort’s defenders were dead; trogs didn’t take prisoners unless they wanted the meat fresh for later. That made the third tree fort. On the bulk of it, losing only three forts up to this point was good news, but more alarming was how Rock Lichen had fallen. The trogs had studied its exposed position with little flanking archery fire. Exhibiting spontaneous battlefield planning, they planned a determined rush. They’d gone up the tree in a blitz while the defenders shot their bows, dropped their rocks, and stabbed down with their spears easily wounding a half-score of the attackers, but the end had come too quick. He went to the plotting table. Surveying the town map, he tapped his finger on Archwood. It anchored the southern end of a line of four forts and formed the corner pivot into the east-west fort line. He fingered it again, saying to no one in particular, “If I were them, I’d go for Archwood next and try to pick off each fort in line.” He considered the attack from every direction. “Send ten warriors from the Twelfth to reinforce Archwood,” he ordered.

“Sir! Sir! The Paleowrights are here! They’ve come to help!”

Sedge stared at the messenger in confusion. “Paleowrights?”

“They’re on the wall.”

He spun and went to his telescope and trained it on the gate. Three Scarlet Saviors stood atop the wall and watched as two more opened the gate, which up to that point the trogs had been content to go over. Spying through the scope, Sedge saw a company of Paleowright Church pikemen march through and form up, a line abreast three ranks deep. “What sort of treachery is this?”

“Sir?” asked someone from behind him.

“Surely they’re here to help,” another said.

Sedge snorted and wheeled on them. He looked from face to face, their hope draining away in the heat of his gaze. “We just fought the bastards in front of Murali’s, down there,” he stabbed toward the floor. “Interesting timing they should show up now, and with Church troops? And explain to me why the trogs are completely ignoring them?" He looked around at the silent gathering. "Pass the word to all forts and safe houses, engage the Paleowrights as enemies, they are consorting with the trogs."

"Gads" a voice could be heard, "It's Whispering Bough all over again."

Sedge snapped. "The hell it is! This is Wedgewood, and by their blasted Ancients the Paleowrights will learn the difference."

Agent Larech, attached to the two Drakan centuries as Washentrufel observer stood next to Decurion Uloch, the Drakan commander, on the newly captured wall. Behind and below them out of sight, now that the trogs had finally rampaged the last tree fort overlooking the Main Gate, were the decurion's two Drakan centuries, two hundred men. To the casual observer, they appeared to be typical Isuelt mercenary companies: they wore no uniforms, tabards or insignia, and instead donned whatever clothing and armor the man preferred or more likely, could afford. Helmets ran the gamut from simple pot-heads to full-faced bassinets, but Larech was not a casual observer. To his trained eye, the two centuries, arrayed as they were in typical Drakan formation, were as conspicuous as a bull wearing an apron. The armor and clothing may be varied, but the weapon types and counts were all Drakan. Each century had ten scouts-skirmishers, ten halberdiers to form the 'crush' squad, sixty hoplites, and twenty archers, the standard configuration for a front-line century, the basic unit of the Drakan Militarium. Each hoplite was armed with a spear, a medium sword, two javelins, and a full-torso shield. In most cases, they wore greaves and gauntlets and donned either a chainmail hauberk or a leather jerkin studded with iron plates.

"No archers."

"Eh?" Larech puzzled.

"No damned archers. I complained about that to the prelate in Hebert," sighed the decurion.

Larech watched the Church battalion form up for the attack, and right enough, all four hundred men bore pikes. Not a quiver in sight.

A signal sounded and the battalion, crisp in their uniform tabards and tall black boots, their twin standards flying, marched forward arrayed in four orderly ranks, one hundred men abreast. Ahead of them was a line of four tree forts and what appeared to be three heavily barricaded buildings. They marched in silence while the nearby trogs stopped to slaver and gawk, more than few of which sported arrow wounds and sprouted fletchings.

The battalion, in the blue and green of the Hebert Cathedral, with their red shoulder sashes and gold tassels, crossed an unseen line and the defenders in the tree forts, clustered at the railings opened with a barrage of multi-colored feathers, all trailing a cloth-yard shaft and a razor-sharp arrowhead. "Well that answers that question," said Uloch.

Larech grimaced. "The Timmies are ready to fight the Church."

"I hope your commandant has this figured Larech. When Oridia, Lamar, and Mestrich hear of this..."

The agent breathed deep. "Darnkilden and SeaHaven will mobilize."

Shaking his head, the decurion added, "The Church clergy didn't think the Timmies would fight? And that the trogs would do the job?" He watched the arrow barrage. "Paleowright troops attack Wedgewood." He let the ramifications sink in. "This was supposed to be an occupation at the worst."

The first churchmen stumbled and fell, their mates behind stepping around the obstruction and closed ranks. They trod over the fallen troglodytes that littered the town like forgotten trash. Everywhere he looked lay a dead reptile. More arrows rained down. The pikemen held up their shields like turtle shells, but their coordination was haphazard; as they marched gaps appeared in the shell through which the archers poured iron-tipped death. At the closing range and downward angle, the shafts easily punctured the Church chainmail made of soft tin. Polished to look good in Church ceremonies and on parade, but was weak in battle. The first pikemen reached a tree fort and failing to find a way up either clustered about the base or pushed on. Well-placed rocks and arrows persuaded the pikemen to move on. They came to the first hard-point, a granary dug partially into the mountain. Stakes protruded from the ground in front of shuttered and barricaded windows. Crossbow bolts flew out from arrow slits. With more patience than the troglodytes, the pikemen beat at the stout doors and levered and pried at the barred windows all the while arrows plucked and struck down from the forts above. Here and there a window was pulled open or battered in only to be replaced by spear points. Mini battles erupted around each hard-point. Where pikemen gained an opening, they were sometimes dragged in while their comrades listened the man's screaming as he was hacked to death. At one hard-point, a leather goods store, the pikemen forced their way in but were bottled up at the door as three and four defenders stabbed and slashed at every man to enter. The doorway became a gruesome, slippery mess with blood, gore, and dead bodies, blue and green tunics trampled red. The pikemen gave a final surge, and fighting and screams could be heard from outside the store. Finally, the noise subsided, and five of the fifteen pikemen who went in came out.

Larech saw the second Church battalion form up in front of the wall. “Reinforcements.”

Uloch grunted, accompanied by a deep frown.

Then the first battalion sounded recall.

The decurion’s frown eased. “Well, that’s the first smart thing they’ve done.”

From below, the second battalion’s commander called up to the decurion “May I borrow your archers?”

Uloch answered, “All forty? And what will you do then? Scale those trees with your bare hands, in full armor. The lowest branch is thirty feet off the ground!”

The officer looked at the tree forts with renewed attention. Clearly weighing the situation, he called up to the decurion, “ladders?”

“Ladders, grapples, rope, and fire!”

“Eh hem,” Larech cleared his throat.

“What?” Uloch snarled.

“If you read my report you’ll know that Ungerngerist bark is resistant to fire.”

“But...” then he eyed the nearest tree. “But what about the branches and needles, surely they will burn?”

The agent shrugged. “Tis late spring, the dead needles have fallen. It's wet here on the mountain. I doubt a flaming arrow, by itself, would light anything on fire. More’s my guess those Timber tree lovers have already thought of your idea and prepared for it. I would suggest a fireball. Something big, soaked with oil.”

“You’d need a catapult for that,” Uloch responded impatiently.

Larech twitched his lips. “I, unlike our Paleowright allies, never expected this to be quick. At every turn, the churchmen have underestimated the Mearsbirch clan.”

“Catapults,” mused the decurion. Then he nodded. “They’ll take some days to build. In the meanwhile, we can starve the bastards.”

Chapter 39
The Raven

Near Tomis, continent of Isuelt, Dianis

Quorat settled the Intruder in fifty feet of water. This was as far east in the fjord as he could go and still have enough water depth to hide his ship. He was still three hundred miles from the mine site. To close the distance he had to leave the water and fly overland, which he was loath to do. The water dissipated his heat profile, canceled his sound signature, and the surrounding walls of the fjord contained his energy leakage, which was minimal but not zero. Having no better alternative, he launched the recon package.

The laser-communications pod shot out the ejection tube and floated to the surface. The package chamber on the pod opened, and the recon drone lifted off followed by the relay drone. Flapping its wings, the raven-like recon drone rose into the air aided by the lift fan centered in its lower body. Carefully configured for Dianis, the drones and bots in the recon package were camouflaged to appear as familiar avians found on northern Dianis continents, courtesy of published IDB Dianis research.

Rising on the thermals in the fjord, the relay drone synced with the communication laser on the recon drone. To the casual observer, the relay drone appeared to be a hawk, occasionally circling, but rising ever higher and higher, moving eastward to maintain the imaginary apex of the communications triangle. On the way, the hawk relayed the signal from the raven to the laser receptor on the communications pod disguised to look like a large piece of driftwood. At the intended destination, three hundred miles away, the hawk-raven recon package would be near its maximum range.

Quorat settled back. The encoded video and telemetry feeds from both birds were working as designed. It was now a matter of time. Seeking eastward air currents the microprocessor in the raven continuously adjusted fan attitude, wing deflection, and body angle for the optimum speed and energy-conservation setting. The solar receptors on the raven helped recharge the bird's energy cell, but most of the power came from the neutrino charger. He'd have to shut down the charger when they neared the mine site because the IDB ground sensor pods were sure to have energy emitter detectors. From there it would be solar and energy cell operation only. Regardless, the raven could only travel as fast as the real biological version, a design limitation dictated by nature. So Quorat rested. The time-to-target readout indicated arrival in ten hours, given the current prevailing air currents. He could have gone with the standard turbo-fan drone and shortened the process by a factor of ten, but he'd been in the intrusion business for a long time, and the reason his clients kept coming back to him was his repeated record of success, and that success was based on skill and patience. Unnatural-looking, fast moving, noisy turbo-fan drones always attracted attention, and attention got intrusion contractors caught or killed.

"Time to target thirty minutes. Time to target thirty minutes. Time to target thirty..."

"Uh?" Quorat roused himself from a deep sleep.

"Time to target..."

"I heard you!" He slapped the mute button silencing the Intruder's AI. Checking the drone displays he grunted, the raven had made better time than estimated picking up a forty-mile-an-hour tailwind over the mountains. Fully charged, the energy cell status glowed bright green. The sun was setting over the mine site, so he shifted to infrared imaging. Shutting down the neutrino charger, he issued glide commands and stealth-sweep guidelines to the drone. Should he lose line of sight comms with the raven when it dropped lower to investigate, the bird's computer would follow stealth recon procedures, collecting and storing all the data and then climb back up to an altitude where it could reconnect with the relay hawk.

The initial video feed was satisfactory. The mine was right where it should be: a steep pit in a rocky granite gorge with a river running beside the mine road. A precipitous gravel trail led straight down the chasm into the gaping hole. A sluice works ran beside the trail and along the river. Vine covered, the works were well-constructed and looked to be functional. Above the gorge, a mine building stood, more of a conglomeration of tin-roofed shacks tacked together in a meandering construction. Then the video feed cut out. "Blast!" He cursed. He slapped the mute button. "Well?"

"Recon drone sync lost," reported the AI. "Line of sight interruption."

Quorat considered sending a climb command to the relay hawk, but he figured it wouldn't work as the raven was descending deep into the chasm. He'd just have to wait.

"Sync reestablished. Sync reestablished. Sync..."

"Uh?" He woke up.

"Sync reestablished. Sync—"

"Arg," he slapped the mute button and checked the clock. "Three hours!" The bird had hit the maximum time separation parameter and had flown to where it could reestablish communications. He scanned the data streaming in over the relatively slow laser feed. Sending a roost command to the drone, the bird would seek a safe place to loiter and conserve battery power, which was down to sixty-two percent, he said to the AI "Rewind the data feeds to where the sync was lost and play video and audio at 3X."

Scrolling by at triple speed he watched the progress of the bird as it orbited lower and lower into the chasm, and then stealth programming took over and sent it to roost in a tall tree on the rim of the gorge. There it launched three of its recon bots. Tiny, identical to bees, the bots made their way into the canyon. The AI automatically divided the display into the three separate video feeds. Something was bothering him. As he watched the bots descend, his disquiet rose. *Where are the people? It is night, and unless they were running three shifts in the mine, most of the miners should be topside*. That was part of the problem. The mine site, mineshaft, and the mine building were dark. Not a candle, lamp, or other light anywhere. "Stop video. Examine audio feed. Are there any human-generated sounds on the audio feed?"

When the AI failed to respond, but the audio results scrolled by on the screen he growled to himself and slapped the mute button off.

"Negative," came the immediate response. "Ambient noise only."

"Blast!" He cursed, slammed the console, and pushed back. He'd been here before. *A dry hole. But why?* "Which bot went into the mine?" he asked the AI.

"Recon Bot Two."

"Play Bot Two video at 2X from the point it enters the mine."

The display centered on Bot Two's camera and the monochromatic scene scrolled by. Quorat watched. Down, down, into the main shaft, and then into a side shaft. He followed as the clock spun in step with the 2X display. Nearing the three-hour resync parameter, the bot had ceased the recon operation and headed back up to the raven.

Played out. No signs of fresh excavations, new timber framing, loose tools, stored water, or standby lanterns. The mine was abandoned. "Damn," he fumed, "damn, damn, damn." The second payout clause in his contract explicitly said locate and confirm the existence of one of two aquamarine mines, and this mine was abandoned. He could send another bot back down to be certain, but he didn't bother. The surface of the mine site was inactive. Judging by the vegetation growth, it was recently vacated. Anything of value, anything removable, had been taken away. *Hmmm,* he mused, *maybe there had been some sort of business squabble or political troubles that forced them to quit operations?* "Scan the mine site videos and locate largest tailings pile."

He waited as the AI executed the command. Then it reported, "Three substantial tailings piles, one of approximately thirty tons, another of fifty tons, and the third of seventy tons."

"Show me a layout of the site and superimpose the tailing piles on the sitemap."

Quorat cocked his head. The smaller tailings pile was at the top of the sluice works, and the largest, the seventy-ton mound was at the bottom. That was a lot of tailings for an aquamarine mine, especially for one this primitive. The third heap was up behind the building where some form of processing was conducted. The whole setup was odd. Usually, indigin miners didn't build a sluice works three hundred feet long to separate aquamarine. A drain swirl was typical. The layout made sense if they were mining for gold. *Yes,* he told himself, *aquamarine can be found with gold.* It was the third pile that bothered him. *I wonder if that is from a smelting operation?* Grumping to himself, he mentally ran through scenarios on how to maximize his payment. *Even if the mine is played out, or work was stopped I can still get my triple kicker if I get an aqua-5 sample.* "Ack, that would be a lot of work," said aloud.

"Unknown command," came the response from the AI.

"Shut up fool, I'm not talking to you." He zoomed the display in on the largest tailings pile. He really did not want to do it: collect a physical sample. He'd have to leave the water, move to within twenty, or so miles of the mine site, find a place to hide the Intruder, hop on his scooter, drive to within two miles or so of the site, and then walk in. *All for what? The site is shut down?!* In the back of his mind, he worried about the location of the IDB surveillance pods. For certain, the pods would not be in or immediately near the site as there was too great a chance the locals would encounter them. They would instead be positioned in a screen surrounding the site, probably a mile or so out. Trying to rationalize his next course of action, he wanted that triple kicker bonus, but his recon drone was not equipped for sample extraction. "Damn," he smacked the console. He'd have to go in.

"Send the raven down to the main tailings pile."

"We will lose sync if the command is executed. The recon drone will then seek to resync."

The AI had a point. Thinking it through, he said, "I want the raven to land on the main tailings pile, ping it with one A-wave scan, directly down into the pile, lowest setting to scan the top of the pile. One ping only, and then return and resync communications. Verify command sequence for operational integrity." The AI liked it when he asked for command sequence integrity, even though it did it out of habit.

"A-wave ping violates stealth mode programming."

"I know that dammit! I want to know if there is aquamarine-5 in that pile! I'll be damned if I drive all the way there only to get a handful of dirt!"

"A-wave ping violates stealth mode programming."

"Arrrg," Quorat picked up his dented drinking bulb and aimed it at the cockpit camera the AI used to discern facial features. "Then bloody remove the A-wave ping block from stealth mode, or I'll rewrite your circuits so you're a castrated turd."

"Removing A-wave ping block from stealth mode."

"Good. Execute command sequence."

"Executing."

Quorat glanced at the display. The camera view of the raven showed it lifting off and then circling into the chasm.

"Communications sync lost."

Quorat sat back in the command console chair and gave the cabin camera the evil eye.

As if to purposely irritate him the AI said, "At lowest A-wave ping setting probability is thirty-two percent that a standard IDB ground sensor pod will detect the radiation if it is within..."

"Shut the hell up!" He smacked the mute button. "I know all about IDB detection pods." Trying to calm himself, "I said I need confirmation that there is aqua-5 in that pile before I go risking my skin to dig a sample." He looked up at the camera. "Is that too hard to understand?" He reached out and pushed the mute button off.

"Command prerogative understood."

He took a deep breath and settled in the chair. Waiting, he ran through the approach vectors for the second aquamarine mine. It was on a different continent. The orbital survey showed those diggings to be smaller than this one. Not good, but the contract clauses said nothing about quantity or size of the mines, just existence.

He considered taking a stimulant shot or a down tube. He didn't know which direction he wanted to go, up or down, jazzed or asleep. Then the "resync" message from the AI forestalled his decision.

"What you got?"

The AI dutifully showed the results of the A-wave ping on the screen.

Quorat's shoulders sunk. "Whaaaaat?"

"You have a command request?"

"Yea. Yes. Run a diagnostics-check on the bird. Confirm the A-wave scanner is working, but do not fire it!" The last he almost yelled.

"Confirmed. A-wave diagnostics are successful. Recon drone sensor suite is fully functional. No faults found."

He squinted at the screen. His mind churning. "What?" he breathed. Nothing. Not a spec of aquamarine 5 anywhere in the tailings pile. It was totally inert. "Shiren!" He stood and flung the drinking bulb at the bulkhead. It hit the control lever for the landing skids and snapped the toggle clean off then caromed off the console and rolled back to his feet, complete with a new dent. Seeing the broken toggle, he screamed and kicked the bulb sending it spinning and bouncing out of the compartment.

In moments like these, the AI had self-learned the best action to reduce further shipboard damage was to remain silent.

"Damn, blasted, damn!" He gesticulated wildly pumping his fist at the floor and swinging his arms and shoulders. When he'd calmed as a result of exhaustion, he slunk down in the command chair. "Recall the raven," he growled quietly, "best possible speed." He looked up at the cabin camera. "You know what the bastards did." It was a statement, not a question.

"My programming, data on IDB tactics, situational characteristics, and this ship's previous mission logs indicates there is a sixty-two percent probability that the Mestrich mine site is a decoy."

"And why is it just sixty-two percent and not one hundred percent!?" Spittle spumed with his sarcasm.

"There is a probability, uncalculated, that the IDB was incorrect. That the mine never had aquamarine or that the coordinates were wrong from initial capture. You are correct that the probabilities of a decoy site would rise above sixty-two percent assuming the IDB were accurate in their geological data collection."

"Bloody hell." Someone had set a trap, and he had walked straight into it. Did the client know? Did the client suspect? If it were a decoy site, then the sensor system the IDB used would be tighter, more sensitive because they expected someone to take the bait. "Prepare to recall the relay drone and pull in the bubble-pack platform. Calculate maximum range for the raven." He didn't want to leave it behind unless he absolutely had to: it was an expensive toy. However, he didn't want it leading a Ready Reaction squad straight to him. He'd have to set a rendezvous point and recover the drone later. He rubbed his face and ran his fingers through his greasy hair. Not one for showers, he never minded his own smell. *Why would the IDB set a decoy site? If this dig was a decoy, did that mean the other was a decoy as well?* He thought about it. He could ask the AI for its opinion, but he knew the answer. His anger started to escalate again when he realized that the triple-kicker payout was a fool's errand. Worse, if the mines were decoys he could lose the payment on the second clause, and that would cut most of his profit. Issuing a stream of commands to the AI, Quorat considered his next move beyond abandoning the contract and the planet.

As the bubble-pack reeled in with the relay drone onboard, Quorat churned over what he knew.

"Ready to depart."

"Roger," he said. "Execute."

Listening to the drive engage, he continued to stew, and then finally decided to ask the AI for its opinion. "Given that an inert decoy site is a one-time snare and will attract a specific intrusion contractor once, and only once, what does that tell you about the purpose of the decoy site?"

The AI had its answer ready. "Seventy-two percent probability the purpose of the decoy site is to lead intruders away from active sites."

Quorat nodded. "Not to purposely trap off-worlders, but to redirect away from true locations."

"Affirmative."

So there is a real aquamarine mine, but where?

Chapter 40
Frustrations

Tivor

The embed in Achelous's thigh tingled with an incoming message.

"There are bats everywhere! One landed in my hair!" Patrace complained to Marisa. They were having a debate about the sulfur dig in the cavern.

Achelous waited for the message code.

Marisa, not fond of bats either, looked concerned. "In your hair?"

"Eh hem," Eliot interrupted, "it swooped past your ear."

Patrace wheeled on him, "How would you—" and so her tirade went.

The three-part message-code told him he had a text message on his multi-func, it was from Baryy, and it was urgent. He turned and walked slowly out of the converted flour mill not wanting to attract attention.

He opened his multi-func and read the message: *Wedgewood under attack. Trogs. Scaled the wall and in town. We are uptree in forts. They work. Busy ATM. Will call.*

A chill constricted his chest. *Troglodytes in Wedgewood? That's not good. That's very, very bad.* He walked away from the mill. Baryy indicated the defenders had taken to their tree forts. *That's a disaster! That meant...* his mind shied away from what it meant, but he forced himself to think about it. *That implies the clan defenders have been unable to keep the troglodytes away, or out of the town.* "Shiren. How long did that take? This is his first message? How many bloody trogs are there?" he asked aloud.

Marisa came out of the mill, "Why does everything have to be such a challenge?" She fumed, rolling her eyes and shaking her head. She stopped cold. Atch's face was ashen; he was holding open his Auro Na bible. The bible he was never without. The one he never quoted from but always drew his intense interest. He stared off into the distance, worlds away.

Her diminishing patience with Patrace forgotten, she edged to the left to get a better look at what he was reading. Her brow creased. Trying to get a better look she walked up beside him, but then the page in the bible shimmered. *What?* She shook her head not understanding what she saw. Reaching out she took the book from him and looked at it, the text was in the language of the old Auro Na, and she couldn't read it. For that matter, she didn't know of anyone, other than Achelous who could read it. "Dearen, what does it say?"

"Trouble."

His voice sounded old, defeated. She studied the greying stubble on his face. He hadn't shaved in three days, but she let it go. Closing the bible, she asked, "What trouble?"

Baryy and Outish are in Wedgewood. What can I do? He ran through all the options.

"Atch," this time she dropped the *Dearen*, "what is wrong?"

He grimaced, shook his head, and kept shaking it. He turned and walked away.

Marisa's eyes widened. Not accustomed to being ignored she wanted to demand an answer, but then Patrace came storming out of the mill, "I am not going to be the one to wade in bat guano and tell the diggers what the best poop to dig is!"

Marisa whirled, "Shut up!" Her snarl so quick and uncharacteristic that Patrace, wild grey hair, and greasy leather apron, came to a sudden startled halt.

Marisa stabbed a finger at the mill, and Patrace took the hint. "Arg!" The alchemist spun on her heels, stomped the ground with a heavy boot, and stalked back to the mill.

Achelous came to it finally. The only thing he could do was call the IDB and request an extraction. The gig would be up of course. Maybe they could get there in time, maybe they couldn't, but the whole plan to defend Dianis against the Nordarks would be undone, ruined. It didn't matter though, as bad, as terrible as that might be, he couldn't just let Baryy and Outish die. They were his... He thought about it, they had become his friends, not subordinates. He'd have to save them whatever way he could.

"What's wrong?" Marisa demanded from behind him.

He turned.

She blinked. The Achelous she knew was back. The narrow, determined glare told her.

"Wedgewood is under attack. It's been overrun by troglodytes. Baryy and Outish are there."

She looked at the bible.

"And where there are troglodytes, there are Paleowrights. Those bastards are behind this."

"How—" she asked, holding the bible.

He came to her and took it gently from her hand. He considered going to the Auro Na temple and shifting to Wedgewood, but he dared not go alone. There would be trogs everywhere. He'd need an escort, a big one.

He opened the bible and told her to stay there.

She watched him walk away, turn his back to her, and do something in the bible. Finally, that done, he said, "We need to go back to the hall. If something happens, we need to be with Boyd."

Riding hard Achelous suddenly pulled up. Marisa, Eliot and the five guards slowed and turned, looking for an explanation. They were within fifteen minutes of the hall. "Eliot, take the guards back to the hall. We are safe here. Marisa and I have an errand I just remembered."

When Eliot looked to Marisa, she nodded once and rode to Achelous.

When the guards had left, he said, "How bad is it?"

"How bad is what?" replied Marisa.

He held up a hand and pointed to his ear. A gesture completely lost on her.

"That bloody figures," he said exasperated.

She glared at him and cocked her head.

"Sorry, Baryy, I have Marisa here with me, and she has no idea that we are talking to each other." He paused, waiting. "Well, what am I supposed to do?" He ignored Baryy's complaint about letting Marisa know they could talk via A-wave. "I have one choice, and that is call for extraction."

"Extraction?" she asked.

"The Paleowrights have invaded Wedgewood," he told her. "There is a pitched battle going on. Baryy says they are hurting the troglodytes and Paleowrights, but it is a close thing." He cupped his ear, and held up the other hand to Marisa, "What's that?" Listening, he finally responded, "You sure you don't want extraction? I mean Baryy," his throat caught, "if there is something I can do to save you two I will do it. Period." He listened, continuing to cup his ear, "Okay, yes I know it would ruin everything. Yes, it may be bigger than two lives, but those two lives are you and Outish, and I," he choked.

He nodded. Dipping his head. “Fine,” he whispered. “I’ll let you go.”

He dropped his hand, signaling his conversation with Baryy was over. “There is nothing we can do. Baryy says he and Outish will fight it out with the Timberkeeps.”

Still befuddled she urged her mount next to his. “They’ll be alright.”

He laughed a short, bitter laugh. “That may be true, maybe. But those damned Paleowrights are going to be the end of us all. They are after the aquamarine mine, and just like Tomis, and the Archbishop in Linkoralis, and sending the pirates after you, the Paleowrights will not give up.” In frustration, he spurred Echo away. Sorry that he may be offending Marisa, but the Paleowrights were about to ruin everything he fought for. The stupid, blind idiots were about to destroy the planet’s single best chance to defeat Nordarken Mining and the flood of corsairs that was sure to come, and with that loss so to would go any chance of Uplift. So much at stake and the Paleowrights were interested only in maintaining their own pathetic status quo. It was hard enough, impossible enough for him and the provincials to fight Nordarken Mining, but now they had to fight the Paleowrights, pirates, and troglodytes too.

He slowed Echo to let Marisa catch up. He so much wanted to focus on the Nordarken threat, but now the Paleowrights, provincials he was trying to protect, were the paramount danger. When Marisa caught up, he looked at her. “We need to hurt the Paleowrights. I don’t know how, but anything we can do, we must do. They are putting at risk the defense of this world.” Usually, the thought of intervening and influencing local politics would have been abhorrent to him. He believed in ULUP. Up to now, his struggle had been focused on keeping Nordarken Mining off the planet, but now that the Paleowrights had intervened in Wedgewood and could kill Baryy and Outish, things were different. Adding to his woes, Ogden, the foundry, the rifle plans, and prototypes were all in Wedgewood.

Chapter 41
For the Second

Wedgewood

"They're retreating sir," an aide said hopefully. Sedge nodded and leaned on the railing for the command loft. The view still unobstructed because they as yet had no need to drop the wooden arrow blinds. The streets and woodland paths of Wedgewood were strewn with enemy dead. Here and there a Timberkeep lay, mostly on the wall, and along the bloody retreat down Wide Lane. He estimated over a thousand trogs had assaulted the wall and now approximately half of those were roaming about in lose bands ransacking bivvies, toppling latrines, and rooting in unguarded shops while collecting an arrow or two for their efforts. Some had already left the town for prey in the countryside. Grimmer were the casualties inflicted on the battalion of churchmen. He doubted seventy pikemen made it back to the gate. Against that slaughter, they paid with the loss of two ten-man hard-points.

"Where're their archers?" he called to his operations officer. "Surely the Paleowrights have archers?"

The captain shrugged. "None reported, none seen sir. I've asked. The front line forts have been instructed to lower their arrow blinds when the archers arrive."

Sedge didn't like having to use the arrow blinds. They converted the fort into an enclosed turret, but the blinds drastically reduced visibility and limited the archer's ability to provide supporting fire to the redoubts and hard-points around them. However, if it came to an archery duel, the blinds could be a decided advantage.

Lettern climbed up through Perrty's trap door and pulled up the rope ladder. "Oi, all's quiet on this side of town. There's a fresh Parrot battalion lined up at the gate, but they're not moving." She was excited. Her quiver empty save for two arrows. Today she had exacted revenge for Mergund's death.

“How many battalions do they have?” asked Pottern, a nervous edge lilting his voice. Noodles stood on a branch over his head engaged in a chattering duel with a chipmunk in the next tree.

She shook her head. “No one seems to know.” They let silence curtain the implications. Then Baryy broke it by asking “Have you seen Outish?” there was a nervous edge to his voice as well.

Lettern paused, her face blank. “I—No, I was in the archer’s nest atop Murali’s. Why? He’s not here?”

Baryy looked away and gave a short shake of his head.

“Shiren,” she hissed, not the second of her friends. “This is his rally station for the ward. He should be here.”

Baryy nodded, staring at the trog bodies on the path below. Some moved and twitched feebly, a few moans and guttural raspings added to the alien presence. In a day’s time, the dead lying in the sun would begin to bloat and stink.

Lettern looked to the west; the sun was sinking, two fingers above the shoulder of Mount Mars. “We’ll be mounting a foray to recover our wounded...and dead, at last light. We’ll search for him. He may have made it to a hard-point.”

Baryy ground his teeth. At first, he feared for the success of their ‘project’ if the astrobiologist were killed before they had all their data, but then, the more he thought about it, the more he didn’t care. Grudgingly, he admitted to himself that Outish, as odd, goofy, and impetuous as the Halorite was, he’d become his friend, his comrade in arms, a co-conspirator in a great plot. Those odd and impetuous behaviors were exactly the attributes that endeared the astrobiologist. Not having Outish around for him to shake his head at was like missing an emotional foundation, an integral part of their Wedgewood existence, he swallowed. Stashed in his cabin was a FiPWiS, a Field Portable Wound Stabilizer. Markedly less capable than a full autodoc, it was nonetheless very good at doing one thing, inducing a trance-like state that slowed all bodily functions to a crawl and stopped bleeding through point-focused coagulation. Autodocs were equipped with a FiPWiS unwind program that actuated functions to reverse the stabilizer effects, but in order for that to happen they’d have to find Outish, alive, stabilize him, get him to the shift zone -- a day’s hard ride away – and then shift to the repair bay at Isumfast where the autodoc sat. “I’m going now,” he said.

“What? No, you can’t. We’re to remain uptree until we’re called to muster.” Lettern’s tone brooked no debate.

Baryy shouldered his way past and reached for the trap door.

The old, grizzled fort-warden stepped on the door. "Sorry laddie, we dropped the ladder for Lettern because she's assigned here. Otherwise, it stays up till I get orders."

"Fine." Baryy jumped on the railing, grabbed the repelling line, and before they could snatch him, leaped into the void. He'd never used the repelling line before but saw it in action. He held on for dear life as he sank like a stone and his stomach lurched into his chest; the cable drum paying outline on an ever-tightening spring. He pivoted just in time to take the hit against the trunk on his shoulder. Spinning, the rebound swung him away from the tree as the ground came up fast. Rather than hit the tree again he let go of the line and fell the last few feet, rolling in a heap. By then the drum spring had bound tight and latched, reducing the impact. He stood, swaying, and looked up. The warden was shaking his head, but not surprised, Baryy had cast his die and now had to live with it. Pottern gawked, his eyes wide as saucers, but Lettern fumed.

Disengaging the latch pawl and setting the retrieval brake the fort warden let the drum recoil. Baryy watched his safety line snake out of reach. He loaded his handbolt and secretly checked the laser charge status. "Don't go! We'll send down the line," Lettern called out, but Baryy waved with a dry grin that held no humor and set off quickly before he was spotted by trogs. Reaching the nearest building, he hid behind the cabin and peaked around the corner.

"The way's clear to Wide Lane," Pottern called.

He held up his hand in acknowledgment and saw Lettern scampering across the footbridge to Broomstick fort. *She's going to rat me out to Odgen,* he guessed. Pushing away from the wall, he darted to the next hut in a low crouch. Out of sight, he opened his multi-func and issued a low energy ping. If Outish were nearby, his embed would respond. They'd had to disable most of the embed's location functions otherwise the Matrincy could turn the embeds against them. On Wide Lane in front of him lay the first bodies from the shield wall. Judging by their armor, two were mercs, and one was a Timberkeep. Peering down the street the nearest mobile trog -- that he could see -- was at the gate, a fair distance away. There was no response to the ping. Dread sunk heavy in his stomach. *Maybe...* He scuttled to the nearest Timberkeep body and turned it over. It was Bagonen. "Damn," he cursed. The man's lifeless eyes stared up at the sky. He closed the branch warden's eyes and felt sick. Choking down vomit, he wiped his mouth on his shoulder. A palpable, chest-crushing fear seized him. Up in the tree looking down, he'd been safe, relatively. Here on the ground amongst the dead and dying...he realized this was going to be way harder than he thought.

"What is the problem with the chieftain?" asked Uloch when Larech returned from eavesdropping on a heated conclave between the troglodyte chieftains and the Church commanders. Viscount Helprig was nowhere to be seen though he'd been on the wall when the first battalion attacked. "They're upset that the churchmen have stopped their attack. They want them to attack now. They think the Paleowrights are either snake piss liars or muck bottom cowards."

The commander laughed. "They may be right, but they're an impatient lot nonetheless. We've been fighting for all of a half day. The trogs have no sense of strategy other than direct, brutal assault. If they can't club and eat it, they're confounded."

"No," replied Larech, finding himself in the odd situation of praising the reptiles, though like many humans he found them viscerally repelling. "They do in fact understand tactics. In the open field they can be devilishly cunning, but this town warfare, with tree forts no less, in what is beginning to look like a siege they're lost. Siege warfare is beyond them. If they can't skulk and maneuver about, plotting ambushes and sudden charges they will generally refrain from combat. I dare say they're having a hard time adjusting if they can. They're lizards after all."

The commander grunted, it made sense from what he'd seen, and so far the Washentrufel agent's guidance had been accurate. The man appeared to know middle Isuelt, whereas this was Uloch's first foray beyond the Darnkilden frontier.

"The head chieftain says he's lost half of his warriors. The Paleowrights promised him an easy victory and lots of Doroman meat to drag back to the swamp."

With a snort, the decurion waved his hand at the tree forts. "The only easy meat to be had here is raw reptile on a Timmy arrow."

"Perhaps you should join the conclave, your council would be useful." Larech looked at the decurion, respectful yet challenging.

Uloch returned the look with disdain. "You preach futility. Every step of the way here the churchmen ignored my suggestions. No archers, no fodder for the mounts, no scouts, no grapples and ropes, no scaling ladders, and a single point of attack. Bah, you were there Larech, why do you suggest more folly?"

"They are building the catapults, and perhaps their mood has changed, and the reality of war will persuade them to listen to your professional opinion."

His brows dripped scorn, and he turned to watch the Timmies in the nearest bastion lean idly on their railing, strung bows propped beside them, arrow bundles draped on the boles like moss streamers. "Yes, the catapults will help, but let them send a messenger requesting my counsel. Until then don't annoy me with daydreams."

"I hear you have news for me Brookern." Sedge straightened up from the planning table, pouring over situation dispatches.

"I do my lord."

Sedge ignored the honorific, he'd grown tired of correcting people. It didn't seem to matter to the Timberkeeps that he'd refused the lordship the King of Mestrich offered him.

Brookern, the self-appointed leader of Clan Mearsbirch voyants, stood tall for a Doroman, wearing his long brown hair tied back, and a suede coat over a white linen shirt buttoned tight to the collar. A wide black belt cinched his pants to his wire-thin frame; his grey eyes were watery. "We've convened a conclave of town sensitives and are seeking to ken the nature of the disaster that has befallen us. To that end, we are in agreement as to many visions we are seeing. Our voyants, dreamers, and pathics concur on related and intriguing aspects." To a voyant, it was important that their personal visions be compared with others to separate simple temporal dreams from those real images spawned from astral inspiration.

For Sedge, a man of no sixthsense ability, a man of the physical realm where he trusted what he could see, believing the adepts was a leap of faith, and he had little patience for their fretting. "Good. Is it any different from what I can see with my own eyes?" He pointed in the direction of Wide Lane. "We have four, maybe five tribes of trogs, and two probably three or more battalions of Paleowright Church troops in possession of our Main Gate. What can you add to that?"

"Yes my lord. There are, we admit conflicts in what we augur, and often the visions are blurred. There is a great deal of turmoil in the ether here. It can be hard to concentrate while under duress. The people, their spirits assailed by fears, believing their lives at risk, send much energy and anxiety into the ether. There is much hostility, as you can see, coming from the minds and souls of those here in the town and beyond the wall, both human and alien. It can be confusing—“

“Yes, yes, I understand,” Sedge ran a hand through his grey hair, “but I don’t need excuses, I need information. Now tell me what you have.”

The voyant cast his expression down and ordered his thoughts. “We see seven distinct groups, or what you call formations, obvious enemies to Clan Mearsbirch judging by the images they project.”

“You can read their thoughts?” he asked.

Brookern quickly shook his head. “No, I can’t, but we’ve been comparing our own senses with those of the pathics. They draw the same picture.”

“And that is?”

Brookern cast about and saw the town map laid out on a planning table. He went to it and put his finger on the Main Gate. “We can see this group of hostiles visually, and they have proved helpful in gauging the size of the other groups we see through our visions. Some bodies are weaker in energy; hence we can interpret size and numbers. Only one group is stronger than the body at the Main Gate in its emotions and imagery.” The group at the Main Gate was the fresh Paleowright battalion arrayed in four neat ranks just out of bow range.

“And that larger group is?”

He moved his finger to the area near Hollowmeade tree fort. “The troglodytes, they— they are most bizarre, alien.” He shuddered.

“Good,” replied Sedge, his caustic tone biting off the word. “So far you’re two for two.”

Brookern put his finger behind the gate. “Here stands another formation of these same men,” comparing the group behind the gate to the Church battalion in front of the it. “They have pious thoughts of the Ancients but bear ill will towards us nonetheless.”

“Funny that,” Sedge quipped dryly.

Then Brookern moved his finger to the south of Wedgewood, a short distance beyond the wall. “And here, another group of Ancient worshippers, but they are moving.”

Sedge leaned on the map. His bosses crowded closer. “Moving you say?”

“Yes, heading west along the wall. When we perceived this, we decided I should hazard the trip here to convey the message directly.”

The fortifications engineer tapped the map with his pointing foil. "They're heading for the Timber Hall gate."

Sedge nodded. "They can scale the wall anywhere they want, we've pulled the wall defenders back. It's just a wooden palisade the farther west you go. That tells me they want to attack Timber Hall directly. Bastards know it is the seat of the clan. What else?"

"Another group, perhaps half in size, comprised of Drakans has set off to follow them."

"Drakans," someone exclaimed. Sedge's head rose from the map. His gaze pierced Brookern. "How do you know?"

"One of our voyants had a clear vision of their faces. They are Nakish. Moreover, they think images of a land that can be none other than the storm cliffs south of Ompo. They emanate pictures of their true uniforms. They are Drakans."

The captain of Scouts cleared his throat. "Half the size of a full Paleowright battalion? If it is Drakans, then that group is probably comprised of one or two centuries. They follow their command structure rigorously and build their units based on a hundred-man century."

Sedge swallowed the implications. The plot deepened. "First trogs, then churchmen, and now Drakans? All just for Wedgewood? What else? I count five formations."

"The sixth group is greatly diminished, a mere shadow of itself and emits much pain." He tapped the Ungern Road. "We can sense they were once proud, but now humiliated."

"More churchmen?" the warlord asked. The voyant nodded.

"Probably the remains of the Church battalion we clobbered," surmised the operations captain.

Sedge let out a breath. "And the seventh unit?"

"They were one, but of late split into two groups, neither very large." He pointed behind the Main Gate, to the southeast corner of the wall near the Drakan formation. "And they are?" asked the scout's captain.

Brookern looked up, a pained expression on his countenance, "You've met them before, and we have sensed them here at Murali's. Most definitely Scarlet Saviors," he said distastefully. "Haughty, arrogant men, with thoughts of Ancients and vengeance. Our visions of their rachiers are clear."

Sedge lingered over the map, analyzing the enemy positions and movements. "Scouts," he addressed the Scout's boss, "send pickets to confirm what the voyants are reporting. A quick look beyond the south wall please." He sighed and straightened. "I count at least twenty-two hundred troops facing us, compared to our seven hundred." He recalled the images of the fight for the Tannery hard-point. "But that does not include our remaining townsfolk who have acquitted themselves well. They may be our hidden strength."

He straightened, stretching his back. Speaking to no one and yet everyone, "Hopefully, unknown to our visitors is Perrin's merc company at Wayland's Farm. They've reported in via pathic and await my orders. We've received messengers carrying dispatches from two Plains wards on patrol in the lower foothills. Refugees from the surrounding farms alerted them. They want to know if we need their help. I sent runners back with instructions for them to rendezvous with Perrin. It's too early to hear back from the Plains or Rock clans elders, but I've sent word to them of our situation and asked them to raise all their wards, which they will not do unless they know our situation here is dire. It's the planting season for them, and their folk will be in the fields and outland hamlets."

"But by the time they--, we could be—"

Sedge held up his hand. "Be that as it may. For the moment we are stuck with it. The other Timber clans, except for Red Elm, are even farther away and will be of less help. Red Elm, having a pathic of their own has responded. They are marching. But it will be two days before their lead wards arrive.

"On the plus side," the captain of operations supplied, "our Sixth Ward is returning from patrol. They have a telepath with them and are moving with haste to join Perrin."

"Right," noted Sedge. "That accounts for all of our fighters. With the aid of the Plains wards, we're up to nine hundred effectives." He traced a finger to where the Church battalion marched towards the Timber Hall gate. "These must be stopped. There are only four tree forts in range of the Hall. Assuming we keep them from taking the Hall that still leaves them in possession of the gate. If the enemy blocks the gate, they not only block our main supply route but also our retreat." At the mention of retreat, there was a stirring amongst the officers and mumbled comments.

"Yes, yes, I know," he said tersely. "But a commander who has a route of retreat has a route of attack. Men fight better when they're not worrying about how or if their wives and children can escape. Fetch me the Ascalon. I have a task for her."

Baryy checked the body, a female shield-bearer. Putting two fingers on her neck, his urgency doubled. He shook the woman, slapping her face. She moaned. He leaned close and whispered into her ear. "Stay still. Trogs are roaming about. I'll send help."

The woman licked her lips. "Water," the word came out like a breath from a grave. "I'll fetch some," he said. She made the third alive but gravely wounded fighter he found, and he'd not checked the mercenaries.

There was one last group of bodies to investigate, but they were the closest to the gate. "Spirits Outy, you would have to fall on the first stand." The sun had settled behind Mount Mars, and twilight began to deepen. There was a hard-point up ahead. He darted to the left out of sight of the gate and ran up to the building. His chest heaving, he nearly leaped out of skin when the shuttered window popped open.

"Baryy, how many have you found alive?"

"Huh?"

"We've been watching you all along. Is that Territern? Is she alive?"

He peered past the shutter and saw the familiar face of the teamster who'd hauled his trade supplies. "Yea," he said hoarsely. "She needs water."

He heard voices inside, then a shuffling and grinding noise. The door beside the window opened, and three men sneaked out. "Get in, quick. We'll go for her." One of the men peered around the corner watching the gate. He made a hand gesture, and the two others bolted up the street. Baryy waited outside with his handbolt ready while the two rescuers grabbed the warrior by the arms and dragged her back. The trogs at the gate and a small band outside a sacked hard-point took notice, but then a white and brown-fletched arrow *twacked* into the dirt in front of them, a cloth-yard reminder of what awaited them. The troglodytes peered up at the tree fort and held their ground.

Baryy followed the men into the dimly lit building that became darker when the door closed, and the window shutters were pulled tight. The room smelled of sweat, blood, and urine. From what he remembered, the building was a knitting parlor. Someone lit a lamp in the darkness, and sure enough, there were the two looms disassembled and neatly stacked in a corner. Someone hissed about the light, "It be dark soon. Trogs can see better'n at night than we can and that lantern won't 'elp."

The lantern was dimmed, but not snuffed. Baryy spied an empty bench and sat heavily. A water bottle was thrust at him, and he drank deeply. "You're either a damn fool or a brave man," a voice said in the gloom. There was a chuckle. "Probably both," said another. "Fine line between a fool and a brave man."

"What? Were you looking for a customer? Trader--" Laughter ran around the dark room, gallows humor the only humor they had. "Must have owed you a lot of money!" More laughter.

"No," said Baryy heavily, gulping down the water. "I was looking for a friend."

The room went quiet.

"He was in the Second," he added, tears threatening to well up.

Silence.

"Yea," said another, "We all got friends out there. We've been sneaking out and dragging them in whenever we can."

Baryy sat up. "You have?"

"Sure. Who you looking for?"

"Outy, I mean Outish."

Then a woman's voice said blithely, "Oh sure. We got him alright; he's in the big room being tended by Elmern. Got clubbed clean on the head when the shield wall was right in front of us. His pot helmet--" The woman said something else, but Baryy stood and asked, "Where? Where is he?"

Outish lay on the floor amongst the other wounded. The bandage wrapped around the top his head showed red on the cranium. Baryy knelt beside him. "Outish? You alive?"

Elmern was a young woman with a fresh, bright face just now showing the wear and cares of life, and dressed in a long woolen robe in a brown-checkered pattern. She shut the door and turned up the lantern in the chamber. "I need light to see by. There are no windows in here; so it won't attract the greenies."

Outish's eyes were open. He gave a caricature of a smile. "Ula, Baryy, I got thumped something good on the head."

Baryy chuckled, "Spirits Outy, I'm just glad you're alive. When you didn't report back to Perrty, and my pings failed I began to think the worse."

"Oi," chimed Elmern, rubbing her hands on the blood-stained apron tied around her waist, "a tad bit harder and that awful swamp ape would have crushed his skull."

"Is he..."

"I have healing skills and applied energy to the wound," she let her voice trail off, "but before today I never had to work on so many, and not with these injuries," she paused. "I think his head will be okay. Whenever he complains of pain or headaches, I apply more healing, but I need Mbecca here to help me. Until then I'm doing what I can."

"I'm sure you are," Baryy heartily replied.

"What about Ogden and the foundry?" asked Outish.

Baryy shook his head. "Ogden is up in Broomstick. I saw him climb up. He's okay."

"But the foundry, who's guarding it?"

Shaking his head, Baryy asked, "Why? The foundry is not a hard-point."

"No—" Outish looked as if he wanted to say more, he tried to lift himself on his elbows, but collapsed back down, closing his eyes.

Baryy leaned in. "What?" Outish reached up, felt for Baryy, and pulled him close. He whispered, "Ogden left the plans for the rifle on the table. He told me. When Lettern sounded the bugle call from the forward watch post, he dropped everything and marshaled the ward. The plans are still sitting there, in the open."

"Shiren." He looked at Elmern who concentrated on a wounded merc, then back to Outish. "You may not know this, but the Paleowrights are here. They've sent in at least one battalion of Church troops. We beat them back, but there's for sure more to come. If they get to the foundry..." he thought about it. "We've no choice. I have to go to the foundry and retrieve the drawings."

Though his head pounded like a gong in an outhouse, Outish managed a firm nod.

Night had fallen. Wide Lane was as murky as a ghost's hollow; the customary street lanterns and porch lights were not lit, the cheery glow from windows was gone. Lonely Soul had yet to rise, and when it did, a bare sliver would mark its trek across the velvet night. Baryy moved more by memory than sight. He snuck through the empty stables across from Murali's, the eenus and burnos gone, herded up to the mines. Through the back door and across the next street sat the foundry, huddled in its own cloak of darkness and foreboding. He stepped carefully across the hay-strewn floor, stifling a sneeze from the thick aroma of eenu dung and grain dust. It wasn't eenus he smelled for, but the thick musk of troglodytes.

Approaching the rear door, he contemplated how to open it without making a noise when, "Don't open it," came from the dark. He nearly leaped out of his skin. His heart pounded madly, at once relieved and chagrined he'd not used his multi-func to scan for heat and aural signatures. "Who's there?" he hissed, raising his handbolt.

"Kiltern, Second Ward. Lettern's hereabout somewhere. We came looking for you and Outish. Ogden thought either you or Outish might be in the foundry."

"You saw me coming?"

"Oi, only a Timber leaves the Knitting Mill hard-point, and only a fool by the name of Baryy the Trader walks this night alone."

"Aye," Baryy exhaled, lowering the weapon and de-cocking it. It would be just their fortune he'd trip in the inky blackness and shoot someone. Sidling up to the door, he sensed three others there with him, one peering out a crack into the street. "A group of swampies came through a while back. Bastards are looking for food. They're eating dead churchmen and Woodies alike. Seems like we all taste the same."

"Ugh," replied Baryy. "Where's Lettern?"

"Right here," and Baryy jumped at the harshness in her voice. "I'm not talking to you Baryy. You scared the needles off my tree when you jumped off the fort on the repelling line. Honestly Baryy, you should think before you leap." A snicker came from behind him. "Did you think we'd let you come out here alone? I brought a squad to search for you. We're all in danger."

She sounded genuinely hurt and maybe something more.

The voice called Kiltern said, "Be thankful you found us and not the trogs or the Parrots." He used the derogatory name for the churchmen as the Timbers had taken to calling them. Their uniforms resembled the plumage of a Uralda Parrot.

"Did you find Outish?" Lettern asked moving close.

He nodded but realized she couldn't see it in the dark. "Yes. He's got a nasty bash on the head, but he's alive and being tended to in the Mill."

"Great. Then we can get back to Perrty." Lettern grabbed his arm and made to haul him away.

What to tell her, thought Baryy. His night's work was not finished. He stood firm. "Uh, Lettern, Og's been working on some prototypes for Achelous, you know, new weapon designs like the handbolts we supplied to Sedge."

"Oi, and good ones too," remarked Kiltern. "Handy things," by the sound he made a motion and held one up in the dark. "They load fast."

"Killed a couple of trogs climbing up Perrty with one," said another warder.

"Right," said Baryy. "The plans are safe from the troglodytes. They wouldn't know what to make of them. But if the damned Paleowrights find them, we face the danger of their monks turning them against us. Og left the plans and prototypes for other ideas in his drafting room."

"Oh," Lettern's voice was quiet and close to his ear.

He knew she held Ogden and his work in high regard.

"You sure?" she questioned. "Ogden didn't say anything about plans."

"I'm sure," he replied firmly. "He'd want them, and I was willing to come get them by myself."

After a pause, "Alright then." She turned her back, and her ponytail brushed across his face as she stepped to peer out the door. After a day of fighting, he could still smell rose water in her hair, mingled with sweat and fear. It reminded him that she was a woman.

"We'll need to cross the street. I'll go first." She tapped Kiltern who slid the large door back on its wheels, magically not making a noise by lifting up on the handle and forestalling the wheels a reason to squeak.

Baryy watched her lithe form dart across to the foundry slipping into a coal-black shadow. Time passed, each second a minute. Finally, seemingly at leisure, she leaned out and in the lesser darkness waved her arm.

The five of them ran across, and two warders bumped each other, their shields and axes, gnashing in the night. One cursed and the other shushed him. Lettern held open the entry door in the giant wagon doors. Baryy found himself in the pitch-blackness of the foundry.

Kiltern unshuttered his beacon lantern, and the wan glow seemed brilliant against the dark reaches of the foundry. "Over here," Baryy instructed Kiltern, and they made their way to the drafting room. Outish told him that Celebron had locked the drafting and gunroom doors before they left, but under general orders from Tall Lofty, the Silver Cup guards were forced to leave the foundry and go to their designated hard-point. Lettern's rebuke burned in his ears. If he'd thought before he took to the repelling line, he could have asked Celebron and the Silver Cup bravos to help. In the dark, he searched for the spare keys hidden in a kindling tin behind a false wallboard. The Timberkeeps watched him in silence, the air charged with intrigue.

Finding the keys and opening the door, he went in. Inside the room, unmolested on the drafting table sat a notebook opened to what Baryy recognized as the design for a trigger mechanism. It rested on top of a free-hand sketch of a second-generation rifle; Ogden's pencil notations of dimensions, metal composition, annealing characteristics, and concerns about blast pressures scribbled in the margins. "What is it?" asked Lettern standing beside him. Someone found a candle lantern and lit it. The smoke from the burning wax made him sneeze. "That is our future. But for now it is a secret, and you must all swear to me you'll not speak a word of this." He looked around at them in the dim yellow glow, shadows playing across their dumb faces as they had no idea what the drawing showed. "Swear it!" he barked, "Swear on Mother's Life."

They nodded meekly, making the sign of Infinity over their hearts. "Oi," Kiltern said.

"But what does it do?" asked Lettern confused. Her brown eyes shimmering in the lamp glow.

"Don't worry, you'll find out soon enough." He said it to mollify them, little did he suspect Fate agreed with him. He rummaged around looking for a pack. "Quick, anything that looks important stuff in this bag."

Next to the table, he opened the chest whose lock hung open on the clasp. He sought the black powder manual Achelous had replicated using the synthesizer at the Isumfast repair bay. He searched more, scouring the room, but it wasn't there. Could he have hidden it? Baryy hadn't paid close attention to the instructions Achelous had given Ogden in regards to the book. He wasn't positive that Ogden even had it. Satisfied there was nothing more of value, "Next door, we need to go to the new workshop," known to those privileged few as the *gunroom*. The gunroom had been added on to the foundry in the past week. The strong resin aroma of newly sawn pine timbers nearly overwhelming the subtler smells of coal, iron, coke, and baked brick. Baryy unlocked the door. In the room was Ogden's growing repository of specialized tools and equipment for making firearms. Bullets molds, a bore reamer, a new rifling jig, a lathe, stocks of annealed iron and steel, sand castings in all stages of completion for making firing pin hammers, triggers, and casings sat on ordered shelves. Baryy ignored it all and went straight for the three rifles that rested in a gun rack against the far wall. Two he recognized: the original smoothbore musket and the first rifle. The third one appeared to be another rifle but with a longer barrel.

"Shss! Someone's coming."

Kiltern immediately shuttered his lantern and Baryy did likewise with the candle. The room plunged into complete darkness. He could hear the Timberkeeps in the foundry jostle their way into the dark gunroom. By the sound, someone shut the door and fumbled with the catch. "There be a whole troop of them out the back way," a male voice said.

"Parrots or trogs?" Lettern asked.

"Parrots."

A bump, followed by a thump came from along the wall outside the gunroom facing on the narrow lane behind the foundry that ran between the tannery and stockyard. Then the unmistakable sound of a door being kicked in, a crash and a swinging bang. It came from the foundry.

Tension rose in the room as everyone held their breath.

"Quiet you moron! Did you have to kick in the blessed door?! The Ancients themselves are waking up. Was it even locked?" The voice beyond the gunroom door carried the lilting accent of Herberians.

"You'll bring the stinking rep-tiles down on us for sure." A second male Herberian voice said.

"What?" A third complained. "They're helping us!"

"You're a moron as daft as they come. They don't care who they eat."

Another voice, "I heard they were sent to the farms to pillage."

"Oh go blow your sack, there's plenty of them greasy geckos roaming about."

More voices and murmurs could be heard; the foundry seemed to be filling up. "Well, it ain't much, but it beats sleeping with goats. It's cold enough to snow."

"It's not winter you dumb fool."

Kiltern edged to Baryy. He whispered nervously, "Sounds like they're looking for a place to sleep. What do we do?"

"Good question. Wait for them to go to sleep?"

By the way Kiltern didn't immediately respond, Baryy guessed he was thinking the idea through. "All of them?"

Baryy frowned, unseen in the dark. It did sound like a lame idea. "Go ask Lettern."

While Kiltern did that, Baryy cracked open the candle lantern. In the dim glow, he eyed the gun rack. Trapped in the gunroom with a host of enemies just beyond the door forced him to something he thought was far off in the future, and belonged to someone else. He never expected to be the first person to use them. A Timberkeep watched him with interest. Baryy carefully opened the powder chest and pulled out a sack of black powder. Finding a measuring horn, he pulled the musket from the rack and poured the powder down the barrel. There were two sacks of round balls – bullets -- in the chest. He examined the first, wrapping the ball in a cloth patch. He'd never actually loaded a musket but had seen it done often enough. Placing the ball at the end of the barrel, he pushed it down with the ramrod. He silently cursed when the rod scraped against the barrel as he pulled it out. All eyes in the gunroom turned to him.

Carefully, acutely aware of the proximity to the candle, he primed the flash pan. Setting the musket aside, he loaded the first rifle. This time the ball fit tighter, and he had to apply pressure to the rod. Pulling the rod out it again scraped inside the barrel, and a voice said outside the door, "Ay, quite everyone."

"What?" asked someone.

"I thought I heard a noise."

"Yea, you heard Meggins blowing hot squishy ones."

"Not me," a churchman replied. "I didn't fart."

Baryy waited until the noise beyond the door resumed, and the voices spoke of the day's trials, the warmth of the forge, and who had the better sleeping spot. He reached for the third rifle and poured the powder down the barrel. Judging by the lock mechanism and the raw, bright steel at the throat of the muzzle the weapon had never been fired. He gave the ramrod a firm push and seated the ball squarely. Out of the corner of his eye, he saw Lettern making frantic waving motions. Hastily he dashed priming powder into the flash pan and slapped down the shutter on the candle lamp.

The double doors to the gunroom shoved open. Framed in the soft glow of a match-light stood a man in the door. "Anyone in here?"

Baryy raised the rifle and brought it to his shoulder. It was heavy, awkward, and unbalanced to the front. He couldn't see the sights in the dark, but he didn't care, the shadowed target clearly outlined. He pulled the hammer back. The double click sounded distinctly like a loud cricket.

"Huh?" The man in the door said, "Eh fellows, there's..."

Baryy pulled the trigger. The flint hammer struck the pan, and the spark ignited the powder. The flash lit the room, but the explosion that followed eclipsed everything. A jet of flame three feet long stabbed from the barrel. For an indelible instant, the room was lit in a strobe of history. The five Timberkeeps stood transfixed at either side of the doors, their axes and swords reflecting silver-bright. The churchman's green and blue uniform stood out clearly, eyes glowing orange in awe.

Then the ramrod Baryy had left in the barrel cartwheeled past the man's head and the forty-caliber bullet hit the churchman square in the chest. He fell back, nearly blown off his feet. Baryy in his haste had overcharged the barrel. The blast shocked the foundry into an absolute stillness, his ears ringing; acrid smoke billowed out of the chamber to the forge. The stricken churchman lay on the floor and cursed the silence with a gut-deep moan. Someone at the forge knocked over the match light; the tiny light went out.

Adrenalin, fear, and random impulse spurring him, Baryy grabbed the two other guns and screamed. He ran to the door and roared at the top of his lungs. At first, as a sociologist, he just wanted to scare the churchmen, but then his fears and anger took control. His rage at seeing Bagonen's lifeless eyes, of the dead Timberkeeps he found, then the tension of the night all churned for release. Remembering Outish with his head nearly caved in twisted a wrench in his mind. His primal emotions came welling up and gave a raw edge of hysteria to his voice. He cocked the gun in his right hand and holding at his side, fired it. The blast and tongue of flame strobed the foundry chamber again. A churchman screamed, "Aiyee. I, I, I'm hurt! Help me!"

In the black, the room burst into chaos.

Into that chaos, Baryy wailed and screamed. "Die, churchmen! Die! Fear Mother's Wrath!" He cocked the gun in his left hand with his thumb and pulled the trigger not caring where the bullet went, but with soldiers leaping up from bedrolls and dragging on coats he couldn't miss.

"Arrg," a gurgling cry came from the center of the room. A body fell, and other bodies stumbled over it.

"Die!"

Explosions, flames, screams, and smoke drove the foundry to an apoplectic frenzy. Baryy went after anything in the room with the butt of a rifle. The back door was thrown open, and churchmen jostled and shoved falling through. More soldiers surged towards the door. Baryy ran at the door bashing and flailing at anything that moved.

"Second Ward! At 'em!" Kiltern bellowed.

Lettern screamed, "Get them!"

Pandemonium reigned as the churchmen's panic was complete. They stampeded the door and were crushed by their fellows.

Every dim, dark shadow that went by Baryy smashed with his rifle butt. Then someone grabbed him from behind. "Back lad. Out'a me way. I've something better to use." He was veritably flung backward. A man wailed pitifully in concert with the gruesome sound of an axe slicing through cloth and sinew.

Lettern stabbed with her sword, but then a Timber axe errantly knocked her blade from her hand. She gasped and dove for the floorboards. The sweep of a axe head made a hollow whooshing noise over her. She scrabbled in the gloom searching for her sword and came up ready.

"For the Second!"

"For Wide Lane!

"For the Shield Wall!"

The five Timberkeeps made butcher's work of the churchmen trapped in the foundry. Some, no telling how many, made it out alive, but a half score were hacked down.

Lettern helped Baryy to his feet where he sat against the wall stunned and spent. "I didn't mean to kill them," he mumbled. "I just wanted to scare them. Get them out so we could leave."

"Scare them? Mother's fire Baryy, you scared me!" she said softly holding his elbow, her voice soothing his raw nerves. "Whatever that contraption is, it did what you wanted. We're getting out of here now!"

Chapter 42
New Contract

Near Tomis, continent of Isuelt, Dianis

"Incoming message," the AI announced.

Quorat grunted. The raven lay disassembled on the workbench in the equipment room. Removing the primary lift fan, he checked the fan bearings. "Who's it from?"

"Anonymous AX009012"

The contract broker for this gig. He recognized the A-wave address pseudonym. *That didn't take long.* He'd sent a message requesting instructions via tight-beam laser only five hours ago.

"It is a new contract."

"Yea, and what about payment for the first contract?"

"They have deposited payment for Job One, Intrusion Testing."

Quorat looked up at the equipment room camera. The live indicator glowed red showing the camera was active. "And?"

"Claims against Job Two and Job Three have been disallowed."

"Why?" he snarled.

"Job Three is incomplete, and Job Two did not meet the terms of the contract. It was not an aquamarine mine."

"Those bastards! I knew it!" He banged the workbench with his fist careful not to touch any drone parts. "Not my bloody fault!" He glared up at the camera. "They're the ones who said it was an aquamarine mine, not me!"

The camera just glared back.

"Aaack." He shoved both hands on the table and looked down at the floor thinking. "What are the terms of the new contract?

"It lists twelve sites on this planet that you are to visually inspect and provide a three-sixty, ground level videograph from within fifty meters of the target site with the target clearly in focus. A bonus is payable if the videograph is captured within one meter of the target center."

Quorat gripped the table with both hands and pressed until his fingers turned white. They were asking him to do precisely what he did not want to do: conduct a physical on-site inspection of what he presumed were the hits from an orbital A-wave surface scan. His standard, safer approach was to send in a recon drone to do the videograph, but he knew there would be a clause B. "And the clause B?"

"Collect mineral samples from within fifty—"

"Bah!" Quorat kicked the metal cabinet door beneath workbench leaving a satisfying dent in the door. He eyed it critically and wondered if the door would still open. He didn't have a drone that could collect mineral samples, at least not from three hundred miles away. He had the standard turtle crawler drone that could be configure-camouflaged as any number of objects, but the thing took forever to get anywhere and was prone to attracting attention. He'd have to get within a quarter mile to use the piece of junk, or it would drive him nuts waiting for it to crawl in.

"There is a bonus attached to clause B."

"Yea, does it have anything to do with the sample testing positive for aquamarine-5?"

"Affirmative."

He shook his head. He wanted to punch the monitor screen in front of him, smash the multiplex display and rip it off the bulkhead, but instead commanded, "Show me the list of the twelve sites."

Peering at the list, he recognized the report format. He'd been engaged by that contract-mining outfit before. *They want feet in the dirt. They want me to do their dirty work. They know I won't leave the planet now that I'm here, successfully intruded, not just for the payment of an intrusion test. Bastards.* The report showed the geo-coordinates of each suspected aquamarine-5 site. It also listed the signal band of the A-wave reflection detected and the signal strength. Some of the target sites were a collection of smaller sites, meaning there were multiple hits of an A-wave signal rebound from within a mile radius. A-wave orbital surveys, even aerial surveys were notorious for ground scatter where the A-wave ping broadcast would echo and bounce from object to object before rebounding. The dispersion resulted in false positives. "Open Site Four."

The AI displayed the data for the three sub-sites for Site Four. Quorat stared at the signal strength for sub-site two. The type of A-wave rebound signal detected was "point specific."

Studying the data for Site Four, his mood began to change. He squinted at the signal strength for the point-specific reading. Becoming very calm, he considered the size of the measurement.

“Really?” he whispered. If that point-specific signal was accurate, there was enough high-density aquamarine-5 in that single location to make him a wealthy man. He leaned back. Of course, the mining outfit would know that too and would be watching his actions very closely when he neared that site, like a recon-bot stuck on the end of his nose. "Where exactly is Site Four?”

A hologrid projection appeared above the workbench. It showed the planet Dianis, his location, and the location of all twelve sites with Site Four highlighted. Squinting at the globe, “I can’t read that. Zoom in on Site Four’s location.”

The globe resolved itself into finer and finer detail until he said, “Stop!” Site Four was centered on a town in a mountain range only sixty miles from the decoy site in Mestrich. “Hmm, that’s curious.” He cocked his head to read the label of the town. The aerial image of the town and mountains looked like it came from high-resolution IDB survey scans. No telling how old the image was, but it clearly showed a mine complex set outside the town coinciding with one of the diffused hits in the scan. The image showed some sort of smelting operation that matched with the third sub-site of Site Four. It looked promising. Just by glancing at the geological formation of the mountain he could tell it was the right type of granite formation. The high-density, high-reading point-specific source, however, was going to be a problem. The geo-coordinates put it dead center in a building, dead center in the town. A drone would be useless for that. “Translate the name of the town.”

“Translating, searching probable languages.”

Waiting, he pondered what he would do if he got his hands on a sample of what was in that building. *I can pack enough out to be set for life, but what sort of fail-safes does the contracting outfit have in place? Does the owner of the seed contract know? They would be the ones I need to watch for.*

“Translation confirmed. Name of the town is Wedgewood.”

Chapter 43
Christina

Wedgewood

Dawn bade definition to the eastern foothills. The chatter of birds in the alpine woodland heralded the new day, a day destined for conflict and strife. Christina crouched low threading her way along the line of Perrin's mercenary company. They were hidden in the tree line south of the town palisade. She'd ridden in the early evening to rendezvous at Wayland's Farm with Perrin, two wards from the Plains clans, and the Timberkeep Sixth ward. Refugees were flooding into the farm known to be the rally point for Wedgewood and Doroman forces dislocated in the fighting. The homeless came with stories of rampaging troglodytes freed from the attack on Wedgewood to wreak havoc in the countryside. Christina suspected the Paleowrights wanted the reptiles out of the way now that their initial shock value was past. They'd be more useful terrorizing the outlying communities and causing disruption, distraction, and angst for the Wedgewood leadership. The thought of the growing body of refugees fleeing south at the mercy of the troglodytes chilled her. Hearing of a ward of Rock Doromen on their way to aid Wedgewood she asked Perrin to divide his company. Half to march to Wedgewood and the other half drive east against the reptiles and scatter them. She left a message for the Rock ward to guard Wayland's to protect the refugees and provide Perrin's southern merc detachment a base of operations.

Leaving the farm was painful. The farmer's wife with two younglings on her hip pleaded with her to stay. She blessed the children and said she would return, and then told Wayland who stood behind his wife, a pained expression on his sun-beaten face, that if Wedgewood fell his farm would drown in the Paleowright backwash. They had to save the clan before they could recover the countryside. So they left the steading, marching through the moonless, star-filled night Christina had led the half-company of mercs and the three wards. She intended to attack the camp of a Church battalion before dawn, but scouts reported a Timberkeep counterattack at the foundry had kept the churchmen awake and edgy. The news lifted the spirits of the Sixth Ward, their clan was alive and fighting.

Bands of trog routiers foraged in the dark and the further east the column marched the higher the chance of detection. So Christina had changed plans and opted for their current ambush site. If the churchmen indeed planned to attack the Timber Hall gate and behind it, the Timber Hall itself, as Sedge suspected, then the battalion would march past on the road in front of her. It was a broad track, cleared on both sides to offer a field of view for sentries on the palisade parapet. Lately, market traffic had taken to using the road, bypassing the growing crowds on Wide Lane, but this morning only rabbits and squirrels hazarded it.

She crouched beside a merc sergeant. Judging by his accent, he hailed from Taldamar far to the west. "Be our turn to attack and take the battle to these knuckle Parrots." His breath steamed in the chill morning air.

"Attack is but a good defense in disguise," she whispered, her voice husky, kneeling with her armor on, concealed by the verge bushes. She'd heard the talk amongst the mercs as they marched in the night. "But yesterday was no defeat."

"No," the sergeant agreed with a heavy voice, "But I hear Barrigal lost twenty good men in the Shield Wall."

"They fought well and accomplished their purpose. Because of them, we are here today." She didn't tell him she had stood in that wall and dragged one of her own, one of their very few Defenders, wounded to a hard-point. She bid the sergeant good luck and moved on down the line.

"Scouts report the churchmen are on the move, sir. They'll be at the Hall Gate in thirty minutes."

Sedge merely nodded. He'd managed a few hours of fitful sleep in his loft above the command deck. What the hundreds of other soldiers in the tree forts did for rest he could well imagine. Most of the Ungerngerist redoubts were built purely for fighting and had no accommodations for sleeping, eating, or other bodily functions. "Christina's in place?"

"Yes sir, they're set."

He stood up and stretched, his body stiff from the cold, stiff from bending over the map table, stiff from pouring through field reports in the dim lantern light, and stiff from the constant tension. "Then we shall see if surprise and nerve can make up for the churchmen's three to one advantage."

Christina, crouching low, darted from tree to tree. Sighting Perrin, she crept up to him, mindful of the churchmen battalion marching past their ambuscade. "Any sign of the Drakans?"

"No, Alon. The last word from the scouts said they were breaking camp. Their skirmishers came out, spied our scouts and chased them." He squinted at the rising sun. He and his men were drained from the night's march, but the sight of the enemy spurred them with fresh energy. "To be expected, the Drakans know their business. The Timber scouts are good, especially in the forest, but them hoplites are used to fighting Darnkilden Rangers, so they know all the tricks."

She took a deep breath, resting her gauntlet on his armored shoulder. She knew she was asking much of the mercs and warders who had hustled from Wayland's to get here, but much depended on this attack: Timber Hall, the hundred families that sheltered there, the councils, and perhaps even the fate of Wedgewood. Moreover, she did not want the Drakans to spoil her surprise, not now. Without the Drakans to bolster the churchmen, she hoped to land a heavy, surprise blow. Perhaps even rout them. "Prepare your men. I will give the command."

Perrin passed the hand signal down both sides of the line. He gripped the wire-bound hilt of his long sword but kept it sheathed, and snugged his shield tight to his arm.

Christina whistled the call of a blossom bird, high and carrying across the field. At once the mercenaries leaped up and charged through the trees. Ninety men in black tabards, burnished steel shields, polished steel helms, and gauntlets. They ran without a word brushing aside the bracken. In two lines they came into the clearing at a dead run charging four hundred Paleowrights.

The nearest ranks of churchmen just gawked, uncomprehending. In the early morning dew, they marched in their ordered rows of pikemen as if their body as a whole were unassailable. These strange men came from the left, not from Wedgewood, and they were not dressed nor equipped as Timberkeeps, their swords still sheathed. They came without the screams and yells and insults of attackers, so was there ill intent?

The Zursh mercenaries covered the open ground swiftly and at the last moment drew their pale swords, streaks of grey in the wan light. Only when the first Paleowright, watching as the sword descended, had his helm split in one awesome blow did the others blanch and raise their shields, and yet the battalion continued to march oblivious.

"*Aregen et marinar!*" a sergeant uttered the age-old Zursh war cry, and the spell was broken, and the blades fell. As one, the company roared "Aregen et marinar!"

Christina hit the organized Church ranks and slashed her way through the first two rows of surprised pikemen, slamming a shield here and bashing a shoulder pouldron there running straight for the commander's standard.

Hoarse cries rose. The Paleowright soldiers nearest the banners stopped their march and turned alarmed to face the assault of the liveried professionals. The black and silver tabards a stark and ominous contrast against the green and blue tunics. Christina knocked an enemy sergeant flat with the boss of her shield and cut the standard-bearer's arm in half, severing the staff, dropping the battalion colors into the dirt. The battalion major screamed a challenge and launched himself at her.

A cheer arose from the head of the solidifying Paleowright line. But it was a strange cheer, not one the churchmen understood.

Alex, his Defender's shield raised above his head, rose up out of the ravine the road approached. Behind him came a ward of Plains Doromen. They assaulted the head of the Antiquarian column in a crash of shields, splintering pikes, and the cries of warriors thrown to the turf. Just as the battalion began to adjust to the two-front attack, another cheer carried above the din and the second Plains ward launched themselves to the left of their compatriots in an attempt to swing around the north side of the churchmen.

The major and his command sergeant faced Christina. Behind her, three mercs fought feverishly to keep her from being surrounded. She swung her long sword in a feint at the command sergeant, but then spun, battering the major with a series of blows. Every minute he fought her was another minute the churchmen lost cohesion and direction. The Paleowright company captains, without orders, were stricken by indecision.

It started as a trickle at first. The Zursh mercenaries, inflicting a fearful toll on the front rows of surprised pikemen began to roll up the southern flank of the battalion. Churchmen in ones and two's began to shuffle towards the rear, and then run back to the Main Gate.

A horn sounded, the familiar clarion of a Timberkeep ward. It blew and blew again, and then a ward came charging out of the forest. "The Sixth!" They bellowed. "Meeeeear-biiiirch!" Like crazed dogs long straining at the leash the Sixth struck at the Paleowright line right where Christina entered. Exasperated, their clan, their town, and their families assaulted while they were out on the southern parks, the axemen vented their frustrations with every cleave and hammer of their weapons.

More churchmen fell back sensing a trap, others--the faint-hearts-- threw down their pikes and shields and ran.

A core company of stalwart soldiers held on defending the battalion colors. The fight was now a brawl, a wild melee with the opposing sides intermingled, and more than one blow struck friend instead of foe.

Christina notched her sword against the fine steel of the major's heavy cutlass. He'd held her off with help from the command sergeant until she flung her shield up, stamped down hard on his foot, whirled and caught the sergeant on the temple with her gauntleted fist that held her sword. The blow staggered him, and a maddened Timber warder bowled him over. Both men sprawled on the trampled, blood splattered gravel.

The major made to stab Christina in the back, but she kept turning and brought her sword neatly around. His exposed neck lay open to a clean killing stroke. She angled the blow up slightly and caught him on the back of his helmet ringing his bell as sure as a clapper in an Antiquarian church. The major went down in a heap. He lay there dazed. Christina hooked his leg with her boot and rolled him over. He opened his eyes to find the Ascalon's sword at his throat. "Yield." She ordered. "Yield or we'll slaughter your men." While it was a boast, a calculated exaggeration, the major laying bloodied in the dirt knew it not. He nodded weakly.

"He yields!" roared a Timberkeep. "The major yields!"

"Do you surrender?" asked a merc. It was one thing for a soldier to yield on the battlefield; it was another for a commander to surrender his entire force.

Word of the major's fall riffled through the ranks. Some dropped their weapons, but others, whole companies fearful of capture turned and ran. The battalion broke. As a body, they flooded to the east, back the way they'd come.

"Did they surrender?" ask the Warden of the Sixth. "No," said Christina, heavy in her heart for she knew what would follow. The major, having given his parole, lay there dazed and blank.

The warders and mercs ran after the fleeing Parrots, hacking, slashing, striking them down from behind.

"That was the horn of the Sixth, sir. They're on the attack."

"Aye." Like everyone else in Wedgewood who heard the horn blow, Sedge looked to the south. Through the telescope from Tall Lofty, he could just see over the palisade, but the fighting was too close to the wall to see much of the action. Instead, he had to rely on reports. That the Paleowrights were stopped and being driven back was plain.

Christina saw the line of rectangular shields marching towards them. Churchmen fled towards the moving wall and when it refused to open for them flowed around either end.

"Back!" she called. "Back!" Seeing the Zursh trumpeter, she grabbed him. "Sound recall." He looked at her with a quizzical expression. She seized the trumpet hanging on its lanyard and shoved it at his face. "Blow it. Sound Recall. Now!"

Startled, the bugler raised it hesitantly, not used to taking orders from anyone but Perrin. He blew tentatively.

"Louder!" she demanded. "And keep blowing it until I tell you to stop."

A Timberkeep hot in pursuit suddenly found himself faced with the tip of a leveled pike and was cut down with a swift thrust to the throat. Another died with a spear in his belly. The shield wall marched over their bodies, trodding them into the muddy ground.

"To me!" Christina yelled at the top of her voice waving her arms while the bugler blew his horn beside her. More warders fell to the advancing barrier, but the mercs were returning and forming their own wall.

The horn of the Sixth, and now that of the Plains wards began to blow. The Doromen, like a pack of bounding wolves, skidded to a halt, appraising the advancing phalanx stunned. Then heedful of the clarion calls they turned and begun to run back but not before more of their fellows were cut down. And still the wall of rectangular shields marched forward.

"Drakans," breathed Christina, her blood racing.

Perrin spat. "Bloody hoplites." He left her and went to form his ranks. "Right lads. We've seen these bastards before. You know what to expect. So square up. Shields tight, blades low." An era earlier the Empire of Lamar and the fledgling Drakan Empire had been at odds. The Lamarans, of which Zursh was the capital, soundly thumped the upstart in their many border skirmishes, but since then the Empire of Lamar had collapsed, and Nak Drakas rose to ascendency. In place of the Lamaran Empire, a loose federation of city-states attempted to fill the void. Each contributing troops to the eastern frontier to keep the Drakan menace at bay. They fought shoulder to shoulder with the Rangers of Darnkilden and the Marines of the SeaHaven League. It was in those numerous brushfires that Perrin's company had faced, fought, won, and lost lonely battles on that bitter frontier. Today was to be another meeting between Lamarans and Drakans, only in a pristine woodland far to the south and west where no Nakish army had reason to be.

Christina watched the last of the warders shuffle into line either side of the Zursh mercs. "Back!" she called. "Perrin, order the line to fall back to the other side of the ravine." The two wards of Plains fighters were on Perrin's left, and the Sixth was on his right. The whole formation executed an about-face and jogged back across the hard-fought ground they'd just won, giving it up, along with scores of blue and green-coated dead and wounded. Christina ran past a churchman sitting, holding his eviscerated entrails, glazed eyes seeing death. A Timberkeep from the Sixth was bent over, nursing a bandaged, bloody stump of an arm. She grasped him under his good arm and dragged him up. "Come." He struggled to move his feet, his face pale from a loss of blood. She gave him a grim but steady smile. "That'll have to be your shield arm from here on out. You'll learn to wield an axe with your other hand before the snows fall."

"Recall sir. The horns are sounding recall!" There was a general commotion on the command deck. Woodwern, who'd made the perilous trek from Timber Hall to meet with Sedge, asked, "What does it mean? Have they—have we lost?"

Sedge shook his head. "No. Tis neither rally nor retreat, but a command to gather her troops." He swiveled the telescope to the left and let the chairman look. Just over the sharpened wooden logs of the palisade, Woodwern could see the end of a line of spearmen marching with precision, a neat double line moving from east to west. He inhaled, not quite a gasp, "Are those?"

"Drakan hoplites," Sedge completed for him. "Two centuries. Two hundred foot. We knew they were there. It was a calculated risk."

"What do we do?" The chairman looked closely at Sedge's drawn face.

In light of Woodwern's concern Sedge forced himself to laugh. "What else my good Chairman." He clapped him on the shoulder. "We fight them!"

"Bloody hoplites," Perrin growled.

Christina studied the advancing line. "How many archers do they have?"

"With two centuries they'll have forty. Twenty skirmishers; that be the fellows on the ends, with twenty halberdiers. Nasty tough buggers those are. They'll be the best he's got." Perrin nodded at the decurion who marched behind the double line of soldiers under a bare guidon. "I see he's keeping them in the second rank center. Watch for the bastard to try and send them around the right or left flanks once we're into it."

"And your archers?"

"Mine? I've eighteen."

She twisted her lips. "So we won't win an archery duel."

Perrin scoffed. "No, we won't. And their soldiers are fresh. We've just finished fighting a whole battalion. We've maybe a hundred eighty fighters, they have a solid two hundred." What he didn't say, but was lurking in the back of both their minds was the ability of the wards to face seasoned Drakan professionals. The Timber and Plains warders were effective, they'd acquitted themselves well against the churchmen, but the Warders were primarily farmers, millers, and miners. They carried axe and shield as their wards were called upon, but they did not make their living waging war like the Drakan hoplites before them. Which was why Sedge and his two merc companies had been hired to bolster the ranks. The Doromen wards practiced fighting in the shield wall, but the Drakans were experts at it. Perrin had no qualms his Zursh mercenaries could stand toe-to-toe with the Nakish and perhaps give better than they got, but that still put Doromen wards on his left and right flanks.

Christina turned to peer into the west where the Timber Hall Gate, a quarter mile away stood closed and barred. She thought about it, an idea forming.

"What?" Perrin glanced over his should at where she stared. "What you thinking, Alon?"

"Alex." She waved him over. While the Drakan centuries closed the gap to the ravine, Christina explained her idea to the two warriors.

"Well if we're to be about it we'd best fall back now, their archers are readying a volley," Perrin stepped forward. "Shields up!" The order was seconded by squad sergeants and wardens down the line as a rain of forty arrows fell from the sky.

Alex took off at a dead run heading for the Hall Gate.

"Back, double time!" Perrin ordered.

"Look how they run!" smirked a centurion. "Cowards."

Uloch sniffed. "No," he drawled, "I doubt they are cowards." Resting his hand on his sword pommel. "You see that woman leading them?"

The centurion laughed, "How can you miss her, she's a head taller than the Timmies."

"She was in the shield wall yesterday with those Timmies you mock. They fought three and four times their number of trogs in a backwards fight over a half mile. Somehow I think she and her Timmies are not cowards. Have you not noticed her shield?" He signaled a halt, waiting for a group of more stalwart churchmen to form up and join the ranks.

Squinting, the centurion finally said, "A Defender?"

The decurion turned to him. "Yes. And the pagan guardian is up to something. I can feel it. I half thought they'd stand and fight at the ravine. But no, they continue to retreat." He tapped his command rod in his hand. "We'll play her game. For a bit more." He turned to a runner. "Find the acting Church commander and inform him that if he should so deign, now is an opportune moment to rejoin our line."

Waiting for the blasted churchmen get their quailing livers back to the front, Uloch kept his emotions tightly in control. It was bad enough for them to run like squealing school girls, but to keep him waiting was worse. Unfortunately, as the senior Drakan commander, he had to maintain an air of decorum with his allies. The Emperor through General Biornach had given explicit orders that he was to keep his two centuries in reserve. Well, he'd now seen a thousand troglodytes scattered and two full Church battalions routed. He now had a plausible excuse to engage. The sight of the Zursh colors only whetted his appetite.

Chapter 44
Outish

Wedgewood

"You took a risk coming here just now. I assume it is important." Larech watched Baldor Prariegrass pull back the hood of his cloak. "No time like the present to deliver information." In fact, Baldor seriously worried he'd be scooped on his secret if he didn't sell it right away. He peered nervously at a troop of Scarlet Saviors marching by in a column of twos carrying unlit torches. The last two men hefted a brazier of hot coals between them. He'd never seen so many of the Red Britches in one place before. He wondered if they'd empty the Hebert Cathedral. To his quick, hungry eye the torches meant that either the Britches intended to fight in the dark, and with the sun climbing, he doubted that, or they planned a burning. Turning his mind to greedy thoughts of silver, "I heard your churchmen had a spot of trouble last night." It was more a probing question than a conversational opening.

Larech, the Washentrufel agent, thumbed through a sheaf of dispatches and handed the stack to the Paleowright runner.

"You know, at the foundry," Baldor prodded.

When the agent failed to show any interest, Baldor worked his jaw, wondering if he had indeed been scooped, or whether the agent just didn't care. "Odd thing about the flames and explosions that killed your men."

"They aren't my men," Larech replied sourly. "What of it?"

"Well, I know who is responsible for it."

Larech scoffed. "So do I. The fools, as I heard it, walked into a Timmy hard-point and were ambushed. Buckets of hot coals from the forge fires were thrown at them, and the Timmies dumped sulfur on the coals causing smoke and an explosion. The rest of the story is the embellishment of their imaginings and fear. They were scared witless at being attacked by axemen in the dark. No real mystery there Prairiegrass, just churchmen trying to hide their shame behind a glorified explanation as to why they were summarily routed, yet again."

Baldor blinked at the agent's blind ignorance and unquestioned acceptance that nothing more than fear and embarrassment lie behind the tale. Then he sputtered, "But, so—you think they just threw coals?!" He was so incredulous that Larech gave pause. His brow furrowed. "They were attacked in the dark in a Timmy stronghold. Small events take on enormous aspect when fighting at night. Confusion reigns." He decided to go along with this farce a minute more. "But if you have the Timmy side of the story I'll note it for the battalion commander."

Baldor told him what he knew, up to a point.

"And?" demanded Larech.

"Five Lamaran silver for the rest."

The agent squinted in the morning sun, the din of battle sounded from the west. Judging by the stream of churchmen returning from the attack, their uniforms bloodied and disheveled, some without pikes or shields, the battle was not going well. It was of no account; the two Drakan centuries in support of the churchmen would settle the issue. "Very well, three Lamaran silver or I'll send you to nearest trog chieftain to clean his teeth."

Baldor ignored the threat and rubbed his hands as he did when money came close. Three silver was what he expected to get. "You see your churchmen—"

"They're not my churchmen," the agent's voice rose, and he didn't care who overheard.

"Right, well the foundry is where a Wedgewood blacksmith has been working on new weapons."

"What new weapons?"

"Well, they've already sold fifty new handbolts to Lord Sedge the almighty. And handy little things they are indeed. I saw a Timmy cock and fire ten quarrels in a minute!"

Larech doubted it was that fast, but he'd seen the compact crossbow in action through his field glass. What bothered and intrigued him was only recently had the Paleowright archivists shared the discovery of a new longbow with roller wheels. He'd not seen the contraption, but the thought of the Timmies having a new weapon of their own bothered him. "Prairiegrass, I'll not pay one bent copper for something I already know."

"The blacksmith is working on a new contraption, and they used it last night. It spits fire and thunder and knocks men dead with one touch."

Impatient with the turncoat's dramatics the agent growled, "And what of this contraption, tell me, man. So far I have flash and bangs in the night." He shook his head and flapped a hand in exasperation.

"Well," for once Baldor's confidence flagged, and he seemed lost for an explanation. "That's all know," but he hurried on when the agent's impatience took the shape of a brewing tirade "but I know who's behind it. I don't know the secrets of the weapon because everyone's tighter than a splitting wedge in knot-wood, but I can say that Tivorian trader, Achelous, is the one with the ideas and he's been working with the blacksmith to build them."

"Achelous again?" They'd confirmed that the Achelous here in Wedgewood was indeed the same Achelous from Marinda Merchants, but with the debacle at the tavern when the viscount attempted to confiscate the aquamarine treasure, there'd been no opportunity to interrogate the trader.

Baldor ducked his head, a greedy gleam in his eye. "He travels between here and there. I've not seen him lately; others say he's back in Tivor now."

Larech gave the tale of a new weapon a modicum of credence. The Washentroufel didn't have agents in far Tivor so distant it was from the empire's preoccupation with the Darnkilden frontier. He'd have to speak with Viscount Helprig. The Paleowrights had inquisitors and examiners all across Isuelt. They would be most interested in anything that appeared to compete with their archivists. He made up his mind. "Baldor, if you have played me false I will have you hunted down and fed naked to troglodyte hatchlings."

Baldor, taken aback by the threat, swallowed.

"An interesting thing about troglodyte hatchlings," Larech went on ghoulishly, "when fed male captives they go straight for the genitals." He smiled like an opossum eating dung. Baldor quailed. "They consider human skin a delicacy. They'll fight each other for the privilege, devouring the skin first, shredding it off the meat. You'd be alive the whole time. It's amazing how long a man can live while being skinned."

Baldor's hand shook as Larech dropped three silver coins in his palm. For the barest second, he considered refusing the boon, but the weight of the silver strengthen his greed.

Larech walked to Helprig's command tent deep in thought. After their debacle here in Wedgewood the Church hierarchy was in a foul mood, and they were searching for any way to save face. The presence of the Drakans made them a possible and convenient target, so he was loathe to be around them, but he'd at least make an effort to ask the predicant if he had connections with inquisitors in Tivor.

As fortune would have it, Captain Irons and a subaltern were in the command tent. Larech loitered until he caught the captain's attention.

Irons, taking the hint, gave instructions to the subaltern and sent him away. "You have something?"

"Hmm," Larech let the tent flap close, casting the tent into the gloom of diffused sunlight through the canvas walls. "I've just received a tip from our informant here."

The captain waited for Larech to get to the point.

"The Tivorian trader Achelous has been here again."

Though it was gloomy in the tent, Larech could tell by the tone of the captain's voice the captain was frowning. "Ah yes, unfinished business."

"New business I might think. My informant says the man had something to do with the fight at the foundry last night."

Irons moved to stand in front of the agent. "What did he do at the foundry?"

"Prairiegrass can be confusing, but whatever happened there, the explosions, fire, whatever, may have been caused by something the blacksmith and trader are working on." He paused, then "you have inquisitors and examiners in Tivor. Have you learned more about this man? Could it be they've traded for artifacts or Ancient secrets from Linkoralis and brought them here?" The last was sheer speculation on his part, but he liked to prey on Paleowright paranoia. It always elicited a response.

The captain's response was disappointing for his lack of emotion, but illuminating for its information. "No." Irons moved to the tent flap to peer at the preparations for their next attack. "The pirates are succeeding, at least for now. We've no word that any Linkoralis cargo has made it to the Tivor docks." Then he looked back at Larech, "But we have learned something about this Achelous. Something interesting indeed. When his imminence heard it, he tasked me with a new mission." Looking back out the tent, "Something I will do once we are finished here."

Larech hated begging Paleowrights for information, so he waited. At first, he thought the captain might leave before saying more.

Then finally, "This Achelous is something more than just a trader. Our examiner in Tivor has always been suspicious of him."

Larech could understand that. Examiners, the people responsible for finding, testing, and sequestering Ancient artifacts were always suspicious of traders. They hounded them like ticks on a dog.

"As it turns out, this Achelous is the father of Marisa Pontifract's child."

Larech's eyebrows arched. Considering the implications, he quipped, "That adds a new twist."

Irons nodded. "It does. It does."

"And your new mission is?"

Irons shook his head. "That my Drakan friend is strictly Paleowright business. But first, we must scour this squirrel's den of its vermin." He pulled the flap open, and sunlight swarmed the interior. Stepping out, he let it close.

The Perrty tree fort stood a hundred paces west of Tall Lofty. The string of collapsible suspension bridges hung in an unbroken chain from the remaining tree forts nearest the Main Gate, through Tall Lofty, through two other forts, past Perrty, and finally to the Bitter End forts overlooking Timber Hall. Messengers, carrying missives to and from posts, ran thumping across the swaying bridges whose centers drooped with the weight of the passing couriers. The steady tromp-tromp of the messengers on the planks heralded their approach, and the fort garrisons need not be told to clear the way. In repayment for moving aside the messengers passed along snippets of the battle. It was from one such courier Ogden heard the news he dreaded. "They've broken the southern wall and are setting fire to tannery row." The messenger ran past and hit the next suspension bridge without breaking stride.

Ogden dropped down from his hammock slung between two huge branches above the fighting deck. He scanned the buildings to the south. Smoke rose from Morgat's Tannery. "Damn," he cursed. The Perrty garrison crowded the railing murmuring and pointing. Flames appeared above the buildings in front of Morgat's; one of those buildings was the foundry. The tannery to the east of Morgat's and directly across the lane from the foundry began to billow smoke. "Bastards," he cursed pounding the pine railing. Dense black roiling smoke rose in a thick plume, punctuated by the harsh flare of jetting flames. Caught by the wind, the choking smoke and fumes carried west amongst the buildings nearest the wall.

"Fire brigade?" Pottern asked, "shall we get our buckets?"

Ogden leaned over the rail to get a better view of Tall Lofty. If they were to form the fire brigade and dismount from the tree forts runners would come with the orders. He watched for a flurry of departing messengers from 'Lofty.

"Smoke from the saddlery," a captain said, his voice even but dry.

Sedge had a decision to make, and the longer he waited, the more devastation Wedgewood suffered. Debating with himself, the fire was either a ruse to draw him down from the forts, or a serious attempt to destroy the town. If they didn't act, the Paleos would become more emboldened. Businesses were afire.

"Sir!" A messenger came running and skidded to attention, breathing heavily, "It's Scarlet Saviors. Nearly fifty of them!" The dread in the woman's voice told all. After the fight at Murali's all the wards had come respect and fear the prowess and brutality of the red and yellow-armored paladins. That the Paleowright commander chose now as the time to unleash them told Sedge the height of the attack was approaching. "The trogs," he turned to his captain of Scouts, "where are they?"

"Still in the countryside, sir, attacking the farmlets and villages," he said pain evident in his voice.

Sedge couldn't worry about that now. If he couldn't save the town, he couldn't save the farmsteads. "You're sure?" The captain gave a quick nod.

"So we know where the Drakans are, and two of the Church battalions. Fetch me Brookern, quickly. I must know where those remaining Parrot battalions are."

Outish peered out the arrow slit of the Knitting Mill hard-point. The entire garrison was at the windows smelling for smoke, alert, bows ready. His head pounded and dizzy spells came quickly, his vision fractured. He assumed he had a concussion at the minimum. His stomach churned, and his hand trembled holding onto the table, but he'd not lay on the floor in the death room while the hard-point was attacked. In his other hand, he held the handbolt cocked and ready. He'd seen a Scarlet Savior duck around a corner of a building across the way and knew they were brewing trouble. The bastards had killed

Mergund. While the others in the room thought of them with dread, Outish only felt hate, a long, low lingering hate typical of Halorites. He wished one of the Scarlet Britches would come within range.

Smoke swirled heavy and thick along the street obscuring the view across Wide Lane. On the far side was the granary hard-point. With the loss of the three forts facing the Main Gate and the leather goods hard-point, the granary anchored the southeast corner of the defense. Exposed, it had repeatedly been assaulted by the trogs and churchmen during the first day. The Parrots had even managed to burst a barricaded window or two, but each time the attack had been repulsed. Now the smoke often concealed the three-story building in a swirling black cloud. Outish could only imagine what it must be like inside. From time to time the wind carried the plume their way, and he and his fellows would duck to the floor coughing.

From his perch, Sedge watched the archers up in Archwood send volleys of arrows at Scarlet Saviors as they ran in and out of the smoke attempting to set the granary hard-point afire. When the devils exposed themselves their superior armor and shields often thwarted the arrows. More than one Savior sported multiple arrows sprouting from their shield. They ran about flaunting the trophies as tokens of their invulnerability.

He listened to Brookern's summary. Then made his decision. "Dismount the Second, Third, Eighth, and Tenth Wards." Sedge said to the operations captain. "Sound the call for the Fire Brigade." He issued more commands and instructions. "And mount the ballistae. I've had enough of this. No point in saving our surprise for any longer."

Receiving the signal, the defenders of Archwood lowered their four massive crossbows from their racks in the branch rafters and mounted them on the pedestals at each compass point of the fort. It took a crew of three to operate the ballistae: a loader, cranker, and archer trained to aim and shoot the unique device. The loader slotted a three-foot-long bolt as thick as two fingers and fitted with a massive, razor-sharp arrowhead. The quarrels were expensive to make, and only the best archers who trained with the weapon were allowed to shoot it. That Trishna was neither a Timberkeep nor a permanent member of the Archwood garrison mattered little. Her prowess with the ballistae became apparent to all when Ogden had let the foundry security team test his latest innovation.

"Set!" the cranker latched the pawl and stood back.

Trishna watched the corner of the burning leather goods hard-point. There was a squad of Britches lurking in the smoke. She bided her time. "There! There!" multiple calls came of potential targets, but rather than chase fleeting ghosts she wanted a real enemy. She wanted one of the cocky paladins who brandished their arrow-studded shield like a trophy.

A billow of smoke concealed the gap between the granary and leather goods store. Three Scarlet Saviors darted out, all with their shields up, one carrying torches. She could see arrows shoot from the second story arrow slits of the granary. Smoke blocked her view, but she was positive one of the Britches had been hit.

Then the wind whipped away the veil just as a Savior threw a torch at the roof of the granary. Covering for him was a Savior with a nest of fletchings stuck to his shield.

The *ka-chunk* of Trishna's ballistae shook the mounting pedestal and railing. A yard long, the bolt split the Savior's shield like so much tin and kindling. It penetrated his layered breastplate, leather jerkin, and punched through his body flinging him hard back against his fellow. "Reload! Quickly!"

She could hear and feel through the deck the *ka-chunk* of the other Archwood ballistae and the ballistae from Spotted Frog to their west. Smoke and the smell of burning shellac wafted through the fighting deck, but Trishna ignored her watering eyes and waited for the "Set!"

Two Scarlet Saviors shields up, ran into the clearing, followed by two more, to pull back their brothers who, staggering, guards down, were being shredded with arrows from the granary. *Ka-chunk.* The bolt struck low on a shield, spun the Savior about, and knocked him down to the smoking pine needles. Fletchings on the end of the shaft protruded from his thigh.

Outish saw the Savior fall. The hard point heard the call to dismount the wards, and he'd convince the knitting mill captain to let him out to join his friends, bandaged head and all.

"Go!" said the captain and flung the door open. Outish darted out weaving slightly, his head pounding. The sudden motion gave him an intense bout of vertigo. Instead of turning right and running up Wide

Lane to the Second's muster station, he ran across the street towards the granary.

Trishna, from her Archwood post behind knitting mill, saw a bandaged, helmet-less warder run at the granary. The warder raised his handbolt, and she recognized him. "Outish!" Over the roar of the fires and bellows of defenders, her voice was lost.

A Scarlet Savior blocking for his comrades readied his rachier. Outish, his Halorite craze boiling, ran forward. A ballistae bolt scarcely cleared his head as it slammed the Savior in the chest.

Outish skidded to a stop and fired. He cocked the bolt and shot again. Ballista darts from three separate ballistae arced past him. He cocked and fired. Anything that moved was fair game. A dense, white wall of smoke enveloped him. He turned, choking and coughing, holding a hand over his mouth while he spun about holding his handbolt at the ready.

From the gloom came a distinctive red and yellow helm followed by an upraised arm holding a rachier sword-axe.

He dove for the ground. The rachier descended, but the Savior fell over him. Outish took the man's armored knee on the chest, and then the Savior rolled away in the smoke, was up, and back at him.

From his sprawl, Outish fired point blank over the Savior's lowered shield. The quarrel at three paces punched through the sternum plate and lodged in the warrior's chest. He stumbled and fell clutching at the shaft. Outish pulled his arm away from the descending axe but not before blood squirted from his hand. The searing pain convulsed him. So hot it dimmed the banging in his head. Yowling and groaning, he rolled over clutching his hand in his lap. Blood, warm and sticky was everywhere. He dared not look for fear of what he might see. Fumbling with a quarrel, he managed to slot it with his mangled hand. Holding the handbolt between his knees, he cranked the lever with his good hand. A form came through the acrid gloom, and Outish raised and fired the hand bolt. Pinioned in his left side, the Scarlet Savior staggered and struggled to grasp the fletchings sticking from his lower back.

His hand numb, Outish managed to hook another quarrel with two fingers from his hip quiver, and it miraculously fell, with Mother's sweet blessing, into the bolt track. Cocking the lever, he struggled to stand. The Scarlet Savior saw the source of his agony and came at Outish.

Outish fired, and the two collided. Down to the dirt, both he and Savior went.

Somewhere in his daze, he managed to roll the Savior off his chest. All he could think of was the hand bolt and the need to reload.

Timberkeep voices sounded from the gloom. Outish coughed and coughed. Gagging, the pain made him wretch. A shadow loomed above him axe held high, "Oi! It's one of ours! Help me with him." Arms grabbed him. "Up lad! The granary's on fire. We're leaving before we're all cooked gristle."

Chapter 45
The Gate

Wedgewood

From their position before Timber Hall Gate, Christina watched the black cloud boil ominously into the blue sky. Her double line of mercenaries and warders stirred and chaffed at the sight. Fire punctuated the billowing smoke. She knew what the Paleowrights were doing and hated them for it. They'd taken the coward's route. Turning her thoughts to the approaching line of Drakans and churchmen, she pushed growing fears and images of flaming buildings to the recesses of her mind. She had her own battle to wage.

"Ready lads!" Perrin called. Shields along the front rank of the wall locked. "Brace for it!" Having retreated across a quarter mile of ground, harassed by archers the entire way, they could withdraw no further without surrendering the gate and direct access to the rear of Timber Hall.

Perrin barred his teeth as he looked in the eye of a hoplite whose spear came questing for an opening. He glanced at the enemy commander behind the center of the opposing line. Though the man wore clothing and armor reminiscent of a free company he could tell by the man's stance and the orders he barked that the decurion was all Drakan. Why they were out of uniform with a bare guidon, he could only guess. Word of a Drakan force this far west behind the frontier bore dire ramifications. How had they gotten here? How had they avoided the blockade? Was the defense still in place? Was there a breach in the frontier? Were there other Drakan units operating incognito waiting to turn and strike Lamar from the south? A spear dug its point into his shield and Perrin tilted the buckler, letting the spear gouge the surface and then slide up and over the top. Spears versus swords and axes, the Drakans held the length advantage, but they'd have to drop the spears if they wanted to get close.

"Back two!" Christina ordered, running down the line. On her left, the Plains wards anchored their line against the palisade wall, but on her right, the Sixth dangled and had to curl back to keep a scratch company of churchmen from outflanking and rolling up the line. The churchmen, a bare hundred rallied from the routed battalion, sensed blood and wanted revenge from their morning drubbing, but they were wary of getting close to the sharp and swift axes. "Back two!"

Up and down the line they clashed. Here and there a defender fell or stumbled in their backpedaling, but soon....

"The gate is almost ours!" echoed a centurion. Uloch eyed the empty ramparts. Waiting for an unseen enemy to pop up and start slinging arrows, but the fires behind him attested to the overwhelming demands on the enemy forces. "Once we clear the gate heave the grapples and send the skirmishers over the top to open it. We'll hold the Lamarans here while we send the churchmen in." A Paleowright messenger waited behind the decurion assigned as runner to Viscount Helprig. The viscount held a Paleowright battalion in reserve ready to follow up on either this attack or the Scarlet Saviors assault on the southern wall.

"Back two!" Christina called, and Perrin sensed the moment had come. "Make the signal" she ordered the mercenary bugler.

Uloch heard the call and paused, the chill of foreboding crept up his spine, "Hold! Hold the line!"

Suddenly the Hall Gate swung open, and a cheer arose from inside. A mass of Timberkeeps sallied forth led by a group of mercenaries.

"Ach--" Uloch wheeled, "skirmishers and halberdiers to the right! Quick men, move!"

Alex ran with Barrigal –limping mightily--, Ogden, and the captain of the Timber Hall garrison. "This is no time for finesse. We'll be straight at them. Hit them hard and collapse their shield wall from behind. When I sound Rally have your troops fall back to the gate and form the shield wall. Expect Christina to send a runner with new instructions." Ogden nodded, a smolder in his eyes. He waved his arm and his remaining twenty warders charged.

Horns--Plains, Timber, and merc-- blared from beyond the gate. "That's our call people!" The Hall garrison captain yelled.

Ogden settled his dented and scarred shield on his arm and raised his axe. He'd used a whetstone to take the notches out, it was crude work compared to what he could do on a proper grinding wheel, but the foundry was on fire. The Second Ward crashed into a wave of skirmishers.

“Right!” said Alex, and waved his sword. He ran past the gate cross bars laying on the ground. Barrigal’s mercs came behind and raised the Zursh cheer “Aregen et marinar!” Aiming for the rear of the Drakan line Alex met a tall halberdier. He raised his shield high so all could see. To some, it was a thrilling sight, to others their dismay.

Ogden cleaved the shield of a Drakan who came to face him. He followed through with a shoulder and bowled the man into the skirmisher next to him. Another Drakan charged him but Ogden just kept moving before the Drakan’s spear could complete its arc. The end of the Drakan line dissolved into a melee. Suddenly a herculean warrior bearing an equally heroic halberd loomed above the squat Dorman and brought the massive blade down. Ogden’s initial reflex was to bring his shield up, but his fighter’s sense kept the guard low, and he dove at the Drakan’s feet lest the halberd crush his shield and forearm with it. The long blade thudded into the dirt behind him, and he jammed his axe into the Drakan’s groin, up under the chainmail hauberk. The assailant grunted with a loud, “*Whoof.*”

The shield wall in front of Perrin began to fall back. For a moment, he had no assailant. “What now?” he called to Christina.

“Keep your line together and drive them. Drive them hard to the ravine. Don’t let up. We need to break them.” She hacked and hacked, using her height, aiming to dent and ring helmets. A rivulet of sweat ran from her helmet and glistening down her cheek. “I see Ogden and his Second. We keep on the Drakans until we lose the advantage.”

“Tell those damn Paleowrights to attack!” The decurion shoved a command sergeant in the direction of the churchmen. “No more dancing around. Attack now!” His right century had initially faltered, but the left was holding firm, keeping the Zursh mercs at bay. He’d had to sacrifice his skirmishers and some of his halberdiers to save the right century, but the line was firming. He fumed. The pagan bitch had lured them into a trap, at a closed gate no less, which they marched right past.

Alex angled a squad of mercs towards Ogden but the Drakans were reforming, and isolated targets were few. “Hold there weapons master.”

Ogden swung at a shield but struck only air as the hoplite pulled back. The entire length of Drakan line was back-peddling fast. The horn for the Sixth sounded recall. He stopped, his arms burning.

Looking to the right, he saw Christina gathering the Timbers on the right after apparently smashing a gaggle of churchmen.

The whole Wedgewood force came to a stop at the ravine, but the Drakans kept retreating. Barrigal came to Alex. With the lull, he kneeled down heavily on his fair leg and grimaced. He unbuckled his greave exposing the bloodied bandage. "How be your leg?" asked Alex.

"Throbs like a bloody war drum. Be that as it may, this fight is over." He nodded at the still retreating Nakish. "That decurion is no fool. He could probably fight us good for the rest of the day, but why bother? Who's he fighting for? Helprig? And where is that pompous ass?" Barrigal stretched his wounded leg out and sat on the trampled ground while runners passed orders to dress ranks and take a knee. Barrigal watched the Drakan formation with a detached professional eye. "He's conserving his force."

Chapter 46
The Matrincy

The planet Avaria

"You're sure?"

"We've looked everywhere."

"What have you checked?"

"We've pinged his embed. Signaled his multi-func. Scanned the A-wave channels for any traffic relating to him. We even did an orbital aural scan of the entire planet, not just the Farless Islands."

"You pinged the transponder on his embed, and it did not respond?"

When she didn't hear a voice answer the question, she could imagine he was shaking his head. The matriarch continued to stare out over the city. Her sanctum suite was on the hundred and eleventh floor. Councilor Breia and Margrett, seated on the divans behind her continued their conversation. She lost herself in the ebb and flow of the aural energies emerging from the city below her. She let her mind wander across the currents, the whispers of dreams, the cries of desires, and the woes of fears. Her thoughts soared to the darkness of space and then floated, descending, spiraling back down in ever-widening circles seeking, always seeking, searching for a cause, a signal, an arm waving in the crowd. Ever restless, her prescient awareness perpetually searched, it never stopped. She could only ignore it, mute it against the background of conscious activity.

Turning from the panoramic view, the lights of the city winking on against the encroaching night, the most powerful person in the Avarian Federation and therefore in Human-controlled space, glanced over her shoulder. "The embed did not respond?"

Breia paused and turned from Margrett. "Yes, Matriarch." She was wearing a slim-fitting gown, black. Always black. She had the figure of a twenty-year-old holovid model, and her pale skin, thanks to gene therapy, showed not a single line. Her hair, also black and unbound, hung to her shoulders. Breia understood her hair to be natural.

"Is it functioning?"

"I'm sorry your Matrincy, but we believe it should be."

“You’ve tried calling his communicator I assume,” asked Councilor Margrett.

Breia shook his head. “No. I have it here.” He donned special, aural insulating gloves and opened a sealed steel tube, and withdrew an aural-sealed evidence bag.

Intrigued, the matriarch walked over, a long leg exposed by the slit in her dress. “He didn’t take it with him when he went on leave?”

“No Matriarch.”

The smallest hint of emotion played on her perfect features. “Do you think that odd?”

“Absolutely,” Breia nodded emphatically.

“If he ever used it,” added Margrett, noting the contents through the clear evidence bag. “It’s a Spark Constellation. When was the last time you saw one of those?”

Searching, seeking, always searching, the Matriarch asked, “Have you handled it? Will it augur?”

“No your Matrincy. I am a telepath,” answered Breia

She lifted her chin acknowledging him. Then she asked, “Margrett?”

The Special Envoy to Dianis was a counterpoint to the matriarch. Where the matriarch always wore black and had black hair, the councilor always wore white and had blonde hair. Both were elegant in their own distinctive way. “No your eminence. I think a prescient should have first try.”

The matriarch dipped her chin acknowledging Margrett’s logic. Margrett was a dreamer, divination her art. Whereas the matriarch a voyant, a mystic, was the one with farsight. Moreover, the matriarch was famous for being a rarity: A single person who could demonstrate no less than three of the six sixthsense skills, telepathy, clairvoyance, and precognition. Though she readily admitted that clairvoyance was by far her most proficient skill. Breia, she was confident, was a more sensitive telepath, and Margrett -- a dreamer -- was able to reach, not only into the distant past but the near future as well. “Where did you find the communicator?”

“It was found in the inspector’s office in Central Station Dianis, Matriarch,” Briea responded.

“And how long has it been since,” she put it delicately, “he disappeared?”

Margrett answered. “We agreed to give him a month leave at which time he would contact us.”

"And when should he have contacted you?"

"Ten days ago, standard."

A perfect eyebrow arched to a point, but for any other movement, the matriarch could have been cut from marble.

The councilors waited. Breia and Margrett eyed each other, barely breathing. They were waiting. The master voyant was weighing her decision. Would she choose to scry the communicator herself, or pass on the event? The matriarch had many heavy responsibilities and weighty decisions to make. That she had taken an interest in the fate of Dianis and its inhabitants told Margrett how vital the world was, but she already knew that.

As if the sealed packet were an illicit drug or perhaps a venomous animal the matriarch stayed well away from the table where it lay between the two councilors. Taking a deep breath through her nose, her nostrils flaring, she finally held out her bare, gloveless, hand.

Briea picked up the packet and handed it to her.

The matriarch's eyes narrowed, and she treated the zippered seal as if it were a malodorous bug. Examining the package, she mentally tested it for any residual auras, but Breia had processed it correctly. Finally, with two delicate fingers, she unzipped the seal and slid the communicator out onto a psychic insulator plate sitting on a tall table next to her hologrid desk.

She circled the table like a cat prowling an unwitting bird. Finally, she reached out to pick up the communicator. Her eyes grew wide, and she immediately dropped the device back on the block. "Well," she said emphatically "your chief inspector is certainly still alive. And," she said with more emphasis, "he was in an agitated state of mind when he last used that device." She walked over to her desk. "I don't think he liked it. Nuisance is the word that definitely comes to mind." She pulled up the hologrid. Images of Chief Inspector Achelous Forushen immediately circled in the air. She scanned the facts and details of the man. Whispering more to herself than to the councilors she said, "Well chief inspector, who are you, where are you, and what are you about?" Sitting in the chair, she watched the images circle. The face, somewhat gaunt but handsome in a weathered sort of way, rotated. She clicked on a view of him obviously in-country on eenu back. Another image, in-country as well, sitting at a table with a team of IDB agents. The image did not say they were IDB, but she knew they were. Piercing blue eyes and an analytical expression predominated his visage. "Did you notice our chief inspector never smiles? At least not in these pictures. And he shaves, what, once every three days?"

The two councilors shook their heads.

"Hmm yes. He is a serious driver-analytic. His record says he is a cultural anthropologist. Interesting. He's missed his calling."

Margrett knitted her blonde brows. "And what is that?"

"A father." She paused, entering a command, "Or has he?" More data scrolled on the screen. "No. No record of children. His wife of fifteen years died ten years ago." She looked at them. "Did you know that?"

Breia cleared his throat. "Yes, Matriarch, we did."

Then she saw Clienen Hor was his director. "Have you spoken with Director Hor yet?"

"No. He's been reassigned to IDB Uplift Monitoring."

She nodded her head absently. Years ago, when Clienen was first posted to Dianis and the matriarch was a docent councilor she had interviewed him for the post. She remembered his answer to the question, "If you had to do what was right and it was wrong, would you do it?"

Again taking a deep breath through her nose, she stood and approached the table with the insulating block. "Well Achelous, tell me, where are you?" She reached out her right hand and extended her index finger. She touched the communicator and this time pressed her finger down hard. Closing her eyes, she let Achelous's aural signature, the residual psychic energy of his being flow into her. It was powerful. Even though the device had not been handled within the last three months or so, she could tell it was fresh with the aural scent of Achelous Forushen. She absorbed the signature, draining the aura from the device. Images of him, its owner began to swirl, take shape, fade, coalesce, disintegrate. She sent her mind to Remus IV, specifically the Farless islands.

For a voyant to see a distant land, it was common practice for them to travel there. Once an adept had "bonded" with the images of the venue, they could be anywhere, at any time and call up a perspective of that place as it was that day. For that purpose, she made it a habit of traveling to all worlds in Avarian-controlled space, when her schedule allowed.

Her mind roved around Remus IV. Like many of the Federation elite, she'd not only been to Remus but had vacationed there at length. It was a remote, pristine world renowned for not being "connected."

The corner of her lips turned down. In her mind, she spun the planet around. Opening her eyes, she looked at the councilors. Then, one more time, she closed her eyes and sought the world, but knew what she would find.

"He's not there," she said finally. Remus IV world was cold, devoid of his life force.

Breia and Margrett started talking, asking questions, but the matriarch kept her finger on the Spark. Images of Achelous came to her, and she said, "Oh." Somewhat out of sorts, she almost lifted her finger but kept it in place. New images came vibrant, and she wondered why. She didn't intend to be a Peeping Tom, but yet there they were, Achelous and his lover, in the throes. Startled, she pulled her finger.

"What?" asked Margrett, unconsciously dropping the matriarch's honorific.

The matriarch felt oddly flushed. There was something about the woman that Achelous was with. She either knew her or would come to know her. For certain, she was no ordinary woman. Psychic energy swirled about his lover like a gathering storm. Chief Achelous Forushen was an intriguing, but somehow the Spirits, Fate itself had led the Matrincy to the woman who lay in his arms. Who was she?

"What?" Margrett again asked, but this time a different question.

Taking another breath through her nose, the matriarch said, "Our chief inspector has not missed his calling after all." The three matronens shared glances. The matriarch nodded. "Yes. I have seen the mother of his child. Wherever our good Achelous is, he is not on Remus, and he is involved." She walked away from the table and sat on the divan next to Breia. "I can see one reason he does not want to be contacted, his child is not listed in his personnel file."

"But we need him, or at least Agent Baryy to testify before the ULUP commission," Breia complained.

Margrett added, "One of them is needed in Wedgewood to help us with the adept selections. They know the population. They can give us a head start on the environmental contamination theory."

The matriarch mused, "Ah yes, Agent Baryy Maxmun."

Margrett narrowed her view. They'd not mentioned Agent Maxmun to the matriarch until just now.

"He's with Achelous. That much is certain." The matriarch leaned back on the divan, psychically drained. She'd consumed all her essence to do the reading, and it would take time to refill her cup of sixthsense energy. One thing nagged her: Dianis. The planet. She'd never been there. It was a Class E world. Her mind wanted to go there. She could feel it, but it repelled her senses like a black veil. Chief Inspector Achelous Forushen was somewhere, alive and well, and he was evading attention. She could feel that too. Moreover, he was protecting a woman, that woman. The matriarch stood and stalked to the table. Peering down at the old Spark, *Achelous Forushen, why you are hiding this woman? Who is she?* Pondering a while more she considered the alternatives and options. Then a secret smile crossed her lips.

Achelous's eyes popped open. He rose up on his elbows positive someone was in the room with them. The kindling candle near the cold wood stove cast dancing ghosts on minute air currents. He threw off the blankets and rose naked. The candle fluttered in the breeze.

"Hmm, what is it?" Marisa purred, disturbed from soft dreams.

"I—" he hesitated, "I—" he felt someone watching him, watching them, but now it was gone. "Did you hear anything?" he asked, conviced a sensitive had just scried him.

"No," she murmured. "Come back to bed. The night watch has dogs, good dogs."

Still hesitant, he walked to the dresser and searched for his bible. His embed was quiet, no alerts, yet he just couldn't dispel his feeling of disquiet.

Not bothering to hide it from Marisa, he activated the backlight on the multi-func and swiped the pages. There were no messages for him. He set the display to route the short-range signal to his optic nerve embed and darkened the bible's screen. In his mind's eye, he scrolled through the alert screens and event monitors. Everything seemed fine. Then he stopped. He was using the anonymous account. When they'd gone in-country, on their supposed sabbatical, he and Baryy had set up anonymous A-wave messaging accounts so that they could get inbound communications without being tagged to the IDB network. Theoretically, they made all the correct connections, spoofing as they called it, to route the messages from the IDB Dianis monitoring system, such as it was, to their anonymous accounts. Of course, all the orbital and aerial systems were gone, but the ground-based systems were still intact. Frowning in the candlelight, he wondered why he'd not received one single notification from the ground sensors. The systems were not foolproof, transient spikes in magnetic fields caused by earthquakes, for example, would trigger alerts. Volcanic activity, even electrical storms, and lightning would trigger a false alarm, but he'd received nothing ever since they shifted to the anonymous accounts. *Now, why is that?* Thinking carefully, *can I log into my Achelous Forushen IDB account and not trigger an event log entry? Probably not, but does it matter?* He stood up and walked to the window. Parting the curtains, he peered out into the dark night. A lantern, mounted in a sconce on the hall's wall-walk, glowed below the window. Right enough, a night watch tread the planks with his trusty hound. He turned. Marisa watched him from their bed, her black hair a dark mass on the white satin pillowcase. Her black eyes dark pools on her pale skin. She said nary a word, just watching, waiting.

Turning back to the window, he looked down at his bible. He needed the full user interface of the multi-func to execute the next set of commands. "Jeremy, I have a question?"

"Yes, Achelous."

He turned to Marisa and pointed at his ear indicating that Jeremy was talking and she, of course, could not hear him.

"Can you connect to my IDB account without triggering an access log entry?"

"I have systems administrator's permissions to the Central Station Interconn server. I can access your account as a scheduled maintenance activity."

"Oh. Scheduled maintenance?"

"Yes, there is a system update scheduled in thirty-two minutes."

"Ah," Achelous said.

"What is it you want me to do?"

"Check my account to see if any event triggers have been posted. I've not received any in my anonymous account."

"And why do you think event triggers posted to your IDB account would be routed to your anonymous account?"

The question caught him off guard. "Well, because we have it set up that way."

"Yes, I detect an agent sitting on the message queue. I presume the purpose of the agent is to copy and route event messages to your anonymous account?"

Feeling slightly embarrassed that the AI had so easily discovered Baryy's little bit of hacking subterfuge, he said, "Ah yes, that is correct."

"I can modify the signature and behavior of the agent so that it cannot be detected without an enhanced, five-pass heuristic, but that will not fix the disconnect."

Suddenly Achelous's knees felt weak. He sat on the bed, the iron springs creaking. "What do you mean disconnect?"

"Your message routing will not work as intended."

His alarm spiked; he could feel sweat breaking out on his forehead. "What do you mean?"

"Your transponder has been disabled. The messaging system does not know where to route the alert messages."

"Shiren." It hit him like a plasma blast to the head. When he'd asked Clienen to disable the transponder in his thigh embed he'd done it so he couldn't be tracked. Couldn't be tracked by anyone, including, apparently, the message routing system. "Well how do we fix that?" he asked the easy question first.

Jeremy explained a series of patches that it would have to implement.

"How long will that take?"

"It can be done in the next maintenance window, twenty-nine minutes from now."

"Okay," and now he asked the question he dreaded the answer to, "and will I then get all the previous messages sent to my anonymous account?"

Marisa saw him nod his head, close the bible, and then collapse on the bed next to her.

"Who's Jeremy?"

"Huh?"

"Who's Jeremy?"

"Ah, he's an assistant."

"Like Baryy?"

"Uh, sort of, but he's not human." Laying there in the night staring at the ceiling, it was a good place to have this kind of conversation. No visual frame of reference. Impossible to pick up in a memscan should they come after Marisa.

"What, a reptile?"

He sniffed at the thought of having a reptile field agent. Although...that would help with uplift and relations with the reptilian nations. It was an idea. "No. He's an off-worlder. An extra-solar."

She seemed to accept the explanation without mystery. Then, as if she too was a galactic, she asked matter-of-factly, “What is wrong with your message routing?”

He was instantly on alert. She’d been listening, and moreover, understood a conversation of which she only heard half. A conversation between extrasolars a half millennium in advance of her own culture. Relaxing, he admitted he was all-in with Marisa, his lover, his partner, the mother of his child. “I’m afraid we screwed up. I know we screwed up.” He explained to her, in general terms what they tried to do and how they had apparently failed.

“So in twenty-five minutes—“

“Twenty three.”

She stirred. Drawing the covers aside she slipped out of bed. His eyes tracked her naked form in the gloom to where she retrieved her discarded nightgown. “It’s early yet. Let’s go down to the kitchen and wait.”

In the kitchen, she poured him a glass of wine from the tapped-cask sitting on a trestle by the free-standing chopping block. He sipped it. A rare treat; it was a superb Tomis heart-red, a one-of-a-kind cask that Marisa had made an exclusive barter for. Between the two of them, they were doing their best to drain it.

The kitchen staff was gone. Boyd was sound asleep, and only the night watch stirred. He confirmed it with an aural scan of the surroundings. Preparing for the results of the maintenance window, he routed the audio feed of the multi-func to the nano-configured speaker so Marisa could listen in.

For the first time, she heard Jeremy’s voice. “There is another sentient presence, human female, in the room with you.”

Marisa locked eyes with him.

“Correct,” he said. “Confirm aural signature.”

“Marisa Pontifract,” came the voice from the multi-func.”

Her eyes widened to saucers.

Achelous smiled. “Jeremy knows all.” Getting serious, “What do we have?” He routed the video feed to his optic nerve embed not wanting to give a visual reference to the discussion.

He sat back stunned. “Oh...” The alerts scrolled by, row after row, record after record, event after event. “How many are there?” he asked, his throat dry.

“Two-hundred nine.”

Even Marisa caught the significance of the number. "Are those— "she tried to ask, but Achelous waved her silent. "Filter and correlate against probable environmental events."

"That eliminates one hundred and fifty-three alerts as probable extraneous events," noted Jeremy.

"Shiren." That still left fifty-six unaccounted for. "Scroll the list slowly." He saw a pattern in the early alerts from when they first vacated Central Station. A few of those alerts either he, Baryy, or Outish probably triggered inadvertently. Picking those manually out of the list he was left with...

"Thirty-six alerts."

He took a deep breath, *something about them...* "Identify possible patterns and propose a correlative hypothesis."

Jeremy had his answer ready. "Thirty-two of the alerts follow the standard orbital search pattern for aural signature rebound for surface deposits of aquamarine-5."

He stared at Marisa. In his mind's eye, he could see the date and time of each trigger. They started at the southern pole and ran sequentially upward to the northern pole as if the surveyor was peeling an apple. "All thirty-two of our ground monitoring zones were scanned." He explained the data to her, what he was seeing. "They run sequentially with each trigger about an hour apart."

"So they scanned the entire planet?" she asked, guessing, struggling with the concept, but it was an unnerving guess.

"They did, two days before we officially closed the station. Bastards. They didn't even wait for the IDB to leave."

"The last four alerts are for site M 23 Alpha," Jeremy reported.

"That's a decoy aquamarine mine in Mestrich we seeded our reports with," Achelous explained, not expecting her to understand the details. "The sensor readings in the alerts indicate one for ultrasonic noise, two for neutrino power cell emissions, and the fourth for a close-range aural scan. It was low power and isolated which tells me, along with the other alerts that a recon drone was used to investigate the site."

She gave him a blank look. "Is that bad?"

He looked away. "It means they, whoever they are, were here, on the planet, less than two days ago." Considering the ramifications, he asked Jeremy "Any movement or signal traffic from IDB assets in response to the incursion?"

"Negative."

He grimaced. "Damn."

"What?" she asked.

"Jeremy, do the alert profiles match either IDB, Matrincy, or contract mining equipment?"

"Negative. I've analyzed the neutrino emissions and the micro-turbine fan noise and have determined that they fit any number of widely used recon drone models."

"It's not the IDB or Matrincy," he said to Marisa. "We don't know who these extrasolars are, but we do know they did a full planetary scan for aquamarine, something I, as IDB Chief Inspector, was never authorized to do, and that they bit hard on our decoy." He took a deep gulp of his wine. Setting the glass down carefully, "They also now know that Mestrich mine was a ruse."

She sipped from her own glass. Looking down into the deep burgundy. She set the glass carefully on the table. "Will they know about Wedgewood? Murali's? The mine there?"

"Most certainly. That huge aquamarine pegmatite would have lit up their scan like a sun."

"Then we have another reason to go to Wedgewood." She gathered her robe about her. "I will make arrangements. I need to speak with the aorolmin again. To finalize the terms of our offer." Standing, she hugged herself tightly. "These would be corsairs? The ones..." She harkened back to the day in the farmer's field when they first fired the wooden cannon, to when she asked why they needed it and he had answered with a cryptic description of some ominous threat.

"Yes."

"And they are the dangerous ones?"

"Yes." He paused. "Sorry Lace, but we're all dangerous."

She took a deep breath. "Then so it begins."

Chapter 47
Tolkroft

Wedgewood

At dusk, a lone Church soldier, a sergeant, baring a white flag at the end of a spear traipsed nervously into Wedgewood. He'd been ordered to do it after no volunteers came forward. Carrying a flag of truce on the end of a weapon, under these conditions, was an intended slight. The sergeant feared the archers in the tree forts would shoot him out of hand; a flag of truce on spear meant one thing: a demand for surrender. After the fighting of the past two days, the sergeant saw no reason why the Timmies would surrender. He'd fought them, twice, south of the wall and had been beaten both times. He'd heard the stories of the foundry. The clergy and his fellow churchmen, with the trogs, vaunted Scarlet Saviors, and even the Drakans had failed to capture the town, or blockade it. Yet he did as he was ordered, or else.

The buildings in the southwest corner of the town were smoking ruins. Surely this added to their anger. He flinched when a burning frame crumbled, sparks swirling into the dusk like so many fireflies. Flames still licked at charred timber skeleton, a ruined granary. A tavern, judging by the wrecked barrels, silo tanks, and twisted tubing, was the building nearest the business center to have caught fire. It sat as a gutted shell amongst the buildings saved by the fire brigade. He'd watched as the Dorman bucket brigade, under cover of their archers managed to stop the tide of the blaze there. Ash covered the pine needles like dirty snow except where sparks started one of many secondary fires that smoldered in a hodge-podge pattern to the west and northwest. Had the wind shifted from out of the south the damage would have been much, much worse. As it was the thick smoke had backfired on the Paleowright plans for advancing behind the wall of flames. The smoke had choked and scattered the ranks of the battalion destined to carry ladders to the next line of tree forts.

Checked at the Timber Hall gate and driven back before being reinforced by the last remaining Church battalion, the attacking force south of the town fared no better. It was that current state of affairs that forced the clergy to order him to carry a message. Taking stock of their limited accomplishments the Paleowrights and decided on an approach they were unaccustomed, diplomacy.

Sedge dispatched the captain of operations to speak with the emissary. When he returned, the captain smirked and said, "The bastards didn't even send an officer," He unrolled a parchment and began to read. "Viscount Helprig accepts your penance as a misguided heathen and will absolve you of your sins once you confess. In the interim, we have until dawn to surrender, or they will unleash the full fury of the Ancients and destroy us utterly, man, woman, and child, with no quarter. We are idolatrous vermin and deserve no consideration of mercy. However, though his duty demands our total destruction, his conscience desires to show us sympathy." The captain waved his hand dismissively and looked away. "And so it went. I'm impressed that poor sergeant remembered it all. He said he wasn't allowed to write it down. They didn't want us to have a written text of it. But I did write it down." He handed the parchment to Sedge.

Sedge read the rest of the message and snorted, following it up with a sardonic grin. "When your opponent resorts to brow-beating, he's whipped. The tongue starts flapping when the sword quits swinging." The warlord moved to the railing and looked east in the fading twilight. "They're running out of troops. Moreover, they're running out of stomach to fight. The whining churchman is desperate."

Woodwern rose from his chair at the warlord's table. "Wayland's Farm is overflowing with refugees from the trog attacks. We need to send wards to defend them and drive the troglodytes back. We've lost most of our grain stocks and will have to send our livestock to the lower elevations and wild pastures, and that will put them further at risk to trog depredations." He went to stand by the railing, "By Mother's Peace, Sedge, they've burnt half our town!"

He didn't need to be reminded of the damage though the clan chairman exaggerated the devastation. Most of the homes were still extant; it was the business quarter that took the brunt of the fires. Food, however, would become a problem. Depending on the havoc wreaked by the trogs against the farms, they could be faced with a substantial dislocation of their population just when the spring planting should be progressing. "I hear you Woodwern. If the Paleowrights stay here, we'll be able to hold them off, but we can offer only scant aid to the lowland farms. We have a great many people to feed, and we'll need to retake the captured farms and salvage what we can."

"What do you suggest?" Woodwern eyed the warlord, exhaustion washing over him. The past two days had taken its toll on the heavyset Timber. He'd not slept, and the torment of watching his clan suffer was almost too much to bear.

"As we spoke this morning. We take away the reason for them being here."

"But what of the trogs? They're not here for the aquamarine."

Impatiently, Sedge stepped back from the railing, his unbound grey hair caught in a clean breeze. "Once we drive the Paleowrights away we can deal with the troglodytes by themselves. The Plains and Rock clans are sure to send more wards, and Red Elm is coming. My concern is they don't bring their own food."

Woodwern pondered for a moment, his ruddy complexion darker than usual. He seemed to resolve himself, gripping the rail, staring down at worker rolling a partially blackened barrel out of the wreckage that had once been Murali's. The barrel hadn't burst, and by the struggle of the worker the barrel was still full. He idly wondered if it was ale or whiskey. "You really think it will work?"

Sedge laughed, a hard, brittle sound. "If they had triple, even double the men, probably not. But with what they have now, yes. I think it will work."

Woodwern took a deep breath and watched the worker, with the help of his mates set the barrel on its end and use an auger to bore a hole into the barrel. A spout of amber liquid issued from the hole. The worker quickly captured the stream in a tankard while another worker pounded a bung into the hole. It was too far to hear, but he saw the worker sample the cup, nod vigorously, and pass it around. "Very well. Proceed. It is my decision, and I will inform both councils."

"Ops, tell the envoy that we will parley at the mining camp at high noon tomorrow. I shall look forward to meeting with the viscount in person." Sedge placed a hand on Woodwern's shoulder. "Do you want to be there, or shall I deliver our message?"

Woodwern watched the workers pass the cup and guffaw. "Oi, you can deliver the message. But I will be there to see how he takes it. I hope it sticks in his throat like a Ungerngerist pine cone."

"You going to set up your holofield?" Baryy watched Outish fumble with his multi-func. He held it in place with the bandaged hand that looked more like a cloth club than an appendage.

"Yes," he grumped. Baryy felt for the kid. His head was draped in a bandage turban, his hand was useless, and he'd just spilled a cup of kdel tea in his lap. He managed to get his multi-func open and connect to one of the orbiting recon bots. Manipulating the display grid with his healthy hand, he transferred the visuals from the multi-func to a holofield. He sat the multi-func down on the kitchen table across from Baryy's so that they now had two opposing holofields in action, each one connected to a different recon bot.

"Send yours to track the viscount's coach."

Outish stabbed the holofield with a finger, spun the recon bot about in an arc and sent it skimming through the trees on an intercept course for Viscount Helprig's caravan. "There, that good?" he grumped again.

Satisfied they were ready, Baryy stood up from the table, "I'll make you another cup of tea," he said as a peace offering. It was dark in the cabin with the windows shuttered and boarded, their own mini hard-point. Ogden had at first balked at letting them return to the cabin, but it sat under the watchful eaves of the Bentwood tree fort, and that area of the town with its hermit bivvies and small family lodges had seen little troglodyte depredation. A few of the bivvies had been pushed over and ransacked, more out of curiosity, but the findings were meager for hungry reptiles. Baryy told Ogden he could better care for Outish in the cabin. Outish was unfit for duty, and Baryy was exhausted after spending a tense night in the foundry and the whole day fighting fires with the fire brigade. The only place to rest on Perrty were the benches that ringed the tree.

Moving by the dim light of the holofields he put the tea kettle back on the stove. "How's the hand?" He'd treated Outish with the field medpack which included inserting a neural dampener astride the median nerve in the wrist.

"Doesn't hurt," he replied with evident relief. "Do you," he hesitated, "do you think we can fix it?"

Baryy came back to the kitchen table and watched on Outish's holofield the viscount's procession approach to the Tolkroft mining camp. "You tell me. You're the astrobiologist."

"We need the autodoc to do reconstruction."

He nodded. "It's at the repair bay."

Outish peered at the bandage. He didn't want to think about what remained of his hand. He also didn't want to think about how and when they would be able to shift to Isumfast.

Viscount Helprig and his coach arrived at the mining camp a half hour late escorted by two columns of Scarlet Saviors. At first, Woodwern fretted that the viscount's tardiness would spoil their surprise, but the mine superintendent consoled him. "Tis an inexact thing you ask of us Woodwern. We've no good idea how long it will take." In the end, Helprig's feigned tardiness worked to the Timberkeeps favor.

Arrayed behind Sedge were the mine superintendent, Woodwern, Margern, captain of operations, captain of Scouts, Christina, and Alex. The operations captain noted the obvious, "We told them this be a truce parley, yet they bring their Scarlet Britches."

Sedge rolled his shoulders and straightened his back, his body stiff from too little sleep and too much pacing on the command deck. "Take care of it when the time comes captain. You know what to do." Again he was thankful to Mother the Paleowrights were so predictable. Their dogma of righteous superiority would never allow them to respond outside of the ecclesiastical box they built for themselves. Church doctrine demanded they invoke the eminence of the Ancients and anything less was a sign of faithlessness. They simply could not leave their paladins, their icons of their power, behind.

The column of Scarlet Saviors on matching chestnut brown eenus split to the left and right, followed by the coach which skewed to a stop twenty paces in front of the Wedgewood leaders. The Saviors turned their mounts to face the party, remaining saddled. The calculated display intended to intimidate and instill awe in the power and glory of Diunesis Antiquaria.

A churchman sergeant climbed down from his seat next to the teamster and lowered the retractable coach steps and opened the door. The first person to exit the coach was the predicant, followed by a civilian who the captain of Scouts murmured "Washentrufel." A soldier in a mercenary's nondescript but functional armor stepped down and behind him the viscount.

"The merc is the Drakan decurion," Alex said clearly. The decurion sought the voice in the assemblage and caught sight of Christina. Their eyes locked. A bare smile flickered crossed his face. He nodded to her.

Christina inclined her head, assuming a squared posture. Her face impassive as stone. In recognition of the moment and in comradeship with the Zursh mercenaries, her long flaxen hair was coiled in a twisting braid, in distinctive Lamaran fashion.

Alex leaned close to Christina, not caring who heard, "I think he likes you."

Her eyes twinkled, and she answered, "Weakness."

Stepping forward and adjusting his vestments, not deigning to look Sedge in the eye as if he were a loathsome rodent unworthy of his attention, the viscount delivered his terms directly and not through his aide. He began without preamble, "Our terms are thus, you will abandon your tree houses and march your remaining rabble to the Main Gate whence we will disarm them. This is to begin in one hour. You will then evacuate each of your earthen huts and march those dwellers to the Main Gate likewise--"

Sedge interrupted him. "You can save your words for your Ancients, Helprig. We're not surrendering."

During the exchange, the mine superintendent noticed a growing discomfiture on the Washentrufel agent's face; the superintendent could barely suppress his grin. The agent drew the predicant close and whispered something in his ear while the viscount fumed and spewed at Sedge. The aide's eyes grew wide as he looked directly past the mine super up the hill at the Tolkroft Mine entrance. He stepped to the viscount and attempted to gain his attention, but the prelate would have none of it.

"You wood chopping, slug-kissing miscreants, will be trampled beneath our steel-shod feet you fool—What?!" he slapped the predicant away. "Do not interrupt me while I dress down these heathen idiots. Not surrender! You are daft!" The viscount fairly shook. "I can bring the full might of Diunesis Antiquarian down upon your head."

Sedge let the viscount rail. Woodwern was shocked. The viscount's calm, calculating demeanor, so carefully practiced at the council meeting, shattered like crockery dropped on stone.

Margern pulled Woodwern close, "I do think our dear viscount has himself in a spot of trouble."

"Oh, how so?"

"Instead of the easy victory, we assume he's promised the archbishop, he is instead finding himself in the position of having to negotiate. He's used to bullying, and it's not working. Whatever he committed to Hebert it is surely in need of reconsideration, which belies a misjudgment and when do the Antiquarians ever misjudge?" she asked rhetorically, an arch to her eye. "Imagine what it will mean to his reputation if he goes back to Hebert beaten for the second time." She paused, "By us, simple wood chopping, heathen squirrel lovers." The wicked smile lightened Woodwern's spirits after the two days of brutal fighting.

"Indeed," Woodwern agreed, "and you can add slug-kissing miscreants to that list. Have you ever kissed a slug? I have not. Who would have thought such a motley bunch could bring the Church so low?"

A flicker of Margern's eye caught him, and he sensed the sudden silence, a break in the viscount's tirade.

"Burning? What do you mean burning?" Helprig snapped. "The whole town has burnt." The aide drew Helprig aside and whispered in a highly animated manner, ending his monolog with one arm pointing at the Tolkroft Mine entrance.

The viscount stared up the hill and blinked. His mouth moved, but no sound came out. Finally, he said in a low, strangled voice, "Why is," his voice trailed off, and he shook his head, "What has happened to the mine?" A thick column of smoke disgorged from the entrance, drifting into the trees and dispersing through the forest. Accustomed to the sight of burning buildings and smoking ruins Helprig had paid it no mind.

"Uh, um," the mine superintended spoke up. "Uh, that be our fault, your Excellency. You see we were cleaning up the mine and all, sort of sprucing it up when one of the lads knocked over a lamp in the storage room. I'm mean accidents in mines will happen of course, but this is a wee catastrophe. There isn't a worse place in a mine to knock over a lamp than in a storage room with lamp oil, candles, quicksilver, spare timber frames, and what not. Once the fire got started, it was the most we could do to scramble our arses out of there before the smoke overcame us." The superintended nodded his head with the most apologetic, buffoon-like expression he could manage, and even doffed his cap and wrung it between his hands. Sedge looked up at the sky feigning interest in a passing bird while Margern turned Woodwern around and they stepped a few paces away in huddled conversation. Christina gave the decurion a wry twist at the corner of her mouth, and the decurion arched an eyebrow in return. The look on Larech's face turned sour as he traded a glare with the Scout's captain's benign shrug.

"Fire! Why you moron you have to put it out!" Helprig wailed.

"Is that so?" Sedge rejoined, a steel edge to his voice." He took two steps towards the viscount and the twenty mounted Scarlet Saviors drew their rachiers. The operations captain blew a whistle. "Put it out?" hissed Sedge, deadly menace punctuating his words.

"Oh oh," Baryy said watching the holofield. His recon bot had recorded the Timberkeep's earlier preparations. He reached for his handbolt. If he ran, he could be at the mine in ten minutes.

Suddenly the doors of the nearby mine buildings and bivouacs were thrown open, and three wards of Timberkeeps rushed out. The Scarlet Saviors whirled their mounts about. The Timberkeeps arrayed themselves into three separate double-line ranks surrounding the enclave. Confused at which threat to face first, the eenumen finally directed their mounts to form a protective circle around the small party of churchmen and Drakans.

"Wait," called Outish before Baryy could fling open the door. "Alon isn't moving. She has this handled."

Uloch watched Christina closely. Her disinterest in the mounted warriors confirmed his fears. The Timmies would not be bluffed. Properly led, the Timmie warriors would spear the horses and pull the riders from the saddles. It would be short work.

Sedge pointed towards the town, "You will put out every fire you have started, and you will rebuild every building that you have incinerated before we pour one bucket of water down that mine." He hooked a thumb over his shoulder at the smoke billowing from the mine mouth.

Helprig stuttered then caught himself. His face dawning in realization and then he squinted, grinding his teeth. "You did this on purpose. You deliberately set fire to the mine."

Sedge snorted derisively, "Did you seriously think we were going to let you have the mine? Here in Wedgewood? After what you've done? We don't need the aquamarine, so rather than have it be a bane to this forest, to these people, and to this town, we've destroyed the mine to, as you say, protect it for when the Ancients return--"

Suddenly there came a deep rumbling from underground. They all turned to look at the mine. The vibration set the eenus to piping and stomping, the low resonance of the sound seemed as if the mountain were turning in its sleep, fretted by a nightmare. A whoosh of hot, black smoke issued from the opening in a sudden massive belch. More noises, this time of falling, grinding rock, and splintering timbers nearer the entrance echoed from the shaft. The shaking of the ground stopped, and the last dirty, dusty gasp of air came from the hole. All stared in subdued silence.

Sedge looked to the mine superintendent. For a man who'd just lost one of his life-long accomplishments he appeared unconcerned, "Oi, those ironwood timbers finally went. I always wondered how long they'd last. Though truly I expected them to go long before now." He stared at the viscount. "I'm heartily thankful the viscount was here to witness it. Otherwise, he'd be wanting to go in to see for himself, and then he might be hurt, and we can't have that."

"Arrrgh!" The viscount raised his hands in claws and made to attack Sedge but the predicant, assisted by the Washentrufel agent, seized him by both arms.

A thin smile creased Sedge's lips. "Let the viscount go. He and I can settle this here and now." But three Scarlet Saviors dismounted. One, Sedge recognized as Captain Irons from Murali's, worked to usher the viscount back to the coach. The other two stood before Sedge while the others boarded the coach. "This is not over!" the viscount yelled from a coach window. "You shall pay dearly for this you Ancient-cursed heathens!"

With the departure of the coach, Decurion Uloch approached Sedge and gave short bow at the hip. "I believe our conclave is over. Given the situation with the mine, I am sure the clergy will not be mollified. Are we to assume that hostilities will resume?"

"You are," Sedge stated formally.

The decurion nodded and glanced towards the Defenders, then back to the warlord, resignation heavy on his shoulders. "Very well. Nothing good will come of this. Certainly, nothing has so far." He saluted Drakan-fashion, flat of his right hand over his heart. "In the morning we will settle this."

With the Paleowrights gone, Alex asked Sedge "Are you sure collapsing the mine will dissuade them? Seems it has only sparked the prelate's incoherent ire from which all logic has fled. And to what benefit? Yonder mine is now in ruins and so your source of gold."

What he didn't say, but was thinking, was Sedge and his mercenaries required gold for their payment.

Sedge gave him a sly grin, "Superintendent, what say you to that?"

"Oi, we've been digging in that mountain now for forty years. I'm itching to be down there and see what's happened, but I can tell you Tolkroft Mine has five shafts, all of which are connected at multiple levels. This be the first and original shaft, and so it be known as the Tolkroft Mine entrance. But there be others. Tis true this is the shaft where the aquamarine deposits are, but our richest gold lode is off the Quarry shaft, up and around that shoulder there."

Alex lifted both brows, and then he started to chuckle. "And the look on that pompous priest's face? Oh, Mother's fair breath, that be priceless."

Margern gushed "Wasn't it now though! I was fit to be tied, shame on me. It was doubly hard to contain myself knowing it was only the aquamarine we buried."

"And good riddance too," added Woodwern soberly. "We aimed to take the heart out of the Paleowright attack, and I think we have done that. They may still want to fight for spite and hate, but there's no margin in it for them now. They'll come to their senses soon enough; continuing the attack will gain them naught but blood and misery."

"Baryy, maybe with the aquamarine buried the Nordarks won't bother with this mine, and maybe the corsairs won't come." Outish peered around the holofield looking for Baryy's agreement.

"Huh?" Baryy grunted watching the recon bot track the viscount's coach. Their stock of charged bots at the cabin was down to a handful. They needed to get to a decommissioned IDB supply station to restock, or to the repair bay to recharge their units. He punched the recall button to bring the bot back to the cabin. The logistics of operating as clandestine extrasolars were crimping their methods. Normally, he would plug the bots into a neutrino charger but it radiated a traceable signal, and near Wedgewood he couldn't deploy a solar array.

Looking away from the bot control display, Baryy asked, "What does collapsing the mine have to do with the Nordarks not coming here? The coordinates they have are for a mine in Mestrich."

"But eventually, won't they figure out there is no aquamarine in Mestrich? And when they do, won't they come looking for the real mine?"

Baryy collapsed the holofield and set his multi-func aside. By the tone of Outish's question, Baryy realized his friend had been worrying over a potential hole in Atch's plan. "Wait, rewind. How is burying the mine supposed to make it harder to find?" he asked, dropping his usual sarcasm.

Out of his depth, unsure of the geological consequences, the astrobiologist thought about it. "Well, there won't be a mine. How can they get in? It's buried under tons of rock."

Baryy slowly shook his head. "It's not like corsairs would use the Tolkroft mine entrance even if they did find it. They can deploy A-wave transponders, and if they get a hit, they'll send in a robo-miner. It digs its own hole. It doesn't need a Doroman mine shaft to get in and out."

"But," Outish searched for words, "it has to help."

Baryy shrugged, "Maybe, though I doubt it. I know you can scan for the aural reflections of aquamarine-5 from low orbit." He thought about the pegmatite the fire brigade rescued from Murali's, soot-covered and chipped, but otherwise undamaged. It sat stashed in a bivvy, hidden under a heap of blankets. Safe, perhaps, from marauding trogs, but not Nordarken Mining.

On their way to Timber Hall Sedge asked, "Have they finished their catapults yet?"

The Scout's captain stirred at his commander's question, turning away from a party of workers building a makeshift eenu corral in place of the stables. "Two of them are ready now. Three others will be ready over the next two days."

Sedge sniffed. "They'll not be wanting to leave until they've tried their new toys." He turned to the operations captain. "We can't let them deploy those catapults against us." Musing over an idea, "I say we borrow them."

The Scout's captain gazed at the warlord with an open expression. "What do you have in mind?"

Instead of answering her question he pointed, "We have guests."

Sedge stopped at the top step in front of Timber Hall, and stuck out a hand, "I'm Sedge, commander of the Clan Mearsbirch wards and the Wedgewood militia. Glad to have you here." The few walk lamps competed fitfully with the darkening night, but one of the Red Elm Doromen held a torch so he could see the chieftain's face clearly.

"Oi, glad we got here before those damn Paleo's toasted you. I'm Ordern Smoothgrain, Chieftain of Red Elm." A ward of Clan Red Elm marched past, followed by more in the gloom as they came in through the Hall Gate. "Stinking loglards are everywhere. Where did you drag those from? The bloody Great Swamp is way that way." The chieftain jabbed a thumb over his shoulder. He was a barrel-chested man with a red beard that reached his chest. He wore a conical helm with a nose guard and earflaps. Unlike the Mearsbirch wards, he wore a breastplate and carried a long sword. The armor was unpolished, leather sleeves worn smooth with no attempt to pound out the dents and gouges. The torch cast a yellowish glow, but Sedge could tell the man had reddish skin, lined and scared. His typical prominent Doroman nose sported a big mole.

"Yes, well sorry about that," answered Sedge. "They came as guests of the Parrots. Near a thousand of them. Flooded over the wall like the sea at high tide. It was a bit touch and go there for a while."

The chieftain rocked back. He hooked his thumbs into his sword belt. The news settled on him like a fresh cut tree hitting the ground. "The Paleowrights brought them?" His voice hoarse. "I thought they were," he stopped, "I, we knew the loglards attacked you, but no one said the loglards were working with the Paleowrights. How can that be?"

"Chief, the Paleos have hatched an evil scheme with the trogs that I thought was just folklore. I knew about Whispering Bough, but never did I think it possible they could coordinate an attack with the lizards, but they did. Ill is the day those two married."

Chief Smoothgrain nodded once. "Mother forbid the spawn from that coupling."

"Come into the Hall." He started up the steps. "When your runner came in this afternoon Woodwern bade us meet as soon as you arrived. We had a parley with the Paleo clergy at noon." Sedge led Ordern through the high doors.

"Oi, and how did that go?" anger and skepticism dripping from his every word.

Sedge stopped to give a hard smile. He liked the chieftain. "Arrogant bastards. They wanted us to surrender." Before Ordern could interrupt as he saw the man about to launch Sedge held up his hand. "By noon tomorrow, we'll see who is surrendering. Come upstairs, Alon and our Scout's captain will brief you on our plans."

"Alon?" he asked as they headed for the grand staircase and Woodwern's chambers.

"Hmm, yes, Christina is here. She's been leading the fight." When Sedge sensed Ordern had stopped he turned to look. "What?"

"The Ascalon is here?"

He smiled. "In the flesh. In the armor. And in Mother's spirit. She's as good as they say Ordern. Have you met her?"

"No." He looked down. "I never expected I would."

Sedge laughed. "She's human, just like you and me. Come, let's go up."

They gathered around an impromptu diorama arranged on a table In Woodern's chamber using pinecones, inkwells, feathers, buttons, and whatnots to represent Timber and Paleo positions. The Scout's captain adjusted the pieces, and the ops officer outlined the operation. "Chief, we know you've marched hard, and had to fight trogs on the way, but it will be a big help. With your wards here, we can assign more of our wards to the attack. If you can position your five wards behind the wall, held in reserve, we won't have to worry about the Drakans trying something sneaky."

Ordern nodded. He'd left his four other wards at Wayland's Farm to help the Plains wards sweep the foothills and upper pastures clear of the troglodyte vermin. "What time will you need them in place?"

"Three hours past midnight."

"So be it. I will send word for the troops to get what sleep they can, but to muster at three hours past." Weary from the road and the day's fighting, Ordern pulled up a chair and sat, heaving a sigh and stretching his legs. "Even if we beat them here," he said to Woodwern, "the bastards will not let this lie. They're pernicious cones. They'll be back."

Woodwern swallowed. A look passed between him and Margern.

"How big an army can they muster?" The Red Elm chief asked. "With what they have here, in Hebert, and everywhere else?"

Sedge inclined his head to the Scout's captain, a cue to share their collective wisdom. "The four battalions they've sent at us here are from the two standing Hebert regiments. The Paleos can be cheap bastards. They hoard silver like a squirrel hoards nuts. The only troops they really like paying for are the Saviors. But now that we've bloodied their nose and trashed their fake honor, I dare say they'll pry open their purses and build themselves more regiments. They can draw from Dorthunia, Quarden, Dairned, and a whole slew of other parishes. Our best guess is they could muster five thousand in five months."

"Five thousand?" Ordern grimaced.

More if they take more time," added Sedge.

"But five thousand?" Ordern shook his head. "Even with Floral, Tough Nut, Burr, and all the other Timber clans, we'd barely notch four thousand warriors."

"We'd have to ask the Plains and Rocks for help," said Woodwern.

Christina stepped back from the table.

Ordern had been respectful of the Alon's silence and thought not to encroach; focusing instead on Sedge's briefing, but now he openly appraised her. She bore an erudite expression. Ordern noticed her hair was done in a braid of the Northwren. He did not know she was Lamaran. In her simple leather britches, white linen blouse, leather vest, and wide leather belt, there were few things to give away her prowess as a warrior, except for her height and the muscles in her neck and shoulders. Muscles common from wearing a helmet, heavy armor, and wielding a sword. There were, of course, the scars, the old short scar over her right eyebrow and the recently healed one low on her left cheek. The rumor he'd heard walking through Wedgewood was she was beautiful; he'd be propagating that rumor himself now. Inwardly he wondered how such a creature could be an Ascalon. He banished the thought. Mother was life.

"How far and to whom we call for help depends on the Drakans," Christina spoke. "A Paleowright army of five thousand will embolden the archbishop. He'll want to use it, and strife will certainly follow. It will benefit the Empire if we are fighting here in middle Isuelt. Oridia, Mestrich, and SeaHaven would all be distracted. If the Paleowrights were to make such mischief, the Drakans would time their own assault on the Stronghold of Darnkilden and the SeaHaven to coincide the Paleowright move. Is that not true master of operations?"

"It is, Alon. Between the Drakans and the Ompeans, they easily have ten thousand troops, some say twenty thousand. If they coordinated with the Church, whose forces lie to the west of the Drakan frontier, deep in the heart of the West, the whole defense of the West could be undone."

"Mother's spirit," Ordern hissed. "It would be war, across all of Isuelt. What has that fool Helprig done?"

For the first time, Margern spoke, "Ordern, the Drakans have been biding their time. They are getting bold. Helprig is certainly a fool, but he is a pawn as well. We can blame this on the Paleowrights, but the Drakans are their sponsors."

"They are," agreed Scouts. "It's worse. I've conferred with Perrin and Barrigal. They think the Duchy of Neuland will side with Nak Drakas."

Woodwern jerked. "But they were part of the Lamaran Empire?"

"They were, but the new duke is weak," said Scouts. "The duchess is Lamaran, but the duke's mistress is Ompean, as is the sage-rose she supplies to the court. It's as rotten as a termite den. One good blow and the whole duchy could drop to Nak Drakas."

Ordern breathed a heavy sigh. "What of Mestrich and Oridia? Surely they are committed to the defense."

It was Sedge's turn to respond. They all knew he had close ties to the Kingdom of Mestrich, a neighbor to Oridia. "Oridia, the SeaHaven League, and Darnkilden are all Eldred. Oridia sends squadrons to the League against the Drakans. So they will fight as one. But," he shook his head slowly, "King Isip of Mestrich is an isolationist. He thinks he can sit behind the Darnkilden-SeaHaven wall and not worry. Isip does not believe the Lamaran-Drakan feud is not his fight. And why should it be? Mestrich was never officially a part of the Lamaran Empire. And if you want to know the truth..." he looked around the room. "The king has gotten very fat and lazy. Some say it takes four men to carry him. I've not seen Isip since I left their service, but I hear from his steward. The king's army is not what it once was." He did not say that many in Mestrich blamed the king's decline on Sedge and his departure. "Regardless. The SeaHaven and Stronghold need to be warned of what has transpired here. Oridia is now on the front line, and the alliance now needs to look south as well as east."

Chapter 48
Shift Zone

Tivor

Akallabeth lined up his five bravos on their eenus as instructed. Achelous checked the field generator status on his multi-func. Control and power were set to local. Theoretically, there would be no alerts on any IDB or Transportation Authority monitoring boards of the transmission. The system was in on-planet, point-to-point mode. It was a narrow, low-level emission akin to blinking a flashlight on and off, three times in a very big and dark forest: easy to miss.

"Are you nervous?" he asked Marisa. She nodded once, short and sharp. "Yes." It was cold that morning at the Auro Na temple. Frost lay like a heavy white blanket. Her teeth chattered. Bundled in her fur cloak, woolen garments, and her amber face framed by the fur hood she should be warm.

Akallabeth spoke quietly with his team. They occupied the shift zone and waited for Marisa and Achelous to join them. They were seasoned professionals. Two ex-Darnkilden Rangers, a former Oridian Lancer, and the other two ex-Tivor marines. Hard men, ready for a hard fight. They were mounted on the swiftest eenus the Silver Cup could buy. They brought with them three remounts in case one came up lame for this would be a quick ride. Three leagues straight to Wayland's Farm. No stopping. From there they would meet up with a full ward of Red Elm warriors for an escort into Wedgewood. Baryy had arranged the escort with Sedge who grudgingly agreed once he heard a mission from the aorolmin of Tivor was coming with an offer of a possible alliance. But first Akallabeth and his bravos, with Achelous and Marisa as their charges, would have to thread the needle through the farm and forestlands torn by troglodyte raiding parties. In the end, they'd all decided the best approach was to ride fast, ride straight, and not stop. That was why for this morning Marisa rode Echo rather than Achelous. Of the seven eenus only Echo had been through a field shift. It was the least likely to panic and acknowledged to be the fastest. Marisa had repeatedly complained about Achelous giving up Echo, but he was firm. Marisa carried the message from the aorolmin to Clan Mearsbirch. She was the one entitled to negotiate on the aorolmin's behalf.

The field generator status turned green: coordinates validated, energy level confirmed for seven humans, their gear, and ten eenus. Achelous set the transmit timer and closed the bible.

"What?" she asked, seeing his grim smile. Her black eyes peering from the dark shadows of her hood.

"It was a stroke of genius for Sedge to destroy the aquamarine mine." He reflected a bit. "That will take the stuffing out of the Paleowrights," he said it more to himself.

"Will it?"

He looked at those eyes. His smile flattening at their truth. "For a while. Either way you cut it, it was a major victory to force the Paleowrights to a parlay and then have them see the mine destroyed. The fight isn't over, but Wedgewood has survived, and that, I am sure, is a major defeat of the Church. That they couldn't crush the Timberkeeps with a thousand trogs in one swift blow has to be a severe setback to their plans." The destruction of the foundry was a significant setback to his plans, the plans to defeat Nordarken Mining, but thank the Spirits Baryy and Outish survived, and with Ogden, they would be able to rebuild. Now with the aorolmin's help, and the galvanized Clan Mearsbirch, perhaps progress would even be accelerated. His hopes were once the Paleowrights were driven from Wedgewood -- if they could be -- that he and Baryy would once again be able to focus on the main threat, the threat to the entire planet, not just the danger to Wedgewood or even Marinda Merchants.

The sun cracked the eastern horizon. Achelous edged his new mount a bit closer. "Ready?"

The fur-trimmed hood bobbed.

He trotted into the shift zone.

"Remember," he called to the entire party, "the shift will be sudden. One second you are here, next second somewhere else. The new smells, temperature, scenery may freak your eenus. So just concentrate on staying in the saddle and then calming them. Echo has done this before. She will recognize where she is at. Marisa will point her at the trail and give her the spurs. That steed won't need much encouragement so she will be flying. I've found with nervous eenus the best thing to do is give them something to do, like ride fast. Once we're moving in good order, Akallabeth will take the lead using the map I've given him." He looked around. "All good?"

There were nods all around.

"Very well," he heard the countdown timer tick in his ear implant. "Here we go."

Marisa's hood blew back. Echo hit the trail unerringly, dug hard to the left and galloped. There was the smell of smoke in the air. Trees flew past. She glanced behind. The trail full of galloping riders, billowing cloaks, pounding hooves, flying dirt clods, grim faces low over the heads of their mounts. The trees were a blur. They were whitish-green. *What kind are these?* She wondered. Then Echo came upon a dark form lying prone on the trail. Jumping it easily Marisa looked down, it was a human, a woman by the hair. She almost pulled up, but then Echo jumped another prone body, this one was a— *Is that a troglodyte?* I was big, mottled green, and had scales. She shivered. *That's the closest I've ever been to a trog! Thank Mother it is dead!*

"Go!" She heard Achelous yell from behind, so she lowered her head and rode. Akallabeth was supposed to take the lead, but Echo had the bit, and Marisa just let the eenu fly. Another clearing came and went. A downed log loomed. Vaulting it neatly the party rode hard.

"Pull up Lady, let me pass," Akallabeth called.

Marisa considered easing Echo's hard pace, but then they burst into a broad clearing. A farmstead off in the distance to the right was a smoldering ruin. A mounted troop of human warriors, red trees painted on their shields, charged a nearby tree line. The world was in chaos. Fires dotted the fields set by human defenders.

A band of trogs, live ones, crossed the prairie a fair distance ahead where the trail widened into a road. Marisa reached down and freed her marine cutlass in its sheath. It wasn't the brutish boarding cutlass used by seamen, but the lighter, faster officer's cutlass designed for point-work rather than bashing and hacking.

The band of trogs was attacking a barricaded farmhouse. More reptiles were scattered about seemingly disinterested in the assaulting the hard-point until they saw the galloping troop. One, a hulking brute, took sights on Marisa and started swinging something.

Holding the reins in her left hand, she drew the cutlass and swept it back, carrying the point low over Echo's rump. The trog started running to cut her off, it was swinging an object above its head.

"Pull up Lady!" Akallabeth's call came from immediately behind.

Oh, it's a flail! she realized. The spiked ball whirled around and around connected by a chain to the staff. Her pulse pounded in alarm: she'd never trained to fight an opponent with a flail; they weren't used on ships. The trog opponent was big and fast.

"Pull up Lady!" beseeched Akallabeth.

Achelous fumbled in the folds of his cloak for his whistle, the eenu call. *Gads, we're too close!* In a moment he was about to see his love die. The world slowed to excruciating slowness. Marisa pounded straight at the trog, her cloak flowing behind, the curved cutlass glinting dimly, held straight back. Having no other choice, he raised his handbolt.

Marisa struggled with what to do, but then the trog settled it for her. Instead of aiming for her, she could see it swinging the spiked head at Echo's muzzle. Yanking hard left and jamming her heels forward, she commanded Echo, at full gallop, to curl like a huge ball. The spikes whistled past the eenu's head, grazed her thigh in a flash of searing heat, shredded her cloak, and whipped past. One instant she was in the saddle and the next--

Akallabeth came fast. The spiked ball swung back around in a whistling arc as he dodged left and then leaned right, slashing down with his sword hitting something hard and bony.

Achelous, next in line, shot the beast with his handbolt. The quarrel flew true, straight into the snout. Then he was past, diving for Marisa.

The next in line, a Darnkilden Ranger, riding low, wrist-flicked his saber and opened the trog's throat in a spray of gore deep to the spinal cord.

The next in line, the Oridian Lancer, for good measure cleaved the troglodyte's head clean from its shoulders.

Achelous leapt from his saddle. Marisa lay in a sprawled heap, her limbs askew, her hair undone, her cutlass far from her hand. He dropped to both knees and cradled her head. Dimly he was aware of Akallabeth ordering their escort: forming a skirmish line.

"At them boys!"

Achelous paid no heed to the eenu charge; Marisa's eyes were open, unfocused, staring past him to the stars. Her porcelain cheeks were smeared with dirt, her lip bleeding heavily. Blood and earth were in her hair. He cursed this day. He cursed this life; he cursed the troglodytes, the Paleowrights, the IDB, and everything else that came to mind. Pressing her unfocused faced close to him, he cried. He just rocked back and forth, holding her tight. Flashes of memory assailed him: Boyd, Marinda Hall, her smiling face from the time they first met to now. His loves, fears, and anger all vied for attention. What was he doing here on this desolate plain with dead Marisa?

Then finally, he sensed someone beside him. "Oi, we'll need to bandage that leg." Akallabeth, having driven the trogs away, had come back, dismounted, and held a wrapping in his hand.

Achelous looked at her thigh. There were bloody torn gauges where the spikes of the flail had hit her. He wanted to scream and cry, unable to think, unable to call up the med-bot he had in his pack.

"Dearen?"

He looked down.

"Dearen?"

It was the most beautiful face he'd ever seen or held in his life. It was her face, his love, his life.

"Yes," a tear dropped on her cheek.

"You can let me go now. You're suffocating me." Her eyes, clear, black, were on him, not the stars.

He snuffled. "You have to be alive for that."

Chapter 49
Catapults

Wedgewood

Ogden swayed on the rope ladder as he groped his way down in the dark. The trick for him and four hundred other warriors was to make it to their muster points without undue noise. A shield or helm dropped from a tree fort would clatter like a copper milk kettle carrying far in the night. Many of the warders were living on little sleep; they were stiff, aching, bruised, and a substantial number sported bandages, but they made their muster points without alarm. The thinnest sliver of Lonely Soul rose in the east, dawn three hours away. Eight full wards and the effectives of the two mercenary companies formed the attack force. After two days of battle and casualties, it was the absolute most Sedge dare put in the field, counting on Red Elm to defend the town wall.

"You have the farthest to go," Sedge whispered to Christina, "you better get a move on. We're going through the front gate in ninety minutes, whether you're in position or not."

Christina looked to Perrin in the gloom of the lantern-less gathering. She would lead the mercenary companies in an attack along the outside of the south wall past the southern sentries of the Paleowright camp, and straight at the catapults. Her orders were to capture them and only set them afire if she couldn't hold them. Sedge himself would lead the eight Timberkeep wards on a frontal assault of the camp. The first hour of the attack would be in complete darkness and pandemonium would reign. He counted on it.

Pulling on a gauntlet, she stood composed. "Are you finished with your checks? We want no jingling or scraping."

"Yes, Alon," replied Perrin. "The men are ready."

"Then let Mother guide us." She held out a mailed hand, palm down. Sedge, Perrin, and the other commanders stepped in and placed their hands on hers to hear her blessing.

"The world turns. The sun rises, the moon sets. We live, we love, we cry. In spring the snow melts, in summer the grass grows, in autumn the leaves fall, in winter the hearth fires glow. Such is the wheel of Mother's life. We are all on the wheel. Together we roll it forward. Tonight we roll it forward to an uncertain future, but it is a future of our making. Mother calls to us. Protect the world, protect life, and defend all that is good for there is evil in our world and it would undo our good work. Tonight we fight the evil that has brought fire and death. Mother calls."

"Mother calls," came the chorus.

Christina dropped her hand and touched Perrin on the shoulder. "We go."

Outside the charred palisade, a young, female Timberkeep scout waited. Following behind Perrin were a hundred of the fittest men of Barrigal's and Perrin's companies. Perrin was Christina's mercenary leader as Barrigal's wound kept him, grumpy and complaining, on the command deck as Ordern's advisor.

The woman explained the route to their destination and the column set off. Down through the Ungerngerists, on the thick carpet of needles, the scout led them at a fast walk downslope, then when well below the shoulder of the mountain they cut left. Their course took them parallel to the main road into Wedgewood that the Paleowrights were camped astride. A distance further the scout signaled a halt. "From here we go uphill to our position."

"Where are the sentries?" Christina whispered, gazing into the distance through the forest at the near-death campfires of the churchmen camp. The Paleowrights were struggling to burn newly cut wood she noted, live pine needles still on the limbs. She held much sympathy for the anger and shame that coursed through the Timberkeeps. The Paleowrights greatest insult came not in the slurs they used, the demands they made, or even the ruin of Wedgewood, but in how they villanized the forest. Of all ironies the Paleowrights greatest affront was least appreciated by them; they had little notion of the ill they wreaked and the shame for the Timbers the wanton forest destruction caused. Until now, the stewards of the forest had been powerless to stop them. Until now. Christina uttered a long sigh. Among the many wrongs to be righted this night not least of which was purging the forest of this malodorous ilk.

The scout made a hand motion of a finger across her throat.

Christina acknowledged. The two nearby Parrot sentries were dead. "They won't come to check on them?" she asked.

The scout shook her head and crept closer. "They're lazy. We've been watching them for two nights now. Their watch rotation is the same. They post the sentries for four hours, but no one inspects them until their relief arrives. These are city troops, they mount a night watch like they are on a wall."

Christina looked back at the scattered fire pits, embers glowing in the dark. Clearly, the churchmen were not experienced campaigners, more accustomed to bullying village citizenry and marching in parades. "Where are the catapults?"

Pointing, the scout whispered "Through there, two longbow shots. Maybe two hundred yards."

Perrin swallowed. They were about to charge into an enemy of over a thousand soldiers. The Alon crouched close, then asked, "We're set?"

"Yes."

Watching the camp for signs of movement she said, "We wait for the message from Sedge." Their telepath, a teenager, kneeling behind them, shook his head at the implied question when Perrin glanced back. No word as yet from the main force.

Time crawled like a slug on a forest trail. Seconds slowed to minutes, minutes slowed to hours.

"Is this your first battle," Christina asked the telepath. He wore no helmet in the style of other pathics. His long brown hair hung lank on his leather jacket. Mail links peeked out along the neckline. His longbow was the stout variety and matched the muscles in his shoulders. He carried two quivers full of the green and white fletched arrows of his ward.

"No, Alon. I fought on Hallow Meade and then Archwood."

Perrin grunted in satisfaction.

She nodded. "Tough fight at both."

"Heard Archwood gave uppance to the Britches." Perrin watched for signs of movement.

The lad nodded earnestly. "We did. The smoke, fire," he swallowed, "the Britches thought it would help, but we shot them anyway." The pale whites of his eyes dim rings around the black pupils.

"How old are you?" she asked.

"Sixteen summers, Mam."

She breathed at that, feeling her chest expand in her armor. "Who is your partner?" Telepaths operated in partner-pairs, the familiarity between the two critical for connecting across the trackless ether.

"My sister, Alon. She is one of five with Sedge."

Five? She'd not expected Sedge to have five pathics with him in the attack. "And how old is she?" she asked fearing the answer.

"Eighteen. My younger sister is a pathic at Timber Hall."

At that Christina smiled. "The talent runs in your family."

The pathic raised his hand and dipped his head. "The First Ward is through the Main Gate."

She set her jaw. Standing, her greaves creaked, binding at the ankles. She bent and undid the buckles, laying the plate and leather guards aside.

"What?" asked Perrin, seeing her strip them off.

She shook her head. "Speed my good captain. Speed. They'll slow me down."

Taking a step forward no hue or cry heralded her presence. Perrin made a signal, and to either side, the Zursh mercenaries emerged. They quietly drew their weapons from padded sheaths and muffled slings. A long line of silent, dark shapes.

Christina raised her sword high. Then swept it down and with no preamble launched into a sprint. She ran, the cold air flowing through her armor. Peripherally she sensed the black and silver shapes of the mercs slicing in, compressing behind her like a long wedge narrowing as she charged forward. Like a Barrens Leopard, fluid grace, following the undulations in the ground, Christina ran trusting her night sight and innate senses. In a breath, she swept past the first fire ring of orange coals. Amongst the enemy tents, she dug into the soft loam, flashing past tent stakes, guide ropes, and stacked pikes. Her armor, shield, and sword mere feathers to a hawk. Wind rushed through her helm to carry her flaxen braid out behind. To the rear the company pounded, chain mail crinkled and chinked, greaves and gauntlets rattled, but not a word uttered. Where she was the mist, the men were the rain. A churchman in a tent said, "Hey? What's up?" Another groggy voice answered, "What, I'm trying to sleep, leave me be."

Christina ran.

"But someone ran past our tent."

Christina ran.

"Well then go and look."

Christina ran.

"Ach, that's the sergeant's job. I'm not interested. If they need us, they'll get us."

Christina leaped a pair of crossed guide ropes and angled hard to her left where an angular shaped squatted in the greater darkness. More by sense and intuition than by sight, she headed for a second hulking shape. A churchman stepped from a tent to relieve himself. She came up from behind at full tilt and drove her sword elbow into the base of his head sending shivers up her arm. The man shot forward and slammed to the ground.

She drew up in front of what was indeed the second catapult, stopping hard in the pine needles and spinning round in search of a sentry. The man she clocked lay still, thirty feet away, his tent dark and silent. Her telepath arrived, hard on her heels. He quickly notched an arrow.

Perrin met her. "Anyone challenged us?" she asked quickly.

He shook his head, his eyes wide at their good fortune. Christina stared at him, at a momentary loss of what to do next for she had expected to fight their way in and face a melee around the machines. "Well then," she breathed a cloud trying to catch her breath. In the cold air, she was sweating rivulets. "Organize the men into three platoons. Station one," another breath, "to the east, one to the south, and one here in the center. The center platoon will be the reserve for wherever the fighting is heaviest."

"As you wish, Alon."

With Perrin gone she asked, "What is your name?" The young telepath held his longbow low and level, ready to draw. "Mitchern, Alon."

"Well then Mitchern, tell the command pathic we've captured the catapults with no casualties, and as yet the Paleowrights have not challenged us.

The lad searched the darkness, "I have."

Hoarse cries sounded in the distance to the west. The distinct clamor of metal clashing against metal carried to them. A Paleowright bugle sounded briefly before it abruptly cut off. Christina listened. "I expect we'll have company soon. Can you sense any interest in us?"

Mitchern stood still, his gaze straight. "They are waking up. All around us. Many of them. There are tremors, an edge of rising fear, or", he sought a description, "warning or alarm."

"Tell Perrin I'll be over there," she pointed to the westernmost catapult hulking black in the night. "You stay here with the company command. There'll be deserters fleeing Sedge, and we'll need to divert them, give them a fright on top the one they just had." She tapped a command sergeant and a runner to come with her.

The Paleowright battalion camped outside the Main Gate ceased to exist. Three hundred clansmen struck the camp which in the Paleowright hubris had no defensive works to protect it. They cut down anything that moved and did not have a conical Mearsbirch helm or white cloth streamers tied around their arms. Those few churchmen lucky to emerge from their tents and have the wits to immediately run survived. Those that came out with spears and attempt to fight were hacked down.

The camp near the catapults began to come alive. First one lantern then another lit the inside of the large troop tents, casting shadows on the walls of men rising from their billets and pulling on breeches. A figure came striding out of the darkness, his silhouette instantly recognizable by his fluted helmet and shoulder boards. He walked past the catapults several wagon lengths away, oblivious to the silent men of the eastern platoon. They dared not stir lest the magic of their invisibility dissipate with the Savior's attention. "You in there," the Scarlet Savior demanded of a tent shadow, "did you hear a horn blow?"

"Uh, no, I was asleep. But someone else said they heard men running past."

The fluted silhouette, caught against the wan glow of a tent lantern, paused, "You," he pushed on the tent corner, "did you hear a horn blow?" The tent walls were so thin the man's shadow could be seen to buckle on a belt. "Aye, I heard something, but it was cut off. I was going to check." The silhouette grumbled and began to move past the catapults, but then by premonition or curiosity turned and approached the silent line of warriors, stone boulders for all that they moved. "You there! Speak up! By the Ancients, you stand there like statues. You heard my question." The Scarlet Savior walked right up to the line of warriors. The man before him stirred, and in his heavy Lamaran accent, stark against the Herberian lilt from the tents, said, "Horn? I didn't hear no horn. Howbout you fellas?"

A cheerful chorus rippled amongst the black statues, "No, uh, not me. No horn." Then another "Who'd be daft to be blowing a horn and waking all the yonder sheep?"

The Savior's intake of breath rasped like an axe on a millstone.

Swords sprouted from the dark statues, and the paladin fell gurgling in a mass of black shapes. A cry of alarm came from the nearest tent.

"At 'em boys!" the eastern platoon launched themselves at the tents, cutting guide ropes and bodily heaving themselves onto the canvas like children jumping on beds. They flattened the tents into death traps where anything that moved or uttered a sound was stabbed.

Mitchern, with a message from the command sergeant, found Christina with her sword drawn, waiting for the enemy to form a counter attack. "Eastern platoon killed a Scarlet Savior," he hurried. "The platoon is attacking the tents near the third catapult."

She whirled to the east. Shadows, shapes, men running, and a growing commotion brought her no comfort. "Runner!" she called out, not caring who heard. "Get to the eastern platoon and tell them they are ordered to stand fast." She sought Perrin and found him with the reserve platoon. He was tense, staring in the direction of where the eastern platoon should have been. "Are we undone?" she asked.

"Aye," he said tonelessly, "we've been discovered, and the eastern platoon is attacking."

"Trees and leaves," she cursed. "Take the reserve to where the eastern should be and have them stand their ground. Then do your best to extricate the eastern if you can." She spun on Mitchern who was close at her heels. "How soon till Sedge is here?"

He covered his ears with his hands and concentrated. "The command pathic is running – wait he's stopping. I'm getting his attention." Mitchern fell silent, then said, "He doesn't know. Maybe five, ten minutes."

"Have him ask Sedge if we can attack. We still have the initiative." She thought about it. Many of the churchmen were just now rousing from their sleep. Done right, they could corral the hapless ones force them to surrender.

"Wait," Mitchern said, "he's trying to find Sedge. Seconds drained away. More Paleowrights were emerging half-dressed from their bivouacs and grabbing pikes. She could hear the eastern detachment clashing with spears and hacking at shields, bashing anything that moved which was easy as they were in the midst of a full battalion of pikemen. Eventually, the thirty warriors of the east platoon would have to fall back or be overwhelmed.

"No. We're to stand and hold. They are coming."

She glowered in the dark, then made up her mind and ran back to the southern platoon anchored dutifully where she'd left them. "Sedge will be coming from the other direction. If the churchmen organize a counter-attack, it will come from the east over there, or here. So follow me. We'll cover both."

Finding the line of the reserve platoon, she arrayed the southern detachment beside them, and formed a semi-circle about the catapult, unfinished, its basket missing. She looked up through the trees to see a purple glow lighting the east. Dawn approached.

A bewildered line of pikemen began to form to her front. More churchmen came running only to be stopped by the tableau. Men from the eastern platoon began returning by two's and three's with Perrin as the last, supporting a wounded Lamaran.

More pikemen arrived on the other side. As yet they were unorganized, but one or two officers with maybe a squad of Saviors were calling orders. Soon the mercenaries would be outnumbered, by a lot.

Grimly, Christina shook her head. "We have to attack."

Perrin agreed, "It's that or fall back. They'll be on us as soon as the Scarlet Britches wise up."

"Sound it."

Perrin lifted his sword in the dwindling night. "For Zursh! Aregen et marinar!"

The battle cry went up, and they charged.

Sedge heard the cry. A hundred hoarse voices in the dawning light. He knew Christina would do as ordered and not attack unless things were desperate. He could see the looming shape of a war machine, a trebuchet of some sort. "Go! Go!" he called to the younger, faster warriors. There would be nothing fancy about this fight. Just a straight up brawl. "Go!"

Captain Irons came up with ten squads. Decurion Uloch followed with his two centuries, but the pikemen were breaking. Over two hundred churchmen were being scattered. "Close order!" Irons called. "Trumpeter! Sound it!"

Uloch watched the Saviors array in a line abreast and shook his head in disgust. Their pikemen brothers were running like so many frightened cattle. He looked left and right at his ordered double line.

Shields held perfectly slanted to the left ready to lock, spears pointed level, each step measured, all heads forward.

Irons slowed his pace to let the Drakans gain on him. Paleowright officers with two squads of Savior enforcers on each flank attempted to stem the pikemen route, herding them into groups. Then he saw the cause of the flight. A force of black and silver-clad Zursh mercenaries were striking down the last of the churchmen stragglers. How had they gotten this far?

Marching forward, the steady beat of fifty Saviors keeping pace, Uloch watched as a tall warrior in brown with a painted aegis called the mercenaries back into a line that shook itself out neatly along a low rise. Then he recognized her as the first dawn rays struck her shield. At every step in the battle, she'd been there: the shield wall, the Hall Gate, the mine collapse, and now here deep in the Paleowright camp wreaking havoc. Well, he'd just have to fix that and put an end to her exploits.

Alex shouldered his way in beside Christina. "Look at all them Saviors. You'd think it was a Church reunion."

"There's more of them. These are just the ones that aren't hung over." She watched as the Saviors halted, then began to shift left making room for the approaching Drakans. On either flank, the Paleowright officers were having some success at organizing the pikemen into two separate formations.

"There's a large tribe of trogs coming back from fighting the Plains and Rock wards," Alex said. "The Timber scouts are watching them. The trogs are to the south. Could be more." He listened to a Timberkeep ward horn sound rally. Then another, and another. "Going to be a hot day."

Uloch's eyes narrowed as more Timmy wards formed up on either side of the mercs. "Larech!" he called, then looked back to where the Washentrufel agent loitered with a pair of Church clergy. "How is it the Timmies feel free to send all their wards against us? Who's manning the forts?" But the answer presented itself on the left of the Wedgewood line. Two new wards, with strange devices on their shields, formed up. One, a red tree, and the other a house on a field. "Reinforcements," he muttered.

"Should we attack?" asked the Scout's captain. Sedge, Christina, Perrin, Ogden, and the bosses stood back from the line in a conclave. "We have the numbers on them, and the town is secured by Red Elm."

Christina replied, "No."

Sedge agreed, "We've achieved our purpose and more. We've captured the catapults, driven the Paleos back and sustained minimum casualties. We hold here."

"But I'm sure we can crack the churchmen on either flank. Drive them, scatter them, and that would leave the Drakans or Scarlets to pivot. We could surround them." Perrin saw an opportunity and wanted to finish the battle decisively. "We've broken the pikemen three times in three days. We can do it again."

Christina shook her head. "We'd lose more warriors, many. We've been blessed by Mother so far. It is one thing to ask Red Elm and the Plains and Rock clans to come to our aid, but it is another to take them into a war. And yes, we've broken the pikemen before, but they were not prepared."

"Aye." Sedge flexed the muscles of his sword hand. "We broke them when they attacked our tree forts. We broke them in the ambush south of the wall. And we broke them in our attack here at the catapults. In all those cases they were not prepared. If they are going to stand their ground and fight it will be here and now, set as they are with the Drakans and Scarlets to bolster them." He gripped the sword pommel. "No, we will wait for them to attack." Turning to peer at the war machines that lay behind them. "But I do think we should try out our new toys."

Sedge ordered the mercenaries to turn the catapults around to face eastward, and Perrin assigned a crew of men to each of the three functional machines. Huffing their way to where the line had formed, squads of ballistae-bearing Timberkeeps manhandled their weapons into position between the catapults. They raised whicker screens as protection from an archery duel.

"Your surprise night attack was a good move," remarked Christina. "With Red Elm maybe we should have hit the churchmen harder."

Sedge shook his head. "No good. The scouts weren't sure of the Drakan camp, and they said the Red Britches were up and about. Seems the bastards never sleep. No, we've accomplished our purpose for the moment." He patted a trundling wheel of one of the catapults.

"Maybe it's time to test our new found artillery against that vaunted Drakan shield wall."

"If they are smart they would withdraw. Certainly, the Drakan is no fool."

Sedge snorted. "We should be so lucky. No, Alon, they will not run away. Pride and arrogance have been their undoing since they came to Wedgewood and it will be Paleowright pride that undoes them again." He patted the wheel. "They'll want their catapults back. And without any good idea of how strong we are, they will at least come have a look see. That's why I'm ordering half our fighters back into the forest. I don't want what's left of the Paleos to be too timid to attack us."

"I'm ordering you to counter-attack decurion." Viscount Helprig growled at Uloch.

"I don't take orders from you count. You know that as well as I do."

"Cowards. That's what you are and the lot of your men. You hide behind your emperor like a babe behind his mother's skirts."

Uloch stood facing the prelate. Though his mouth twisted, his eyes bore no umbrage at the slight. The viscount's tactics were patently obvious. Without turning from Helprig, he ordered: "Optio, relay the skirmisher's scouting report."

"Sir." The light-troop commander snapped to attention. "The enemy has manned the catapults and is preparing them with scattershot. They've moved six ballistae into position and are concealing them behind arrow screens."

"And how many warriors do they have?" he queried, never taking his eyes from the viscount's fuming face. "Between three and six hundred, sir. Could be more. They've moved two or three companies into the forest to the north and have taken up flanking positions along our probable approach."

Nodding once, Uloch dismissed the officer and then tilted his head. "Let us take a tally, shall we your lordship? You came to Wedgewood with a thousand troglodytes, sixteen hundred pikes, and one hundred—"

"I know all that. Are you going to fight like a Drakan warrior or are you going to stand there and whimper!"

Unfazed, the decurion continued, "You now have none of your troglodytes at your disposal having seen fit to send them into the countryside to terrorize the citizenry, and of your pikemen, you have barely three hundred remaining. Many of those are demoralized, beaten men, and to show for it you have nothing. The Timberkeeps have destroyed the mine and retain control of Wedgewood. Moreover, they have captured your siege engines. I dare say, sir," and nodded his head at Captain Irons standing next to him, "If it were not for your seventy Scarlet Saviors you'd have no effective fighting force at all."

The viscount's eye's narrowed to slits in the morning sun. "I will lodge a formal complaint with the archbishop, decurion. We will take your matter of refusal and gross cowardice all the way to the emperor!"

"As you may," the decurion replied. "I see no further purpose in continuing this attack. You cannot achieve your stated objectives, or what was promised to the Empire and that was an operating base here in Wedgewood." What he did not tell the prelate were his orders to husband his force. Once successfully infiltrated behind the SeaHaven-Lamaran frontier he was to take every opportunity to establish a secret base, at Wedgewood or not, from which to carefully build the Drakan presence until one day it could be launched at the rear of the Western Alliance in a coordinated assault with Nak Drakas itself. Every soldier he lost to the Timberkeeps was a sword that should be fighting Sea-Haven or the Stronghold of Darnkilden. Not some loggers halfway across Isuelt. The waste sickened him.

"We cannot achieve our goals because you will not attack!" Helprig stamped his boot though the effect was lost on the thick carpet of pine needles as if the forest mocked him.

Uloch turned to the Larech, the Washentrufel agent. "Our business here is concluded."

As the Drakans walked away, the viscount rose both fists into the air shaking them. "We will be back. We will wait for them to dig out their mine, and then we will unleash the fury of the Church and restore the honor of the Ancients. This is a blot on their legacy that must not stand!"

The decurion called back over his shoulder, "And when you do return count, I suggest your first order of business be to capture the mine." Continuing to walk away, he said to no one in particular, "And not stroke your ego by trying to crush the Timmies." Without the mine and the gold, the allure of the town would fade, and the population dwindle, thus accomplishing by economics what they couldn't by arms.

Helprig ignored the Drakan and instead glared into the distance. He would need someone to blame the disaster on. Surely it couldn't be the troglodytes since they were his idea. The decurion was an obvious candidate, but Helprig was no fool. Leveling blame on the Drakans would draw the ire of the emperor, and the damned Washentrufel agents would give their account. Undoubtedly, a healthy dose of incriminations would be heaped on the hapless battalion commanders, but he needed a better scapegoat, someone, or something out of his control. "Captain Irons."

"Yes, your eminence."

"The archbishop will require a battle report upon our return to Hebert."

"Yes my lord."

"You will write it."

Irons looked out the corner of his eye at the predicant who turned away.

"You will note how the entire Doroman nation, clans from across Isuelt were raised against us, including battalions of Life Believers from Lamar and all of the Mother's precious Defenders. Write with particular attention the despicable deed of the Timberkeeps. How they destroyed the mine in desperation, and we, in retribution, razed the town. And a final point, the Timberkeeps were aided and abetted by stolen Ancient technology carried here from Tivor no less, and that Marisa Pontifract of House Marinda had a personal hand in supplying the new weapons. That we have identified her chief spy and will endeavor to bring him to justice."

Irons inclined his head to the prelate. "As you command my lord. Am I to assume that after we deliver the report to the archbishop that I am to pursue and apprehend the trader Achelous from Tivor?"

Helprig straightened his back, peering loftily into the distance. "Yes, and you will deliver the battle report to the archbishop yourself. I have other pressing business to attend. Make my excuses to his lordship for my absence."

"You were right," Sedge said, watching the Drakans turn about and march away.

A cheer went up along the Wedgewood line. Timberkeep, Plains, and Lamarans clashed shields with weapons and gave a celebratory salute, raising their swords and axes high into the air. For many of the warriors, there had been no sleep for three days and the loss of many comrades. Wedgwood was saved. The Paleowrights were quitting the field. The last churchmen remaining were ten squads of Scarlet Saviors, tempting, goading the Timberkeeps to attack.

Sedge ordered a single catapult fired. The shot, a boulder, sailed clear over the elite churchmen. Soon they too turned and left.

"You sound disappointed, Sedge." Christina glanced over her shoulder as she congratulated Perrin's men.

"I am. I'd like to kick all their asses here and now, but that is not to be. The Paleowrights are learning, and that is not good."

Chapter 50
Council

Wedgewood

Trishna turned at the sound of the voices as they entered Baryy's cabin. With the loss of the two inns and numerous lodgings in the blackened business section of town, sleeping quarters were at a premium in Wedgewood. She was temporarily bunking with Baryy and Outish while the other Silver Cup bravos squeezed in with Celebron. Sleeping in hammocks in the treeforts worked during the siege, but they were cold, damp, and breezy.

Her mouth gaped. Marisa Pontifract stood in the low-ceilinged bungalow, her jet-black hair done up in a riding bun. She looked wan and tired, her lip healing from a cut. She wore an expensive leather duster over riding britches and supple knee-length riding boots. A slim, curved sword hung at her hip. She smiled at Trishna's surprise, a shy blush on her cheeks though her tired, ebony eyes twinkled with mischief.

When Trishna had last touched with the telepath in Tivor two days ago, Marisa had been with Achelous relaying messages to the aorolmin. Akallabeth walked in the door behind her, followed by Achelous himself. Trishna's surprise turned to shock. *All three of them?* It was a three-week ride between Wedgwood and Tivor, two if you rode to exhaustion with remounts.

Akallabeth seeing Trishna's discomfiture and Marisa's embarrassment hurried to clear the awkward silence. "Ah, Trishna. We've just come from Celebron. We-- well, he had a similar reaction as you." Baryy, having met them at Wayland's Farm with the Red Elm escort, slipped past, and sat down in his bentwood rocker in the corner. Watching the exchange, the sociologist in him was fascinated by the reaction of the provincials as one attempted to explain to another the existence of dimensional shifting. He wondered how well Akallabeth grasped the concept. Outish, standing behind Trishna in the small kitchen purposely hid from view. He dreaded his first meeting with Achelous. Much had transpired since and during the Paleowright assault, and Achelous's repeated warnings of Dianis being a dangerous place range in his ears.

Achelous shut the door to the cabin so the six of them could have their discussion in private. With the crowded bungalows and bivouacs, people no longer honored the little fences and boundary stones that partitioned the cottages.

Akallabeth continued, "I know you be wondering how we've come to be here seeing that you just touched with us in Tivor!" He laughed a hearty laugh, and bent to slap his knee. "I still can't believe it myself, but here we are, and if it weren't for a day's ride from Wayland's Farm it would have been a blink!" and he snapped his thumb.

Trishna stood holding the crockery she was drying from the morning's breakfast. Judging by her frozen expression of dismay Akallabeth had substantial explaining to do.

His laughing diminished to a chortle, and he rubbed a tear from his eye. "I knew Celebron would be shocked, and he was, mind you, but your reaction is better!" and his chortle threatened to escalate back to the belly-busting laugh when Marisa touched his arm. "May I?"

"Hu? Oh, my pleasure lady," he said and folded his neckerchief.

Marisa limped to Trishna and relieved her of the crock, concerned the pathic would drop it. "We've come here by an Ancient network. I don't profess to understand it. But the Ancients in all their glorious mystery constructed what Achelous calls shift zones across the continents. It's what they used to move about the planet. Some of them are still operational, and Achelous has learned how to use them." Trishna's pale green eyes darted to Achelous who stood watching her intently. Suddenly, with a shiver, she realized she was the only one in the room who did not know. In the first instant, a flash of anger came when she thought they were playing a trick on her, but neither Baryy nor Achelous were smiling. Somehow this comforted her and cooled her irritation.

"We literally can step across the continent, from one shift zone to another, in an instant. It has to do with the astral plane," Marisa waved her hand in the air, and Trishna noticed the nails were polished a deep maroon though she wore no rings. Rings would catch on the lining of a mailed gauntlet, but the polish would scratch from days of hard riding, and here they were, perfect. "The same dimension through which you communicate."

Trishna gave a single dumb nod. All pathics eventually learned of the astral plane through their guild instructor.

Achelous came forward. "Trishna, there are very few who know this secret. It falls under your Silver Cup oath to divulge nothing of client information."

Akallabeth turned serious. "Aye."

"We do not treat this lightly. You can see the devastation the Paleowrights have visited on Wedgewood. They are willing to do the same upon anyone who holds either knowledge or technology of the Ancients. It is best for your safety and those around you that if you are confronted by anyone you are to steadfastly profess ignorance and report it to Akallabeth or I. Anything less, and we are all at risk. The Washentrufel and Inquisitors can be anywhere."

The telepath closed her mouth, her expression set. "I understand." As a telepath, she relayed many sensitive messages, and her ability to keep a secret was almost as important as her ability to send them.

Achelous nodded, satisfied. Trishna was the least of his security concerns. He went to set his pack on the kitchen table. It was then he saw Outish lurking in the corner, his back against the cupboard. Achelous stared at the fresh bandage that covered half of the biologist's head and then at his hand, similarly swathed in white wrappings. "What happened to you?"

Outish looked away and shrugged. He mumbled something, and Achelous asked, perhaps a bit too loudly, "What?"

"Shield wall I said!" Outish snapped. "I fought in the shield wall. There, you happy?" Outish glared at him, pain in his eyes. Achelous stood back, dismayed.

Trishna, unaware of the relationship between the two, chimed in, seeking relief from her own shock, "And that's not all he did." Outish shook his head, his eyes pleading with her.

She paused, uncertain. Outish kept shaking his head like an agitated chipmunk. She pivoted to face Achelous, "Sir, you must understand, we've fought a pitched battle for three days. It was life or death for us all. The trogs didn't care if you were a trader or a Timber; we were all fresh meat. Everyone had to fight, and some of us," and she looked squarely at Outish, "fought with great distinction, your runner for one."

Achelous softened his expression, absorbing the bandages and intern's apprehension at seeing him. A fear he did not wish to heighten considering all the trials they had just faced. No matter what fool thing Outish had done the former-chief inspector was heartily glad to see him alive--if bandaged at least whole. Baryy's multi-func messages to him omitted any mention of Outish's wounds. He'd have to discuss that with the sociologist.

Achelous stepped forward and hugged him. Stunned, Outish stammered and stood rigidly. Achelous separated, holding him at arm's length, grave concern on his face. "I haven't lost—" he wanted to say more, but with the provincials in the room he went on lamely, "I am very glad you are alive. I feel responsible for—"

"Don't worry boss," Outish said huskily, "I, well, like you said I'm alive."

Achelous shook his head with a mixture of sadness and frustration, a tear welling in his eye. Outish understood the look. If it weren't for the presence of Trishna and the others, he'd be hearing the 'Dianis is a dangerous place' lecture.

Baryy rose from his rocker in the corner. "We should meet with the chairman soon before he makes up his mind and goes to the full council. There are competing interests vying for his and Margern's attention. One proposal before them is to attack Hebert," he said it to highlight the extremes in arguments facing the councils in the wake of the Paleowright attack. "He knows you are bearing a message from the aorolmin. I told him that you and Marisa were already on your way here and were in 'touch' with the aorolmin during your travels. Our work with Mbecca before the attack has convinced her of the dangers in the soil. She's prepared to help us plead our case."

After the travelers changed from their traveling clothes and freshened, Baryy led them to Timber Hall, collecting Mbecca along the way. Her face was drawn, and her eyes bloodshot from a lack of sleep, but she shooed off their attention when they doted on her limp. Her grey-streaked hair was wild, but her smock and ankle length dress was clean and wrinkle-free. "We've fifty two wounded in the lodge," she told Achelous, "the infirmary is overflowing. The conditions are ghastly, but we're coping. There are two other hospitals setup, the largest is in the Hall itself. "We're dealing with all manner of injuries. Spear wounds, burns, trog bites, nasty putrefying claw rakes...." She plodded along beside him, her head high, but the weight of the victims clear upon her.

"We've brought bandages and medical supplies from Tivor," Marisa said. "We, uh, suspected there would be trouble when we set out." Marisa omitted that she had paid for them out of her own purse.

Achelous glanced at her, pride in his heart. While he felt sheepish that she'd been forced to lie, as he did, he felt a huge relief that she was now his confidant. There appeared to be no end to what she could do. He wondered how long and through how many of his deceptions she had peered? The irony being she was only scratching the surface. Layers and layers remained before she knew the whole truth.

"Thank you, we gladly accept all you bring. We are using a combination of both physical medicine and sixthsense. We reserve our healing energy for the most egregious injuries."

They met Ogden at the base of Perrty which was the muster point for Second Ward now that the foundry was destroyed. Achelous asked if they could see the ruins, so they picked their way through the charred stables to the blackened rectangular plot that outlined where the foundry stood. Rising from the scorched foundations and skeletal timbers the chimneys for the tempering oven and the two furnaces sat in silent mockery of the once bustling shop that forged raw iron into live metal, articles of man. A cold drizzle began to fall from the grey sky, the drops sputtering and sizzling in the patches of dying coals dotting the wreckage. Odgen stepped in and kicked a rafter beam that disintegrated into pieces of charcoal. His face reflected the gloom of the surroundings. The foundry had been his life. He'd taken it over from his father, as did his father's father when he came from Whispering Bough.

A deepening sense of shame weighed on his shoulders that it was during his turn at the anvil that the foundry was destroyed. Oh, how his ancestors must be stewing at their hearths. "The building may be razed," Marisa waved her gloved hand across the scene, "but the creations of the master are spread across the land bearing witness to the hand that made them. The knowledge of that hand yet lives within the master and his craftsmen. The furnace will forge anew, it is but bricks and mortar that even I can lay and mix. But a simple nail," she bent to pick one up, "I have no skill to make." She studied it for a moment and placed it in her pocket as if it were the bones of a dead friend. "Ogden, think of all the shields, swords, axes, hinges, plowshares, pots and hammers at service here in Wedgewood. They care not if the foundry stands for they still do their work. There is need of more, much more to rebuild the town. The first priority of Wedgewood should be to rebuild the foundry."

Odgen took a deep breath. "Oi, and the stables, and the granary."

"The stables and granary will need accouterments from the foundry. With no auger to lift the grain, hands from the field will be needed to carry the grain, and they are better suited for the harvest."

"The issue is not in doubt." Achelous picked up a door lock, burned free from its door, the screws bent and corroded, the carbon sucked away by the intense heat. "Elliot has replied to our message. He's engaged the builder we spoke of. Elliot can order the land to be cleared when we give the word."

Marisa found it most useful that Elliot had been brought in on the secret of the shift zones. She didn't worry, as Achelous had with her. She kept few secrets from Elliot, and they shared many of the same suspicions. As her authorized household agent he could act on her behalf without being questioned. He didn't need to explain where Marisa was or how she got there.

Achelous found a partially molded gun barrel in what had been the gun room. To the uneducated, it could be just another blacked piece of foundry iron, but to his expert eye, he discerned its real application. He tossed it back into the ashes and turned to Baryy, "You managed to rescue everything?"

Baryy nodded mindful of Mbecca who stood near the stables with Outish. The healer did not know of the foundry's secret work. "I have the dubious distinction of being the first man to kill with one of Odgen's rifles."

Ogden grunted and grinned, not the jovial smile that usually split his face, but the smirk of professional pride that stewed at low ebb. "He got three of them he did."

"Three?" Achelous had heard there was a fight in the foundry, but with all the other news the tale had been truncated.

"Yes," Baryy admitted. "The Parrots had us trapped in the gun room. There were five of us and maybe twenty or thirty of them, it was dark, and they didn't know we were there. I had to load the rifles in the dark with a lantern", he chuckled at Achelous's expression. "But we didn't need a lantern when I fire the guns, the muzzle flashes lit the room like lightning. You should have seen those Parrots run." He'd come to terms with having to kill what he considered innocent men. Individually, the churchmen hadn't marched to Wedgewood to rape and murder, they hadn't come because they hated the Timberkeeps, but because the Church clergy order them to it. After watching them fight, he was convinced the pikemen would sooner be standing a boring watch on a rampart in Hebert than campaigning in the wilderness bringing heathens to heal. Those in the foundry that night just wanted a warm place to sleep. *No,* he mused, *it's the zealots who are responsible for this. They put those men in front of me and dared me to kill them.*

Cheering up, oblivious to Baryy's own gloom, Odgen clapped him on the shoulder. "And I'll make you more lad." He strode to where the anvil lay overturned. He kicked it with the familiarity of an old friend. I'll be taking this with me. It was my grandfather's from Whispering Bough. I'll be needing it to shape more barrels."

They filed into Timber Hall, and Ogden hung his shield and axe on a crowded weapons rack inside the Hall's double doors. Many of the shields, aegis, and targes resting there were from his shop, and they bore fresh dents, gouges, and dark stains. Marisa made to unbuckle her cutlass, and Ogden stayed her. "Noi, no qualms Lady. The ban on weapons in the Hall has been lifted for now. You may wear your weapon if you wish. We hang ours here, so we don't have to carry them."

"Thank you, Ogden, but it'll just get in the way, and I'd rather not mar your fine woodwork." She craned her head peering at the rafters and the family banners that decorated them. "It's a marvelous place. I'm so glad it wasn't damaged."

The armorer rested a beefy hand on the richly lacquered rail leading up the broad staircase. "Oi, I can rebuild something as crude as the foundry, but rebuilding Timber Hall can only be done by generations of feet buffing these steps."

Knocking on the door, open to Woodwern's private chambers, Baryy saw Margern, and she waved him in. Rising, Woodwern, Margern, and Ordern Smoothgrain made introductions, and Woodwern bade them sit. Seating was plentiful and cushioned, and tea was sent for. Outish gawked out the window, a double-wide glass frame, that from the third floor had a clear view over the palisade and down into the valley to the southwest where the forest gave way to extensive parks and farmsteads. Farms that were now being reclaimed by their families. He saw in the distance a mounted half-ward patrolling a wood line.

"Sir," Baryy led off, "we have a proposal from the aorolmin of Tivor." He turned to Marisa, who picked up from there. "The aorolmin has been apprised of your circumstances here on Mount Mars and is offering a permanent holding to Clan Mearsbirch in the

Ungerngerist forest on the flanks of Mount Epratis. It lies within a half day ride from Tivor proper, and he is offering the holding as a county with all the rights and warrants that implies, including mutual defense."

Sitting at his desk, Woodwern considered Marisa, attractive and refined. Her boots, riding breeches, and riding cloak were cut and tailored from choice leather and berga wool. She wore no jewelry yet carried herself with the confidence of a leader, but in what role he knew not. Her bruised mouth and limp attested that she too had suffered in the fighting. "Are you empowered to speak on the aorolmin's behalf and negotiate his terms?" he asked.

A tall, flaxen-haired woman, dressed in simple brown buckskins and a white linen blouse appeared at the door. She smiled at Outish, inclined her head at Sedge and locked eyes with Marisa. The two women weighed each other. Achelous, who'd never personally met the woman, guessed by her dress, the deference the others in the room paid to her, and from Outish's fidgeting that this must be, "Christina?" He moved to clasp hands, Timber style. He'd not used her formal title as Baryy had briefed him on her preferences and he'd watched the hologram recording from the Tolkroft parlay.

She shifted her gaze from Marisa and leaned forward to grasp his hand. "Yes," she smiled warmly. "And you must be Achelous, master trader, friend and partner to Ogden, our good weapons master."

Achelous shook her hand, and then the Alon stepped towards Marisa's seat. When Marisa made to rise, Christina said, "Sit, please. I've heard of your ride to Wayland's Farm. You are Marisa Pontifract, of the House Marinda," she said.

Marisa blinked, taking the offered hand. "Al suri Alon, I'm sorry I missed you in Tivor, I was at sea. "

"Yes, I know. Never fear, we can catch up while you are here. I would know of your tribulations with the pirates and Paleowrights. I seldom travel farther south than Tivor, and the Warkenvaal and their pirates are a mystery to me." She let the lady's hand go, appreciating the sword handling callouses on a hand manicured with nail polish. "And you are here for?"

"That was part of Woodwern's question. I am here as both the aorolmin's chief trade councilor and special envoy to Wedgewood."

Woodwern nodded slightly. *Trade councilor to the aorolmin.* That meant she was a trade negotiator working for the ruler of the second largest port in western Isuelt.

"She's come from the aorolmin offering a steading," said Margern. "A free steading?" Margern asked Marisa, never the one to miss a detail.

"Yes, a free steading. No land purchase necessary. The land lies empty and unused. The aorolmin would rather have it occupied and productive, generating marginal taxes. He's not needful of a buyer, but he does wish to strengthen trade and commerce. I've," and she glanced at Achelous, "we've convinced him that the Timberkeeps are of a like mind, and people of your forest ethic would be a welcomed addition as neighbors."

"And what would be the taxes on this new steading?" Margern pursued. The two women took stock of each other. Each saw a business counterpart, savvy in the ways of negotiating.

"Taxes would be to our mutual agreement and can be assessed on personages, improvements, goods, or acreage. The aorolmin is prepared to make the terms most fair."

Woodwern stirred his bulk in the chair. "And why would he do that? An Ungern grove is highly prized."

"Oi," agreed Ordern. "You've been perched in this grove of yours for years while my clan makes due with oaks, hickories, and maples." Though anyone who'd been to the Red Elm holdings knew the majestic thousand-year Silver Oaks rivaled the greatest Ungerngerist. "Time to share the wealth." He peered at Marisa, "We are fairly bursting at the seams in Knife Branch. The Floral Cedar clan is growing as well." Looking at Woodwern, "The Timber Clans are growing Wood. This may be an opportunity for all of us."

Marisa smiled, her lips quirking at the corners. "There is a saying I'm sure you've heard, Ungerns without Timbers is a forest without squirrels."

The chairman laughed, "Oi, I've heard it."

"And if I may be candid sir," Marisa paused to stretch her wounded leg.

"Please do," interjected Margern.

"The Ungerngerist forest has long been the property of the aorolmin, but to date, he has made the vast bulk of his revenues through trade, and those principally by sea. A steading on the shoulders of Mount Epratis would create a trading partner, a tithing source, and an ally to guard the southern roads. The pirates have lately become bolder and are matched by increasing brigandry on the south roads. We think the two are linked. A Timberkeep holding in the Ungerngerists would necessarily force the bandits from those havens and extend the aorolmin's reach to the west and south. Today, his cavalry patrols those reaches, but the populations are sparse and the way-stations few." She left unsaid her fear of the growing Paleowright threat against Tivor.

"But as you can see," Margern, said, "Wedgewood survives, and the Paleowrights have been beaten. Why should we leave the forest that is our home and move yet again?" the memory of Whispering Bough the unspoken backdrop to her words.

Achelous smiled inwardly. He'd learned much of the Timbers, and though they cherished their Whispering Bough ancestry they'd become besotted with the Ungerngerist forest, so much so that a vocal minority in the clan openly advocated to seek out, colonize, and protect all Ungerngerist forests on Isuelt, no matter where they were. Achelous chose not to capitalize on that sentiment, and instead pursued the obvious: "We came through Wayland's Farm. We saw the destruction the trogs have wreaked on the countryside. There are as many refugees at the farm as you have residents here in Wedgewood. Moreover, their situation grows more precarious every day. Food, sanitation, and clean water will become a problem. Spring planting is nearly at an end, and many of the farms are sacked or defiled, their livestock slaughtered or scattered. You will have a hard enough time feeding and housing your population here in Wedgewood. The Paleowrights may have suffered in their assault, but what the Church clergy failed to achieve by arms they may yet achieve by the desecration they wreaked on the surrounding lands."

Woodwern stirred. "There is no cause to abandon Wedgewood. We will survive." He said the last with a fervency that brooked no argument.

"Yes sir, I am sure Clan Mearsbirch will survive and flourish." Marisa's tone was conciliatory. As a practiced trade negotiator, she understood how the more powerful human emotions could override even harsh economic realities. Pride could take precedence over feeding a family, for a time. "It is not our intent to suggest the relocation of the entire clan, nor imply that Wedgewood -- after your hard-fought victory here-- should be surrendered to your enemy's ghosts amongst the blistered ruins. Nay, our proposal is of, shall we say, a distribution of risks. When I make an investment in a new venture, I hedge my risk. If you were to establish a colony at Mount Epratis, however small, you would gain numerous advantages. The first of which is to ease the burden on your food stocks and provide shelter for those who are displaced. I know by speaking to a warden of the Rock ward at Wayland's that the Rock clans would take in your refugees—" Ordern interrupted, "As would Red Elm."

"But I also perceive a Doroman rivalry between the Rock, Plain, and Timber that preclude you from becoming beholden to one another, you have a fierce notion of self-reliance. You have all now acted in the mutual defense of another, but I suspect having Mearsbirch clansmen housed in Rock dens or Red Elm lodges, for even a single winter, is not a burden the clan wants to foist. Am I right?"

Woodwern frowned at the notion, an unspoken word passing between him and Ordern. "We will rebuild here, we can provide new homes."

"Yes," agreed Achelous, "but Tivor is close to Mount Epratis. Tivor will help you build there too, and there is plenty of food. The trade routes carry it down from the north shore."

Ordern came to their aid, "Wood, I don't see the point of worrying over this. You can move as many people down there as you want. As chieftain of Red Elm, I will take this offering if you do not. We can partner in this, together!" He waved his hand in the air. "What's more important, as we discussed at Tolkroft, is the Paleowrights amassing an army. Helprig is insane and vindictive. There'll be no more trading with Hebert. You, we, are at war with them. And what of the troglodytes? Do we expect them to just go back to their swamps and live peacefully hereafter? Mother's wisdom, the Drakans have crossed the frontier. They may be outfitted as mercs, but they are here, you fought them! War is coming Wood. You, we, are going to need every friend we can find. Take their offer," he pointed at Marisa. "I'll talk to Floral, Cedar, and the others. We need to start marshaling our forces. If Tivor is willing to help, then Mother be blessed. Although," and he looked at Marisa, "Do we know the aorolmin really understands what he is signing up for?" Ordern shook his head, as if it didn't matter. "Be that as it may. The Ungerngerists in Tivor may make a bastion of last resort for you or all of us to fall back to." Ordern left it hanging the dire conditions they would be in if the Timberkeep clans had to retreat to Tivor.

Sedge stirred. "He brings up a good point, Woodwern. We need to move our defenses forward. Watch posts on Ungern Way are no longer enough. We need to garrison Lycealia. Probably other posts on the eastern slopes as well. If we don't, we'll always be under threat of a surprise attack."

"And we may need more than just new allies," said Margern. "There may not be enough of them. We need to rebuild, quickly. Hebert has not been hurt, we have. If Tivor can help us with construction..."

"Oi. You are right Margern," Ogden agreed hurriedly, "I need to rebuild the foundry here. Expand it to a proper iron works." Ogden debated how much he should tell the chairwoman of his intentions, "I can have my day foreman begin rebuilding the foundry here, while I hurry south to supervise the construction of another iron works in Tivor. Between the two larger foundries, I'll have the capacity needed to supply the rebuilding of Wedgewood and the new colony. As you know Margern, I have," he sought the right words, "special projects. Like the new handbolts Sedge requisitioned and that Outish and Baryy carry."

"Special projects?" Margern asked. The way she asked the question made Achelous wonder if she were being coy. Achelous interjected, "You'll forgive Ogden, please, but he's under oath to me to not divulge the nature of these projects. It is my fear that should the Paleowrights learn of our work they will hound and harass us. They are tenacious and annoying when it comes to new inventions."

Woodwern grunted. "You mean they are jealous and covet anything new."

Marisa put it more directly. "They believe any invention of note must be inspired by the Ancients and if they interrogate the inventor, they can prove it." She left unsaid what everyone knew: Paleowright interrogations were ruthless and often amounted to innocent victims tortured into bearing false witness. Facts and truth were irrelevant.

Margern stood from her chair. "It doesn't matter what the Paleowrights learn, we are at war. May Mother frost them to their core." She looked from Marisa to Odgen. "I hope Clan Mearsbirch will benefit from these special projects. We are beset by formidable enemies." She stared him in the eyes. Without shifting her gaze, she raised a hand at Baryy. "He unleashed your secret project on the churchmen that night in the foundry, that much Cordelia and Brookern have seen. What the fire-sticks are Woodwern and I care not, but we do care they are used to defend the clan. You, the foundry, this hall, we are all of the clan."

At the mention of Cordelia and Brookern, Baryy stole a glance at Achelous who caught the look and used a hand-signal: They would talk later.

Ogden nodded gravely. When his grandfather built the foundry, the clan had loaned him – interest free -- the money, materials, and labor. So it would be again. "Oi, that is our plan. Achelous and I have agreed the defense of Wedgewood comes before all else."

Margern moved to Woodwern. She gave him the curious head bob only Woodwern knew the meaning of. He straightened in his chair, gripping both armrests. "Marisa, we shall take your proposal to the full clan council and recommend its approval. We will seek a joint endeavor with Red Elm, Floral, and any other Timber clan that wants to join us."

"Will you come with us to Tivor, Alon? To Mount Epratis?" Outish followed Christina down the staircase, the attendants to the meeting with Woodwern breaking into their own small groups. He trailed after her like a loyal acolyte. At the head of the stairs, off to the side, Baryy and Achelous watched.

"No Outish. My mission I fear takes me to the east." She moved slowly down the stairs, in no hurry to leave.

"To the east?"

"Yes. I've been in contact with our Faithful. The six missing adepts have been seen in Nak Drakas."

Outish kept his hand on the railing as he negotiated the steps. "Who has them?"

"The Washentrufel. Of that, there is no doubt." She paused on a step, looking over her shoulder at him. "Life continues on, and into Nak Drakas it goes. Mother asks that we save all her children, so to Nak Drakas I shall go."

He absorbed the news, the gravity of the import struck him at the knees. Momentarily distracted by the torchlights reflecting off her hair, he sought to say something relevant and blurted, "I hear that Racheal will be apprenticing with Alex." Standing above her he could smell the rose water in her hair. It was popular with the women warriors in the clan, they all bathed in it.

She took another step and another. "Yes. Though Rachael will be staying here with Feolin until he is able to travel. While he is recovering, he will instruct her in the sword ways of Mother, and he will test her."

"Test?" he asked confused.

"Yes, of course," she replied without turning. "Just because someone wants to be a Defender, does not mean they can be a Defender. They must test." Then she added, "But Rachael comes with high recommendations. She fought against the Paleowrights at the Battle for Wedgewood. She came to our aid, unbidden."

"I fought at the Battle for Wedgewood," he protested. "Someday I would like—"

She stopped and turned to look up at him. Her leaf green eyes gone dark to the color of tree bark. "Yes, Outish, you are certainly brave enough, and you have fought shoulder to shoulder with Timber and Defender. But are you a Life Believer? You must tread on Mother's Wheel to be her Defender." The Alon peered past him up the stairs to Achelous and Baryy. "Or are you something else, Outish." It was a statement, not a question. "Or are you something else entirely." Those eyes gazed through his psychic defenses and plumbed the depth of his thoughts. A crinkle of a grin softened her inspection. "Come. In celebration of rebuilding the tavern, Murali is holding a social. I hear the grain spirits survived the fire in rare form. You can be my honored guest."

Baryy watched the pair from the balcony. "Did you ever think how Christina resembles an Amazonia from Heklo IV? She's an Amazonia if I've ever seen one."

Achelous heaved a breath, tired and drained, musing over Odern's portent of war and the revelation that the clan's sensitives were informing clan leadership of their prescient visions. *How far did that go? What had they seen? What will they see?* He pulled himself away from the dark hole of paranoid uncertainty. If the Timberkeep adepts could scry Ogden's work, then perhaps they could spy the actions of Nordarken Mining? Casting his introspection at Christina, he answered, "No, but I bet I know who *is* an extrasolar."

Baryy craned his head around. "Who?"

"Sedge."

Baryy held still, his hand tight to the balustrade. The way Achelous said the name made the assertion incontrovertible. "How do you know?"

"You mean what gave him away? Other than his lack of history before Mestrich? His contract to an aquamarine-mine owner? The way he acted when Ivan appeared in the nick of time? Sedge's lack of real interest in handbolts? His very real interest in the source of

Ogden's experiments, and Sedge's idea for the treeforts and other innovative military tactics?"

Baryy considered the data points. "Yea," he drawled.

"You mean what really gave him away?" Achelous offered a sad smirk. "He did let his hair go grey, and his skin pigment mottle, but he kept his perfect teeth. They always do."

Baryy glanced to Woodwern's chambers where the clan leaders were conversing with Sedge. "Hmm. Yes, that's not fair. His teeth are better than mine."

The End

Preview
The Matriarch

IDB Central Station

"Gear check by squads." Ivan Darinarishcan triggered the charge indicator on his hand-bolt. It glowed a cheery seventy. The Dianis Central Station transport bay was crowded with troopers: two squads of Ready Reaction troopers from the former IDB Dianis command and three squads of Special Forces infantry, all to guard their high-value package. They wore an array of in-country armor and clothing typical of free-company Isuelt mercenaries. The kind of mercenaries that Sedge, militia commander of Wedgewood and Clan Mearsbirch, would appreciate. The difference being the weaponry the guard carried in their baggage. Between the clouds of nano-bots, array of battle drones, and count of plasma rifles, those ten Special Forces soldiers could hold off a Turboii swarm for hours; they needed only three seconds for the cruiser *Alexis* to shift the high-value package clear of any perceived danger. The in-country weapons the ULUP commission temporarily sanctioned for this expedition were insignificant compared to the power of the Avarian task force in orbit.

Councilors Briea and Margrett wore the black, cowled robes of Auro Na priests. Margrett pulled her hood forward covering her blonde hair and waited for her personal escort of two Ready Reaction troopers to check the saddle girth of her eenu and lead it toward the field generator platform. The first squad of soldiers, astride their mounts, vanished from the platform, their sudden disappearance causing the typical inrush of air filling the vacuum.

Ivan turned to his high-value package, "Your last chance, matron. You can still back out. Your special envoy and planetary councilor should be able to handle this." His eyes bore amusement, but his voice was serious."

Margrett, standing aside, smiled, expecting the response.

A laugh came from the high-value personage, whose head was covered by the hood of their black robe, a garment indicative of an Aura Na high priestess. "My dear chief, I am on sabbatical, albeit short. And who, in my role, would pass up the invitation to explore a pristine world, vibrant with unique peoples, ripe with intrigue, and a former Lock Norim colony no less? My curiosity would never let me rest, I am enthralled to see how the human population has evolved. And these troglodytes and wryvern and earlking— sentient reptiles; I would so love to meet them."

It was Ivan's turn to snort a laugh. "Ula. Troglodytes will be the last thing you'll be meeting."

"Ula?" The high-value package asked. Her long black hair, covered by the hood, blended into the ebon darkness matching her eyes, contrasting starkly against her flawless, alabaster skin.

"It means, loosely translated, *ouch* or *oh no*," Ivan replied. "Did the matron take her injection learning with Wedgewood cultural sensitivity? We made a special program for you and the councilors."

"I did, I just didn't expect you to slip into their language so soon."

He shrugged. "It comes from practice." He sighed and appeared distracted.

"You love Dianis."

He gave a wan, slow grin that had seen many days filled with sun, life, and pain. His forehead bore care lines, his nose was abused by the sun, his thin lips bleached pale. He had bushy eyebrows that had witnessed more than their share of rescues. "You are reading my mind matriarch. That's not nice."

She shook her head, the hood stationary. "No chief, I don't need to read minds to hear what is plainly told."

"And what is it, if I may ask, that brings you here to Dianis, other than sabbatical?"

Briea and Margrett watched the interchange silently as their escorts went about the business of shifting gear, mounts, and themselves in-country.

The matriarch waited to answer, time stretching on. Finally, "I've come for two things, three perhaps, maybe four." Pausing, "Certainly I need to know this world. If I am to see it in my prescient visions, I need to be here, to explore it, to know it. I need to connect with this world."

"And?" he gently prodded; one did not press the most powerful human in the galaxy without hazard.

"And I am truly on holiday. I seek a respite, a hiatus from the turmoil and stress of Avaria. I do so love the wildings, the life, the living. It is simple and honest."

Ivan smiled in spite of himself. "And?" He knew he was tempting the ire of one or more of the councilors or the matriarch's guard captain.

"And...and I come in search of your friend."

That surprised him. Ivan knew that Briea was interested in Achelous, but for the chief inspector to gain the personal attention of the matriarch? "Okay. So Atch has been annoying. He could have done better than just run off on leave, without a trace, but the federation owes him. He's done his time. I know he is needed on a half-dozen worlds, but why look for him here? Surely you don't think?"

Her ageless black eyes appraised him.

Then the field generator operator called, "Chief, your group is the last. All squads are in-country and waiting for you."

Ivan ignored him. "You don't think? Atch is--"

She answered his first question, "And I come in search of a woman."

"A woman?" he leaned forward as if not hearing correctly.

"Yes." The matriarch slipped an arm through Ivan's, drawing him near. "Shall we go in-country?" She looked to the shift platform.

He obliged and led the matriarch and the two councilors to the platform. "What woman?" he asked when they stepped into the shift zone.

"The woman your friend will lead me to."

The field generator ready light flipped from *Standby* to *Ready*.

"Atch? What woman? Who is she?"

The matriarch peered up at him testing his innocence. "Yes, a woman. Tell me chief, what do you know of the Life Believers and their Mother?"

"What do you mean?"

"Have you thought their Mother might be a suitable metaphor?"

The field operator actuated the shift cycle.

"Metaphor for what?" Ivan asked, puzzled.

"Uplift. The way to uplift Dianis.

Air swooshed into the platform, filling the void.

Acknowledgements

I'm not the first person to say it takes a village to publish a book, and *The Foundry* proves that. The finished manuscript was a long time in coming. No point in counting the years, except to honor my friends who followed the book's progress on the long journey. Those stalwarts who accompanied me on the trek are Terry Mihm, Jeff Hay, David Hough, Sarah Korte, Nick Korte, Susan Ring, and my master cartographer, Jerome Mooney. I laugh when I remember the early state of the first manuscript. Uf da, the village elders can be patient and forgiving!

Special thanks to Ina Felsheim who relentlessly compelled me to excellence. To Steve Felsheim for his repeated applause (there were times when I needed it). To Danya Dravis who faithfully read every word, no matter the version. To Tom Harron who gave me such great, detailed feedback that the work was transformed. Tom, being a software engineer, was demanding in plot cohesion. To Allison Krzych for helping me bring *The Foundry* and its social media platform to market.

Lastly, to Kim for being patient and understanding when the den door was closed, alternative rock was blaring, and Frank was in the groove writing. No, I don't think the music bothered the dogs, they've gone deaf, as you feared.

About the Author

Frank lives along the Mississippi River, and has leveraged his many life experiences to write The Foundry, the lead story in the Dianis, A World In Turmoil chronicles. He was born and raised in Detroit, Michigan where he and his father cruised the Great Lakes. His father often chose to go out on the lake when it was empty, on the roughest days. Frank spent six years in the US Navy chasing Soviet submarines during the Cold War. His love of the sea is reflected in The Foundry, and again in The Matriarch, a love he has shared with his wife and two girls.

As a hunter, Frank has taken game with a variety of weapons, including the muzzleloader, the device modeled in *The Foundry* and used as the weapon against the pirates in *The Matriarch,* and against the Drakans in *The Citadel.*

He assists his wife in her passion for horses as stable hand and the sole rider of Shaboom their willful appaloosa. Equines appear regularly in the Dianis series, just not as horses, but as eenus.

Frank's care for our Earth and the stewardship of their land in Wisconsin is emulated in the culture and ethos of the Timberkeeps.

He has two degrees, a Bachelor of Computer Science and a Master of Business Administration. Those degrees have been integral to his professional life where he has worked in a variety of roles from software engineer, to marketing executive, to chief information officer, at such prominent firms as SAP and Organic Valley. The technical and scientific acumen he gained through those endeavors is demonstrated in the series in the effort to make the Dianis brand of science practically possible somewhere in the galaxy.

Social Media

For current information on the Dianis a World in Turmoil series please visit us on Facebook at
https://www.facebook.com/thefoundrybookone
where additional maps, character info, details behind key concepts, and the status of both *The Matriarch* (book 2) and *The Citadel* (book 3) will be listed.

You can follow the author on Twitter @FrankDravis.

Most importantly, if you like the book please write a review on Amazon. Frank is an indie author, and the community of independent authors need your reviews!